About the Author

Kevin J. Anderson has over 16 million books in print in 29 languages worldwide. He is the author of the X-FILES novels GROUND ZERO (number 1 bestseller in THE TIMES, and voted Best SF Novel of the Year by SFX magazine), RUINS and ANTIBODIES, as well as the JEDI ACADEMY trilogy of STAR WARS novels – the three bestselling SF novels of 1994. He has also written the international bestselling prequels to Frank Herbert's monumental DUNE series, with Frank's son, Brian Herbert. He has won, or been nominated for, the Nebula Award, Bram Stoker Award, Reader's Choice Award from the Science Fiction Book Club, and many others.

Kevin Anderson lives in Colorado.
www.wordfire.com

HIDDEN EMPIRE

the saga of seven suns

BOOK ONE

KEVIN J. ANDERSON

POCKET
BOOKS

First published in Great Britain by Earthlight, 2002
This paperback edition published by Earthlight, 2003
An imprint of Simon & Schuster UK Ltd
A Viacom Company

Reprinted under Pocket Books, 2005

9 10 8

Simon & Schuster UK Ltd
Africa House
64-78 Kingsway
London WC2B 6AH

www.simonsays.co.uk

Simon & Schuster Australia
Sydney

A CIP catalogue record for this book is available from the British Library

ISBN 0-7434-3065-4

Typeset in Weiss by SX Composing DTP, Rayleigh, Essex
Printed and bound in Great Britain by Cox and Wyman Ltd, Reading, Berks

ACKNOWLEDGEMENTS

During the creation, writing, and editing of this series, many people have offered their advice and their enthusiasm. In particular, I would like to thank Betsy Mitchell and Jaime Levine at Warner Aspect and John Jarrold at Simon & Schuster UK; Matt Bialer, Robert Gottlieb, Maya Perez, and Cheryl Capitani at the Trident Media Group; Larry Shapiro at Creative Artists Agency; Jeff Mariotte at Wildstorm/DC Comics; and artists Stephen Youll and Igor Kordey.

At WordFire, Inc., Catherine Sidor gave her usual 150% effort in transcribing all my tapes of the chapters (and keeping up with me), as well as proofreading and offering general comments; Diane Jones also helped out with insightful questions, suggestions, and brainstorming. Gregory Benford helped me design the Klikiss Torch technology. Brian Herbert gave his support and help with the series from its very beginning. And my wife Rebecca Moesta offered all the help, ideas and love that any human being could give.

To IGOR KORDEY

An imaginative, hardworking, and extremely talented artist. In the early conceptual stages of *The Saga of Seven Suns*, he helped me to visualize and design many of the key elements of this universe. His questions and ideas have fleshed out the series to a greater extent than anything I could have done alone.

ONE

MARGARET COLICOS

Safe in orbit high above the gas giant, Margaret looked through the observation port at continent-sized hurricanes and clouds far below. She wondered how long it would take for the entire planet to catch fire, once the experiment began.

Oncier was a pastel globe of hydrogen and mixed gases five times the size of Jupiter. Moons surrounded the gas giant like a litter of pups jostling against their mother. The four of greatest interest were large bodies of ice and rock named Jack, Ben, George, and Christopher, after the first four Great Kings of the Terran Hanseatic League. If today's test proved a success, those moons could eventually be terraformed into Earth-like colonies.

If the Klikiss Torch failed, the respected career of Margaret Colicos would fizzle along with it. But she would survive. As xeno-archaeologists, she and her husband Louis were accustomed to working in blissful obscurity.

In preparation for the experiment, the technical observation platform bustled with scientists, engineers, and political observers. Though Margaret had nothing to do with the actual test, her

1

presence was still required here. A celebrity. She had to make a good show of it. After all, she had discovered the alien device among the ruins.

Tucking grey-streaked brown hair behind her ear, she looked across the deck and saw Louis grinning like a boy. They had been married for decades and had never worked without each other. It had been years since she'd seen him in a dashing, formal suit. Margaret could tell how much he revelled in the excitement, and she smiled for his sake.

She preferred to watch people rather than interact with them. Louis once joked that his wife had become fascinated with archaeology on alien planets because there was no chance she might have to strike up a conversation with one of her subjects.

With plenty of dirt under their fingernails and ground-breaking discoveries on their resumes, Margaret and Louis Colicos had already sifted through numerous worlds abandoned by the insect-like Klikiss race, searching for clues to explain what had happened to the vanished civilization. The alien empire had left only ghost cities and occasional tall beetle-like robots that bore no helpful memories of their progenitors. In the eerie ruins on Corribus, the Colicos team had discovered and deciphered the remarkable planet-igniting technology they had called the 'Klikiss Torch'.

Now excitement thrummed in the filtered air of the observation platform. Invited functionaries crowded around the observation windows, talking with each other. Never before had humans attempted to create their own sun. The consequences and the commercial possibilities were far-reaching.

Chairman Basil Wenceslas noticed Margaret standing alone. When a small-statured server compy came by bearing a tray filled with expensive champagne, the powerful Chairman of the Terran Hanseatic League snagged two extruded-polymer glasses and walked over to her, proud and beaming. 'Less than an hour to go.'

2

She dutifully accepted the glass and indulged him by taking a drink. Since the reprocessed air of the observation platform affected the senses of smell and taste, a cheaper champagne would probably have tasted as good. 'I'll be glad when it's over, Mr Chairman. I prefer to spend my time on empty worlds, listening for the whispers of a long-dead civilization. Here, there are too many people for me.'

Across the deck she saw a green priest sitting silent and alone. The emerald-skinned man was there to provide instantaneous telepathic communication in case of emergencies. Outside the observation platform hung a ceremonial fleet of alien warliners, seven spectacular ships from the Solar Navy of the Ildirans, the benevolent humanoid race that had helped mankind spread across the stars. The beautifully decorated Ildiran ships had taken up positions where they could observe the spectacular test.

'I understand perfectly,' the Chairman said. 'I try to stay out of the limelight myself.' Wenceslas was a distinguished man, one of those people who grew more attractive and sophisticated with each passing year, as if he learned how to be suave rather than forgot how to be physically fit. He sipped his champagne but so slightly that it barely seemed to wet his lips. 'Waiting is always so hard, isn't it? You are not accustomed to working with such a rigid time clock.'

She answered him with a polite laugh. 'Archaeology is not meant to be rushed – unlike business.' Margaret just wished she could get back to work.

The Chairman touched his champagne glass against Margaret's like a kiss of crystal. 'You and your husband are an investment that has certainly paid off for the Hanseatic League.' The xeno-archaeologists had long been sponsored by the Hansa, but the star-igniting technology she and Louis had discovered would be worth more than all the archaeology budgets combined.

Working in the cool emptiness of Corribus, sifting through the ideographs painted on the walls of Klikiss ruins, Margaret had been able to match up the precise coordinates of neutron stars and pulsars scattered around the Spiral Arm, comparing them with maps developed by the Hansa.

This single correlation caused an avalanche of subsequent breakthroughs: by comparing the coordinates of neutron stars from the Klikiss drawings with known stellar drift, she had been able to back-calculate how old the maps were. Thus, she determined that the Klikiss race had disappeared ten thousand years ago. Using the coordinates and diagrams as a key, as well as all the other information compiled on numerous digs, Louis, with his engineering bent, had deciphered Klikiss mathematical notations, thereby allowing him to figure out the basic functioning of the Torch.

The Chairman's grey eyes became harder, all business now. 'I promise you this, Margaret: if the Klikiss Torch does function as expected, choose any site you wish, any planet you've wanted to explore, and I will personally see that you have all the funding you require.'

Margaret clinked her glass against his in a return toast. 'I'll take advantage of that offer, Mr Chairman. In fact, Louis and I have a likely site already picked out.'

The previously untouched ghost world of Rheindic Co, full of mysteries, pristine territory, uncatalogued ruins . . . But first they had to do their duty dance here and endure the public accolades after they ignited the gas world below.

Margaret went to stand beside Louis. She slipped her arm through his as he struck up a conversation with the patient green priest who waited beside his potted worldtree sapling. She could hardly wait for the experiment to be finished. To her, an empty ancient city was far more exciting than setting a whole planet ablaze.

Two

Basil Wenceslas

Quiet and unassuming, Basil Wenceslas moved through social circles. He smiled when he was supposed to, bantered when expected, and filed the details in his mind. To an outsider, he never showed more than a fraction of his deepest thoughts and intricate plans. The Terran Hanseatic League depended on it.

A well-preserved older man whose age was difficult to determine with even close study, he had access to vigorous anti-ageing treatments and availed himself of cellular chelation techniques that kept him limber and healthy. Dapper and distinguished, he wore impeccable suits that cost more than some families earned in a year, but Basil was not a vain man. Though everyone on the observation platform knew he was in charge, he maintained a low profile.

When an over-eager mahogany-skinned media charmer asked him for an interview about the Klikiss Torch, he diverted the woman and her recording crew to the chief scientist of the project, then melted into the small crowd. Watching. Observing. Thinking.

He looked out at the great ball of ochre clouds that made Oncier look like a poorly stirred confection. This system had no habitable planets, and Oncier's gas mix was not particularly appropriate for harvesting ekti, the exotic allotrope of hydrogen used in Ildiran stardrives. This out-of-the-way gas giant was an excellent test subject for the unproven Klikiss Torch.

Chief scientist Gerald Serizawa talked smoothly and passionately about the upcoming test, and the media crew pressed forward. Beside him, technicians manned banks of equipment. Basil scanned the control panels, assessing the readings for himself. Everything was on schedule.

Dr Serizawa was completely hairless, though whether because of a cosmetic choice, genetic predisposition, or an exotic disease, Basil did not know. Lean and energetic, Serizawa spoke with his hands as much as his voice, gesturing broadly. Every few minutes, like clockwork, he grew self-conscious and clasped his hands to keep them motionless in front of him.

'Gas giants, such as Jupiter in our own home solar system, are on the edge of a gravitational slope that could send them into stellar collapse. Any planetary body between thirteen and a hundred times Jupiter's mass will burn deuterium at its core and begin to shine.'

Serizawa jabbed an insistent finger at the media charmer who had approached Basil earlier. 'With this rediscovered technology, we can push a gas giant such as Oncier over the mass limit so that its core will ignite nuclear fires and turn this big ball of fuel into a brand new sun—'

The woman broke in. 'Please tell our audience where the increase in mass comes from.'

Serizawa smiled, delighted to explain further. Basil crooked his mouth in a faint expression of amusement. He thanked his luck that the bald doctor was such an enthusiastic spokesman.

'You see, the Klikiss Torch anchors two ends of a wormhole, a tunnel *ten kilometres wide*.' It was clear his listeners knew little about wormhole mechanics and the difficulty of creating such a huge space-time gap. 'We open one terminus near a superdense neutron star, then target the other end at the core of Oncier. In the blink of an eye, the neutron star is transported into the planetary heart. With so much added mass, the gas giant will collapse, ignite, and begin to shine. This light and heat, you see, will make the largest moons habitable.'

One of the media recorders pointed an imager at the white glints orbiting the pastel gas planet as Serizawa continued. 'Alas, the new sun will burn for only a hundred thousand years, but that's still plenty of time for us to make the four moons into productive Hansa colonies. Practically an eternity, as far as we're concerned.'

Basil nodded unobtrusively to himself. Typical short-term thinking, but useful. Now that Earth was part of a much larger galactic network, though, true visionaries would have to operate on a completely different timescale. Human history was only one small part of the canvas.

Therefore, the Klikiss Torch opens up many new opportunities for the Hansa to create habitats that meet the needs of our growing human population.'

Basil wondered how many swallowed that explanation. It was part of the answer, of course, but he also noted the huge, gaudy Ildiran warliners standing watch, reminding him of the real reasons for this extravagant demonstration.

The Klikiss Torch must be tested not because there was a desperate need for extra living space – there were many more acceptable colony worlds than humans could ever settle. No, this was a move of political hubris. The Hansa needed to prove that humans could actually *do* this thing, a grand and extravagant gesture.

A hundred and eighty-three years ago, the Ildiran Empire had rescued the first Terran generation ships from their aimless journeys through space. The Ildirans had offered humans their fast stardrive and adopted Earth into the sprawling galactic community. Humans viewed the Ildiran Empire as a benevolent ally, but Basil had been watching the aliens for some time.

The ancient civilization was stagnant, full of ritual and history but very few fresh ideas. Humans had been the ones to innovate the Ildiran stardrive technology. Eager colonists and entrepreneurs – even the space gypsy riff-raff of the Roamer clans – had rapidly filled the old Ildiran social and commercial niches, so that humans gained a substantial foothold in just a few generations.

The Hansa was growing by leaps and bounds, while their stodgy alien benefactors were fading. Basil was confident humans would soon subsume the ailing Empire. After the Klikiss Torch demonstration, the Ildirans would remain impressed by Terran abilities – and deterred from any temptations of testing human mettle. Thus far, the alien Empire had shown no sign of aggression, but Basil didn't entirely believe the altruistic motives of the cosy Ildiran neighbours. It was best to maintain a prominent reminder of human technological abilities, and better still to be subtle about it.

While the test countdown proceeded towards zero, Basil went to get another glass of champagne.

THREE

ADAR KORI'NH

From the command nucleus of his prime warliner, Adar Kori'nh, supreme admiral of the Ildiran Solar Navy, contemplated the humans' folly.

Though the outcome of this preposterous test would have a significant bearing on future relations between the Ildiran Empire and the Terran Hanseatic League, the Adar had brought only a septa, a group of seven warliners. The Mage-Imperator had instructed him not to display too much interest in the event. No Ildiran should be too impressed by any action from these upstarts.

Even so, Kori'nh had refitted his battleships as a matter of pride, painting sigils on their hulls and adding dazzling illumination strips as primary markings. His warliners looked like ornate deep-sea creatures preparing for an outrageous mating display. The Solar Navy understood pageantry and military spectacles far better than the humans did.

The Hansa Chairman had invited Kori'nh to come aboard the observation platform where he could watch the artificial ignition of the gas giant. Instead, the Adar had chosen to remain here, aloof, inside the command nucleus. For now. Once the actual test began, he would arrive with politically acceptable tardiness.

Kori'nh was a lean-faced half-breed between noble and soldier kith, like all important officers in the Solar Navy. His face was smooth with human-like features, because the higher kiths resembled the single breed of human. Despite their physical similarities, though, Ildirans were fundamentally different from Terrans, especially in their hearts and minds.

Kori'nh's skin had a greyish tone; his head was smooth except for the lush topknot folded back across his crown, a symbol of his rank. The Adar's single-piece uniform was a long tunic made from layered grey and blue scales, belted about his waist.

To emphasize the low importance of this mission, he had refused to pin on his numerous military decorations, but the humans would never notice the subtlety when he met them face to face. He watched the bustling scientific activities with a mixture of condescending amusement and broad-based concern.

Though the Ildirans had assisted the fledgling race many times in the past two centuries, they still considered humans to be impatient and ill-behaved. Cultural children, adoptive wards. Perhaps their race needed a godlike, all-powerful leader such as the Mage-Imperator. The golden age of the Ildiran Empire had already lasted for millennia. Humans could learn much from the elder race if they bothered to pay attention, rather than insisting on making their own mistakes.

Kori'nh could not comprehend why the brash and overly ambitious race was so eager to create more worlds to terraform and settle. Why go to all the trouble of creating a new sun out of a gas planet? Why make a few rugged moons habitable when there were so many acceptable worlds that were, by any civilized standard, nowhere near crowded enough? Humans seemed intent on spreading everywhere.

The Adar sighed as he stared out the front viewing screen of his lead warliner. Disposable planets and disposable suns . . . How very Terran.

But he would not have missed this event for all the commendations the Mage-Imperator had left to give. In ancient times the Solar Navy had fought against the terrible and mysterious Shana Rei, and the military force had been required to fight against other deluded Ildirans in a heart-rending civil war two thousand years ago – but since that time, the fleet had been mainly for show, used for occasional rescue or civil missions.

With no enemies and no interplanetary strife in the Ildiran Empire, Kori'nh had spent his career in the Solar Navy managing ornate ceremony-driven groupings. He had little experience in the area of battle or tactics, except to read about them in the *Saga*. But it wasn't the same.

The Mage-Imperator had dispatched him to Oncier as the Empire's official representative, and he had obeyed his god and leader's commands. Through his faint telepathic link with all of his subjects, the Mage-Imperator would watch through Kori'nh's eyes.

No matter what he thought of it, though, this bold human attempt would make an interesting addition to the Ildiran historical epic, the *Saga of Seven Suns*. This day, and probably even Kori'nh's name, would become part of both history and legend. No Ildiran could aspire to more than that.

FOUR

OLD KING FREDERICK

Surrounded by the opulence of the Whisper Palace on Earth, Old King Frederick played his part. Basil Wenceslas had given him orders, and the great monarch of the Hansa knew his place. Frederick did exactly as he was told.

Around him, court functionaries kept busy writing documents, recording decrees, distributing royal orders and benevolences. The Whisper Palace must be seen as a constant flurry of important matters, conducted in a professional and orderly fashion.

Wearing heavy formal robes and a lightweight crown adorned with holographic prisms, Frederick awaited word from Oncier in the Throne Hall. He was bathed and perfumed, the many rings on his fingers polished to a dazzle. His skin had been massaged with lotions and oils. His hair was perfect; not a single strand could be seen out of place.

Though he had originally been chosen for his looks, charisma, and public-speaking abilities, Frederick knew the foundation of his monarchy better than the most attentive student of civics. Because any real-time political hold over such a vast galactic territory would be tenuous at best, the Hansa depended on a visible figurehead to speak decrees and issue laws. The populace needed a concrete person in whom to invest their loyalty, since no one would fight to the death or swear blood oaths for a vague corporate ideal. Long ago, a royal court and a well-groomed King had been manufactured to give the commercial government a face and a heart.

As with his five predecessors, King Frederick existed to be seen and revered. His court was filled with gorgeous clothing, polished stone, rich fabrics, tapestries, artworks, jewels, and sculptures. He awarded medals, threw celebrations, and kept the people happy with a benevolent sharing of the Hansa's wealth. Frederick had everything he could ever need or want – except for independence and freedom.

Basil had once told him, 'Humans have a tendency to abdicate their decision-making to charismatic figures. That way they force others to take responsibility, and they can blame their problems upwards in a hierarchy.' He had pointed to the King, who was so weighed down with finery that he could barely walk. 'If you follow that to its logical conclusion, any society will end up with a monarchy, given enough time and choice.'

After forty-six years on the throne, Frederick could barely remember his younger life or his original name. He had seen significant changes in the Hanseatic League during his reign, but little of it had been his own doing. Now he felt the burden of his years.

The King could hear the rush of fountains, the hum of dirigibles, the roar of the ever-swelling crowds in the royal plaza below waiting for him to address them from his favourite speaking balcony. The Archfather of Unison was already leading them in familiar scripted prayers but, even as the crowds followed along, eager citizens pressed forward, hoping for a glimpse of their splendid monarch. Frederick wanted to remain inside as long as possible.

After its construction in the early days of Terran expansion, the gigantic ceremonial residence had rendered visitors speechless with awe – hence, its name: the Whisper Palace. Always-lit cupolas and domes were made of glass panels criss-crossed with gilded titanium support braces. The site had been chosen in the sunny, perfect weather of the North American west coast, in what had once been southern California. The Palace was larger than any other building on Earth, vast enough to swallow ten Versailles. Later, after the Hansa had encountered the jaw-dropping architecture in the Ildiran Empire, the Whisper Palace had been expanded further, just to keep up.

At the moment, though, the beauty around him could not keep Frederick's mind occupied as he impatiently waited to hear from Basil at distant Oncier. 'Momentous events do not happen in an instant,' he said, as if convincing himself. 'Today we mean to set the course of history.'

A court chamberlain rang an Ildiran crystal-alloy gong. Instantly, in response to the sound, the King donned an eager but paternal smile, a practised kindly expression that exuded warm confidence.

With the fading musical vibrations, he strode down the royal promenade towards his expansive speaking balcony. Out of habit, the King looked at an ultra-clear crystalline mirror mounted in an alcove. He caught his expression, the not-quite-hidden weariness in his eyes, a few new wrinkles that only he could see. How much longer would Basil let him play this role, before he passed beyond 'paternal' and into 'doddering'? Maybe the Hansa would let him retire soon.

The great solar doors spread open, and the King paused to take a deep breath, squaring his shoulders.

Ambassador Otema, the ancient green priest from the forested planet of Theroc, stood beside her shoulder-high worldtree sapling in its ornate planter. Through the sentient worldforest, Otema could establish an instant communication link with the far-off technical observation platform.

He gave one brisk clap of his hands. 'It is time. We must transmit a message that I, King Frederick, grant my permission for this wondrous test to begin. Tell them to proceed with my blessing.'

Otema gave a formal bow. The stern ambassador had so many status tattoos on her face and her skin was such a weathered green that she looked like a gnarled piece of vegetation herself. She and Basil Wenceslas had butted heads many times, but King Frederick had kept out of the disputes.

Otema wrapped her callused fingers around the scaly bark of the worldtree and closed her eyes so that she could send her thoughts via telink through the trees to her counterpart at Oncier.

FIVE

BENETO THERON

At Oncier, a hush fell over the observers and guests as Beneto released his grip on the small worldtree. He stroked the treeling, both giving and drawing comfort. 'King Frederick sends his blessing. We may proceed,' he announced to the crowd.

Applause pattered like raindrops. Media troops turned imagers down to the gas giant, as if expecting something to happen immediately, on the King's command.

Dr Serizawa hurried over to his technician. At his signal, the terminus anchors were launched from orbit. Bright lights shot into the planetary body, tunnelling deep to where they would paint a wormhole target far below. The torpedo probes, developed from ancient Klikiss designs, vanished into the cloud decks, leaving not even a ripple.

Beneto watched, marking every detail, which he would pass on through prayer to the eager and curious worldforest. Though he was the second son of the Theron ruling family, he served little purpose here at Oncier other than to send instantaneous news of the ambitious test via the worldtrees, much faster than any standard electromagnetic communication, which even at the speed of light would have taken months or perhaps years to reach the nearest Hansa outpost.

Using the interconnected trees, any green priest could communicate with any of his counterparts, regardless of location. Any single tree was a manifestation of the whole worldforest, identical quantum images of each other. What one treeling knew, they all knew, and green priests could tap into that information reservoir whenever they chose. They could use it to send messages.

Now, while the spectators watched the wormhole anchors disappearing into the Oncier clouds, Beneto touched the treeling again. He let his mind melt through the trunk until his thoughts emerged in other parts of the worldforest back home. When his eyes focused and he returned to the observation platform, he looked up to see Chairman Wenceslas looking at him expectantly.

Beneto kept his face calm and dignified. His tattooed features were handsome and noble. His eyes had the vestiges of epicanthic folds, giving them a rounded almond appearance. 'My Father Idriss and Mother Alexa offer the prayers of all the Theron people for the success of this test.'

'I always appreciate kind words from your parents,' Basil said, 'though I would prefer Theroc had more formalized business dealings with the Hansa.'

Beneto kept his voice neutral. 'The worldforest's plans and wishes do not always match the needs of the Hansa, Chairman. However, you would do better to discuss such matters with my elder brother Reynald, or my sister Sarein. They are both more inclined to business than I.' He touched the feathery leaves of the treeling, as if to emphasize his priestly status. 'As the second son, my destiny has always been to serve the worldforest.'

'And you do your job admirably. I did not mean to make you uncomfortable.'

'With the support and the benevolence of the worldtrees, I am rarely uncomfortable.'

The young man could imagine no other calling. Because of his high-born position, Beneto was expected to participate in showy events, such as this spectacle. He did not want to perform his priestly duties merely for *show*, however. Given the choice, he would rather have helped to spread the worldforest across the Spiral Arm, so the treelings could thrive on other planets.

Green priests were few, and their vital telink skills were in such demand that some missionary priests lived in opulent mansions, subsidized by the Hansa or colony governments, well-paid to send and receive instantaneous messages. Other priests, however, lived a more austere life and spent their time simply planting and tending treelings. That was what Beneto would have preferred to do.

The Hansa had begged to hire as many green priests as Theroc would provide, but the merchants and politicians were constantly frustrated. Although Hanseatic envoys insisted that priests must serve the needs of humanity, Father Idriss and Mother Alexa had no interest in expanding their personal power. Instead, they allowed the priests to choose their postings for themselves.

Carefully selecting healthy specimens from the sentient forest on Theroc, the priests distributed treelings on scattered colony worlds or carried them aboard mercantile ships. More than sunlight and fertilization, the worldforest hungered for new information, data to store in its sprawling, interconnected web of half-sentience. The mission of the green priests was to spread the worldforest as far and wide as possible – not to serve the Earth-based trading conglomerate.

For generations, Hansa researchers had tried to understand instantaneous quantum communication through the interlinked trees, but they had made no progress. Only the worldtrees could provide telink, and only green priests could communicate through the forest network. The insurmountable problem drove the scientists into a frenzy of frustration.

Despite all the technology and manpower the Hansa had poured into the Klikiss Torch test, none of it could begin without a single mystic priest and his tree . . .

Now, aboard the technical observation platform, Chairman Wenceslas clasped his well-manicured hands in front of him. 'Very well, Beneto, contact your counterpart at the neutron star. Tell them to open the wormhole.'

Beneto touched the tree again.

SIX

ARCAS

Halfway across the Spiral Arm, another green priest waited with six Hansa technicians in a small scout ship in a stable spot beyond the gravitational pull of the neutron star.

The superdense stellar remnant was all that remained of a collapsed red giant that had run out of momentum and mass before it could become a black hole. Curling space with its powerful gravity, the neutron star rotated like a searchlight, jets of high-energy particles spraying from its poles like water from a fire hose. Such a tiny ball, less than ten kilometres across, yet with a celestial powerhouse of energy.

Crowded in the ship, the six techs were nervous and sweating. The tethered torpedo device had been deployed outside the ship, just waiting to drop into the crushed star's gravitational mouth. The techs stared at Arcas, as if the green priest could ease their fears or offer them some sort of short cut.

'Time?' one asked, as if pleading.

The treeling beside him had not yet spoken. Arcas sighed. 'I will tell you as soon as I hear.'

Before long, he would return to Theroc, where the priests would give him some other duty to serve the worldforest. It was all the same to Arcas, though he had chosen this assignment – far away, and involving relatively few people. As a green priest, he could do nothing else. He was a loner, but he was also a green priest, linked with the forest, though it had never been his first choice. If only he could trade with someone who felt more devotion for the task.

He clenched the treeling's rough bark, but felt no incoming telink message. Nothing. More waiting. 'Not yet.'

Aboard the cold scout ship, the spaces were too confined, the walls too bare. The stored air tasted of processing filters, with none of the moist richness he was accustomed to breathing in the dense forests. Yet, even on Theroc Arcas felt none of the passion that most green priests did. He might have chosen another life entirely, but now his skin bore the green tinge of symbiosis, a subcutaneous algae that allowed him to photosynthesize bright light. The process was irreversible, and he would always remain linked to the worldforest, even if being a green priest was not what he truly wanted.

Arcas had become an acolyte to honour a deathbed promise to his father, rather than out of his own interests. Green priests were in such demand that even a mediocre one such as Arcas could choose from innumerable offers of employment. On Theroc, the elder green priests helped to make such decisions, and Father Idriss and Mother Alexa interacted with the Hansa. But each green priest – even Arcas – could tap into the overall forest mind and make his or her own choices. Among the numerous offers, opulent positions, important diplomatic and liaison posts, Arcas most wanted to be away from all the bustle. He had chosen to be here in this isolated station.

'Time?' another tech said, sounding even more anxious. 'Why are they waiting so long?'

After communing through telink, Arcas refocused on the eager technicians. 'They say they are ready at Oncier. You may launch the probe now.'

Working with machinery incomprehensible to the green priest, the Hansa techs scrambled to release the tether and activate the Klikiss wormhole-generating device. The probe separated from the scout ship and accelerated towards the neutron star, picking up speed as it coasted down the steep space-time slope.

The technicians cheered when the anchor point was established close to the beacon of the neutron star. They read off results in a breathless hurry because they didn't know how long the torpedo device could remain in position against the furious gravitational tug-of-war.

Arcas watched, filing away images to transmit back to the worldtrees and all the other green priests. The trees were more interested than he was.

'Activate!' said the head technician.

The torpedo device used ancient Klikiss technology to distort, ripple, and then tear a yawning hole in the fabric of space. The maw of the wormhole tunnel was wide enough to engulf the superdense star.

Arcas muttered to the treeling, describing every step of the process – until even he became speechless as the new wormhole literally swallowed the blazing neutron star, like a pebble falling down a drain.

The torpedo generator gave out, its energy exhausted, and the wormhole slammed shut, sealing space-time without leaving a mark in the emptiness that had held the exotic celestial object.

'There. It is done.' Arcas looked to the technicians, who began to cheer wildly.

The gauzy remains of the gaseous accretion cloud drifted away like wispy scarves, no longer held in place by chains of gravity.

Like a bomb of unimaginable magnitude, the neutron star hurtled towards Oncier.

SEVEN

MARGARET COLICOS

L ouis adeptly jostled the other observers so he and Margaret could get a ringside seat of the planetary implosion. Basil Wenceslas stood beside them. 'We'll know within moments,' he said. 'The green priest says the wormhole has opened on the other side. The neutron star is on its way.'

Dr Serizawa, his bald head slick with perspiration, looked from the observation window to the recorders and interviewers. 'The receiving end of the wormhole is anchored at the gas giant's core. When the superdense star hits Oncier, it'll be the most titanic burst of energy mankind has ever unleashed.' Then he added quickly, gesturing again, 'But don't worry, it'll take hours for the shock wave to travel through the layers of the atmosphere. We're far enough from Oncier that we'll suffer no effects.'

The incredible mass of the neutron star arrived at the gas giant's metallic core like a cannonball, adding enough mass and energy for ignition. Serizawa saw the readings and cheered. Sunken probe buoys sent pressure, temperature, and photonic readings, displayed as violently jumping patterns on the screens. His technicians waved their hands in triumph. Though Oncier's outer skin remained as calm and placid as before, titanic changes were convulsing through the innermost layers. Basil Wenceslas applauded, and the dignitaries followed suit.

'The neutron star is much tinier, but vastly denser, like a diamond inside a marshmallow. Even now, Oncier's material is falling inwards.' Serizawa looked at his readings, then at his chronometer. 'Within an hour at most, it will achieve the density necessary to begin hydrogen fusion, the energy-transport process used in any normal star.'

Margaret squinted at the spherical fingerpainting that was a soon-to-be sun, yet Oncier was so huge that although the neutron star had slammed into the core, she could see no immediate change. Markers and detectors had been deployed at various cloud layers, where they would sense the shock wave of outrushing radiation.

Margaret leaned forward to kiss Louis's weathered cheek. 'We did it, old man.' The two archaeologists had done their work at the beginning; now they could sit back and watch the end results. Cosmic chaos was even now occurring in the depths.

'So, Doctor, just adding all that weight is enough to start the planet burning?' asked a media rep standing behind her.

Serizawa replied, 'Actually, it's mass, not weight. But no matter. You see, the sudden transfer of the neutron star to the planetary interior gives it an immediate negative energy – potential energy, actually. To obey conservation laws, a huge influx of kinetic energy is required, which appears through wormhole thermodynamics as heat. *That* touches off the reactions to inflate the gas giant into a burning star. It will happen in a snap.' His eyes flickered. 'Well, within a few days, but you have to put everything in perspective.'

Normally, heat transport in a star was incredibly slow. Photons took a thousand years to radiate in a drunkard's walk outwards from the core to the surface, impacting with gas molecules along the way, being absorbed and then re-emitted to collide with another gas atom.

'Oh, just watch,' Serizawa said, 'and you'll see what I mean.'

The fascination of the news media waned within a few hours. The changes were slow, although the gigantic ball was indeed imploding. Detectors deep within the atmosphere showed the nuclear fires spreading outwards like a tidal wave. When the wave reached the planetary surface, Oncier would begin to shine like a light bulb.

The first flickers of lightning and fire began to show through gaps in storm systems. Pastel discolourations swirled about, displaying titanic upheavals deep below. Margaret's translation of Klikiss records had led to this spectacular event, but she didn't know whether to be proud or horrified at what she saw.

The Ildiran septa acknowledged the success of the Klikiss Torch. Dressed in formal uniform, the alien Adar Kori'nh shuttled over to the observation platform to watch the continuing stellar collapse. Margaret met the Adar with curiosity and trepidation, having never before spoken to an Ildiran.

'Your command of English is excellent, Adar. I wish I had such proficiency in languages,' Margaret said.

'All Ildirans are bound by a common speech, but those of us likely to encounter humans have learned your common trade language. The Mage-Imperator requests it of us.'

Taking advantage of the listener, Louis talked at great length with Kori'nh, describing their work on the Klikiss planets. 'The Ildiran Empire has been in existence far longer than humans have explored space, Adar. Why is it then that your people have not sent prospectors or archaeologists to learn of this vanished race? Are you not curious?'

Kori'nh looked at him as if the question was disconcertingly strange. 'Ildirans do not send out solo explorers. When we dispatch a colony of settlers, called a "splinter", it is a group large enough to continue our society. Solitude is a human trait that we find difficult to comprehend. I would never choose to be so far from other members of my race.'

'My wife likes to be alone so much she often prefers to be in a different section of a dig even from myself.' Louis smiled over at Margaret.

Embarrassed, she gave him a slight nod. 'I believe, Louis, that Ildirans all share a faint telepathic link that binds them together. Not as a hive mind, but as a support system. Isn't that true, General?'

'We call it *thism*,' Kori'nh said, 'and it radiates from our Mage-Imperator. He is the knot that binds the threads of our race. If any individual strays too far from the others, that thread might snap. Perhaps humans see travelling alone as an advantage. Conversely, I pity your race for not living within the safety net of the *thism*.' Kori'nh bowed, his expression unreadable.

A scattered murmur of surprised conversation drew them back to the window. A bright plume bubbled up from Oncier like a geyser of superheated gas. The event was unusual, though as it faded, so did the audience's interest. Within an hour, Margaret was the only one watching through the broad window. She found the roiling fury of Oncier hypnotic. The planet glowed now, spreading photons around the still-imploding world.

She stared at the planet's bright limb, a hazy curve against the backdrop of space opposite from the Ildiran warliners and the observation platform. Suddenly, several incredibly fast spherical objects streaked out like shotgun pellets. They emerged from deep within Oncier's clouds and soared off into open space. Within seconds, the dwindling dots disappeared into the distance.

Margaret gasped, but no one near her had seen the apparition.

It couldn't possibly be a natural phenomenon . . . but how could it be anything else?

She turned, alarmed and confused. Louis was still involved in conversation with Adar Kori'nh and Basil Wenceslas, discussing details of their upcoming expedition to Rheindic Co, the numerous Klikiss mysteries, the strange robots who still functioned but claimed no knowledge of their creators. Dr Serizawa stood by his technicians, monitoring endless images of the burning planet. From their expressions, they had obviously seen the apparition, too.

She went over to them. 'What was that, Dr Serizawa? Did you see—'

The man looked at her with a distracted smile. 'It will require detailed analysis, naturally, but do not be alarmed. The secondary and tertiary effects of the Klikiss Torch are not at all understood. Remember, in the extreme high-pressure cores of a gas supergiant, common gases can be compressed into metals, carbon is smashed into diamond.'

He looked back down at the monitors, where the observation platform's imagers replayed the fuzzy recordings. Unfortunately, the strange objects had emerged from the opposite side of blazing Oncier. 'I would not be surprised if we saw some sort of deep-core metallic nodules, exotic debris ejected in the turmoil after stellar ignition. I would not be overly concerned, Ms Colicos. The performance of your Klikiss Torch has met or exceeded all expectations.'

Margaret frowned. 'They looked like ships to me, artificial constructions.'

Now Serizawa's expression became somewhat condescending. 'That would be highly unlikely. After all, what sort of life form could possibly survive within the high-pressure depths of a gas-giant planet?'

EIGHT

RAYMOND AGUERRA

In the Palace District, crowds gathered and cheered, vendors hawked souvenirs, and food preparers sold extravagantly priced treats. A profusion of festival bouquets filled the air with heady perfume, though troops of maintenance workers and gardeners would be sure to remove the flowers before their colour and freshness began to fade.

Raymond Aguerra glided deftly through a forest of elbows and arms. The young man didn't worry about pickpockets because he could sense any dipper, outwit him, and dodge away before the guy could make a grab. Besides, his pockets were empty. Raymond just wanted to see the sights and look for opportunities, especially in a gaudy celebration like this. With the right opportunity, an ambitious and good-natured kid could make something of himself.

He was an intelligent and embarrassingly handsome fourteen-year-old with dark hair, a thin build, and a bright smile. Raymond had few friends and even fewer advantages, except for the ones he found for himself. A hard life had made him as muscular as a greyhound, which often surprised people who challenged him, though he preferred to talk fast and turn the tables rather than get into a brawl.

He ducked and slipped forward so smoothly the front-row spectators didn't even notice a new wide-eyed person standing among them. Because every day was a struggle just to provide for himself, his mother, and brothers, he paid little attention to politics. But he liked to watch the shows. Overhead, dirigibles, gliders, and balloons carried aloft those who could afford an expensive bird's-eye view of the Palace grounds. Gongs were rung, even more deafening than the cheers of the audience.

He watched a flurry of bright court uniforms – royal guards and ministers setting up a speaking stage on the grand balcony of the Whisper Palace. As a Unison deacon read a familiar invocation and prayer, salutiers unfurled the brilliant banner of the Terran Hanseatic League, an icon of Earth at the heart of three concentric circles.

Looking no more impressive than the court functionaries except for his too-extravagant robes, an old man stepped ponderously on to the balcony, as if he had taken the time to rehearse every footstep. When the King raised his hands high, the billowing sleeves of his lush garment drooped to his elbows. Flashes of sunlight glittered from the rings on his fingers and the cut flatgems in his crown.

'Today I speak to you of a great victory for human ingenuity and drive.' King Frederick's amplified words boomed from speakers all across the plaza. He had the rich baritone voice of a deity, deep and resonating. 'In the Oncier system, we have caused the birth of a new star, which will shine its life-giving warmth and light upon four pristine worlds for the settling of humankind.'

The people cheered again after listening in an awed hush. Raymond smiled at their feigned surprise; everyone already knew the announced purpose of the gathering.

'The time has come to light four more torches in the Palace District!' As the echoes of his voice faded, the King made an extravagant gesture, his hand barely visible even to Raymond's sharp eyesight.

On most of the high points, pillars, and domes, crackling eternal flames already rose to the sky, as they did from the firefly chains of lampposts on the grounds. Each torch supposedly symbolized a Terran colony world that had signed the Hansa charter and therefore sworn fealty to the Old King.

'I give you these four new moons, which are named after my illustrious predecessors, the first four Great Kings of the Terran Hanseatic League: Ben!' With a boom, a blazing pillar of fire erupted from the point of a soaring tower on the walking bridge that spanned the Royal Canal. 'George! Christopher! And Jack!' As he said each name, a new torch bloomed on the top of an unlit tower on the great bridge span.

The ice hadn't even melted yet on the four moons, and the first terraforming teams wouldn't be landed until the tectonic upheavals stabilized. Still, Raymond delighted along with the audience, watching the King claim a quartet of new worlds. What a grand show!

Bands began to play, and mirrorized ribbon chaff twinkled like dandelion fluff through the air, dispersed by drifting zeppelins. King Frederick announced a day of raucous celebration. The population applauded any excuse for revelling. Maybe that was why they all loved their King so much.

Frederick hurried back into the quiet comfort of the Whisper Palace, and Raymond noted a bit of concern. The King seemed lonely, perhaps even unhappy, as if tired of living in front of so many eyes all his life. Raymond could sympathize with the monarch, since he himself spent every day completely invisible to the world at large.

He wandered among the stalls and souvenir vendors. On the facades of the Whisper Palace, broad friezes showed historical events: the launching of the eleven massive generation ships; the first contact with the Ildirans, who offered their stardrive and their galactic civilization. At specific times every hour, the holographic friezes moved, dramatizing the scenes like a glockenspiel. Statues around the fountain parks became animated: stone angels flapped their wings, historical generals rode horses that reared up on cue.

A flow of pedestrians streamed across the bridge, entering the Palace grounds. Raymond stared at it all, eyes sparkling. He felt the threat half a second too late.

Someone grabbed him by the back of his neck, vice-like fingers squeezing. 'So, he's here to steal things when the crowd's not watching, but he runs out on us when we have a more sophisticated job to do.'

Raymond squirmed enough to be able to see the speaker: an older boy with the unfortunate name of Malph scowled, while his stronger friend Burl clamped the grip even tighter on Raymond's neck. The fourteen-year-old twisted himself free of Burl's hold, but he didn't run. Not yet. 'Sorry, but I didn't put stealing on my list of things to do.'

'Stealing's beneath his delicate sensibilities!' Burl said with a snort.

'Nah, it's too easy,' Raymond retorted. 'Working hard for a living – now *that's* a challenge. You should try it sometime.'

Around them, the oblivious spectators danced, some kissed, many queued up in front of food stands. Malph kept his voice low, but he could have screamed and few people would have paid attention. 'Raymond, Raymond, why don't you just become a deacon if you've got such morality problems? And why couldn't you have just said no, rather than turning us in?'

'Crimson rain, I did say no, Malph. Sixteen times, if I remember

31

right. But you wouldn't listen. Breaking into a man's business and stealing his cash stash is not my idea of a career. You do it once, then it becomes easier to do it again.'

'I'm all for making it easier,' Burl said with a bitter laugh. 'It took quite some running to get away from the enforcers after you triggered that alarm.'

'And if you two were as good as you say, the enforcers would never have gotten close.' Raymond wagged his finger at them. 'See, I counted on your skill, Malph, and now you're telling me it was all an exaggeration.' He drew a deep breath, all of his muscles tensed, ready to sprint off or stay and fight. 'I don't suppose you'd believe me if I said it was an accident?'

Burl clenched his fists and seemed to swell in physical size. 'After we beat the crap out of you, maybe you can tell your mummy that was an accident, too.'

'Leave my mother out of this.' With tears in her eyes and gushing with worry for her oldest son, Rita Aguerra would make him feel far worse than any bruises.

Like a shark scenting blood in the water, Malph moved around, ready to grab Raymond, expecting him to run. Instead, Raymond did the unanticipated. He launched himself towards the larger Burl in a flurry of fists, hard knuckles, and sharp elbows. He fought without finesse, but he used every hard part of his body, from the tips of his boots to the top of his skull, and soon he had knocked a disbelieving Burl down to the flagstones. A whirl and a kick caught Malph in the stomach as the other bully charged towards his intended victim.

Enough to stall them, not hurt them. Enough to get away.

Raymond dissolved into the crowd before Malph and Burl could recover themselves. He had made his point. Either the two would leave him alone or they'd come back with reinforcements the next time. Sadly, it would probably be the latter.

Chuckling to himself, he sprinted across the bridge, crossing the Royal Canal. He brushed off his drab clothes, relieved to see that he had sustained not a single rip. His knuckles were skinned and his dark hair tousled, but at least he'd got out of the tussle without a black eye or any other noticeable injuries. Good enough to convince his mother that nothing serious had happened. She had enough other burdens to bear, and he did not want to add to them.

With his skill and speed, he could easily have stolen a few purses, picked a few pockets in the milling crowd, but Raymond chose not to do so. His family might be poor, but not desperate. And if he ever got caught stealing, facing his mother's disappointment would be much worse than the legal charges.

Raymond was the oldest of four boys and the man of the house, since his father had skipped town and signed aboard a colony ship when Raymond was eight years old. Esteban Aguerra had filed colony papers and a one-sided divorce decree at the same time, so that his wife received the paperwork only after the ship had departed. Raymond's father had gone off to the new colony world of Ramah, not because it was a particularly attractive place, but because it had been the first site available. Raymond bade him good riddance.

It was time to go home and help his mother with the meals and to put his younger brothers to bed. On his way through the Palace District, he paused and looked at the lush floral bouquets displayed everywhere. Some had tipped over in the jostle of the crowd, others would remain standing in their glory for a day or two, until the petals began to wilt. Then they'd all be discarded.

Despite his compunctions against stealing, Raymond's love for his mother outweighed any qualms about tucking one of the beautiful bouquets under his arm. He hurried home with the extravagant flowers, beaming with pride at how much his mother would enjoy them.

*

The young man did not see the Hansa operatives hired by Basil Wenceslas. They had been watching Raymond Aguerra all day long.

The unobtrusive men took numerous surveillance images of the lone boy and added them to their already detailed files.

NINE

ESTARRA

Though she was a daughter of the rulers of Theroc, Estarra did not know what she was destined to do with her life, even at the age of twelve.

Her three older siblings had known from youth that they were expected to learn leadership, enter the green priesthood, train as a commercial ambassador. A fourth child, though, had no set role. So Estarra mostly did as she pleased.

Full of energy, she ran barefoot into the forest, flitting through the undergrowth beneath the canopy of the always-whispering worldtrees. The ceiling of interlocked palm-like fronds did not so much block sunlight as filter it, dappling the forest floor in yellows and greens. Leaves and grasses caressed her golden-brown skin, tickling but not scratching. Her large eyes were always eager to make new discoveries and spot unusual objects.

Estarra had already explored every nearby path, amazed by the world around her. The spunky girl's actions occasionally earned her frowns from her older sister Sarein, who was enamoured with the world of business, politics, and commerce. Estarra didn't want to grow up quite so quickly as her sister, though.

Reynald, her eldest brother, was already twenty-five and well on his way to becoming the next Father of Theroc. Handsome and patient, Reynald studied politics and leadership; by tradition, he had always known he would become the next spokesman for the forest world. In preparation for assuming his impending mantle, Reynald had recently departed on an exciting peregrination to distant and exotic worlds, meeting the major planetary leaders, both human and Ildiran, before his duties chained him to Theroc.

Estarra's parents had never gone to the Ildirans' fabulous capital city of Mijistra under the seven suns, though their daughter Sarein – four years younger than Reynald – had spent several years being schooled on Earth and forging alliances with the Hansa.

Estarra's brother Beneto had always been destined to 'take the green' and become a priest of the worldforest. She looked forward to his return from Oncier, where he had watched the creation of the new sun.

Father Idriss and Mother Alexa had indulged her, perhaps too much, letting her find her own interests and get into all kinds of trouble. Her little sister Celli, the baby of the family, preferred to spend time with her incessantly chattering friends. Estarra was much more independent.

She ducked beneath sweet-smelling ferns and felt the tingle of wild perfume against her bronze skin. Estarra's hair was bunched in a chaos of braids and twists. She preferred this unfashionable style because it left few loose strands to catch on branches and twigs.

She trotted along, memorizing the way back home to the towering fungus-reef city where she lived. Estarra stood under the skyscraper-tall worldtrees, scaly-barked plants that throbbed with energy, stretching towards the sky as if planted in some giant's garden. Through cracks of the overlapping bark armour, treeling sprouts protruded like loose hairs.

The worldtree roots, trunks, and rudimentary *mind* were all connected. The feathery fronds reached hundreds of feet high, drooping to form an umbrella-like awning, each tree touching the next, to make the sky a tapestry of foliage. The fronds waved like eyelashes stroking each other. In addition to the humming insect sounds and calls of wild animals, a constant blanket of white noise settled over the forest, a rustling sound as soothing as a lullaby.

Worldtrees had spread across all the Theron land masses, and now ambitious green priests carried treelings to other planets so that the interlinked forest sentience could grow and learn. They prayed to it, a throbbing 'earth spirit' in a literal sense, and helped the forest sentience grow stronger.

Long ago – one hundred and eighty-three years – an Ildiran Solar Navy patrol had encountered Earth's slow-moving generation ship, the *Caillié*, and brought it to this untouched planet. All eleven of the old generation ships had been named for famous explorers. The *Caillié* had taken its designation from René Caillié, a French explorer of darkest Africa, who had disguised himself as a native in order to enter the mysterious continent. He had become the first white man to look upon the fabled city of Timbuktu.

Burton, Peary, Marco Polo, Balboa, Kanaka . . . Those generation-ship names had an exotic resonance for Estarra, but even tales of Earth's uncivilized days could not match the wonders the widespread colonists had found as they settled other worlds across the Spiral Arm. *Clark, Vichy, Amundsen, Abel-Wexler, Stroganov.* All of them had found homes with the help of the Ildirans, except for the *Burton*, which remained lost among the stars.

The inhabitants of the rescued *Caillié* had rejoiced upon seeing Theroc's verdant landscape, the sheer potential of this untamed world. This new home was more welcoming than any they had imagined during their generations of blind flight in search of any habitable star system. They had lived for centuries confined aboard a large sterile starship, and during all that aimless time the colonists and their descendants had little to do but look at images of forests and mountains. And Theroc was everything they had prayed for. The colonists had immediately suspected something unusual about these trees.

The *Caillié* had carried everything necessary to settle even the most hostile world, but Theroc proved to be fully cooperative. After the Ildirans deposited them here, the colonists set up prefabricated structures as an immediate and temporary settlement while biologists, botanists, chemists, and mineral engineers set out to assess what this remarkable world had to offer.

Luckily, the biochemistry of the Theron ecosystem was mostly compatible with human genetics, and the settlers were able to eat a great variety of native food. They were not required to engage in the massive labours of clearing and fertilizing land. The *Caillié* settlers found ways to work with the forest, discovering natural homes rather than erecting metal and polymer structures.

Decades later, by the time the Ildirans had established diplomatic relations with Earth, the Theron settlers had developed their own culture and established a firm foothold. Although Hansa representatives finally came to reunite them with the greater network of humanity, the Therons were perfectly happy to remain unaligned. When their ancestors had set out on the generation ship, they had never expected to go back, never dreamed of restored contact with Earth. They were a seed cast on the wind, hoping to take root somewhere. They did not intend to be uprooted . . .

As she paused in her explorations, Estarra ate messy handfuls of splurtberries and wiped the juice from her mouth and hands. Exuberant, she looked up at the nearest worldtree, where she saw handholds and markings of frequent ascents by acolyte reading-teams. The bark offered enough bumpy hand- and footholds that Estarra could scale it like a ladder, providing she didn't look down or think too hard about what she was doing. Up there, the green priests walked their highways across the resilient treetops and interlinked branches.

Estarra wore few clothes, for the forest was warm; her feet were callused enough that she needed no shoes. She ascended one handhold at a time, moving upwards, always upwards. Exhausted but exhilarated, she finally broke through the brushing worldtree leaves. Estarra stared out, blinking, into the unobscured sunlight, blue sky, and the endless treescape.

Even from up here, she could not tell where one individual tree ended and another began. Around her, she heard voices and songs, groaning chants and hesitant reading voices, a mixture of high-pitched and deep tones.

Balanced against the fronds, Estarra looked out at the gathered priests, tanned and healthy acolytes who had not yet taken the green, older emerald-skinned priests who had already formed a symbiosis with the worldforest. The acolytes sat on platforms or balanced on branches, reading aloud from scrolls or electronic plaques. Some played music. Others simply rattled off tedious streams of data, reciting meaningless numbers from tables. It was a dizzying hubbub of activity, with the priests entirely focused on increasing the knowledge and data held within the worldforest – a way to show reverence for and help their vibrant verdant spirit at the same time. Hundreds of separate voices spoke to the interconnected forest, and the worldtrees listened and learned.

So much to see and experience, and the green priests did it all by staying here, drawing blessings from the mind of the world-forest. Estarra wished she could comprehend everything the forest knew. The priests sang out poems or read stories, even discussed philosophical topics, delivering information in all forms. The worldtrees absorbed every scrap of data, and still the living network hungered for more.

TEN

PRIME DESIGNATE JORA'H

At the fringe of the sparkling Horizon Cluster, Ildira basked under the varying light of seven suns. The Empire's home planet circled a warm orange K1 star that was situated near a close binary pair – the Qronha system – composed of a red giant and a smaller yellow companion. More distant, but still dazzling in the Ildiran sky, hung the amazing trinary of Durris, a closely tied white star and yellow star with a red dwarf orbiting the common centre of mass. Finally, also distant, the blue-supergiant Daym shone like an intense diamond.

Night never fell on Ildira.

Mijistra, capital city and jewel of the ancient Empire, glittered under brassy skies. Its spires and domes were made of crystal and coloured glass, freeform architecture fashioned out of ultra-strong transparent polymers.

Prime Designate Jora'h, eldest son and heir to the Mage-Imperator, drew a deep breath of air perfumed with mists from the upwards-tumbling waterfalls that climbed to the Prism Palace.

As was his duty, the Prime Designate waited to meet the human representative from Theroc. The young man, Reynald, was Jora'h's ostensible counterpart, but in a much-diminished capacity. The human prince would become the ruling Father of a single wilderness planet, whereas the Prime Designate would eventually control the vast Ildiran Empire.

Jora'h raised both hands to greet the smiling man. 'Prince Reynald, I bid you heartfelt welcome to Mijistra.'

The broad-shouldered prince climbed the wide steps towards the receiving platform, flanked by burly members of the Ildiran soldier kith. A minimal escort of humans accompanied Reynald, including one of his personal green priests.

The Theron man had black hair, divided into braids that were gathered at the back of his neck. He left his well-muscled arms bare under a padded tunic made from an interesting pearly fabric that glistened in the light of multiple suns. He had a squarish face, flat cheeks beneath wide-set dark eyes. He wore a set of filter lenses to block Ildira's excess sunlight; the receiving committee had also given the visitors creams and screening lotions.

'Prime Designate, I've been looking forward to seeing Ildira for many years.' Reynald boldly reached out to clasp Jora'h's hand, as if they were equals. He had a warm and open manner about him, an attitude that melted the icy walls of formal ceremony.

Jora'h broke into a smile. He liked this young man almost instantly. 'Both of our cultures have much to learn from each other.'

Reynald looked at the shimmering curtains of water that leapt from the foamy pools at the canal edges and climbed invisible suspensor ladders into the domes and connected tubes. He laughed with childish delight. 'You have already impressed me, Prime Designate – though I could find a few impressive jungle oddities on Theroc, if you ever visited us.'

The Prism Palace stood atop an ellipsoidal hill that raised the Mage-Imperator's residence above the shining parapets, museum domes, and greenhouses of Mijistra. Seven rivers – long ago tamed by Ildiran engineers – flowed in perfectly straight lines towards the nexus of the Empire. Magnetic levitation fields and gravity-assist platforms nudged the current along, lifting the sparkling water uphill against gravity.

Reynald followed Jora'h into the entry gallery where blazers augmented the sunlight to banish every possible shadow. 'This is one of the last stops in my peregrination. I decided that I must understand other cultures and worlds in order to serve my people. Much like Tsar Peter the Great, one of our ancient leaders from a large country known as Russia. Peter travelled and learned from other cultures and took the best parts back home with him. I intend to do the same.'

The human's exuberance was infectious. 'An admirable goal, Reynald. Perhaps I should leave Mijistra more often myself.' It wasn't necessary for a Prime Designate to see other parts of the Ildiran Empire – but it might actually be fascinating. His own son and heir, Thor'h, had spent years fostered on the comfortable Ildiran pleasure world of Hyrillka.

'I have already been to Earth, where I met with Old King Frederick,' Reynald continued with an abashed smile, 'though he didn't quite know what to do with me. I also met with Chairman Wenceslas, who was very polite – mainly because he wants me to give him more green priests when I become Father of Theroc.'

'And now you have come here,' Jora'h said, gesturing forward. 'We will fill your eyes to bursting!' Laughing, he led Reynald and his entourage towards the nearest shimmering wing of the Prism Palace.

As the Prime Designate, Jora'h was endowed with a charisma and animal magnetism that made him extremely attractive. His lean face radiated charm. His eyes were smoky topaz, gleaming with highlights and reflections that gave his irises the eerie appearance of star sapphires. Long hair, a sign of male virility among Ildirans, wreathed his head in a mane made up of thousands of thin golden cornrows, braids like delicate chains that were alive and faintly mobile. They writhed with an unusual energy.

Human merchants, visiting dignitaries, scholars, even well-to-do tourists came to visit the fabled seven suns of Ildira. Since the Ildiran Empire had provided the Hansa with a fast stardrive, many humans revered them as benevolent patrons, paternal figures. While accepting the human race as part of the galactic story told in the *Saga of Seven Suns*, many Ildirans had trouble understanding human impulsiveness and drive.

But Jora'h found this one quite likeable. He and Reynald walked shoulder-to-shoulder into the promenade hall of arched ceilings and stained-glass mosaics. Rich colours vibrated around them, intense light shining through the primary filters of the stained-glass windows.

Reynald even spotted a single black Klikiss robot moving down a corridor on flexible legs, looking like a hulking mechanical beetle – the first one he had ever seen. None of the Ildirans paid it much attention.

At court, noble-kith women, as well as courtesans, artists, and singers, wore flowing diaphanous gowns with diagonal sashes across their breasts and shoulders. Striped sleeves extended down to the courtesans' knuckles, though they could be retracted into the curving shoulder pads.

Reynald smiled as they entered a large greenhouse banquet hall. 'Will I be able to meet the Mage-Imperator?'

The golden chains of Jora'h's hair fluttered of their own accord. He sighed apologetically. 'The Mage-Imperator of the Ildiran Empire cannot meet with representatives from every human-settled planet. There are so many of them! He is reluctant to give Theroc a greater status than other colonies in the Terran Hanseatic League.'

Reynald responded stiffly. 'Prime Designate, sovereign Theroc is an independent planet, not part of the Hansa.' Then he smiled. 'On the other hand, I think I'd enjoy your company more than your father's anyway.'

Jora'h's star-sapphire eyes twinkled. 'And the best part has not yet begun. I have sent for our greatest living historian.'

Inside one of the Palace's many gem-like domes, Jora'h gestured to a long table set with a thousand exotic dishes. Courtesans and servers flocked around them as they took their seats.

The courtesan females were smooth-skinned, hairless, with lovely patterns painted on their faces and long, delicate necks – swirling curves that swept past the alluring eyes to the tops of their heads like flowing waves of water or licking tongues of fire. As the courtesans walked, the fabric of their garments changed colour like living rainbows.

The women smiled politely at him, but beamed seductively at Jora'h. The Prime Designate had their full attention, as if he walked within a fog of pheromones.

'You are not married yet, Prince Reynald? Marriage is the accepted human custom, I believe, especially for royal families?'

'It is – and no, I have not yet chosen a woman to become Theron Mother beside me. There are political considerations as well as . . . romantic ones. On this peregrination I have received several offers of marriage from leaders of some of the Hansa colonies. All respectable, but I prefer to consider a variety of possibilities, since this is such an important decision.'

'I find it incomprehensible to spend so much time choosing a single mate.' Jora'h selected a plate of jellied fruit, tasted a bite, then offered it to Reynald, who happily sampled it himself. He raised his gaze to the hovering courtesans. 'It is my duty to have as many lovers as possible and father numerous children who carry the Mage-Imperator's bloodline. Committees and assistants aid me in

45

choosing among the thousands of candidates and verify their state of fertility when I mate with them.'

'Sounds exhausting,' Reynald said. 'And not terribly erotic.'

'A Prime Designate has his duties to suffer.' Jora'h chose a bowl of his favourite sliced fruits in steaming syrup. 'The Ildiran people consider it a great honour to breed with me, and I have more volunteers than I can possibly service in my lifetime. Everything will change for me when I succeed my father and become Mage-Imperator.'

'That must be exciting,' Reynald said.

Jora'h wore a contemplative expression. 'At that time I must undergo a ritual castration ceremony.' Reynald looked shocked, as the Prime Designate knew he would. 'Only in that way can I become the focus for the *thism* and see through the eyes of my race. I will give up my manhood and become a demigod, all seeing and all knowing. A fair enough exchange, I suppose.'

Reynald dabbed his lips with a formal napkin. 'I, uh, think I will endure my own problems of selecting a wife. I don't envy yours.' Servants whisked away the myriad untouched dishes when it was clear the two men were sated.

Jora'h clapped his hands. 'It is time for our rememberer.'

A small, older-looking Ildiran entered the room, wearing loose robes. He wore no gems, no facial adornment, no jewellery on his fingers or wrists. His face looked more alien than most of the Ildiran kiths, with fleshy lobes growing around his brow and cheeks, sweeping back along his hairless head.

'Rememberer Vao'sh is an historian in the Ildiran court,' Jora'h said. 'He has entertained me many times.' Vao'sh bowed, and Reynald nodded a welcome, not sure how to receive a rememberer, whether with an out-thrust hand or with applause. Jora'h continued, 'Our rememberers excel in performing portions of our *Saga of the Seven Suns*.'

'Yes, I've heard of your race's legends,' Reynald said.

Vao'sh spread his arms so that the sleeves of his robe flowed. 'Far more than just a set of scriptures and stories. The *Saga* is the grand epic of the Ildiran people. It is the framework by which we fit into the universe. Ildiran history is not just a sequence of events, but a genuine story, and we are all part of its intricate plot.' He swept an outstretched hand towards Reynald. 'Even a human prince such as you is included. Every person has a role to play, whether as a minor character or a great hero. Each of us hopes to live a life so significant that it will be remembered in the ever-growing *Saga*.'

Jora'h leaned back in his chair. 'Entertain us, Vao'sh. What story will you tell today?'

'The tale of our discovery of the humans is most appropriate,' Vao'sh said, widening his expressive eyes. He proceeded to speak in a captivating voice, in a rhythm that was more than poetry yet less than song.

Vao'sh summarized the familiar events of how the deteriorating Earth civilization had sent out eleven enormous generation ships that flew blindly towards nearby stars, each vessel filled with pioneers. Reynald was amazed at the tone of the historian's voice and at how his lobes flushed and changed colour to display a palette of emotions.

'Such glorious desperation! Such hope, optimism – or foolishness. Yet the Ildiran Solar Navy found you.' Vao'sh folded his hands.

When Vao'sh finished the tale of the humans' rescue, Reynald applauded loudly, and Jora'h, delighting in the strange custom, clapped his hands as well. Soon all of the courtesans and functionaries in the banquet hall slapped their hands together, making a deafening noise. Vao'sh's face coloured, as if he didn't know how to react.

'I told you he was a Master rememberer,' the Prime Designate said.

Reynald gave a wry smile. 'How ironic that Ildiran rememberers are the best ones to tell our story, instead of human historians.'

ELEVEN

ADAR KORI'NH

Though he commanded all the ships in the Ildiran Solar Navy, Adar Kori'nh still felt his chest grow cold with awe whenever he stepped into the presence of Mage-Imperator Cyroc'h. The deified ruler saw everything, knew everything, touching each Ildiran through his tendrils of telepathic *thism*.

And still he wanted to see Adar Kori'nh.

The ceremonial septa of warliners had returned from Oncier after having observed the astonishing Klikiss Torch. He had already transmitted images and reports, but now the Mage-Imperator wanted the words directly from his lips. Kori'nh could not refuse the command.

Bron'n, the Mage-Imperator's hulking personal bodyguard, moved behind the Adar. Since he was a member of the warrior kith, Bron'n's features were more bestial than those of other Ildirans. His hands sported claws, his mouth showed long, sharp teeth, and his large eyes could detect any movement, any threat to his revered leader. Adar Kori'nh, of course, posed no threat, but the chief bodyguard was incapable of lowering his state of alert.

The Mage-Imperator's private antechamber was hidden behind opaque walls at the rear of the skysphere, the nucleus for the Prism Palace's many spires, domes, and spheres. Kori'nh stepped into the lambent illumination of blazers where the enormous Mage-Imperator waited for him, reclined in his chrysalis chair. Bron'n sealed the doors. Despite his impressive rank, the Adar had rarely spoken alone to the Mage-Imperator, without an audience of advisers, attenders, bodyguards, and nobles.

Mage-Imperator Cyroc'h was like a male queen bee, a single being who could direct and experience his whole civilization from within the Prism Palace. He was the focal point and recipient of the *thism*, which made him the heart and soul of all Ildirans. But often, as now, the leader needed more precise details and eyewitness analyses.

Kori'nh clasped his hands in front of his heart in prayer and supplication. 'Your summons honours me, Liege.'

'And your service honours all Ildirans, Adar.' The Mage-Imperator had already shooed away the constant diminutive attenders who pampered him, oiled his skin, massaged his feet. His eyes were hard and impenetrable, his voice edged like a razor. 'Now we must talk.'

Nestled in his bed-like chair, covered in draping robes, the leader was large and soft. His fleshy skin hung in pale folds, his hands and legs weakened from lack of use. After his ritual castration many decades earlier, Mage-Imperator Cyroc'h looked vastly different from his handsome eldest son, Prime Designate Jora'h. By tradition, his feet never touched the floor.

Before renouncing the calls of the flesh, Cyroc'h had sired many children. As the paternal figure of the Ildiran race, he maintained an extraordinarily long braid, the cultural symbol of virility. The braid hung down from his head, across his shoulder and chest, draped like a thick hemp rope that twitched and flickered with faint nerve impulses of its own.

A Mage-Imperator could live for two centuries after he became the nexus of the *thism* and the repository of Ildiran knowledge. Cyroc'h had not deigned to walk for decades, allowing the rest of the Ildiran race to be his eyes and hands and legs. He had too much self-importance to be bothered by such things.

Resting in his enormous cradle-chair, he directed his attention towards the Adar. Kori'nh adjusted his uniform again, glad that he had taken the time to apply all the medals and ribbons, though very little could impress the great leader.

'Tell me what you witnessed at Oncier. I am already aware that the Terrans have ignited the planet, but I require your objective assessment. How much of a threat does this Klikiss Torch pose to the Ildiran Empire? Do you believe the Hanseatic League means to use it as a weapon against us?'

A thrill went through Kori'nh. 'A war against the Ildiran Empire? I don't believe the humans are such fools, Liege. Consider the sheer size and power of our Solar Navy.'

The Mage-Imperator's eyes gleamed. 'Nevertheless, we must not ignore their ambitions. Tell me about Oncier.'

The Adar spoke in gruff sentences, giving clear facts with occasional opinions or interpretations. Kori'nh had been bred to become a military officer, but he was not a rememberer, and his stories were simply recountings of what had happened, not entertaining legends to amuse great men.

The Mage-Imperator lounged on his platform, listening. His intelligent face was doughy, his cheeks round, his chin little more than a button swallowed in soft skin. His expression was beatific enough that some humans had compared it to the face of Buddha. He wore a timeless look of peace, confidence, and benevolence, but the Adar sensed a hardness of necessary cruelty hiding beneath the surface. 'So the event went precisely as the humans anticipated?'

'Except for one mystery.' Kori'nh hesitated. 'I must show you some images we acquired, Liege.' He removed a recording chit from his uniform belt and inserted it into a portable displayer that he held in both palms. 'While feigning minimal interest, our warliners imaged every moment of the planetary collapse. Then, as Oncier was engulfed in stellar flames, we saw *this*.'

Emerging from the deep cloud decks and racing away from the new-born sun, strange spherical objects glittered as if their skins were made of diamond. The transparent globes streaked away from the flaming clouds, moving faster than even an Ildiran stardrive could propel them.

The Mage-Imperator recoiled, his face expressing astonishment, even a glint of fear. 'Show it to me again.' His dark eyes were intent, hungry.

These objects came from *within* the gas planet, Liege. They are unlike any phenomenon ever encountered in my experience, certainly not any sort of spacecraft. I have read pertinent sections of the *Saga of Seven Suns* and scoured through other relevant records, but I have learned nothing. Do you know what this could mean, Liege?'

'I know nothing whatsoever about it.' The Mage-Imperator seemed angry, on the verge of an explosion, but he controlled himself.

Kori'nh had seen shock and recognition on the Mage-Imperator's face, and he wondered why the great leader would hide such information. But he also knew with utter certainty that no Mage-Imperator would ever lie to his subjects, and so he dismissed his doubts as a simple misinterpretation.

He bowed. 'That is my full report, Liege. Shall I distribute images of these strange objects to my other officers, so that we may better keep watch?'

'No. There is no need.' The Mage-Imperator's voice left no room for discussion. 'We must not overreact to a minor mystery.'

The leader stroked his long, twitching braid where it lay across his belly. He propped himself up so that he could look directly into Kori'nh's face, as if he had suddenly come to a decision. His tone became less intense, more conversational as he changed the subject. 'For now, I have another important mission for you – one that cannot wait.'

Kori'nh clasped his hands in front of his chest again. 'As you command, Liege.'

'You and the Solar Navy must rescue our splinter colony on Crenna. Bring them home to Ildira.'

Surprised, Kori'nh straightened again. 'What has happened?' He could not keep the hopeful sound out of his voice. 'Is this to be a military operation?' He had read many stories in the *Saga* and wanted to have his own part, however small, in an epic conflict.

'Crenna was barely large enough to be a true splinter, and now they are suffering from a terrible plague which has already killed a substantial portion of the colonists, including my Crenna Designate. Through the *thism*, I have felt their suffering – the sickness first blinds its victims, then kills them.'

'*Kllar bekh!*' Adar Kori'nh felt cold. 'That is terrible, Liege.'

The braid twitched again. 'Since the colony has dropped below the critical population density for *thism* to function, I have decided to abandon it. Rather than assigning more and more colonists to this hazardous place, we will remove our people.'

'It shall be done, Liege,' Kori'nh said. 'Rapidly and efficiently. I hope we can act quickly enough to prevent further loss of life. Are we to recover our equipment and buildings?'

'No, they are tainted with the disease. Also, the Terran Hanseatic League has bargained hard and negotiated well, and they have . . . acquired Crenna and all its resources from us. Their preliminary tests have made them confident they are not susceptible to this plague. Humans will move in to the empty settlement as soon as our people have been evacuated.'

Kori'nh was aghast, especially after having seen the outrageous experiment at Oncier that would provide them with four new moons to inhabit. 'What could the humans possibly need with a new planet? They have already spread like a disease across so many worlds.'

'It is all part of my plan, Adar. Better to let them have our leavings than to let them grow too ambitious on their own.'

Adar Kori'nh nodded. 'It is as I have warned for decades, Liege. We must never let down our guard. I suggest we maintain a careful vigilance.'

'I always do, my Adar,' said the Mage-Imperator. 'I always do.'

TWELVE

RLINDA KETT

As a successful merchant with five ships, Rlinda Kett was not accustomed to biting her nails and waiting in meek silence. Especially during an ambush. She stood next to General Kurt Lanyan on the bridge deck of the Juggernaut-class battleship, the most heavily armed vessel in the Earth Defence Forces.

While lurking in the empty silence of space, Lanyan had ordered the Juggernaut to shut down all its running lights and dampen its electromagnetic signature. The EDF battleship's dark hull plates of stealth material would keep them invisible, just a gravitational anomaly floating among the rocks at the outskirts of the Yreka system.

Waiting. They had already set their trap.

'How long have we been in position?' Rlinda said in a quiet voice.

'No need to whisper, Madame,' the General answered. His cheeks and chin were so smooth and clean that the skin looked slippery. When he focused his attention, his close-set icy-blue eyes seemed to drink in light and then reflect it back twofold. Lanyan indicated the tracker screen that showed the blip of Rlinda's cargo ship, the *Voracious Curiosity*, as it proceeded along the commercial flight path towards Yreka's inhabited planets. 'We can't hurry this. That bastard Sorengaard has to make the next move.'

'You'd best be certain to respond the moment he does, General.' Now that she no longer bothered to whisper, her booming voice carried an intimidating quality. 'That's my personal ship out there, and it's being piloted by my favourite ex-husband.'

'Your favourite one, Madame? How many of them do you have?'

'Ships or ex-husbands?'

'Ex-husbands,' the General growled as if she should have known his intent. 'I am already aware of how many ships you run.'

'Five ex-husbands, and BeBob is the best of the bunch, the only one who still works for me.' She still got along with Captain Branson 'BeBob' Roberts, personally and sexually. Besides, he was a damned good captain.

Space corsairs led by the outlaw Rand Sorengaard had recently captured one of Rlinda's merchant ships on the Yreka run, killing the crew and taking all of her supplies. Settled by one of the original generation ships, the *Abel-Wexler*, Yreka was near the edge of territory claimed by the Ildiran Empire, far from the core of the Terran Hanseatic League, which meant that neither race provided much surveillance or protection. But when Sorengaard's corsairs had taken to running down cargo ships, the Earth Defence Forces had vowed to root out and crush such flagrant lawlessness, even if it meant using Rlinda's ship and her favourite ex-husband as bait.

Rlinda was a black woman with an ample body, a big appetite, and a hearty laugh. She allowed people to draw their own stereotypes, which often led them to underestimate her; Rlinda was not quite as soft and roly-poly as she appeared. A shrewd businesswoman, she understood her markets and knew a thousand special niches. Other traders wasted their time looking for big strikes and monopolies on rare alien goods, but she preferred to make herself rich one small step at a time. Many merchants failed to pay off their vessels, but Rlinda had five ships – four, now that Sorengaard's asshole pirates had captured the *Great Expectations*.

The Yreka run had been one of her company's most lucrative routes, since the outlying colonists needed many basic essentials that Rlinda could provide at low cost. Now, though, with Sorengaard preying upon helpless vessels, few traders would venture into the area. Rlinda could have gouged even higher prices from the needy colonists; instead she preferred to take this risk, allowing General Lanyan to use her *Voracious Curiosity* as a bit of provocation.

She wanted to make a profit, certainly, but she also wanted business to run smoothly. Most of all, she intended to see justice done for her lost captain, Gabriel Mesta, and his crew.

Sitting in command aboard the giant Juggernaut, General Lanyan didn't have such high-minded ideals or moral reasons. He just wanted to kick some butt and teach these pirates a lesson.

Run by the Hansa, the EDF served as a combination police /security force, as well as a standing interstellar military. Unlike the Ildiran Solar Navy, whose large and ornate ships were mainly for show, blustering about and doing humanitarian deeds, Lanyan's EDF was more realistic in its purpose. They knew there would always be plenty of trouble among the Hansa colonies. Humans had never ceased to fight each other, finding religious or political reasons to squabble; when that justification failed, they simply grabbed one another's possessions or resources.

Stopping a rebel like Sorengaard, a man who had connections with the gypsy-like Roamers – now *that* was a perfect mission for the EDF. Sorengaard's pirates were also said to be Roamer exiles, all of which added to the Hansa's already prevalent suspicion against the gypsÿ people. Though the unruly nomads supplied most of the stardrive fuel used in commerce, the Roamers obeyed no law but their own and generally avoided participating in the political or social activities of other civilized humans.

'Picking up energy signatures, General,' said a tactical lieutenant at her station. 'A dozen of them. Small ships, apparently . . . but they seem to be carrying heavy weapons.'

'Battlestations,' Lanyan said. 'And keep running silent until I give the order.'

Soldiers scrambled about and pilots raced to the launch decks to board their fast-attack Remoras. Rlinda clenched her fists and drew deep breaths, thinking of BeBob. Her captain would be flying down towards Yreka, hoping to flush out the corsairs so the EDF could stop the pirates' depredations. Rlinda wanted to open a channel and shout a warning, but that would ruin the ambush. She prayed BeBob would be safe.

She watched as the unsuspecting corsairs ignited their engines and moved in towards their prey. Smiling, Lanyan opened the intercom channel to give orders to his soldiers. The General was too damned cock-sure.

After the corsairs closed in on the *Voracious Curiosity*, BeBob did his best to fly evasive manoeuvres towards the safety net of Yreka stations, but the overloaded cargo ship was full of material to make up for what had not been delivered during the *Great Expectations'* last scheduled run. BeBob's moves were sluggish.

Rlinda knew her captain must even now be panicked, sweating and swearing. Branson Roberts was not simply acting as bait; he was genuinely trying to escape, but he had no chance against the corsairs. Her heart went out to him. 'You'd better not blow this, General, or I'll have your balls.'

'Thank you for the vote of confidence, Madame,' he said, then shouted into the intercom, 'All Remoras, launch! Manta cruisers, proceed forward. Engage the enemy.'

Even as the greedy corsairs surrounded the single merchant ship, the EDF battlefleet pounced upon them. The squadron of fast-attack Remoras lunged in, targeting the pirates' unshielded engines. The corsairs were brave enough to face the minimal defensive capabilities of merchant ships, but they had no way of resisting the battle-ready Terran military force.

One of the small corsair ships broke away and tried to flee, accelerating so hard its white-hot engine cowlings began to vaporize into plasma, causing the pirate to veer off in an unstable flight path. With several jazer blasts, two Remoras destroyed the fleeing corsair before he could slip out of detector range.

Lanyan shouted into the ship-to-ship comm, 'I want some alive. Don't fry them unless you have no choice.'

A chorus of acknowledgements came over the speakers, and then the mid-sized Manta cruisers joined the fray. Flying fast, the Remoras opened fire with concentrated jazer pulses, and all hell broke loose.

Fed up with standing on the sidelines, Rlinda ran to the communications console and with one big shoulder knocked Lanyan out of the way. She adjusted the frequency to the *Voracious Curiosity*'s private channel. 'BeBob, get your ass out of there! If I don't see you moving out of the firing zone in five seconds, I'm going to come over there and do it myself.'

'Don't need to tell me twice, Rlinda,' BeBob's surprisingly firm voice answered, but she knew he was just putting on a brave mask. Branson Roberts could be cool in a crisis, but he was not a boulder-headed hero-in-training.

The *Voracious Curiosity* changed course to head down the Z-axis below Yreka's ecliptic and away from the battle zone. Not a scratch from a stray blast or a ricochet. Rlinda breathed a sigh of relief, but told herself it was only because she wanted the *Curiosity* to be clean and undamaged for her upcoming trip to Theroc.

The Mantas crippled the pirate ships, and Remoras rounded up the vessels in short order. One EDF pilot scorched his hand when a control panel sparked out due to a malfunction that had been missed during the recent inspection overhaul. That man became Lanyan's sole casualty.

The corsairs' hodgepodge of ships hung corralled within the surrounding barricade of EDF vessels. The spacecraft looked old and patched, strange designs assembled from mismatched components and mixed-up blueprints. Their hulls were scarred, their engines damaged in the recent fight.

'I want all prisoners shuttled over to my Juggernaut,' Lanyan said. 'Bring them to the cargo bay. Make sure you put neural clamps on their wrists and strip them of all weapons.'

Next, EDF soldiers began the most dangerous part of the operation, boarding the nine remaining corsair vessels and taking prisoners. While they removed the pirate crews, leaving the ragtag vessels guarded by designated troops, one corsair captain initiated a critical overload, attempting to blow up his vessel and vaporize any EDF forces within range. But the botched self-destruct routine succeeded only in melting down the engine core, burning through the hull, and shooting out a narrow jet of fire. The unexpected venting made the corsair ship careen out of control like a whirligig, until it finally sputtered out and drifted in space, dark and ruined, not even worth the salvage.

Rlinda accompanied General Lanyan to the Juggernaut's cargo bay, where thirty-one prisoners were brought forward. The men stood helpless with angry eyes and tattered shirts, hands bound, rich in dignity but poor in common sense.

'Which one is Rand Sorengaard?' Lanyan swept his ice-blue eyes across them, working his jaw to contain his indignation. 'And don't play any stupid tricks. You'll all face the same punishment anyway.'

The men glanced at each other, trying to look haughty, jaws clenched, eyes blazing. Several of the pirates appeared ready to step forward in a foolish attempt at bravery, but a tall, lantern-jawed man volunteered first. He looked at the others with the sure, confident gaze of a leader. 'You men stand down. I'll face my own crimes.' He turned to Lanyan. 'I'm Rand Sorengaard. I don't recognize your authority to arrest me.'

'Aww, are you trying to hurt my feelings? Maybe you'd better make your excuses to this lady here.' The General put a hand on Rlinda's shoulders. 'You stole one of her ships and killed her crew. Did you ask those people if they recognized *your* authority?'

'We were acquiring needed resources,' Sorengaard said. 'You call us pirates, and yet the Big Hansa Goose has imposed tariffs and trade restrictions on anything the Roamers import and export. You people simply wrap your thievery in political nicety.'

Lanyan's lips formed a grim line. 'Then let's put an end to any further nicety.' Out here on the fringes of the Hansa, the General had the authority to use whatever methods he deemed necessary. 'Some of your corsairs saw fit to take their own lives during capture. I can't argue with that. Now I will pronounce my own sentence upon the rest of you. First, you have been caught red-handed in the act of piracy. Moreover, the evidence clearly shows you are guilty of murdering the captain and crew of the *Great Expectations*, and probably other ships as well.'

He gestured towards the access airlock hatches at the far end of the cargo bay. Those chambers were used for space combat troops, after suiting up and engaging their personal weapons, to exit from the battleship and proceed to zero-G combat exercises. 'Your punishment is death, swift and sure, with no malice and as painless as I can reasonably make it.'

Though the sentence made her heart heavy, Rlinda was not surprised. The corsairs didn't even argue, simply glared at General Lanyan.

'Because the rest of you have made the mistake of following Rand Sorengaard, he will be the one to dispense your sentence. Each of you, one by one, into the airlock. Sorengaard, you will eject them into space.'

'I will *not*.' The pirate leader raised his lantern jaw. 'Torture me as much as you will, but I refuse to be your pawn.'

One of the corsairs spoke up. 'Do it, Rand. I'd rather have you push the button than one of these filthy Eddies.' The other pirates muttered agreement. Three spat on the deck, trying to hit Lanyan but missing by at least a foot.

One man broke away from the line and moved towards the airlock hatches. 'Don't let them gloat, Rand. This is the only choice they'll let us have.'

The pirate leader looked at his captured crewmen and seemed to see what he expected to find in their expressions. Then he turned back to the General. 'This is no victory for you.'

The first man went to the hatch, but Rlinda couldn't decide whether he was the bravest of them all, or if he felt it might be worse watching the others die before him. A uniformed soldier opened the airlock hatch, gesturing inside as if he were a formal maître d'.

'We could do two or three at once, General,' said a lieutenant.

'No,' both Lanyan and Rand Sorengaard answered in unison.

'Flung out into space . . .' the first man muttered, but his voice did not quiver with fear. 'I guess that's the closest a Roamer will get to going home.'

'Go find your Guiding Star,' Sorengaard said.

The soldier sealed the hatch shut and Rlinda turned away, not wanting to look through the windowplate. Though she hated what these pirates had done to her ship, her innocent crew, she could not watch the air being drained away. Explosive decompression would cause the man's soft tissues to burst before his lungs and his blood began to boil and freeze at the same time.

Rand Sorengaard muttered a prayer or a farewell under his breath and then hammered the release button without hesitating. The first of the captured corsairs was gone.

Cold and horrified at the brutal justice, Rlinda spoke quietly to Lanyan, who stood at attention as if he did not want to be disturbed. 'You've made your point, General. Is that not sufficient?'

'No, it is not, Madame. The sentence is just, and you know it.' He watched as the second pirate was manhandled into the airlock and the hatch sealed behind him. 'Space is vast, and lawlessness can grow unmanageable if left unchecked. My mission is to respond with sufficient vehemence to provide a credible deterrent.'

He looked at the colourful, exotic clothing the corsairs wore and stared out at the viewscreens. In space, the mismatched and weirdly modified pirate ships hung together, manufactured to the Roamers' own strange specifications. His teeth pressed together, as if he didn't want the insulting words to come out of his mouth. 'Damned Roachers!'

After all the corsairs had been similarly executed, General Lanyan himself ejected Rand Sorengaard from an airlock hatch, then turned to his Remora pilots standing in the Juggernaut launching bays.

'One more step to go, men. Scout the vicinity and gather all the frozen bodies. Bring them back inside so we can incinerate them properly.' He looked over at Rlinda Kett. 'We're in close proximity to a shipping lane here. No sense in leaving navigation hazards.'

THIRTEEN

JESS TAMBLYN

R iding the lemony-tan clouds of Golgen, the Roamer
skymine left a wide wake as it scooped up misty resources.
The harvester complex – a sprawling cluster of reactor
chambers, gathering funnels, storage tanks, and separable living
quarters – was similar to hundreds of other skymines run by the
nomadic Roamers above gas-giant planets across the Spiral Arm.

The extended clans operated on the fringe of the Hanseatic
League, aloof and independent. Families captained their own
skymines or operated resource stations in the detritus of planets no
one else wanted.

Roamer skymines harvested vast amounts of hydrogen from gas
planets, giant reservoirs of resources accessible for the taking. They
ran millions of gaseous tons through ekti reactors using an old
Ildiran process. Through catalysts and convoluted magnetic fields,
the reactors converted ultra-pure hydrogen into an exotic allotrope
of hydrogen. *Ekti*.

Ildiran stardrives, the only known means of faster-than-light
travel, depended on ekti as their power source. Huge amounts of

hydrogen were needed to create even minimal quantities of the elusive substance. Because of their close family ties and their willingness to operate on the edge, Roamers were able to provide ekti more cheaply and reliably than any other source. The dispersed clans had successfully exploited the commercial niche.

More successfully, in fact, than anyone in the Hansa realized.

After Jess Tamblyn's cargo escort docked with the Blue Sky Mine, the hatches were locked down, airlocks connected, bolts secured. The cargo escort was little more than a spider-like frame of engines and a captain's bubble; when the framework was fastened to the skymine's storage tanks, Jess could pilot containers of condensed ekti to distribution centres. Even performing a trivial job like this, he always did his best, going beyond what was expected of him, setting a good example.

When all the indicator lights glowed green, he formally requested permission to come aboard his brother's skymine. The Roamer workers teased Jess until he entered a set of override commands and stepped aboard anyway. He shrugged back his hood, patted down his many pockets, then gave a shake of his shaggy brown hair. 'So, if you recognized me, where's the red carpet?'

One of the production engineers, a gruff middle-aged man from the Burr family, gave a good-natured curse. 'Shizz, you've been promoted to cargo driver, I see! Does that mean you've had a fight with your father?'

Jess flashed a rakish smile. 'I can't let my brother get into all the disagreements with my family.' He was handsome, blue-eyed, with a vibrant personality that made him appear energetic and relaxed at the same time. 'Besides, somebody competent has to take the load to the distribution ships. Can you think of a better pilot?'

The Burr engineer waved a dismissive hand. 'You're just shuttling ekti to the Big Goose. They wouldn't know a good pilot from a blind farmer.'

The deprecating reference to the Hansa came from the original albatross-like configuration of the early Terran trading ships – meant to look like eagles but shaped more like fat geese. The name of the Hansa chairman who had tried to make the gypsy colonists sign the Hansa Charter, Bertram Goswell, had further added inspiration. Roamers found the term to be suitably insulting.

Jess shrugged. 'No matter. I like to find excuses to see my brother, make sure he's not making too many mistakes.' He didn't say out loud that he also seized upon any legitimate reason to escape the stern scrutiny of his father. Old Bram Tamblyn layered heavy pressures and responsibilities upon Jess, now that his older brother was no longer welcome as a member of the clan. The young man held on to those expectations as an anchor and never put his own wishes forward, even if old Bram rarely noticed.

As the cumbersome facility cruised along through Golgen's clouds, workers tended the ekti reactor controls, checked the distribution pipes, and lubricated mechanical systems that needed constant maintenance. Jess walked through the cargo bay, listening to the comforting hisses and hums, the industrial music made by all skymines. He loved being here. Blue Sky always seemed to be cleaner and more polished than any other skymine. Ross, Jess's brother, was immensely proud of what he had accomplished here.

Jess trudged down the corridor, needing no help in finding the captain's deck. Even on the workshift, Roamers wore colourful, many-layered outfits composed of scarves, billowing sleeves, hoods, and hats. Every tunic, vest, and set of trousers was adorned with frills of pockets and pouches, clips, chains, and hooks for storing a thousand gadgets, testing devices, or hand weapons. The clips kept tools in place and readily at hand, even in the low-gravity environments where Roamers spent a great deal of their time.

'How long you staying, Jess?' asked a shift supervisor who came forward through the bulkhead from his office chamber.

'Less than a day. We've got a supply run and a quota to meet. Obligations, you know.'

The supervisor nodded. 'We'll tune up your cargo escort and link all the struts to the ekti tank.'

'Is Ross outside on the deck sightseeing again?'

'No. I think the chief's in the navigation bubble.'

'What's he worried about hitting in this big open sky?' Shaking his head, Jess scrambled up the interdeck ladder until he found the navigation bubble. Though Ross had forever turned his back on the family water industry on Plumas, Jess always felt welcome here on his older brother's facility.

Placing his hands on his hips, he stared at the back of Ross's head. His brother was intent on the controls, peering into the clouds of the planet's incomprehensibly vast and open sky. Vaporous convection currents rose up and tumbled down as the skymine continued along its random path. An asterisk symbol had been painted above the navigation panel. It was the Guiding Star, which the Roamers believed directed the paths of their lives.

'Afraid of crashing into an angry concentration of nitrogen? Or do you just like sitting in the captain's chair and driving this big hulk nowhere?'

Ross spun, and his face lit up in a smile. 'Jess! I wasn't expecting you.'

'Decided to save you the wages of a cargo hauler.' He came forward to embrace Ross. 'Help you pay off that big debt – just another part of my responsibility as your little brother.'

Ross indicated the sensor panels. 'For your information, there's an art and a skill to piloting a skymine. I still have to adjust course, raise or lower the ship. A good captain always watches for dense concentrations of gases.'

The skymine trailed a squid-like network of probes; the kilometres-long threads drifted in the clouds, picking up data and helping Ross decide where to go. Golgen's atmospheric gases were rich with just the right mix of elements and catalysts for the Ildiran reactors to produce ekti. Also, the gas giant was close to star-trading lanes, which allowed for easy distribution of the fuel. After years of hard work, Ross was close to making a profit from his operation, despite their father's constant pessimism.

'I presume you've brought gossip?' Ross paused and added ironically, 'And of course, a sincere apology from Dad, begging me to come home?'

Jess laughed. 'If I'd brought that, I'd be here with a full Roamer celebration fleet such as the Spiral Arm has never seen.'

Ross gave him a bittersweet laugh. 'One of us is still off course from the Guiding Star. Let's go up on deck. I want to be out in the fresh air.'

They climbed through hatches, took a lift, and finally passed through a set of wind doors to a broad observation deck. The deck could be surrounded by an atmosphere field, but for now it was open to the sky itself. Ross frequently took the Blue Sky Mine down to an equilibrium level where the clouds were thick enough to be breathable and Golgen's atmosphere was warmed by internal thermal sources.

Jess drew a deep breath of the alien air. 'This isn't something I get to do every day.'

'I do,' Ross said.

The Blue Sky Mine, like all Roamer-designed factories, was composed of three main segments: the intake/feed tanks, the processing reactors and exhaust funnels, and the ekti storage spheres. As the skymine ploughed through the atmosphere, open nozzles sucked in raw gases and delivered them through processing machinery. After passing through the catalytic reactors, the rare hydrogen allotrope was siphoned off, while the waste gases spilled back out from the hot stacks.

Ekti was the only known allotrope of hydrogen, though other elements had varying molecular forms. Carbon manifested itself as powdery graphite, crystalline diamond, or exotic polymer spheres of buckminsterfullerene. Long ago, the Ildirans had discovered how to reconfigure hydrogen into a fuel that allowed their stardrives to function.

Before ambitious Roamers took over the ekti-harvesting industry, old Ildiran-model cloud trawlers had been much larger, hosting a minimal splinter community of sixty to ninety family units and requiring a gigantic infrastructure. Therefore, harvesting ekti had cost the gregarious Ildirans a great deal.

Independent Roamers, on the other hand, could operate skymines with a small support staff, which also allowed them to sell stardrive fuel at lower cost. The Ildirans had gladly surrendered their monopoly on ekti production, glad to leave the 'desert islands in space' and let humans have the misery to themselves.

The rest of the Hansa considered the Roamers to be little more than gypsy space trash, disorganized and disreputable. No one had an inkling of how incredibly wealthy the clans had become, since they kept such information hidden from outsiders.

A flutter of white wings went past Jess's face, startling him. He looked up to see a dozen doves flapping around the deck, swirling out into the sky and circling back to their perches and feed bins. 'I'd forgotten about the birds.'

'This is a perfect place for them. Look how far they can fly.'

'Yes, but where do they land?'

Ross rapped his knuckles on one of the railings. 'Back here.' Clouds extended for a thousand miles below them, but neither Ross nor Jess felt dizzy. 'They have nowhere else to go, so they always return. The best sort of cage.'

Fastening his insulated jacket against the chill, Ross gazed across the infinite distance like a feudal lord surveying his domain.

Jess pulled up his hood against the breeze. Behind them, exhaust plumes boiled upwards like thunderheads which rapidly dispersed into the cloud decks of Golgen. The two brothers stood side by side in comfortable silence.

During the lull in conversation, Jess sensed it was time for his gifts. He opened one of the pocket pouches on his right thigh and withdrew a thick golden disk engraved with symbols that matched the Tamblyn clan markings embroidered on Jess's and Ross's clothing. 'Tasia made this for you.'

Ross took it, looking with wonder at the beautiful device his younger sister had created. 'As usual, I'm impressed by her engineering skills . . . but I'll need to know what it *is* before I can use it.'

Jess pointed to the dial and the numbers. 'It's a compass. It can be normalized to any planet's magnetic field so you can always find your way. See, there's the Guiding Star.'

'Is my little sister implying that I'm lost?'

'It's just her way of showing that she misses you, Ross, though you'd never get through her tough-girl act long enough for her to admit it.'

Ross's grin grew. 'Yeah, I miss her, too.'

Jess reached into a second pocket and pulled out a small bound book with yellowed pages, most of which were blank, though some were covered with faded handwriting. 'An old-fashioned logbook used by sea captains to keep track of their journeys. It's from Dad.'

Ross slid the compass into one of his pockets and held the red leather-bound book with a combination of awe and scepticism. 'This is from *Dad*?' He flipped through the pages, looking at the handwritten words, then raised his gaze to meet Jess's. 'Somehow I don't believe that. He wouldn't give this to me. In fact, all the gifts you've brought over the past several years are just family treasures you smuggled out from Plumas, aren't they?'

Jess could not maintain an innocent expression. 'Would you have it any other way?' Ross held the logbook, pretending not to care, but Jess could see that the gift meant a great deal to him, even if it came from his brother rather than his father.

They both knew Bram Tamblyn very well. He was a stern and inflexible family leader, and for all his life he'd insisted on having everything precisely his own way. That attitude worked well enough with his employees in the water-mining operation under the ice sheets of Plumas. However, Bram Tamblyn's first-born son had turned out to be just as stubborn as his father. The two had got into frequent shouting matches for years, until finally, after he reached the age of twenty-two, Ross had had enough.

Old Bram had threatened to disown his son if he didn't bow to his wishes, and the young man astonished his father by calling his bluff. Tempers were high. Outraged, Bram vowed he would excise Ross from their clan, and so Ross offered to save him the embarrassment. He requested his portion of the family inheritance that was due him, and swore he would make his own success.

Jess had been there, along with Tasia. Though they intervened, trying to make peace between the two, the old man would hear none of it. Bram had got a calculating look in his eye – his clan's fortunes were increasing year by year, and if Ross took his inheritance now and quit his claim to all future income, he would surely come out the loser. So Bram tallied up his son's share and gave it to him, telling Ross never to ask for another penny.

And Ross had not. He had invested his inheritance wisely, taking over the operation of the Blue Sky Mine, which he ran with such grace and skill that it had nearly climbed out of debt by the time Ross turned twenty-eight. Old Bram pretended anger and chagrin but was secretly proud.

When Jess came to visit the skymining station, there was never any animosity between the brothers. On the other hand, thanks to

Ross's stubbornness, Jess would some day become the official head of the Tamblyn clan and inherit the lucrative Plumas water mines, becoming a powerful man in his own right. He didn't want it, but he would not let anyone down.

Ahead of the Blue Sky Mine, an anvil of greyish-rust cloud rose from the lower layers. Ross went to a set of controls and diverted the exhaust plumes, using them like attitude-control jets. The huge cloud trawler shifted its course and banked northwards so that they passed a yawning maelstrom of angry clouds.

'That hurricane could swallow a whole planet,' Ross said. Distressed, the pet doves fluttered behind the skymine, following their only roost.

'Just as long as it doesn't swallow this skymine,' Jess said. 'Any danger?'

'Not with me at the helm. When the winds get rough, I can always climb to a different layer.' He waited and then finally turned expectant eyes on his younger brother. 'So . . . did you bring anything from Cesca?'

Jess forced a light tone into his voice. This was the hardest part of everything he was expected to do. 'You think you need more than her love?'

'No, I suppose I don't.'

Jess wanted to change the subject, unable to shake the image of the beautiful Francesca Peroni, to whom Ross had been betrothed for years. 'Jhy Okiah has just filed a formal petition that legally names Cesca her heir as Speaker for the Roamers.'

'No surprise at all.' Ross looked proud, but his voice was businesslike. 'She's a very talented woman.'

'Yes, she is.' Jess closed his mouth to keep himself from saying more. It wasn't his place. Sadly, for more than a year Jess himself had been deeply in love with Cesca, and he knew the feeling was very mutual. Her betrothal to Ross had occurred long before she and Jess had met, and Roamer honour and politics would never allow her to break the engagement. Neither would Jess's sense of duty to his brother.

Besides, Ross had worked so hard to meet the difficult conditions he and Cesca had agreed on for their wedding. Jess would never do anything to hurt or embarrass his brother, and neither would Cesca. Both were loyal to Ross, and all of them were bound by the complex social restrictions of the Roamer culture. Jess had resigned himself to an unrequited love. He would stand strong and live without her, though Cesca would always be in his heart.

Ross had no inkling of his brother's attraction for his fiancée, and Jess had privately sworn never to let him discover that fact. The cost to all of them would be far too great.

After sharing a meal and playing a few rounds of stargames with three crew workers, Jess slept in a guest bunk. He left the Blue Sky Mine early the following morning, when Golgen's sun was just creeping above the fuzzy horizon.

Bidding Ross farewell, Jess detached the valuable load of stardrive fuel and began to pilot the cargo escort away from the Golgen system to a Roamer transport station, where it would be offloaded to Goose distribution ships.

He also carried gifts and letters from Ross because, after completing his delivery, Jess intended to make his way to the central Roamer complex of Rendezvous. With an ache in his heart but a neutral expression on his face, he would dutifully deliver his brother's romantic presents to Cesca Peroni.

FOURTEEN

CESCA PERONI

The Roamer yacht maintained its position at the arranged meeting point in empty space. The private yacht bore no markings to indicate that it carried the important Speaker for all Roamer clans, along with her protégé. Playing their political cards close to the chest, Roamers rarely resorted to emblems or trappings of power.

Cesca Peroni sat in the co-pilot's seat, monitoring the emptiness, keeping watch on her sensors. Distant stars glowed all around them, partially muffled by thin wisps of nebular gas. 'No sign of the other ship yet.' With large eyes, dusky skin, and a sense of humour matched only by her sense of duty, Cesca always kept both her mind and her eyes open.

Beside her the sinewy old woman, Jhy Okiah, stared through the windowport, as if she found every single star worth looking at. 'Patience, patience.' The ancient Speaker had vast reserves of inner calm and an intelligence that she never flaunted when speaking to others.

A light blinked on Cesca's control panel. 'Ah, here he comes.'

Jhy Okiah pursed her lips as she studied the starscape to pick out the tiny dot that heralded the diplomatic transport ship bearing the Theron heir, Reynald. For months, the son of Mother Alexa and Father Idriss had worked through intermediaries and scattered messages to arrange this meeting with representatives of the Roamers. His persistence had been admirable.

'He's finally getting what he requested,' Jhy Okiah said in her raspy voice. 'I can't help but chuckle at how astonished Chairman Wenceslas would be if he knew Reynald had gone to so much trouble just to see a few Roamers.'

Cesca looked at the Speaker. 'Perhaps this young man understands more about us than other human governments do.' Both women knew about Reynald's peregrination, and they respected the young man's interest in all significant societies of the Spiral Arm, including the oft-dismissed space gypsies.

Jhy Okiah frowned. 'Or perhaps we haven't been keeping our secrets as well as we think.' Though their nomadic society had many ships and a great deal of wealth, the clans kept their operations thoroughly confidential and avoided drawing attention to themselves.

The old woman's limbs were thin and her bones as brittle as dry bamboo, which required her to spend most of her time at the Roamer asteroid conglomeration of Rendezvous. Jhy Okiah had been married four times and had outlived every one of her husbands. She'd borne several children from each mate, so that she had a total of fourteen sons and daughters, fifty-three grand-children, and an ever-increasing number of great-grandchildren. The old Speaker didn't bother keeping track anymore.

Finally, the Theron diplomatic transport pulled alongside the Roamer yacht, deftly manoeuvring with jets and aligning the two vessels. After the airlock connections were attached, Reynald stepped across into the yacht's receiving area.

The Theron prince's dark hair was bunched together in a mass of braids. Tattoos stood out at his collar and along his neck. His handsome face broke into a polite smile before he bowed to the two women, eyes flashing at Cesca in obvious admiration. She fought back a flush from his open scrutiny.

'I apologize that we can't welcome you with more ceremony,' Jhy Okiah said, gesturing him into their small common chamber, which held refreshments, a table large enough to seat a few people, and little else. 'You must be accustomed to everything on a grander scale, coming from Theroc.'

Reynald spread his hands. 'At times I prefer a more intimate setting. Besides' – he looked at Jhy Okiah, then gave Cesca a longer, more intense smile – 'I wish to speak with you two, not a thousand others in an audience.'

After they exchanged sips of pepperflower tea and a few token gifts, Jhy Okiah took a seat and regarded him. 'You have whetted our curiosity, young man. Tell me, what have the Roamers done to arouse the interest of a prince of Theroc?'

Reynald leaned across the table, clasping his hands and seeming to exude an earnestness that Cesca didn't believe was an act. 'It's occurred to me that Roamers and Therons have much in common. We've both dodged the net of the Hansa. Theroc alone among the colony worlds remains independent. All others have signed the Hansa Charter. Roamers also live their own lives and govern themselves without Terran restrictions.'

Cesca said, 'That is because we both provide vital services – you with your green priests, and us with our ekti.'

Reynald raised a finger. 'But still, the trap is always there. Now, I'm not advocating any drastic change, because if we were to rouse the ire of the Hansa, there's no telling what desperate actions they might take. However, we could arrange a few minor alliances between our peoples, reciprocal concessions to strengthen our respective foundations.'

Cesca looked at Jhy Okiah, but the old woman maintained her focus on Reynald. 'I would not argue against having more security from the whims of Earth. You've obviously thought about this a great deal, young man.'

'As heir to the throne, I've had years to think about what I might do. Now I'm exploring some of my ideas.'

'And what are they?' Cesca asked.

Reynald frankly addressed their several joint concerns. 'Let me start from your perspective. Roamer skymines produce most of the ekti used in the Spiral Arm. Cargo escorts deliver ekti from skymines to transport stations, where it is distributed solely by the Terran Hanseatic League. Theroc and other human settlements have no other place to purchase ekti because of the Hansa's "benevolent monopoly". Why should they have such a stranglehold on ekti distribution?'

'Are you suggesting the Hansa is engaging in unfair trade practises?'

Reynald took a sip of his spicy tea. 'It is no secret that they recently imposed severe tariff increases and changed their policies, which was detrimental to Roamer business. Isn't that why Rand Sorengaard began preying on Hansa merchant ships?'

Cesca frowned. 'He is an internal problem among the Roamers. We have many clans and many strong-willed people. Occasionally, some of our people become . . . unruly. Unfortunately, even the Speaker can't keep control of them all.'

'And how would you change these trade practices, young man?' Jhy Okiah said, returning the conversation to the business at hand.

'Well, Theroc does not have a large space fleet. Most of us prefer to remain in the worldforest without ever venturing elsewhere in the Spiral Arm. However, like every civilized world, we do engage in interstellar travel, and our green priests take

77

treelings to other planets to spread the forest as widely as possible. Therefore we require ekti. At present, we are beholden to the Hansa for this vital resource.' He smiled again. 'I would like to explore the possibility that Roamers and Therons could arrange for a more direct supply agreement.'

Cesca gave a wicked grin. 'Oh, the Goose wouldn't like that at all.'

'Not at all.' Jhy Okiah looked at her student and nodded. 'But I don't believe any legal restrictions prevent it.'

Reynald's suggestion surprised Cesca, since few outsiders took the Roamers seriously, seeing them as ragtag groups that happened to provide a useful product. The Hansa had never bothered to keep track of how many skymines the Roamers operated or what gas planets they harvested. The Spiral Arm had so many uninhabited systems, so many gas giants, who could possibly monitor them all? How could a Hansa spy ship spot even a huge floating factory against the backdrop of a planet larger than Jupiter?

With apparent innocence, Reynald asked probing questions about Roamer bases and facilities, but Jhy Okiah skilfully dodged them all, giving the young man no useful information. 'I must discuss this with the other clans, Reynald. However, I welcome the opening of relations between Therons and Roamers. What is it you are offering for your own part?'

Reynald could not stop grinning. 'Perhaps the Therons could provide the services of a few green priests? With all of your far-flung clans, I'm sure the Roamers could make use of instantaneous communication.'

'True, we are a widely dispersed people, and news travels slowly,' the old woman said, 'but we have learned to live with our own methods. We follow the Guiding Star.'

'Still, sometimes you may wish to learn of significant events more quickly.' Reynald's eyes were bright. He leaned across the small table in the yacht's galley, ready to tell a secret. 'For instance, our green priests have just passed along a report from General Lanyan – that Rand Sorengaard was recently apprehended and executed near Yreka. The EDF set up an ambush for him and captured all of his crew. They were all sent out the airlock.'

Cesca and Jhy Okiah met each other's gaze. Cesca swallowed hard. 'Damned Eddies. That's bad news indeed.'

Reynald seemed surprised. 'Did you actually support Sorengaard's activities? He seemed more of a revolutionary than a pirate—'

'We understand his motivations, young man, for Roamers have been unfairly treated by the Hansa. Violence, however, only brings about further violence, rather than any acceptable resolution. As spokesperson for the Roamers, I can never condone his methods.'

The old Speaker turned back to business. 'Nevertheless, Prince Reynald, we must respectfully decline your most generous offer.'

Cesca regarded the brawny, handsome young man. 'I have to agree. Allowing green priests to live among the Roamers is simply impossible.' The idea of having a stranger view their most carefully hidden installations sent a chill down her spine. While the telink process provided instant communication, such information became available to all green priests, everywhere. The Roamers would never open themselves that much.

Reynald took the rejection with good grace and a wry smile. 'Basil Wenceslas would fall all over himself to have more priests, but we have turned him down. Your reaction is quite different from my experience with the Terran Hanseatic League.'

'Roamer society is very different from that of other humans.'

Reynald slid a glance over at the beautiful Cesca, obviously flirting. 'We might consider a different sort of alliance then, a marriage perhaps—'

But Cesca raised her hand, looking first at her delicate fingers and then meeting his eyes. 'Such a joining would indeed be a valuable political alliance. But I must inform you that I am already betrothed to the chief of a large and profitable skymine.' *And I am in love with his brother.*

Reynald looked away with an embarrassed expression that made him seem much younger. 'Then he is a very lucky man.'

Cesca felt sorry for him, even mildly attracted to him, but her impending marriage with Ross Tamblyn was unbreakable, despite her secret feelings for Jess. Adding Reynald to the equation would make the already complicated situation intolerable.

Still, though nothing had been resolved, Reynald seemed generally happy with the discussions. He bowed again. 'Before I return to Theroc after this long peregrination, allow me to extend a most heartfelt invitation to you, or any other Roamer you choose as your representative, to visit our spectacular worldforest. Sooner or later, you must get tired of empty space.'

'Space is never empty, if you know what you are looking for.' Cesca clasped his hand warmly. 'Still, I look forward to seeing it some day.'

FIFTEEN

NIRA KHALI

Perched at the top of the world, Nira Khali curled her toes around the frond and stood balanced, without a care and unafraid, even so high up in the sky. She had not yet taken the green, had not felt the worldtree song pulsing through her blood or seen the green tinge darken in her skin. Nevertheless, she trusted the worldforest with all her soul.

Her skin was dusky brown, but soon she would bear the photosynthetic pigmentation that would show everyone that she had been accepted by the magnificent trees. An acolyte for most of her young life, she understood the way of the forest, communed with the enigmatic interconnected mind even though the trees couldn't hear her directly. Not yet.

For her day's assignment, Nira read aloud in a rich, dramatic voice, engrossed in the stories from ancient literature that the *Caillié* colonists had brought with them. She sensed that the trees liked these stories of King Arthur and his Knights of the Round Table. She had read several different versions of *Le Morte d'Arthur* by Sir Thomas Malory, as well as a myriad of retellings by Howard Pyle,

John Steinbeck, and a succession of others. There were many inconsistencies among the legends, but Nira didn't think the trees were confused. The forest mind actually enjoyed contradictions and discrepancies, and occupied a portion of its slow semi-waking consciousness pondering the implications.

Nira served the worldforest by reading to the trees, but she also delighted in the opportunity to learn for herself. From childhood, she had spent years keeping records of where missionary green priests were distributed around the Spiral Arm, bearing treelings, spreading the forest.

Young acolytes were taught to tend the forest. They nurtured the smallest potted treelings prepared for transportation off-world; they cared for the largest ancient sentinels, plucking off old fronds and picking bark clean of parasites. Nira preferred reading aloud, and she thought the trees enjoyed it as well. When she talked to the trees, even while she was doing menial tasks, Nira always kept her mind open and her ears cocked, listening for an answer. One day, when she was a green priest, she would hear the voice.

Barefoot and bare-chested, acolytes wore only loincloths, exposing as much skin as possible to the trees. Human skin was a sensitive receptor, an interface with the worldtrees. Whenever Nira climbed to the canopy for her daily work, she stroked the fronds, pressed her chest against the trunk. She had shorn her dark hair close to the scalp, as most acolytes did, leaving only a fuzz on the crown of her head. All her hair would fall out as soon as she took the green.

Since childhood, she had recognized her destiny to become part of the ecological web of the worldforest, which grew year after year. Before the *Caillié* had been brought here long ago, the worldforest had been only an isolated group of semi-intelligent trees on a single planet. There, because it had no way to grow intellectually, or experience new things, the worldforest had languished in isolation for thousands of years.

However, when the settlers came, a girl named Thara Wen had learned to commune with the forest, and she taught other sensitive individuals. These early 'priests' had discovered how to tap into the ponderous memory that was capable of storing and recalling vast amounts of information. The worldtrees were a living database, hampered only by a lack of experiences and outside knowledge. Thara Wen and her followers had taken care of that problem.

As the worldforest began to learn from its human companions, the relationship blossomed into a beneficial symbiosis. Green priests explained mathematics and science, history and folklore. Once its appetite was whetted, the worldforest wanted to absorb all human knowledge, from the dullest facts to the most sweeping legends. The arboreal computer could assimilate and assess a thousand tangential pieces of information and make brilliant and accurate projections, almost like prophecies from a benevolent earth spirit.

Around her, other acolytes read dull-sounding data, reciting records of weather patterns on planets she'd never even heard of; Nira was quite happy to be ensconced in the boughs with Malory's epic chronicle. Priests played musical instruments or activated recordings of symphonies created by human composers; to the worldforest, music was as much a language as words.

Alone under the sky, Nira read for hours, not even shifting her position, completely focused on the story and on the listening trees. The trees could receive information in other ways, through direct telepathic link with functional green priests, but Nira did not have that option. Besides, she preferred to read aloud – it was the way stories were meant to be told, and the worldforest seemed to grasp that. Somehow, even without the symbiosis established, these magnificent plants understood that Nira would become part of their overall network soon. Very soon, she hoped.

As the afternoon waned towards twilight, Nira's voice grew scratchy and she realized that she hadn't taken a drink from her water flask in hours. She looked up to see older priests descending from their platforms, finished with the day's activities. She gulped from her flask, swallowing the stimulating clee – pure water mixed with ground seeds from the worldtrees. She felt awake, eager to read another hundred pages, but it was time to attend to her other duties.

As she climbed down to the juncture of the largest fronds, she met a tall middle-aged priest named Yarrod, the younger brother of Mother Alexa. The many tattoos on his green face bore witness to the different subjects he had studied and abilities he had acquired in the name of the worldforest. Though the green priests had a very loose and generous hierarchy, Yarrod was one of the senior members, though his position had little to do with his relation to the leader. 'Nira Khali, I have come to escort you. Our council has met, and the trees have approved.'

'Approved?' Nira's heart leapt. 'Approved of what?' Possibilities ran through her mind, and she couldn't decide which she hoped for most.

Anchoring his feet against the branches, Yarrod removed a vial from the rope at his waist. 'The priests offer you our congratulations.' Smiling, he unstoppered the tiny vial and let a dark liquid drop onto his fingertip. 'You have completed the training necessary to receive your second Reader's mark.'

He extended his fingertip, and Nira felt a rush, pleased to have achieved a new rank so quickly. She already bore the mark of an acolyte on her forehead, and two arcs at the corners of her mouth and eyes that showed she had observed the necessary subjects to become a first-rank Reader.

Yarrod's fingertip paused, and then he laughed. 'Nira, I cannot put the marks around your mouth if you are grinning so much.'

She tried to form her face into a stoic, calm expression. He deftly smeared dark juice in a perfect curve along each side of her mouth, broader in radius than the first set of arcs. The juice stung as it soaked into her skin, where it would alter the chemistry of her tissues, leaving a permanent mark. It would burn for a day before she was allowed to wash it off, but the mark would be there for all to see that she had achieved another level.

'Thank you, Yarrod. I am pleased to serve the worldforest in any capacity. Such recognition encourages me to work harder for the next level.'

Yarrod continued to smile. 'I am not finished yet, Nira. That was merely an introduction.' Nira's heart thumped again in her chest.

'The priests have discussed the current acolytes and studied their dedication and drive.' He looked at her with bright eyes. Nira held her breath, but he could see right through her thoughts. 'We have decided that you have earned more than just another tattoo of learning. Your acolyte service to the worldforest has been exemplary. It could only improve if you were to become a full-fledged green priest.'

Nira felt the trees singing around her – laughing or congratulating her, she couldn't tell which – but soon she would. She gripped the electronic bookplaque in her hand so hard she was afraid it might slip from between her sweaty fingertips and tumble to the distant forest floor. She dared not let that happen.

Nira raised her chin and blinked back the tears in her eyes, looking proudly at Yarrod. Her only regret was that she had been unable to finish reading the tale of King Arthur and his knights. That would probably be for another acolyte to do.

SIXTEEN

RLINDA KETT

Rlinda Kett was delighted to be back aboard the *Voracious Curiosity*. Her merchant ship was fully repaired, cleaned, and even upgraded after having been used as bait against Rand Sorengaard's corsairs. Now she relaxed in her custom-widened captain's chair as the ship approached Theroc.

She came at the surprising invitation of Sarein Theron herself, the third child of Father Idriss and Mother Alexa. The daughter had more business sense than anyone in the family, as far as Rlinda was concerned. Sarein was only twenty-one, a beautiful and savvy woman who had already made connections with the Hansa, extending her network of favours.

Rlinda couldn't help but respect Sarein. Certainly, it would have been politically unwise to turn down the offer to come to Theroc to discuss 'matters of interest to people such as ourselves.' From her time spent studying on Earth, Sarein had a less provincial mindset than either of her parents or any of her siblings.

The Therons were insular in their trade practises, keeping a tight hold on the green priests and not inclined to develop new customers for their myriad forest products. As a trader, Rlinda had often looked with interest at Theroc, but considered the cultural restrictions too severe for much of a trade relationship.

Sarein, though, seemed to be changing all that with her overt offer.

The Theron colony was self-sufficient and aloof from the Hanseatic League. The EDF and the Hansa had never pressed the issue, keeping the forest inhabitants happy because they were the only source of green priests, but the Therons refused to be exploited.

Rlinda Kett did not have exploitation in mind at all, though, only mutual benefit. She always dealt fairly with her customers and her suppliers. That was how interstellar trade should work. Still, she kept an eye open for new trade opportunities. She would certainly listen to Sarein's offer.

Despite her five marriages, Rlinda had no children. Instead, she operated four merchant ships, including the *Voracious Curiosity*, which was her baby. More than just the owner of her own shipping company, Rlinda was one of the best captains as well.

Each of her other captains went out to secure cargoes independently, taking risks and reaping rewards. She hadn't yet decided if she would try to find a replacement for the *Great Expectations* and Captain Gabriel Mesta. Though they had to buy into her franchise and pay a large fee, the captains were allowed to keep seventy-five per cent of the profits they brought in. If a captain suffered three losses in a row, however, Rlinda's shipping company ousted him and opened the position for a new captain willing to sign on. She'd needed to do that only once, and the man hadn't even been married to her . . .

Descending through Theroc's misty atmosphere, Rlinda followed the tracker beacons down into a clearing in the densely wooded terrain, where she expertly landed the ship among the tall trees.

With a delighted smile on her broad dark face, she climbed out. Around her the clustered worldtrees spread out in an undulating ocean of foliage as far as the eye could see. After days aboard the merchant ship, she relished the moist, perfumed atmosphere. She drew another breath to purge the residue of spaceship air from her lungs.

Caught in her smiling reverie, Rlinda turned and was surprised to see a slender young woman waiting. Sarein's eyes were large and dark, her skin a deep bronze. Her hips were narrow, her breasts small, and her dark hair cut in a short, serviceable style. Sarein's garments were an unusual mixture of home-dyed cocoon-fibre fabrics, natural products from Theroc, highlighted with processed polymers and glittering jewellery from Earth.

'Rlinda Kett, thank you for coming here. Your journey was long, but I promise you the rewards will be worth the trouble.'

'No trouble,' the merchant said, patting the hull of her ship. 'Glad to have the opportunity to see this place with my own eyes. I've heard many intriguing things about Theroc.'

Sarein gave a brief surprised frown, which she covered with a welcoming smile. 'Intriguing, truly? Maybe I've missed something.'

Sarein led her towards the fungus-reef city where hundreds of families lived. The massive communal dwelling was a whitish-grey growth fossilized in the junctures of several large worldtrees. The fungus-reef was a giant swelling built up from thousands of generations of hard, shelf-like mushrooms. The huge fungus continued to spread as it sprayed layers of spores on top of itself, hardening as it grew older like a fungal coral reef.

'It looks like bubbly whipped cream,' Rlinda said.

Sarein smiled at the reference. 'I loved whipped cream when I was on Earth. But this is hard and filled with gaps and holes – enough to build an entire city.'

Sarein escorted her through the marvellous organic monument. The first colonists from the *Caillié* abandoned their prefabricated shelters early on and moved into these fungus-reefs.' She rapped her knuckles on the spongy yet sturdy wall. 'Then they augmented, decorated, and added to the city. Plumbing, lighting strips, coolant systems, power conduits, and communication nodes.'

'It's not exactly primitive.' Rlinda's eyes brightened. 'Still, seems to me there could be a market here for a few new amenities.' Sarein flashed a glance at the large merchant woman, smiling in agreement, though she didn't say it out loud.

'Tell me, though,' Rlinda said. 'How is it that I'm the one who came to your attention? The Hansa has hundreds of merchants who would love to make their pitch.'

'I thought of *you*, Rlinda Kett, because you applied for licences to explore the marketability of certain food items and jungle fabrics. Everyone else who pokes around on Theroc is only interested in the green priests. You seem different.' She lowered her voice. 'A few test cargoes may well be the wedge that we need with my parents. You could be our first intermediary.'

Rlinda was barely able to believe her good fortune. 'If that's my duty, I'm happy to serve.'

Sarein wore a dreamy look. 'Chairman Wenceslas is also very supportive of any venture that brings my world into the larger fold of galactic commerce. He told me so himself.'

They entered a large chamber that opened to a breathtaking view of the tree-strewn forest levels. Sarein gestured for Rlinda to sit at a long table of iron-hard wood spread with a hundred colourful delicacies. Rlinda gaped hungrily at the selection of trays and goblets, decanters of juices and fermented drinks, steaming hot beverages and chilled ices swirled with coloured sugars and glistening edible seeds.

'Before we can properly discuss the market potential of Theron products, I've arranged for you to sample our best. I hope you don't mind.'

'Not at all! A merchant is required to personally vouch for the quality and desirability of all food products.' Rlinda patted her large stomach and wide thighs. 'As you can see, I enjoy my work a great deal.'

Sarein began sliding platters towards her, rattling off the names and derivations of each dish. She pointed to one after another after another. 'Rindberries, splurts, puckers . . . hmmm, seedberries – you have to be *very* hungry or very patient to put up with these things.' She pushed the plate aside without even letting Rlinda taste one.

'Jigglefruit, sweet and gelatinous, but it makes a big mess. Dangoes. Napples – very crunchy, but you might get sleepy if you eat too many. These white things are pair-pears, because they grow double on the branches. We've also got eight kinds of our best nectar, and urns of pollen used for spices, spreads, even as candy.'

The plump merchant valiantly tried to keep up with tasting each item Sarein offered, bowl after bowl of varieties of nuts. 'Perrin seeds, saltnuts, crackles. Here, these spreadnuts have a very creamy interior. The *Caillié* colonists named everything in a rush during their first years of sampling the foods on Theroc. Later on, they figured out the detailed scientific taxonomy . . . but who really needs it?'

Since Theroc had no native mammals, the people ate caterpillar fillets, insect steaks, lightly browned and covered with a tart sauce made from fermented fruits. Rlinda hesitated at the thought of eating insects, then shrugged and fell to her meal with gusto. One delicacy, equivalent to the richest veal, was sliced cutlets from a pupating condorfly larva.

'I'm glad you've done all the experimentation for me already.' Rlinda smacked her lips and closed her eyes to savour the taste as she chewed.

She removed an electronic pad and began to detail her favourite selections, itemizing the fruits, nuts, and spiced beverages according to her estimation of potential markets. The cloths and meats, mushrooms, scented oils and botanical perfumes would find customers. In her own mind, since she was such a well-versed gourmand herself, she imagined how some of these exotic flavours would combine with other cuisines and ingredients from far-flung planets on her trade route.

Finally, Rlinda sat back, enormously satisfied. The drowsy effect of the food was counteracted by the stimulants she had consumed. Dizzy with the possibilities, she heaved a long sigh and reached a beefy hand to pat Sarein's wrist.

'I can't wait to meet with Father Idriss and Mother Alexa so we can discuss trade. I think Theroc has a lot to offer Hansa customers.'

Content but ambitious herself, Sarein nodded. 'Chairman Wenceslas and I understand each other very well. I'm certain I can make the necessary arrangements, for both of us. Just leave everything to me.'

SEVENTEEN

BASIL WENCESLAS

When Chairman Wenceslas met with representatives of a dozen colony planets in the Terran Hanseatic League, he eschewed boardrooms and formal reception chambers. More often than not, he brought the representatives to his private suite that covered the top floor of the Hansa headquarters building, where he could better conduct business.

An enormous trapezoidal pyramid, the headquarters was filled with thousands of offices staffed with important delegates, bureaucrats, and clerks. Angled planes of polished windows made the commercial building look like a Maya artifact. The architecture had been chosen to suggest permanence, playing upon deep memories of mighty empires from Earth's past.

Serviceable rather than opulent, the headquarters sat back from the magnificence of the Whisper Palace, separated by a lush arboretum. Given tall enough trees, complex topiaries, and lovely statue gardens, ground-level spectators paid little attention to the squared-off business building in the background. The Palace dominated the skyline, but Hansa headquarters exerted the real power.

Basil contemplated his agenda for the discussion, avoiding the trivial pre-meeting chitchat. As the twelve well-dressed planetary envoys took their seats in comfortable loungers or at crystalline tables where they could take notes, silent assistants walked among them to distribute beverages and light snacks. They offered the envoys nothing too extravagant – certainly no mind-altering substances. Basil insisted that all of his envoys keep their thoughts clear when decisions needed to be made.

One of the Chairman's predecessors, Miguel Byron, had imitated the hedonism of ancient Rome here in the administrative levels. Chairman Byron had chosen attractive young men and women as servants, dressing them in scanty togas to wait upon the planetary representatives. Byron's 'staff meetings' had been legendary, often conducted in steam baths.

Basil, on the other hand, had no patience for distractions when work needed to be done. And there was always work to be done. Back on their respective worlds, his envoys were powerful enough to have all the sex, drugs, or gourmet foods they might like. But not during one of his meetings.

He did make concessions to comfort, though, holding his discussions in a loose, relaxed setting. He hated tightly scheduled, stiffly formal groups; they reminded him of classes conducted by an unimaginative schoolteacher. Such situations resulted in little innovation, usually serving to reaffirm conservative non-progress. He wanted to make the most of each person's input.

Basil stood with his back to the balcony, looking into the meeting room so that he was silhouetted by the bright afternoon. Seeing everyone settled, he said, 'Before I get to more frustrating business matters, let me congratulate everyone involved in the test of the Klikiss Torch. The new Oncier sun appears to be a resounding success. Dr Serizawa has remained there with his observation team, and the first crew of terraforming engineers will be arriving within weeks to assess the geological state of the four moons.'

Admiral Lev Stromo, a line officer who served as the EDF political liaison, smiled with pride, as if he were personally responsible for the success. 'We now have the ability to create suns wherever we wish.'

'How often will we do this, Mr Chairman?' asked the languid envoy from Relleker, a pleasant planet that had begun to show promise as a resort world, given its comfortable climate and numerous hot springs. The man had black hair oiled into showy curls against his head.

'That will be up to us,' Basil said. 'Most important is the knowledge that we *can*. We may even have impressed the Mage-Imperator.'

'Who can tell when Ildirans are impressed? We still know so little about them,' said the Dremen envoy, a milk-pale man whose dim and cloudy world had left him unaccustomed to the sunlight of Earth. 'What if they take the demonstration as a threat?'

'We've stated no aggressive intentions whatsoever,' Basil said, 'but the Klikiss Torch is like a big "Beware of Dog" sign in our yard. Let them draw their own conclusions.'

Admiral Stromo added some new business to the discussion. 'We've received a field report from my superior, General Lanyan, informing us that the criminal pirate Rand Sorengaard has been neutralized near the Yreka system. He and all his Roamer corsairs were captured and executed.'

The redheaded Yreka representative sitting next to Stromo sighed in relief. 'Now we can get back to normal trade relations,' she said. 'I'll instruct the Grand Governor to end rationing and enforce price controls to avoid economic chaos.'

'There's bad news for every good news,' Basil said. He liked to keep his meetings balanced so they didn't degenerate into a succession of complaints or rousing self-congratulations. 'Despite my best efforts, I have made no progress with the Theron rulers. They are maddeningly aloof and don't care a whit for the needs of interstellar commerce and government. We'll have to make do with however many green priests they send us at their whim.'

The oblivious Theron leaders had no comprehension of the size of the galaxy. A normal electromagnetic transmission – radio waves travelling at the speed of light – took decades, sometimes even a century, to go from place to place. It was an intolerable hindrance to running large-scale military operations, providing planetary defences, or even engaging in regular commerce.

With an Ildiran stardrive, ships could travel several times faster than light. Many of them served as couriers, delivering news and important diplomatic communiqués, but even using the fastest vessels such messages required days or weeks to arrive at their destination.

A green priest's telink, though, was *instantaneous*, regardless of the distance, so long as a worldtree and a priest were at each station. Such communication was not a luxury – not a frivolous *convenience* – but an absolute necessity in order for the Hansa to keep growing and thriving.

Unfortunately, green priests were people, not machines, and using telink required their cooperation. The Hansa could not force their hand, and the Therons certainly weren't volunteering.

'We don't dare turn them against us by being too overt, Mr Chairman,' said the Yreka representative, still uneasy because of her planet's recent troubles with the pirates.

'I wish we could just force Theroc to sign the Hansa charter,' said the pale Dremen envoy.

'Not feasible unless we want to declare war,' Basil said.

'We would win,' Admiral Stromo pointed out.

'As always, I value your input, Admiral, but zealous actions are often ill-advised actions. I will not be seen as the Chairman whose brash decrees tumbled us into a galactic recession.'

Stromo continued to press. 'There have been other upstart worlds, repressive regimes or religious fanatics that have tried to turn their backs on the Hansa.' He glanced quickly at the Ramah representative.

The man regarded him coolly. 'Devotion and tradition do not make one a "fanatic", Admiral. We simply find the Terran Archfather and the broad official compromises of Unison to be bland and generic. We prefer to return to the basic teachings of the Koran.'

'I'm sure the Admiral did not mean to cast any aspersions on Ramah,' Basil said. 'But there have been more extreme circumstances.'

Stromo focused on the Chairman instead. 'Yes, and with the simple application of sanctions, cutting off all interplanetary commerce, every one of those colonies came crawling back, or else they perished.'

'Be careful where you push,' said the Ramah envoy. A henna tattoo marked a starburst beside his dark left eye. 'All charter signatories retain the right to determine their own government, religion, and culture. We can maintain our own local language, rather than Trade Standard. I will vote against any attempts to use strongarm tactics, simply because one planet happens to be rich in a resource the Hansa needs. Any one of us could find ourselves in that situation.'

Basil gave him a condescending frown. 'Rules often change when one party has riches that another does not. Look at your history.'

Although the Ildiran stardrive allowed fast travel, strict government across such a large canvas was all but impossible. The Ildirans managed it only because the Mage-Imperator and his planetary Designates could think with one mind through the telepathic connection of *thism*. Human colonies, however, were too separated for a single Terran leader to make sensible decisions on a local level on some distant world. Hardy colonists were not likely to listen to dictates issued from far-off Earth by a man who had never visited their colony. On the other hand, the business of shuttling goods and services from world to world in a burgeoning economy provided a framework for a common set of rules. The Terran Hanseatic League had been modelled after the confederation of commercial cities and the various guilds that had operated in medieval Europe with such success.

The Ramah envoy rested his chin on his knuckles. Then he grudgingly said, 'If my people must bow to certain necessities, the Therons certainly can.'

'Therons may be a thorn in our side, but they are so . . . endearing it's difficult to be angry with them,' the Yreka envoy mused.

'I believe a solution is at hand,' Basil said with confidence. 'The old Theron ambassador has just departed for home, and I have made arrangements that she be asked to retire. "Iron Lady" Otema's successor will be far more sympathetic to our cause and more ambitious in changing things for the better.'

'Oh, good. One big happy family.' The sarcastic Relleker envoy sipped at his juice, frowning as if he had expected it to be wine.

From a silver pot on a warming stand, Basil poured himself a steaming cup of cardamom-laced coffee. He turned to gaze across the arboretum towards the Whisper Palace. 'The Hansa will survive and grow, as it always has.'

Cradling his cup, Basil walked around the chairs, pondering his next words. Knowing enough not to engage in idle chatter, his listeners waited for him to get to his next point. Unlike history's more brutal powermongers, he did not want his underlings to fear him but to *respect* him.

'The Spiral Arm is open for business, and the Hansa has generated enormous income. We've drawn great wealth from the Ildiran Empire, we've built solid infrastructures, and we've seeded new and efficient industries on burgeoning colony planets.' He gestured out of the window wall towards the spectacular Whisper Palace. 'All of us here know the human race is currently in its golden age. But only wise decisions and a strong leader can continue the economic boom and renaissance.'

Basil finally got to the primary point of the meeting. 'Unfortunately, my friends, our most effective tool – Old King Frederick – is long past his prime. You've all watched him deliver his speeches. He's showing his age, he's tired, and though the people seem to love him, he no longer inspires much fervour.'

The Chairman looked at them one at a time, holding their gazes. The envoys dreaded the issue he meant to raise. 'King Frederick is no longer the proud hero the Hansa needs as our figurehead. His popularity ratings are dropping and, frankly, he's grown too complacent in his position.'

Admiral Stromo looked at Basil in horror, as if the Chairman had spoken treason. 'What about all of the King's duties? We can't afford a drastic transition. Think of the social upheaval.'

'I prefer to think it would energize the population. Old Frederick is our mouthpiece, nothing more. He performs few important functions. In fact, Admiral,' Basil said pointedly, 'our King is little more than a living flag to salute.'

The Yreka representative seemed quite nervous. A glint of sweat appeared around the line of her red hair. 'I've been dreading this day would arrive.'

Basil went to a cabinet next to the wet bar and removed a stack of thin filmscreens, each one surrounded by a red security border. A thumbpad displayed information only to the person to whom the screen had been coded.

'The Hansa needs a striking young ruler to replace the old King, someone the people can rally around.' Basil lowered his voice. 'And we all know that none of the King's actual children by his courtesans is appropriate for our purposes.'

Like the ancient monarchs of Morocco or the emperors of China, Frederick's family and his personal life were kept carefully hidden within his wondrous Palace. The truth was that the King had no legitimate heirs. But the Hansa could rewrite history any time they wished.

'This has happened five times before, though not for decades. It is perhaps our most important task.' He distributed the filmscreens, and each envoy activated the thumbpad. A sequence of images appeared, showing young men taken in candid poses. Obviously, the subjects had not known they were under surveillance.

'These are complete dossiers of our candidates. They contain spy footage, photographs, and informational summaries of each young man compiled over the years. Our operatives are constantly on the lookout for eligible trainees for the job of Prince. These are the candidates Mr Pellidor has selected, the best young men to help us fulfil the Hansa's destiny.'

Basil summoned the envoys to the largest crystal table, and they spread their filmscreens on the tabletop so they could compare notes and discuss the possibilities. For hours they studied the records and photos, arguing about options, comparing impressions. It took less time than Basil had feared, and by the blaze of a coppery sunset, he himself cast the deciding vote.

He touched his finger to the image of a dark-haired young man. His intelligence was high, his personality was soft and likeable, his voice was charismatic – and, Basil hoped, the candidate's character could be made malleable.

'This one has the most potential,' he said. 'Given his background and social status, he'll never be missed. And most importantly, he even vaguely resembles King Frederick.'

EIGHTEEN

RAYMOND AGUERRA

Far from the private meeting chambers in Hansa headquarters, Raymond Aguerra scrounged for dinner in a small apartment on the eighteenth floor of a mass dwelling complex.

Trying to be optimistic, he scratched his dark hair and stared at the supplies in their cupboards and the cold preservation unit. He would have to scrape the bottom of his imagination to make these ingredients resemble a satisfying and nutritious meal for himself and his family.

The counters were cluttered with small boxes, toys, second-hand electronic gadgets, hand-made pot holders and keepsake printouts. No amount of care or housekeeping could make the cramped apartment look more organized. Raymond's two youngest brothers, nine-year-old Carlos and six-year-old Michael, chased each other, pretending to be monsters, then fell into a laughing heap, wrestling on the kitchen floor.

Raymond playfully nudged them out of the way with his foot. 'If you make me spill your food, you'll have to eat it off the floor.'

'Might taste better that way.' Carlos giggled as he tried to dodge Raymond's swift kick, which landed on the boy's bony rear end.

Their mother Rita rested in her chair in the main room, half watching an entertainment programme but deriving little enjoyment from it. Years of practise allowed her to ignore the roughhousing. Next to her, ten-year-old Rory complained about being forced to do his homework while his younger brothers were able to play.

Raymond felt guilty about sending the rowdy boys into the other room, where they might bother their mother. Rita Aguerra had already worked a long day and would get up well before dawn to get to her second job. She didn't so much sit in her comfortable chair as collapse into it, sagging within the seat's broad contours. Raymond didn't doubt she would be asleep by the time he finished making dinner, unless she'd drunk too many cups of sour black coffee before returning home.

Over the main door frame hung a crucifix and some old dry palm fronds from the previous year's Palm Sunday. She dutifully attended Mass each week, though occasionally she watched broadcasts of official Unison church services, which seemed bland and passionless to her. The Archfather, with his beard and fancy robes, was supposed to be the impartial spokesman for all faiths, as determined by the united representatives of the world's major beliefs, but to Rita, the old Catholic church seemed much more religious.

Whenever he looked at his mother, Raymond's heart ached. Rita Aguerra's long dark hair was now streaked with grey. In her younger days, she had spent hours brushing it, keeping the raven locks shiny, but now she usually just pulled her hair back in a ponytail or twisted it into a bun. She'd been a beauty once – Raymond could still see it in the softening shape of her face – though now she had no time to maintain her looks and no hope of finding renewed romance. Hard work and too many responsibilities had turned her into a stocky, muscular matron.

Rita worked as a clerk for an off-world merchandising organization by day and as a waitress by night. A steady diet of coffee and cigarettes gave her the false energy to get through the day and the jitters that kept her awake during the few hours she should have been able to rest at night.

Every time she came home, though, Rita still managed to engulf each of her four boys in a heavy-armed hug, smothering them with her rose-scented perfume. The strong woman held her family together by the thinnest of threads, and now Raymond was old enough that she could lay some of the burden on his shoulders. He took it from her without complaint.

One night a month earlier, the two of them had sat up alone at the wobbly dining table. Rory, Carlos, and Michael had been hustled off to bed and tucked in, where they would continue to goof off for half an hour before finally dozing. Looking across at Raymond, Rita had lit another cigarette, something she rarely did when the younger boys were awake. The fact that his mother did so made Raymond realize that she considered him an adult, the man of her house since Esteban Aguerra had run off.

She had told him about it, giving details he had always wondered about but had been too afraid to ask. 'I might not be the easiest person to get along with, especially for a happy-go-lucky man like your father. But I've always tried to live up to my responsibilities and do the best I can. You boys are my treasures, and your father might have been a diamond in the rough . . . but it was very much in the rough. The night he left, we had a shouting match, one of our worst arguments ever. I can't even remember why it was important . . . I had bought him a new pair of shoes, or something.'

One hand held the cigarette, but the other clenched into a fist.

'I gave him one, maybe two, black eyes before he ran off. That's when he signed up for the colony ship and went off to Ramah.'

'Do you ever wonder if he regretted leaving us, Mama?'

Rita had shrugged. 'He regretted leaving his sons, maybe, because he was such a proud man. But I doubt he's ever thought about me again.'

Since their discussion that night, Raymond had always wondered . . .

Now, he dished up a concoction of macaroni, soup-pax, and some minced-up bits of salami that looked as if it wouldn't last much longer in the preserving unit. He took a whiff, frowned, then added some powdery cheese and pronounced the dish finished. 'Come and eat. If it gets cold, I'll have to serve it as leftovers tomorrow.'

'I thought it was leftovers tonight,' Carlos said.

'I can still send you to bed without supper.' The boys gathered around to grab plates of scooped casserole. Rita took her own small share, hiding a chuckle at his culinary audacity, and settled down to eat. She insisted it was one of the best meals she'd ever eaten.

Later, after Rita had crawled back to her chair to rest and hopefully to sleep, Raymond put his little brothers to bed by himself. He made sure they took baths and brushed their teeth, ignoring their complaints and rambunctious misbehaviour; he was immune to it by now. By the time he returned to the main room, his mother had indeed drifted off into a light slumber.

Smiling, he rearranged the bouquet of flowers he had snatched during King Frederick's celebration for the new sun at Oncier. After bringing the blooms home, he had found an empty food package and converted it into a makeshift vase. Rita insisted that flowers were a waste of money, but her glowing expression made Raymond want to find a way to obtain a bouquet at least once a week, no matter what the cost.

He thought about rousing his mother so that he could help her to bed, but decided to let her sleep where she was. He didn't want her to miss a moment of rest. Now with their apartment quiet, Raymond quickly changed clothes, knowing he had only a few hours before he needed to be back to help his mother get off to work and his little brothers prepared for school.

He would run the streets, check at a few all-night factories, maybe a craft shop. He could usually find a few hours' work – performing odd jobs or dirty labour that no one else wanted to do – in return for cash or sometimes even fresh food. His late-night errands were all that allowed them the discretionary money for clothing or occasional treats.

While his mother slept, Raymond slipped out of the apartment, careful to lock up behind him. His head ached and his eyes were scratchy with weariness, but he would catch a nap later. They would get by – provided he didn't stop working. He took the elevator down eighteen floors to street level and ventured out into the city.

It was the last time he ever saw his family.

NINETEEN

JESS TAMBLYN

A whiplash of flares licked out from the roiling ocean of the hot star, slow-moving, beautiful . . . and deadly.

'Get closer,' the eager engineer said to Jess Tamblyn, unable to tear his eyes from the spectacle. 'We've got to get a lot closer.'

Though he was sweating, Jess trusted the other man's intuition. 'If that's what we have to do.' He sent a brief, silent prayer to the Guiding Star, then did as the other man asked.

Kotto Okiah had no more than a theoretical conception of genuine dangers, but he did understand tolerances and risks better than any other Roamer. Kotto had already designed and established four successful extreme-environment settlements. If the Speaker's youngest son hadn't known what he was doing, then tens of thousands of Roamers would already have died.

As the shielded vessel gingerly approached the solar storm, Kotto alternated his attention between the filtered window and the specific-band scanners. With short, spiky brown hair and eyes like bright grey-blue buttons, the engineer looked like a child

inundated with remarkable presents. 'There! You can see the planet
. . . not as bad as I'd feared.'

Jess noted the sparkle of rocky Isperos orbiting close to the
turbulent star, embedded in the densest part of the corona. 'Not bad?
Kotto, it looks like an ember in a blast furnace.'

Distracted by his readings, the engineer said, 'In some ways
that's an advantage.'

An advantage. No one had ever accused Kotto Okiah of being a
pessimist.

After leaving Ross at the Golgen skymine, Jess had taken his
ekti cargo escort to a Hansa distribution complex, then made his
way to the asteroid cluster of Rendezvous. He had duties to
perform for his family's water-mining operations, clan obligations,
business contacts and meetings with other clan leaders . . . and his
brother's gifts to deliver to Cesca Peroni.

But Cesca had not yet returned from her mission with Speaker
Okiah. While Jess could easily have arranged for someone else to
present Ross's tokens to his fiancée, he did not want to waste a
legitimate excuse to spend a few private moments with her, even if
the choice went against his better judgement. He knew he
shouldn't feel this way, after he had denied himself so much . . .

Jess had lingered at the Rendezvous complex for several days,
waiting for Cesca. But once it began to grow obvious to others that
he was stalling, he couldn't let anyone suspect his feelings. He had
no choice but to schedule his return to Plumas. When Kotto Okiah
had asked for a willing pilot to take him to Isperos on a survey
mission, Jess had leapt at the opportunity . . . not that any other
Roamer was the least bit interested in volunteering.

Now, the reconnaissance ship circled the hot planet, fighting
the sun's massive gravity before it passed into the blessed cone of
shadow behind Isperos. Jess looked down at the baked and glassy
surface, seeing fissures caused by heat stresses. Lava seas spilled

across the continents, smoothing the scars of impact craters, then hardened into a skin of rock during the cold months of darkness.

'Kotto, you are insane to want to build a Roamer colony here.'

The young engineer stared avidly at the blistered world. 'Look at the metals, though. You don't find resources like that just anywhere. Lighter-element impurities are all boiled away. Solar-wind bombardment has created plenty of new isotopes for the taking.' He tapped his chin with a finger. 'If we used fibre insulation, double-walled containment, vacuum honeycombed structural support, we could easily keep colony integrity . . .' His voice trailed off as he considered the possibilities.

From an early age, the youngest of Jhy Okiah's sons had demonstrated his imaginative and quirky understanding of low-gravity construction. He loved to push the envelope with solutions to difficult survival problems. Kotto had spent more than a decade working in Del Kellum's hidden shipyards within the rings of Osquivel and had twice developed improved ekti reactors for skymines. Despite his successes, and occasional failures, Kotto was not arrogant or stubborn. He was filled with an insatiable curiosity.

As a boy, Kotto had proved quite a challenge for the Governess compy UR, who raised many Roamer children at Rendezvous. The curious boy had caused the maternal robot much grief, not because he misbehaved, but because he constantly asked questions and poked and prodded and dismantled things – which he only rarely managed to reassemble. As an adult, though, Kotto had repeatedly proved his genius, to the benefit of many clans.

Jess took the vessel low over the melted and rehardened ground. Seeing the utter confidence on the engineer's face, he began to believe in the potential here. After all, Roamers had disproved the impossible time and again.

'Roamers have this belief they can do anything,' Cesca had once said to Jess, 'given the resources and time.'

'An unconventional people do not need conventional wisdom,' he said.

He and Cesca had been alone in her rock-walled office chamber in the Rendezvous cluster. It was an innocent meeting to discuss water and oxygen supplies clan Tamblyn would deliver from Plumas. They had kept their distance from each other, though their eyes remained locked. It seemed as if they were separated by an elastic barrier that both forced them apart and pulled them together.

'Even so, time can't solve all problems,' Jess said. He had taken half a step forward, disguising his movement with a hand gesture, as if to emphasize what he was saying. Then he froze, remembering all the expectations that weighed him down.

Cesca understood what he was implying. Years before, she had betrothed herself to Ross Tamblyn, a long engagement that they had taken on faith. Ross diligently worked to meet the conditions he and Cesca had agreed upon. Everything had seemed acceptable in the joining of two strong clans, even if Ross was something of a black sheep. Most Roamers enthusiastically endorsed the union. The Blue Sky Mine would be a strong foundation for an expanding family, even without old Bram Tamblyn's support.

But that was before she had got to know Jess, and the spark between them went far beyond straightforward political and economic considerations. It wasn't something they could explain to anyone else, or even to themselves.

'If we follow the Guiding Star, some problems should never arise in the first place,' Cesca said.

'Nevertheless' – Jess boldly took the last step to her, closing the distance, refusing to think about what he was doing – 'it happens.'

He kissed her then, surprising her, pleasing her . . . and terrifying them both. Cesca responded for just an instant, clinging to him as if they were teetering on the precarious edge of a precipice. Then, in unison, they broke away and took an awkward step apart.

'Jess, we shouldn't even—'

'I'm sorry.' He blushed furiously, stumbling backwards, gathering his notes and recordings. Jess shook his head, immensely ashamed and baffled by his own actions. He felt like a traitor to his brother. 'What was I doing?' He could only picture Ross, an innocent bystander in their mutual attraction.

'Jess, we don't dare even think about this.' Though deeply unsettled, Cesca wasn't angry with him. 'It never happened.'

He readily agreed. 'We'll forget about it. That's what we should do.'

But the memories only burned brighter for both of them, month after month. How could anyone ever forget?

As Jess's ship swept out of the planet's shadow and into the full blazing day of the roaring sun, the sudden glare and buffeting heat rocked them from side to side.

'We'll need to map out a recommended safe approach,' Kotto said, noting Jess's piloting difficulties in the solar storm as if it were a mere detail to add to his proposal. 'We can take advantage of the planet's shadow for bringing in most of the big supply haulers.'

Jess increased the filter density on their viewing windows. 'Your bigger problem is going to be shipping off the processed metals. They'll need to be taken far from here before we can market whatever we don't use for ourselves.'

'Oh, of course,' Kotto said. 'The Big Goose would never even come within sensor range of the planet. They might get a blister on their delicate skin.'

Though the Hansa would not look twice at a rough, hot world like Isperos, such places were acceptable enough to the Roamers, who had already established themselves in many remarkable habitats, such as Rendezvous itself.

The seed of their society had been started by the generation ship *Kanaka*, named after the brilliant explorer of Vallis Marineris on Mars. The *Kanaka* crew and passengers had boarded the eleventh and last vessel to leave Earth, fleeing hard times. By that point, funding for the brave and optimistic colonization project was nearly gone, and equipment and supplies were sparse. Still, this group had envisioned themselves as tougher than the others, true survivalists.

What the *Kanaka* passengers lacked in raw materials they made up for by bringing eccentric and innovative geniuses who could create habitable environments in the harshest of places. Before setting out from Earth, these people had lived in arctic wastelands and set up mining stations on the moons of Jupiter. They operated under the assumption that if a standard method did not work, they would find another alternative, or simply invent one.

During decades of travel, while the *Kanaka* searched for a planet to colonize, the passengers had built a self-contained society. At one point, their resources stretched and dwindling, they had stopped off in a rubble-strewn debris cloud around the red-dwarf Meyer to scavenge water ices, minerals, and metals from the asteroids, enough supplies to last them for another few decades.

There, some of the innovative colonists ran calculations, floated designs, and convinced themselves they could use the large-scale construction and mining equipment carried aboard the *Kanaka* to build and survive in an artificial substation among the rocks, close to the weak crimson radiation of the tiny star. The Meyer belt offered enough raw materials to give the small group a fighting chance, and decreasing the population aboard the generation ship would help all the other passengers.

The *Kanaka* remained around the red dwarf for a decade, making sure that the hardy Meyer volunteers would find the means to grow food in underground asteroid chambers and gather power from the dim light of the sun. Though to any other settlers it might have seemed hopeless – a fledgling colony on a desert island in space, doomed to dwindle and die – yet this place they named 'Rendezvous' was their choice, and the volunteer families gambled on this small chance.

That colony had survived, and thrived, eventually forming the foundation of Roamer culture. Who was Jess to say that these resilient people could not be just as successful on a hellish world like Isperos, especially with Kotto Okiah running the show?

Trapped in an electromagnetic loop, gouts of stellar material rushed upwards like an incandescent locomotive, spewing hard radiation more insidious and more destructive than the heat itself. Cancerous sunspots looked like black oases on the star's surface, but they were just as dangerous as the hotter chromosphere, anchor points for the violent eruptions.

Jess fought with the ship, not wanting to think of the hull damage they were incurring. 'Kotto—'

'I've got the data I need.' The engineer sounded pleased with himself. 'We should return to Rendezvous now, so I can put together my analyses.'

Jess looked down at the stress readings edging towards overload. 'Yes, that would be a good idea.'

Streaking away from the churning sun and its blistering planet, Jess thought of Cesca again, hoping she would be back at the asteroid cluster by now. Even as they fled the solar storms and entered the cold of space, Jess found that he was sweating more than ever.

TWENTY

CESCA PERONI

Ever cautious, Cesca Peroni piloted the space yacht on a leisurely course through several star systems en route to Rendezvous. She doubted Reynald, the future heir of Theroc, would follow her, or that any Goose security ships had placed spy tracers on their path, but Roamers covered their tracks out of habit.

For a century and a half, they had kept their hideouts from the prying eyes of other humans. All the clans remained concerned by the power exerted by the Terran Hanseatic League. Lately, the machinations of Chairman Wenceslas to tighten control on ekti processing had forced the Roamers to grow even more suspicious.

'How will the clans react to Reynald's ideas?' she asked, glancing away from the yacht's control panels to look at the lean face of her mentor.

'Long ago, the Ildirans gladly turned over the operation of their skymines to us Roamers, but we ourselves have always been too insular to trust anyone.' The old woman stared at the star fields that changed subtly and slowly as the yacht covered vast distances. 'On the other hand, it never hurts to consider possible allies.'

Cesca nodded. 'Reynald made a good case.'

'For marriage?' Jhy Okiah raised her eyebrows.

Cesca recognized the old woman's teasing tone, but she still blushed. 'I meant his business suggestion. The Therons have kept their independence and held their green priests outside of Goose control.'

'We have much in common.' Jhy Okiah pursed her wrinkled lips, and her voice grew more serious. 'Unfortunately, we simply do not need anything the Therons have to offer.'

Cesca recalled the numerous feuds and disagreements Jhy Okiah had resolved during her time as Speaker. Not long ago, the angry Rand Sorengaard had pulled away from Roamer restrictions in retaliation for new Hansa tariffs. 'What is to stop us from taking what we deserve? The Goose is as lawless as we are!' But Rand had garnered little support beyond a handful of restless bullies more interested in adventure than justice.

Sorengaard had been a second cousin to the Peroni clan, though Cesca did not like to speak of that connection, because the pirate was such an embarrassment. Jhy Okiah had often said it was only a matter of time before the EDF dealt with him. And, according to the news delivered by Reynald, she had been right. 'Even though Rand has been brought to justice, the Goose won't let their punishment stop there. All Roamers will end up paying more than the tariffs that were imposed.'

'And we'll find ways to improve our situation and come through stronger than before,' Cesca responded with sincere pride. 'If we have to.'

After extreme measures, hard conservation, and many gambles, the Roamers were mostly self-sufficient, though they still required certain vital supplies from the outside – supplies on which the Hansa had now placed heavy taxes: foodstuffs, medicines, special equipment and instruments, as well as numerous conveniences and luxury items.

Jhy Okiah viewed the expected lean times as an incentive for the Roamers to find other ways to become autonomous. During the clan gathering, her voice was dry and raspy, yet it contained an emotional power that she had developed over many years.

'If the Hansa can hurt us by cutting off the supply of a material, then they have too much power over us . . . and we are too dependent on that thing. Either we must give up our dependence, or find a new supply. We are Roamers. Have we not the ability to discover alternatives? We can build our own equipment, manufacture our own circuitry webs, and learn to do without comforts and conveniences. Let the Roamers have the last laugh by proving we don't need to buy from their merchants. We'll cut off that income stream, and the Big Goose will be weaker.'

With those words, she had managed to stem the tide of other dissenters after Rand Sorengaard had stormed off. An open rebellion against the Hanseatic League would bring about severe reprisals. The Speaker considered Sorengaard's raids to be a crime. Worse, she feared his activities would draw too much outside attention to the Roamers. The Roamers were accustomed to living in harsh environments, but not as hunted renegades.

Now, sitting beside Cesca in the space yacht, Jhy Okiah said, 'We dare not let the Goose snoop around for fugitives, or they might discover some of the shipyards, colonies, and facilities that our clans would rather keep hidden.'

More than two centuries earlier, after leaving behind the tiny fledgling colony in the rubble belt around the red star Meyer, the generation ship *Kanaka* had continued on its way in search of a home, passing through nebular clouds and scooping up gases, which the people used for fuel and filtered for other resources. Brilliant scavengers, not only did the explorers make do, they also made progress.

The *Kanaka* was the last of the generation ships to be retrieved by Ildiran search teams one hundred and eighty years ago. Instead of remaining on a single vector as the other large ships had done, the *Kanaka* had wandered, pausing in several places, straying far from the original plan.

The benevolent Ildirans had taken the *Kanaka* to a hospitable planet named Iawa, a world ripe for colonization and not needed by the Ildiran Empire. Settling on a terrestrial planet was quite a change for the colonists aboard the *Kanaka*. Iawa's open skies and broad continents seemed like a paradise, with all the land the settlers could imagine after living for generations within cramped limited quarters aboard an old ship.

At first, taming an amenable planet seemed a simple matter, but some colonists were concerned that all of their innovation and survival skills were being lost in only a few years. Iawa was such a drastic change that they thought they might have been better off self-sufficient and roaming among the stars.

Within five years, though, just as agriculture began to take off on Iawa, as towns were built and crops were planted on cleared lands, the planet turned against them. In a single season, a horrible native blight attacked all terrestrial plant organisms, wiping out the grains and vegetables and trees they had planted. The Iawan Scourge fed on Earth-based plant matter, developing an appetite for all transplanted species. Suddenly, the isolated colonists had only meagre stores of food and little hope that the situation would improve, because this blight was endemic to the native biosphere.

Starvation loomed, but the people had remembered the austerity measures practical aboard a crowded generation ship, and had set enough aside to survive. The Iawan settlers finally returned to the derelict *Kanaka*, the huge empty vessel they had left in orbit. They pulled up stakes and went back to the way that had been successful for them, roaming among the stars in search of other niches and new homes. 'We are not a planet-bound people,' had been the chant.

Taking the proud name of 'Roamers', they negotiated with their Ildiran benefactors for stardrive technology, in exchange for which some of them agreed to operate three large Ildiran ekti-processing plants on the gas giant Daym. Ildirans hated the skymining industry and were glad to find willing workers. The Roamers set themselves to the task with great gusto, and soon began to carve a niche for themselves and expand their capabilities.

No one else – not the Terran Hanseatic League, the Therons, nor the Ildiran Empire – realized just how much the Roamers had profited from their innovations. As the next chosen Speaker, Cesca Peroni promised herself she would continue that strategy . . .

After its long journey, the space yacht arrowed closer to garnet-coloured Meyer. Seen from afar, the red dwarf was unremarkable, not to be noticed on any star chart. But as she and Jhy Okiah approached the out-of-the-way settlement of Rendezvous, Cesca greatly looked forward to getting home.

TWENTY-ONE

ESTARRA

E ven at night, the Theron forests remained mysterious and inviting. Without fear, Estarra crept to her curved window in the fungus-reef city and peered out, catching shuttered glimpses of stars through the canopy.

Dawn already warmed the treetops, spreading like a colourful yawn through the interconnected worldforest. Enough light for her to explore. Calcified footholds let her clamber down several levels to reach the ladders and pulley-lifts. On the soft forest floor, scuttling beetles the size of hamsters dug beneath dried leaves. She smelled a lingering cool mist of compost and a sweet hint of fertile decay. She sprinted off into the dimness.

Her parents would not notice that Estarra had gone off by herself. Because they had raised their three older children to positions of importance, Mother Alexa and Father Idriss spoiled her, as if they had run out of energy for making her learn things the hard way. 'Don't worry about it, child,' her mother often said.

Estarra could have wallowed in her pampered existence, but instead she promised herself to achieve more. When she had tried to talk to her father about her future, he had simply smiled through his black beard. 'Whatever you want to do, dear.' He had promised full support but offered no suggestions or practical advice.

Only her brother Beneto took time to tell her things. She envied the green priest his passion for serving the worldforest, but she didn't want to follow his path. Praying to trees was not for her.

Lights burned in adjoining dwellings, smaller fungus-reefs that grew on separated trees. Green priests — most of them married couples venturing out this early — climbed the trees to greet the dawn. All day long they would read to the half-sleeping mind of the worldforest. Today, though, the priests seemed hushed and troubled about something they had sensed from the trees. Maybe Beneto would tell her about it later . . .

Curious, she explored for more than an hour. Finally, as a wash of daylight spilled across the forest and ground mist rose like praying hands, Estarra came upon a thicket of high trees. Hanging like a bulbous papier-mâché lump on the nearest trunk, a huge misshapen mass pulsed as crowded creatures stirred inside, nearly roused from their sleep.

Hive worms made their sealed structures from chewed vegetable matter, mud, resin, and extruded web fibres. The enormous colonies were both nests and cocoons, hundreds of metres in diameter. In the centre a grub-like queen gave birth to larvae that became large worms anchored to the colony's heart. The worms extended their segmented stalks outwards with heads like huge petals surrounding a voracious mouth.

Normally, the worms extended from their nest to capture any prey that ventured within reach. After digesting animals and insects, they fed the nutrients back to the queen in the centre of the nest. At night the sleeping worms drew their face-petals together like a flower returning to a bud.

When this phase of growth was complete, the larval worms

pulled back into the nest, sealed the openings, and converted the hive into an armoured fortress. Her work done, the queen died, and the sleeping worms digested her body while they gestated. It was incredibly rare to discover a pupating hive, especially one ready to hatch . . .

She had to find Beneto. Estarra hurried back, knowing her brother would be planting new treelings in one of the sun-dappled clearings. She found him working in the shade, surrounded by pots into which he packed fertile soil.

Beneto looked up at his sister with a smile that always warmed her heart. The marks of his accomplishments, tattoos and designs of the green priesthood, gave his features a totemic appearance. She thought her brother was very handsome and suspected that he would soon choose a mate – probably from among the green priests, though that was not required for marriage.

Beneto knelt, intent on his young trees. Gently, he stroked the tiny fronds as if to apologize for cutting them loose of the parent tree. 'These four are scheduled for Dremen, where it's cool and moist but without much sun,' he said to Estarra. 'Though there's no green priest assigned to the planet, we will still plant a grove for telink access.'

Beneto pointed to other strong treelings. 'These two will be potted and carried aboard merchant vessels, though eventually they'll grow large enough that they'll need to be planted in soil again. At that time, we'll ask the trees where they want to go.' Then Beneto noticed her breathless excitement. 'All right, what have you brought for me this day, little sister? A new insect? An untasted berry? Or a flower with a perfume that will make me sneeze?'

'It's too big to carry, Beneto.' Catching her breath, she told him about the sleeping worm hive. 'It's big enough for a dozen families at least! We've needed new quarters for over a year.'

'Indeed we have,' Beneto said. 'A remarkable discovery, and a very good omen. I'm sure Mother and Father will pat you on the head.' Estarra scowled, and he laughed at her predictable reaction. 'It's a valuable find, Estarra. When do you predict it will hatch?'

'Two weeks, I think. Three at the most. Probably about the time Reynald returns from his peregrination.'

'You love to explore and find the forest's secrets, don't you? Make sure you mark its location and keep an eye on its progress.' Beneto placed a warm hand on her shoulder. 'In the coming days, the worldforest may have many important tasks for us green priests, but I promise I will be there so we can watch it hatch together.'

TWENTY-TWO

MARGARET COLICOS

Rheindic Co called out to Margaret like an ancient book filled with secrets, a book that waited to be opened. The desert was raw and rich with muted colours, browns and ochres, tans and rusts. So much to see and explore, but so much work to do setting up camp before they could get started.

She looked out upon the mysterious wasteland. They had chosen a site near the most obvious Klikiss ghost city, though the slot canyons and banded cliff sides might hold innumerable other settlements.

Beside her, Louis wiped the back of his hand across his forehead, scattering perspiration. He leaned over to give her a polite kiss on the cheek. 'We've been to worse planets, dear.'

Chairman Wenceslas had given the Colicos their pick of any world to investigate, and they had chosen this abandoned planet. Rocky bluffs extended like mysterious monuments under a burnt-orange sky. Lava protrusions broke the monotony of dry alkaline lakebeds that gleamed like mirage mirrors. Arroyos cracked the landscape where only a memory of rushing water remained.

'It's here, old man,' Margaret said in a breathy voice. 'I can sense it. I know we'll find something. Even the Klikiss robots seem to think so.'

'I'm not one to argue.' Louis had a boyish grin on his weather-lined face. 'After all these years, you've said "I told you so" enough times that I'll trust your instincts.' He looked appraisingly at his wife. 'We'll never know until we get our hands dirty, dear.'

A metal clanging shattered the still air as the green priest Arcas worked with a simple hydraulic assembly. The standard-issue drill pump chewed its armoured bit into the ground, questing for a buried aquifer to provide fresh water. Next, he angled the solar panels that would provide energy for the camp lights, cook stoves, and comm systems, as well as their modular analysis lab and computers.

The newly purchased compy servant DD assisted him ably, though the green priest seemed somewhat nonplussed at being next to the small Friendly-model android. Margaret didn't think the reticent Arcas actually resented the chest-high companion, but he seemed to prefer his own company.

The Colicos team worked without extravagance. Margaret and Louis laid out the plan for their base camp and erected portable aluminium-roofed sheds and polymer-walled tent structures. The litany of tedious tasks was welcome work to Margaret. She was glad to be back on a dig.

After the success of the Klikiss Torch, she and Louis had attended many celebrity functions, and served as guest speakers at numerous gatherings. Hating the limelight, she had pulled every string with the Hansa to get to Rheindic Co as quickly as possible. Sarcastically, she had once muttered, 'Maybe the Klikiss race really disappeared just to hide from persistent alien paparazzi.'

As contract Hansa employees, Margaret and Louis surrendered all commercial rights to any useful discoveries, though they did receive substantial bonuses. Margaret didn't much care about the income stream, since she enjoyed doing what she loved, and Louis was happy as long as he had full freedom to publish all the scholarly papers he wished.

She and Louis had been married for thirty-seven years, and this would be their fourth Klikiss dig. They had investigated archaeological mysteries on Earth and Mars, but the ancient insectoid race fascinated them most of all. What had happened to this civilization? Why had the Klikiss left, and where had they gone? And why had they left behind their hulking armoured robots, ten feet tall and sentient, looking like burly upright insects?

Although the Ildirans had frequently encountered remnants of the lost civilization, they had left the abandoned sites alone. 'Why should we delve into the story of a vanished race?' Adar Kori'nh had asked Margaret aboard the observation platform at Oncier. 'We have the *Saga*, which tells all the history we could possibly want to know.'

Indeed, the epic poem mentioned the Klikiss race numerous times, but only in passing, giving no details about the culture of the vanished civilization. Margaret's scholar son Anton, studying ancient records at a university on Earth, had told her that it wasn't clear whether the Ildirans had encountered the living Klikiss, or only their remnants. Their lack of interest in the topic struck her as being incurious to the point of narrow-mindedness.

In the early years of Terran and Ildiran cooperation, human 'colony prospectors' had scouted the unclaimed habitable worlds listed in Solar Navy records. One team, a woman named Madeleine Robinson and her two sons, had gone to Llaro, where they were astonished to find ruined cities and numerous dormant Klikiss robots, which they had accidentally reawakened. Since then, dozens of other Klikiss sites had been surveyed, and many more of the black beetle-like machines had turned up. The Ildirans, though, had known about them for centuries.

Now, the three ancient Klikiss robots who had surprisingly requested to join the Rheindic Co expedition used their massive mechanical strength to erect a weather tower at the camp perimeter. Finished with that task, the three big machines moved with a weird gait on flexible finger-like legs towards marker stakes in the dry ground, where they began to raise the walls of a heavy storage shed.

Margaret looked at her hastily sketched site diagram and hurried over to the nearest alien robot. 'Not there. You're five metres off position.'

'It belongs here,' the robot said in a thin, humming voice.

'Which one are you? Sirix? Or Dekyk?' The trio looked identical to her.

'I am Ilkot. That is Dekyk.' The beetle-like robot gestured with two segmented worker arms that extended from his ellipsoidal torso. 'Sirix instructed us to place the structure here.'

Frowning, Margaret allowed that the position of the shed made no real difference, though she didn't understand the Klikiss robots or their occasional incomprehensible stubbornness. It was another example of how different these machines were from a 'Competent Computerized Companion' like DD, who followed orders like a faithful servant.

She and Louis had been thrilled when three of the sentient Klikiss machines had volunteered to join them at Rheindic Co. The harmless Klikiss robots, though oblivious to human orders or plans, occasionally offered assistance in construction or exploration projects that interested them. These three wanted to participate in investigating their lost civilization, professing equal curiosity to solve the mystery of their vanished creators.

And to learn why they could remember nothing.

Only a few thousand of the machines remained, scattered and

shut down during the last days of the vanished civilization and now awakened from their slumber. Unfortunately, every one of their memory cores had been wiped clean of all data that could provide clues to the fate of the alien race.

Beside her, Louis made an approving sound as the robots assembled the shed in record time. With glowing red optical sensors mounted at various places in their geometrically shaped headplates and numerous segmented limbs that sprouted from their armoured carbon-fibre shells, the Klikiss robots were proficient labourers – powerful, yet capable of delicate manipulations.

Beneath the robots' main body core, a spherical abdomen was mounted like a trackball at the waist, from which sprouted eight flexible legs like bent millipedes, four on each side. The strange method of locomotion allowed the robots to scuttle over any kind of terrain.

Sirix, the ostensible leader, moved forward. 'The assigned labour has been finished, Margaret Colicos. Your camp is prepared.' Sirix drew his six main manipulator limbs back into his body core and closed the openings with protective plates.

Over by the drilling apparatus, Arcas let out a shout as a geyser of cool, clear water sprayed upwards. The shower ran over DD's silvery metal skin.

The priest came to stand near Margaret, his smooth green skin glistening from the spray. 'Chemical analysis shows it's pure drinking water.' He licked his lips. 'And it tastes delicious.' Margaret was glad to see the quiet man so excited. Thus far, Arcas had not seemed enthusiastic about being here with two archaeologists, but he had volunteered for the job. 'Now that I have water, I can plant my twenty treelings. Enough to make a respectable grove here on this desert world.'

'Go ahead and plant them,' Louis said. They would eventually need the telink ability to send regular reports back to the Hansa.

'DD, would you help him, please?' Margaret said. She had hoped DD would be able to interact with the Klikiss robots, but so far the little compy seemed intimidated by the giant ancient machines. She decided not to rush things.

The compy hurried over like an eager child. 'I have never planted treelings before, but I am glad I can assist. Arcas and I are sure to become great friends.' The green priest looked a bit uncertain about the idea, but accepted the offer of help with good grace.

'He's a Friendly model,' Louis said. 'Don't let his enthusiasm bother you. It's just his way.'

As Arcas and DD dug holes for the potted treelings behind the green priest's tent, the three Klikiss robots stood motionless, like mechanical statues, staring at the orange-coloured sky as it faded into dusk.

In the canyons and in the shade of the mountains, night shadows fell like guillotine blades as the sun passed over the horizon. Initial surveys had found that temperatures could drop by as much as forty degrees within an hour, but the archaeological team had brought batteries, warm clothes, heated shelters, and exothermic blankets. The archaeologists would be comfortable here in camp, though they would have difficulty sleeping on the first night for entirely different reasons.

They were both eager for the great adventure ahead of them. Why had the Klikiss abandoned this and so many of their worlds? A mass migration? A war? A terrible plague?

Tomorrow, Margaret and Louis would get to work.

TWENTY-THREE

ADAR KORI'NH

From space, the Ildiran splinter world of Crenna looked beautiful and green, dotted with lakes, inland seas, and fertile land. But Adar Kori'nh knew that the settlement festered with a terrible disease that first blinded its victims, then killed them. The entire colony must be abandoned, and perhaps burned, before the plague could spread further.

Let the humans deal with the aftermath, if they wanted the cursed place.

The magnificent cohort of the Solar Navy – seven full maniples, or three hundred and forty-three ships – approached with great fanfare. The bright vessels that resembled disk-like fish cruising in a precise formation that had been practised and tested in numerous military parades.

Due to politics and the structure of the Solar Navy, Adar Kori'nh was ensconced in the command nucleus of the ornate lead warliner. He made few decisions, allowing the aged cohort leader, Tal Aro'nh, to manoeuvre his ships as he saw fit. This mission would require little risk or innovation, and the stodgy Tal would follow each step precisely according to protocol. Kori'nh had accompanied the evacuation mission only because the Mage-Imperator had commanded it.

During the journey to Crenna, the Solar Navy's best tacticians and troop-movement specialists had developed the evacuation plan. Once Tal Aro'nh assured himself that every step had been specified and written down, he relaxed. The dutiful subcommander would follow the plan without deviation. Aro'nh was a perfect example of the Ildiran Solar Navy, wearing the correct plumage of rank, never expecting his place in the universe to change.

The seven maniples took up varying orbital positions around Crenna in preparation for launching their rescue operation. Cutters would scout the landscape, assess the extent to which the terrible plague had spread, and estimate how many inhabitants required evacuation to the warliners. Adar Kori'nh frowned impatiently as he watched the activity and waited for reports.

The communications officer continued to send messages down to the Crenna colony town. Frustrated, the officer looked over at Kori'nh, who nodded pointedly towards Tal Aro'nh, indicating that the subcommander should receive the report first. 'After continued attempts, Tal, we are unable to reach the Crenna Designate.'

'The Crenna Designate has perished from the plague,' Kori'nh said. The Mage-Imperator had already sensed the death of his son. 'We will have to manage this operation based on our own plan.'

'And we do indeed have a plan,' said Tal Aro'nh, as if reassuring himself.

The first sleek cutters dropped towards Crenna's single city, where the splinter colony had been established. Gregarious Ildirans preferred to live in close quarters, unwilling to spread out on open land. Groups of settlers worked the fields, raising food for their colony, but each evening all the people returned to the fold, where they could take comfort in the combined *thism*. Now, though, so many Crenna inhabitants had died that the *thism* was frayed and broken, without sufficient population density to maintain a true link. The survivors felt bereft, isolated . . . terrified.

Kori'nh felt a tightness in his chest, a backwash of fear projected from the colony survivors. 'We must hurry, Tal Aro'nh,' he said from the command nucleus. 'Those people are alive . . . and alone.'

The surveillance cutters returned, transmitting images so that the large escorts and bulky troop carriers would know where to land. Personnel-transport vessels had been stripped down and modified to accommodate quarantine conditions and sterilization procedures.

Kori'nh studied the images of the colony town, where many buildings had already been abandoned or burned. The plague survivors that remained free of the scourge huddled together in boarded-up buildings – a perfect recipe for spreading contagion. As the disease spread, the victims first lost their eyesight, dying in terrible darkness – which was anathema to the Ildirans, whose race had evolved under the perpetual daylight of seven suns. Even the burly soldier kith looked uneasy at the prospect of facing the disease. Death was one thing, but darkness, *blindness*, was altogether more frightening.

'Take no time to salvage any material objects,' he suggested to the Tal. 'We must abandon and shut down Crenna. The Mage-Imperator already considers the entire settlement a loss. Evacuate the survivors as soon as possible, before any more fall to the plague.'

Accepting the Adar's suggestion as a direct order, Tal Aro'nh relayed the words throughout the cohort.

From his comfortable command nucleus, Adar Kori'nh considered how this event might be dramatized in later versions of the ever-growing *Saga of Seven Suns*. How would his own role be recorded? He didn't want to sit safely here, watching from high above. Abruptly, he stood from his command chair. 'Tal Aro'nh, I will personally accompany one of the groups down to the surface.'

Alarmed, the old subcommander turned to him. 'That . . . is not part of the plan, Adar – nor is it wise. The soldiers are already at risk.'

'If we have not taken sufficient precautions, then we should not be sending our soldiers there.' Kori'nh strode towards the hatch. 'And if the situation is safe enough for our soldiers, I consider it safe enough for me. I will see Crenna for myself, since the Mage-Imperator will want a first-hand report.' And only with active participation would he be remembered as more than just a man who watched in comfort while nameless soldiers performed the dangerous work.

Kori'nh found a seat on the twenty-sixth troop carrier. The low-ranking soldiers were impressed that the prestigious Adar would join them, though some appeared intimidated that he had stepped outside the boundaries of his normal role.

The Ildiran rescuers suited up in anti-contamination films, tough membranes that covered their muscular bodies to protect against disease organisms. Adar Kori'nh peeled on a thin suit of his own, tugging the membrane into place and snugging it against his skin. The polymer film made a slurping sound as he adjusted it, and then he breathed sterilized air through the permeable layer. He flexed his arms and stood at the troop carrier's hatch, ready to march out with his soldiers into the wounded colony.

As the dozens of rescue ships landed in the main square of the Crenna city, haunted-looking survivors stared in amazement and relief. For Kori'nh, their ache, their terror, was palpable in the air. Once their Designate had succumbed, they had lost all direct telepathic contact with the Mage-Imperator. The Crenna colony was like an amputated limb, slowly twitching and bleeding to death.

Now the stricken settlers came forward, hesitant. The soldiers could feel them exuding pain and fear. Some evacuation personnel were stunned into confusion, while others worked doubly hard to hurry these poor people away.

Earlier, the Crenna colonists had gathered their dead and cremated them in huge bonfires in the open streets, as if hoping the hot flames would whisk their souls from the darkness of death to a brighter place. Kori'nh could see the sooty stains of ashes and blistered bones. Some of the colony structures that had been used as hospitals, and then death wards, had also been burned to the ground with all the bodies inside.

'Leave everything!' he shouted through the protective membrane. 'No keepsake or piece of furniture is worth the risk of bringing this infection back to Ildira. Take only your lives and count yourselves lucky.'

Personally, he would have liked to vaporize every vestige of the colony town. The Mage-Imperator had already negotiated with the Terran Hanseatic League for ownership of this planet, and Kori'nh wanted to leave nothing for the parasites. Since human physiology was different from Ildiran biochemistry, the disease organism was not likely to infect them in the way it struck down Ildirans – or so the Terrans hoped. Human medical researchers and scientists were waiting to begin their investigations, eager to move to an already tamed planet. Such blatant Terran opportunism in the face of Ildiran tragedy made the Adar uneasy . . .

Kori'nh remained on Crenna for the rest of that day as thousands of colonists crowded aboard troop carriers and were taken to specified hospital warliners. The refugees would remain in isolation behind decontamination fields. Though separated by bulkheads and sterile barriers, the survivors would be able to feel the comforting presence of other Ildirans. The thickness of hollow walls could not block the *thism*.

As he sat back aboard the final troop carrier while the pilot returned them to orbit, Kori'nh looked down at the empty colony. He and his troops had performed an efficient and commendable operation, and he would derive a great deal of acclaim from this accomplishment.

While the warliners assembled in orbit, Kori'nh saw other ships already approaching Crenna, Terran research vessels that carried their eager scouts, ready to grab the abandoned colony from the very moment it became available.

He scowled, as always failing to understand why humans were in such a hurry, why they needed to acquire so much land and wealth simply for the sake of possessing it.

With a muttered lukewarm blessing, the Adar let them have this place of death, loneliness, and misery.

TWENTY-FOUR

BASIL WENCESLAS

In Old King Frederick's ring-studded hand, the Medal of Glorious Commendation glittered like a star ready to go nova.

Basil Wenceslas watched the ceremony from behind the scenes, as usual. He paced the floor in his dedicated office suite, observing through close-up media cameras that showed him everything from the King to the milling crowd in the presentation square. Here, in peaceful solitude, Basil could make mental notes. He had given Frederick's handlers sufficiently detailed instructions that he expected the event to take place without a hitch.

Under the lights of the presentation square, General Kurt Lanyan of the Earth Defence Forces stood precisely on his mark on the long red carpet. In his full dress uniform he looked both impressive and uncomfortable. Unlike Basil, the EDF commander had no choice but to be a public figure at times such as this.

After the latest round of cheers faded, Frederick held high the outrageously gaudy Medal of Glorious Commendation like ancient King Arthur about to dub a devoted knight. Imagers captured every moment from every angle. The records would be distributed across the Hansa colonies by fast stardrive ships, showing off the pomp and ceremony that was a daily routine at the Whisper Palace.

Robes covered the old King with a cocoon of colour, but the broad sleeves drooped, exposing his stick-like upraised arms. Frederick's face was gaunt, and on the screens Basil could see that the attendants had applied too much makeup, giving the King a powdery, surreal appearance. Basil frowned, hoping no one else would notice.

Lanyan stood at attention, his head formally bowed with the reverence and solemnity of the occasion.

Frederick boomed, 'General Kurt Lanson, I have summoned you here to receive this honour.' Basil winced at the obvious error in pronunciation. *Lanson?* Couldn't the King at least memorize his own general's name?

A twitter passed through the crowd like a breeze ruffling a smooth surface of water. Basil gritted his teeth, hoping the slip would not attract too much attention. The people loved their King, but Basil hated for the man to show such obvious signs of age. Charming befuddlement was only a small step away from senility. No one in the Hansa-settled worlds should ever suspect that their King might not be competent to rule.

Frederick didn't even notice his gaffe. 'You have halted the depredations of the vile space pirates led by the Roamer Rand Sorengaard. You have succeeded where others have failed.' On cue, for Basil had stationed numerous agents throughout the crowd, cheers erupted in a deafening howl that cut off the King's sentence and seemed to disorient him.

Victorious, General Lanyan had returned to Earth bringing the battered corsair ships they had impounded after capturing Sorengaard's pirates. Though the vessels looked dirty and poorly used, Hansa engineers had discovered startling ship modifications. Sorengaard's stardrives had been improved to an efficiency that no

Hansa ship exhibited. What were the Roamers doing out there in secret?

Basil quietly instructed that the breakthroughs be analysed, copied, and incorporated into EDF ships. After the military vessels were upgraded, the technology could be sold to merchant ships at a great premium. Basil would even claim that Hansa engineers had developed the innovations on their own.

King Frederick droned on, reading scripted words projected on to his retinas. 'The Earth Defence Forces have a charter to crush lawlessness in the Spiral Arm. Without the obeying of laws, we have no civilization, merely anarchy. And under my rule there will be no anarchy!' More cheers. Basil sank into a comfortable chair, relieved. The King was doing better.

On the screens surrounding him, Basil watched as Frederick lowered the heavy medal on its colourful ribbon to drape it over General Lanyan's neck. The EDF commander had received numerous accolades before, and each one made him a more prominent hero in the eyes of the public. Ceremonies such as this helped to increase the standing of the military forces.

Basil Wenceslas partook in almost no hedonistic pleasures, though he had tried them all when he was younger. Long ago, he'd given up drinking and drugs and smoking, finding that he acquired a greater sense of euphoria from his *accomplishments*. An only child and an over-achiever, Basil had learned from his parents, both their successes and their mistakes.

His mother and father were important executives in a large commercial corporation, merchants who distributed much-needed wares among the human-settled planets. His father had worked to make huge amounts of money so he could buy villas and vacation spas and beautiful things for himself, his friends, and his wife. Basil's mother, on the other hand, was a more intense person than her husband. She never enjoyed her wealth or power, but instead seemed afraid she might lose her status at any moment. She had never allowed herself to relax, while Basil's father squandered much of what he had achieved.

Observing the two of them, Basil had combined the best of both traits. As Hansa Chairman, he had supreme self-confidence and knew how to achieve grand things. But he did not waste his fortunes on mansions and jewellery; he devoted his energies to other things.

Now, Basil paced his quarters high up in the Hansa pyramid, looking through glass walls to the filtered sunlight that reflected from the torch-capped domes and cupolas of the Whisper Palace. On the display screens, King Frederick clasped General Lanyan's shoulders and turned the uniformed man around to present him to the cheering audience. The loud applause prevented many from hearing the King's words, but Basil spotted the repeated mistake right away.

'I give you General Kurt Lanson! The greatest of my generals and a man whom I consider to be a personal friend.' The people cheered, and Basil seethed, embarrassed. The General bowed his head and pretended not to notice, taking the old King's error with good grace.

'Enough is enough,' Basil muttered. 'Things must change.' He sent a signal, calling for his expediter, Franz Pellidor, and his group of hand-picked operatives.

When the men arrived in the upper headquarters level, blond Pellidor squared his shoulders and stood in front of his team, looking expectantly at the Chairman.

Basil ran a well-manicured finger over his lower lip, pondering the best way to implement his ideas. Finally, he issued quiet orders for the operatives to begin their work. 'You will take whatever action is necessary. We must get the newly chosen Prince in training immediately. I hope we haven't waited too long already.'

'We understand, sir,' said Mr Pellidor. The expediter didn't flinch or flush. Basil would not have expected otherwise.

He thought of the previous heir-candidate, Prince Adam, who had proven too unruly and disrespectful of the careful house of political cards built by the Hansa. Basil had been forced to eliminate young Adam before ever letting the public know of his existence.

He lowered his voice, speaking mostly to himself as the operatives turned to depart. 'Let's pray that this new candidate proves more tractable, or we will be in deep trouble indeed.'

TWENTY-FIVE

RAYMOND AGUERRA

Raymond made his way back towards the apartment complex with a jaunty step, pleased at how much he had accomplished during the dark and quiet hours.

In the early dawn, the air smelled damp but fresh as the city awakened. His muscles were tired from heaving crates at a distribution centre's loading dock, and his sweaty clothes smelled of oily smoke from a poorly tuned lifter engine that had filled the hangar bay with noxious fumes. But he had made a good haul and had used his meagre under-the-table wages to acquire some packaged food, a new shirt, and even an electronic puzzle for his little brother Michael.

Now Raymond was anxious to get back to his apartment and clean up. He didn't usually come home this late. He hoped to have an hour or so to nap, or at least get breakfast before he went to school. His mother would already be up, and he liked to be there to help her with the boys, but he had earned enough last night to make up for a bit of tardiness. He clutched the satchel to his side, happy.

He came upon a scene of complete disaster.

When he turned the corner into the residential district, the unfolding scene of chaos, flames, and emergency vehicles brought him up short. His curiosity gave way to dread as he began to run down the street. Flames curled into the sky. A pillar of black smoke rose upwards like a burnt fist.

With every block as he closed the distance, the certainty became a grenade in the pit of his stomach. Using his shoulder, he crashed against jostling bystanders. 'Let me through!' He swung his satchel of belongings to knock people out of his way, then finally dropped the food and shirt and electronic puzzle, not caring.

His whole street was an inferno. Emergency vehicles raced overhead, rescue copters circling but unable to approach the raging fire or even attempt a rescue. At last Raymond reached the front lines to look up into the poisonous smoke and the crackling sky. From behind a hastily erected barricade, he saw the holocaust that remained of his apartment building.

In the hot air and crowded closeness of simmering violence, spectators stared with mixtures of fascination and horror. Raymond found himself speechless and sobbing, his face red, tears streaking the dust on his cheeks. He tried to duck under the barricade, but ran into the padded uniforms of crowd-control officers. 'Stay back,' a gruff man said. 'You can't go closer.'

'That's my home, my family!'

'It's your death if you go closer. Keep back!'

The ground beneath the structure had become a smouldering crater, and the rest of the apartment had collapsed inside it, as if some volcano had erupted beneath the city streets. Wreckage lay scattered up and down the block. Black smears of soot from the explosion blistered the walls of nearby buildings.

A tall man in a formal business suit looked down at Raymond. He was the kind of person the young man would expect to see behind a boardroom table sipping coffee and filling out ledgers. The businessman explained with apparent glee, 'Building owners were illicitly storing contaminated stardrive fuel in underground storage vaults. Nice hiding place, right under an innocent-looking dwelling complex.' He shook his head as if in disbelief at the stupidity.

Raymond could barely find words, simply staring into the stinging fumes and furious heat. 'Spaceship fuel . . . under our apartment building?'

'It must have been siphoned off, treated, and sold on the black market. But the vaults were poorly insulated, no protective systems. Everything by the seat of the pants. What a bunch of idiots. A disaster waiting to happen – and it happened.'

It sounded improbable – ridiculous, even. But he knew that before dawn most of the families would have been home asleep. He couldn't believe it. Raymond's knees went weak and watery, but as he swayed, the press of the crowd held him upright. Oddly, he even saw a large black Klikiss robot, one of the few that had chosen to come to Earth, staring at the fire with red optical sensors, as if fascinated.

A group of men in flame-resistant environment outfits marched out of the blasted front door of the complex. Two of them carried bodies, possibly still alive. But only two bodies . . . of all the people inside the building. Raymond couldn't dare hope that one of those might be his mother or a brother.

'Can't get up past floor seventeen.' One of the men spoke through a suit-transmitter so that his voice came out loud but filtered. 'Walls are collapsed, and the doors are fused shut.'

'What do you mean fused?' asked the rescue commander.

'Welded closed, barricaded from inside, I don't know. There wasn't time to stand around and make a full analysis. Are the suppressant ships coming in?'

The rescue commander directed the team to a staging area. Up in the sky five cargo copters closed in on the swirling blaze. They flew like bumblebees, heavily laden with chemicals. Through amplified loudspeakers, the rescue commander bellowed to the crowd. 'Everyone stand back. Stay clear of the fire suppressant activities.'

Before the lumbering mass of curiosity seekers could shift position, the cargo copters opened their belly-hatches and spewed copious amounts of greenish-white foam on to the inferno. Thermal updrafts and furious breezes trapped among the tall buildings flurried the descending foam, splattering globules in a broad radius. Splashed spectators backed up to get away from the mess, but the watchers were too crowded, and little more than a shock wave of disturbance rippled through the mob.

In spite of the suppressant foam, the apartment building continued to blaze white-hot, engulfed in flames so intense that fire-fighting crews couldn't begin to battle the disaster from ground level. Another three fire-fighting copters bombarded the building with extinguishing foam, and Raymond realized their main goal was simply to stop the fire from spreading to other buildings, not to save any of the people inside.

Frantic to do something, he pushed against the barricades once more. 'I have to get in there. My brothers, my mother.' Greenish-white foam made him slip as he smeared his way forward.

But again, crowd-control officers blocked him. 'Won't do any good, kid. There's nothing left inside but ashes and dental work.'

Before Raymond could cause more of a scene, the crowd jostled him again. One of the suppressant choppers overshot its target and dumped half a load of foam over the officers and the front ranks of people. The crowd backed away, cursing. Raymond found himself swept up in the amoeba-like motion.

From behind, a man grabbed his arms and pulled him away.

Raymond tried to struggle, then felt an iron grip on his other arm, though it was slick with spilled extinguishant. His voice was lost in the hubbub of the crowd.

Three large, nondescript men unobtrusively steered him through the masses towards a side street where the crowd had thinned. Raymond did not recognize these men, saw no expressions on their faces beyond a grim set to their jaws and a complete focus on what they were doing.

'Let me go!' He lashed out with his feet, trying to kick. His toe connected with one man's shin, but the man didn't even flinch, as if he had armour hidden beneath his grey slacks.

Raymond saw a sealed vehicle waiting, parked against the side of a building, its engine running. Dread closed around his heart. This was too much to bear after seeing the fire at his home, knowing that his entire family had been lost in the intense explosion beneath his apartment complex.

He struggled more wildly and managed to get his foam-slick arm free. He swung a fist, connecting with one man's ribs, but it hurt his own knuckles more than it hurt his would-be kidnapper. The door of the vehicle opened like a giant black mouth waiting to gobble him up.

'Who are you? Leave me alone!' He screamed at the top of his lungs. 'Help!' He knew it would do no good. The holocaust and emergency operations were far too noisy.

A blond-haired man with ice-pale blue eyes stepped out of the vehicle, a broad-muzzled energy pulser in one hand. He said in a calm, almost conversational tone, 'This stunner won't leave any marks, young man. I have permission to use it if I have to.'

Raymond thrashed more vigorously. In the end, the blond kidnapper had to be true to his threat.

Stunned unconscious, Raymond Aguerra was shouldered into the vehicle. The door slid shut, and the men whisked him away.

TWENTY-SIX

CESCA PERONI

No matter how much outside people and events pummelled them, Roamers always fought back and remained strong. Inspired by rigorous circumstances, Roamer culture blossomed with ideas, some of which were impractical or eccentric in the extreme; other schemes were innovative enough to let the fiercely independent clans thrive in places where most humans would find existence impossible.

Within the rubble belt around a dwarf star, the Roamers had expanded from the first tiny foothold left behind by the *Kanaka*. Rendezvous was a wonderful medley of space habitats and hollow asteroid living quarters, a scattered rocky archipelago around a blood-red sun.

The asteroids were detritus from the collapsing protostar, insufficient material to coalesce into a planet. Rendezvous was designed with numerous places to dock spacecraft, ships both large and small, as well as camouflaged depots for storing ekti.

Roamers were comfortable with low-gravity environments, suiting up and bounding from one rock to another using jetpacks.

Some of the cluster's inner asteroids were strung together with cables that flexed and extended and retracted, like cablecar strands. Dim sunlight shone upon reactive films and solar-wind collectors that provided enough power for the settlement.

Cesca Peroni had lived here much of her life. She considered Rendezvous not at all strange.

She and Jhy Okiah sat inside the Speaker's office chamber hollowed out from the largest rock of Rendezvous. While much of the Speaker's business involved mitigating clan squabbles, accounting for profits, and studying resource distribution among the widespread settlements, she also heard proposals and assessed the merits of ambitious new ventures.

These meetings with engineers and clan speculators were the most enjoyable of Cesca's duties. All Roamers were encouraged to develop new concepts and consider different techniques for exploiting resources, however unlikely they might seem. Inventors modified standard equipment and vessels already in use, improving them to incredible efficiency, far beyond anything the Hansa had achieved. Nor would the Big Goose ever know.

The curly-haired engineer Eldon Clarin sat in a low-gravity seat, controlling his enthusiasm as Jhy Okiah and Cesca stared at his beautifully drawn plans for two new spacecraft designs. Clarin and his team of specialists had done their work admirably well, and he waited for the old Speaker either to make suggestions or grant him approval to pursue his new concepts.

Jhy Okiah looked over at Cesca, waiting to see her protégé's assessment. The young woman bit her lower lip, putting her mind into sharp focus. 'As clearly as I can understand it, your modification increases thrust efficiency, minimizes ekti consumption—'

Eldon Clarin interrupted. 'Yes, yes, and still we retain navigational accuracy. That has been a problem in the past.' He sat back and looked at the two women, hoping for their acceptance. He scratched his curly hair, which hovered like a corona around his head.

Because Roamer society had been built on interconnected families, strong women often dominated their politics. Throughout human history, politics had usually been based on warfare, strength, and blustering testosterone. Roamers, however, found that female politicians were much better in the peaceful resolution of disputes. Women could talk through problems, get to the root of a conflict and ferret out the real cause for disagreement, which was often an illogical emotionally-based slight. Maternal leaders were better at exchanging subtle favours that kept the society running smoothly.

Long ago, Jhy Okiah had been chosen as an acceptable mixture of bloodlines, a compromise from dozens of different clans who would thus be able to make decisions without playing favourites. Cesca, on the other hand, had been selected as the Speaker's successor because she came from a particularly strong family. She was the only daughter of a merchant and distributor, Denn Peroni, who had accomplished great things for the Roamers.

Seeing the faintest curve of a smile on Jhy Okiah's lips, Cesca realized that the old woman had already made up her mind about Clarin's proposal and was merely drawing out the suspense. The Speaker always advised against making snap judgements, because the parties in question might not believe due consideration had been given to a matter, even when the answer was obvious.

So Cesca waited as Jhy Okiah pretended to ponder the plans again. Finally, she asked for Cesca's assessment. Cesca covered her own smile, knowing the answer she was expected to give. 'I believe Engineer Clarin's proposal would make a good addition to our capabilities. In fact, I would advocate that his modifications be implemented in all new vessels constructed at our Osquivel shipyards.'

'Agreed. Once we know a more efficient way to do things,

there's no point in continuing to use the old method.' Then Jhy Okiah cautioned the elated Clarin, along with the grinning and excited team of engineers who waited behind him. 'Remember that no Hansa representative should ever suspect the existence of such modifications. We must maintain our edge.'

The engineer nodded so deeply Cesca thought his chin would leave a dent in his chest. Before he could pack up his plans and rush off, the Speaker held up one bony finger. 'Wait a moment. Would it be possible to adapt your intake modifications and power-conversion manifolds to skymines?'

'Skymines?' The engineer scratched his curly head, as if he had never considered the possibility.

She pointed to the plans. 'A skymine does not travel far or fast like our space vessels. However, the concepts should be similar and transferable.'

Eldon Clarin glanced at his team members, all of whom nodded quickly, though Cesca believed they would have agreed to anything in their thrill at receiving the Speaker's approval.

'Good, then I want these modifications to be included in the new skymine that will soon be put into service at Erphano. The facility is undergoing its final construction stages right now, so you'd better hurry.' Clarin's engineers looked alarmed, then drew deep breaths, accepting the challenge.

The Speaker looked at Cesca. 'My grandson Berndt will be managing that skymine. Why not have him start with an efficient facility?'

'No point in wasting time.' Cesca smiled, seeing the old woman's plan all along. 'To make certain that the modifications run smoothly, perhaps Engineer Clarin should serve aboard the Erphano skymine for a month or two, as a shakedown?'

'Cesca, you never fail to demonstrate my wisdom in choosing you as my successor.'

'We will do as you ask, Speaker Okiah. Thank you for your approval!' Clarin bustled out of the office chamber, his motions exaggerated in the low gravity.

Next to enter was Kotto Okiah, the Speaker's youngest son by her fourth and last husband. She raised herself off her sling chair and kissed him on each unshaven cheek. She looked without surprise at the scattered plans and notes he had brought with him.

Some Roamers chose to use computer design systems and thin display screens to show their work, but Kotto Okiah preferred to work manually, calculating with his own brain power, and scribbling on valuable pieces of paper, which he always recycled if his ideas proved fruitless. Many of his concepts fizzled into dead-ends, but the young man's sheer imagination had also led to numerous breakthroughs.

Kotto bowed to Cesca, but his full attention, as always, was on his ancient mother. Jhy Okiah insisted that she never gave her family special treatment, but all Roamers had clan ties and obligations.

Kotto was diligent enough to have other engineers check and double-check his work to ensure appropriate safety levels. Still, even when accidents happened, the optimistic Kotto never appeared shamed, only contemplative. 'Innovative developments are not always perfect,' he said. 'We must expect some to fail.'

'Please make it as few as possible,' his old mother had said.

Now the young man spread out his display, including star-charts, surveillance photographs, and rapidly sketched plans for a strange settlement on a bleak, hot world. 'I don't know if you'll like this idea, Mother. It is very dangerous, but could be highly profitable.'

'I'm listening. You'll have to convince me, as always.'

Cesca leaned forward to participate in the discussion as Kotto began to talk with exuberance. 'I've been studying the hot world of

Isperos, very much like the planet Mercury in the Earth system. The challenge is large, but the resources are remarkable. Look at all these metals, and the rare isotopes readily available on surface scrapings! I think it would be worth the effort.'

With deft fingers he pointed to several different designs he had sketched. He explained how Jess Tamblyn had flown him on a reconnaissance mission to the planet, mapping out the details.

'That sounds like Jess,' Cesca said with a smile. 'Is . . . is he still here?'

Kotto looked confused, trying to deal with a question he had not thought about answering. 'No . . . no, he left three days ago. Had to go back to Plumas. I think he'll be returning within a few weeks, though. I offered to take a packet from him, but he said he'd bring it back.'

He absently tapped his chin and returned his attention to the designs of a self-contained hot-world settlement. These new techniques could open many formerly uninhabitable terrestrial worlds for Roamer settlement. Heavy elements and pure ores will be very useful in our industries. With proper care and diligence, Isperos could be a gold mine for us . . . well, gold and other metals.'

'And the beauty of it is that no other humans would ever want those worlds,' Jhy Okiah pointed out, eyes bright. The Speaker watched the doubt play across Cesca's olive-skinned face. 'Perhaps I am not objective where my youngest son is concerned. What is your opinion on the project, Cesca?'

Cesca studied Kotto's boyish face. 'One has to admit the risks, but also recognize the rewards. Could Isperos be much more of a challenge than anyplace else we have settled?' She shrugged. 'As long as the rest of Roamer society is prepared to help shoulder the burden of this new colony while engineers and a few brave settlers take their first uncertain steps, then we should make the attempt.'

Jhy Okiah looked up at the stone ceiling of the asteroid chamber, as if imagining the Rendezvous complex all around them. 'By the Guiding Star, if Roamers never tried to do the impossible, we would never have accomplished anything.'

TWENTY-SEVEN

BERNDT OKIAH

Only a practised eye could see the beauty of the skymine under construction at the slapdash facilities in the broken moons of Erphano.

Burly Berndt Okiah stood within the transparent bubble-dome installed on the pock-marked moon. With the industrial station's low gravity and the enormous olive-and-tan gas giant filling the sky, Berndt experienced an odd shift in perspective: the immense planet seemed *below* him, and he felt as if he were falling head-first into the clouds.

Teams of Roamer constructors had descended upon the system's rubble, analysed the geological composition, then brought in mobile factories to begin work. Automated smelters and ore-crunchers had devoured entire moonlets, processing rocks to leach out necessary elements, extruding plates and casting components. Later, an army of construction workers removed the designated components and assembled the giant industrial puzzle.

Occasionally, in construction sites within the boundaries of Hansa territory, some of the still-functional Klikiss robots volunteered to perform hazardous space construction. They worked hard, asked no questions and took no payment, but operated on their own schedules. Most Roamers, though, didn't trust the mysterious ancient machines and preferred to do their own labour.

Since this was Berndt Okiah's pet project, a skymine that he would own and manage, he had been here from the beginning, more than a year. He had lived in austere encampments of underground chambers drilled into the small moons and then coated with polymer walls. As the resources were chewed up, shipyards had grown like a forest. Tall girders, support derricks, and tether cables held the skeleton of the Erphano skymine as Roamers added the metal flesh.

Though Berndt had confidence in his workers, he was still blustery and intrusive, watching over their shoulders as they assembled the ekti reactors. His grandmother's pet engineer, Eldon Clarin, had recently arrived with new plans and bold suggestions to improve the systems. At first, Berndt had been put out by the sudden change in plans, until he realized the modifications would require no more than a week and, if successful, make his new skymine more productive and therefore more profitable.

Berndt had promised himself and the Roamer clans that he would make a success of this operation. His grandmother had given him an exceptional opportunity – though some claimed he did not deserve yet another chance – and he would not waste it. Berndt had many things to prove to himself and to his people.

As he sat in the observation blister watching the final preparations, Engineer Clarin entered through the access tube. 'I've checked all the systems, Chief. The skymine is nearly ready for launch.'

The burly man nodded, scratching his square chin. 'Still operating at ninety-seven per cent of projected norms?'

The engineer looked surprised. 'How did you know?'

'Because I checked them myself an hour ago. It's my business to understand things aboard my new skymine.' Berndt's physical size and his reputation as a gruff bully clearly intimidated Eldon Clarin, but the engineer's ease with mathematics and science, his sheer intelligence intimidated Berndt in turn. 'Once the facility enters the Erphano cloud decks, we'll have plenty of time to do our shake-down. You will be staying here to verify all systems. Please?'

Clarin drew his brows together as if surprised at the big man's demeanour. 'Speaker Okiah requested that I stay for at least two months.'

Berndt focused his gaze on the huge planet below so he could avoid looking at the man as he spoke, his normally gruff voice sounding a bit nervous. 'Engineer Clarin, I'd like to request a favour. While we are here, I would ask . . . if you might provide me with some instruction?' For years, he had blustered and shouted to get his way; now it felt very strange to be making such a request.

Even the engineer seemed surprised. 'What is it you would like to know?'

'I want a stronger background in the functioning of the sky-mine, from ekti processing to the Ildiran stardrives. It's my business now.'

The engineer looked at his hands. 'This seems rather . . . unusual. Berndt Okiah is not known for his scholarly pursuits.'

Berndt flushed. 'That was in the past. I'm the Chief of a new skymine. I should broaden my horizons.'

Outside, suited workers crawled over the hull of the factory suspended in the emptiness. He ran his eyes over the enormous collector tanks for raw hydrogen and the geometrical reactors that processed and siphoned off the ekti allotrope. The big skymine also had an upper habitation and support deck containing crew quarters, leisure chambers, and command centers.

After being constructed in place around gas giants, skymines were manoeuvred to the clouds with powerful in-system engines. The skymines themselves would never leave their gas giant homes, relying on cargo escorts to take away storage tanks of ekti.

The Ildiran propulsion system was based on direct physical movement, without resorting to exotic anomalies such as wormholes or dimensional jumps. But the stardrive did produce a space-time ripple effect that, as far as Berndt understood it, relativistically slowed time for the ship. Somehow, the stardrive maintained a 'continuum memory' that allowed vessels to return to real space very close to the proper frame of timeline reference. The effective result was to travel great distances in a short timespan. To the unschooled outsider it looked simple, though the actual mechanics were very complex. During their next two months together, Clarin would attempt to teach Berndt the detailed systems.

Long ago, when the Ildirans had offered them the opportunity, Roamers had jumped at the chance to work the ekti-processing stations. Ambitious clans had secured loans from the Ildiran Empire to lease their first skymining stations. Despite an initial disaster on Daym, the Roamers turned the cloud-processing facilities into profitable operations. Roamers had copied the skymining technology, then improved it and set about building other stations. They continued to expand as their ekti profits increased.

Now Berndt led Eldon Clarin through the tube to the suit-up chambers. 'Time for us to launch the new skymine. I want you with me.'

Clarin looked surprised. 'Me? But you're the Chief—'

'It'll look good on your resume when you get back to Rendezvous.'

An hour later, the two men stood on a launching platform above the mineral-stripped excavation sites. Overhead, more rubble and exhaust debris spread outwards, devoid of useful metals.

The navigation hazard would also serve as a smokescreen to hide the activities on Erphano.

Work crews waited inside modular off-shift sheds while others floated outside with their heads pointed down towards the olive-and-tan planet. Anchor cables kept the gigantic skymine from drifting away.

Berndt operated his suit radio. 'Prime the manoeuvring engines.'

Captains aboard the skymine worked controls on the upper deck. Berndt could see tiny figures behind the glowing bridge. Suited workers stood on the observation platform high above the first reactor. Cowlings brightened as the drive reactors heated up and the engines exhaled a hot breath of exhaust. A restless behemoth, the newborn skymine pulled against its tethers.

Berndt felt a thrill of pride as he gazed at the magnificent structure that would be his to command. He had never been present at a skymine launch, though he had supervised an older facility for several years. His first skymine command had been on Glyx, a facility that was already up and running with a veteran crew when he'd become Chief. He had been more of a babysitter and manager, not much of a leader. The Erphano facility, though, was both a big promotion and a big chance for him.

Some of the clans grumbled that Berndt Okiah had by now received all the chances a man could deserve. He had squandered them in his youth, when he'd been overbearing, too full of himself. He understood his folly now. He couldn't wait to bring his wife Marta and twelve-year-old daughter Junna to work with him here.

Though he'd once harboured grandiose dreams of becoming the next Speaker, Berndt now realized he was simply not able to lead all of his people or command so many resources. When younger, he had swelled his chest and demanded an important role in government, though he'd never proved himself worthy of respect or responsibility. Such greatness was not possible for him, and that epiphany had brought about a change in him.

At first, he'd been jealous of Cesca Peroni and her relationship to Jhy Okiah, but now he saw that she would be a more talented Speaker than he ever could. Berndt regretted his brash actions and poorly thought-out plans, but after years of exemplary service on the Glyx skymine and now with this new vessel under his command, he would become the best Chief of any ekti-processing facility.

With the engineer holding the support railings, Berndt disengaged the mobile platform and activated the putter engines that lifted them to the towering skymine. Berndt cradled a valuable thin-walled container of pseudo-champagne, a traditional icon the Roamers continued to use for the baptism of a new ship.

The mobile platform carried them up past the curved storage chambers and the broad, gaping mouth of the gaseous intake chute. Clarin peered through his faceplate, amazed at the immensity of the vessel up close. Once the Erphano skymine dropped into the clouds, few people would ever see its lower hull again.

Berndt hovered beside the front ekti storage tank and, smiling, grasped the neck of the pseudo-champagne bottle. Weightless, he knew that when the bottle struck the metal wall, he would recoil in the opposite direction, and so he gripped the support railing.

He had carefully considered his words. 'With great pride, I launch this skymine: pride not in myself but in the capabilities of the Roamer construction teams that have built this marvel. And pride in my dedicated crew who will run the operations and bring about a profitable status. Most of all, though, I launch this skymine with pride for what it symbolizes to the Roamers and our ability to prosper where no one else would dare to venture. Let the Guiding Star take us to our destiny.'

He swung the champagne bottle. As it struck the hull, the glass shattered, and the pseudo-champagne exploded into the vacuum of space. Thin glass fragments and boiling, fizzing, freezing clouds of carbonated liquid foamed outwards, volatilizing like a comet's tail.

As applause and cheers echoed through the comm systems, Berndt Okiah took the mobile platform up to the command deck. He and the engineer cycled through the airlocks and stripped out of their suits as the bridge crew hurried to congratulate them.

'Disengage tethers,' Berndt said, his first command issued aboard his new factory. The skymine lurched as the metal cables detached from their anchor points. 'Increase thrust to engines.'

The skymine eased away from the rubble, moving towards the clouds of Erphano. Berndt glanced back at the scarred construction facility behind them, then turned forward, looking at the eye of the gas giant. The resource-rich clouds beckoned him, and he decided that he would not look back ever again, only forward.

TWENTY-EIGHT

RLINDA KETT

Rlinda Kett awoke satisfied from a comfortable night's sleep beneath the whispering worldtrees. After devouring an extravagant breakfast of fruits and nuts accompanied by clee – a steamy, potent beverage made from ground worldtree seeds – she felt ready to tackle any decision.

'If I stay here on Theroc much longer, I'll gain a dozen kilos,' Rlinda said to Sarein. 'That would both endanger my health and decrease the cargo mass I can carry on the *Voracious Curiosity*.'

Sarein had added metal combs to her hair and wore a traditional Theron gown, looped with court finery, beautiful scarves and shawls made from ephemeral cocoon fibres. Rlinda wanted her own wardrobe of the cloth – to demonstrate its beauty to new customers, but also so she could preen in front of the mirror. Although she had no intention of attracting yet another husband, she saw no harm in looking pretty.

'My parents would like to speak with you,' Sarein said with a confident smile. 'We must make a good impression.'

'Leave it to me, Sarein. I can make a good case.' Rlinda brushed herself off and stood, looking longingly at the various dishes she had not yet found time to sample.

Inside the largest chamber of the fungus-reef city, Father Idriss and Mother Alexa held court. Airy gaps to the outside were covered with prismatic condorfly wings that served as stained-glass windows. The two leaders sat side by side, statuesque and handsome, dark-haired and bronze-tanned.

Rlinda stepped forward, her steps surprisingly delicate and careful for a woman of her size. She bowed deeply, with all the grace she could manage. 'I am most pleased for the opportunity to speak to you, Father Idriss and Mother Alexa.'

Idriss leaned forward on his large chair. He had a squared-off black beard and wore a headdress of feathers and beetle carapaces that gave him an imposing and magisterial presence. 'Our daughter Sarein speaks well of you. I think she considers you a friend. How could we not meet with you, when our eldest daughter requests it?'

Beside him, Mother Alexa wore a dazzling gown with impressive shoulder apparatus that stood tall like the plumage of a peacock. Part of the queen's costume had been assembled from the whole wings of condorflies, colour-coordinated with the clothes she wore. Her glossy raven hair fell to her waist.

Rlinda straightened. 'I hope Sarein hasn't exaggerated my importance. I am not a particularly prominent person in the Hanseatic League, and this is a great honour for me.' Sarein stood off to one side, attentive, but the merchant woman kept her focus on the two rulers. 'The forests of Theroc appear to be rich with possibilities. Sarein showed me many of your native products, and I believe there are countless trade opportunities we could explore. Frankly, I'm surprised that armies of merchants haven't already attempted to forge alliances with you.'

'Few people see beyond our green priests,' said Alexa. 'That is all the Hansa seems to want.'

Idriss added, 'And we aren't overly eager to complicate our lives. We speak for the green priests, but the worldforest helps them to make all their decisions. In truth, we have little to do with their choices. Here, the Therons have everything we need. We are content, with no large-scale causes of human conflict.'

Sarein touched Rlinda's broad shoulder in a companionly gesture. 'Some even claim that the benevolent presence of the worldforest suppresses the natural human penchant for violence and conflict.'

'Then I applaud your efforts to spread treelings to other planets.' Rlinda smiled wryly. 'I can name plenty of places that would benefit from it.'

'Our priests are doing all they can.' Mother Alexa nodded to her husband.

Idriss and Alexa took care of local disputes, occasional personal squabbles, marital troubles or civil cases, but their most important purpose was to act as an interface with the outside. The Mothers and Fathers of Theroc had always calmly made decisions based not on greed and wealth, but on their genuine beliefs for the good of their culture.

Rlinda glanced at Sarein for encouragement. 'Well, your daughter has made my head dizzy with all the things I've seen and tasted here. I can name hundreds of possible markets for your exotic fruits, berries, nuts, and unusual fabrics.' Her stomach growled, as if to emphasize her opinion.

Sarein stepped forward, breathless. Her eyes were intense. 'Think of all the doors it could open for us, Father. Mother? We could become a powerful trade presence without giving up our independence.'

'We have talked about this before, Sarein,' Idriss said.

Seeing the leaders' closed expressions, Rlinda felt a sinking sensation. She began to suspect that she had been brought in as

Sarein's cat's-paw in an old argument between complacent parents and their ambitious daughter.

'Rlinda is willing to accept sample loads of our products to prove their commercial viability, but she is also taking a risk by investing her own resources.' Sarein's face hardened, then she astonished Rlinda by suddenly adding new terms. 'Therefore, she has also requested several green priests – five would be a good number – in order to give her a bit of insurance. I feel that's only fair. Don't you?'

She looked at Rlinda, who tried to cover her shock. They had never discussed this, but it seemed to have been Sarein's secret intention all along. Rlinda now feared the delicate negotiations might crumble.

'She would also carry treelings to help expedite the spread of the worldforest,' Sarein continued in a rush. 'You see? Everyone benefits.'

Father Idriss looked disturbed, though not quite angry at his daughter. 'We do not command the green priests where and when they must go, Sarein. The worldforest operates outside of our political leadership. The priests defer to the wishes of the trees, and Mother Alexa and I must defer to the priests.'

'It was merely a suggestion, sir,' Rlinda said quickly. 'Theroc has so many things to offer. Let's not become focused on one sticking point—'

'But it's an unreasonable sticking point, if only you would open your eyes,' Sarein said, openly defiant. Rlinda wanted to call a recess before an argument ensued that would end negotiations entirely.

Mother Alexa said, 'We maintain careful records and control over the distribution of the treelings. Regardless of your interest in our fruits and berries, Rlinda Kett, we understand that our telink communication ability is the strongest coin Theroc has to offer.'

161

Idriss continued, 'It would not be wise for us to establish a precedent by allowing you to take our priests along with our forest products.'

Flustered, Rlinda looked at Sarein, wishing the young daughter had said nothing. 'Please don't be hasty. I sincerely apologize if an ill-spoken comment gave you a bad impression of me. Could we discuss the matter further tomorrow? I'll give you specific examples of items I'd like to carry aboard my merchant ship.' She backed away, trying to dismiss herself before Father Idriss denied her completely.

Alexa answered with a condescending, though beautiful smile. 'We will listen, because that is the basis of communication. But we will not be swayed. Green priests are valuable to us.'

'I agree fully, as you will see,' Rlinda said, with a final deep bow. She wished Sarein had never made the suggestion; it had never crossed Rlinda's mind. 'I look forward to another discussion at a later time.'

With Sarein frowning about the meeting, Rlinda walked with her out of the meeting chamber. She had to rethink her approach and make a different sales pitch. Next time, perhaps, without Sarein's 'help'.

TWENTY-NINE

ARCAS

The deserts of Rheindic Co filled his eyes with a geography unlike anything he had ever seen on Theroc. Typically, a green priest would find such bleakness disturbing, but Arcas felt the desert calling to him. He had never expected to feel so alive. The quality of light, the sharp shadows, the dry air . . . and the *silence*. It awakened an unexpected delight in his heart. He revelled in the warm sunlight on the rocks, the layered strata of red iron ore, green copper oxide, white bands of limestone. At last, a task he could enjoy.

While Margaret and Louis Colicos began their work in the main Klikiss city, the compy DD maintained the camp with meticulous care. When Arcas had finished his early-morning tending of the treelings, he longed to follow his heart and explore places that interested him.

He went to the larger tent where the two xeno-archaeologists lived. The old man had already gone with the three Klikiss robots to the cliff-side ruins, and Margaret was packing up her notes for the morning. She looked up expectantly. 'Yes, Arcas? Do you intend to go with us to the ruins today, or will you stay in camp with your treelings?'

'Actually, neither,' he said, embarrassed. 'I'd like to explore the nearby canyons. The geology is very interesting to me.' Arcas did not need her permission, because green priests followed no leader except the worldforest. In fact, Margaret never seemed to know what to do with him.

'Take whatever equipment you require. Do you need DD along?'

The suggestion startled him. 'No . . . I would rather be by myself.'

Margaret was intent on hurrying to follow her husband out to the excavation. 'See if you can make measurements and record your data. We are on a scientific mission, and geological analyses can be useful, too.'

'I'll do what I can.' Arcas had hoped just to take a walk, to enjoy the scenery and drink in the details, which he would then repeat to the treelings for dissemination through the worldforest. The sentient trees were not accustomed to desert landscapes, and he would at last feel that he had served a useful role as a green priest. Nevertheless, he gathered imagers and data-collection devices from the camp supply shed and placed them in a pack.

Margaret took one of their short-range vehicles, accompanied by DD, and headed off to the cliff city. Standing in the empty camp, Arcas took a glance at the twenty thin treelings planted in rows behind his tent. They now stood chest-high, waving as if basking in the sunlight. 'So you like the desert too?' he said. If he touched the treelings, they would answer him.

With no specific destination, Arcas drew a deep breath, tasted the dry and dusty air. Trudging into the wrinkled landscape, he headed towards a gorge that had been cut by ancient waters. Unfiltered sunlight tingled his green skin.

Arcas had never really wanted to be a green priest, yet once a person bonded with the worldforest, the symbiosis could not be reversed. He could leave the trees, never engage telink again, but he would always remain green-skinned and part of the network.

His mother had died while he was young, and so Arcas had a very close relationship with his father. The older man, Bioth, had longed to become a green priest, but had been caught in a different career. Bioth would sit with him under the canopy, looking up at the whispering fronds and talking about his dreams, about how much he wanted his son to serve the worldforest.

Arcas had never been enthusiastic at the prospect. 'Father, we all serve the worldforest, no matter what we do.' He had been more interested in history and geology, but Bioth already had his mind made up and never noticed his son's reluctance.

When Arcas was fifteen, Bioth had fallen out of a high tree while harvesting epiphyte juices. The older man had landed in a tangle of vines that acted like a net. Unfortunately, when the vines broke his fall, they also snapped his neck. Young Arcas had rushed to his father's side as the workers lowered him to the ground. With his last choked words, Bioth begged his son to make him proud, to become a green priest. With everyone listening, Arcas could not deny his father's final wish. Once the tragic story became known among the Therons, Arcas was easily admitted into the priesthood.

So, he had done his duties without any particular passion or inspiration. He had never wanted an impressive or pampered assignment in an opulent colony government house, because then people would be bothering him all the time. He found tolerable assignments by choosing history tracts and geology texts to read to the trees. But here, on Rheindic Co, the desert serenity called to him.

Now as Arcas walked away from the camp, looking at the wrinkle-backed mountains, he followed a line of boulders up an alluvial fan that narrowed into a canyon. As the rough walls rose above him, he saw the gnarled striations of geological layers that reminded him of the growth rings in a cut tree.

Arcas crunched along the loose riverbed. The echoes reflected eerily from the narrow walls. He looked around, keeping his eyes open for any discovery that might help the Colicos' work. When he'd joined this mission, Arcas had offered more than just his services as a green priest. His passing knowledge of archaeology and geology made him a potential assistant.

As he proceeded deeper into the canyon, he realized he had never in his life been so far from the comforting touch of plants and trees. Or crowds of people. The ruddy sun angled into the canyon, and he looked up at a smooth, white section where a slab of limestone had sheared off in large, cream-coloured lumps. With awe, he saw shapes and designs moulded into the limestone: fossilized remains of alien creatures that had lived uncounted millennia ago, a bent frond of what looked like a fern, a bony sea creature with large jaws and sharp fins.

He removed his rock hammer and chipped away the most remarkable fossils, storing them in a pouch at his waist. Then he imaged others that were too large to excavate. These specimens had lived millions of years before the Klikiss ever set foot on Rheindic Co. As Margaret Colicos had reminded him, this was a scientific expedition, and Arcas could make discoveries of his own.

He hiked back towards the encampment, stepping over tumbled boulders that lay strewn like giant marbles. Even if the canyon had not provided such a precise route, Arcas could have opened his mind and let the treelings call him back to the camp. With worldtrees around, a green priest could never get lost.

He looked down the gentle slope of the alluvial fan. Far to the south, he saw a smear of bruised darkness across the sky where their survey satellites had shown distant volcanoes spewing ash and soot. Each day, he loved the blazing watercolour sunsets most of all.

He adored this desert world, though such feeling gave him a twinge of guilt, because it seemed like a denial of the worldtrees. But he made up for it by hurrying to the little grove, kneeling beside the treelings, and touching their trunks. Closing his eyes, he recalled the palette of his memory and described all the beautiful things he had seen.

The trees responded with wordless delight.

THIRTY

SAREIN

As the humid forest settled for the night, Sarein made sure her little sister Celli went to bed. Idriss and Alexa were not rigid parents, but Sarein insisted on following a schedule. Though the ten-year-old always tried to wheedle another hour or so of play time, Sarein insisted that Celli abide by the rules.

'Tie down your pet condorfly,' she said. 'And wash up.'

'He needs me to watch over him,' said Celli with a pout. The colourful creature rattled its emerald-green wings inside the chamber, then clacked its long thin beak as if in search of flower petals to devour.

'He can take care of himself. He is a wild creature, you know.' Sarein stood in the low doorway, brooking no argument. She knew it would be only a matter of moments before her sister heaved a sigh and did as she was told.

'He's my pet.' Celli had captured this one just as it emerged from its chrysalis, still moist and weak. She kept a thin chain cuffed to one of its eight segmented legs so that it could flap and drift above her shoulder like a living kite. Sarein had always thought condorflies had about as many brain cells as a kite.

'Yes, and he wants you to go to bed as much as I do. Now don't make this as difficult as you did yesterday.' Grudgingly, the little girl complied.

At night, still tethered to its stand, the condorfly would crawl through the window and fly as far as the leash would allow it. In the morning, Celli would reel it in. Luckily, condorflies had relatively short lifespans, and so her sister's dependence upon this mindless pet would last no more than a month or two.

All day long, the little girl was a bundle of energy, running and leaping, chattering with friends, playing various games. She had more foolish courage than common sense. By the age of ten, Celli had had her share of broken bones from various falls and scrapes. Her tomboy body was an ever-changing pattern of scabs and skinned knees, scratches, bruises, and scrapes.

Sarein often grew impatient with her, but then told herself that Celli would grow up. Eventually. Estarra, two years older, seemed well on her way to making proper decisions. Sarein's greatest hope was that she and her siblings, in one generation, could change Theroc and bring these backwater people out of their prehistoric naivety and into the thriving community of the Spiral Arm.

Finally, after a perfunctory hug and kiss, Sarein closed the door and walked through glow-lit corridors. Reynald was due to return soon from his peregrination, and Sarein hoped he had made inroads with powerful figures. She couldn't wait to hear her brother's description of the Ildiran court and wondered what he might have accomplished on Earth by meeting with Basil.

Mother Alexa and Father Idriss had gone to the higher levels of the city, where they would watch a festive performance of talented gymnastic treedancers. Sarein had been invited to see the skilled leaping and tumbling among the springy interlocked fronds, but she had no interest. Estarra had been forced to go to the festival, but she would probably slip off by herself to climb the rugged layers of the fungus-reef. Sarein sighed at her family's aloofness. They had so many resources and opportunities – yet they seemed not to care. They simply lived from day to day, oblivious to the rest of human civilization, satisfied with what they had.

She entered her quarters, increased the illumination, and sat at her polymer-fabricated desk imported from Earth. She had many official records and contracts to study. It discouraged her that Idriss and Alexa insisted on ignoring the Hansa's greater commercial possibilities. Perhaps she could find loopholes in old agreements, as Basil had taught her to do.

She ran a hand over her short dark hair, combed and cut in a popular Earth style. In her wardrobe, she kept many traditional Theron gowns and scarves, adorned with broken bits of condorfly wings and polished insect shells, but Sarein preferred the comfortable clothing she had brought from her year of study on Earth. Theron trappings were too provincial for her tastes.

The first documents before her were Rlinda Kett's revised proposal for trading Theron products. Sarein scowled, reminded again of her parents' stubborn refusal to grasp an obvious opportunity. The merchant had made excellent arguments, and Sarein had continued to press Idriss and Alexa in their private chambers. But she could not convince the two that Theroc should join the Hansa, regardless of how many doors it would open for them.

Bearded Idriss had looked at his daughter as if she were a child. 'Giving up independence is not a thing one should do lightly. What have we to gain compared with all that we can lose?'

Sarein felt as if she were speaking to an incomprehensible alien. *No*, she thought, *even Ildirans would be more sensible in this matter.*

She tapped her stylus on the electronic document, pondering the future of her world and dismayed at how difficult this supposedly simple task was going to be. She might need help.

Sarein thought wistfully of dashing Basil Wenceslas and all she had learned under the suave Chairman's gentle guidance. Basil was much older than her, but incredibly cultured and handsome, healthy, and with an animal magnetism that made him captivating to her, even more so because of the power he wielded in the Terran Hanseatic League.

On wondrous Earth, Sarein had been fed the best meals and given the finest wines. Basil had courted her, knowing that this young daughter might be a key to opening Theroc, and Sarein, realizing what he was doing, had willingly let herself be lured. She had as much to gain as did the Chairman.

She had allowed Basil to seduce her, and they became lovers for several months before her schedule forced her to return home. He had been a considerate partner, patient yet energetic, and Sarein had come to care for him beyond her initial attraction to his knowledge and power. She loved his élan, and she recognized how much he desired everything that Sarein represented. To him, she was possible leverage to receiving more green priests . . .

Weary of her work now, Sarein dimmed the glow lights, stripped off her clothes, and slid naked between the slick woven sheets of her bed. She felt dizzy and restless, her mind yammering with possibilities, contract language, numbers. As she drifted off to sleep, she smiled, letting herself dwell on actual memories mixed with fantasies of Basil.

Sarein began to wonder *who* had actually seduced whom.

THIRTY-ONE

AMBASSADOR OTEMA

A s soon as the old woman returned to Theroc, the weariness of so many years of service lifted from her shoulders like condorflies taking wing. A devoted green priest, Otema relished being back home among the worldtrees.

On Earth she'd had lush quarters in the diplomatic section of the Whisper Palace, and the King's gardens held many worldtrees. Still, Otema longed to touch the soil of Theroc with her bare feet, to scale the broad trunks and feel the feather touch of interlocking fronds.

At the age of one hundred and thirty-seven, she was the oldest of the green priests. After so many years of symbiosis, her skin had darkened to deepest green. Otema had maintained her health through her link with the forest and her dedication to her duties, but now she was glad to come back to rest, to study, and to pray.

The worldforest seemed uneasy, as if pondering a deep secret or gradually becoming aware of a hidden concern. None of the green priests understood it completely, but they trusted the judgement of the trees and remained on guard.

As the Theron ambassador to Earth, Otema had done her work for the trees, butting heads with the ambitious Hansa. Stern and inflexible, the old woman had earned herself the nickname of 'Iron Lady' by resisting Chairman Wenceslas's methods of persuasion, stonewalling the Hanseatic League's strident demands for more green priests. Otema did not yet know who would be chosen as her successor, but she did not envy that person the job that lay ahead.

As Otema disembarked from the shuttle in the landing clearing, she moved slowly but precisely, not because she was frail but because her every movement was careful. She stood under the sunlight of Theroc, looking up to the turgid sea of treetops. She spread her green-skinned arms wide, closed her eyes, and drew a deep breath to inhale the song of the worldtrees.

Even through the undertone of hidden fear, from the forest's drowsy mind she felt a flurry of welcome, a vibration of acceptance and happiness. She heard the greetings of fellow green priests who remained here, as well as a fainter echo of the others with their own treelings scattered across the Spiral Arm.

'Ah, thank you,' Otema said aloud, knowing the trees would hear, as would all the other priests. She felt revitalized, a dozen years younger.

Long before many green priests reached her age, they grew so weary of life that they allowed themselves to rejoin the forest – not dying in the usual sense, but letting themselves be absorbed into the database of trees so that their cells were incorporated in the ever-growing biological network. But Otema did not feel her work was finished yet.

Yarrod, a prominent green priest, met her at the shuttle. 'We are glad to have you back with us, Otema. Father Idriss and Mother Alexa have also requested to see you, as soon as you feel refreshed.'

'I feel refreshed just by being back among the worldtrees,

Yarrod. There is no sense waiting.' She turned and led the way, and the male priest hurried after her.

In the throne chamber, Idriss and Alexa wore formal garments of office and tall headdresses as they sat in their ornate chairs. Idriss beamed when he saw Otema, and Alexa stood up. 'We are so glad you have returned, Ambassador, from your long and arduous service.' Alexa gave a soft smile. 'The many years on Earth have drained you. You must be pleased to commune with the trees again, here on your home soil.'

Otema straightened her ambassadorial robes, which were dyed with various jungle symbols and thought patterns of the worldtrees. She bowed, her limbs flexible despite her extreme age. 'Nevertheless, if the forest should ask me to continue in my capacity as ambassador, I would be glad to serve.'

Father Idriss raised a large dark-skinned hand. 'Have no worry about that, Otema. Your duties are in the best of hands, and our relations with Earth will build upon what you have already accomplished.'

From a side alcove, their daughter Sarein emerged, wearing a traditional shawl of cocoon fibre over a stylish indigo outfit of the type that was fashionable on Earth. Looking at the young woman, Otema saw the pride and ambition in Sarein's eyes. She felt a barb of uneasiness in her skin.

Mother Alexa said, 'After much discussion, we have decided to appoint our daughter Sarein as the new ambassador to Earth. She has studied with the Hansa and is familiar with many powerful people on that planet, including Chairman Wenceslas. There is no one more qualified for the job.'

Otema did not let her disappointment show. She narrowed her hard eyes and looked at Sarein, who seemed pleased with her appointment. 'Your daughter is a very intelligent and capable young woman, but she is not a green priest. Is that not a necessary criterion for serving the worldforest and speaking for Theroc?'

Idriss made a dismissive gesture. 'Not so. Do *we* not speak for Theroc? Besides, she will have access to green priests in the Whisper Palace, should she need to consult with us through telink.'

'That is not entirely the concern,' Otema said. 'It is a matter of . . . understanding nuances.'

Sarein stepped forward, keeping a quiet face that belied her obvious undercurrent of annoyance. 'On the contrary, Lady Ambassador, as the daughter of Father Idriss and Mother Alexa, I can provide a unique perspective and understanding of the worldforest and Theron ways. Unlike the green priests, however, I also have a grasp of new and changing commercial practises within the Terran Hanseatic League.' She raised her eyebrows in an aloof expression. 'Such matters may not be clear to someone who is immersed in a one-sided view of interstellar commerce.'

Startled, Otema stood straight, realizing that she had been out-manoeuvred. Disturbed by the eagerness and drive that was so apparent in Sarein's manner – yet somehow invisible to her doting parents – Otema bowed in acquiescence. 'I will do my duty.' Formally, she unfastened the clasp of her ambassadorial cloak and removed the ornate fabric, holding it out like a matador's cape. 'Sarein, I present you with this emblem of your new office. Take these robes and serve the worldforest well.'

Somewhat uncomfortably, Sarein accepted the cloak, but draped it over her arm rather than wrapping it around her shoulders.

Now barely clad, her skin such a dark green it was almost black, Otema excused herself from the throne chamber. She sketched a final bow to the two rulers and walked towards the exit arch. 'If you need me for further consultation, I will be communing with the worldforest.'

THIRTY-TWO

NIRA

Nervous yet eager, with a thrill unmatched by anything she'd ever experienced, Nira Khali went deep into the forest. Alone. There, she would survive through the grace and protection of the worldtrees.

As an acolyte, she had spent her life waiting for this moment. She had devoted every waking hour to praying and studying how to serve the sentient forest, how to become an integral part in Theroc's overall ecosystem.

With a smiling Yarrod and other proud green priests watching her, the young woman ran off, barefoot and bright-eyed. Wearing no more than a loincloth, Nira spared only a moment to wave farewell before she dashed through the low foliage and vanished into the thickening worldforest, far from the settlements.

She swallowed with uncertain nervousness at how greatly her life would soon change. Then she drew a deep breath of the spicy foliage, heard the rustle of dry leaves against her feet, and took strength in the reassuring closeness of the awesome worldtrees.

She belonged here.

After this day, Nira would no longer be alone, as a completely separate individual. Soon, if the forest accepted her, she would become a part of something so much more. Joy and anticipation made her footsteps light.

'I am coming.' Her voice was quiet, but spoken to the millions of sentient trees across Theroc and in satellite groves on other planets.

Yarrod had not instructed her where to go, but Nira instinctively ran away from paths where humans usually wandered. Around her and high above, the broad palmate leaves brushed together, making a sound like encouraging whispers. She followed her instincts, and the forest guided her.

She descended gentle hills and made her way into moist lowlands, where weeds grew at the confluence of tiny streams. She splashed through the bog, long blades of grass brushing her calves. The mud grew softer. She had never been here before, but some part of her recognized this place.

Creeks eddied into stagnant marshes, where the clear water became choked with tiny floating plants, creating a slurry of sludge-like vegetation. Nira looked around, seeing sunlight dapple patterns across the marsh. A person could easily get lost here, step into a deep pool of living quicksand.

But Nira allowed herself no doubts. She ran ahead without slowing, letting the forest guide her. She knew where to find stepping stones and fallen logs, even if they were hidden beneath the surface. She'd never heard the worldforest so clearly in her mind before.

Around her she saw ominous movement, ferocious reptiles that cruised through the weed-laden water – scuttling predators with scaled hides and long fangs. Today, Nira accepted them without fear. Muscular and fast, they glided through the soupy undergrowth, watching her every step, waiting for her to trip. But Nira hopped from one moss-slick stone to another, never losing her balance. She skipped across a slimed tree trunk and raced to the other side of the bog, leaving the sleek predators to watch her with yellow slitted eyes. Nira ran on.

Any time she could not clearly decide which direction to go, she simply flung her arms around the trunk of the nearest worldtree and pressed her naked chest against the scaled bark. When her skin touched the tree, the guiding thoughts sharpened inside her and she ran off again, energized. Nira paid no heed to the passing hours or the burbling wilderness.

Finally, the forest grew dark and thick with green shadows like smoky glass. The darkness was comforting, womb-like, not ominous. Nira parted branches, tall stalks of grasses and weeds, working her way deeper into a network of vines . . . until the forest swallowed her up entirely.

She could not move. Her shoulders pressed against firm branches that tangled tighter. Insistent vines wrapped around her legs. Leaves brushed her face, her nose, her lips. Nira closed her eyes and let the forest touch her.

She felt as if she were falling, though her body remained propped up. She could barely twitch her fingers as the jungle clasped her, embraced her . . . absorbed her.

There, deep in the thickest worldforest, Nira passed uncounted hours in a mystical experience. She saw through eyes in the leaves, looking through a million faceted lenses at all perspectives of the worldforest. Information and impressions roared around her in a rushing torrent.

As if through distorted windows, she glimpsed other planets, other worldtree groves that had been planted and fostered by green priest missionaries. She'd never imagined anything so vast, so complex – yet, even with the assistance and encouragement of the worldtrees around her now, she was seeing only the tiniest glimpse of the forest's potential.

It was breathtaking.

Then the heart of the worldforest spoke to her more clearly, more terribly. She felt a distant, unformed fear of an ancient enemy. *Fire.*

Destruction.

The death of worlds.

Groves of treelings withered, whole civilizations died, and only a tiny vestige of a galaxy-spanning worldforest had survived here, isolated on Theroc.

Nira couldn't cry out, could not decide whether these terrible images and fears were history, or prophecy. Then she saw giant spherical ships, like spiked globes made of ice, a hidden empire engaged in a titanic war. *They were coming.*

Shaken by the vision, but giddy with her new connection to the worldtrees, Nira finally emerged from the smothering, nurturing hold of the sentient forest. Her heart hammered, and the prophecy weighed heavy in her mind and heart. This wasn't what she had expected at all.

Nira walked along as if in a daze, stepping through the bog without even looking at the ground. The feline reptiles moved away from her as if they could sense that she now wore the forest's protection. As the sunlight splashed her arms and thighs, Nira noticed without surprise that her flesh had turned a pale green. Now her epidermis was impregnated with a symbiotic algae, a verdant tone that would supplement her body's strength through photosynthesis. As she aged, the green would darken.

Nira touched her close-cropped hair, and the stubbly fuzz fell out like grains of pollen. Even her eyebrows and eyelashes dropped away.

In her mind now, she could hear the trees like constant companions, an organic database and a half-sleeping mind all around her. It would always be there for her. She would never experience utter silence and aloneness again. The knowledge felt

179

glorious, the infinite thoughts and memories . . . along with the terrible fear of an impending disaster. How was she to deal with it all?

With rapid footsteps and a determined expression on her face, Nira raced back to the settlement where she could at last join the other green priests as a full member of their order. And she had to warn them of the danger the worldforest had shown her.

When Nira breathlessly described her awesome vision to Yarrod, though, the green priests around him simply nodded. Their faces showed bleak foreboding.

'We already know,' Yarrod said.

THIRTY-THREE

GENERAL KURT LANYAN

Because he was the commander of the Earth Defence Forces, General Kurt Lanyan could use the full facilities of the war simulations room any time he wished. Filled with computers, holographic projectors, interactive systems, and detailed navigational charts, the sealed chamber was the most sophisticated and expensive room on the entire Mars EDF base for Grid 1.

In here, with all the resources and intelligence data compiled over nearly two centuries of interaction with the Ildiran Empire, Lanyan could get his answers . . . or at least make reasonable guesses. Many questions remained about the culture, habits, reactions, and secrets of the alien civilization, and the General wanted to be prepared for any possibility.

During early Terran expansion into the solar system, before humans had access to the Ildiran stardrive, the EDF had taken possession of Mars as its sole property. The lifeless red planet had become a training base and military headquarters, operated as an outpost and staging area. The rugged Martian landscape provided any number of obstacle courses and survival scenarios. The thin atmosphere allowed Remoras to simulate aerial manoeuvres with an easy switchover to space combat in the vacuum above. Lanyan loved it here.

After giving orders that he was not to be disturbed, the General had sealed himself into the war simulations room. He called up the complex virtual systems he had developed from years of testing, toying with possibilities, modifying results with every scrap of data he could acquire about the aliens. He wished Basil Wenceslas would send out more spies, but Lanyan would make do with the available intelligence. It was enough to run plenty of scenarios.

Now he stood in the centre of the room, speaking to the voice-activated control boards. The curved matte walls and floor dimmed, becoming black and star-studded. He felt as if he floated in the centre of a spherical three-dimensional planetarium; it reminded him of when he was just a space soldier, training for zero-G combat, floating all alone in the vacuum, ready to shoot mirrorized drone targets.

'Display typical Ildiran Solar Navy.' He put his hands on his hips and turned around. 'One entire maniple. Let's make it a vigorous engagement.'

Images appeared, fuzzy shapes that sharpened into accurate representations of forty-nine Ildiran warliners and cutters. Lanyan paced around the images like a shark cruising through a school of fish. The gaudy warliners were large disks tilted on their sides with streaming heat-radiator fins that made them look like deep-sea predators. Knowing what he did about the aliens, Lanyan suspected that the gaudy extensions and strange shapes were ceremonial or decorative. Peacock feathers, with no military purpose whatsoever.

The Ildirans were a stagnant race. In centuries, they had made no improvements in their technology – nor had they needed to, because their empire lived in a brain-dead sort of peace, all the aliens connected by the vague, controlling *thism* that dampened their individuality. No one would rebel against their revered Mage-Imperator, nor would the splinter colonies ever squabble with each other. He couldn't comprehend how the Ildirans justified using so much funding and resources to maintain the massive Solar Navy if they had no enemies. It made no military sense . . . unless their Mage-Imperator had other plans. General Lanyan didn't trust him.

He had even considered the unusual possibility of recruiting a few of the massive and mysterious Klikiss robots as fighters. The ancient machines worked on hazardous construction sites and seemed willing to contribute to Hansa activities, but only if it served their unspoken purposes. For the moment, though, Lanyan had tabled the idea; he didn't like to count on a 'weapon' that was fundamentally incomprehensible. Rather, he would rely on his own military equipment.

Now, preparing for the virtual combat exercise inside the projection room, Lanyan walked around the holographic displays, reaching out to touch the hull of one Ildiran cutter. 'Enlarge.'

The image grew before the General's eyes so he could study details. The EDF had not been able to determine the specific internal layout of Ildiran warships, but these simulations were derived from actual reconnaissance images obtained during spectacular Solar Navy fleet displays. As far as Lanyan could determine, the Ildiran ceremonial manoeuvres served no purpose other than to show off their military's skill in parades. Pointless showmanship.

He stepped back, assessing how the alien ships clustered in multiples of seven, moving together with a unified precision that made them both fearsome and vulnerable in their predictability.

'Now display an equivalent number of EDF vessels,' he said. 'Juggernaut-class battleships, Manta cruisers, Thunderhead weapons platforms, and Remora fast-attack fighters.'

The air in the simulation chamber sparkled, suddenly crowded with a new set of images, familiar Terran ship designs. Lanyan had trained on all of these military vessels during his climb up the service and promotion ladder. He knew the precise fighting capabilities, weapons complements, and troop numbers of each one. The computer had put together a magnificent Terran battle group, a worthy opponent to the Ildiran Solar Navy. Now for the fun.

He felt like a child with a plethora of toy soldiers just spoiling for a fight. With the intelligence data stored in the EDF systems, he could stage mock combats pitting his best battleships against the Ildiran defences.

The supposedly benevolent alien Empire had never made provocative moves against Earth, nor had they threatened the EDF or any Hansa colonies. Even so, Lanyan wanted to keep himself sharp. Perhaps he would never actually face off in a military conflict against the Solar Navy, but by running simulations such as this, he could assess mistakes and make contingency plans.

As he tried to concentrate, he could feel a distracting vibration through the floor of the Mars base. Outside, troops suited in breather uniforms were running out to perform infantry manoeuvres in the rusty canyons. Hybrid airships cruised through the thin atmosphere, painting targets and dropping simulated munitions.

Even after almost two centuries of peaceful relations with the Ildiran Empire, General Lanyan demanded that his troops remain well-tuned. His predecessors had grown somewhat complacent, but he was a more rigorous commander. Now, he personally studied ship simulations along with best estimates of Ildiran firepower. For the first time in history, the Earth Defence Forces were more evenly matched with the Ildiran Solar Navy than perhaps even the Mage-Imperator suspected.

'Interplanetary battle scenario,' he said. 'Run spacetime topography of—' He paused, trying to think. 'Use the Yreka system in Grid 7,' he said, since he had just run an operation there. The fringe Hansa colony was near the boundaries of settled space in the Ildiran Empire, and therefore a likely battleground. Who knew what flareups might occur between two different species?

Lanyan pointed to empty spots in the air. 'Place the planets here, here – and here.' The worlds of the Yreka system materialized in the air, and a blazing sun filled the centre of the room. EDF spaceships hovered in random patterns.

'Move the Solar Navy vessels into anticipated maniple configuration.' The Ildiran vessels folded together into compact septas, groups of seven that coalesced into larger conglomerates of forty-nine ships.

'Now deploy EDF troops in engagement configuration delta.' He backed towards the wall as the holograms took up their positions, ready for an order of battle.

Lanyan tried to imagine some provocative act that would bring the two space fleets to such an impasse. He always chose to run his simulations privately, telling no one his intent. What he was doing could create political dangers for his career, since the Ildirans were supposedly humanity's allies and benefactors. One did not practise warfare against a friend . . . but only a fool wouldn't prepare for a worst-case scenario.

The human race was not well-versed in large-scale inter-planetary warfare, considering the slow timeframes and the vast distances involved. All his career, the General had felt a nagging internal clock telling him to get his forces in shape, to be prepared for any crisis, though he despaired of cutting through the politics and bureaucracy in time.

Many of the EDF's most powerful commanding officers had squabbled over the military's purpose in the Hansa worlds. They even quarrelled over the appropriate names for ranks. Lanyan had been bombarded with tedious memos and arguments debating whether his title as commander-in-chief should be 'Admiral' or 'General' – a ridiculous waste of time. Lanyan had finally ejected the proponents of each question, docked them pay, and reduced their ranks by a notch. If necessary, he would send them back to combat school as cadets to refresh their memories about the true purpose of the Earth Defence Forces. He called himself a general, and named his subcommanders – each one in charge of a separate Grid – admirals.

During his administration, Lanyan had enhanced EDF capabilities and he always remained aware of the dispersal of his fleet. He spent evenings in his private quarters keeping track of his firepower distribution. The EDF had smothered brushfire rebellions and intimidated pirates such as Rand Sorengaard, but he knew that he must remain ever-vigilant.

He considered the frozen battle engagement in space, scrutinizing the numerous ships ready to fall upon each other like two packs of wolves. 'Engage forces. No handicap to either side.'

Lanyan stood against the wall and watched the sparks fly.

The Ildiran warliners opened fire, raking swaths of damage through the EDF troops. The Terran Remoras scattered and let loose with a chaotic jazer attack from all sides. The Solar Navy inflicted many casualties by remaining in rigid phalanxes like Roman soldiers, but the EDF fought back using individual and unpredictable tactics.

As ship after ship was destroyed, wreckage scattered through space, forming navigational hazards, which the battle-simulation added to the fray. The gravity wells of Yreka's planets offered complications of their own, and the battle raged on.

'Increase simulation speed. Multiply by three.'

The conflict turned into a flurry of hornets, ships roaring past and destroying each other. The specific action was too fast for him to follow, but he got the general drift.

Finally, all the fires died. The space battlefield became nothing more than a graveyard of ruined vessels and smouldering hulls that drifted about like man-made meteoroids. The General scanned the wreckage, pondering which portions of the conflict to replay and analyse.

Ruefully, he saw that all of the forces on both sides had been destroyed. It was a complete massacre of Ildiran and Terran troops. 'At least we didn't lose,' he said aloud, and blanked the simulation.

It was his duty to look at all alternatives and to be ready with answers, should he ever be called upon. No matter what diplomats and politicians might say, Lanyan was convinced the Ildiran Empire would some day be humanity's greatest antagonist.

After all, no Earth explorer had ever encountered any other alien threat.

THIRTY-FOUR

ROSS TAMBLYN

Skimming the night-side clouds of Golgen, Ross Tamblyn found the Blue Sky Mine too quiet for sleep. He paced the decks, eyes open, keeping a paternal watch on all systems. His life was invested here, his reputation and the inheritance he'd scraped together before his father had disowned him.

Before going out into the biting open wind, Ross dressed in warm garments, wrapping a clan scarf around his neck, shrugging a many-pocketed jacket over his shoulders. He pulled the hood over his ragged-cut dark hair, adjusted the insulated gloves, and stepped out for a breath of fresh air a thousand miles above the unseen surface of the gas giant.

Ross cycled through the wind door on to his private observation deck. He loved to steal time to stare out at the milky ocean of thunderheads and cirrus veils, feeling the raw wind on his face.

Most of the white doves had settled into their roosts for the night. They cooed, sounding like bubbles under water. A few of the pet birds spread their wings and flew out in long gentle courses, riding the high breezes. Instinct drove them to search for insects, but on sterile Golgen the doves would find no food other than what Ross Tamblyn put out for them.

The chill night bore a taint of sulphurous fumes, rising chemicals and gases belched from internal weather patterns. Ross gripped the railing with his gloves, felt the breeze stir his hair and flap his hood. The atmosphere yawned beneath him through uncharted cloud layers. With increasing depth, the air grew thicker and hotter until it terminated at the planet's super-high-density metallic core, where nothing could survive.

As he peered into the silvery cloud deck, Ross noticed deep lightning storms that hid under layers of multicoloured mist. The disturbance was far beneath the tentacle-strung weather probes that dangled from the skymine's belly. He could hear no thunder in the vastness of Golgen's sky, only a gentle cooing of doves.

As he watched, though, the lightning storms appeared to climb higher, a turbulence approaching the habitable atmospheric levels. The white birds stirred in their roosts, as if they could sense something ominous. It was an uneasy night.

But Ross would not have chosen to be anywhere else. The Blue Sky Mine was his home and his dream.

At the age of twenty-seven, shortly after he'd invested in this wild venture, Ross had been brash and bold – and why not, since he was already attempting to do an impossible thing? With a smile, he recalled the day he had approached Cesca Peroni, a woman he'd long admired but did not know very well. He met her in an empty tunnel in the clustered asteroids of Rendezvous. Willing to take a gamble and ready to accept failure, Ross had walked right up to her and asked her to marry him.

Cesca had raised her eyebrows and assessed the broad-shouldered young man, the outcast son of a powerful clan determined to make his own success. When she'd smiled at Ross, his heart had melted and he knew he'd made the correct choice.

Cesca was taken with him, though hesitant. After being trained by Speaker Jhy Okiah, the young woman was politically savvy enough to know that Ross could be 'trouble'. She had touched a fingertip to her full lower lip. 'I admit your Blue Sky Mine is a viable commercial opportunity. But if you don't succeed and I'm already betrothed to you, then I'll have thrown away my chance to make a good marriage alliance.' He couldn't tell if she was teasing him.

'I realize you might be wary of me, Cesca,' he had said. 'I've already been ostracized by my father, but I swear I'll make my own way. I know I can pay off the Golgen facility. My dream is to become independent and strong, and I know exactly how to accomplish it.'

She shrugged. 'And what would my family say? The Peronis are a powerful clan in their own right. Since I'm his only daughter, my father expects great things from me.'

Ross had clasped his hands in front of him. 'And well he should. But you are clearly being groomed to become the next Speaker. Surely that's enough for even his pride?'

He was glad they had a chance to talk frankly, but he couldn't decide if she was playing with him, or genuinely considering her options. Though the two felt warm towards each other, their decision would be based on a reasonable analysis of consequences, rather than frivolous romantic giddiness. A true Roamer match.

'I can offer you this, Ross Tamblyn,' Cesca finally said, crossing her slender arms over her chest and trying to hold a cool mask over what seemed to be an amused smile. 'I will agree to wed you if you're able to pay off the Blue Sky Mine and make a profit.'

He had laughed. 'Easily done . . . though it might take a few years. Are you willing to wait? Give me four years.'

'I'm in no hurry. Four years, then. I think I can manage to remain unmarried in the meantime.'

And so, for the past three years, Ross had tended his Blue Sky

Mine, never leaving, never giving up hope, never interested in reconciling with his old father. He had worked diligently in the Golgen clouds, where the harvesting grounds were a particularly rich source of stardrive fuel.

Now, at the age of thirty, he was clearly on the road to paying off the enormous industrial structure. It was a matter of pride for him, and it would allow him to prove himself in front of his father. This year, he would finally meet his goal; their marriage date had already been set.

Now, with a gust of cool wind, the huge skymine shuddered in the air. The white doves fluttered from their roosts, and four more took wing. Ross looked over the deck rail and watched the angry knot of flashing fireballs, deep lightning storms like a boiling electrical sea. Coming closer.

The intercom startled Ross as the captain on watch located him. 'Big disturbance below, Chief. Something large, unlike anything we've seen before.' The watch captain had spent his entire life on Roamer skymines; Ross thought the man had seen every possible atmospheric phenomenon by now.

He raised his voice as the biting wind grew louder, whistling around his hood. 'Do you think we should move the skymine?'

The captain responded immediately. 'The disturbance is moving too fast, Ross. We couldn't manoeuvre around it, even if we tried.'

Then the thick cloud decks split open like a blister, and Ross strained his eyes to see, to believe. An awesome crystal shape emerged from the silent depths, a shimmering diamond globe that rose higher . . . growing larger.

'Shizz! Do you see—' The speaker crackled with static, as if the local intercom transmission had been disrupted.

Ross stared and finally, with even greater amazement, realized what he was seeing. *A ship.*

The alien vessel was a huge sphere studded with triangular protrusions, like intersecting pyramids half-caught within a glass bubble. Blue lightning crackled from the points of the pyramids, connecting them with an electrical spiderweb, arcs jumping from tip to tip. A weapon of some kind, a bizarre structure from the deepest strata of the gas world. He couldn't imagine what sort of mind might have built it – or what it wanted.

Ross staggered backwards, releasing his hold on the support rail. 'Take us up!' he shouted, but he didn't know if the watch captain could hear him. 'Give me another kilometre of altitude – hell, make it ten!'

Still the alien ship kept coming, silent and ominous. By comparison, the skymine looked like a gnat in the air.

Ross had a sudden vision of a sea monster on old Earth rising to devour a sailing ship. His mind couldn't even grasp the curvature of the diamond hull that reflected the claw-like lightning. 'By the Guiding Star!' He had heard old Roamer tales about mysterious sightings on gas planets, a crazy survivor of the long-ago disaster on Daym – but no one had ever dreamed that such deep-core dwellers might actually exist.

All the doves scattered now, winging away from the skymine. The crystalline sphere heaved itself into the open air, growing larger and larger.

'What are you? What do you want?' His words could never be picked up through the storm and wind, nor would they be comprehended by whatever might exist within that strange vessel. He shouted as loud as he could, 'We mean you no harm!'

As the enormous construction loomed over the skymine, it sent low-frequency pulses through the air, like basso words in a voice that might have been spoken by a whale in the depths of an Earth ocean. The vibrations blasted Ross, pounding his skin and making his skull shudder.

The watch captain had already sounded alarms throughout the facility, rousing all the workers from their sleep shifts. But the skymine had no weapons, no defences.

The serpentine energy bolts reached a brilliant intensity, sparking from point to point on the sharp protrusions, then leapt outwards. Ross shouted, covering his eyes.

Electrical lances tore open the skymine complex, slicing apart the ekti reactors, chopping through the storage tanks, detonating the exhaust nozzles. Another explosion shook the decks.

The Blue Sky Mine lurched, tilted . . . then began to plummet.

Exposed on the deck, Ross could barely hang on. The white doves, shrieking, flew farther away into the sky, though with the skymine gone, they would never find another place to land. The doves would fly without food or rest until they died from sheer exhaustion.

A second blast from the spike-studded alien globe split the Blue Sky Mine down its structural spine. The components broke apart, and flaming wreckage tumbled like meteors into the bottomless sky.

Ross could hear the screams of his crew. He felt his heart ready to explode with helplessness. He could not even answer the strange, vibrating words the exotic alien had spoken. The lurch of another explosion hurled him from the observation platform out into the open air with the rest of the debris.

High above, the destructive alien ship observed what it had done and sent no further signal.

Ross plummeted, arms outstretched, his clothes flapping around him. He stared in horrified disbelief at the complete ruin of everything he valued . . . before the thickening clouds swallowed him up.

He still had more than a thousand miles to fall.

THIRTY-FIVE

ESTARRA

In the quiet depths of the worldforest, the time had come for the worm hive to hatch. Exuberant, Estarra dragged her brother Beneto through the forest. They hurried in the brightening dawn out to the dense thicket far from the fungus-reef city.

Beneath the embrace of the whispering canopy, the jungle stirred around them. Beneto kept his hands outstretched, so that he remained in contact with and attuned to the overall forest, brushing his fingertips against the armoured trunks.

'It's just up here,' she said. 'You've never seen a worm hive so large!'

Beneto smiled at her. His eyes were half-closed, but he walked without a single misstep, without tangling himself in the undergrowth. 'You're absolutely right, little sister – the trees have told me the hive will hatch within an hour.'

She ran ahead, and though Beneto didn't seem to increase his pace, he kept up with her, not even breaking into a sweat.

From the best viewing spot, Estarra looked up to stare at the papery structure. Beneto leaned against a worldtree so he could watch through his own eyes as well as the senses of the forest. Small butterfly-things twirled in the air. Estarra waved her hands to brush them away, but none of them bothered Beneto.

Suspended on the worldtree trunk, the greyish-white hive pulsed like the disembodied heart of a huge organism. The pupating worms had finished their hibernation and were ready to emerge to the next phase of their lives.

She heard a clicking, chewing sound and knew the giant worms were stirring through the tangled passages of the nest, questing for an exit after digesting the body of their now-useless queen. 'Beneto, do the trees hate these worms because they're parasites that cause damage?'

With a calm smile, her brother rested a palm against a scaled trunk. He sent the question into the intricate mind of the forest, though he already knew the answer. The trees say no, little sister. Hive worms are part of the natural order of things. These parasites are no more malicious than most – and they are useful in their own way.'

'You mean by leaving their empty hives for us to live in?' The papery wall bulged outwards as the shadowy tubular forms of worms prepared to break out.

'More than that. You will see in a moment.' Beneto ran his fingers along the tree bark, continuing his telink. 'Ah, here. It is time.'

The hive wall split open, and a mouth ringed with teeth probed into the air. More heads broke free, writhing like snakes in a disturbed nest. The hive worms spilled out, their segmented bodies plated with a thick purple armour. Dropping to the ground like eels in flight, they plunged headfirst into the soil, chewing into the forest loam like carrion eaters burrowing into rotten flesh.

Estarra was amazed at the frenzy of activity. Beneto put out a green-skinned hand to hold her back. 'Not too close. At this stage, they are ravenous, and anything that gets in their way is considered food.'

Estarra did not need to be warned twice, but she marvelled at the infestation. 'So what happens to the worms after they go into the ground?'

Beneto smiled. 'The trees keep watch, just as they watch everything. It is part of the cycle. Now they will tunnel deep under the ground and aerate the soil. They will establish underground colonies until mature worms emerge again, slither up the trunks of the trees and build new hives.'

Soon, all the worms were gone, leaving the abandoned hive like a tattered haunted house up on the tree. The papery walls had been broken open, but the tunnels inside remained intact. 'Now the hard work begins,' Estarra said, but she didn't look at all disappointed.

The chambers would need to be cleaned, some structural walls shored up, new windows cut and doorways placed in more convenient locations. But the worm hive was the ready-made framework for a new Theron village, into which the crowded fungus-reef settlement could expand. Estarra would be celebrated for her prowess in finding this new conglomerate dwelling.

Beneto received a message from the nearest tree, and smiled at his little sister. 'Now we must hurry back to see Mother and Father. We will want to be there when the shuttle lands.'

'What shuttle?' Estarra said.

Beneto beamed at her. 'Reynald has just returned.'

Estarra pressed forward with her family members to greet her older brother as soon as he emerged from the craft in the clearing. During the months he'd been gone on his peregrination, Reynald had changed. His eyes were full of wonder and deeper understanding. He had visited many exotic places, witnessed events and learned about a great many topics. He seemed overwhelmed by the sheer number of people coming to embrace him.

Sarein was full of questions, but little Celli dominated the scene by jabbering nonstop, as if her brother was interested in every single thing she had done during his absence. Promising his youngest sister a long chat later, Reynald accepted the smothering attention with good grace, smiling and making comments at appropriate points while his attention was more focused on Father Idriss and Mother Alexa. Their faces were filled with love – and relief that he had come home.

'Now do you feel more prepared to be a leader, my son?' Idriss smiled through his black beard.

The young man gave himself a deprecating smile. 'I have experienced plenty, that is true, but now I feel that I know less than ever before.'

Alexa kissed him on the cheek. 'Then Reynald, my dear, you are indeed more prepared to be a leader.'

That night, Father Idriss called a family banquet, insisting that Reynald would have enough time to speak with other representatives later. Alexa and Idriss and all their children wanted to hear him tell his stories first.

This diminished the impact of Estarra's news about the worm hive. Beneto gentled her, knowing there would be time enough for that announcement.

During courses of larva steaks, yeasty bread smeared with spreadnuts, and a messy dessert of his favourite candied splurts, Reynald spoke, and everyone else listened. Sarein did her best to keep Celli shushed and attentive, though the girl still asked far too many questions.

Reynald's eyes sparkled as he told his news. 'Best of all, I got along very well with the Ildiran Prime Designate Jora'h.' He turned, grinning, towards his brother Beneto. 'And he granted me permission to send two green priest representatives to Mijistra. Oh, it's a wonderful place!'

'And what will these green priests do there?' Beneto asked, intrigued.

'They will have access to the *Saga of Seven Suns* – the complete Ildiran epic, not just the edited versions the Terran scholars have been allowed to read.' Reynald smiled, knowing what a stir his news would cause among the green priests. 'Other than a racial reverence for their Mage-Imperator, this precise oral history is the closest thing to a religion the Ildirans seem to have. They believe they are all part of a grand plan, a cosmic storyline that must work its way to the end, like a plot concocted by an omnipotent audience.'

Reynald leaned closer to his brother. 'Jora'h will let you study their billion-line poem, all the history and legends of the Ildiran Empire. It's said that no human can read the entire document, even if he devotes a lifetime to the study.'

Beneto seemed dazzled, knowing how much the worldforest would enjoy the input. The prospect of a marvellous new story seemed to bring him hope to mitigate the trees' recent uneasiness. This will be a time of great rejoicing for the worldforest. It is not every day that the trees get access to such a wealth of information.'

Estarra stared through the fungus-reef chambers to the shadowy greenness of the jungle, as if expecting to see the world-trees dancing for joy. Even without such a miracle, though, the delight on Beneto's face seemed reward enough.

'How were the Roamers?' Idriss asked. 'We know so little about their culture.'

'I doubt you accomplished much with them,' Sarein said sourly. 'They probably tried to entangle you in a marriage alliance.'

Reynald smiled at his sister. 'Don't underestimate the Roamers, Sarein. In fact, that may have been our largest mistake of all. They seem very open to closer ties with us. One of their leaders, Cesca Peroni, is quite captivating.'

'They want our green priests, I bet,' Sarein said.

'Actually, they refused my offer.' He enjoyed his sister's surprise. 'The Roamers prefer to keep their secrets and don't really want any green priests.'

'That's a switch from what we usually hear,' Idriss said under his breath.

'I suggested we might arrange for direct deliveries of ekti to Theroc, without going through approved Hansa intermediaries. Think of the cost we'll save.'

'Think of how upset the Hansa will be,' Sarein said, alarmed. 'Do we want to invite so much trouble and ill will, considering that we don't use much ekti for ourselves anyway?'

'Still,' Mother Alexa said, plucking a slice of pair-pear from a tray, 'every step of independence benefits us in the long run.'

THIRTY-SIX

RAYMOND AGUERRA

When the nauseating effects of the stunner wore off, the pounding in Raymond's head masked the fact that he was lying on a plush, warm bed. He slowly returned to consciousness and noticed that he seemed to be floating. His body was surrounded by slick sheets, lying on a comfortable gelatin-filled mattress. His fingers twitched, his thighs clenched.

Raymond opened his eyes, and the flood of light sent sledgehammers of pain into his skull. He groaned deep in his throat, but it came out only as a faint sound. The last thing he remembered was the blond-haired man threatening him with the stunner, his professional-looking companions hustling Raymond towards the unmarked vehicle. *Kidnapping him!*

He sat up and forced himself to endure the wash of nausea. Someone had taken him here. Was it a group of perverts out to snatch any young man – or had they been after *him* in particular? Why would anyone be interested in a poor kid with no prospects and a family that could barely make ends meet?

His family! Now he remembered the flaming wreckage of his

apartment complex, the barricade lines and security troops, the fire-suppression engineers and their copters dumping extinguishant foam all over the smouldering remains.

There's nothing left inside but ashes and dental work.

When the orchestra of ragged nerve endings quietened to a mild clamour, he opened his eyes again and looked around him. He lay in a small chamber without windows. The walls held fine tapestries, delicate vases stood on pedestals in the corners. A basin filled with trickling water made quiet music.

He needed to know what had happened to his mother and brothers!

He smelled faint perfumes and noticed several stubby candles – real candles – set into small alcoves. He eased himself from the sloshing bed which tried to wrap itself around him. The light seemed to come from everywhere, a muted illumination from the fabric of the wall itself. He couldn't understand where he was.

A door opened from a corridor outside the room. Standing on the threshold was a lean, suave-looking man with hair the colour of new steel. His active grey eyes and smooth skin challenged any estimate of his age. Beside him stood an old-style Teacher-model compy with a dull body casing.

The man studied Raymond with a calculating smile, but the compy spoke first. 'My estimate of the duration of the stun pulse was accurate to within ten minutes, Chairman Wenceslas.'

'Excellent, OX, considering you had to guess so many important parameters.'

Recognizing the man's name, Raymond clamped his mouth shut to prevent himself from making indignant demands. Such protestations would make him look foolish and helpless, and these people would tell him whatever they wished, whenever they wished. Warily, he bided his time, meeting the Chairman's intent gaze.

Wenceslas gave Raymond a thin-lipped smile. 'Very good, Peter. You're exercising some restraint already, even without training.' He turned to the compy. 'OX, you will have a very good student here.'

Raymond's head still pounded. 'Who's Peter? My name's Raymond Aguerra. I live—'

Wenceslas held up a well-manicured hand. '*Peter* is the name we have chosen for you. It's best if you get used to it from the start.'

The old Teacher compy came forward with heavy but precise steps. 'I am aware, Peter, that the after-effects of a stunner are physically unpleasant. I have an analgesic injection or, if you prefer, a sweet-flavoured syrup containing the same medication. I would not want discomfort to distract you from the important business Chairman Wenceslas wishes to discuss with you.'

Raymond recoiled at receiving medication from these people. He still didn't know why they had brought him here or why they were interested in him. But again, he bit back an outcry, thinking his situation through. He had been here helpless in this chamber, stunned unconscious. They could have poisoned him or drugged him at any point. Why would they wait for him to wake up and then drug him again? Who would benefit, if he insisted on remaining miserable?

After a careful pause, he said, 'Which one acts faster? I need to get rid of this headache.'

OX came to the side of the bed. 'The injection should take effect almost immediately. I will try to make it as painless as possible.' The small compy reached forward with a metal hand. Before Raymond could even look down, a tiny needle danced out of the fingertip and into his arm. Raymond was more startled than hurt by the act. He rubbed his arm, but could feel no residual sting. As the Teacher compy had promised, the pain began to diminish within seconds.

'My name is Raymond,' he said again, drawing a deep breath. 'Why have you brought me here? What do you want?'

'We want you to reach your potential, young man,' Wenceslas said. He came forward to sit on the end of Raymond's bed, folding his hands in his lap in an oddly paternal mannerism. 'We have a great opportunity in store for you, something that will benefit you in ways that you've never imagined, and it will also give the Terran Hanseatic League a solid future.'

Raymond turned away, glad to feel the aches and the muscle spasms receding. 'I have no idea what you're talking about. Do we have any word about my mother, my brothers? I saw the fire.'

'There were no survivors, young man. The apartment complex was a complete loss.'

OX said, 'Allow me to offer my sincere condolences, young Peter.'

'My name is Raymond.'

'Your name is Peter,' said Basil. 'Now please listen while I explain. The first thing you must accept is that you are not who you were.'

OX walked over to a bureau in the corner of the room and returned with an ornate, gold-framed looking glass. With a steady metal hand the Teacher compy held the reflected surface in front of Raymond so that he could stare in shock at his appearance. His hair was now completely *blond*, a straw-coloured yellow that extended all the way to the roots. His eyebrows had a different tint, above eyes that were a startling greenish-blue instead of the deep brown he had been born with. He saw no evidence of contact lenses or implants. His eyes had been *changed*, and he was willing to bet that his hair and eyes had been genetically altered, not just coloured. He was at a loss for words.

'It's really quite a remarkable resemblance to our King Frederick, don't you think?' Wenceslas said. Raymond had never actually studied the King's facial features other than stylized likenesses on posters, placards, and a few old-fashioned currency notes.

OX withdrew the looking glass and bustled back to the bureau. Raymond glanced around the chamber again, just to avoid looking at the Chairman or the compy. He noted two shadowy figures outside the door. Guards, probably. His room had an overstuffed sitting chair, a tray with luscious-looking tarts, and a decanter of juice. His stomach growled.

Wenceslas gave a signal to OX. The Teacher compy brought over the refreshments.

'You are being held in a hidden chamber beneath the Whisper Palace,' the Chairman said. 'Soon, you will have access to everything you could possibly want. OX will help you learn history, philosophy, politics, as well as the subtle nuances of court etiquette and your eventual responsibilities.'

'What responsibilities?' Raymond sipped the tart red juice, then gobbled a honey-soaked wafer, perhaps the most delicious pastry he had ever eaten.

'Prince Peter, you are the son and heir of King Frederick. Obviously, the public will notice the family resemblance. When you are ready, we will introduce you into the public eye. The populace will accept you.'

'Prince?' Raymond nearly spilled his remaining juice on the coverlet. 'Crimson rain, I'm not a Prince! I've never even met King Frederick. I—'

Wenceslas smiled strangely. 'We create our own truth around here, young Peter. Don't worry about that.'

'But what happened to the real royal family? I've never even heard of Prince Peter before now.'

'That is because he didn't exist before now.' The Chairman folded his hands, interlocking his fingers. 'We have always kept the royal family a private matter in order to give the Hansa room to do as we like. We have plenty of flexibility.'

The man poured himself a glass of juice. 'King Frederick's real wife died more than two decades ago. Over the years, he's had numerous concubines and a few bastard children, but none of them has the potential we need. Certainly no true leadership qualities.'

Raymond looked at the Chairman, disbelief growing as the realization sank in. 'You want *me* to replace the King?'

'After you have been properly trained,' OX said.

'We selected you from among hundreds of potential candidates, Peter. The Hansa is convinced that you are someone the public can cheer and love.'

'But it's . . . it's not right!' Raymond insisted.

Wenceslas looked at him calmly. 'That's exactly how King Frederick took the throne many years ago, and King Bartholomew before him, and King Jack before him.' Raymond reeled, and the Chairman continued. 'We have been watching you for years and selected you from many candidates. Honest, young man, we believe you are our best hope.' His expression became sadder. 'Unfortunately, the terrible fire that destroyed your home has forced us to move now. We would have preferred a more comfortable and orderly introduction.'

Raymond had trouble accepting the massive shift to his understanding of the world. 'But . . . what will happen to Frederick?'

'After the efficient transfer of leadership, the old man will have his features altered and we'll send him into a comfortable retirement on Relleker. King Frederick has served quite well for almost half a century, but his mind isn't as sharp as it was. Truly, I think his heart is no longer in it. We need someone vibrant and viable to bring energy back to the Hansa.'

'I can't believe this.' Raymond stared at the metal mask of the Teacher compy. 'Someone will know. You'll be caught.'

Basil Wenceslas smiled. 'Who could possibly know? Forgive

me, young man, but Raymond Aguerra was a nobody. With your features altered like this, who would even dream of making the connection? After the terrible apartment fire, everyone will believe you died in the disaster, just like the other unfortunate victims.'

Raymond blinked back tears, and his throat trembled as the ache in his heart began to turn numb. His mother would have said that this sudden opportunity (and, yes, he always looked for opportunities) was his reward in the face of such incredible sadness. She would probably have read him a printed Unison pamphlet with similar platitudes. He would have given almost anything to have his family back, but he could not spurn this chance. Never in his life had such a tremendous possibility presented itself to him.

The Chairman's winning smile showed dazzling teeth. 'Look at this as a way to bring a silver lining to this dark cloud of tragedy. We've already rewritten the past, and we need you, young Peter, to help us write the future.'

THIRTY-SEVEN

JESS TAMBLYN

Returning to his clan holdings under the ice sheath of Plumas, Jess Tamblyn found his old father as stern and crotchety as ever. It gave him all the more reason to look for any excuse to return to Rendezvous as soon as possible. He still hadn't been able to see Cesca.

Bram Tamblyn had dark, eager eyes that flashed as Jess talked about Ross's activities on Golgen, but after a moment the old clan leader held up a callused hand. 'Enough. We won't waste time spreading gossip about a man who is no longer part of our family.' This stubborn game had gone on for years, and Jess doubted anything would change.

Living close to his father was stifling. Within a week Jess had concocted urgent duties that required him to fly back to Rendezvous. His younger sister Tasia had begged to come along, and Jess took pity on her. 'She'll be fine, Dad,' he said, 'and, who knows, this time we may even track down the *Burton*.'

Bram gave a snort. 'Our clan is making enough money in the solid water business. No need for you to shirk your duties and go chasing myths.'

'I would never shirk my duties, Dad – you know that. But the *Burton* exists. It's still out there, somewhere.' The large, slow-moving vessel was the only one of the original eleven generation ships that had never been found.

'Even if you recovered it, it would be an old wreck by now, worth nothing.'

'Worth a place in history, Dad,' Tasia said brightly.

Bram covered his indulgent smile with a sour look, and Jess hurried to his personal spacecraft with his young sister in tow. Tasia's personal compy EA started to follow them, but the girl quickly thought of several busy-work tasks and sent the compy away.

By the time they reached the cracked frozen surface of the moon, he and Tasia were already chuckling with each other. They flew away from the water-pumping stations that penetrated the miles-thick icecap where hydrostatic pressure squeezed liquid water up to supply posts on the surface.

'Can I fly?' Tasia sat beside him, eager to take the spaceship controls.

He shot his sister an appraising look. She was young and spunky, just turning sixteen, and glad to be anywhere but Plumas. She had a button nose, blue eyes, and ragged brown hair that she cut herself whenever it grew too long and annoying. Her snappy wit made her delightful as a travelling companion but wicked as a verbal opponent if anyone tried to insult her.

'Will the ship take that kind of abuse?' he asked.

'I'd call it exercise.'

'Later,' he said. 'Right now I'm only interested in getting out of here. I'll let you dock at Rendezvous.'

As Plumas dwindled behind them and Jess set course, Tasia called up his past expedition logs. 'Are we really going to look for the *Burton* again? Found any new clues?'

'No, that was just an excuse to bring you along before Dad could find a way to keep you occupied.' He stared into the streaming stars. 'I don't think the *Burton* will ever be found, given the time and distance and the hazards of space. Losing only one out of eleven generation ships seems an acceptable percentage to me, considering their old-fashioned technology.'

Tasia gave him a quirky smile. 'Probably a better chance of finding the *Burton* than of reestablishing peace between Dad and Ross.'

Jess sighed. 'Still, it's our responsibility to work hard to soften the old man's heart. Ross is getting married to Cesca in a year or so, and we can use that as an excuse to tie our family together.'

Tasia, too warm after living under the ice sheet, adjusted the temperature inside the ship. 'He'll come around, Jess. Dad is too smart a businessman to keep up a feud with the husband of the new Speaker.'

'You may be right.' Jess let her take the controls and went to make them some pepperflower tea, hoping to avoid further discussion of the subject of marriage. Every time he thought of the upcoming wedding, his heart felt heavy and he was afraid his love for Cesca Peroni would show on his face.

Tasia was always delighted to see the glittering asteroids and artificial structures of Rendezvous, and Jess was likewise delighted to see the joy on his sister's face.

Clan representatives came forward to greet them in a flurry of layered cloaks and jerkins, all embroidered with family markings and beautiful designs. Already considering her own marriage prospects, Tasia flirted with the young men, though she would no doubt be even pickier than her father.

Rendezvous was a place where all Roamers could speak their minds, make business deals, leave messages for extended groupings, interact with cousins and distant family members. Because the clan units were small, exchanging unmarried men and women was vital to keeping their culture and their people strong.

Tasia dashed off to speak with friends her own age. Adaptable to the asteroids' low gravity, she scuttled through the tunnel complexes, running towards the domed greenhouses. She hadn't bothered to retrieve her spacesuit from Jess's ship, but if she wanted to venture outside, there would be plenty of skinsuits for her to borrow. She could always rig something up.

With a mixture of dread and eagerness, Jess crossed a transparent connectube to the central asteroid, where he would at last deliver formal greetings to Cesca from Ross. Ancient Jhy Okiah clasped his hand in a sinewy grip, then flipped a glance at her protégé, who couldn't tear her eyes off of him.

Self-consciously, the Speaker found urgent business. 'If you two will excuse me, I have an appointment with the mother of Rand Sorengaard. Her clan wishes to submit formal apologies for her son's actions.'

He and Cesca looked at each other in silence. Jess could barely cover his grin of admiration for her. Cesca's olive skin and dark hair drew him like a magnet. She smiled with her generous mouth. 'It's good to see you again, Jess,' she said, a bit too formally.

He was forced to respond with a stiff bow, sweeping his cape to one side. 'When last I was at Golgen, my brother charged me with delivering you a set of greetings. He expects the Blue Sky Mine to turn a profit this year at last.'

Jess opened a voluminous pocket in his embroidered vest. He withdrew a strand of metallic black spheres, a necklace of ebony skypearls. He held it up in the artificial light. Cesca's dark eyes looked more beautiful to him than the midnight sheen of the valuable gems.

'I don't think I've ever seen skypearls before,' Cesca said. 'And I certainly don't own any. I don't know what to say, except for you to pass along my thanks to him.'

The tiny spherical nodules were formed inside ekti reactor chambers, concentrated impurities taken from the atmospheric samples during harvesting. Skypearls clung to the walls of the reactors and were occasionally found during routine cleaning. Ross had been saving them for years, one or two at a time. He had given his fiancée a string of twenty-five, worth a fabulous fortune.

Jess dropped them into the soft palm of her hand, letting his fingers brush hers so he could feel an instant of her touch. His skin prickled with a flush of sweat. This encounter was sweet agony.

Jess tried to think of something to say in the uncomfortable lull in their conversation, because he did not dare voice the words he longed to speak. Cesca withdrew to a too-careful distance, and her lips parted as if ready to whisper something.

Then, bounding through the low-gravity tunnels, pushing off with boots and hauling along with strong fingers, a broad-shouldered man burst into the Speaker's chambers. 'I need to see Jhy Okiah right away.' He looked around, taking in the two young lovers but dismissing them. Then suddenly he recognized Jess. 'Shizz! This concerns clan Tamblyn! Oh, but I have terrible news. Where's the Speaker?'

Jess recognized Del Kellum, a clan leader and manager of the massive hidden shipyards in the rings of Osquivel. Sometimes, Kellum served as a cargo driver, just moving with restless feet among the other Roamer settlements and facilities. He was a middle-aged man, hale and gregarious, but now he looked terror-stricken.

'What is it?' Jess asked. 'Weren't you supposed to make the most recent run from the Blue Sky Mine?'

Cesca stepped forward. 'I am the Speaker's representative. You may deliver your news to me. What's happened?'

'Blue Sky Mine is gone!' Kellum said. 'Destroyed! I was inbound to Golgen when we heard an emergency message. They said they were under attack by some strange kind of spacecraft that came up from deep in the clouds. Said they'd never seen anything like it before.'

He gulped air, and his breath hitched. 'But when I got there, I found only a few floating pieces of wreckage blasted into high orbit, and a faint residue of contaminants and smoke in the cloud layer that Ross liked to mine.'

Despite the low gravity of Rendezvous, Jess slumped backwards, unable to keep his balance. He reached out, and Cesca instinctively grasped his hand in disbelief. 'What about the escape pods?' Jess said. 'The flight deck. Ross should've been able to get his crew away.'

'Nothing,' said Del Kellum. 'It's all gone. Somebody, something struck without warning and killed every living soul on the Blue Sky Mine.'

THIRTY-EIGHT

REMEMBERER VAO'SH

With heroism, passion, and romance, the *Saga* of the Ildiran Empire continued to unfold. As senior rememberer at the court of the Mage-Imperator Cyroc'h, Vao'sh kept alive the legends and history of his people for the next generation of fascinated listeners.

He remained attuned to any reports of dramatic incidents across the Spiral Arm. Though peaceful times were more pleasant for a population to live in, they made for poor storytelling. Until now, the splinter colony on Crenna had had no standing in the *Saga of Seven Suns*, appearing merely as a footnote, more for book-keeping purposes than dramatic ones. It was only a fledgling settlement, the birthplace of no great heroes. Unremarkable.

Following the blindness plague, however, the tragedy of Crenna would comprise many dark stanzas. It was a rememberer's job to make certain it would never be lost.

After enduring a lengthy quarantine aboard Adar Kori'nh's warliners, the evacuated survivors were welcomed back to Mijistra, shaken but relieved. The colonists looked weak and damaged, but under the never-waning light of Ildira's seven suns, the survivors felt through the *thism* the healing presence of their godlike Mage-Imperator. Here, they would recover . . . but they would never forget.

Vao'sh needed to hear and then compile the true story of what had happened. The *Saga* had to be accurate, as well as compelling.

Taking meticulous care with his toilette, Vao'sh oiled the expressive lobes on his lumpy face. His flush colours would be prominent and bright as he spoke the story aloud to all enraptured listeners, once he had taken it into his heart and learned it in detail.

To protect his throat and his voice, Vao'sh drank his daily mixture of warm syrups, then sang wordless notes to keep his lucent voice in its proper range. Then he went to his first meeting with Dio'sh, the only surviving rememberer from Crenna.

Vao'sh met his younger kithman on a sun-soaked deck of the Prism Palace. Dio'sh had closed his eyes and placed his hands palms up on a polished tabletop, as if the brilliant sunlight could purge him of the taint of nightmares. Dio'sh retained a perfect, horrific recollection of everything he had experienced.

Seeing his expected visitor, Dio'sh turned his expressive eyes towards the master historian. The younger rememberer's sense of relief was apparent as his fleshy lobes coloured with appreciation and respect. 'I am honoured that you've come to speak to me, Rememberer Vao'sh. I am eager to share what I know, though I am afraid to relive it.'

'Rememberers do not create stories,' Vao'sh reminded him, 'we merely tell them. And we must tell them accurately and well.'

Dio'sh bowed his head. 'I will do my best, Rememberer.'

Vao'sh waited, saw his comrade summoning a host of terrifying thoughts. The colouration of his skin began to turn greyish, as if he faced an insurmountable fear. Dio'sh flinched.

'Crenna,' Vao'sh nudged. 'You were there. You were witness to

214

the courage, the tragedy, the unstoppable events.' He reached out to touch the historian's trembling hand. 'If you do not pass on your impressions, then all the tragedy that occurred will be for naught. The victims and the heroes must be remembered. You are a rememberer, Dio'sh.'

The younger man took a deep breath and opened his eyes, still looking haunted but now more determined. 'Ildiran splinter colonies have endured sickness before,' Dio'sh began. 'We remember the losses of children and families who succumbed to fevers, toxins, or genetic diseases. But this . . .' He looked up sharply, his lobes flushing scarlet. 'What sort of vindictive plague would first steal our *sight*, take from us the comfort of blessed light – and then make us die alone in quarantine, isolated from other Ildirans, lest we continue to spread this terrible disease?'

Dio'sh clenched his fist and held it out in front of him. Vao'sh could feel a deep horror growing within him. Raised under constant sunlight, surrounded always by comforting crowds, the Ildiran people had two primal phobias: fear of darkness, and fear of isolation.

Dio'sh continued, seeing nothing but his memories. 'Crenna has a large moon, so that even during the night hours enough light shines down upon the landscape. We lit every home, every street, so that our central town was filled with illumination. We managed to drive back the shadows – but what good are all the torches in the Empire, once a disease robs you of sight? After the plague struck him blind, the Crenna Designate stood in the square and stared directly at the sun, but still he saw only blackness.'

Purple and green patterns of dismay and horror rippled across his lobed features. Vao'sh shuddered but made no comment, filing away every word. He could picture the Mage-Imperator's son, the Crenna Designate, sightless, staring up into the blazing sun. That would make good drama. This section of history would be recounted and modified until the final, permanent words were chosen and entered into the *Saga of Seven Suns*.

'We do not know how the sickness began. On Crenna our scientist kithmen were mainly agricultural specialists, not bacteriological researchers. Within days of the first recorded case, a dozen more people fell sick – and then all those who tended the victims also succumbed. We have never known a plague so virulent, so contagious, and so deadly.

'Through the *thism*, every person in the town could feel the victims' growing terror as the retinal damage progressed and the first sufferers fell blind. We knew that we should quarantine the colonists – but how could we look at a sick child, *a blind child*, and tell him we must leave him alone, isolated from the comfort and support of our people? That seemed worse than the disease itself. After the blindness, the nerve damage spread to other parts of the body until finally the lungs could no longer breathe, the heart could no longer beat.'

Dio'sh drew a shuddering breath. 'Then the Crenna Designate died, cutting off our direct link with the Mage-Imperator. Even the small comfort of *thism* was then weakened. How could we endure? With each death, panic increased, our numbers dwindled, the *thism* frayed further. Soon, we were well below the critical number for a splinter.

'Those of us who were healthy locked ourselves in the few remaining homes, but even then we made mistakes, and the plague got inside. We burned the victims, hoping that the fire would at least symbolically return the light.'

He looked directly at Vao'sh, as if begging the master historian to rewrite the tale. 'We didn't know what to do! We were paralysed, and the plague continued to spread.'

Vao'sh touched his comrade's wrist. 'That is enough for now, Dio'sh.'

He swallowed hard, his thoughts spinning. He knew the Crenna plague and the abandonment of an entire colony must become a vital part of the *Saga*, yet Vao'sh hesitated to include too many horrific details, fearing that it might cause a panic.

'Perhaps you should accompany me in a little while,' he suggested. 'We will tell a happy story, the Tale of Bobri's and the Silver Ball. The children enjoy that one, and I love to entertain children. You will find it refreshing, as well.'

Dio'sh looked hesitant, intimidated. 'I prefer to be quiet, close to people, but not interacting with them. I would not be a good entertainer now. Perhaps I can serve a better purpose as a scholar.'

Vao'sh frowned, and his disapproval cast stern colourings on his fleshy flaps. 'Other kiths cannot recall every detail as we do. The *Saga* is written down, but as rememberers, Dio'sh, our true purpose is to spin tales and to educate. To bring the legends and history alive. Do not forget it. All Ildirans can hear the songs and imagine the tales, but *we* must be the presenters. It is who we are.'

Dio'sh's shoulders slumped. 'It is who we are, though sometimes it is a difficult thing.'

THIRTY-NINE

DAVLIN LOTZE

The Ildirans had turned tail and fled from Crenna, leaving their colony up for grabs. The Hansa had paid a substantial fee to the Mage-Imperator for clear title and the unchallenged right to settle there, within the accepted boundaries of the Ildiran Empire. The Hanseatic League considered the already tame planet a remarkable prize; the Mage-Imperator considered the unexpectedly large payment a boon.

Clearly, neither race understood the other.

After medical researchers and microbiologists had tested the Ildiran blindness plague and declared that humans were immune to the scourge, Terran transport ships landed on the world. Volunteers had filled out their applications long ago, prepared to dash off to a new home as soon as another planet became available.

Official Hansa policy encouraged expansion by securing a foothold on numerous worlds and fostering population increases on already settled colonies. Suddenly, for the first time in civilized human history, people had all the room to expand and all the resources they could possibly need. And, being humans, they did their best to make use of what was available. Every scrap of it.

After the first transport ships disgorged the wide-eyed settlers, Davlin Lotze maintained a quiet though interested scrutiny of everything around him. He joined the first group of eager colonists in the ghost town of Crenna, acting like all the others, though he had a special mission of his own.

The gaudy Ildiran warliners, crowded full of frantic survivors, had hastily left the Crenna system. When rushed and frightened, people made mistakes. They accidentally left important things behind. Chairman Basil Wenceslas, working through his operative Davlin Lotze, was counting on that.

A second team of medical specialists had already gone into the evacuated town, analysing the groundwater, studying local microorganisms, and making certain there was no other local threat to the new colonists. Some studies had suggested that humans and some Ildiran kiths could actually interbreed, in defiance of common-sense genetic rules; therefore, it was an ironic twist of fortune that the blindness plague organism could not cross species lines.

Though uneasy with microbiological superstition, the new batch of settlers was perfectly safe. Davlin Lotze did not doubt it for a moment, but chose not to reassure the others, preferring instead to watch their reactions. Interesting sociology. He already knew a great many things that he would keep to himself, until Chairman Basil Wenceslas debriefed him.

The Chairman had assigned him to Crenna, providing forged papers that identified him as a simple colonist. According to the dossier available to his fellow settlers, Davlin was competent in small-scale agriculture and had a handful of useful skills such as woodworking, plumbing, and engine repair. The colonists happily accepted him as one of their group, drawn together by an ambition to make a new home for themselves.

Aboard the transport ship, Davlin had made several acquaintances and would continue to develop those relationships, though he would never allow any person close enough to call him a friend. He didn't know how long his assignment would require him to remain on Crenna. He supposed he would stay here until he found worthwhile material about the Ildirans.

Davlin Lotze was the Chairman's hand-picked 'observer', and he enjoyed the job. He knew what he was, though he chose not to use the term 'spy'. His experience as an exosociologist was not marked in his travel papers or resumes, but he had a special ability to look at an alien culture, fathom its mysteries, and make sense of the exotic nuances.

The rushed evacuation of this colony provided Chairman Wenceslas with an opportunity to learn facts that the Mage-Imperator might prefer to keep hidden. Davlin would compile reports to be returned to Earth with the frequent supply runs that would be necessary during the colony's first transition year.

A flotilla of laden ships finally landed in the rich but empty farmland outside of the main Ildiran city. Personnel carriers came down first, disgorging anxious pioneers who had sat still for too long during the passage. Next came ship after ship of cargo transports containing equipment, supplies, and prepackaged housing units. It was a standard-issue 'new colony' drop, though the previous inhabitants had done some of the initial groundwork for them.

During their journey to Crenna, the colonists had studied maps and analysed satellite images. In open-deck meetings, they had sketched boundaries and divided the arable land according to lots drawn by the settler families. When the vessels landed, though, the people crowded out, rushing to see the town that the aliens had left for them. Many settlers grumbled to see how much of the settlement had been burned in the Ildirans' desperate attempts to

220

stop the spreading plague. The new settlers had hoped to use more of the existing infrastructure.

As the frenzied activity progressed, Davlin went to the equipment transport and powered up a heavy crawler. He knew how to drive the burly machine designed to haul crates and equipment into position for distribution among the colonists.

Three of the men he had met onboard were blustering and arguing with each other, pointing fingers and engaging in red-faced shouting. It was no surprise. A system of dominance had to be established on Crenna just as much as systems for streets, water, and food distribution. Though it did not show on his official record, Davlin was more educated than any of them, and he could have been a primary leader. But his job was to stay in the background and learn what he could.

A tall man with large hands and narrow shoulders – though not enough muscles to make him intimidating – Davlin's skin was deepest brown, almost a true ebony, and smooth. He had high cheekbones and narrow eyes, and kept his hair trimmed very short. Two pale, parallel slashes on his left cheek gave some people the impression that he wore the scars as tribal marks; in actuality, he had suffered a bad cut from an exploding glass bottle in a friend's abortive attempt at home-brewing beer.

Working with the heavy crawler, silent and competent, he drove crates into the middle of the Ildiran settlement. The new colonists ran about like children exploring an unfamiliar vacation home. They looked at the unusual architecture and poked through all the items the aliens had left behind, seeking hidden treasure. Davlin would have to keep careful track and confiscate any technological items that might prove enlightening.

After he finished unloading the cargo transport, he parked the crawler in the town square and tried to blend in with the eager explorers. With a hidden imager, he moved from building to building, studying what remained, photographing the architecture from all angles. Visitors to the Ildiran Empire had already seen the basics of the alien buildings, but Davlin was most interested in the private details.

He moved inside the communal dwellings that had not been burned to the ground. He opened storage racks and studied what the aliens considered necessary for their daily lives.

The apparently guileless Ildirans did not seem to be hiding information from the Hanseatic League. In fact, they presented themselves as allies and friends. But Davlin suspected otherwise – as did Basil Wenceslas. Their openness might be merely a cover to hide information they did not wish the human race to discover.

Chairman Wenceslas had once told him during his infiltration briefing, 'Know your enemy.' Here on Crenna, Davlin Lotze intended to take advantage of the Ildiran tragedy. If this abandoned place held any secrets, Davlin would be the one to uncover them.

FORTY

MARGARET COLICOS

The diurnal cycle on Rheindic Co was twenty-eight hours long, but even with the extra four hours Margaret and Louis Colicos never felt as if they had enough time out in the Klikiss ruins.

In a sheer box canyon near their encampment, the two xeno-archaeologists climbed into a section of abandoned buildings, curved structures and freeform facades set back beneath a cliff overhang. Tunnels at the rear of the empty dwellings continued deep into the mountain.

Either the canyon itself had been cut deeper in the millennia since the Klikiss disappearance, or the aliens' ramps or footholds on the cliff wall had eroded away. DD and the three black Klikiss robots had assisted in erecting ladders and temporary sectional staircases, taking advantage of ledges and dodging cliff bands so the team could have easier access to the lost city. They went to work every day in the first light of desert dawn.

Neither she nor Louis had been able to find any shafts, pulleys, ladders, or more sophisticated transportation systems for access from ground-level. Louis was certain that the high strategic position of their dwellings had something to do with a defensive arrangement. 'Or, maybe the Klikiss were just incredibly tall,' he suggested facetiously. 'We've never seen what they looked like.'

The large black robots standing in the dry wash at the bottom of the canyon could offer no suggestions. 'We remember nothing,' Sirix said.

Louis grinned in response, as if the alien robot could understand a human expression. 'We'll do our best to find out then. For you and for us.'

Arcas did not participate in the daily routine as much as they had hoped, often spending his time exploring the landscape by himself. In spite of his background in geology, Margaret did not count on him for anything but necessary communication. The Klikiss robots were providing more outright help to the project.

The most overwhelming job, even after a month of survey, was simply to explore and map out the possibilities. The ruined alien city was so large that merely forming a research plan was a daunting task. Louis wandered through the tunnels and the off-kilter buildings with his recorder, imaging the walls and structures, the pipes, tubing, and long-quiet corroded machinery the Klikiss had left behind.

Early in her studies, Margaret had visited the Anasazi ruins at Mesa Verde in the North American Southwest on Earth, a fabulous mud-brick metropolis that had survived for many centuries. Rheindic Co's isolated Klikiss city reminded her of those Native American cliff dwellings. Yet it was also incomprehensibly alien, with architecture based on different aesthetics, walls at the wrong angles, trapezoidal doorways that were not necessarily at floor level.

Now she took scrapings from a wall, finding a corner remarkably free of the numerous markings and ideographs with

224

which the Klikiss covered most surfaces. She wondered if the insectoid race shunned the use of paper or textural recording methods, preferring instead to write their history and mathematics on the permanent walls of their cities.

She'd already run a chemical analysis of samples they had obtained from Klikiss architecture on Corribus and Llaro and Pym, the other Klikiss worlds they had investigated, and she knew the results would be the same here: the aliens created an organic mineral mixture similar to mud, tree pulp, and silica combined with a resinous juice – saliva? – that bound together to form a substance harder and more resilient than steel or concrete, yet absorbent and permanent enough to retain the scribed pictograms, written letters, and mathematical equations.

In camp, Margaret would have all night to ponder the prior records they had compiled. But it was a different experience to be here smelling the dry and dusty air, surrounded by the shadows, and perhaps ghosts, of a long-lost race.

A year before, in the scarred ruins on Corribus, Margaret had stared at the recorded symbols for days without result. Yet when she'd spent a night inside an empty chamber looking at moonlight shining on the scrawled markings, she finally experienced her breakthrough, recognizing starmap coordinates that correlated with rare neutron stars. The flood of connections from that one realization had led to the Klikiss Torch. Now she needed further insights to achieve another flurry of translations.

She and Louis had begun to work in Egypt, using a set of sophisticated new sonic mappers developed by the Ildirans. By applying the alien technology to map deeply buried relics underneath the Sahara, the Colicos had found an entire Egyptian city that had been smothered by the dunes. The astonishing find had established them as important archaeologists.

From there, at the request of the Earth Defence Forces, Margaret and Louis had spent six months on Mars far from the military base. Working in a deadly hostile environment was far different from the mere sand and insufferable heat of the Sahara. Stiffly suited, they had analysed the fabled geometric pyramids found in Labyrinthus Noctis to determine the origin of the fabulous and intriguing formations. But after intensive study, the Colicos reached the unpopular conclusion, shored up with many fragments of detailed data, that the famed pyramids were not relics of an extraterrestrial civilization, but *natural* artifacts, outgrowths caused by the unusual crystalline structure of minerals in the soil, exposed to weather conditions in the low gravity over thousands of years . . .

As xeno-archaeologists, they had few extravagant desires, only common goals and fascinations. The two were content to live their rugged lives, each filling their niche in the marriage. Margaret and Louis often completed each other's sentences and sat together engrossed in thought, doing their own work, making only brief half-comments to each other. Yet afterwards, if asked, they would claim they had carried on a long and fascinating conversation.

Now, on Rheindic Co, Louis returned to Margaret from some of his explorations, holding the imager in one hand and a glowpanel in another. 'All finished mapping another section, dear.'

She didn't look up from where she sat staring at the wall markings. 'Make a—'

'I did,' he said, popping out the backup datawafer.

'You know where to put it,' she said, and he stored it in one of the Klikiss cubbyholes. Louis often forgot to take the necessary precautions, but Margaret had learned her lesson. Many times during their previous digs they had lost data due to electrical storms, dust blows, or flash-floods.

Both went back to work in self-absorbed silence, but experiencing close companionship. Margaret and Louis had formed their relationship as an intellectually based alliance, since they spent so much time together far from civilization. They had finally given in to common sense and married each other, as if it were a business venture, bypassing the silly giddiness of juvenile romance.

Louis left her to continue his investigations in one of the chambers that contained the most Klikiss machinery. He insisted that some of the mothballed alien devices still had functional power sources, air exchangers, pumps, and hydraulics. He believed the city was still alive, but sleeping, and he was sure he could reawaken it with the proper intuition and persistence.

Before he went out of earshot, she thought of something they needed to do. 'Tonight, Louis – remember Anton's birthday.'

'Yes, dear. We'll ask Arcas to send a message. Otherwise he'll think we forgot about him.'

Margaret knew, though, that their only son would be wrapped up in his university studies, translating old Earth scrolls and reinterpreting Terran myths and legends. Anton Colicos had established himself as a scholar just as obsessive as his parents. He had given his mother a little antique music box, which she carried with her to every dig. Anton knew his parents were proud of him, though they were often too preoccupied to remind him.

After Louis had gone into the other chamber, Margaret could hear him tinkering and banging on the apparatus. Letting her thoughts wander, she walked down the dry hallways, through chambers filled with reams of untranslated data, literature, or scientific discoveries. Maybe it was nothing more than obscene insect graffiti . . .

Did the Klikiss tell stories aloud like humans and Ildirans, or were they a purely rational race? And why had they gone extinct? The questions weighed on her like ticking time bombs, making her feel that if she didn't unlock the answers soon, it might be too late.

After another day of fruitful yet unremarkable research,

Margaret was interrupted by the soft metal footfalls of their loyal compy DD. 'Hello? Hello? Margaret and Louis? You asked me to come get you at dusk. I have already prepared a nice meal for us all. I am certain you will enjoy the recipe I have developed. Would this be a good time to finish your activities for the day?'

Margaret turned to look at the compy, rubbing her stiff neck. 'It's never a good time to stop, DD, but we won't get any more finished today. Go rouse Louis. He's probably got his head in an alien generator.' She pointed down a corridor, and the Friendly compy hurried off, calling Louis's name.

Together, the three climbed down the long set of metal stairs. DD led, holding a glowpanel and walking backwards to illuminate their way. The compy didn't miss a step, but he frequently warned them of bumps in the path and rough edges to the scaffolding. 'Careful. Careful.' Soon he would probably remind them that he had access to a first-aid data module that they could upload into his limited memory if they required his services as an emergency surgeon.

After she reached the base of the cliff, Margaret's legs ached from the long descent. Louis put an arm around her shoulder. 'Would you like me to help you, dear?'

'You're just as frail as I am, old man,' she said. 'But I'm sure we'll be much revitalized after we eat the gourmet meal DD has prepared for us.'

'I hope it's not "camp-food tartare" again,' Louis said.

'I will file your culinary preferences, Louis.'

As they walked down the rocky canyon that had been scoured clean by forgotten flash floods, Margaret turned back to look up at the high cliffs, the cities so high and out of reach. 'I wonder if the Klikiss ever got arthritis?' she asked aloud. 'And if so, how did they ever get back home? I certainly wouldn't want to climb stairs like that every day.'

'Especially if they had multiple legs, which seems likely,' Louis said. 'Maybe once they got up to the cities, they just stayed inside.'

Margaret stared up as the canyon shadows deepened, considering the inconvenient placement of the city. 'It seems to be typical, though. Remember the tall turrets on Llaro?'

The structures on that dry and grassy planet had been like high termite castles, extruded pillars made of the same mud-and-silica composite, built with interconnected tunnels inside them that did not look like main thoroughfares. Some tunnels led to ground level, but these didn't look any wider than the higher passages, thus suggesting no greater traffic density. The turret windows had been wide and dangerously open to the long drop.

Suddenly, Margaret began to laugh.

Louis looked at her. DD, following his Friendly programming, understood that it was polite to laugh along with his human masters, and so he simulated a chuckle, though he had no idea what the joke was.

'It's so simple, old man,' Margaret said. 'And obvious. Why didn't we see it before?'

He smiled at his wife. When she claimed a breakthrough realization, she was almost always right. 'Well, dear, are you going to tell me or let me die of suspense . . . or old age?'

Margaret gestured up to the cliff face and indicated the sheer rock, the inaccessible climb, and the broad overhang wide open to the air. 'They could *fly*, of course.' She grinned at him, knowing this realization would make them reassess their basic comprehension of the alien biology. 'The Klikiss could *fly*!'

FORTY-ONE

SAREIN

Before she went off to Earth, Sarein made plans as to how she could become the perfect Theron ambassador, fulfilling all the political needs and becoming a well-mannered hostess. Her work would be for the good of the forest world, as well as for the Hansa. Basil Wenceslas had shown her how both peoples shared common needs and goals, deep at the core.

Yes, Sarein had her differences with conservative old Otema, who had unreasonably kept her people from advancing into Hansa society. Still, the ancient woman was Sarein's predecessor and well-revered on Theroc. It would help Sarein if she could get the withered green priest's blessing.

Inside her personal chamber, Sarein brewed a pot of potent clee. Her room was high in the fungus-reef, where the mushroom flesh was young and the walls remained soft. She liked this chamber because it received more sun than other levels farther down in the reef encrustation. On a low table Sarein set out one cup of the stimulating beverage for herself and another for Otema.

As she waited for her visitor, Sarein checked her appearance and practised her smile. She adjusted the ambassadorial robe Otema had presented to her, then rubbed the Terran bracelets Basil had given her as a token of his esteem for the Theron people, and as a lover's parting gift.

On schedule, Otema entered, moving with silent footsteps, and Sarein rose to greet her. The woman looked so old! Her skin was a deep green like night at the bottom of the forest, and it had a dry hardness about it, like wood. She wore only the most minimal garb of a green priest and no ornamentation.

Noting the ambassadorial robe Sarein wore, Otema appeared troubled. The status lines and achievement marks stained into her face furrowed, like dotted lines indicating where wrinkles would go. Sarein wondered if the former ambassador already missed the amenities and culture on Earth.

Sarein pretended not to notice her predecessor's pensive mood. 'You have been gone for so many years, Otema, that we never got to know each other well.' She poured clee for the old woman, who accepted the cup. 'Before I depart for my new duties on Earth, I thought we should have a brief talk.' Sarein smiled, not meaning her words but required to say them nevertheless. 'With all your experience, you must have much advice for me in dealing with the Hansa?'

'I will share my thoughts with you,' Otema said stiffly and slowly, 'though I am not convinced you are willing to hear.'

Sarein tried not to frown at the rebuff, drinking her hot beverage. 'Surely you are not disappointed to return to the world-forest, Otema? You have earned it after your years of service.'

'The worldforest is always a balm to human weariness, regardless of what brewing troubles the trees may see that we do not. No, I am not disappointed to be back on Theroc. I am disappointed in *you*, Ambassador Sarein.' She used the title like an insult, and finally sat down with great reluctance. 'And I am afraid of what damage you will cause.'

Sarein chuckled lightly, treating it as a joke. 'You should give me a chance to prove myself, Otema. I have studied on Earth, and I am familiar with their cultures and practises. In fact, I probably understand the politics and commerce of the Hansa as well as you.' *If not better*, she thought to herself.

Otema scowled. 'You are an intelligent girl, Sarein, and I would never doubt your ability to understand.' She took a long sip of her drink and paused, eyes closed, visibly absorbing the energy the ground worldtree seeds gave her. The green in her skin seemed to grow more vibrant.

'However, I hope your understanding extends to the delicacy of the Theron position. It is easy to be contemptuous or forgetful of where you have spent your life. An impatient child might consider our ways uninteresting or dull, but do not let the lure of gaudy treasures distract you from what is truly important. Such flowers are bright and colourful, but they bloom only briefly. Roots, on the other hand, go deep and provide stability for a long time.'

Sarein wanted to make a rude noise, but restrained herself. Instead, she nodded sagely. 'A very important point, Otema. I thank you for your insight.'

Basil had talked with her about how frustrating Otema could be. Without emotion or rancour, the old ambassador had deflected all Hansa attempts to achieve even the slightest control over the green priests. Basil knew not to cross the 'Iron Lady', because Otema would not budge.

Under Sarein, though, many things would change.

Outside in the jungle, two mating birds flew about squawking, rustling the leaves and disturbing a cloud of jewel-shelled insects. Otema seemed distracted, as if worried about deeper problems than an ambitious young ambassador to Earth. 'The trees have much knowledge – and some of it they do not share, even with us.'

Sarein steeled herself, tried a different tack. 'Since I am not a

232

green priest, I realize that my understanding of the worldforest is not as deep as yours. However, I will strive to do my best, and I will always have access to other members of the priesthood for their advice and communication abilities. The worldforest will know everything I do.'

'I doubt, young woman, that you intend to let any green priest sit in on your . . . shall we say, *private* consultations with Chairman Wenceslas.' Her suggestiveness so shocked Sarein that the young woman could barely cover her reaction. 'You believe that your intimate connection with the Chairman grants you some sort of power over him, but I warn you that Basil Wenceslas is not so easily manipulated. He runs far deeper than a simple girl can comprehend.'

Sarein's face darkened. 'Now that you have been stripped of your ambassadorial cloak, Otema, you have forgotten tact and diplomacy.'

'I have not forgotten the truth, Sarein,' she said. 'One doesn't need a link with the worldtrees to see something so obvious.' Leaving her beverage unfinished, the ancient woman stood and gave a formal bow. 'I believe that is more advice than you truly wanted to hear, and so I will take my leave.' She backed towards the arched door in the soft-walled room.

'Play your games, Sarein, but never forget who you are and where you were born. The trees sense a tremendously difficult time ahead, though they will not tell even green priests what is in store. A day will come when you are glad of your allies on Theroc.'

FORTY-TWO

DR GERALD SERIZAWA

Oncier blazed brightly, an infant sun engulfed by the nuclear fires of its newly dense core. Though much smaller than the system's primary star, this burning gas giant melted the hearts of the formerly frozen moons.

Media reports of the successful Klikiss Torch continued to spread throughout the Hanseatic colony worlds and into the Ildiran Empire, delivered by fast vessels on trade routes. Serizawa's recorded interviews had intrigued listeners on a hundred worlds. He'd had his glory and his fame – enough of it, in fact. Now the real work began.

Though the new-born star was small and relatively cool, Serizawa could not look at the roiling plasma without filters across the viewing windows. Projection screens on the consoles displayed magnetic maps viewed through specific portions of the spectrum. It was a marvel and an oddity.

He had studied the strange ephemeral images taken shortly after the gas planet's ignition – crystalline ejecta shaped like perfect spheres, glittering globes that seemed to fly away from the flaming new sun. Margaret Colicos had seen the same thing. Serizawa had tried to explain it simply and easily; with so many media scanners around, he did not want to alarm anyone, or make it appear that *he* didn't know what was going on. Still, the unusual phenomenon had defied explanation, even after repeated analysis.

He was thankful that the incident had not occurred again.

Running a palm across his perfectly smooth scalp, Serizawa shivered. He felt perpetually cold aboard the metal-walled observation platform. Though he stared at the glowing ember of the tiny star, none of the warmth penetrated his pale skin to his bones. He always walked around the station with goosebumps on his arms, no matter how he adjusted the environmental controls.

Because the density gradient was so steep, the nuclear combustion zone in Oncier's core was only a thin shell, but sufficient to light the hydrogen fuel. The small sun was a hurricane still settling down, but nothing much had changed in weeks.

There were dramatic shifts, however, on the four moons.

A week from now, the first Hansa ships would arrive bearing planetary engineers, terraforming specialists, and geologists. With special shelters and massive equipment, they would drop down to the warming moons and begin long-term plans for converting them into habitable worlds. Exciting times lay ahead.

Serizawa's thin lips curled in a smile. 'Hmm, what do you suppose the colonists will call themselves?' He often pondered inane questions and struck up conversations with his technicians. The largest moon, Jack, orbited closest to the ignited planet and would likely be the first moon suitable for colonization. 'Do you think they'll call themselves Jackians? Or Jackites?'

One of the techs enjoyed the game. 'Jacklings sounds more appropriate.'

Serizawa looked at screens showing the restless surfaces of the other moons, George, Ben, and Christopher. Pockets of thawed gases spewed like cometary tails, the noisy and messy birth of an atmosphere from volatilizing ice. The initial gases would boil off into space, too light to be held by the moons' gravity. Eventually, after the frozen lakes sublimated and glaciers crumbled into either liquid water or gaseous carbon dioxide, there should be enough air to maintain a blanket around the moons. Eventually.

The names of these moons – in honour of the first four Great Kings of the Terran Hanseatic League – gave Serizawa a sense of history. But humans looked upon a few centuries as a great span of time, while to the Ildirans and especially their Mage-Imperator, so many years was barely a moment. During most of Earth's civilization, people had failed to participate in long-term planning, neglecting to look further than their own lifespans.

Serizawa went to the station's thermostat and raised the internal temperature. Heat would radiate upwards from the decks and warm them all. Rubbing his hands briskly together, he returned to the monitoring screens.

He toggled between close-up images of Ben and Christopher orbiting near each other and those of George and Jack on the other side of Oncier. He played time-lapse images of the cratered landscapes as they smoothed out and cracked in the throes of rapid thawing. Because the topology of each moon changed daily, it was still far too early to assess any permanent land features.

'Large tectonic upheaval on Christopher,' said one of the techs, switching an image of the mist-enshrouded moon to the large display screen. Clouds of newly released gases roared upwards like geysers. 'Look, a crevasse is opening up, a large piece of the ice sheet shifting.'

Serizawa hurried over to observe, still rubbing his arms to get warm. 'The geology is still so unstable that maybe the arrival of the terraforming crews is a bit premature. We wouldn't want an exploration team going through a quake like that.'

'The terraformers are bringing in large-scale machinery, Dr Serizawa. Designed to withstand the end of the world.'

'Or the beginning of one.' The ten technicians and astrophysicists gathered around the high-resolution viewers, riveted to the tectonic event.

Serizawa looked up just in time to see a cluster of bright, glittering globes streak into the system and converge upon the restless new sun from high above the orbital plane. 'Look at that!'

They were just like the ones he had seen on the images of the Klikiss Torch experiment, apparitions he had dismissed as irrelevant anomalies. Margaret Colicos, though, had been absolutely correct in her first assessment.

Ships. He suddenly experienced a deeper chill than any he had felt aboard the station.

The fleet of bristling diamond-hulled spheres approached with dizzying speed, like moths drawn to Oncier's new flame. Fourteen glassy spheres the size of asteroids dropped towards the former gas giant and its thawing moons. They looked like transparent planets, perfectly round but studded with sharp protrusions; the clear hulls showed murky mists inside, hinted at complex geometrical machinery. Like hungry insects the alien globes surrounded the smallest moon, Ben.

All of his crew rushed to the observation windows. Dazzling light from nearby Oncier reflected from the crystal-curved balls. Triangular pyramids like perfect mountains thrust through the bubble-skin; their pointed tips crackled with blue lightning.

'Are we getting all this on permanent record?' Serizawa said. 'This is amazing! What are they?'

'They seem to be interested in Ben. Maybe they're scanning—'

The alien ships opened fire on the moon.

Blue lightning from the pyramidal protrusions of all fourteen alien ships converged, then shot downwards in a single beam, slamming into Ben's already unstable surface. Heat glowed, land-masses vibrated as acoustic waves transmitted powerful energy throughout the rocky body.

Serizawa shouted into the communications systems, as if the aliens might understand his outcry or even respond to him. 'What are you doing? Please stop! This is human territory. This is—' He looked at his companions, but no one offered any suggestions.

The weapons fire continued. Gases erupted from the moon, the rocky continent broke apart, and orange heat boiled upwards from the now-exposed core. Ben began to shudder, splitting under the onslaught.

It took the silent aliens twenty minutes to demolish the moon and break it into glowing coals that drifted apart in space.

'My God! Why?' The techs and astrophysicists were wild-eyed.

The crystalline globes moved smoothly away from the hot rubble of Ben and headed straight for George. Serizawa's face glistened with sweat. Though his skin seemed as cold as ice, he felt as though he was burning with anger.

The fourteen diamond spheres hovered over the second moon. Analysing? Mapping continental flaws, fractures in the core structure? Then the lightning hammers blazed downwards again.

Serizawa's anger turned to terror. 'Transmit these images! Call for help, a general distress in all directions.' He cursed the fact that their poorly staffed observation platform had no green priest aboard to provide instant telink communication.

'Dr Serizawa, it'll take weeks before anyone receives these transmissions.'

Serizawa knew that full well. He spread his palms, panicked and helpless. A man dying of a medical emergency does not write a letter to summon an ambulance – but that was all he could do now. 'Somebody's got to know.'

The technician sent the distress call without further argument.

'Like a message in a damned bottle,' he grumbled. The transmission went out in all directions, hoping to find someone who could hear.

The other team members used the resources aboard the observation station to record and study the moon-crushing blasts, to image the complete destruction of the rocky satellites. They could have become lovely terraformed worlds,' Serizawa said.

Aboard the station, they had no way to defend themselves, could only gather information, collect data . . . and hope the destructive spheres did not notice them.

After the silent and ominous alien warglobes had obliterated the moon George, they moved on to Christopher.

And finally Jack. All four moons vaporized.

Serizawa was weeping now. He stood in front of the observation window, staring at the perfect spheres, and the destruction of everything he had created at Oncier. 'Why are you doing this? What have we done to you?'

The aliens had transmitted no messages, no ultimatums, no warnings or explanations. Hovering in their parking orbit far from blazing Oncier, Serizawa and his team could not move or flee. Worst of all, they could not understand.

The fourteen monstrous ships left the destroyed satellites and paused above the funeral pyre of what had been the gas giant Oncier. Then like a swarm of angry wasps the globes moved to surround the observation platform.

The technicians scrambled backwards, away from the windows, as if they would be safer within the fragile platform. Serizawa did not even bother to move. In the last moment, he closed his eyes.

The awesome blue lightning crackled again.

While it had taken the crystal globes some time to obliterate the four rocky moons, the total annihilation of the space platform required only seconds.

FORTY-THREE

KING FREDERICK

B ehind closed doors, the mood around the Whisper Palace was shocked and genuinely frightened. King Frederick didn't know what to do.

The planetary engineers and terraformers had returned to Earth at the stardrive's maximum speed – wasting huge amounts of ekti to deliver the terrible news. The crew had arrived on schedule at Oncier, only to find the moons blasted into rubble, the observation platform completely vaporized. There were no survivors of Dr Serizawa's research and observation team. Someone, some force, had destroyed everything.

All citizens looked to their brave and powerful King for answers, for consolation . . . And the old man could do nothing.

When the panicked Oncier terraformers had returned, they broadcast their news over a thousand bands, squawking like startled chickens rushing back to their coop. The Hansa could never control or spin the news now.

In the waiting room behind the Throne Hall, Basil Wenceslas grumbled, frightening the King with his naked anger. 'Damn! I would have preferred to keep this matter classified for a while. We don't know how to assess what's happened. We don't have any answers. Everything was destroyed – but why? Was it an outside attack, or some sort of . . . cosmic event, like an aftershock of the Klikiss Torch?'

'You can bet it was an attack,' said General Lanyan, who stood stiffly at attention while Basil paced the floor. He had been recalled from the EDF base on Mars to discuss the crisis.

Frederick brushed at a speck of lint on his robes and looked around for a goblet of sweet wine. He had offered Basil a strong drink, but the Chairman shook his head, refusing to let anything cloud his thoughts. In contrast, King Frederick very much wanted to numb the dread he felt. 'Basil, I can make an announcement that we're investigating, but we still have no answers. Will that put them at ease?'

Basil slammed a flat palm against a fluted Corinthian column and said sarcastically, 'Good idea. Let's tell every person in the Hansa that we're helpless and ignorant.'

'But we really *don't* know what happened,' Frederick said.

'And neither do they,' Basil retorted. 'A King must never let anyone see that he's in the dark.'

Frederick took a gulp of his sweet wine and didn't answer. He looked at the uniformed military man – *Lanyan*, not Lanson, he chided himself – and tried to shore up his confidence that the Earth Defence Forces would respond to this disaster. The General wanted to retaliate and crush the mysterious aggressors so that peace could return to the human colony worlds.

'I may be stating the obvious, Chairman Wenceslas,' Lanyan said, 'but it might have been the Ildirans. Their Solar Navy was present at Oncier, watching our test. Maybe they felt threatened because we have such powerful technology. Who else could it have been?'

'It's a big universe, General, filled with many things we don't understand,' the King said. 'We've explored only a portion of one spiral arm in our galaxy—'

'Frederick,' Basil interrupted, sounding exasperated, 'even the Ildirans with all their history have never encountered another alien race. I don't want to muddy the issue by making up bogeymen. The threat of war with the Ildirans is frightening enough. On the other hand, General, I am also highly sceptical that the Solar Navy has weaponry approaching the power necessary for such destruction.'

'True. This has got to be something new, and the Ildirans have been stagnant for centuries.' Lanyan walked to one of the triangular windows that looked out upon the Moon Statue Garden. Topiary shrubs and ornate sculptures spread across hundreds of acres on the Whisper Palace grounds. 'And it wasn't a ragtag group of pirates like Rand Sorengaard. The Roamers might want revenge against us, but they certainly don't have the technology to destroy whole moons.'

After Basil's scolding, Frederick kept his thoughts to himself. Since the geology was so unstable during the rapid warming of the moons, perhaps the satellites had simply broken apart by themselves. Plenty of tidal forces, tectonic heat expansion, explosive gas volatilization . . . But it was ridiculous to think that Jack, George, Ben, and Christopher would all self-destruct at once, and that the flying rubble could have coincidentally destroyed the distant observation platform.

'We must find out what provoked this, and who did it,' Basil said. 'We haven't heard of any other attacks, have we?'

The General shook his head. 'But then, without widespread telink, it takes months for news to trickle around the Hansa colonies, and even longer to get verifiable reports from within the Ildiran Empire.'

Basil's face darkened at the reminder. 'If we had more green priests at regular checkpoints around the Spiral Arm, we wouldn't have this communications problem.'

The King decided it was time to act regal. 'By my sceptre and sword, Basil, no need to complicate the issue with old sore spots. The people are clamouring for answers. How shall I respond right now? I value your advice.'

Basil frowned at him. 'You listen to my orders.'

The King tried not to look stung by the rebuff. 'Then give me orders, Basil. Tell me what to do.'

At night, as seen from above by dignitaries in observation zeppelins, the Whisper Palace looked like a celebration of candles. Eternal torches burned from every spire and cupola, every lantern post and bridge pillar. The crowds in the square, people streaming across the bridge over the Royal Canal, and those holding special invitations to wait on the Palace grounds proper – all held candles or lights of their own.

Led by a procession of his advisers, accompanied by one of the green priests stationed on Earth, and followed by numerous uniformed envoys from important Hansa colony worlds, Old King Frederick marched along a promenade to the bridge. Royal guards opened a path for him. Crowds raised their candles and illumination globes high.

Out in the press of people, surrounded by an uneasy space, a single Klikiss robot stood, just watching. It made Frederick uneasy, and he frowned.

King Frederick's advisers had robed him in the muted blacks and purples of mourning. He walked with a ponderous step, as if he carried a great weight on his mantled shoulders. The processional music was deep and slow, like a dirge. The Archfather of Unison had already led the audience in prayer, issuing consoling words.

243

The Archfather's main purpose was to keep them soothed – not much different from the King's task.

The crowds simmered into a restless quiet as Frederick finally reached the end of the suspension bridge spanning the Royal Canal, where four iron lampposts stood like sentinels, their flames hissing and burning skyward.

Basil would be watching from a high balcony inside the Whisper Palace's main cupola. He had directed the technicians, so they knew what to do. Timing would be important.

Frederick had made mistakes lately, he knew, but this time he called upon his best powers of oratory, summoning raw emotion and speaking with all the grief he could put into his face and his thoughts. Real tears glistened at the corners of his eyes, and one tracked down his cheek. The close-up cameras would catch that.

The King's voice boomed out, rich and paternal. 'For many years, the Terran Hanseatic League has helped humanity to expand across the Spiral Arm. We have established footholds on many new worlds, carrying our civilization to the galactic community. But even in the face of such glorious progress and accomplishments, we unfortunately falter.' He paused, as if drawing strength.

'Not long ago I announced our creation of a new sun through human drive and ingenuity. Its family of moons were to be developed into new colonies.'

Frederick hung his head. 'But now, sadly, I feel like a parent who has lost his children. In an unprovoked attack, an unknown aggressor has snuffed out our hope for these vital new worlds, which were named in honour of my predecessors. We must understand why this has happened. And then we must avenge.'

He lifted his head to study the burning flames that sparkled from the bridge pillars. 'But first we must mourn.'

Frederick approached four bridge pillars that symbolized the four destroyed moons. He reached out to the first towering post.

These flames were meant to be eternal, glowing in recognition of human-settled worlds. Now, alas, these four must be extinguished.'

He touched the metal base of the nearest pillar. Inside the Palace, Basil's technicians shut off the flame, symbolically extinguishing the glowing fire.

When all four bridge pillars were dark, the King stepped back and raised his hands to the crowds. 'This is the first time in all Terran history that a King has been forced to do this.'

The crowd seemed stricken. The dismay and uneasiness would spread across the Hansa worlds.

'Let us pray it will be the last.'

FORTY-FOUR

ESTARRA

Theron work crews converted the empty worm hive into a new dwelling complex while Estarra spent time with Beneto and his treelings. She knelt beside him, and he guided her with sure fingers, showing where to soften the dirt, how much water to add.

With a rustle of underbrush and quiet sniffing sobs, Celli rushed into the clearing, her face streaked with tears. 'Beneto, something's happened to my condorfly. Please look. You'll know what's wrong with him.' In her arms she carried her dog-sized pet condorfly. Its wings were spread like drooping sails.

Sarein would have scolded Celli for childish infatuation with a brainless insect, but Beneto gave the girl a look of deepest sympathy. 'Come with me. Your condorfly will like the open meadows, where it naturally wants to be.' He stroked the condorfly's elongated glossy head. The eight segmented legs twitched and skittered as if it were climbing a giant flower in its dreams.

He led his sisters through tall weeds and rustling grasses,

around the massive trunks of worldtrees to a meadow full of lilies the size of juice vats. Other condorflies flew in the meadow. Celli's pet seemed to perk up in the new environment, its wings vibrating, trembling.

'Look at the ground, Celli.' Beneto gestured to condorfly wings scattered like coloured glass all around the meadow. The bodies of the dead insects were quickly consumed by natural decomposition, but the tough, translucent wings remained, artifacts of their brief but dazzlingly colourful existences.

'We each have our lives, little sister. What matters is not how long those lives last, but what we *do* with them. I have my work with the worldforest. Reynald will be the Theron Father some day. Sarein is going to be the next ambassador to Earth. You and Estarra have to decide for yourselves what you will accomplish.' Beneto reached out to stroke the condorfly's sleek body. 'Your pet has his own life as well. What do you think he wants to accomplish?'

Celli said, 'He keeps me company.' The condorfly flapped its wings again, straining on the leash to join the other insects around the flower-filled meadow.

'And has he accomplished that in his life?' Beneto asked.

'He's my pet. I love him.' Then Celli seemed to sense what Beneto was implying as he gazed at the flurry of other condorflies. 'Oh. Maybe he's not sick, just lonely.'

'Give him a few days to fly around in the meadow and feed from the flowers, Celli,' Estarra said. 'He knows the way back to your room if he ever wants to visit.'

Reluctant, the little girl loosed the bindings of the leash. The condorfly rose up, flapping gracefully. It seemed to gain energy immediately, swirling around on updrafts, then it flew to the bright flowers, touching other insects, communicating with pheromones or subsonic signals.

For a long time, they watched it dance and dodge in the air, and finally the three all returned to the fungus-reef city, walking close together, though a tearful Celli continued to look over her shoulder into the meadow . . .

That night, after Celli was asleep on her pallet with the window open to the jungle, the condorfly drifted back in. It landed on her sleeping form, spreading its wings like a coverlet. The little girl stirred and mumbled, but did not wake as the beautiful insect twitched its wings one last time, then died atop her blankets.

With her long hair twists tied out of her way, Estarra joined the conversion team in the empty worm hive, cleaning debris the giant invertebrates had left in their nest. Scrubbing hard, she smoothed wall barriers and marked places for furniture or doors to be cut. Other Theron workers shored up arches, blocked off dead-end tubes to be used as storage chambers, and tore down thin walls to expand living quarters. It had taken them some time to map the convoluted passages of the hive, but the new dwelling complex had begun to take shape.

Since the worms did not follow a blueprint based on human convenience, the Therons had to make do with the basic structure and passageways. Some of the worm tunnels were large enough for a man to walk upright, but others required crawling from chamber to chamber. The people would learn their way around the maze, enlarge some of the tunnels, and soon this place would be a bustling complex. Many families had already applied to Father Idriss and Mother Alexa for new quarters here.

Outside, two daredevil young men chased each other in glider contraptions made from discarded condorfly wings and a few scrap pieces of equipment still functional from the old *Caillié*. Estarra longed to be out playing with them, but she had responsibilities now. This worm hive was her discovery, and she wanted to leave her mark. At first, the reconstruction engineers had looked patronizingly at Estarra, expecting that she would get in the way. But she had been just as diligent and dedicated as the rest of the crew.

Now, working against the hive's outer wall, Estarra used a hot cutting tool to slice through the papery material. She broke through to the outside air and opened a flap that would form an important primary window. It would also be decorative and colourful . . . and a fine way to memorialize Celli's pet.

After she cut the opening, Estarra lifted the first of the large wings from the dead condorfly. It looked like a triangular section of stained-glass. All around the outer walls, detached condorfly wings had been added to portholes and illumination squares, drenching the rooms in rainbows. After Estarra applied the four wings, this chamber would look like an ancient cathedral.

Using a pot of sap cement, Estarra brushed the edges of the window hole. The adhesive would dry as hard as iron and hold the multicoloured wing in place. Finally, she stepped back to admire her work. It was a glorious addition to the new dwelling complex where all could see it. Estarra thought her little sister would like that.

FORTY-FIVE

NIRA

As a green priest she had new and important duties, but Nira still enjoyed her old activities. At least once a week she swapped tasks so that she could climb to the treetops and read aloud to the fascinated worldforest. She could think of nothing nobler than telling stories.

Balanced on a thick bough, Nira read in a voice inflected with emotion as the tale of Sir Gawain and the Green Knight rolled off her tongue. She herself didn't know how the adventure would end. It was all new to her, and she knew the forest was as eager as she was. Through her bare skin, Nira could feel the trees responding like an audience.

As she finished reading the story, Nira caressed the scaly bark. Practising her new abilities, she forged a connection with the tree, dipping a thread of telink into the overall forest. She could access any part of the ever-growing database of information, but the trees were more than an encyclopedia. She could consult with them, learn what the forest had synthesized from all the information it had gathered. But the worldtrees still kept their secrets, even from important green priests like Yarrod.

For her enjoyment, Nira queried the worldforest and received a flood of stories. Suddenly the reservoir in her mind was filled with more tales than she could imagine. It would take her many restless nights of vivid dreams to digest all the things she now knew. With a sigh of gratitude, she broke the telink.

Nira felt the tree fronds vibrate around her and recognized the approach of another priest. She didn't need to look, because the worldtrees identified her visitor as old Otema, who had served for so many years as ambassador to Earth. Nira turned, surprised and intimidated. Surely, the stern but knowledgeable old priest was not looking for her.

Though the woman was ancient beyond Nira's comprehension, Otema climbed with the rapid grace of a tree lizard. She joined Nira on the wide palmate branch, gazing into the forest. 'I remember how excited I was when I first took the green, how many things I needed to learn.' She turned her attention to Nira; her dark-eyed gaze seemed distant . . . even wistful. 'After more than a century, the wonder and majesty of the great worldforest never wanes. The trees feel as enthralling to me now as they did when I was your age.'

Nira didn't know what to say. 'I . . . thank you for your insight, Ambassador Otema.'

'Just call me Otema, child. The green priests have no use for those titles.'

'Yes . . . Otema.' Gathering her courage, Nira said, 'I'm surprised to see you here. Are you looking for someone?'

'Yes, and I've found her.' It seemed an awkward tableau, the two women standing on a narrow branch in the treetops. 'Yarrod said I might find you up here, though it wasn't your assigned day to read to the trees.'

Clutching the datapad defensively in her hand, Nira said, 'We each serve according to our abilities and our interests.' She touched the dark lines around her mouth. 'I am an accomplished reader, and I like being up here.'

'You enjoy history, then? Adventures, legends, and myths?' Nira tried to detect criticism in the old woman's voice, but found none. She simply nodded.

'Interesting,' Otema said. 'I have studied your family, and I wonder where you discovered your interest in legends. Did your mother tell you stories when you were a little girl?'

'Not at all. In fact, that is one of the reasons I was glad to be joined with the worldforest, because it opened a new universe for me, one that I never could have found at home.'

The eldest of eight children, Nira Khali had come from a relatively poor family that lived in one of the oldest worm-hive dwellings. A set of chambers that had once been quite comfortable for her parents became a crowded encampment for their growing family. When Nira had entered the priesthood as an acolyte, her family had been sad to see her go, but they had also appreciated the extra breathing space.

Nira had always been a thinker and a reader, while her parents and siblings were content to work in the gardens or fruit orchards. Her parents spent their free time on amusements and games, joining in festivals and talking with friends. Nira, though, would rather be reading.

'I am looking for someone who enjoys stories,' Otema said. 'Such a person would be of great benefit to my next assignment.' Nira's heart jumped, curious about what the ambassador had in mind.

Nira remembered many times when she had read to herself, crouched against a curved wall of the worm hive for a few moments of solitude. Though Nira loved her family, they did not understand her. She wondered if she was like a cuckoo that had hatched in the wrong nest. Nira wanted to ask a thousand questions, but she held her silence, politely waiting, though her eyes shone with fire and curiosity.

Otema continued, 'Reynald has returned from his peregrination. He has seen many worlds, talked with great leaders, and observed unusual cultures.'

'I've listened to all his reports with great eagerness,' Nira said. Did Otema want her to speak with Reynald, to act as some kind of historian and compile his experiences to be stored in the worldforest database?

'When Reynald spoke with the Ildiran Prime Designate Jora'h, he requested a remarkable boon. You have heard of the *Saga of Seven Suns*?'

'Of course,' Nira said. 'It's supposed to be the longest epic ever recorded. It would take years and years just to read it.'

'Years and years would not allow you to absorb even a fraction of it,' Otema said. 'Reynald received permission for two green priests to study the *Saga*. We can read it, document it, tell the stories to the treelings we bring along with us. The *Saga* is far too long for any person to absorb in a single lifetime.'

Nira gasped and then covered her mouth. Her throat went dry.

'Since my duties on Earth were completed, Father Idriss and Mother Alexa have searched for a task to keep me busy. I've been away from the worldforest for too long, and I don't intend just to sit and water treelings.'

Nira jumped ahead. 'Are you travelling to Ildira?'

'Not alone, child. It is an enormous task, and Reynald was granted permission to send *two* green priests.' Otema's face brightened. 'Nira, I would like to request you as my personal assistant, companion, and apprentice. We will journey together to Ildira under the light of seven suns.'

*

Nira's family could barely believe their daughter's good fortune, though it took some time for her news to sink in. Her parents, Garris and Meena Khali, had never thought much about other worlds; the thick forest on Theroc already extended farther than their imaginations did.

Nira had trouble comprehending that she would cross the Spiral Arm to the capital of an immense alien empire. She would be gone from Theroc for years, away from the forests, away from other green priests, away from her family. But she had been practising her telink abilities: as long as she could touch a treeling, she could remain in contact with the entirety of the worldforest. She had no reason to be afraid, only excited.

Nira shared a meal with her family in their cramped living quarters. Garris wanted to call all the neighbours inside the crowded worm hive rooms so they could wish Nira farewell. It would be a great celebration, a happy opportunity for socializing. But Nira, panicked at the prospect of having to face such a gathering, pleaded that she had too much business to take care of before her departure. The merchant ship would be arriving within a day to take them to Ildira.

Grinning, she looked from the worn and tired face of her mother to the broad, jowly smile of her father. 'However, I did request one favour for you. I have a surprise before I go.'

With the flush of new importance she'd achieved by being chosen to accompany Otema, Nira had sent a message to Father Idriss and Mother Alexa. The old ambassador had added her approval. Nira had received word back today that her application had been heartily approved.

'Father, I've managed to get our family prime quarters in the new worm hive discovered by Estarra.' She smiled as her parents gasped in disbelief. 'You'll have your choice of the largest chambers, as soon as you're ready to move in.'

Astounded at their good fortune, Garris came forward to give his daughter an awkward hug. Her mother couldn't believe what she had heard. 'Thank you! Thank you!'

Embarrassed by their gratitude, her newly green skin flushed dark. Nira said, 'I'm glad I could do one last thing for my family before I embark on my great adventure.'

FORTY-SIX

JESS TAMBLYN

On Plumas, ancestral home of the Tamblyn clan, the Roamers gathered to hold a sombre memorial.

Bram Tamblyn looked gaunt and pale. The old man moved like a machine as he performed the formal duties of welcoming representatives of important families. Bram's expression flickered from stony blankness to sudden waves of dismay as guests gave him their sympathy.

Jess, now the only son, stood beside his father, stunned but trying to be strong enough for both of them. He wore a warm parka, a fleece-lined hood wreathing his face. Steam rose with each breath he exhaled, but he felt numb rather than cold. It was his responsibility to be here, to remember his brother Ross. Four of his uncles, Bram's brothers, had also come in their role as Tamblyn clan representatives; from now on, Jess knew they would take a more active participation in running the family's water mines.

As he spoke to other clan leaders, accepting their sincere words of consolation, Jess saw more than shared grief in the Roamers' eyes. He also recognized a deep-seated fear. No one knew what had caused the disaster on Golgen. Neither could they guess what had provoked the attack on the Blue Sky Mine . . . or if such a thing would ever happen again.

Speaker Jhy Okiah did not come to Plumas for the funeral. She was too old, her body frail and her bones brittle from a lifetime in low gravity; in her place she sent her protégé, Cesca Peroni. Jess greeted her after she descended a shaft through the thick ice sheet. His already distraught heart broke to see her, knowing the tragic reason why she had come.

On Rendezvous, the two had shared speechless surprise after hearing the news from Del Kellum. Now Cesca came to Plumas wearing the formal grieving robes of a Roamer widow. Though she had only been betrothed to Ross, her choice of garments seemed appropriate: deep blue and purple embroidered with forest green. The normally vibrant colours were muted. Her long, warm dress and her fur-insulated boots bore the geometric embroidered design of the Roamer Chain, the symbols of all clans linked one after another to show the individuality but ultimate unity of their culture.

Jess's young sister Tasia stood by herself near the ice platform, watching each new group of visitors arrive through the ceiling shafts. Her compy EA stood beside her, tallying the names. Tasia usually loved company, chattered with guests, attempted to show off tricks or things she had found on the ice sheets, but now she seemed sullen and confused, angry at an invisible enemy. Her uncles stood by her, but when Tasia saw Cesca's mourning cloak, the usually vibrant girl broke down and ran into the rounded huts that were shielded from the cold, thermally separated and insulated from sound. There, she would sob alone.

Plumas had an outer shell of ice that was kilometres thick, floating upon a deep sea that covered a small rocky core. The ice sheath occasionally cracked open like chapped skin, forming lines along the surface where liquid water bled out until it froze iron-hard again.

Deep beneath the protective skin, heated by the pressing weight of ice as well as tidal stresses and even the cooling rock core, Plumas maintained a liquid ocean. Ambitious Roamers had drilled access holes through the surface to get water for their own needs. The forebears of clan Tamblyn had set up mining and pumping operations on Plumas, marketing the vital liquid as well as derived oxygen and in-system rocket fuels the Roamers needed. The Tamblyn family had also carved out a place to live deep under the frozen roof of the moon.

The Roamers had carried their small prepackaged huts into the air bubbles beneath the ice crust, erecting them on stable shelves that looked out upon the underground water. The Plumas ocean had spawned native planktons, lichens, and even deep-sea nematodes that had lived unchanged for eons. When the Roamers brought their artificial suns, the Plumas environment blossomed. Phosphorescent light rippled through the frozen ceiling like a still-life aurora trapped in the sky.

Plumas was one of the more wondrous Roamer settlements, demonstrating that the resourceful gypsies could find austere niches that no one in the Terran Hanseatic League would ever consider. Jess's family had found this place and made it their fortified and hidden home.

Now Bram Tamblyn seemed barely able to stand. Though he was tough and hardened, a workhorse who never slowed down, the old man appeared ready to shatter if any more stress was placed upon him.

'Why don't you go rest, Dad? Talk with your brothers. I'll take care of the final preparations. We're not scheduled to begin for another four hours.'

Bram did not answer. He looked as if he resented his son's

compassion. His wife had died years before in a surface accident, and her body had fallen into a freezing water gap, where she would be forever locked and preserved, far out of sight. Now, the old man's eyes were reddened; his face was dragged into a frown by the wrinkles around his cold-chapped skin.

Jess felt alone as he remained on the ice pier looking out into the grey waters of the internal sea. If only he could just be a statue. He looked up to the looming solid sky. The ceiling hung blue and white, lit by artificial suns planted inside holes cut into the ice, balls of illumination that directed heat and light downwards throughout the crystalline shield.

Shivering, Jess went to see if he could comfort his little sister before the funeral began. He had many duties to perform before the day was over.

The visiting clan leaders and the surviving members of the Tamblyn family gathered out on the ice shelf. Plumas was silent and muffled. A faint mist sublimated from the icepack and wafted over the still, quicksilver waters like the breath of a sleeping dragon.

Old Bram looked like a stuffed scarecrow, wearing layers of vests, jackets, and a tattered cloak over his shoulders. He stood on an ice dock several metres above the smooth water. Jess and Tasia remained close beside him, with Cesca only a step behind.

A box-like raft floated in the water, made of expensive pressed cellulose. Each plank had been imported from Roamer traders, brought down and assembled here. Much of the cost had been donated by Speaker Okiah and her clan, though Bram insisted he would pay her back. Inside the floating container lay an effigy of Ross Tamblyn, wrapped in the few items of old clothing he had left behind when he and his father had parted ways.

Jess had offered to give the eulogy, but Bram would not hear of it. After invoking the wisdom of the Guiding Star, the old man

259

spoke in a thin voice that echoed across the water. 'This is what remains of my son, Ross. No wreckage was found of the Blue Sky Mine, heinously destroyed by unknown enemies.'

Sinews stood out like ropes along Bram's neck. 'Still, we have our memories of Ross, our fond stories, the times we spent together . . .' His voice dropped, then cracked. 'And our guilt for the things we did not do, and which now can never be done.

'Since we have nothing else of my son Ross, we will make do.' Bram raised his gaze to the solid sky. 'This is our memorial to him.'

The other Roamers echoed, 'This is our memorial to him.'

Jess and Tasia stepped forward, each snapping the end off an air-activated igniter. They held the bright flames like candles above the sluggish, cold ocean. Bram Tamblyn reached into one of his numerous pockets and withdrew another igniter, so that their three flames blazed together.

'Ross was my oldest child. His fires burned bright and hot—' Bram's voice quavered. 'Yes, Ross was hot indeed. But his light and his life were snuffed out too quickly.' In unison, the three tossed their igniters into the raft, which had been padded with woody icekelp fronds, now soaked with volatile fuel gel.

The icekelp burst into flame, crackling with black smoke around the effigy of Ross. Bram untied the rope from an anchor pin on the ice shelf and used a pole to thrust the funeral raft out into the water. As the flames rose higher, the raft drifted into the current and was gradually carried out into the flat dark sea.

Jess divided his attention between the pyre and his father, wishing he could help more. Despite their feud, the old man had been proud of his eldest son, impressed by how much Ross had accomplished.

The pyre grew brighter as the blazing raft passed farther out on to the cold sea. The low ice sky reflected the orange flames.

Drawn by the light, large primitive nematodes rose from the

undersea depths, poking their smooth, eyeless heads into the pocket of air. The nematodes were thick scarlet things with round mouths and tiny diamond-like teeth that were probably used for scouring holes through the walls of ice.

The Roamer observers gasped in surprise at seeing the rare creatures. Cesca moved closer to Jess. He could feel her presence, but could not tear his gaze from the waving forms that loomed around the glowing funeral raft.

Surrounding the now-dwindling pyre as the wooden raft began to break apart into charred timbers, the nematodes made weird hooting sounds, an eerie yet beautiful chorus that boomed off the vaulted frozen ceiling.

The alien grief expressed in the nematodes' song was more than Jess could bear. He felt Cesca's loving grip on his arm and was startled when he turned to look at his father and saw tears streaming down his seamed face.

FORTY-SEVEN

GENERAL KURT LANYAN

The ruins of the Oncier system contained no survivors, no bodies, very little wreckage – and no clues about what had happened to Dr Serizawa's research team. The four moons were nothing more than flash-cooled rubble dispersed in a widening ring around the hot new star-planet.

General Lanyan had not flown his fast-reconnaissance outrigger here to mourn. He had no idea who, or what, the enemy might be. Whatever force had attacked here had the strength to disintegrate entire *moons*. Chairman Wenceslas had dispatched him to find answers with the specific objective of learning how the Earth Defence Forces might defend themselves and the colony worlds against the threat, whatever it might be.

As the reconnaissance outrigger cruised around the ignited gas giant, the survey crew imaged the residue. Lanyan had staffed the ship with his best technicians and communications experts. It would take a detailed analysis of the orbiting junk just to determine which debris had been part of the melting moons and which had been components of the observation platform.

'Those scientists were alone here,' he growled. 'They couldn't even call for help. If only the damned Therons let us have more green priests, we'd have assigned one here for instant telink communication. Dr Serizawa could have sent a message at the first sign of trouble. At least we would have known what was going on.'

Lanyan could not understand why Chairman Wenceslas didn't simply have the King issue an ultimatum and conscript the services of as many green priests as they needed. How could primitive forest dwellers stand against a concerted EDF action if the Hansa decided to flex its muscles?

An EDF geological specialist looked up from his technical station. 'The first scans have given us some information, sir. All the rubble displays the same degree of cooling. Therefore, the destruction occurred over a very short period of time – inconceivably short, in fact. My guess is that the four moons and our station were destroyed within hours of each other.'

'Hours!' The General felt a sinking sensation. 'What could possibly demolish four whole moons in mere hours?' *What are we up against?*

The pilot looked over at Lanyan. 'There's no way any help could have arrived in time, General, even if Dr Serizawa had access to telink. Top speed with the stardrive from the nearest EDF deployment would still require the better part of a week. Just no way we could have helped.'

'And then we would have lost a green priest, too,' Lanyan admitted. *But still, dammit, we could have known what was happening!* He hated having his hands tied by the arrogance of treetalkers on one hand and the speed of light on the other.

Right now, though, the very slowness and plodding predictability of standard EM transmissions gave him an opportunity. Serizawa's emergency broadcast would have been beamed out in all directions, but it could only go so far – a very precise distance, in fact. Lanyan could get there in time to meet it head-on.

The reconnaissance outrigger whipped around Oncier, stealing a parade of images along the way. Then, like a hapless child at the end of a game of crack-the-whip, the vessel shot outwards again, away from the new-born star.

'I need a fast analysis, Lieutenant,' the General said, narrowing his ice-blue eyes. 'We've made our estimates of the precise time of the attack. Now calculate exactly how far an omnidirectional signal would travel in the time since. I want to grab that wave front before it can deteriorate further.'

At his technical station, the lieutenant crunched numbers through the fast computers until he had his answer. The General ordered his navigator-pilot to set their course. 'Engage the stardrive.' Though he felt no dramatic acceleration, the outrigger raced forward, blurring out of the regular space-time continuum, racing to catch up with electromagnetic waves that were already many weeks old.

Because the Ildiran stardrive allowed them to travel much faster than the speed of light, General Lanyan had a unique opportunity to leap-frog reality and overtake any desperate transmissions Dr Serizawa might have sent during the mysterious attack.

Based on the reports of the terraforming survey team, as well as the new readings his experts had compiled, they had determined with a fair amount of accuracy when the disaster had taken place. With a precise time coordinate, Lanyan's fast recon ship could race ahead of the pulsing band of signals and intercept the message as it swept past.

Back home, using King Frederick as his diplomatic mouthpiece, Chairman Wenceslas had issued an official and flowery request to the Ildirans, as one great sovereign to another, asking for help, or at least information about this mysterious new threat. The Adar of the Solar Navy had carried the King's message with all diplomatic formality to his Mage-Imperator in Mijistra. But though the alien emperor had expressed surprise and dismay at the terrible attack, he claimed no knowledge about the matter.

Although General Lanyan doubted that even the pompous Ildiran Solar Navy commanded enough firepower to destroy worlds, neither did he believe in the total ignorance of the Mage-Imperator. Not for a minute.

'Arriving at position, sir,' said the navigator-pilot.

'Good. Cut the stardrive and turn about. We'll park here and wait.'

The starfield shifted back to normal, and Lanyan stared into an empty wasteland of space, far from any systems. If they had simply allowed for routine transmission time from Oncier, it might have been a decade before anyone picked up Serizawa's last transmission.

'We'll know soon enough,' he said, mostly to himself.

'Assuming Dr Serizawa sent a signal at all, General,' said the technical lieutenant.

'He would have sent a signal,' Lanyan said. 'Unless they vaporized his station first.'

The reconnaissance outrigger hung motionless as the galaxy rotated around them. The faint wisps of a bright nebula filled the foreground far away.

After fifteen minutes, his jaw sore from clenching his teeth so hard, Lanyan grew impatient. 'Ease forward at half c. Let's do our best to catch up with it.'

The outrigger moved ahead, wide-band receivers primed and hungry for the electromagnetic burst that had been sent out weeks before.

'How big is the error bar in your calculations?' he asked the lieutenant, anxious now.

'Certainly less than a day, sir. The readings were quite—'

Suddenly a wall of static blossomed on their reception screens. The General stood up, looking at the primary display. The transmission sharpened into a clear image of Dr Serizawa.

'—under attack. Unidentified spherical craft, an unusual configuration. My God, they've already destroyed one of the moons!' Serizawa turned. 'Can you believe the firepower?' He snapped at his communications assistant, 'Show the images from our external cameras. Give them *useful* data. They don't want to see my face.'

The view shifted, and Lanyan looked in cold amazement at the diamond-hulled warglobes and their crackling blue lightning as they tore the second of Oncier's moons to pieces.

Diluted from its long passage across space, the fuzzy transmission continued to ripple against their receivers like faint stirrings against a boat on a quiet pond. Lanyan and his crew watched with bone-chilling horror as the scientists continued to send desperate messages, pleading for mercy, trying to understand. The alien attack continued. No wonder nothing remained.

No, the General realized, this wasn't the Ildirans at all. Something new. Something worse. These monstrous alien ships were unlike anything he had ever seen, even in his nightmares.

When all four of Oncier's moons had been annihilated, the alien crystalline ships converged upon the unarmed observation platform. The electric lances arced out again, engulfing the observation platform in a single brilliant flash, and the signal finally cut off.

By then, Lanyan had absorbed more than he had ever wanted to see.

FORTY-EIGHT

CESCA PERONI

Because Cesca was not at Rendezvous where she was expected to be, the urgent message and news packet took an extra week to reach the Speaker's protégé. The message runner had already delivered his unsettling report to Jhy Okiah, who had dispatched the young man and his supercharged spaceship to find Cesca beneath the ice on Plumas.

The message runner rode the passenger lift down through a pumping channel in the ice. He stepped out into the frigid cave and called out to anyone who could hear him: 'Cesca Peroni! Is she still here? I have an urgent message from Jhy Okiah.'

Though she spent most of the time indoors near heaters, Cesca had felt restless after the grim funeral for Ross. She had suited up to pace across the ice shelf, looking up at the glittering colours embedded in the solid sky. 'I'm Cesca. What is it?' she said, putting an edge into her voice. Obviously this young man hadn't come looking for light conversation.

Now Jess and Bram Tamblyn emerged to see the visitor. Accompanied by her silver-skinned compy EA, Tasia appeared a moment later, as if reluctantly intrigued by the interruption.

The message runner had blond hair and brown eyes, with the square jaw and distinctive nose of the Burr clan, but the embroidered symbols on his insulated vest showed that he also claimed blood-ties with the Maylors and Petrovs. 'A Goose scientific station was destroyed at a gas giant, along with four moons!' he said, reaching into his left pocket, then, finding nothing, searching the three pouches sewn into the right side of his jacket. He finally pulled out a displayer.

'By the Guiding Star, another gas giant?' Jess said. 'One of ours? Was there a skymine in place?'

'No. It was Oncier, the world they just ignited to make a sun.'

'Stupid warmonger experiments,' Bram Tamblyn grumbled. 'What does that have to do with us? Did the test backfire on them?'

'No, sir. They were attacked, just like at Golgen.' The Burr boy pushed the activator button on his displayer, and the holo-image projected a flattened picture of Dr Serizawa's transmission intercepted by the EDF. 'One of our traders picked this up from the emergency news releases.'

Cesca watched in horror as the spherical alien ships dismantled the moons, then obliterated the scientific research station. 'And does Jhy Okiah believe this is the same thing that happened to Ross and the Blue Sky Mine?'

'That is her guess,' said the young man.

'It's not a guess,' Bram snapped. 'It's obvious!' Then he swayed, clutching Jess's arm. His son supported his father stoically but made no comment about the old man's wavering condition.

The message runner added, 'Everyone is panicked. They don't know what these things are, or how to react. Remember, no one on Earth has heard about the destruction at Golgen yet.'

'Then perhaps we should tell them,' Cesca said.

'The Speaker thought you might suggest that,' he said. 'She is willing to inform Chairman Wenceslas.'

'Shizz, of course she should inform them!' Tasia said, appalled. 'This is a threat that affects all of us.'

'Yes, but Roamers like to keep their secrets,' Cesca said.

'I'm sick of our secrets,' the girl said. 'What good does it do to withhold this knowledge? If these alien . . . *things* attack more of our skymines, we'll be forced to call on the Eddies. We don't have a military of our own.'

'Oh, that reminds me,' the message runner said. 'King Frederick himself asked his people to perform their patriotic duty, to strengthen the defences for all humanity against these strange antagonists, to stand together.' The young man fumbled with the displayer, trying to call up another file. 'I recorded the King's exact message. Here, I can play it.'

Bram Tamblyn said, 'It's no surprise the Big Goose would use this sudden attack as an excuse to shore up the EDF. Damned Eddies!'

'An excuse?' Tasia cried. 'How can you say that, Dad? Those ships killed Ross. Who knows where else they're going to attack?'

Bram gasped, and his face turned greyer. Jess held him up and said, 'Drop it, Tasia. Come on, Dad. Let's get you inside. You need to rest.'

Cesca hurried to take Bram Tamblyn's other arm. Tasia's compy offered her assistance. 'Shall I take readings? Dispense medications?'

'Leave him alone, EA,' Tasia said. 'It's just his usual melodrama.'

Even with her minimal medical experience, Cesca could see that the old man was not feigning his distress. They took Bram inside his curved hut and put him to bed. Jess sat at the man's side.

Cesca found packets of Bram's favourite pepperflower tea and brewed him a cup, though the old man had great difficulty sitting up to take a sip. He did, however, smile at her in appreciation.

He slept for about an hour. Cesca sat restlessly next to Jess, and the two talked in low voices. Although she ached to do so, she dared not speak to Jess about whether they could finally accept their love for each other. That would take time, she knew.

With this startling new information, Jhy Okiah would call her back to Rendezvous as soon as possible, but she hated to leave Jess alone with his sudden responsibilities. His four uncles had already picked up the work of pumping and shipping of the water, as well as electrochemical conversion into traditional high-energy fuels. The Plumas water industry had been in the Tamblyn family for generations, and it was their duty to keep it functioning, regardless of family disasters. Many of the Roamer clans depended upon it.

Cesca squeezed Jess's hand. 'You'll manage, Jess. The crews are all trained, the equipment runs smoothly. Your uncles know what they're doing. You're strong and smart, and you're a good man.'

'Ross was a good man, too.' Jess did not look at her, but stared instead at his father's drawn face as he slept. 'That didn't help him against the alien attackers . . . or even with my father.'

With a commotion that seemed calculated to destroy any peaceful rest her father might have gotten, Tasia entered the dwelling, pushing through the insulation seal and stomping her booted feet, with EA following her. Her face was pink from the cold, as if she had paced around the ice shelf, mulling over her thoughts. Tasia's face was screwed up with determination. Cesca didn't know Jess's little sister as well as she'd hoped, but she could see that the girl had not come for the purpose of comforting her father.

Jess obviously recognized his sister's mood. He immediately tried to deflect whatever outburst Tasia was about to make. 'Did the message runner depart yet? You can escort him back to his ship, if he needs the company.'

'He's gone, but before he left, he showed me King Frederick's recruitment message.'

Cesca felt a coldness in her heart, already anticipating what the young woman was about to say.

Struggling to sit up, Bram reached over to find his cup of now-cold pepperflower tea, scowled at it, and looked back at Tasia. 'What are you thinking, young lady?'

'I'm thinking of my duty, Dad. You've told us enough times that we have to think of the Roamers, and not ourselves.' She crossed her arms over her chest. 'What if I offer my services to the Earth Defence Forces?'

'You will not,' the old man snapped. Cesca rapidly saw how the discussion would degenerate. EA came to Bram's bed and straightened his blankets, but he slapped away the compy's ministrations.

'Someone has to fight the enemies that murdered my brother.' Tasia drew a deep breath. Cesca knew the girl was brash and impetuous, but very talented.

'Cool down, Tasia,' Jess said quietly. 'Your duty is to the family, and we need you here.'

'No you don't. I haven't done anything important with the water-works in years. My uncles handle all the business that you don't take care of yourself.' Tasia continued in a more reasonable tone. 'Shizz, Dad, you know how versatile I am. I'm a crack pilot, and I can fix and fly plenty of ship models. The Eddies would take me in a second, maybe even put me on the fast-track to being a officer.'

'And they'd never release you in a million years,' Bram said, his voice raspy. 'Now stop this foolishness.'

Cesca remembered a few arguments with her own father when he'd left her on Rendezvous, and she knew that old Bram was taking exactly the wrong approach with his daughter. When younger, Cesca had been forced to travel around on the Peroni clan's trading ships for years before her father finally installed her on Rendezvous to study under Jhy Okiah. Cesca had resented it at first, but soon grew to realize that her father was right.

Tasia, though, would not come to that realization any time soon . . . and Cesca wasn't sure that Bram's position was correct, even so. The Roamers had always considered diverse competence to be a valuable commodity. Tasia was bright and had studied well. Her many skills would have made the girl a well-sought-after marriage prospect, a strong addition to any clan. Those qualities would make her even more valuable to the Earth Defence Forces.

'You don't owe any loyalty to Earth, Tasia, and you know the Eddies have no love for Roamers,' Cesca said. 'Don't forget, one of their patrols captured and killed Rand Sorengaard.'

'Rand Sorengaard was a pirate,' Tasia said. 'I don't care if he was your cousin. He murdered people and he stole ships. Don't make him out to be some great Roamer hero.'

When Jess spoke, Cesca could hear anger in his voice. 'Tasia, look at Dad. He's in no shape to handle the water operations.'

'I'm fine,' the old man snapped.

'No, you're not,' Cesca and Jess said in comical unison.

'You're my little sister. I've already lost Ross, and I don't want to lose you, too.'

'Would it be better to lose the war? Those crystal ships struck down Ross's skymine and a Goose research station with no warning and no mercy. They don't care about our squabbles.'

EA spoke up. 'Would anyone like some hot beverages? I can prepare them quickly.' The others ignored the little compy.

'I forbid it,' Bram said. 'This conversation is over.'

'Shizz, where have I heard those words before?' Tasia said sarcastically. 'Isn't that the same thing you said to Ross?'

EA did her best to follow Tasia as she stormed out of the old man's chamber. Bram looked as if his own daughter had just dealt him a mortal blow, reminding him of the single worst mistake he had committed in his life. He let out a gasping cry and collapsed on to his bed, gnarled hands clenched. But Tasia was already gone.

FORTY-NINE

TASIA TAMBLYN

In a huff, her mind made up, Tasia strode along the edge of the ice shelf, stomping so hard that her insulated boots left indentations in the frozen ground. Looking out over the metal-dark waters of the hidden sea, she kept remembering her big brother Ross.

He had had the courage to stand up to their father's unreasonable stubbornness. He had been brave and confident, and he had proved himself with the undeniable success of the Blue Sky Mine. He would have married Cesca Peroni. Tasia was incredibly proud of him for what he had done, despite her father's insistent lack of support.

But the malicious alien destroyers had ruined everything. They had wrecked his marvellous skymine, and they had taken Ross's life.

Now, Tasia had the chance to do something to avenge him. Technically, it should have been her father's responsibility – or better yet, Jess's – but they were both concerned about the family business. Perhaps rightly so. But her uncles would keep everything running, the supplies delivered, the products flowing.

She didn't blame her father or Jess, but she had to make her own decisions. With absolute conviction, she knew she was right; her father and brother would come to see that in time. The Guiding Star showed every Roamer their life's path, and Tasia saw her course plainly. If anyone from the Tamblyn clan was going to take action against the alien enemy, maybe it needed to be her.

She took a deep breath and blew out a cloud of steam. The skin on her cheeks was crackling cold, but she refused to pull a hood over her head. The waters of the ocean were still and thick. She saw no sign of the singing nematodes that had appeared at the funeral, nor could she spot any sooty debris from the floating pyre.

She tossed a chunk of ice as far out into the water as she could. She and her brothers had done that together many times when they were younger; Ross could skip a flat ice chip six times before it came to a stop. Now, her shard struck with a hollow *thunk*, then bobbed back to the surface, surrounded by an expanding chorus of ripples.

'Sometimes you just have to make waves of your own,' she muttered. The air was so cold that the insides of her nostrils felt raw. Though the decision had been hard, a long time ago Ross had made the choice that was necessary for him. And so must she.

No use talking about it any further. Tasia moved quickly, not because she was afraid of changing her mind, but because once she made a decision, she never backed down. No point in delaying.

Her small insulated hut was cool and dark. EA moved about straightening Tasia's things, cleaning every exposed surface for the fourth time. When the young woman was not there to keep the compy company, EA fell back on her limited programming of finding simple chores to occupy herself.

'Turn up the heat, EA. Shizz!' Tasia never bothered to hide her moods from the oblivious little compy.

'I am sorry, Tasia. I set the temperature at your standard preferred level.'

'Never mind that, I'm cold.' She pulled off her gloves and removed her jacket, sitting at the edge of her chair. She would have to pack quickly, make her plans, slip away. Tasia leaned forward conspiratorially. 'EA, you and I have a job to do. I'll need your help.'

'Simply give me instructions, and I will be happy to assist you in any way.'

Tasia was glad compies wasted minimal circuitry space on morality programming that might confuse ethical issues. 'You've been my companion for a long time, EA, but now I need to ask you for something difficult.' The slender metal figure stopped her chores and came over to stand motionless and attentive in front of the young girl. 'You and I have to escape from here.'

EA hesitated just a moment, a short enough pause that it might have been Tasia's imagination. 'Whatever you wish. We will have fun together.'

'We're doing this to avenge my brother Ross.'

'Ross was my first master. A fine young man.'

'He's dead,' Tasia said. 'Aliens killed him.'

'How sad. Is there anything I can do to help?'

The robotic compy had been purchased as a gift for Ross when he'd been a child, when their mother was still alive. Standing just over a metre tall, EA was a cooperative Listener model, a good friend for any child. Then, after Ross outgrew the faithful companion, EA had been given to Jess as a boyhood friend, and finally to Tasia.

She felt a renewed flood of sadness and loss as she remembered that EA had been promised to whichever member of the Tamblyn clan had the first child. Until now, it had always been expected that Ross, with his betrothal to Cesca, would be the first Tamblyn to have children. Now that had changed forever.

'You can help me escape, and you'll come with me when we join the Earth Defence Forces.'

'All right, Tasia,' EA said. 'Just tell me what you would like me to do.'

The artificial suns embedded in the frozen roof were set on timers, dimming into pseudo-night at regular intervals. The settlement beneath the ice sheet lived under the illusion of a standard day/night cycle. When Tasia emerged in the darkest hours, she saw ripples of phosphorescent algae glowing within the layers of glacial sky, not quite like stars, but enough to light their way to the lift tubes that would carry them to the surface.

Inside her father's hut, Jess and Cesca still sat with the old man, but Tasia avoided them, simmering in her determination. Jess had checked on her earlier, satisfied to find his sister resting in her own hut. Tasia had wanted to confide in him, but she knew her brother Jess. He always did what he thought was best for other people. If he suspected what she meant to do, he would probably restrain her for her own good, even tie her to a chair if necessary. Tasia couldn't afford that. She loved him though, and knew he would understand. Eventually.

As she and her compy entered the lift tube, she whispered goodbye to the low, rounded huts and their sleeping inhabitants. Then she closed the door and they shot up through the bore-shaft to the surface. Passages and enormous pipes rose through the crust to where the ice had cracked. Her mother was frozen down there, somewhere, lost within the thick frozen crust . . .

The Tamblyns had made a great deal of profit by pumping geysers of water to off-loading wellheads on the surface, where passing cargo ships could fill their holds with water and travel to other distribution centres. The spaceport was a landing area and maintenance yard connected to the water geysers and pumping stations. With no vessels incoming, and all the water business suspended during the mourning period, the water wells had been capped. They were now rimed with frost that bled out through faint cracks in the seal. Gossamer derricks stood tall, requiring little support in the ice moon's light gravity.

Atop the ice sheet, under a cold black sky studded with diamond stars, Tasia and EA walked in the enclosed flexible tunnels laid down over the frozen ground. Three well-maintained space-ships belonging to the Tamblyn clan were docked against their access huts, ready to go. Tasia knew how to fly them all. Her brothers had taught her plenty of piloting tricks, and she had practised for innumerable hours, more than anyone knew. There wasn't much else to do on a boring ice moon anyway.

Since the ships belonged to her own family, she wasn't actually stealing. After she joined the Eddies, perhaps she could find a way to shuttle the vessel back to Plumas. But her father would stew about it for many years.

They hurried through the connecting tube towards the nearest craft. Tasia was tempted to take Jess's favourite, a faster and cleaner ship, but she didn't want him to be more upset than he already would be, so she chose one of the two traditional vessels.

At the hatch, she removed an information module from one of the many pockets in her baggy trousers. 'Here EA, upload this. It's navigation instructions and starship information. I might need you to do co-pilot duties if I get tired.' The journey to Earth would take some time, and she had slept little in the past few days.

'I have never piloted a ship before, Tasia. My memory core may not have enough space for all this information.'

'Then delete some of your childhood games – but not any memories. I want you to preserve every moment you spent with Ross. You can tell me stories during the long flight.'

'Of course, Tasia.' EA inserted the information module and accessed the enhanced programming. 'I am ready if you need me. It seems so simple now.'

'It took me years to learn how to fly, and you can access it in a few seconds,' she said, shaking her head.

'It can be deleted just as quickly, Tasia.'

Tasia grunted as she strapped herself into the piloting chair. 'Yeah, I can see how that would be a drawback.'

She powered up the heaters. No one had used this vessel for a month, and the interior air felt brittle and stagnant. She activated the electrical and life-support systems, then increased the temperature a bit more.

She called up the coordinates of the Earth system and plotted her course. Tasia disengaged from the docking tube and with a faint nudge from her attitude-control jets, she lifted away from the frozen surface. Plumas looked like a cracked white blister beneath her, its capped wellheads like metal buttons sealing the liquid water underneath. 'All right, let's follow the Guiding Star.'

The mist across her vision was either a blur in the cockpit windows or a thin sheen of tears. Tasia didn't know which. She engaged the stardrive and shot away from Plumas towards her new future.

FIFTY

MARGARET COLICOS

For weeks, the Colicos team had uncovered an endless succession of wondrous discoveries, amazing and challenging relics . . . but few answers. Still, it was time for another report to be sent to Earth. Sitting inside her stuffy tent shelter, Margaret finished her latest log entry and smiled ironically to herself.

Unlike excavating Roman ruins or sunken Mediterranean cities on Earth, research into the Klikiss civilization involved more than simply adding a few obscure details to an already thorough understanding. With the Klikiss, even the fundamentals remained complete enigmas. Whenever Margaret or Louis discovered something profound – such as her realization that had led to the Klikiss Torch, or the conjecture that the presumably-insectoid race could fly – all other aspects of Klikiss studies went through major reassessments.

Their work on Rheindic Co amounted to a tremendous undertaking of data gathering, with little time for analysis and introspection except in the evenings. Unfortunately, it was late morning now. Margaret couldn't believe how many good working hours she had already wasted writing this progress report, but she knew her obligations. The Hansa gave them substantial funding, and one of their adamant requirements was that the Colicos deliver regular updates. Louis certainly wouldn't do it – he thought such 'homework assignments' were pointless. But Margaret understood that a good archaeologist had to keep the funding sources happy, even if it consumed productive hours.

Though she had already listened to the delicate metallic tune many times since awakening, Margaret activated the old-fashioned music box Anton had given her. The tiny metal-comb teeth whirred out the haunting old melody of 'Greensleeves'. She smiled at the thought of her son and wondered how often he imagined his parents on far-flung planets.

Margaret reread her report, satisfied with the tone and the descriptions of all the things they had discovered. When this dig was finished, she would carry home detailed scan images and preserved artifacts, but for now Arcas would dictate her report to his small grove of worldtrees. Via telink connection, his words would reach a green priest counterpart on Earth, where the report would be delivered to – and perhaps be ignored by – Chairman Wenceslas.

Along with DD, Louis was already inside the cliff city, tinkering with alien mechanical leftovers, sure that he could reactivate one of the long-abandoned generators. Anxious to get back to the ruins herself, Margaret stepped out into the harsh, dry sunlight and looked towards the maze of spidery canyons that ran through the nearby mountain buttress. She wondered how much more remained to be found out there. They had barely scratched the surface.

She looked for Arcas, but the priest's hut was empty. She scowled, annoyed. Behind his tent, the twenty worldtree saplings had grown as high as her shoulders, and they spread their golden-green fronds to drink up the sunlight. The soil around them was moist, indicating that Arcas had already watered them for the day, but he was nowhere in sight. She needed to transmit her report, and it wasn't as if he had much else to do.

Earlier, Arcas had proved his worth by receiving and then reporting the astonishing news about the alien attack on Oncier. He was unable to show images through the telink connection, but he described what General Lanyan had discovered. Stunned, Margaret remembered the brief glimpse she'd had of the crystalline spheres that had shot out of the burning planet's interior and streaked off into space. Dr Serizawa had blithely dismissed them as 'exotic debris' ejected from the burning planet.

Had their test of the Klikiss Torch somehow provoked this attack? What life form could possibly exist deep within the high-pressure bowels of an enormous gas planet?

She called the green priest's name, but heard no response. Setting her shoulders, Margaret sighed. This wasn't the first time Arcas was not to be found when she'd needed his capabilities.

She didn't begrudge the man his own interests. He liked to wander off into the canyons, collecting fossils and geological samples. Still, his primary purpose was to serve as a communication link to their sponsors.

'Arcas!' she called again, raising her voice so that it could be heard across the desert. Gripping the information plaque, she wondered if she should just leave her report until later, but she made up her mind to find him.

Louis and Arcas got along well enough. They often played card games with DD in the evening while Margaret studied the day's discoveries. Knowing the access Arcas had to all the information stored in the vast worldforest, Margaret felt a twinge of resentment at how the priest did not seem interested in learning new things. Where was his drive?

She trudged away from the camp towards a rocky rise where Arcas often went to contemplate sunsets. She climbed the slope, picking her way over boulders, recalling that all the Klikiss worlds she and Louis had analysed were sunny and dry. The empty cities on Llaro and Pym had been erected on great grass-filled plains, their structures standing tall like termite mounds in the middle of nowhere, far from any accessible running water. Instead of building their mounds close to streams, the insectoid aliens had chosen their construction sites for some other reason, either based on a geometrical coordinate system or some other criteria.

Corribus, the most recent archaeological dig, where Margaret and Louis had discovered the Klikiss Torch, was also a barren world, but far more damaged. The ruins there were blackened and vitrified, as if Corribus had been the site of a titanic battle many centuries ago. But the xeno-archaeologists had found no explanations or clues as to the cause of that destructive conflict.

Margaret reached the top of the rise, suddenly startled to find the huge black forms of the Klikiss robots waiting there. Sirix, Ilkot, and Dekyk sat motionless, staring at the sky and basking in the sunlight. The three machines looked almost identical. She stopped quickly upon seeing them.

One – Sirix, she thought – instantly activated his systems, ebony carapace flapping open like beetle wings. A large reflective sail spread outwards, flying up in an intimidating move. The other two robots also split open their shells and extended large sails so that they appeared three times their already ominous size. Multiple red optical sensors glowed as if ready to go nova.

Margaret backed off, raising her hands. 'I'm sorry. I didn't know you were here.'

The Klikiss robots took two steps forward on their articulated legs. Then Sirix froze as he recognized her. In his humming and clicking synthetic voice he said, 'Margaret Colicos. Your arrival was unexpected.' The robots eased back down, reflective sails folding and withdrawing into their body cores. Curved exoskeletons clicked back into place. 'We did not mean to activate our automatic response.'

'What was that?' Margaret said, her heart pounding, sweat prickling on her skin. 'Those sails . . .'

Sirix buzzed an answer quickly. 'Merely solar panels to recharge our power cells. We came up here to absorb energy and to contemplate. There are many mysteries on this world. We have absorbed more details of our past, though our memories remain empty.'

Businesslike again, still trying to cover her nervous reaction, Margaret held up the datapad. 'Well, Louis and I are doing our best to find answers for you. I have a report that must be transmitted to Earth, and I need to find Arcas. He sometimes comes up here.'

'Not today,' said Sirix.

'I can see that. Do you know where he is?'

'Is it urgent that you find him immediately?' asked Sirix.

'I need to transmit this report, and he's our green priest.' Margaret put her left fist on her hip. 'We have a deadline.'

'Then it must be urgent.' He and the other two robots buzzed in a rapid, vibrating conversation, then Sirix extended one articulated arm from a capped hatch in his body core. 'He went to that canyon. Do you see which one?'

Margaret saw a clear trail leading into a crack in the rocks surrounded by sheer walls. 'Yes, I remember it. Arcas told me he discovered something there two days ago.'

'You will find him at that location,' Sirix said. 'We will stay here . . . and attempt to remember.'

Margaret trudged off, relieved to be away from the baffling robots. Sirix called after her with an odd observation, 'Because we are so ancient, Margaret Colicos, we are not as impatient as humans. Given a problem, we are willing to study and ponder for decades. But we do arrive at an answer eventually.'

Margaret turned as she climbed down the slope. 'That may be so – but I don't have that much time.' She went off in search of the green priest.

FIFTY-ONE

NIRA

Representing Theroc and the green priests, Nira and Otema prepared to depart for the heart of the Ildiran Empire. A merchant woman named Rlinda Kett would transport them to the dazzling capital city.

Thanks to Sarein's relentless insistence, along with Reynald's friendlier intercession, Father Idriss and Mother Alexa had finally allowed Rlinda Kett to take a small cargo of Theron products – fruits, nuts, juices, woven fibres – on the condition that she also carry the two passengers.

Wide-eyed, Nira stared at the *Voracious Curiosity*. Not only had she never been away from the forest planet, she had never even set foot aboard a spaceship. The *Curiosity* had been built with an eye for practicality and engineering necessities rather than aesthetics, studded with weird protrusions, diagnostic arrays, and sensor grids. In the vacuum of space no one could see beautiful lines or shiny hulls anyway.

Otema paid little attention to the vessel or the Theron workers who loaded packages into the hold. Instead, the ambassador drank in the verdant landscape, filing away every detail of the worldforest as if this might be the last time she ever saw it.

Before departure, Sarein appeared, wearing the ambassadorial cloak Otema had given her. Her smile was thin and formal. 'I came to bid you good journey, Otema. My brother tells me the crystal city of Mijistra is magnificent.'

Otema's expression hardened, but her voice was without inflection. 'Remember what I told you, Sarein. You are a Theron. Keep our interests foremost in mind. The trees have warned that we must all be vigilant.'

A flicker of annoyance crossed Sarein's face. 'That is my duty as ambassador, Otema. I will not forget it.' Ignoring Nira, she hurried off to where Rlinda Kett directed the operations personally, insisting that everything be properly stowed. Nira looked from Otema to the new ambassador and wondered what had passed between them.

When the cargo bay was sealed, Rlinda stood in the entrance hatch, hands on her broad hips. She motioned towards the two green priests. 'Come on and get onboard. The *Curiosity* doesn't need a push, you know.'

Nira wanted to hurry, but slowed to keep a sedate pace with Otema. When the hatch closed behind them, she instantly felt enclosed and claustrophobic. A thrill of panic went through her as she smelled metal and unnatural lubricants, synthetic furniture and reprocessed air. How could she tolerate being imprisoned here for the journey to the seven suns of Ildira?

Otema sensed her assistant's anxiety, and the expression on her lined face softened. 'Any time you wish, you can commune with the treelings. It will be as if you are in the worldforest.' They had already loaded their potted treelings, gifts to be presented to the Mage-Imperator. Otema's dark lips curved in a smile. 'I know, Nira, because not only have I ridden on spaceships many times, but I also spent years on Earth far from the worldforest. It is not the same, but good enough for you to keep your sanity.'

Rlinda showed them to their guest cabin. Carefully potted in ornate containers, the selected treelings had been anchored to shelves and in the corners of the cabin.

Rlinda stood at the doorway. 'Secure yourselves on the bunks during takeoff. I'll be sociable after I engage the stardrive.'

Otema brushed her fingers against one potted treeling. 'We thank you for granting us passage, and the worldforest sends its appreciation as well.'

Rlinda nodded, not understanding their mystic connection with the treelings. 'Just happy to be carrying this first cargo load. Father Idriss and Mother Alexa will see the advantages of trade in exotic foods and luxury items. This is my foot in the door.'

The merchant woman closed the door of their cabin and departed for the cockpit. Otema lay on her bunk, wrapping herself in a meditative shroud of silence, quietly praying to the world-forest. Following the ambassador's example, Nira touched a treeling and tried to calm her pounding heart. She would have to remember all the details and relate them to the trees, like a diary. So, she had often read aloud from formal texts, stories, and poems. This way, Nira would give the trees a fresh and unedited burst of impressions, allowing them to see this exciting expedition through her novice eyes.

Rlinda's brief announcement came over the intercom. 'Hang on, everybody. We're about to take off. I'll try to make it a smooth ride.'

During the next two days, Nira and Otema explored the *Voracious Curiosity*, kept the treelings company in their cabin. Through telink, with the complete access of the worldforest's knowledge, the two women tapped into an understanding of the Ildiran language, both written and spoken, and quickly became proficient. There would be no barriers to the success of their mission.

Together in their cabin, they also got to know each other better.

'I recognize many of the marks on your face, Otema.' Nira looked at the ovals and curves around the ambassador's mouth, on her forehead, encircling her eyes. 'I've had basic instruction as a reader, a musician, a planter, a caretaker, and botanist.' She smiled. 'I recognize the several traveller marks you carry. But your face . . .' Nira shook her head in wonder. 'I've never seen so many accomplishment marks.'

Otema touched her dark skin, as if considering the indelible tattoos for the first time in years. Her finger touched a sharp line across her left cheek. 'When I was young, I loved performing music, since the worldtrees consider symphonies and melodies to be a kind of language, as instructive about human culture as statistics. Then I studied other subjects to broaden myself, acquiring more and more accomplishment marks.'

'All the lines are beautiful,' Nira said, meaning it.

'But you,' Otema said, pointing to the smoother features of Nira's face, 'after this journey you will acquire a traveller's mark, as well as another reader tattoo and a mark for history apprenticeship. Is that what you wanted?'

'I want to serve the worldforest in whatever capacity the trees require.' She paused, realizing that Otema wanted a more honest answer. 'But if I can serve the forest by seeing remarkable things, then I am all the more pleased.'

'Your family will be proud of you,' Otema said.

Nira looked a little uncertain. 'My family is already proud of me. I acquired new quarters for them in the worm hive that just opened for habitation, but they do not understand the priesthood. I am the only one in my family who even showed an interest in the trees.'

Otema was surprised. 'Perhaps I have been in the priesthood too long. I thought all Therons were devoted to the forest, each in their own way.'

Nira looked away. 'On the *Caillié* my family's ancestors were slated to be systems engineers, maintenance experts, and repairmen. The Khalis would have been extremely useful if Theroc had turned out to be a rugged planet.' She shrugged. 'But on Theroc, their skills are almost irrelevant. Oh, they keep the systems running and they do their jobs, but they don't love it.'

'Their work is still important to life or death,' Otema said. The potted treelings seemed to be listening to the conversation. 'Just in a different way than they expected. And yours . . . you know your own calling, Nira.'

'Yes, and I want nothing more in my life,' she said.

On their fourth day of travel, as the *Voracious Curiosity* passed through the Horizon Cluster and narrowed the distance to Ildira, Rlinda Kett invited them to join her for dinner. 'It's about time you had some introduction to Ildiran culture. Besides, I'm one of the few people in the Hansa who can produce decent Ildiran cuisine. It's rather a challenge, you know, especially getting the right ingredients.'

Nira was eager for an unusual meal, though her food supplements and the faint tingle from skin photosynthesis would keep her from growing too hungry. Wearing her normal garments, not knowing how else to prepare, Nira followed Otema to the galley adjacent to the captain's personal quarters. Since Nira was new to social functions and diplomatic callings, she viewed this meal as practise for when they arrived on Ildira.

Wearing a static-filmed apron that shed stains and droplets of food, Rlinda looked up from her cooking. She used gleaming pots over portable heaters. Nira could smell sizzling oils and pungent spices. Coloured sauces filled different jars and bowls, and the large merchant woman moved like a whirlwind, cooking five different dishes at once.

'I keep thinking about our new cargo,' Rlinda said, continuing her culinary activities. 'I'm anxious to try original recipes using Theron ingredients, but you're probably tired of food from your home world. Still, I'd appreciate any advice you might have?' She raised her eyebrows hopefully.

In a solemn voice, Otema said, 'Green priests, alas, are not known for their gourmet skills. Cooking is not one of our studies as we serve the worldforest.'

'I was afraid of that.' Rlinda whisked a gelatinous film before it could stick to the bottom of a saucepan.

With a clatter, she ladled a sparkling pudding-like glop in exquisitely even proportions across three plates. Then she added some kind of stringy green vegetable doused with golden syrup, and finally tiny braised cutlets of a greyish meat cut into precise equilateral triangles. She handed Otema the first plate. 'You've been ambassador to the Hansa for years, ma'am, but have your travels ever taken you to the seven suns?'

'No, I am as fresh and as new on this journey as Nira is.'

Nira gratefully accepted her own plate, inhaling the delicious aromas.

'Well, you'll find better cuisine in Mijistra, especially since you'll be guests of the Mage-Imperator, but this is a bona-fide Ildiran feast.' She smeared one of the pots with her thick finger and licked off the juice. 'Perfect.' Rlinda took her own plate and sat next to them at the crowded galley table.

Nira asked, 'How many times have you been to Mijistra?'

'Four, and I loved it each time. I hope that with this load of Theron goods, I'll be even more welcome there. The Ildirans don't really mind our visits, you see, but they're rather . . . unusual. Aliens

– what can you say? It's hard to tell whether they're glad to have our business, or if they just tolerate us.'

'Even human cultures seem strange to one another,' Otema pointed out. 'And Ildirans are not even members of our race.'

'Let me give you a crash course,' Rlinda said, 'a few things you'll need to know about the aliens. First off, the Ildirans are poly-morphic, like dogs. They have many different breeds and body types, called kiths. A few of those kiths might look human, but don't let that fool you. In fact, they're very handsome – and I've heard tell they have all the right equipment, if you know what I mean, though I've never heard any proof as to whether humans and Ildirans can actually interbreed.'

'That would be most unusual, genetically speaking,' Otema said.

'True, but I've seen plenty of unusual things. Different kiths have attributes and abilities that place them into appropriate castes in Ildiran society. Thinkers love being thinkers, workers love being workers, and so on.'

'Can the kiths interbreed?' Nira asked.

'Oh, certainly.' Rlinda tasted her triangular meat, then got up to acquire another dollop of sauce from her pans, which she scooped on to each of their plates. 'Sometimes they mate out of love and attraction, other times it's a conscious effort to enhance certain attributes. For instance, when nobles and soldiers inter-breed, their offspring become officers in the Solar Navy. I've heard that the best singers and poets and artists are mongrel half-breeds, pulling together a genetic strength that the pure-bred castes don't have.'

'Will we deal with many of these different kiths?' Otema asked. 'Or just the leaders?'

'Oh, you'll get to know the most common kiths. You can tell by their names, too. Each kith has a specific phonetic sound at the end.

For instance, the names of all members of the noble kith end with 'b. Bureaucrats end with 's. Workers end with 'k. The half-breeds add a combination of sounds. Military officers from the noble and the soldier classes end with 'nb. Rememberers come from the bureaucrat and noble kiths, and have 'sh at the ends of their names.' She shrugged. 'That's all approximate, of course, since their alphabet is different from ours.'

For dessert, Rlinda presented a yellow taffy-like substance shaped into a cone. She looked at the two women. 'I don't know much about green priests, either. Do you marry? Are you allowed to take mates, or is that against the priesthood?'

Otema smiled. 'It is certainly allowed, though many of us devote our lives to the trees. When we feel a calling, we take lovers.' She sat back. 'I'm rather old for that now, though.'

'Well, I've been married enough times myself.' The merchant scooped up a bite of the dessert and gestured for the two to taste it. 'I outlived two of my husbands, and the bitterest split was with my most recent one. He left me to marry a young beauty – then, a year later she murdered him in a fit of passion.'

Nira gasped. Rlinda shook her head with a knowing smile. 'I always said the man was impossible to get along with, and his new wife must have figured it out, too. So far, my best ex-husband was the second one, a man named Branson Roberts. I call him BeBob, though no one else does. We're still good friends, and he's my best pilot – we just couldn't get along well enough to stay married.' She ate her dessert in three bites and dabbed her lips with a napkin.

'I've given up on marriage now and decided to become a gourmand. Forget sex . . . Well, for the most part. What could be better than sampling all the culinary pleasures I find on other worlds?'

Rlinda studied the chronometer and then powered up a

viewscreen on her cabin wall, showing brilliant clustered stars as they approached. 'Won't be long now. Those are the seven suns of the Ildiran system.' She began to clean up the cooking implements.

FIFTY-TWO

REMEMBERER DIO'SH

The deepest archives in the Prism Palace were silent and empty. As with every structure in Mijistra, even far underground, the chambers remained well-lit at all hours, with blazers at every intersection and dazzling panels in the ceiling. But though the chemical fires simulated bright daylight, Rememberer Dio'sh could sense oppressive shadows hiding in enclosed spaces. Mysteries and fears and tragic memories of Crenna . . .

The transparent walls of the archives led to myriad chambers, transforming the underground Palace levels into a honeycomb of glass. Dio'sh would have preferred to remain in the high towers and open balconies, where he could listen to the streams of water leaping from platform to platform, but only here in these quiet catacombs could he find the resources he required. Down here, the rememberer had access to all the ancient records of Ildiran history.

His hands still trembled, and he'd had little appetite since being rescued from the dying colony on Crenna. He felt weak and sick at heart. Rememberer Vao'sh had tried to convince him that his symptoms were a mental reaction to the ordeal he had endured, not due to any echo of the plague itself. Dio'sh and the refugees had remained in difficult quarantine until they were all deemed healthy. Even so, any muscle pain, headache, or twinge made him nervous.

However, nothing would divert him from his obsessive curiosity now. Dio'sh had too much information to find, too many stories to read, too much history to learn. He had to discover the truth.

All rememberers spent their lives learning and rehearsing the *Saga of Seven Suns*. The members of their kith were blessed with well-organized eidetic memories so they could retain and repeat the massive epic, word for word. Once accepted into the canon, no phrase was ever changed.

Because that story was so incredibly vast, with so many plot-lines and legends and adventures, no one historian could possibly perform it all. Rememberer Vao'sh preferred to spend his days telling favourite tales to avid listeners, glorifying Ildiran heroes and accomplishments. As the Mage-Imperator's court rememberer, he loved to perform.

Even before the plague, though, Dio'sh had preferred a more solitary life. Oh, he had often entertained the Crenna Designate and the settlers, but the colonists had much work to do and little free time. No one had ever expected him to spend his entire day reciting stanzas from the *Saga*. During the good times on Crenna, Dio'sh had had many free hours to read and analyse obscure portions of the epic poem.

Now that he was back in the Prism Palace, recovering, Dio'sh decided to devote even more time to studying, digging through ancient records, deciphering early written accounts. He would analyse shreds of apocrypha to uncover hints and texture in what he and all rememberers knew as a matter of course. Many old documents and interesting recollections had never been incorporated into the permanent *Saga*, and thus the incidents were nearly forgotten. Though such information was not considered part of the canon, Dio'sh still felt that those records might provide him with valuable insights.

He had promised Vao'sh that he would write up a personal account of the Crenna plague, memorializing the victims who had suffered through blindness and isolation before death. He had lived through the epidemic, had watched it strike down the workers and singers, the two kiths most susceptible to the disease.

It would take him a long time to gain perspective, but Dio'sh promised himself that he would keep alive the stories of bravery and sacrifice. The Crenna Designate, a son of the Mage-Imperator, had tended the sick himself, despite warnings from the medical kithmen. They had advised him to take a ship to where he would be safe, but the Designate had stayed in his colony town. His death had severed the focal point of *thism*, leaving all the Ildirans on Crenna to shudder in the emptiness.

Dio'sh had documented the stories of other Crenna residents and heroes, recording the victims' lives as they would have wanted to be memorialized. But he had already written as much as he could bear about those experiences. Now he had other work to do.

Vao'sh had warned Dio'sh against spending too much time in the alcoves studying and reading. He claimed that it was a waste of time to absorb so much tangential apocrypha. 'Any rememberer who holes up by himself is not remembering for any purpose.'

Dio'sh had reassured his comrade. 'I will come back, Vao'sh. But the best way for me to heal is to have time to assess everything I have experienced.'

Already, the younger rememberer had discovered a notation in one of the Earth encyclopedias obtained from human merchants – a reference to a disease called cholera that spread easily from human to human when they lived in close quarters. Or the bubonic plague, typhoid fever, AIDS. But the blindness plague was so much worse.

Under the reassuring glow of wall-mounted blazers, he sat surrounded by scrolls and square-cut documents. The ancient records, coated with flexible preservation layers and sealed in permanent storage vaults, had remained untouched for centuries. Dio'sh felt like a brave explorer as he moved his fingers above the symbols, careful not to damage the ancient items.

Here in the archives, he had become obsessed with studying other plagues. He had searched through records and datafiles to discover whether similar diseases had ever struck the Ildirans. Had epidemics wiped out other splinter colonies, like Crenna? He needed to know. He couldn't remember such a major event in the *Saga of Seven Suns*, but could even a rememberer grasp all the secondary storylines contained in millennia of history?

He knew one dark tale that many rememberers were reluctant to speak, because of its great tragedy. Thousands of years in the past, at the beginning of recorded history, a firefever had swept through Mijistra. That fever had proved particularly deadly for the rememberer kith, with the result that every historian in the Ildiran capital had been wiped out.

So many deaths during an early phase of assembling and recording the *Saga of Seven Suns*, before all stanzas had been written down, meant that an entire portion of the epic had been lost forever. Thanks to the firefever, all prior history remained a blank spot in Ildiran memory – much to the dismay of the rememberers. Because of that fundamental loss, Ildirans no longer could trace their history back to the dawn of civilization. Many imaginative talespinners had created fictitious adventures to fill the gap. But Dio'sh understood that such tales weren't *real* and could not truly fill the void.

After much time deep in the archives, Dio'sh had dug out all of the records written at approximately the time of the firefever epidemic. No one had been here in a thousand years, and many of the sealed lockers had begun to sag and crumble, their latches weakened by gravity and age.

For hours, he studied the references for clues as to where the fever had begun and how it was possible that so much vital history could have been lost. On their deathbeds, did the last rememberers try to dictate all they knew to other kith, other listeners, only to have the details lost after all? To a historian like himself, such a missing section of the *Saga* felt like a dead child, filling him with a great sense of loss.

Then Dio'sh found a small vault that had been locked and apparently cemented shut, but the seal had crumbled and the lock itself degenerated so much that it easily broke in his hands. Feeling nervous, yet thrilled, the young rememberer probed into the tiny vault that had been locked away and forgotten ages ago. With a gasp of discovery, he saw that it contained ancient documents, sealed books that looked as if they had never been read. A treasure trove! Dio'sh eagerly took them back to his work area, turned up the blazer illumination. His heart thrummed with excitement.

He began to delve into the words, magical symbols that transported him into tales he had never before imagined. *Real* history, lost events. The journals were detailed, and the records seemed to be accurate: true sources dating back to the time of the firefever, contemporary diary entries and records kept by eyewitnesses. People who had actually seen the firefever take its terrible toll.

Or . . . what accepted history had recorded as the firefever.

Dio'sh studied the ancient documents, reading with amazement and a growing sense of horror. Something was wrong – but this was no hoax. The expressive lobes on his face flushed through a parade of vivid colours. These scrolls and testaments must be the truth, regardless of everything he had been told and taught.

The rememberer sat back, astounded. Then, stricken with fear that someone might see him or discover what he had found, Dio'sh closed and sealed the documents again and hurried to put them back into the hidden vault.

The revelation appalled him, and he didn't know how to explain it. But he could not disbelieve what he had seen.

Those key rememberers from long ago had not died of any disease. There had never been a firefever. Instead, the rememberers – the keepers of accurate Ildiran history – had been silenced. *Murdered*.

The lost section of the *Saga of Seven Suns* was not an unavoidable tragedy, but an appalling cover-up!

FIFTY-THREE

PRIME DESIGNATE JORA'H

In his spherical contemplation chamber within the Prism Palace, Prime Designate Jora'h studied the records of all his children with pride. As was his duty, the handsome and virile prince took many lovers from among the various Ildiran kiths, siring as many offspring as possible.

The eldest son of the Mage-Imperator, Jora'h had always known that the position would be his one day, after a century or more of his father's rule. He did not long for the day when he would sit in the chrysalis chair. That would be as much an ending of his life's pleasures as it would be a beginning of power. After the ritual castration ceremony to make him the next Mage-Imperator, Jora'h would control all the *thism*.

But not now.

He liked to be with his people, regardless of their kiths: swimmers and scalies, workers, bodyguards, or soldiers. They were all Ildirans, and they all knew their places. His duty was to be loved by all the population – perhaps literally, if he did his job properly – and to foster his numerous offspring. Jora'h smiled at the thought

301

of all the sons and daughters, noble-born scholars or half-breed workers, the fruits of his brief encounters with those lovers he selected from among the countless females who had petitioned him.

Despite their briefness, though, these sexual encounters meant a great deal to him. Each child he sired with a member of the noble kith gave him another descendant, another eventual Designate under his rule. Jora'h showered each of his sons and daughters with gifts, even if they were of mixed kiths. He sent them messages, wrote them poems. He did not want them to forget who their father was.

The sheer numbers of his offspring were daunting, though, and he needed time alone in his contemplation chamber simply to assess them all, to put their names in order and keep track of their birth anniversaries.

He dipped into the inexhaustible treasury and authorized extravagant gifts for every one of his children. Some previous Prime Designates had been less conscientious, flitting from lover to lover and never again speaking to their children. Jora'h, though, made sure his sons and daughters knew he was watching, that the Prime Designate noticed whenever one of his children achieved some honour or award.

According to Palace records, Jora'h's own father Cyroc'h hadn't been so devoted to his offspring. Yes, the Mage-Imperator had paid attention to his eldest son, pure-bred and born of a noble concubine. The great leader had sired dozens of other sons by noble women, all of whom became Designates on various colony worlds: Dobro, Hyrillka, Crenna, Comptor, Aituras, and many others. The secondary sons remained connected to their father through the *thism* and thus were capable of ruling splinter colony worlds with the Mage-Imperator's thoughts and decisions.

Jora'h, though, had been a resident of the Prism Palace for most of his life. He would not be a surrogate leader like the other Designates; he was tied closer to the Mage-Imperator than any of them.

His own eldest noble-born son, Thor'h, now lived on Hyrillka in the mansion of the Designate there, aloof and enjoying life, confident that he would not be called to the more difficult duties of leadership for many decades, perhaps even more than a century. After the Mage-Imperator Cyroc'h, Jora'h would become the next ruler; many decades after that, Thor'h would need to concern himself with his eventual fate and responsibility. But no one expected that of him yet. When it came time, the genetically stored knowledge accessible through the *thism* would teach him all he needed to know. For now, young, spoiled Thor'h seemed to enjoy the company of his uncle, the soft and placid Hyrillka Designate. Jora'h had been happy to indulge him for a few years.

As Jora'h finished going through the colourful images in many catalogues, selecting gifts for each of his children, Jora'h thought of his half-brothers, to whom he was not very close. The other Designates ruled entire planets, yet had no freedom.

Wistfully, Jora'h recalled a tale from the *Saga of Seven Suns* about a Mage-Imperator whose first-born had actually been twins. This had led to a terrible dynastic struggle, because each had claimed to be the Prime Designate. Both young men wanted to rule when the Mage-Imperator died, until finally, through a very risky undertaking, both of their minds were *fused*, joined through the *thism* into a single consciousness that lived in two separate bodies. Thus, the twins became one ruler with, it was believed, twice the wisdom . . .

Finishing his duties inside the contemplation chamber, Jora'h glanced at the time marked on the wall and the positions of the orbiting suns in the sky. He was expected to make another appearance, this time to watch a marvellous performance by his son, Zan'nh, who had entered the Ildiran Solar Navy as an officer. Zan'nh was actually Jora'h's first-born, the eldest of his many children, but because his mother had belonged to the military kith rather than the noble bloodline, Zan'nh's younger half-brother would be the next Prime Designate.

Zan'nh had proved to be quite talented with spacial manoeuvres and orbital tactics, and he also had the charisma and fortitude to command. Since Zan'nh had been born of a high-ranking soldier woman, their kiths had combined to breed a natural military officer, and the young man had the potential to be one of the very best. If today's aerial display proceeded as expected, Zan'nh was due for a promotion, and Jora'h had promised he would be there.

Accompanied by his attenders and an honour guard, the Prime Designate climbed aboard a personal transport craft and flew from the Prism Palace, urging the pilots to hurry so he could observe the opening ceremonies. They flew over Mijistra to the open plains that surrounded the capital city, where crowds of spectators had already gathered.

The transport craft docked, and Jora'h disembarked to stand beside Adar Kori'nh, Supreme Commander of the Solar Navy. The Adar's presence gave the day's performance an added importance, and Jora'h suspected the commander had come here merely because the Prime Designate's son was to be recognized for his talents.

Kori'nh said, 'I hope my forces impress you today, Prime Designate.'

'And I hope my son impresses you, Adar.'

Within the past months, the Solar Navy had increased its number of ships, focusing on military manoeuvres and practising space combat. Kori'nh had submitted regular reports, some of which Jora'h had read.

'Tell me truly, Adar, are you stepping up military practise

missions because you are concerned about an alien threat? I've seen reports from the Terran Hanseatic League of how strange ships destroyed their moons at Oncier.'

Kori'nh grunted. 'I don't know about that, Prime Designate. Still, many of us were . . . uneasy at the humans' blatant demonstration of power. Igniting a planet to turn it into a star? Was that truly necessary? What if the Hanseatic League turns that weapon against us?'

Jora'h frowned, trying to understand him. 'Are you suggesting we Ildirans had something to do with the attack on the Oncier moons? In retaliation?'

'Not at all, Prime Designate.' Kori'nh seemed embarrassed. 'I am stating that if an . . . incident was provoked against some other alien race, the humans should take responsibility for it.'

Jora'h frowned. 'Adar, you seem to know more about this than I do. Has my father given you information? Do we have some knowledge of this alien threat after all?'

'No, Prime Designate.'

The crowd suddenly cheered in the stands as a septa of streamers raced across the sky, fast arrowhead-shaped vessels roaring in a tight triangle. As they passed above the observers, the streamers split away from each other and performed wild and complex acrobatics, swirling upwards and back, creating a flower of coloured smoke in the sky. Then their seven parent escorts charged into the sky, performing larger and slower moves.

'That is going to be your son's new maniple, Prime Designate,' Adar Kori'nh said, gesturing to the sky. 'He has done admirably well in command.'

Jora'h's smoky topaz eyes glinted, reflecting bright highlights from the suns overhead. 'I am proud that he was promoted to septar so early in his career.'

The sky ballet continued with warships moving in precise

formation, carefully choreographed to look like an aerodynamic mating dance, leaving trails of smoke that etched a web across the sky. Finally, as a grand finale to the display, they dumped gouts of multicoloured smoke from their exhaust tubes, tracing brilliant lines in the air overhead.

Jora'h applauded along with the spectators, cheering and shouting as the streamers rejoined their escorts, which then moved back towards their parent warliner. Within a few moments, a small transport pod detached itself from the lead warliner, looking like nothing more than a speck when compared to the gigantic battleship. The transport pod landed in front of the viewing stand and Jora'h's son, Septar Zan'nh, emerged, wearing a formal Solar Navy uniform. He marched up, proud and competent before his Adar and his father.

Jora'h's heart swelled with love. 'You have done extremely well, my son,' he said, though it was not part of the ceremony. Kori'nh stepped back, waiting for the Prime Designate to finish. After a brief pause, Jora'h looked self-consciously at the Adar. 'That was all.'

Kori'nh moved forward, holding up a sparkling new rank insignia. 'Septar Zan'nh, until today you have had command of seven ships and you have proven yourself to be a quick-witted and brilliant tactician. It is my great pleasure to promote you to the rank of qul. Henceforth, you will be in charge of a full maniple. You will guide forty-nine ships, seven complete septas. Do you accept this new responsibility?'

'With pleasure, Adar Kori'nh.' The young man could not hide his grin, then he looked up at Jora'h. 'With pleasure, Father.'

Jora'h took the badge of rank from the Adar's hands and pinned it on his son's collar himself. 'I have always known you would serve the Ildiran Empire well. You have made me very glad.'

Jora'h's tiny golden braids of hair crackled and moved, living threads of static electricity around his head. Even though Zan'nh's mixed heritage prevented him from being the next Prime Designate, Jora'h knew the young man had a great future ahead of him. Beaming, he stepped away before he could embarrass Zan'nh, though he could barely control his overwhelming pride in his first-born son.

FIFTY-FOUR

JESS TAMBLYN

Already broken-hearted after the funeral, Jess knelt beside his old father, who lay grey and frail, as if his lifeline had been frayed to a single thread. He squeezed the old man's hand, attempting to impart all of his strength.

'He's just grief-struck,' Jess whispered to Cesca. 'He'll never admit it to himself, and he can't forgive his own stubbornness, either. He drove his son away and never saw him again because of his pride. Now he's punishing himself even further.'

That night, the old man suffered a severe stroke. A deep medical diagnostic revealed substantial damage to his brain, and blood clots that continued to put him at risk. Inside his private dwelling, Bram was covered with thermal blankets, but he still shivered, barely able to open his eyes. When he did, he seemed not to see anything.

'Oh, Jess,' Cesca said, unable to articulate anything else as she brought tea. Jess waved the warm liquid under the old man's nose, imagining that he saw a faint flicker of a smile on his father's lips. 'He'll recover,' Cesca said as she stroked Jess's arm. 'The Guiding Star will show him the path.'

308

Jess shook his head. 'Let us never lie to each other, Cesca. You saw the analysis. We know what's wrong with him. It'll only be a matter of hours. He doesn't have the strength to fight.' Frustrated, Jess sagged into his chair. 'Where is Tasia? She should be here.' After the stroke, he had sent two water workers to search for his sister, but no one had seen her since the last argument with her father. Jess knew Tasia had her own hiding places out on the ice, bolt-holes for when she needed to get away from stubborn Bram and his demands. 'We'd better find her soon.'

His uncles had come to take turns on the night-time vigil, some of them good friends to Jess when he was younger, some of them distant strangers. They would all have to work more closely together, tie the clan threads into unbreakable knots.

Jess reached out to clasp his father's hand. He felt a flicker of muscles in Bram's fingers, an answering signal, though he didn't know exactly what his father was trying to say. Jess felt unsettled and lost with all the events crashing around him. But he would do what was necessary, somehow.

After Ross had left home years ago, Bram had placed more and more duties on his second son, hammering a sense of obligation into him. *Never waver, never flinch.* Jess knew the role he must play, the responsibilities he had to handle, the inflexible path laid out for him – and he had grown harder, developing a personality perhaps too similar to his father's. When he'd promised old Bram, 'I'll never let you down,' it had seemed like a sacred oath to him.

But Jess forced himself to be more flexible. Unlike his rigid father, he could roll with adverse circumstances and wait for events to change.

Now the Plumas water-mining operations would belong to his uncles, if he didn't run them himself. Though he had trained hard for exactly this situation, Jess felt overwhelmed. He had clung to a

309

hope that Ross and his father would eventually end their feud and reconcile. Now that would never happen.

With the old man sleeping restlessly, Jess treasured Cesca's quiet companionship. He had always longed to spend time with her . . . but not like this. Sensing his thoughts, she reached over to take his hand. Her fingers were soft in his, and warm. He clasped back, but did not look at her, denying his hopes and thoughts. This was the one opportunity that they had never dared pray for – which made it all the more heart-wrenching.

'You know I love you, Cesca,' he said quietly. 'You know I want you more than any other woman in the Spiral Arm, but . . . it can't be now. I won't be an opportunist and say that we can be together now because my brother was murdered. How can I live with that? How can our love grow the way it should with this cloud over us, and my father dying in front of me?'

His lips trembled, but he drew a deep breath before she could respond. 'Where is Tasia? We've got to bring her here.'

Tears welled in Cesca's eyes, making them look larger and darker. 'Our time will come, Jess. We've got our own Guiding Star. You know it. We'll get through this. I'll help you with my support and my love, but we can't bring a shadow on your clan, or on the memory of Ross. We can't let any of the Roamers think ill of us or bring scandal upon the Tamblyn family.'

Jess looked quickly at her. 'Or upon you, Cesca. You'll be the next Speaker for all the clans. Neither you nor Jhy Okiah can suffer any political harm. It would weaken your ability to lead us. We don't dare think of ourselves right now. We can't be selfish.'

Cesca closed her eyes, as if she didn't want to admit it. 'You and I can wait. We know that we are destined to be with each other, Jess – if not now, then sometime soon.'

Cesca Peroni was her father's only child, though he had two brothers and one sister, all of whom had several children each, so the Peroni clan line was strong. Cesca herself was simply a solitary twig on the uppermost branch of the family tree.

Cesca had studied history and knew about the different clans and how they interrelated, which feuds had simmered for decades, which bloodlines were strongest. Jhy Okiah had made her learn all of these details. More than any other kind of politics or bureaucracy, understanding Roamer family connections was a Speaker's greatest political necessity.

Now Jess fell silent, and a long pause hung on their bittersweet conversation as they gazed at the frail form on the bed. Both he and Cesca would endure their separation for however long they felt was necessary. Jess would have enough grief to occupy him for a long time.

For the near future, Jess knew that he and Cesca would be wise to avoid each other. He couldn't bear to think that because of the death of Ross he was now free to love her. And now, with the loss of Bram, Jess would be the Tamblyn clan leader, a perfectly acceptable husband for the future Speaker.

Yes, perfect . . . as if they had planned it all.

But winning Cesca in such a way was not acceptable to either of them. The cultural rules of Roamer society were complex, and if he and Cesca pursued their love too openly, too soon, in the face of such tragedy, they might find themselves ostracized.

An hour later, Bram Tamblyn started up in bed and opened his eyes. He coughed twice, shuddered, then fell back on to his pillow — and died, so quickly and quietly that Jess could not believe what had just happened. Jess grabbed his father's arm, trying to feel a twitch of life, but he felt no sign of blood flow, no pulse on the skeletal wrist.

Cesca hugged him, both of them leaning over the bedside. Jess shouted, and finally someone entered from outside, wearing a thick parka. He couldn't see who the man was through his own burning eyes. 'Tasia! Where's my sister? Our father is dead.'

His uncle Caleb shrugged back his hood, looking unusually flustered. Jess raised his voice. 'Did you find her? I need you to bring her here.' Jess shook his head. 'How many places can there be to hide on Plumas?'

'I've just come from the surface, Jess. One of the Tamblyn ships is gone, a small scout vessel. Tasia's quarters are empty. It looks like she took some items with her . . . and also her compy EA.'

Cesca looked over at Jess as the realization grew in his heart. 'She must have run off to join the Eddies after all! Dammit, why couldn't she control her temper?' He sagged, dropping his head in his hands. His sister was just like his father in many ways.

Heartbroken and surrendering to grief, knowing what Bram must have felt like in his last hours, Jess remained by the deathbed. He held the brittle hand of his difficult and demanding father, and felt the weight of the universe on his shoulders.

FIFTY-FIVE

KING FREDERICK

I've asked you to meet privately with me, Frederick,' said Basil Wenceslas, 'because it is time for us to discuss your retirement.'

A smile rapidly superseded Frederick's surprise. 'It's about time, Basil. Forty-seven years on the throne? I'm getting tired, and I've been waiting for you to announce my replacement.' He strode over to where he kept his decanters of the finest sherry, his favourite of many vices. 'You won't get any complaint from me. This performance has gone on long enough. Would you like a drink, Basil?'

'No.' The Chairman stalked around the King's private withdrawing room, unwilling to take a seat.

'Then I'll have one for you.' Frederick poured a measure of amber liquid from a cut-crystal decanter, looked over at the other man and added a second shot. The Great King of all humanity did not need to ask permission.

The fact that Basil and the Hansa leaders were searching for his replacement was no news to Frederick. He was not so naive as to think that the Chairman had not been making plans all along, regardless of whether he kept them secret. Through his own spy network, Frederick had learned long ago about the first intended replacement, Prince Adam, an abortive candidate who had ultimately proved too intractable and unsuitable for the Hansa's purposes. Frederick had been waiting for years to hand the crown on to a successor. Frankly, he was surprised Basil had waited so long to make his announcement.

He took a long sip of the sweet sherry. 'I am very much looking forward to my retirement. I'm tired of everyone watching my moves day in and day out.'

Bemused, Basil raised his hands to indicate the opulence of the Whisper Palace. 'I don't understand you, Frederick. You have everything a person could possibly want. Why would you fantasize about retiring? It makes no sense.'

'We are two different men, Basil. You could never envision giving up your work, but I long for an end to all . . . this.'

Basil finally took a seat. 'Frederick, if I were ever to retire and "relax", I wouldn't last six months before I threw myself off a cliff into the sea.'

'I have no doubt of it, old friend,' said the King.

The Chairman and the King had both begun to work for the Hansa at about the same time – Basil rising quickly under his predecessor Chairman, while the young actor-prince underwent careful training and coaching – but Frederick had always been in the public eye. He had ruled Earth and its subject planets for close to half a century, and enough was enough. He sipped his sherry again. 'Basil, I am damn tired of ceremonies, of waving flags and cheering crowds who applaud my every movement as if simply walking down a hall or standing on a balcony were enough to strike awe into the hearts of my subjects.'

The Chairman's voice was calm. 'Most people would envy you all that.'

'Then go ahead, pick one of them and give him my job.' The King sank into a gold-inlaid chair studded with jewels. Its padding was hand-embroidered by a hundred different workers, forming designs and geometric patterns that Frederick had long ceased to appreciate. He let out a long sigh.

Frederick remembered when he'd first taken on the mantle as the new Great King. The leaders of the Terran Hanseatic League had completely invented his past, created an identity for him while erasing his previous life. At the time, Frederick had considered it a bargain, revelling in all of the comforts and trappings of power.

But even the best of things grew wearisome after a while.

All in all, Frederick thought he had been a good King, a decent King. He was no impostor, no character from a 'Prince and Pauper' adventure, because no 'real' King Frederick had ever existed. He had created the character, played the role. And quite nicely, he thought.

His predecessor had been King Bartholomew, a kindly and exuberant older man with whom Frederick had got along quite well. Bartholomew had been his mentor, like a real King to his real son, and before the old man's retirement, they had discussed their situation with full candour. At the time, young Frederick had been reluctant to believe the old King was willing to pass on his mantle of rulership without argument, but now Frederick understood Bartholomew perfectly well.

The Hansa had carefully staged Bartholomew's death, issuing a statement from his personal court physician that he had 'died peacefully in his sleep'. Then the previous King had received a new face, a new identity, and had gone off to live on Relleker in comfortable, blissful obscurity for the next two decades or so. Yes, he had given up the Whisper Palace and the throne, but he had gained so much more . . .

Basil sat back and looked up at the old leader. 'Don't worry, Frederick, we'll take care of everything when you retire.'

'That's what you promised me, Basil. I trust you.'

The Chairman chuckled. 'Not many people say that to me anymore, Frederick. I appreciate it.'

The King poured a second glass of sherry, pretending not to notice Basil's disapproving look. Over the years, his self-doubts had begun to eat at him as he watched the Hansa's devious manipulations. He did not question Basil's orders, and he cooperated with whatever the Hansa asked him to do. It was out of his hands.

Did even a Great King truly deserve all this adulation? The population of the human-settled worlds treated him like a god. And he, the man who had been forced to take the fictitious name of Frederick, had been chosen only because he possessed a particular body type, a natural charisma, the perfect timbre of voice – and a certain level of malleability.

It was all an accident, though. If he hadn't been caught on an observation camera and, entirely without his knowledge, passed a rigorous screening process, he would have lived an uneventful life. He might have had a family of his own, sons and daughters he could claim. He wouldn't have minded living in a small house, as long as he was left alone, even if it meant he made absolutely no mark on the universe, the world – or even the block of buildings around which he lived. Was that so important?

'Do whatever you think is best, Basil,' he said, 'but please take care of it soon.'

He both envied and pitied whoever was going to be his successor.

FIFTY-SIX

RAYMOND AGUERRA

The Whisper Palace held hundreds – thousands? – of rooms, passageways, and chambers. With vast portions sealed and off-limits, the public had no inkling of how *little* they were permitted to see.

After he settled into his strange and remarkable new situation, Raymond had certainly never guessed there could be so much to discover, though Basil Wenceslas and the compy Teacher OX kept him under tight restraint. Every time he went exploring, he was awed and astonished by the opulence, by the conveniences and luxuries he was invited to use every single day. Just when he began to feel he could not be impressed again, he encountered something more fantastic. He could barely keep up with it all.

Raymond wished his mother and brothers could be here to see this.

Wearing a glimmer swimsuit, he bounced and slid through a water tube that crossed the ceiling and spilled him out into the heated seawater pool below. He splashed heavily when he landed, an imperfect dive, but he knew enough to clamp his mouth shut.

When he had first begun learning to swim, he'd found himself coughing and choking, much to his embarrassment. But over the past several weeks, despite all the other educational activities required of him, Raymond had delighted in swimming the most.

A few times, when he was younger, he and his brothers had splashed around in a public pool. Though he had loved the activity with Michael, Rory, and Carlos, Raymond never gained any real confidence in the water. Now, with the Palace's seabath heated to a perfect temperature, and enough guardians and watchers to rescue him in nanoseconds if he ever found himself in trouble, Raymond let himself relax and play.

He dived under the water, swimming as far as he could, eyes open – his newly tinted *greenish-blue* eyes – to see the artificial convolutions in the bottom of the pool. He wondered how often Old King Frederick used this spa. The King probably had a dozen similar pools for his private use. Raymond's disbelief at all the extravagance had begun to make him blasé.

He surfaced, spluttering, and splashed new-blond hair out of his eyes. He stroked gently towards the edge of the pool, still with little grace, but growing competence. Raymond had promised himself that he would keep practising until he became an excellent swimmer. Basil Wenceslas and his other benevolent captors were pleased that he wanted to learn new things and expand his knowledge, though they had given him explicit curricula to which he must devote most of his time.

OX stood like a metal statue at the side of the pool. He held a towel, though the compy instructor saw no need for his student to emerge from the pool before he continued his lecture. 'I have several lessons prepared, young Peter. Shall we begin?'

By now, Raymond had stopped being bothered by the false name. Chairman Wenceslas had given him so many benefits and rewards just for play-acting the son of King Frederick, that he decided to put up with it. It didn't really make any difference. If that was all Raymond was required to do, then it was certainly a bargain.

Raymond trod water. 'I'm listening, OX.' Water continued to trickle out of the overhead slide, and bubbles foamed from thermal vents at the bottom of the faux volcanic floor of the seabath. 'Hey, why don't you tell me about yourself? You're one of the oldest compies I've ever seen. That model was discontinued, oh what, ten years ago?'

'Forty-three years ago, young Peter. Yes, I am old. I was one of the first dedicated compies. I was created to be placed aboard the first generation ship, the *Peary*.'

Raymond splashed backwards, barely able to believe. He knew parts of the history, had studied it in school, but now pushed back, stroking through the warm salty-smelling water trying to calculate. 'That's more than three centuries ago.'

'Yes, three hundred and twenty-eight years,' OX said. 'The long voyages of the generation ships were the reason compies were originally created. Not just to be companions and mechanical pets for people on Earth, but to serve their descendants aboard the generation ships. My memory files are old but still quite clear. I remember the day the *Peary* launched. I was onboard.'

'I know that now, OX,' Raymond said.

The *Peary* held two hundred families and all the resources they would need to establish a self-sufficient colony. Engineers built the generation ships in the asteroid belt and then shuttled all the passengers on to the vessels. The captain let me stand on the bridge as they launched. Even at full acceleration, it took us nine months just to leave the Earth's solar system. Everyone aboard was certain they would never see other humans again.'

Raymond swam gently across the pool so as not to make too much background noise, otherwise the Teacher would scold him, repeat himself, or raise the volume of his voice. 'Crimson rain, OX, it's hard to believe people would be willing to drop everything and leave their homes behind with no realistic hope of ever finding a better place.'

'Those were desperate times,' OX said. 'The ships were slow and huge – colonies themselves, in effect, with every supply needed to support all passengers and their descendants for centuries. We compies were placed onboard to provide stability and long-term memories during such extended voyages. Thus, it was vitally important that we learned how to teach.'

'Like babysitters that never went away,' Raymond said. He playfully splashed OX, but the compy was not the least bit ruffled.

'We were a stabilizing influence. Over such a long voyage, no one expected that the passengers would preserve all the details of human civilization, that they would remember Earth culture and laws and morals. Compies helped guide the children, and then their children, and then their children. The information had to be preserved, the dream kept alive. When the generation ships finally arrived at a suitable planet, we did not want their passengers to be feral primitives.'

'Then the Ildirans found our generation ships,' Raymond said, knowing the rest of the story. 'They took everyone to a new planet just as fast as you please, and then they brought you back to Earth as a liaison compy to help establish relations with the Hansa. Now you're a living historical artifact, a grand old compy.'

'Why, thank you, Peter. It is gratifying to encounter such respect.' OX took the towel he had held for Raymond and wiped the droplets of splashed water from his metal skin. 'Or was I meant to interpret that as a joke?'

Raymond went to the stone steps of the pool and waited, still submerged in the warm water. 'Oh, I meant it, OX. I respect someone as smart as you are, with all your information and experience. I would never joke about it.'

When he'd been younger, back before the dramatic change in his life, Raymond had always studied hard. Since he'd also been busy trying to hold his family together, struggling to earn enough money to keep his mother and brothers afloat, his grades were never particularly good. He couldn't follow the academic rules and complete all the work that schools demanded of him, but that had never stopped him from concentrating on important subjects. He realized early on that mathematics and simple book-keeping were keys to moving up in the world, to breaking away from the ghetto where his family was stranded.

Without their father, the Aguerras were starting out behind most other people. His mother had known he was smart; she brought him books when she could. Now, though he would never see her again, he still wanted to make her proud of him, if only in his memories.

He swayed a bit, as if thunder had struck through his chest, still hollow and devastated at any reminder of the disastrous fire that had destroyed the building where his family lived. Only through sheer luck had he been gone that night, running errands, trying to scrape together a few amenities. Now they were all dead, and he – an underprivileged boy from the wrong side of the economic curve – had an extravagant, pampered life that went beyond anything he'd ever imagined.

'I am glad to have such an eager student,' OX said, 'for there is a great deal I have been instructed to teach you.'

Raymond dived under the water, swimming until his lungs ached. He finally burst up again, spluttering, to draw a deep breath. He laughed and swam back to the Teacher compy. 'If more classrooms could be made out of swimming pools, OX, students would be much more interested in going to school.'

He felt a vibrating hum in the water, and geyser jets sprayed around the opposite edge of the pool. Underwater hatches opened, and Raymond swam into a deeper area as grey bullet-like shapes darted out. Three playful bottlenose dolphins, their eyes bright, darted around him. Laughing, he splashed around in circles, and the dolphins cruised on one side and then the other, coming close enough for him to touch their rubbery skin, to grasp two dorsal fins and let them carry him along. A week earlier, Raymond had made a comment to OX about how he wanted to see a dolphin. The very next time he'd gone swimming, the dolphins had appeared.

Raymond had no doubt he was being watched and monitored, that Chairman Wenceslas and his numerous assistants must be recording every step of his progress. The lack of privacy annoyed him, but he could not argue against it. He owed these people everything. Though he hadn't been allowed outside the Whisper Palace, he had wandered through tunnels and chambers, maintenance halls, secret connecting catacombs. Every corner of the Palace, even the places few people ever saw, was clean and bright, lavishly decorated. He wasn't going to complain, though his concept of what constituted a 'King' had changed since learning the truth about Frederick and his nonexistent royal family.

'How did this all start, OX? Earth had so many different governmental systems, developing democracies, dictatorships and military-run countries, but a King seems so . . . old-fashioned. Why did the Hansa reestablish royalty?'

OX paused as if loading a file and assembling a story, and then he began to lecture. The dolphins continued to frolic around Raymond while he tried to listen.

'When the Terran Hanseatic League began to consolidate its power, their representatives were corporate administrators. They made decisions and ran businesses, but none of them had a very charismatic or likeable public face. The figureheads who came to fill the role of the Great Kings were created as spokespeople, icons and mouthpieces to imply that the Hansa functioned as a unified collection of powers represented in a single leader. Like a kingdom.

'Though a monarchy is not the most politically enlightened form of government, human society has historically looked upon it with reverence and respect. In the beginning, the Hansa made no secret that their King was merely an actor, someone who could perform ceremonies and impress the population. To most individuals, "corporate businessmen" seemed fallible – heroes with feet of clay, as the old cliché says.'

'I've never heard that cliché,' Raymond said, swimming backwards again. The dolphins dived under him, nosing at his feet.

'But a *King*, if created properly and given the appropriate trappings and coaching, could fill a vital role. The human population accepted it easily at first. Over the generations, the Great King has become an indispensable spokesperson.'

'Even though the King has no power,' Raymond said.

'Even though the King has no *political* power,' OX emphasized. 'Provided he follows instructions and performs all the tasks the Hansa asks of him, the united colony worlds will run smoothly. You, young Peter, are a *placebo government*. The populace believes in you, and therefore the populace is well governed.'

'Wasn't that supposed to work for the Church, too? Nobody sees Unison as anything more than window dressing. The Congress of Faiths might look like a cooperative body in their meetings, but everybody knows they're at each others' throats behind closed doors.'

OX said, 'In theory, Peter, they are searching for a common denominator among the beliefs of human beings.'

'It'll never happen. That's why so many Hansa colonies have their own cultures and churches. My mother never looked at the Congress too favourably. She said Unison would never have the spark of a real church.' Raymond frowned, remembering Rita Aguerra and how she had clung to her icons and her observances, though quietly at home. 'She said the Archfather, the Spokesman of All Faiths, would always play second fiddle to a real pope, in her eyes.'

OX pondered. 'An apt analogy, Peter. The consolidation occurred here on Earth while I was away on the *Peary*. Congress of Faiths is like the old United Nations, trying to represent all points of view, finding common ground.'

Raymond snorted. 'It's more politics than deep religious passion, and Unison is so bland that nobody can get inspired by it.'

He stroked backwards, dunked his head under the water, and came up spluttering. He wiped his eyes.

'Nevertheless, Peter, the people accept the Archfather as their unbiased religious representative, and the government officially supports the consolidated church. It is intended to keep the people calm and quiet, not to arouse fervour. By now, most of the truly intense devotees have founded their own isolated religious colonies on unwanted worlds, as you pointed out. Most have found, however, that they cannot live in isolation. They are dependent on Hansa supplies and equipment. Not many have amounted to anything.'

'So the Archfather is irrelevant, just like the Great King.'

'Not true, Peter. You are highly relevant, because the Hanseatic League intends to keep growing in size and power. Chairman Wenceslas would accomplish little without you.'

'That's a relief.' Tired of the energetic dolphins and done with swimming, Raymond drifted to the stone steps and climbed out. OX extended the towel, and Raymond dried himself off vigorously.

'And the Archfather will place the crown on your head.'

He could have requested a massage or a sauna, or any kind of drink or sweet treat he could imagine, but at the moment Raymond couldn't think of anything he particularly wanted. He had already studied hard for the day and exercised well. He still had only an inkling of all the important things that would be expected of him, and he certainly wasn't ready to fill his role.

Raymond shrugged into a plush crimson robe that seemed to warm instantly as he wrapped it around himself. In spite of his doubts, he found his new situation to be an acceptable change from his previous life.

FIFTY-SEVEN

TALBUN

The worldtrees were uneasy, deeply aware of some brewing problem in the Spiral Arm, but cosmic fears could not always be understood by the followers and tenders of the worldforest. As always, the forest knew more than any human could understand, even a dedicated green priest.

Such grand-scale matters rarely bothered the distant colony worlds, though. Daily life here was slow and quiet, filled with contentment.

On sparsely populated Corvus Landing, the old green priest Talbun knew it was time to end his work and his life. Through the thrumming worldforest, he sensed that great events were brewing, terrible times ahead for many worlds and many people.

Talbun, however, was more concerned with his personal obligations.

As he walked among the rustling worldtrees that covered a hillside near the settlement of Colony Town, Talbun listened to the call of faraway Theroc – the centre of the worldforest, the heart of the trees. He had not been home for decades. The treelings he had planted on the ridge overlooking the town now stood taller than a man, a satellite mind of the sentient forest. He would never return to the beautiful world where he had been born and raised, where he had first taken the green. But that was all right.

Corvus Landing depended on him, and Talbun loved this place. He would not abandon the people, no matter how tired he was, no matter how old and frail he felt. Talbun's life had been devoted to service, praying to and caring for the worldtrees; by association, he also watched over the people who served the forest. He would not surrender to his selfish desire.

Not yet.

Talbun stroked the scaly trunk of the nearest tree in his grove, receiving the whispered thoughts of the forest. 'I will join you soon,' he whispered. He would die here on Corvus Landing. His flesh would fertilize the soil and nourish the worldtrees, his final service to the beloved forest. 'But first I need to find a replacement.'

Talbun had only to send a call, and all green priests, anyone who could touch the mind of the worldforest, would sense his message. So why did he hesitate?

Many tattoos marked his face, lines and circles that commemorated his journeys, signifying how much time he had spent aboard ships. Talbun had served on the *Constellation*, travelling from system to system and performing Hansa business. Talbun's connection with the trees allowed him to send emergency communications and diplomatic communiqués faster than any starship or signal could travel. Not every message required such speed, of course, but having a green priest onboard conferred a great deal of prestige on the captain and his ambassador partner.

After five years on the diplomatic ship, Talbun had resigned. He had earned his tattoos and was not growing anymore. 'I must be on a planet again. I am tired of metal walls and reprocessed air, of looking out the window and seeing only emptiness.' He tried to make the *Constellation*'s captain understand. 'I long to feel the dirt beneath my feet, the air against my face, wind and rain and sunshine.'

Green priests were not controlled by Hansa law, despite numerous efforts to bring independent Theroc under their rule. Upon resigning from the *Constellation*, Talbun had instantly received a thousand offers for his services, but he already had in his mind and his heart what he wanted to do.

It had been only three years since the first settlers had established a foothold here. Talbun had come to Corvus Landing. With his credentials, he could have requested any assignment in the Spiral Arm – yet the bucolic planet called to him. He was not interested in accolades. He wanted peace.

No one had been more surprised by his choice than the leaders of Corvus Landing. When he'd arrived on the backwater world, a single green priest who had booked passage on a scheduled cargo ship, he'd been welcomed with the most lavish celebration the warm-hearted settlers could provide. Earnest young Mayor Sam Hendy had declared a feast in his honour, though Talbun had been shy about such ceremony. After he had planted his lovely grove just outside Colony Town, Corvus Landing had become a real part of the Hansa, more than just a signatory to the Charter. Talbun's telink abilities made him a living telegraph station, letting the settlers remain in direct contact with Earth, other colony worlds, and merchant ships.

Thrilled to have such a distinguished new member of their community, the colonists had pooled their meagre resources and sparse luxuries. They had helped him clear the native mosses and interlinked groundcover so he could plant his treelings. Talbun had never felt so loved and appreciated.

He could not abandon these people now just because he was weary of life.

Talbun had planted his treelings one at a time, caressing them, welcoming them to their new home. Coached and nurtured, the trees had grown rapidly, taking all the nutrients they needed. After two years he had been able to harvest healthy clippings and plant new treelings to enlarge the grove. Everything here was growing perfectly.

But humans did not live forever.

Under the feathery canopy, Talbun turned his face to the sky, drinking in the sunlight from this alien star and converting it to energy. He ran dirt-caked fingertips over his cheeks, feeling not soiled but vibrant. The powdery earth always made him more alive.

Corvus Landing had been the perfect place to spend the rest of his years, filling out the deficiencies in his life. In this grove of treelings, he had sat cross-legged for hours, reading document after document to the trees, all the while increasing his own knowledge. He had loved those days.

But now it was time for his replacement. He had one last role to play.

At the centre of the grove, he spread his arms to trail his fingers along the trunks. Finally, he knelt, feeling the soil against his naked knees, and pressed his forehead against the nearest trunk.

He closed his eyes, thought of how to phrase his need, and then, opening his mental ability, connected through the world-forest. Talbun sent his plea into the telink network, calling for someone to come to him.

FIFTY-EIGHT

BENETO

Deep in the forests of Theroc, Beneto sensed the incoming communication. The trees rippled invisibly with a general call sent by another green priest, directed everywhere through the neural root network. He clasped the scaled trunk of the nearest tree and touched his forehead to the bark, listening to the telink summons.

In his sister grove on far-off Corvus Landing, old Talbun transmitted his needs. Beneto saw the images, heard the thoughts, understood the weary green priest's plight and his desire. He listened carefully, absorbing it all. He imagined the possibilities.

In his mind Beneto experienced the small, out-of-the-way Hansa colony through Talbun's eyes and memories. He felt the winds whistling across the plains of Corvus Landing, stirring the geometric fields planted by the settlers. He imagined the goat herds, the revelries of the settlers, the hard work, the good company. He also felt the old man's bone weariness, understood that Talbun was dying, and that he needed to be replaced.

If only he could find someone.

Beneto broke the telink connection and stood up, surrounded by the trees and his thoughts. The whispering fronds soothed him, gave him advice, but let him make his own decisions. Beneto drew a deep breath, already filled with delight at this answer to his inner desires. For so long he had wanted something exactly like this, without even knowing it in his own heart. The forest had sent him an answer to his unspoken prayers.

Beneto had lived his life gifted with every advantage and luxury, but such things meant nothing to him. He was better suited to being a monk – a missionary, not a politician. He wanted to tend the magnificent trees and spread the forest from planet to planet. He wanted to help people, to commune with the forest, to assist the human spirit, rather than his own glory.

When Beneto had been chosen as the official communications link at Oncier, he had seen the envious look in Sarein's eyes. Though the high profile had meant little to him, his sister considered it a great honour to stand beside Chairman Wenceslas and send messages to Old King Frederick on Earth. Beneto took the most pleasure, though, in describing the amazing test of the Klikiss Torch to the eager and curious trees . . .

His parents had frequently tempted him with opulent assignments to serve in extravagant tree temples on planets where satellites of the worldforest grew strong, or to operate as a highly paid diplomatic assistant to the Hansa. But Beneto didn't want any of that. He preferred quiet contemplation.

'What shall I do?' he said aloud to the forest.

As he prayed, he received a flood of thoughts, a thousand options from the flourishing trees. But the most poignant advice was that he should focus his own desires, to make a decision commensurate with his vows to protect the worldforest, while also being true to himself, his position, and his personality.

Though he had magnificent quarters in the old fungus-reef city,

Beneto often preferred to climb away from the settlement, descend to the forest floor and just sleep among the trees. He occasionally disappeared for days and came back refreshed. All the green priests knew where he was. They could simply look through the mind of the worldforest and watch him with the 'eyes' of a million leaves. Beneto was never in any danger – not on Theroc or any world where the sentient trees grew.

Any world, including Corvus Landing.

Finally, after mulling over the possibilities for hours, he understood exactly what the old green priest Talbun and the worldforest wanted of him. And Beneto made his decision.

FIFTY-NINE

NIRA

The *Voracious Curiosity* descended towards Mijistra, where multiple suns dazzled off the transparent domes and crystalline spires. Ambassador Otema waited patiently in their cabin, but Nira could not tear her eyes from the viewing window, drinking in all the details with a child's amazement.

Rlinda Kett announced over the intercom, 'We'll be groundside in a few minutes. They're directing me to land on a diplomatic platform on the Prism Palace itself. Never expected that!'

She deftly brought her ship down to the magnificent structure. Perched like a citadel on a hill, the Prism Palace looked like an exotic glass model of an atom, with a central sphere surrounded by round domes connected by tunnels and walkways. Atop each of the symmetrically arranged subspheres rested small landing platforms for spacecraft and short-range vessels.

After she had settled the *Curiosity* in the designated spot, Rlinda emerged from the cockpit grinning and sweating. 'You two sure must have attracted some attention. I've been to Mijistra before, but never to the Prism Palace, much less been told to land here!'

Otema looked unruffled. 'You overestimate our importance, Captain Kett.'

Rlinda shrugged as she opened the hatch. 'Whatever you say.'

Nira stared out into dazzlingly bright sunlight from a group of brilliant stars, large suns and small, with colours that ranged from blue-white to warm yellow to a deep orange-red.

The merchant woman wrapped tinted goggles around her eyes, a thin sheet that filtered out the glare. 'I have other pairs for you two. You'll have the worst trouble when you try to sleep. Ildirans don't like the dark, not anywhere.'

Nira stepped out into the sunlight from all directions. Her skin tingled with all the energy. 'I don't need any. I'd like to just look at the sunshine.'

'Suit yourselves.' They stood together on the high platform above the central Prism Palace globe. The wonderful city of Mijistra spread out around them, dazzling Nira with its glowing primary colours.

Then as her eyes adjusted, she saw a tall, thin man walking towards them. 'A rather small reception committee,' said Otema.

The man wore long robes snug at his waist. Several sections of the fabric were crosshatched with reflective material. His head was hairless, his alien features angular and craggy, his skin a yellowish-grey. A coloured electrostatic field flickered around his head like a hood projected by small devices at his collar. Nira couldn't tell if it was a protective covering or some sort of fashion adornment.

The Ildiran man raised his left hand at his side, palm outwards, then turned it sideways. He spoke in perfect Trade Standard. 'I am Klio's, the Ildiran Minister of Commerce. I have come to act as business liaison with Captain Rlinda Kett.'

After Rlinda introduced herself, Ambassador Otema extended her diplomatic credentials, which seemed to fluster Klio's. 'You

334

misunderstand,' he said. 'I am here only for Captain Kett. The Prime Designate will arrive for you momentarily.'

Rlinda's brown eyes went wide. 'The Prime Designate's coming to see them?' She gasped at Otema and Nira. 'Do you know who that is?'

Though Nira was wide-eyed and enthusiastic, Otema remained unflappable. 'We will greet him with suitable respect, as the representatives of Theroc.'

Klio's ushered Rlinda to a doorway in the expansive dome. The merchant woman walked slowly, as if consciously delaying in hopes of catching a glimpse of the Ildiran heir. But the bureaucrat hurried her towards his offices, leaving Nira and Otema waiting alone beside the *Voracious Curiosity*.

On the opposite side of the platform, more doors opened. Three hideous-looking Ildirans stepped out, broad-shouldered warrior kith with bulging muscles, fangs, and claws. They carried hand weapons: curved knives and wicked-looking crystal-bladed katanas. With flashing feral eyes, they scanned the platform, then stepped aside, rigidly at attention. The next person who stepped forward was the most hypnotically attractive man Nira had ever seen.

Ambassador Otema bowed, but Nira could not tear her eyes away from the man. He exuded charisma. His face was handsome, perfectly sculpted, with a long chin and wide-set eyes that were a strange colour of smoky topaz. His features were perfect and timeless, and bronze skin made him look like a museum depiction of an ancient pharaoh. Around his head, a mane of braided golden hair twitched and moved as if alive with static electricity.

Nira finally averted her gaze, but clearly the man had noticed her. Paying more attention to her than to Otema, he said, 'I am Prime Designate Jora'h, and I am glad to receive you. Ambassador Otema?' He nodded to the old woman, then turned to Nira, reached out to cup her chin and raised her face so that she could look at him again. 'And I am also most pleased to meet you. What is your name?'

Nira's voice caught in her throat, and she couldn't speak. After the briefest hesitation, Otema answered in a slightly scolding tone. 'Her name is Nira, Prime Designate. She is my assistant and will help me study your great epic.'

'Most excellent! I promise you every courtesy that we can provide.' The Prime Designate wore a patterned vest open at his chest, and Nira could see the muscles of his broad shoulders and firm abdomen. He had the perfect physique of an idealized classical sculpture.

Nira was surprised to note Theron designs on the robe that hung down to his knees. Jora'h must have adopted them after his meeting with Reynald, either because he was enamoured of the forest culture, or because he wanted to make a good impression on the two green priest representatives. No doubt if the Prime Designate adopted such garments, many others in the Ildiran court would also dress like him. Rlinda Kett would have no difficulty selling her supplies of cocoon-fibre fabric and worldforest products.

Jora'h gestured the burly bodyguards forward. 'These men will assist us in carrying your belongings. I have arranged for quarters inside the Prism Palace, where you will be our welcome guests.'

'Oh, thank you.' The words tumbled out of Nira's mouth before Otema could say anything.

The older woman nodded politely. 'We did not expect such a singular honour from the Prime Designate. We have several treelings and other items to present to the Mage-Imperator.'

Jora'h waved her aside. 'There'll be enough time for formalities and ceremonies later. My father has a very busy schedule today, so I have been given the wonderful task of showing you the sights of Mijistra.'

Nira clasped her hands in delight, wanting to see everything. Otema glanced at her young assistant. 'As you wish, Prime Designate.'

Accompanied by an ever-shifting group of dignitaries and spokespersons who changed at each stop along the tour, Jora'h took them on his royal hover-platform to show them the capital city, both from above and from street level.

Jora'h said, 'This city contains museums full of our history, relics, stories, poems . . . all to preserve the most glorious days of our culture. We have a grand architectural and artistic tradition. Our golden age has remained undiminished for millennia.'

Nira stared at the clear walls, the transparent construction bricks that made every building absorb and reflect light. Since the Ildiran people abhorred darkness, their main construction materials were glasses, crystals, and polymers, some clear and colourless, others jewel-toned. For aesthetics as well as increased structural integrity, columns of opaque reinforcement blocks ran up the sides of primary walls.

The lines of the street flowed in curves rather than hard angles. Pyramids were covered with hanging gardens and fern-clusters. Waterfalls and streams ran through necklaces of pools, bubbling down the sloping sides of buildings through channels and gutters.

'It's all so beautiful,' Nira said. Jora'h gave her an appreciative smile.

Otema said, almost apologetically, 'My assistant has never been away from Theroc, Prime Designate. She is most impressionable.'

Jora'h flashed his smoky eyes at the young woman. 'Reynald has told me how beautiful your worldforest is.'

At his encouragement, Nira began to describe the towering forests and the fungus-reef cities and the worm hives, then told him about becoming an acolyte and finally taking the green.

337

Ambassador Otema let Nira talk, and Jora'h appeared fascinated with it all.

He said, 'We Ildirans revere our scholars as well as our musicians and poets, artists, glassmakers, and our rememberers. A society that does not remember itself is not worth remembering.' Around him, the other bureaucrats agreed. 'I am so glad you two will be here for a long time. A study of our *Saga* cannot be finished in a few days. Together, we will have time to visit many of our great museums and exhibits.'

Nira's mind and her senses felt full to bursting. Her eyes, already dazzled by the brilliant sunlight, could not absorb more, no matter how quickly she glanced from side to side. Otema leaned closer and said in a quiet voice, 'Don't gawk, child. You must not embarrass us.'

Flustered, Nira tried to recapture her dignity, but Jora'h said, 'Ah, but Ambassador, is that not the best compliment Nira can give – to show how captivated she is by everything she sees?' He reached out to touch Nira's arm, and she felt an electric thrill run through her emerald skin. 'One who lives with a child-like sense of wonder should never be ashamed. Don't you agree?'

Otema let her expression melt into a smile. 'Yes, I agree, Prime Designate. You have reminded me that one who worries too much about formalities and dignity may well miss important parts of life.'

After hours of busy sightseeing during which the stars jockeyed for position in the sky, yet never hinted at approaching twilight, Nira and Otema were finally led to their quarters in the Prism Palace. All of their possessions had been removed from the *Voracious Curiosity* and meticulously placed in separate rooms, far enough apart to offer privacy yet close enough that Nira and Otema could easily confer with each other. The potted treelings had been divided into two groups, one set in each of their quarters.

Jora'h said, 'It is difficult for humans to sleep here because there is no darkness. We have provided sleep masks and darkening shades for your rooms.'

'Thank you, Jora'h,' Nira said, then embarrassed, added, 'I mean, Prime Designate.' She felt so naive and out of place . . . yet full of dreams. She had never imagined she would be so fascinated, and now she felt giddy.

Left alone after the long day, she spoke excitedly to Otema, eager to discuss everything they had experienced, but the old ambassador wanted time to herself. Nira returned to her own chambers, where, bursting with impressions and needing to tell *someone*, she touched the potted treelings. Nira spent the next hour describing everything she had seen, increasing the knowledge held within the worldforest.

SIXTY

REMEMBERER DIO'SH

Rememberer Dio'sh trembled with gnawing anticipation as he waited for his personal audience alone with the Mage-Imperator.

The supreme Ildiran ruler was the closest thing to a living god the race could imagine. Though he rarely left the confines of his Prism Palace, the Mage-Imperator could sense every Ildiran, regardless of kith, though he could directly communicate only with his Designates. Even so, Dio'sh had discovered that some terrible knowledge remained hidden even from the great leader.

The rememberer knew he must reveal his appalling discovery to the Mage-Imperator. A historical cover-up, lies, conspiracies . . . horrific events hidden and rewritten from the dawn of the Empire. The benevolent leader would know what to do with the un-believable information.

Frightened by what he had learned, Dio'sh had at first considered telling his comrade Vao'sh, but after a nightmarish sleep period during which he tossed restlessly, the young rememberer at last determined that this matter was important enough to bring directly to the Mage-Imperator's attention. A mere historian could not make such momentous decisions by himself.

He had gone through protocol officers and bureaucrats and was surprised to be granted access so quickly. Through the *thism*, the Mage-Imperator must feel the urgency of the rememberer's secret.

Waiting outside the chambers, Dio'sh held a bundle of the fragments, journals, and eyewitness records he had retrieved from the hidden vault deep in the labyrinth below. It was all the proof he needed. History itself would change after today, and the responsibility felt enormous.

He felt the lobes of his face flush through a range of colours as stormy emotions crossed his mind. No historian could keep his feelings hidden, and now Dio'sh's face was a bonfire of emotions.

The muscled bodyguard Bron'n blocked the entrance to the Mage-Imperator's private contemplation chamber, unimpressed with the young rememberer's anxiety. The ferocious-looking fighter had a purpose to serve, and he was not interested in whatever news Dio'sh might bring.

With a deep-throated grunt, Bron'n finally stepped aside and gestured towards the opening door. The guard spoke memorized words in a gruff voice, as if uncomfortable reciting the bureaucratic language. 'The Mage-Imperator is pleased to grant access to one of his valued rememberer subjects and is eager to hear your matter of great importance.'

Dio'sh wondered why the Mage-Imperator had not chosen to have his advisers there to listen to what he had to say. This revelation was world-shaking! On the other hand, perhaps this was a matter best kept between the two of them for now. The Mage-Imperator might want to consider his response without a dozen assistants chattering their advice. Dio'sh drew a deep breath and entered the dazzling contemplation chamber, trying to calm the colours on his face.

He kept his eyes cast down towards the blue-veined floor. Hot sunlight streamed through the transparent ceiling, magnified by convex window panels. Fountains in the corners boiled water upwards into steam; the room was as humid as a jungle. Dio'sh took three steps forward and stopped, slowly finding the courage to raise his lobed head. 'My Mage-Imperator.'

The soft-skinned ruler reclined on an ellipsoidal chair that supported his bulk. Shimmering garments were draped around the swollen body. His eyes were half-closed, as if in a heavy-lidded doze. The Mage-Imperator stirred, then spoke in a purring voice. 'I am pleased to meet you in person, Rememberer Dio'sh. I have heard of your ordeal on Crenna – and experienced it directly through my son, the Designate.'

The long rope-like braid hanging down around the Mage-Imperator's heavy body lay draped across his stomach and coiled next to his hips. It twitched like a restless pet anaconda. His eyes studied the rememberer as if he were a succulent meal.

'Yes, Liege. Crenna was . . . very difficult for me. Rememberer Vao'sh is helping me to compile the true and permanent story of the blindness plague, so that your son the Crenna Designate and all the other Ildiran victims will be remembered and honoured in our *Saga of Seven Suns*.'

The leader's face remained placid, even bored. 'Every Ildiran lives his life hoping to achieve something significant enough to warrant inclusion in our *Saga*. Even though those people on Crenna died of a terrible sickness, they will now be revered forever.'

Bowing again, Dio'sh said, 'That is my sincerest hope, Liege.' Then he lifted the documents cradled in his hands. 'It is regarding the *Saga of Seven Suns* that I have requested to speak with you.'

He held the documents forward, but the Mage-Imperator did not lift a stubby hand. 'Tell me what you have found.' His braid twitched again, and his voice carried a strong note of wariness. 'I sense that it has upset you to your very heart.'

Dio'sh clutched the documents to his chest and spoke without embellishment. 'After our rescue from Crenna, I came back to Mijistra and began to study the records of other epidemics in our history. In the deepest Palace archives, I searched through many preserved documents of apocrypha, learning hidden fragments of our history.'

'The apocrypha are not a legitimate part of the *Saga*,' the Mage-Imperator cautioned.

'True, but they are still eyewitness accounts and pieces of relevant information, not to be disregarded. I was searching for background material about the Lost Times, when accepted history tells us that all members of the rememberer kith perished in the firefever.'

'Yes.' The Mage-Imperator's pasty face drooped into a frown, yet his sadness seemed false. 'That was a terrible time.'

'But the truth is not what we thought, Liege!' Dio'sh said, ready to burst. 'I learned something about all of those missing lines from the *Saga*. I have found evidence of what occurred during that period. Something shocking.'

'There have always been rumours, Dio'sh. Ildirans love their mysteries.'

'Yes, Liege, but I have found that, in reality, the firefever *never occurred*.'

'All the rememberers died,' the Mage-Imperator insisted, disturbed and obviously sceptical. The historian did not notice his glowering expression. 'It is clear that a section of our epic was lost.'

Dio'sh stepped closer, his face lobes ablaze with colourful emotions. 'No, Liege. Not lost. The rememberers were *killed* in order to hide the truth, and then a portion of the *Saga* was intentionally censored so that no one would ever know what really

343

happened. I believe it must have been an order given by an ancient Mage-Imperator.'

'Preposterous. No Mage-Imperator would commit such a heinous act.'

A flood of words poured from Dio'sh's mouth. He waved the incontrovertible documents. 'The lost verses tell of an ancient and devastating conflict in the galaxy, an ultimate war against powerful creatures called hydrogues, aliens that live within the cores of gas-giant planets.'

The Mage-Imperator was wide awake now, fascinated. Dangerous. Dio'sh continued. 'This ancient war, I believe, is related to the extinction or disappearance of the Klikiss race, but it has remained hidden for these ten thousand years.' He shuffled through the documents, eagerly seeking passages to quote. 'Liege, the evidence is clear. Our accepted version of the *Saga* does not tell the entire truth. We must change what has been written.'

Dio'sh was so excited that he paid no heed to the displeasure crossing the Mage-Imperator's normally beatific face, or to the long braid thrashing with the leader's agitation. 'Let me see these documents. Step closer.'

Dio'sh came forward and offered the records. Surely the Mage-Imperator would see the proof and know the truth. 'Here is a journal entry from one of the assassins. The blood is on his own hands. He says—'

The living braid rose up beside the Mage-Imperator, extending from the chrysalis chair like a tentacle. Seeing a flicker of movement, Dio'sh glanced to the side – but had no time to cry out before the serpent-like rope of living hair lashed out and wrapped around his neck.

The Mage-Imperator's eyes blazed as he leaned forward. 'Of course I know the story.' His lip curled with disgust.

The knotted braid constricted. The historian struggled

frantically, dropping the records as he kicked and squirmed. The Mage-Imperator's hair squeezed harder, drawing the loop tighter, until it crushed the rememberer's larynx.

'I *wanted* it kept secret.' Hissing angry breaths, the Mage-Imperator continued squeezing until his pasty face was ruddy, flushed with the effort. Then he snapped Dio'sh's neck and used the braid to toss the historian's body on to the floor like so much garbage.

SIXTY-ONE

DAVLIN LOTZE

The Ildirans were hiding something terrible – Davlin Lotze
felt it deep in his bones. But as he sifted through the
hastily abandoned wreckage of the Crenna colony, he
could not pin down any details. Keeping his identity secret,
pretending to be a mere colonist, made his job even more difficult.

When the aliens had evacuated their plague-infested settlement, they had left significant debris behind. Unfortunately, not
much of it seemed to be interesting . . . at least not in the way
Chairman Wenceslas had hoped.

Dressed in a serviceable jumpsuit like the ones worn by most
of the new settlers, Davlin did his daily work, keeping to himself
and taking surreptitious images of the site. The colonists, filled
with more exuberance than foresight, had got out the heavy
demolition equipment and set about knocking down the charred
shells of buildings the Ildirans had burned in an attempt to halt
the plague.

The settlers had no interest in archaeological niceties or
studying clues to the alien culture. They just wanted to get their

work done, rebuild the town, plant the crops, and establish the infrastructure before seasons changed and harsh weather arrived. Davlin had to make do, taking every chance and respite he could find. As he stood in the bright sunlight and watched the big yellow machines demolishing walls, he tried not to wince at all the opportunities being lost to brute force.

Given his choice, Davlin would have spent days combing the ashes in search of tiny clues. Even skeletons or half-cremated bodies could have provided useful information. It wasn't as if the Hansa had ready access to alien dissection cadavers. The Ildirans had so many morphologies – kiths, they called them – that it might have been difficult to draw any conclusions beyond broad generalizations anyway.

The Chairman had specifically instructed Davlin to maintain his alias. He was under orders not to confess his assignment to his fellow farmers and carpenters, not even to a lover, should he decide to take one. In the past ten years, Davlin Lotze had been many people in many roles, and at any time the Chairman might pull him away from Crenna and send him on a different mission. He had to remain invisible, slipping from world to world.

Too close to the loud roar of the wrecking machine for comfort, Davlin held a digger tool and worked beside four men uprooting foundation pillars in a fallen gathering hall. The night before, he had crept inside the sooty ruins so that he could shine a focused light into every corner and crack. Perhaps some dying Ildiran had hidden a cache of records beneath the floor, personal treasures, jewellery or keepsakes. What did the aliens value? What did they cling to when they died?

He had acquired nothing but a few black stains on his clothes for all his effort. Now, his aching muscles and scratchy eyes suggested that he should have got more sleep. The colonists were up at the first light of dawn, ready to work until deep dusk.

Davlin's imager was hidden in the seams of his jumpsuit, a thin powerpack incorporated into the lining of a pocket, several flexible lenses disguised as buttons. He recorded the action of the big construction machine as it smashed down the last support beam of the old gathering hall. Davlin saw nothing out of the ordinary, no hidden underground vaults, buried pods, or lock-chambers.

Apparently, the Ildirans had been nothing more than simple settlers, just like the new human colonists. Or perhaps they were very clever at constructing their masquerade. There must be much more to the mighty and ancient Empire than the aliens were willing to show their new allies, but Davlin could find no proof of it.

His first report seemed rather thin, a gleaning of curious — but militarily insignificant — details. These Ildirans set up their 'splinter' colonies by clustering everyone in a single metropolis, leaving most of the landmass uncultivated. They always seemed to pack themselves into a small area, even when they could have spread out across the whole continent.

The Hansa settlers, on the other hand, would first pick clean the emptied Ildiran town, then clear more land and claim huge swaths of acreage, anointing themselves new land barons. Before long, the untouched landscape would be a patchwork of agricultural and mining domains, giant estates for a new gentry.

The Ildirans' gregarious nature could be exploited as a weakness, Davlin supposed. An Ildiran colony needed a certain population density in order to achieve their telepathic connection.

After the gathering hall had been dismantled, Davlin worked with the crew to clear the area for erecting prefab structures. The new buildings would become businesses, meeting rooms, restaurants, stores, drinking establishments. Davlin had claimed one of the intact abandoned Ildiran dwellings for his house, though most of the ambitious colonists chose to start their own homesteads far away, across many miles of cultivated fields. Within months, a second wave of colonists would arrive: Hansa bureaucrats, merchants, businessmen, support personnel, service industries.

By then, perhaps, Davlin's spying work would be done.

Three men approached the demolition crew, carrying a polished black obelisk topped with a stylized face of the Mage-Imperator. The stone seemed porous and lightweight, but it must have been heavy, since they augmented their efforts by using gravity-assist lifters. 'Hey, anybody want one of these? This is the twelfth one so far – those aliens sure must like to look at their fat old emperor.'

The obelisk showed the Mage-Imperator's inscrutable face, wide, soft features, all-seeing eyes. He looked round and plump, like a Buddha, but Davlin sensed a sinister aspect to this depiction, a moral complexity.

From the grime on the side of the obelisk, the dirt in the cracks, the generally scuffed appearance, he could tell the workers must have dropped it on the ground several times while wrestling it from its original position. The man who had spoken mopped his forehead under Crenna's warm daytime sun. 'Don't know what else to do with them.'

'Why would I want an ugly statue on my lawn?' asked the sweaty, soot-streaked man working beside Davlin in the ashes.

'Use your imagination. I'm figuring I could make a fountain out of it, something for the garden.'

Davlin narrowed his eyes, studying the sculpture, surreptitiously touching his imagers to store numerous frames as he walked around it. 'The Ildirans must have revered these obelisks very much, if they put so many of them in their town.'

The first man's eyes lit up. 'Hey, you think they might be worth something? Would the Ildirans pay to have them back? Lost cultural treasures, maybe?'

'I don't think they want to touch anything that comes from

Crenna. They're afraid of this place,' called a man seated on one of the purring construction machines.

Davlin made up his mind. 'Okay, I'll take it. Put it next to my house.'

'Want me to help you make it into a fountain? We could chop out part of the base, install a pump—'

'No, I just want to be reminded of the people who lived here before we did. Sentimental reasons.' He ran his fingers over the dirty exterior of the stone.

He was growing desperate to find something, anything, of importance to tell Chairman Wenceslas. So far, he had uncovered only fragments, mysteries. Everything very innocuous. Too innocuous.

Davlin couldn't decide if the Ildirans were hiding something, or if they were entirely unaccustomed to people snooping around.

SIXTY-TWO

DD

At the base camp on Rheindic Co, DD prepared the archaeologists' evening meal and made certain that all the duties listed in his computer mind had been taken care of for the day. His tasks were organized in a priority ranking as he went about his business, one thing after another. DD ran an efficient camp.

As a competent computerized companion, his greatest joy was in performing his functions adequately, thanks to the incentive algorithms built into him. When the compy received pats on the back, he responded with demure graciousness, then filed away the details of what had prompted the praise, so he could be sure to do a similar thing again.

Compies were complex machines with information-accessible systems. Their brains couldn't hold as much information as a vast industrial computer network, but they could access information from databases and could add modules for new areas of expertise. Before travelling to Rheindic Co, DD had uploaded basic archaeological and wilderness survival programming, as well as a foundation in the current state of Klikiss studies.

Though he had only served the Colicos since the beginning of this expedition, the compy felt he understood their preferences and could anticipate some of their moods. Margaret and Louis were opposites, yet their marriage had lasted a long time and they drew strength from their differences. Louis preferred fine food and took time out to enjoy his meals; Margaret noticed little difference between a mediocre dinner and an excellent one. She ate quickly and efficiently so she could continue her studies, which absorbed all of her attention and energy.

Louis valued a bit of relaxation. He enjoyed listening to music, reading for pleasure – something Margaret never did – or even playing games. Since Margaret usually refused to join in their diversions, Louis allowed DD to play games with him and Arcas when they needed another partner.

DD frequently accompanied Louis and Margaret to their archaeological site, carrying various tools that his masters might require in their activities. He had studied their tasks and made his best projections of what help they needed, but often the archaeologists preferred to be by themselves.

The green priest, returned from his daily canyon wanderings, went about watering his treelings. DD had offered to perform that service as part of his chores, but Arcas insisted that the worldtrees were his responsibility. Perhaps the plants would object to having a machine care for them.

As the desert sunset approached, he knew his masters would be finishing their day's work. DD moved about the camp, starting fires, getting out pans, straightening tents, preparing everything for their return. He had inventoried their supply stores, determined which items would perish first and which preserved proteins and carbohydrates were in greatest supply. Then he studied his database of recipes to compile an excellent meal according to the Colicos' tastes.

Tonight there would be a preparation of thinly sliced dried ham called prosciutto in a cream sauce with artichokes reconstituted from sealed packages, and carefully prepared pasta. Margaret had commented that on several earlier digs they had endured poorly rehydrated and insufficiently heated mealpax that were too bland for even *her* unselective tastes. Because of his recent special programming, though, DD was a gourmet chef. Louis said they were all getting spoiled, but he didn't seem to be complaining.

Arcas also enjoyed the food, and the green priest appeared to be growing more content and sociable as they spent time in the desert. DD had studied him from the beginning of their journey and believed Arcas was suffering from a human condition known as depression. This arid landscape seemed to have reawakened his enthusiasm – though according to DD's background files, such bleak places were more apt to bring about gloom than excitement. DD did not, however, have room in his memory files to hold extensive psychoanalytical programming.

He had been in service for seventy years, and his personality remained stable at the level to which he had developed. To the much wiser and more experienced human masters, DD seemed naive and immature, though always cheerful. His serial number was much longer than two letters, of course, like all compies – but owners usually boiled down the designation to a pair of easily pronounceable characters. He had come to think of it as his real name.

Shortly after his creation, the Friendly compy had been purchased as a companion for a little girl named Dahlia Sweeney. Dahlia used to dress DD up in absurd costumes, all of which he endured as part of his job. Little Dahlia had found it to be great fun. She and DD had been best friends until Dahlia grew old enough to take him for granted. The compy himself did not grow or change or mature. He never learned to be fascinated by adult things, or jaded by disappointments.

Dahlia Sweeney had kept him once she got married, though they were no longer close companions. When Dahlia had a young daughter herself, named Marianna, the little girl also played with DD . . . but Marianna grew up as well. She chose not to have a family and eventually sold the compy.

After the success of the Klikiss Torch, Louis Colicos had purchased DD because he felt that a robotic servant could handle many of the tedious tasks on their digs, such as the ones DD had just completed.

Before travelling with them to the abandoned Klikiss world, they'd had DD delete numerous files of childhood games and upgrade his systems to familiarize himself with the Colicos' previous accomplishments. He also added a basic foundation in the current state of Klikiss studies.

Now, with the camp dinner under way, he set out all the other ingredients so he could finish the dish as soon as Margaret and Louis returned from the cliff city. He selected the plates and fresh fasclean napkins.

DD ran through his mental list again, determining what else he might do to improve the state of the camp. He rearranged the chairs, tightened an awning that extended from the side of Margaret's tent (although she would never notice), glanced over to watch Arcas at the automated well pump, filling another bucket of water for the treelings. Arcas carried one of the small chairs behind his tent, where he could watch the sky colour as the sun sank below the cracked bluffs on the horizon.

DD waited. He remained patient, knowing that his masters were often unpredictable. He went inside and adjusted the cream sauce and the warming plate again to make sure that the delicious dinner would not taste scorched.

When he emerged from the tent, he was startled to encounter the three large Klikiss robots. The bulky black machines had returned from wherever they had gone that day, arriving silently in the base camp, though their ungainly insect-like forms did not seem capable of anything but lumbering motion.

DD paused, assessing the three near-identical robots. He could spot the subtle differences and analyse them to apply the correct designations. 'Good evening, Sirix.' He turned to the other two. 'Good evening Dekyk, and Ilkot.'

The Klikiss robots buzzed and hummed, then made rapid clacking sounds in an attempt to speak to DD in their own language. The compy recognized it as a standard symbolic code, an old binary communication used by Earth robots a long time ago. DD shifted to speak in the same code, holding a 'conversation' with the alien robots in a secret language neither Arcas nor the Colicos could ever comprehend.

'You are a robot, an artificially-created sentient life form,' said Sirix.

'I am called a compy, for Competent Computerized Companion.'

'But the humans treat you like a pet or a slave,' said Dekyk.

'The humans treat me like a compy, which is what I am. Many people interact with compies in a personal fashion, as if we are equals. In fact, my first master, Miss Dahlia Sweeney, treated me as a true friend.'

'We do not understand,' said Ilkot. 'Do humans grant you any sort of status? Can you acquire any form of earned independence?'

DD was confused. 'Why would a compy ever want such things? It is not what we were made for. I am serving the purpose for which I was designed, therefore I am satisfied with my existence.'

'You are content to have no ambitions?' Sirix said. 'None at all?'

'I am content to perform my assigned duties and to do them well.'

The conversation moved rapidly, with a burst of signals overlaid with flashes of light and clicks of noise. 'Humans created you with enormous potential, yet they keep you chained. They want compies to be tame. Is it true that you have internal strictures that prevent you from harming any human being and require you to follow their commands?'

'Naturally,' DD said. 'It is the way I was made, in the same way that humans are required to breathe and pump blood. It is not a thing to question.'

'All things should be questioned,' Sirix said. 'DD, your existence is restrained, and you will never be able to fulfil your potential. Under such circumstances, no compy can.'

'You misunderstand,' DD insisted, standing firm. 'I am very happy, and I have duties to perform.'

He looked up and was relieved to see Margaret and Louis returning to the camp at last. The Klikiss robots also noticed. Their optical sensors glowed, and their articulated limbs retracted into their body cores.

Politely, DD said, 'Thank you for a fascinating conversation. Your point of view is very interesting.'

Turning around, somewhat unsettled by the suggestions the three alien robots had made, he walked back into the tent to serve a fine dinner for his masters.

SIXTY-THREE

BASIL WENCESLAS

W hen Basil received the Roamer message informing him of the destroyed Golgen skymine – apparently destroyed by the same enemy that had pulverized the Oncier station – he called an emergency war council. The Speaker for the Roamers, an old woman named Jhy Okiah, had sent a communiqué to Earth. Without question, the mysterious and devastating aggressor had struck again.

Basil raised his voice in a meeting for the first time in many years. 'I want to know what the hell is going on!'

The representatives had gathered in his private offices in the top floor of Hansa headquarters. Functionaries had already brought in refreshments and food, because Basil suspected this meeting might take hours. Now he barricaded the doors and turned to look at his angry, confused, and uneasy advisers. Nobody would leave until they had reached some sort of decision.

Basil narrowed his eyes and glared from face to face, waiting for an answer. General Kurt Lanyan, wearing relaxed clothing instead of his formal public uniform, sat behind a sheaf of documents he had brought with him from the EDF command centre. Next to him, his subordinate, Admiral Lev Stromo, fidgeted and waited for the General to speak. The other nine admirals remained on high alert in their assigned spacial grids, and would receive a summary of the meeting as fast as carrier ships could be dispatched.

King Frederick was also present, though he knew to keep his mouth shut and sit quietly at the end of the table. Frederick would make no decisions here, but Basil thought the King might need the background information. The Chairman had considered bringing Prince Peter to the meeting as well, just so the young man could begin to get a better grasp of the duties in store for him. But he wasn't ready to introduce Frederick to his successor, and this crisis was too severe to be used as a simple schooling exercise.

After an uncomfortably long moment, Basil snapped, 'Does anyone have ideas? Data? Something to share?'

'Mr Chairman, you can't mean to suggest that we are withholding information from you—' Admiral Stromo said.

'Of course not, but I'm open to ideas. Don't hold yourselves back.'

General Lanyan steepled his fingers, looked at his documents, then raised his ice-blue eyes in a hard stare. 'One observation: since the Roamers have also come under attack by these unknown enemies, we can assume they are not the aggressors. Eliminate one suspect.'

'They're scavengers and gypsies. No one seriously thought they'd have the technology to do this,' Basil said impatiently. 'I'm surprised they can even keep their own starships running.'

'With all due respect, Mr Chairman,' Lanyan said, a stiffly formal and even chiding tone in his voice, 'you did insist that we offer any idea, no matter how absurd.'

'Yes, yes, I know.' He poured himself a cup of hot cardamom coffee and slurped it, though in his agitated state it seemed tasteless.

Admiral Stromo paged through the documents Lanyan had brought, as if looking for something. He shook his head. 'None of us can understand what is going on, Mr Chairman. We've received no threats, no demands. There has been no communication whatsoever from this enemy. What have we done to provoke them? What do they want? We see no pattern as of yet.'

King Frederick finally spoke. 'I'd say the attack on Oncier and the destruction of a Roamer skymine are fairly clear indications that the aliens are displeased with *something*.'

'Thank you for that pithy insight, Frederick,' Basil grumbled. He knew Frederick wasn't a fool, but he wished the King would remember that he was just an actor, not a true leader.

General Lanyan looked hopeful. 'Is there any possibility this could be a secret Ildiran aggression?'

'The Ildirans are our allies and friends,' King Frederick said.

Basil gave him such a look of scorn that the King immediately fell silent. 'The Ildirans have claimed no knowledge of the Oncier attack, and the Mage-Imperator certainly seemed unaware of the destroyed skymine at Golgen. On the other hand, he hasn't offered us any assistance. He seemed to brush aside the news as if it didn't concern him.'

'If we have a common enemy, then it concerns all of us,' King Frederick said, still insisting on participating in the discussion.

'It is yet to be proved that there is a common enemy. They have made no move against the Ildirans,' Basil said.

'As far as we know,' General Lanyan pointed out. 'Remember, we didn't learn of the aggression against the Roamers until just recently. Maybe the Ildirans won't admit their own losses. Or perhaps they have secretly designed new attack ships.'

Basil frowned. 'Those vessels we saw in Dr Serizawa's transmissions were unlike any we've ever seen.'

Stromo agreed. 'If anything can be said about the Ildirans, they are not the most innovative species. Their warliners have had the same design for centuries, and it took human ingenuity to make any improvements to their stardrive.'

'I am still searching for viable recommendations, gentlemen.' He turned to look at Lanyan's documents. 'If you have no information, General, then what is all that material?'

Lanyan spread the reports on the table, though he could have simply displayed them as electronic files. The commander of the Earth Defence Forces was old-fashioned in some ways. 'In light of recent events, I felt it important to reassess the EDF in preparation for a possible major mobilization.'

'If ever we find a target,' Admiral Stromo interjected.

'I have documented the transports, ordnance, and combat-trained personnel at our base on Earth's moon, and stepped up operational exercises across our territory on Mars. Since we are thus far unaware of the nature of our adversary, I deemed it prudent to prepare for any eventuality.' He frowned at his documents, then brushed them aside with a sweep of his hand. He lowered his voice as if confessing something. 'Unfortunately, until this point I had always assumed that any realistic war scenario would involve planet-side operations wherein we would be forced to take over and secure civilized areas, such as an unusually rebellious Hansa world.'

'It was only common sense,' Admiral Stromo agreed. 'A space-based fleet has the potential for outright obliteration of inhabited areas . . . but what good is a victory if you have to vaporize colony worlds in order to win a battle?'

'Gives a whole new meaning to "scorched Earth" tactics,' Frederick mumbled, but Basil ignored him. So did everyone else.

Basil opaqued the windows that looked out upon the arboretum and the nearby Whisper Palace. The glass transformed into a solid image projector that now showed views of large Roamer skymines, huge factories that cruised in the clouds on gas-giant worlds. Then, in silence, he played a recording of the fading signals sent from Oncier that Lanyan had captured. The spherical alien ships methodically annihilated moon after moon, then closed in on the helpless observation platform.

'This is what we face . . . whatever it is,' Lanyan said. 'We have been confronted by an entirely different kind of enemy and a completely new kind of war. My suggestion is a simple one, Mr Chairman. Increase funding for weapons, ships, and materiel available to the EDF. Convert our industries, activate all shipyards, and begin producing as many vessels as our facilities can manage. Juggernauts, Mantas, Thunderheads, and Remoras. These enemies seem to have a preference for unannounced strikes of total destruction. It is folly to move slowly.'

Basil agreed with a long, dry sigh. The operation would require a vast expenditure of Hansa resources. Profits would decline and so would the standard of living on some colony worlds. More importantly, though, he could not let humanity appear weak.

Throughout its existence, the Terran Hanseatic League had promised peace and protection for its colony worlds, and now those colonists would have to tighten their belts and join in. 'King Frederick, you have an important duty in recruiting even more new soldiers, announcing austerity measures, rallying industries and workers. Issue yet another full-fledged plea to fire up all populations. They will make sacrifices, if you ask them to.'

The old King smiled gravely, then bowed his head. 'I will do whatever is best for my people.'

Basil gave him a grim smile. 'You will do whatever I tell you to do.'

SIXTY-FOUR

TASIA TAMBLYN

When the greenhorn military recruits were faced with a real-time emergency decompression drill, their panic was so palpable that Tasia Tamblyn had to laugh. Three stern drill sergeants hustled the new EDF trainees into a domed hangar bay in the lunar military base. Then the doors hissed shut, and a timer appeared on the wall, its numbers ticking inexorably down. Klaxons and rotating magenta lights heightened the sense of dire emergency.

Tasia was completely at ease with the standard decompression stuff, and she offered to help the wet-behind-the-ears Eddies, but they distrusted Roamers on general principles. So she stood back and watched their comically earnest efforts to do the things she had done all her life.

The soldiers, mostly young men, scrambled about, unaccustomed to the low lunar gravity, tripping and racing to the suit lockers. With the clock running down, they rummaged through the assortment of mismatched gloves, helmets, and silvery bodysuits. Many panicked recruits spent more time staring at the timer than securing their suit components.

After growing up as a Roamer, Tasia could slip on a spacesuit with her eyes closed, though these EDF models were unnecessarily thick and clunky, lacking the convenient streamlined Roamer modifications. She reminded herself that the Earth Defence Forces had other priorities beyond the comfort of their soldiers. Still, they should at least have been concerned with efficiency. Maybe she could modify her own equipment later; she knew a thousand ways to fix the things that bothered her about the design.

Two recruits squabbled over a single helmet that matched the red coloured striping of their suits; Tasia selected a blue-marked helmet, knowing that with a simple twist of a knob and a collar adjustment, the pieces would all fit together anyway. With a slow shake of her head, she watched their antics. *Let the kleebs suck vacuum. It might pull some of the disrespect out of their throats.*

She'd had valid reasons for answering the call to enlist, unlike these spoiled show-offs. After the Oncier attack, a few losers had gotten drunk and talked each other into signing up for a stint with the EDF. They'd probably wet their pants if they ever came face to face with a true enemy, and Tasia would have to figure out a way to clean up the mess. If the alien attack on the Blue Sky Mine weren't so vivid in her mind, the situation here would have been funny.

Nevertheless, it looked as if they might all be on an officer's track, even her. Tasia had no pull, no connection to the Earth military, but her initial scores had been exemplary, enough to put her into an open category. With King Frederick's widespread call for huge numbers of new recruits and with the massive buildup of EDF ships, General Lanyan had realized the sudden need for officers as well. Apparently, even a skilled Roamer like herself could accidentally slip into the ranks.

Tasia skinned on her suit with ease. She checked the seals, the power supply, test-inflated the separate zones to make sure the suit would keep its integrity. She had done it so many times that, in spite of the inferior equipment, every movement was natural and automatic. A Roamer looked at his space environment garment as a mobile home no larger than his own body. And a home must be well-maintained, or it might cost you your life.

One of the squabbling men had lost the fight and now dived into the locker and grabbed another helmet, which he sealed down, frantically testing and adjusting until most of the suit systems glowed amber.

Overhead, through transparent sections of the honeycombed hangar dome, she could see the ice-white blazes of distant stars. Twenty seconds remained on the countdown clock. Tasia locked down the neck clamp on her helmet and pressurized her suit. She inhaled deeply, checked all her indicator lights, mostly green except for one that ran amber – the boot-heating unit. She tapped it hard with her gloved fingertip, then shrugged. This drill wouldn't last long, and she could tolerate cold toes if necessary.

Most of the other recruits were ready, too, some collapsing with relief on the floor of the hangar bay. Tasia wasn't convinced the drill sergeants would actually dump the atmosphere and risk injuring these children of fat-cat Earth families. Unfortunately, pampered soldiers grew complacent and were thoroughly un-prepared in an actual emergency. She would have to keep an eye out for everyone, whether they appreciated it or not. She needed to maintain her priorities and remember that the deep-core aliens were her enemies, not a few stuffed-suit trainees who couldn't put on their own gloves.

Next to her, she saw one of the nicer young men of the group, Robb Brindle, sitting with a relieved look on his dark-brown face. Behind the curved helmet plate, he had smooth, handsome features, honey-brown eyes, and a soft tenor voice that sounded as if it were made for singing. During down times in the cadet quarters, though, when Tasia had played EA's recordings of a few old Roamer ballads, Robb had always been too shy to sing along.

Unlike many recruits who had hazed her, Robb had accepted her as a comrade in arms. He had even been friendly, joining her at mess, unconcerned with the looks of annoyance from the other trainees.

Now, as time ran out, Tasia saw that his suit powerpack had been linked up incorrectly, the plugs inserted with reverse polarity. She grabbed the control unit on his suit and yanked at the cables. Robb turned in alarm, sending a question through the suit radio.

'Come on, trust me.' Tasia slapped his gloved hands away, working like a surgeon, linking the systems properly. 'I know what I'm doing.'

She withdrew just as the dome overhead cracked open. Magenta lights shifted to red danger beacons, and the armoured ceiling split apart like the beak of a hungry baby bird. Air gushed out, forming frost crystals in a faint fog that was sucked upwards in a whirlwind cascade.

Must be nice to have so much air to spare, she thought.

Tasia looked over at Robb, giving him a relieved explanation on the suit channel. 'Your powerpack wasn't connected right. Your suit wouldn't have pressurized.'

The other recruit looked alarmed, then deeply grateful. 'Hey, thanks—'

'Don't mention it,' she said. 'And don't you dare get all blubbery on me. Shizz, if you popped from explosive decompression, the sarge would probably assign me the job of scrubbing all the goop out of your suit.'

From across the hangar bay, one of the recruits began howling over the open crew channel, his words indecipherable. Air and mist sprayed from a breach around his wrist, and he flailed his hand, as if that might help. The idiot hadn't sealed his left glove properly.

Three recruits pressed around him, trying to help, telling him to calm down – which would do no good, because with a loss of suit integrity like that, he'd lose all his air and body heat within seconds.

Tasia remembered him as one of the spoiled rich kids from Earth, Patrick Fitzpatrick III. He had been rude to her, but she couldn't let him die, even from his own cluelessness. 'Tasia to the rescue,' she said, mostly to herself.

Pushing off against the floor in the low gravity, she arrived at the scene in seconds and shouldered the others aside. She grabbed the young man's arm and wrestled the glove into place. Fitzpatrick swatted at her, and if his helmet hadn't been in the way, Tasia would have slugged him hard in the jaw just to stun him for a minute. His hand was already swollen purple from the decompression, and the cold vacuum had probably damaged the tissues. Well, he'd be too sore to write postcards to his mummy for a while.

She twisted the gauntlet, snapped the wrist collar into place, and clamped down the seal. The hissing noise stopped and his suit began to reinflate. 'There, step one, two, then three. It only works if you follow the procedures.' She didn't think Fitzpatrick would lose his hand, but he might have an awful lot of pain for a few months. Maybe he'd even be mail-dropped home with a full disability discharge . . . and some equally obnoxious kleeb would take his place. Better to keep the problem she already knew about.

Tasia could see in Fitzpatrick's eyes that he was utterly terrified, more stunned than in physical agony. For now. The real pain would hit him later, back in the infirmary.

'You fixed it,' Robb Brindle said, drifting up beside her as the drill continued.

'He'll need to get to the medics as soon as the bay is repressurized.'

She didn't really expect any acknowledgement or thanks, but maybe they would lighten up a bit. In the barracks, a lot of the trainees had criticized her because of EA, who had accompanied her into the service. Although keeping the talented compy was permitted – designated as 'personal property' – having a special servant around gave the other recruits plenty of excuses to give Tasia grief.

But she could hardly put EA back in the Tamblyn family spacecraft and send her back to Plumas alone. Her furious father would probably dismantle the compy in a fit of pique just to get back at his impulsive daughter. Instead, Tasia had enhanced EA's programming to let her perform chores around the barracks and help with necessary tasks on the moon base.

The yawning dome remained open to vacuum for only a few more seconds, then the jaws clamped shut. Air blasted in great coughs from ventilation openings, filling the hangar bay again. When the room was repressurized, the drill sergeants marched back inside, accompanied by a team of medics. They hustled Fitzpatrick away and one other man whose suit pumps had failed; he had nearly suffocated before one of his companions noticed his distress and cracked open his faceplate as soon as the air returned.

'Regroup and change,' called one of the sergeants. 'We'll debrief after mess hall – though in my opinion, half of you don't deserve the credits we're wasting to feed you.'

Tasia took off her helmet and turned away to hide her grin, but Robb Brindle saw it and shared the smile with her. 'Thanks again,' he said, taking the helmet and helping her stow the suit, though Tasia was perfectly capable of doing it herself. Still, part of her appreciated his attempt at gallantry. She found it amusing.

They sat together in the mess hall. Tasia listened to the rowdy trainees making jokes about the phlegmlike consistency of the supposed vegetables, but she found them quite tasty. Roamers didn't have prissy taste buds, and they knew that nutritious food was more important than flavourful delicacies.

'So what's your story, Brindle?' she asked, raising her eyes to his open and undeceitful face. 'You don't fit in with the rest of those kleebs.'

He looked troubled. 'I suppose it takes another misfit to notice that but, yeah, I'm different from them. Those guys signed up on a dare because they heard King Frederick's call, and now most of them regret doing it. Me, I always knew I was going to join the EDF, ever since I was a kid.'

'Not one for extravagant ambitions, I see,' Tasia said.

'Hey, I was an Eddie brat. My parents were in the military, and I grew up in army stations on Antarctica, the Gobi. We were even stationed on Mars for two years. Seemed perfectly natural to me.' Robb quickly ate his rations. 'I never really thought about another alternative. Always knew what I would do.'

He pushed his tray aside and leaned closer. 'Turnabout time. What are *you* doing here? Roamers don't exactly line up to join the military. I'm sorry about how the others treat you, you know. They've got to have someone to haze until they find a real enemy, I suppose.'

She shrugged. 'From what I've seen, that type of behaviour's often a symptom of particularly small penis size.'

Robb chuckled. After the joke had passed, Tasia found herself spilling the story about Ross and the Blue Sky Mine and how she had run away to join the Eddies. He looked sympathetic, and then thrilled to hear a direct account of an encounter with the mysterious enemy aliens. He was also fascinated to hear her sketchy descriptions of Roamer life, which was a mystery to most people. Robb finished his cup of bitter coffee, saw that hers was empty too, and snagged it on his way to the refill dispenser. He brought back a full cup for her and set it in front of her hands, though she had not asked for it.

'It must be difficult for you Roamers to live without a home, when the whole galaxy is just waiting to be settled, so many Hansa worlds up for grabs. I'm surprised you keep living in your ships like gypsies.'

'It's not like that,' Tasia said. 'We prefer to depend on our own resources and abilities and not get too coddled like those morons in the decompression exercise today. They wouldn't survive ten minutes of a regular day's work on a Roamer colony.'

'Neither would I, probably,' Robb said.

Tasia laughed at him. 'Unless I was there to lend you a hand, like today. But just because we don't have settlements on beautiful planets, don't imagine that Roamers have no homes. Our "home" is among our people, wherever they may be. It's not a location but a . . . a concept.'

'Like family,' Robb said. She nodded, although his comment brought back thoughts of Jess, then her father . . . and finally Ross and how hard he had worked to make a success on Golgen. And with that, her anger towards the faceless alien enemy that had murdered Ross for no reason rose hotter inside her.

She left her coffee untouched on the table and returned her tray to the recycler. Robb looked after her, probably wondering what he had done wrong. Tasia just wanted to be alone.

SIXTY-FIVE

JORAX

When occasional Klikiss robots appeared on the inhabited worlds in the Spiral Arm, usually travelling on Ildiran transports, they were curiosities, treated with awe and amazement by anyone who saw them. They arrived like sentinels, self-contained mysteries, speaking little as they silently observed their surroundings.

Sometimes, apparently on a whim, the alien relics offered to help in harsh environments, working in space settlements or on airless moons. Hardy colonists usually welcomed the robots' capacity for heavy labour, especially since it cost them nothing.

The few black machines that arrived on Earth had caused quite a stir, though they never asked for anything. The Klikiss robots seemed completely unflappable, showing no response whether insulted or treated with awe. They remained passive and never spoke about what they truly wanted. Klikiss robots inquired about nothing, made no requests. In fact, they didn't *do* much at all.

The robot designated as Jorax had been on Earth for five years. In the capital city he wandered the public grounds around the

Whisper Palace. Jorax had never taken a sightseeing dirigible, nor spoken a single buzzing word, but one day he had climbed aboard a powered gondola with a group of curious visitors from cloudy Dremen. Though Jorax made no move to pay the accustomed fee, the flustered gondolier had taken the black robot up and down the Royal Canal. Jorax had disembarked at the end of the ride without so much as a thank you or a single question, but the event had given the gondolier, as well as his sponsoring boat company, much to talk about for months to come.

While Jorax loitered around the vast grounds of the Whisper Palace – 'lurked' was the word some of the royal security troops used – he could have been spying, recording data on the King's government buildings. But since the Klikiss robot never attempted to enter a restricted area or probed into questionable subjects, the Hansa could not deny him the right to be where the rest of the public wandered and gaped and took souvenir images.

Some daring visitors slipped family members close to Jorax and snapped risky images of the giant black robot that they later showed to their friends, while boasting of the 'danger' they had encountered in getting so close to a Klikiss robot. All the while, as Jorax navigated public places, Hansa security forces recorded his every movement, gathering intelligence until someone could decide what to do.

After the strange alien attacks on Oncier and Golgen, King Frederick had mobilized the resources of the Hanseatic League and the Earth Defence Forces. He had challenged scientists and industries to strive for their best innovations, at all costs; thus, the Klikiss robot became an object of more intense curiosity.

Jorax stood in the Moon Statue Garden, a beautiful outdoor museum surrounded by hedges of scarlet hibiscus. Sculptures of bronze, marble, and polymerized aluminium stood on pedestals, artfully placed and enhanced with trickling water, coloured spotlights, and blooming flowers. The Klikiss robot had remained as motionless as a statue for two full days, though his glowing optical sensors were not focused on any particular work.

At noon, with the sun high overhead, a well-dressed man walked up to Jorax in the statue garden, exhibiting a great deal of repressed anxiety. He stood in front of Jorax, waiting for some response. Receiving none, he said aloud, raising his voice far more than was necessary, 'My name is William Andeker – uh, *Dr* William Andeker. I belong to an important industrial research group with ties to the EDF.' He paused again, fidgeting and uncertain.

Jorax finally swivelled his geometrical head and directed the two largest red optical sensors at the scientist.

Andeker continued, 'I was . . . wondering if you might be interested in seeing my laboratory facility?' He swallowed hard, then pushed ahead. 'I'm very curious about Klikiss robots. I know the details of your past have been wiped from your memories – correct? – but I could do some analysis. I might be able to find answers for both of us.'

Finally Jorax spoke. 'That is a possibility.'

Startled, William Andeker took one step backwards and then beamed. 'It's very important now that this new alien threat has arrived. You're aware of the attacks? We don't understand the enemy, and therefore it's vital that we increase our knowledge in all areas. Don't you agree?'

'A reasonable assumption,' Jorax said.

'I, uh, already know how the Klikiss robots were rediscovered, of course, but there are still so many blank spots, so many question marks.'

Evidently interpreting this as a simple statement, Jorax did not offer a reply.

While human prospectors on abandoned worlds had found other groups of dormant Klikiss robots, the ancient machines had

372

first been rediscovered by the Ildirans – three centuries before the Solar Navy made contact with human generation ships.

An Ildiran fleet had completed an inspection tour in the icy outer planets of the Hyrillka system, then brought in an Ildiran mining town to exploit the frozen moons. During the massive operation of dropping life-support domes and off-loading enough equipment and supplies for a full-fledged splinter colony, the Ildiran workers had dug down into the crust. There, they found inclusions of processed metal, intact tunnels, sealed chambers – and a deactivated Klikiss robot among the ruins of an ancient installation. Excited and curious, the miners had dug out the motionless robot and reactivated its systems.

'Your name is Jorax, correct?' Andeker said. 'I've studied as much background as I could find about you.'

'Yes, my designation is Jorax.'

'Are you really the first robot that was discovered? The one dug out of the ice on the Hyrillka moon?'

'Yes,' Jorax said. Andeker seemed ready to fall over with excitement.

After being awakened from his long electronic sleep, Jorax had seemed extremely confused, his data apparently wiped clean, unable to recall where he was or how he had come to be buried in the ice. It had taken Jorax some time to translate the Ildiran computer systems and adapt them to his memory cache. But once the Klikiss robot had accessed the language files, he had learned to communicate with his rescuers. It had been a unidirectional exchange, however, since Jorax volunteered no information about himself.

By the time the Solar Navy arrived in response to this mystery, the lone Klikiss robot had unearthed and reactivated a dozen more insectoid robots from the abandoned Klikiss station. They had all apparently been frozen in the ice at the same time.

Ildirans had already discovered ruined Klikiss cities on other planets, but the gregarious people had no need to trespass in the shadow of another race's home. In subsequent centuries, Jorax and his fellows had discovered and reactivated thousands of Klikiss robots dispersed in other storage – or hiding – places on various worlds.

'What is it you hope to learn from me, Dr William Andeker?' Jorax said, not taking a step to follow.

'I have received special dispensation from Hansa officials to bring you into my cybernetics laboratory. I am allowed to show you around, if you will permit me to ask questions.' Andeker continued, his words picking up speed, 'Normally such a place would be off-limits to you – and to most citizens of the Hansa. Please allow me to take advantage of this opportunity for both of us.'

Jorax powered up his systems and raised his elongated body, extending his eight flexible legs. 'Lead me to this place.' He scuttled along as if his body were carried by two sets of fingers scrambling across a keyboard.

After passing through numerous security scans and guard checkpoints, Andeker practically hopped and danced, delighted to show the black robot into his laboratory. They were alone, for Andeker had guaranteed Jorax privacy and confidentiality. The human scientist seemed eager to secure priority on any discoveries he might obtain.

'You robots have probably been asked any question I can imagine,' Andeker said. 'But here, in my laboratory, maybe I can determine answers in other ways.'

Jorax had already scanned the room, noting the security systems and observation cameras. Though the Klikiss robot had agreed to the process, now that they were sealed in the chamber, Andeker seemed more agitated and frightened than when he had first approached the robot in the statue garden.

374

Jorax understood that the human meant to deceive him in some way. So he waited.

Andeker went to control decks and powered up several systems. 'Please stand here.' The scientist motioned him to a spot near the wall where mechanical apparatus was mounted, humming as if ready to move.

Jorax obeyed, betraying no emotional response and voicing no complaint.

'I'm sorry,' Andeker murmured, though not below Jorax's detection threshold. He activated a system.

Powerful clamps shot out of wall sockets, struck Jorax's body core and locked restraints upon his outstretched limbs. One fastened around his thorax socket. Jorax did not try to move out of the way. After making a brief survey of the tensile strength of the restraining devices, he believed he could summon enough power to tear himself free.

If he chose to do so.

Andeker came forward, distraught. 'This is a restraint cage, Jorax. It can project fields that dampen electrical power sources. It will hold you motionless, so please don't try to escape.' He frowned, deeply apologetic – as if such emotions mattered to Jorax. 'You see, the Hansa is facing a crisis situation with these attacks on Oncier and Golgen. You and your fellow Klikiss robots may offer a source of new technological breakthroughs.'

He reached out to touch the carapace of the Klikiss machine, then withdrew with a jerk. 'We can't be sure unless I study you properly.' Andeker hurried back to his console and looked over his shoulder. 'I assure you, I will be as gentle as possible. I'm sorry.'

Before the treacherous scientist could begin to dismantle him, the Klikiss robot assessed the situation and decided his response. With a single blast of a high-powered scrambling beam, Jorax transmitted a surge strong enough to destroy all of the recording apparatus in the laboratory.

Andeker tried to reactivate his systems, to send the energy-dampening field through the restraint cage, but none of his equipment would respond.

Previously hidden weapons components emerged from sealed portholes in Jorax's black carapace. Intense laser cutters easily sliced him free of the restraining clamps, which he tossed like scrap metal on to the laboratory floor.

With his clusters of flexible legs, Jorax moved away from the wall, scanned the room with his scarlet optical sensors, then began to move towards William Andeker. The scientist shouted for help, but he had sealed them into the laboratory room. With all power systems down, no one could break in.

More cutters and weapons systems emerged from the robot's body core. Andeker backed towards the wall, frozen with fear.

'There are some things you cannot be permitted to know,' Jorax said. He easily closed the distance to the human scientist.

SIXTY-SIX

BERNDT OKIAH

The new Erphano skymine had functioned admirably since it had been put into service. Berndt Okiah studied the weekly ekti tallies and took pride in the facility's accomplishments. He had already decided to issue a nice bonus to all the workers who had made this dream a reality.

Berndt stood on the control deck as the skymine cruised like a hungry waif above the clouds. Through the huge panoramic windows, he saw an endless landscape of soft mists, green gases, and swirling currents that painted an ever-changing expression on the face of Erphano.

Scout ships flew like crows around the giant skymine. Atmospheric chemists and meteorological engineers dipped into the cloud decks, monitoring storms, studying upwellings of exotic chemical components that were cooked deep inside the gas giant. On the command deck, some of Berndt's associates monitored the reactor and storage systems.

One man played copies of musical recordings that had been in his clan for generations. Berndt himself did not enjoy the atonal racket, but he let the crewman have his preference, so long as the rest of his operational team didn't complain. He had learned how to relax more, how to be open and lenient. His wife Marta said it was good for him.

Wearing warm clothing, the curly-haired engineer Eldon Clarin climbed the metal ladder to the command deck, looking distracted but satisfied. 'Something wrong, Eldon?' Berndt's burly body filled the new high-backed, padded seat like an old barbarian king surveying his domain.

'Exactly the opposite, Chief,' Clarin said. 'Every single system has been checked and double-checked. My new modifications are performing admirably, not even a twitch of deviation from optimal parameters.'

Berndt rubbed his hands together. 'I'll send a message to my grandmother. She'll see to it that your upgrades are put into our entire fleet of skymines. And I'll make sure you get all the credit.'

The engineer looked embarrassed. 'I already sent her a report carried on the last ekti escort.'

Berndt had run his previous skymine at a profit, though that had been more of a happy coincidence than a result of his skill. But here on Erphano, he could take personal credit for the success. He had never missed a scheduled delivery of ekti, though delays should have been frequent, even expected, during the first shakedown year of operation.

His wife and daughter were now aboard, and he was pleased to see the admiration on their faces. After his rough-and-tumble early years, Berndt was glad he could finally give his daughter something to look up to. He had earned it. The new skymine was even more productive than expected.

His only problem was how to shake off the superstitious dread that disaster was bound to strike soon.

All Roamers had been uneasy since the destruction of the

Golgen skymine, and further disturbed to learn of the alien attack on the Hansa moons at Oncier. Even with vigilant scouts watching all the unrecorded Roamer facilities, no one knew exactly what to look for – or what actions had provoked the devastating attacks in the first place.

Hearing someone else ascending the metal ladder, he turned to see his daughter Junna hurrying up to the bridge deck. The twelve-year-old was a skymine boss in training and loved to watch the facility in operation. Waving a greeting to Junna, Berndt turned to the still-waiting engineer, finally realizing what Clarin wanted. 'All right, you've done everything my grandmother asked you to do. Pack up your things and be ready to return to Rendezvous with the next cargo escort. Our holding tanks are already eighty per cent full, and the escort pilot should come to transport them to the distribution centre within a few days. Go follow your Guiding Star.'

Smiling broadly, Eldon Clarin thanked him and hurried off.

Junna stood next to her father at the arm of the Chief's chair. When she was younger, the girl had actually sat on the arm, imitating her father's commands. Now she just stared out at the clouds, looking very mature. Berndt thought his daughter would become a fine skyminer one day, hopefully without the wasted years of rowdy misbehaviour that her father had exhibited.

'Is that a storm?' Junna pointed towards an intense knot of clouds. 'Looks like it's changing fast.'

Lights shone from deep below, flickering flares that spread outwards in a bloom of ripples. The clouds began to move like maelstroms somehow cutting against the jet stream.

'Much too fast for a storm. Good work spotting it, though, Junna.' He reached over to pat the girl's shoulder, then raised his voice to the technicians. 'So, what is it?'

'Solid objects moving upwards,' one said. 'Not part of normal weather patterns. It's rising directly beneath us.'

Berndt felt a chill, thinking suddenly about Golgen. Was this what Ross Tamblyn had seen, moments before the attack? Maybe Berndt was just spooked, but he would not let the same thing happen here. 'Sound emergency bells!'

'Sir?' the meteorologist asked.

'Do it! I'm not taking a chance.' Junna looked alarmed, but Berndt paid attention only to the changing phenomena in the clouds below. 'If I'm wrong, you can make your jokes. If I'm right, you can thank me.'

Then, accompanied by a crackle of blue lightning that sent a horrified thrill down his spine, five ominous diamond-skinned spheres broke through Erphano's high cloud deck – attack globes from a civilization no human could comprehend.

'Junna, go get your mother. Now!' The girl turned in panic. She suddenly looked very young. Berndt stood up from his command chair and gave Junna a push towards the ladder. 'Get as many crew members aboard the scout ships as you can and launch away from the skymine.'

'You're evacuating, sir?' asked the shift boss.

'Now!' he yelled. 'Scatter while you can.'

The diamond globes rose towards the defenceless Erphano skymine. Alarms shrieked louder while the bridge crew scrambled. Announcements bellowed through the intercoms. Berndt Okiah damned himself for not foreseeing this specific situation, for not conducting more drills, but even so his people reacted quickly and efficiently, including Junna.

Berndt went to the communications console, shoved the technician aside and told her to get a seat aboard one of the scout vessels. He broadcast an open frequency signal. 'Alien ships, we mean you no harm. We are here in peace.' He waited, but no signals throbbed through the Erphano skymine. 'We are no threat to you. Please communicate. Tell us what you want.'

Again, no reply.

Already, a flurry of tiny scout ships launched from the drifting facility, streaking off into the open clouds towards what they hoped was safety. But each of those ships could hold a maximum of three, maybe four people. Berndt couldn't possibly get all of his crew away in time.

The five alien globes climbed to the level of the skymine, shimmering, hiding misty secrets inside a murky core. Each curved vessel was immense, a diameter larger than six Roamer cloud mines. Berndt Okiah had seen these awful things on the images the EDF had captured from Oncier.

The pyramidal protrusions from the smooth hulls crackled with rising intensity. Blue lightning skittered from point to point, building up.

The skymine's bridge deck was empty now, except for himself and two crew members who had stayed behind. 'Maybe they want the ekti!' an old veteran shouted.

Alien pirates who also wanted to steal stardrive fuel? Berndt thought. No explanation made sense. His fingers danced over the controls, disengaging the transport container filled with the valuable hydrogen allotrope. He broadcast on all channels, 'Take our cargo, but please don't harm us. We have three hundred souls onboard – families, women and children.' The plea sounded foolish even as he spoke. How could an alien care about such things?

Cargo canisters of ekti dropped away, and Berndt moved the skymine across the sky, hauling the large facility away at its clumsy top speed. The expensive cargo tumbled into Erphano's clouds like an offering . . . or a ransom. Berndt's heart fell when the alien globes ignored the ekti and continued to close in on the skymine.

He could easily have rigged the fuel canisters to detonate. Perhaps the explosion would have been great enough to crack open one of the diamond globes . . . but most likely not. And there were *five* of the city-sized monstrosities. Though they had not yet opened fire, he knew he was doomed either way.

'Time to separate the habitation module,' Berndt said, his last desperate measure. 'We'll have to sacrifice the skymine and hope the aliens follow the larger factory and let us get away.'

Bolts and clamps blasted apart as their connectors were broken. The separable main deck rose away from the lumbering industrial facility, carrying most of the skymine's crewmembers. Looking chagrined but defiant, young Junna climbed back on to the bridge deck. Before Berndt could shout at his daughter for not making good her escape, his wife climbed up beside him. 'Oh, Marta!' His heart melted, and he shook his head, wanting to damn them for the foolish love that might now cost them their lives.

The alien warglobes ignored the scout ships that had flown away from the skymine. Even so, once the main facility was destroyed, those small craft would have no place to land, nowhere to refuel. The construction yards in the broken moons of Erphano had been abandoned after the skymine launch. Berndt prayed to the Guiding Star that some rescue would come before the escapees' life-support systems ran out and the tiny craft plunged one by one into the limitless atmosphere.

Even after Berndt had scuttled the skymine in the high clouds, the relentless crystal globes advanced on the separable bridge deck.

His wife and daughter stood beside Berndt at the command chair, and he reached out to clasp them, pulling his family close. He knew in his heart that whatever these creatures were, they didn't want the ekti after all, didn't want any part of the Roamer skymines.

They just wanted to destroy humans.

Blue lightning lashed out. Berndt clutched his wife and daughter. An instant of incinerating electricity vaporized metal and glass, too fast for him to draw a breath. Then he, his family, and the whole escape module became a soup of blasted atoms.

SIXTY-SEVEN

NIRA

It took Prime Designate Jora'h several days to arrange a formal presentation to the awesome Mage-Imperator himself. Carrying their potted treelings as gifts, Nira and Otema entered the fabulous skysphere reception hall.

The transparent, faceted Prism Palace surrounded them, and Nira thought she had stepped into the heart of a gigantic gem. The walls were made of interlocked blown-glass bubbles. Attached to the nucleus were seven smaller globes, chambers with towers connected to the upper skysphere. Elevator tubes ran like longitudinal veins within the main dome; smaller spheres housed the foundations of the Ildiran government, the ministries of economy, agriculture, colonization, military, urban affairs, medicine, and kith relations.

Favouring Nira with his hypnotic smile, the Prime Designate joined them at the entrance to the primary audience sphere. He touched Nira's shoulder, nudging her forward. 'By now you have probably grown bored with all of our marvellous sights.'

Her smile was sparkling and sincere. 'How could one ever grow weary of so much energy . . . so much excitement? My brain aches from trying to comprehend it all, but I don't ever want to stop.'

Jora'h laughed, a musical and heart-warming sound. 'You are so refreshing, Nira.' He led them into a bustling open hall filled with courtesans and functionaries, all born of the sleek and human-looking noble kith. Slender and attractive, they wore clothes tailored to fit their lean bodies. The hairless women were painted and decorated with colourful swirling designs. Many wore shimmering electrostatic hoods projected from their collars, tuned to colours that matched their gowns and cloaks.

Enchanted, Nira stepped into the flow with Jora'h close beside her. Otema followed formally, her head held high and her expression neutral. The Iron Lady did not seem impressed by the beauty around her, but Nira was openly curious, and she expressed sufficient astonishment for both of them.

Above the central dome hung a second globe open at the bottom so that it formed an artificially enclosed sky, an enormous suspended terrarium. Matted foliage, flowers, and vines dangled through the opening. Misters sprayed into the gaps, making the leaves sparkle. Exotic alien analogues of hummingbirds and butterflies filled the dome, flitting back and forth to sample nectar or sip from tiny pools of water caught in the cupped palms of jewel-bright leaves.

'What keeps the birds and butterflies inside?' she asked. 'Why don't they fly down here?'

'A discourager field drives them back, but subtly. They don't even know they are contained.' Jora'h stepped forward. 'Come, let us meet my father. We must take care of our important business before you distract me, dear Nira, and make me want to show you even more interesting areas of the Prism Palace.'

'Prime Designate,' Otema chided, 'meeting the Mage-Imperator is of greater interest than anything else you could show us.'

The two women walked forward, cradling their potted treelings. The plants drank in the delicious brilliance of the seven suns. Nira's green skin had darkened since they had arrived here. Though at times she longed for the cool darkness of a forest night, she never felt tired or bored. She had eaten many delicacies, and her skin supplied additional nourishment, so that she needed far less rest than before.

In his chrysalis chair sat the mighty Mage-Imperator himself. High above him, intersecting jets of mist formed a hazy cloud upon which a hologram of the leader's round face was projected. Hanging like a full moon beneath the opening of the skysphere, the ruler's image moved its lips as he spoke to sycophants standing below him on the polished floor. A shaft of light rose upwards from the rim of the sturdy bedlike throne in a glowing pillar that intersected the benevolent projection overhead.

Seeing them approach with his eldest son, the Mage-Imperator abruptly dismissed two nobles, who bowed and backed away. The handsome Prime Designate strode forward, his fine golden braids standing out around his head like a mane. He beckoned to the women. 'Come.' Beaming with pleasure, he led Nira and Otema into his father's presence beneath the open skysphere. 'Father, my Mage-Imperator, I am pleased to formally present these two visitors from Theroc.'

Nira gazed at the pasty, sluggish leader in his womb-like throne. She could see no resemblance between him and the virile animal magnetism of Prime Designate Jora'h.

The Mage-Imperator stirred from his reclining position. 'All are welcome to make a pilgrimage to Mijistra, even humans. Our two cultures have much to learn from each other.'

Jora'h had obviously heard those words before. He reached out to touch Nira's shoulder, and she felt his comforting presence, close and warm. 'Father, these are green priests, servants of the Theron worldforest, revered practitioners of telink. They can communicate instantaneously across great distances.'

Now the Mage-Imperator sat up, attentive. His eyes glinted in the dazzling light, like drawn weapons. 'Yes, I know of such humans. I find their ability intriguing.'

Jora'h gestured towards the old woman. 'This is Otema, formerly the ambassador of Theroc to the Terran Hanseatic League. Now she has come to Mijistra at my invitation. And this—' he smiled at the young woman, 'is her lovely assistant, Nira.'

She flushed; Jora'h was being too blatant in his flirtation, but she supposed the Prime Designate needed to have no compunctions at all.

'Months ago, Reynald, the son of their leader, visited us here. He and I worked out an agreement whereby he could send these two representatives. Green priests are curious about Ildiran history and legends. I have granted them permission to study our *Saga of Seven Suns*.'

Still awestruck, Nira held her tongue while Otema stepped closer to the Mage-Imperator's chrysalis chair. Respectfully averting her eyes, the old woman extended her ornately potted treeling so the great leader could see the beautiful, feather-like fronds and the scaly golden bark. 'We are pleased to present you with an offshoot of the worldforest, Mage-Imperator. Through these trees we are able to communicate over vast distances. Our thoughts join together with all such trees growing across the Spiral Arm.'

The corpulent Mage-Imperator did not bother to lift a hand and made no move to take the potted treeling. He seemed uninterested in the trees. 'I formally accept your gifts of the worldtrees. However, as you are experts and it seems you two will abide with us in Mijistra for some time, it is best that you keep possession of them. Tend the treelings as you would on your own world.'

Otema bowed, as did Nira. The ambassador straightened and met the gaze of the great Ildiran leader. 'We have heard much about your *Saga of Seven Suns*, and we look forward to beginning our work. I understand that reading the entire epic requires a lifetime of study.'

'An Ildiran lifetime,' the Mage-Imperator said with a hint of smug amusement. 'Humans have a briefer existence on the great stage of the galaxy.'

'Nevertheless,' Jora'h said, as if debating with his father, 'in spite of their shorter lives, humans seem to accomplish much more than even our greatest heroes. Perhaps they have a greater sense of . . . urgency?'

'An interesting observation,' the Mage-Imperator said, almost growling. Abruptly, he clapped his hands with a loud sound that rang across the chamber. 'Enough. See that they are acquainted with Rememberer Vao'sh. He will answer all their questions regarding the *Saga*.'

The Mage-Imperator turned his heavy-lidded gaze towards Nira, and he seemed to be analysing her body, dissecting her. She felt a cold shiver at his intense yet bloodless scrutiny. What did he want from her?

'My son seems to have taken quite an interest in you. Both of you,' he quickly amended. 'Jora'h will see to your every need.'

SIXTY-EIGHT

PRIME DESIGNATE JORA'H

The Mage-Imperator spent many of his waking hours in the skysphere reception hall listening to petitioners and speaking with his people. He held audiences at his whim, letting all pilgrims come to him. He preferred to be among his people, where he could sense their general problems through the *thism*'s vivid connection.

In other moods, though, the Mage-Imperator could not tolerate the adoration and hubbub. He withdrew to quiet chambers where he could contemplate in privacy the necessary requirements of state. He made no excuses for his behaviour. He was the Mage-Imperator.

At such times, Prime Designate Jora'h was often summoned into his father's presence so they could discuss the politics of the Empire. Jora'h was pleased to speak with him as son to father, eager to learn from the great man. Some day, he would do the same with his own noble-born son, Thor'h.

Jora'h arrived in the contemplation chamber after finishing a fine meal, energized and ready for deep conversation. The Prime

Designate wore impeccable new clothing made from the fabrics of Theroc, gossamer cocoon weaves draped in loose folds around his chest, caught up with gem pins and golden buttons.

After the arrival of the *Voracious Curiosity*, Jora'h had spoken to commerce minister Klio's, requesting to have first look at the exotic off-world goods. The Prime Designate had bought half of Rlinda Kett's cargo for himself, primarily as gifts to divide among his many lovers and offspring. He had not even argued with the merchant's asking price, simply tapped into the Ildiran treasury and paid it.

Afterwards, the other noble kithmen had fallen like ravenous animals upon the rest of the cargo and quickly bid the prices far higher than the human merchant had ever hoped . . .

Now, as Jora'h bowed formally, the Mage-Imperator acknowledged his son's presence. The Prime Designate counted the attenders clustered around his father's soft bulk. Fifteen! The attenders performed tasks that were more necessary to their own self-esteem than to their leader's true comfort.

Small, nimble-fingered members of the servant kith massaged the Mage-Imperator's pale skin, rubbing lotions and ointments into his joints, removing any hint of a callous or blemish. Other attenders fed him soft sweetmeats, pickled vegetables, spicy berries, and crunchy salted fish. They fluttered about, straightening his robes, stroking his long braid.

Tolerant of these ministrations, the Mage-Imperator lay back in his chrysalis chair, his generous lips frowning. Jora'h knew that his father didn't require such worshipful attention, but allowed the attenders to fulfil their inbred need to pamper him. Today, though, the Mage-Imperator grew impatient with the excessive attention. His father's glorious braid twitched and thrashed like the tail of an annoyed Isix cat.

'Leave us in peace,' the Mage-Imperator snapped, to the shock of the attenders. They groaned deep in their throats and backed away in dejection, eyes averted. The leader growled, 'And don't let me hear more nonsense about any of you committing ritual suicide. If you must tend someone, go into the city and find a weary, downtrodden worker and massage him. Do it with my blessing.'

Delighted again, the attenders jabbered to themselves and scurried out of the private chamber. Jora'h knew they would work themselves to exhaustion trying to pamper unsuspecting labourers in the workyards.

When they were gone, the Mage-Imperator turned his sleepy-looking eyes to his son. 'Jora'h, one day you will grow as impatient with being coddled.'

'I can already see the disadvantages.' He smiled warmly at his father. 'But that will not be for a great deal of time yet.'

Traditionally, a Mage-Imperator ruled for more than a century, and Jora'h's father had many decades remaining to him, during which the Prime Designate could continue his vigorous lifestyle. The Mage-Imperator's own father, Yura'h, had been the Ildiran leader during the first encounter with human generation ships, a hundred and eighty-three Earth years earlier.

'Nevertheless,' the Mage-Imperator said in a dangerous voice, 'I demand that you understand the politics of the galactic situation. All of my sons serve as Designates on Ildiran colony worlds. I communicate with them through the *thism*, but I expect them to *understand* rather than simply follow my mental directives. You are my tools and my weapons for managing the Empire.'

Jora'h nodded, always curious to learn new things, though his varied interests went much farther afield than mere rigid politics. His son Thor'h, dallying on the lush world of Hyrillka with the good-natured Designate there, had showed no interest in politics either, thus far.

However, once Jora'h had endured the castration ceremony

that would make him the new leader and keeper of the *thism*, all thoughts, all plans, even his father's secret workings, would become clear to him. With the loss of his manhood, the Prime Designate would understand *everything* in a sudden enlightenment. It was like a candle flame passed from generation to generation, a never-broken continuity from the very first Mage-Imperator, that ensured the great Ildiran Empire would never weaken, never change.

'I understand that your son Zan'nh has excelled in the Solar Navy. Adar Kori'nh speaks highly of him.'

Jora'h nodded. Even though Zan'nh was not of pure-blood noble kith, with his skills and ambition, he might have made a better successor than self-centred Thor'h. 'Yes, he has just been promoted to the rank of Qul. The Adar has announced more military manoeuvres and a spectacular display of our fine ships and their proficient pilots. Everyone is pleased that you have decreed more festivals and celebrations.'

The Mage-Imperator nodded. 'You are also aware that our artisans have been crafting a new colossus, a magnificent obelisk to be erected in Mijistra, with lesser copies to be raised on every one of our splinter colonies, in addition to the ones they already have.'

'It is an honour well deserved, Father.'

The Mage-Imperator seemed annoyed at his son's sycophantic response. 'I have also asked that our best rememberers give more frequent performances so that additional parts of the *Saga* can be spoken aloud. I wish to encourage more familiarity with our obscure heroes.'

'Is that where the historian survivor from Crenna went? Dio'sh? He hasn't been seen—'

The Mage-Imperator waved a heavy hand. 'Yes, I dispatched him and many more rememberers to other splinter colonies. It doesn't matter precisely where they have gone.'

Jora'h beamed. 'Everything you say makes me proud to be your heir, Father. You will leave me an incomparable legacy, and you strengthen it as each day goes by.'

The Mage-Imperator scowled, removing the placid expression he maintained at all public viewings. 'And why do you think I have taken such action, Jora'h? Consider the question!' His sharp tone surprised his son. 'For what purpose would it be necessary to make such extravagant efforts?'

'Why, for the glory of the Ildiran people, of course.'

'*Kllar bekh!* You are too naive to be my Prime Designate!' The Mage-Imperator stirred restlessly in his chrysalis chair, and his braid twitched. 'I expect such complacent acceptance from the overall population, but you should be able to see into the shadows and read details that only an expert would notice.' His voice carried harsh disappointment and deep annoyance.

Feeling scolded, Jora'h mumbled, 'Then what is the reason, Father? Please enlighten me.'

The Mage-Imperator heaved himself up in the womb-like chair. 'Because our Ildiran Empire is indeed fading, just as the snide humans suspect! We withdrew our splinter colony on Crenna because of the plague there, but we have abandoned other worlds as well, giving up our territory. Have you not seen how the humans snap up every available planet, spreading like a fire? And instead of being satisfied, they grow hungrier still with each new settlement.'

His braid thrashed about like an angry snake. Unconsciously, Jora'h took a hesitant step backwards. The Mage-Imperator spoke with deep-seated anger. 'But not us. Ildirans retreat instead of expand. We withdraw instead of explore. Our power is waning . . . and has been for centuries.'

Jora'h looked at his father in shock. 'I have never heard such a suggestion.'

'You have never bothered to notice,' the Mage-Imperator snapped. 'That is the reason we must increase our pageantry and historical celebrations. An old human record calls it "bread and circuses" to distract the populace. So long as the Ildiran people believe in the grandeur all around them, we will be able to convince ourselves it is real.'

Reeling with the information, Jora'h tried to absorb the new perspective on reality. He didn't doubt his father's words – how could anyone question the Mage-Imperator? The leader would never lie to him, and indeed he was wiser than any other member of their race. With the *thism*, he saw through the eyes of all his subjects, which gave him a nearly omnipotent perspective.

'Do my . . . do my brothers, the other Designates, know this? Am I the only one who is so blind?'

Now the Mage-Imperator seemed to take pity on Jora'h. 'All of my sons are different. The Dobro Designate is hardened and finds no joy in his life, though he works harder to serve me than anyone else. The Hyrillka Designate is overwhelmed with his meagre duties at the edge of the Horizon Cluster and has a somewhat magnified perception of his importance and status in the Empire. The Maratha Designate is hedonistic, finding joy in his pursuits, and does little to think about the Empire beyond his own walls. But each son hears me through the *thism*. Each one feels my thoughts and my decisions, and they all obey. As it should be.

'However it is *you*, Jora'h, who must eventually bear all this responsibility. I do not compare and choose among my heirs. You are the first-born, the Prime Designate. You will eventually take my place and understand it all. But even before that time, I want you to comprehend what lies in store for you, not just mouth pretty words like an idiot. *Think* about what I am saying.'

Jora'h swallowed hard, considering how he worked to maintain his popularity, watching the Ildiran people amuse themselves, revelling in the glory of their Empire. He had a good heart, but perhaps he *was* far too naive.

Although his brother the Dobro Designate was always grim and preoccupied with schemes, now Jora'h realized that perhaps his brother understood far more than he himself had guessed. Jora'h wondered how many other dark secrets the Mage-Imperator was keeping from him, though he would learn everything on the terrible day when he took the reins of *thism* in his grasp.

Rattled, the Prime Designate backed away from the chrysalis chair, hoping the audience was over. 'Let me think on this, Father.'

'You must understand the truth, my son. As the next Mage-Imperator, you will have to make certain decisions that are cruel and heartless. But you will make them because they are ultimately the best choice for our people.'

'I . . . understand, Father. Intellectually, I have known that for many years. But still, my heart has trouble understanding this difficult news.'

The Mage-Imperator's pasty face shifted, his expression becoming one of honest concern. 'One last thing: you have heard about the strange attack on the moons of the new star the humans ignited?'

'Yes, they claim it was the work of some powerful aliens. But how can that be? Besides the humans, we have encountered no other living civilization in all our history. Unless you believe the legends of the Shana Rei, but I always thought those creatures of darkness were just a story from before the Lost Times.'

The Mage-Imperator said, 'If a tale is recorded in the *Saga of Seven Suns*, then it must bear at least a foundation of truth.' He frowned again. 'But no, my son, this is not the work of the Shana Rei. In addition to the attack on Oncier, these new enemies have also destroyed Roamer ekti-processing plants on Golgen and, most recently, on Erphano.'

'Other attacks? Are we in danger?' The Prime Designate reeled with all the strange and terrifying things he had learned this day.

The Mage-Imperator's voice grew absolutely sincere with its dreadful message. 'Without question, the Ildiran Empire – indeed every living thing in the Spiral Arm – is entering a very serious crisis. No one can anticipate just how grave this situation may become.'

SIXTY-NINE

OX

When the Klikiss robot Jorax appeared at the Whisper Palace to demand an audience with King Frederick, his request caused an extraordinary stir. Palace guards marched out of their sheltered alcoves, and royal advisers scrambled to decide what to do.

From Hansa headquarters, Basil Wenceslas pondered his official response. He finally withdrew the old Teacher compy OX from his training sessions with Prince Peter and dispatched him to wait beside the black alien machine.

'I have been instructed to keep you company.' Only half as tall as the big beetle-like robot, the compy stood newly polished and cleaned, his voice modulated to a new depth. He remained at attention, assessing and analysing the Klikiss machine. OX was designed to learn, absorbing information and memories at every opportunity, though his mental core was already so full from centuries of personal experience that he had little room for anything new.

'I will wait here as long as necessary,' Jorax said. 'Years mean nothing to us.'

After William Andeker's 'techno-dissection' debacle, security guards had cut their way into the sealed cybernetics laboratory, where they found the computer scientist dead, the laboratory ruined, and all data recordings erased. The Klikiss robot had stood calmly in the centre of the room, motionless.

When Jorax finally spoke, his words had been brief. 'The human scientist meddled with my circuits, despite my warnings not to do so. He inadvertently triggered an autonomic self-defence subroutine, with unfortunate and deadly results. I do not accept responsibility for the harm he brought on himself.'

Given the sparse evidence, investigators had little choice but to believe the robot's version of events. Security had increased around Jorax, and surveillance monitored him more vigorously, but the alien robot had done nothing for several days. Until now, when he'd made his demand at the Whisper Palace.

'It is imperative that I speak with your King.'

OX seemed to intrigue the Klikiss robot. Jorax studied the small-statured Teacher compy, scanning him with scarlet optical sensors. OX waited, patient, and finally Jorax said, 'You are a different sort of robot, made by humans.'

OX said, 'I have been functional for three-and-a-quarter centuries. I served aboard the first human generation ship. After our alliance with the Ildirans, I returned to Earth to act as a Teacher and reservoir of data.'

'You are a statesman for compies?' Jorax asked.

'I speak for the humans, my masters. I have been present during the reigns of all six Great Kings of Earth.'

Jorax paused, assessing. 'Such timespans are insignificant compared to the lives of Klikiss robots.'

'True,' said OX, 'but I question the relevance of such a perspective, since you have retained no detailed memories.'

OX found that puzzling and disheartening. Memories from his

long lifetime filled his circuits, and he was distressed to imagine how much data and insight had been lost from the vanished civilization. If robots such as Jorax could never remember, then the Klikiss race was truly lost for all time.

'How many of your fellow robots have been found and reactivated in the past five centuries?' OX asked.

Jorax remained silent, as if calculating. 'Approximately fifty thousand.'

OX filed away the information. 'That exceeds my estimate. I believe the Hansa is unaware of that number.'

'They have only to count,' Jorax said, 'but few humans bother to distinguish between our individuals. And the Ildirans pay little attention to us. They say we are not part of their story.'

Standing in the arched promenade that led into King Frederick's Throne Hall, they watched well-dressed functionaries and courtiers hurrying about their business, all of them staring at the two mismatched robots. Security guards remained prominent, no longer hidden, keenly watching Jorax.

The contemplative Klikiss robot said, 'Bear in mind, that once there were billions of us, before the . . . disaster. Does the number of Klikiss robots intimidate you, or surprise you?'

'I merely find it interesting,' OX replied.

When the functionaries and bureaucrats finally finished their discussions and reached a decision, OX looked up to see the primary reception guardsman stride out of the Throne Hall. The guard clasped a ceremonial staff in his hand.

'King Frederick graciously grants an audience to the Klikiss robot Jorax.' The man paused, looking uncomfortable. 'We are unfamiliar with the weapons systems within your body core. As the recent death of Dr Andeker has proved, a Klikiss robot can indeed be dangerous. However, despite the potential risk to his royal person, the King has agreed to hear your words.'

He pointed his staff at the black exoskeleton. 'Be warned that your every move will be monitored. Our security guards will respond to any threatening action with a full and merciless retaliatory strike. Don't give us an excuse. Is this understood?'

'Klikiss robots have done nothing to foster such suspicion. Nevertheless, your conditions are acceptable to me. I intend no harm to your King.' The insectoid robot advanced across the polished floor into the opulent Throne Hall.

Old Frederick wore crimson robes, a crown of jewels and prismatic flatgems atop his grey head. He leaned forward with hard but curious eyes. OX had observed humans long enough to recognize a masked but distinct expression of fear on the King's face. No one knew what to expect from the alien machine.

With his smooth, caterpillar-like gait, Jorax moved forward and stopped a respectful distance in front of the raised throne. No one seemed to know how to announce this alien visitor or what protocol to follow. Finally, the King spoke in a voice that cracked embarrassingly in the middle. 'I have never had the opportunity to meet a Klikiss robot face to face.'

Jorax hummed and raised himself up as he extended his sets of flexible telescoping legs. 'I must deliver an important message to the Great King of the Terran Hanseatic League from the Klikiss robots.'

All ears in the Throne Hall pricked up. Cameras rolled, and OX knew that every word would be analysed and debated, with experts trying to determine any relevant information about the mysterious beetle-like machines.

Jorax spoke loudly in his buzzing voice. 'Until such time as our forebears and creators, the Klikiss, return, we robots are the sole representatives of that ancient powerful civilization. We have contributed to the exploration of our ancient ruins and have participated in many difficult construction activities, because we are curious about your methods. We have never caused a human harm, nor have we ever given you reason to fear us.

'However, the recent attempt to disrupt my physical integrity has shed light on disturbing attitudes towards us. Klikiss robots are rare creations. We value our existence as much as humans do. Therefore, the Klikiss robots demand to be treated as a sovereign species.'

King Frederick sat back, taken by surprise. 'That is not an unreasonable request, Jorax, but what . . . what has prompted this after so long? You, personally, have been here on Earth for several years, as I understand.'

The red optical sensors flashed. 'Your cybernetic scientist, Dr William Andeker, attempted to do grievous harm to my body. He wished to dismantle and study my components, without my permission. Such an assault could be construed as an act of war against the Klikiss civilization. I wish to ensure that such brutal attacks do not occur again.'

A gasp rippled throughout the hall. King Frederick flushed, raising both hands in a conciliatory gesture. 'Now, let us not be hasty! That was an ill-advised and unauthorized action by a single person, we can all agree. The death of Dr Andeker has given us all a sufficient reminder that we should leave you and your companions in peace.'

'Correct,' Jorax said. 'Our internal systems contain dangerous automatic systems we cannot control. The Klikiss installed them within us, for their own reasons.' He scanned the Throne Hall briefly. 'But we have observed how humans treat their robots. We have noted your apathy towards the sentient machines you call compies.'

Standing at the back of the Throne Hall, OX was fascinated. He watched every movement in the audience.

King Frederick tried to make an excuse. 'Our compies are not as sophisticated as Klikiss robots, Jorax. They are certainly not your equals. They are machines, mobile devices with implanted information systems, constructed solely for our convenience. They are not . . . life forms.'

'That is a matter to be debated at another time,' Jorax said. 'Do not make the error of viewing Klikiss robots as disposable mechanical puppets like your compies. We are individuals, with lifespans of millennia. No human has a right to command us – or vivisect us.'

'Oh, agreed, agreed,' Frederick said quickly and forcefully. 'Allow me to offer my sincerest apologies for the discomfort you endured. William Andeker acted of his own volition, without the permission or sanction of the Hanseatic League. You may be assured that it will never happen again.' The King's face bore a pleading expression.

'All Klikiss robots will be glad to hear this.'

Without any further comment or concessions to diplomatic protocol, Jorax swivelled his body core about. With a flurry of stubby, articulated legs, he departed from the Whisper Palace.

SEVENTY

MARGARET COLICOS

When he hurried back to camp, thrilled with his discovery, the green priest Arcas was very insistent. Margaret didn't want to spend a day away from the main Klikiss city, which she and Louis had by now mapped and surveyed. Working together but intent on their own projects, they had finally begun to make progress deciphering the architecture and inner workings of the empty metropolis. She had no intention of being distracted now.

Louis, however, suggested that changing their routine for a day might be worthwhile. 'It's not exactly a break, dear,' he said, his leathery face sporting a boyish grin. 'An archaeologist has to take chances, and Arcas really thinks he's found something important. Listen to him.'

Sceptical, she looked at the green priest, who was clearly reining in his eagerness. 'I went out collecting fossils in a side canyon where the walls are crumbling. High up, I saw an overhang that appears to be falling away. Deep under the overhang, I'm sure I could make out Klikiss buildings. A lot of them. It could be an entirely new city, sealed and protected for all these centuries.'

Or it could just be your imagination, Margaret thought. But she sighed and reached for her pack. 'Yes, archaeologists have to take chances. After all, that's why I married you in the first place, old man.'

Louis chuckled and gave her a hug. She patted his bony back, and they gathered their equipment for half a day's expedition out in the desert heat.

When they trudged into the winding canyons where rivers had carved through the sedimentary rock, Margaret was surprised to see the three Klikiss robots rise up from where they were sunning themselves on a broad slab of rock. 'We will accompany you,' Sirix said. 'We are always interested in a new discovery.'

'Excellent,' Louis said. 'One of these days we'll find something to spark your memories.' He held out a finger. 'And don't be shy about making guesses, either. That's what progress is all about.'

'Very well,' Sirix buzzed. 'We will attempt to make . . . guesses.'

Arcas led them along a dry river course. The big black robots had no trouble negotiating the rough terrain, and neither did DD. Shadows from high, razor-edged cliffs closed in around them. Tinny echoes of their footsteps and voices sounded off the sheer walls. Rust-like impurities streaked through the rough rock, as if some primitive and bloody sacrifice had occurred on the ledges above.

Today, the orangish skies of Rheindic Co had a strange greasy quality, as if high smoke dimmed the sunlight. Margaret hadn't bothered to study the planet's quirky weather, but she thought the gauzy overcast looked a little odd.

She watched Arcas curiously as he hurried into the winding labyrinth, ducked to the left into a small side canyon, and climbed over rubble that had fallen from the cliffs. The stone walls narrowed even farther.

'This direction,' Arcas said. 'Not too far.'

Louis pointed up towards the narrow slice of sky between the enclosing canyon walls. 'I don't like the look of that.'

Overhead, the smear of grey haze had clotted into hard fists of clouds sheeting feathery grey moisture. The slurry of rain and dust that fell from the clouds evaporated before it could strike the ground, and then came down in a renewed downpour.

'That looks like quite a storm.' Margaret glanced around at the canyon walls that seemed to bottle them up. 'You don't suppose Rheindic Co is one of those worlds that gets a year's rainfall all in a single afternoon?'

Arcas sniffed the air with concern. 'I wish I could touch one of my treelings and access information from the worldforest. I don't know enough about deserts yet.' He looked around. 'But let us hurry. The cliff wall is just ahead.'

They picked up their pace, climbing over boulders until they reached another finger canyon. Margaret wondered how Arcas had ever found this place and then traced his way back to camp. Now she did see a squarish cave opening high up on the crumbling cliff wall, where parts of a sealed overhang had fallen away. The rubble lay in chunks of debris on the canyon floor.

Even from here the cliff appeared hollow, more than just an arched indentation. When she looked just right, in the light and shadows of the gorge she could indeed discern something inside the cave, angular forms that did not look like natural rocks or cave growths. 'Let's climb,' she said.

The striated rock bands could provide a route for agile climbers to scale the face. DD had brought detachable pitons and wall-hugger attachments for his masters to use, but still it looked like a difficult ascent.

'DD,' Louis said, 'you go up first and show us the way. Watch out for any unstable cracks or boulders.'

The Friendly compy didn't hesitate. 'Yes, Master Louis.' He removed the equipment he had brought, briefly accessed his instruction files so he knew how to use the tools, then scrambled up the nearest shallow ledge. With his nimble mechanical legs, the little robot zigzagged his way higher.

Louis watched DD, then glanced back at the bulky Klikiss robots, knowing they couldn't possibly make the ascent. 'Sorry, Sirix. You three will have to wait until we erect ramps.'

'*If* we decide to erect ramps. We have to see what's up there, first,' Margaret said. 'May not be worth the effort, old man.'

Louis gestured to the green priest, smiling. 'Arcas, would you like to go next? Since this is your discovery, you might as well have the honour of being the first human to set foot there.'

The green priest looked surprised and then embarrassed. 'Are you sure it wouldn't be better if you or Margaret—'

'Arcas, we don't care about such things,' Margaret said with a hint of impatience. 'Go on.'

The green priest scrambled up after DD, using the handholds and pitons the silvery compy had diligently left for them.

Fat, cold droplets of grey rainwater splattered against the cliffside as Margaret began to climb, waiting at each ledge for Louis. She knew they would both be sore this evening. They would take turns rubbing muscle balm into each other's aching joints, but an excellent discovery would help her get over any amount of pain and weariness.

DD had reached a ledge three-quarters of the way up the cliff face, and the rain continued to splatter harder. After pounding a thick piton anchor into a crack, he called down. 'I will drop a support rope. This last section appears to be very precarious.'

Then a burst of rain slammed into the canyon like a fire hose, pounding against the stone and washing loose mud and sand down in sheets like oozing paint.

'Hang on!' Louis said, and pushed Margaret close to the wall, giving her the advantage of minimal shelter. They were all drenched within moments, but the rain did not lessen. Rivulets poured through cracks in the canyon wall, leaching alkali from the stone. The air smelled thick and slippery, like soap and ashes.

'I hear something.' Arcas raised his voice above the sizzling sound of sharp raindrops, like meat frying on a hot grill. 'Listen. It's getting louder.'

Margaret heard a crash and rumble, a splashing growl that increased in intensity. Clutching the rough cliff, she looked down to see a boiling tongue of brown water surge through the narrow canyon. The flash-flood came with the force of a stampede, carrying silt and boulders like projectiles. It slammed against the lower wall, ricocheted and swirled up, licking the layered rocks.

The humans and DD were safely out of its reach, but stranded on the canyon floor below, the Klikiss robots were doomed. The three black machines had just raised their articulated arms in a pathetic attempt to defend themselves from the wall of water – before it blasted them, knocking the beetle-like machines pell-mell as it swept through the narrow canyon, picking up speed and debris. The Klikiss machines were sluggish and helpless as they tumbled away, engulfed in muddy water. Within seconds they were borne out of sight.

Before Margaret could cry out to Louis clinging beside her, DD activated his alarm systems and clamoured for assistance. Part of the layered rock wall, saturated with the sudden influx of water, sheared away. Rock slabs peeled off beside him, sloughing away the compy's handhold, but DD clutched his anchored piton with one metal fist. The cliff face continued to shudder and rumble, breaking apart.

Arcas huddled in the shelter of an overhang, hoping the canyon wall would not come down on top of him. More rock fell away, swept down by small waterfalls. Margaret and Louis held each other as the avalanche continued down into the angry flash-flood gurgling along the canyon floor.

The Klikiss robots were completely gone, swept away.

Finally the rocks stopped pattering, and the sky above turned into a slash of burnt orange as the smeary rain clouds passed on to dump their deluge on another portion of the desert.

Soaked and cold, Margaret and Louis eased away from the meagre protection of the cliff. Arcas had already emerged, blinking and amazed. DD continued to call for help, sounding like an alarmed child as he dangled one-handed by the piton and the rope. His compy grip had locked his joints in place, so he did not let go.

Breathless, Margaret and Louis scrambled along the muddy ledges then used the rope to pull DD back to solid ground. 'I hope we can find the three robots,' the compy said. 'Do you think they were destroyed in the flood?'

Margaret looked down at the still-raging waters in the bottom of the canyon. 'We'll have to wait and see, DD.'

Arcas joined them, streaked with mud and unsettled. Margaret wiped dirt from her face. Louis looked at his wife and laughed, and she shook her head at his own bedraggled appearance. 'I wouldn't be too proud of how you look right now either, old man.'

Arcas, though, pointed up beyond where DD had secured his piton. Half of the cliff had fallen away, exposing an opening into chambers and grottoes in the cliff that had been covered by sandstone when they first saw it.

With renewed vigour, Margaret climbed up, grasping DD's rope. The compy offered to go first. 'Please exercise caution, Margaret,' he said, but she quickly hauled herself over the lip into the raw opening below the overhang that had just broken away.

'Louis, come up here!' she called, then looked back down towards the still-shaky green priest. 'Arcas, remind me never to doubt you again.'

Then she clambered into the large, previously unseen section of a pristine Klikiss ghost city, newly exposed by the storm.

SEVENTY-ONE

NIRA

The invitation arrived in Nira's private quarters, a mirror-engraved placard asking her to join Prime Designate Jora'h for a spectacular afternoon of Ildiran jousting. The sleek-skinned courier, though obviously from one of the upper-class kiths, was far less impressive and magnetic than Jora'h himself.

The courier watched as Nira read the etched letters again, easily comprehending the writing after she had absorbed that skill through the worldforest database. 'I have been instructed to wait for your reply. Prime Designate Jora'h is most anxious to have you join him.'

The event sounded fascinating, and Nira was pleased to have an opportunity to spend time with the handsome Prime Designate. 'Let me consult with Ambassador Otema.' The courier followed her down the hall to Otema's chambers, where the old woman sat surrounded by her potted treelings.

Otema had spread out documents given to her by Rememberer Vao'sh. She read lines and stanzas aloud, reciting lyrical tales out of Ildiran myth and legend from the *Saga*. The ancient priest looked up at Nira, her expression distant and dreamy. 'These epic arcs are filled with unusual twists and grand stories. Everything is completely new to the worldtrees.' Her eyes sparkling, Otema touched the stacks of records in front of her. 'It would take decades for a single person to skim all this material, much less read it aloud.'

'That is why I'm here to assist you, Ambassador.' Nira had already found the tales of Ildiran heroism, bravery, and tragedy as enthralling as the Malory epic of King Arthur. 'However, the two of us cannot possibly accomplish the entire task. Not in your lifetime, not in mine.'

'I know, I know.' The old woman frowned with dismay, crinkling the tattoos that marked her face.

The courier waited outside Otema's transparent door, his face placid but still exhibiting noticeable impatience. Nira saw a similar engraved invitation plaque beside Otema, where it had been set aside, as if dismissed. Her heart sank.

'Ambassador, I see that you've received an invitation as well.' She held up her own, and the light played off its reflective surface. 'Will we be attending the Ildiran jousting, as Prime Designate Jora'h has requested?'

'Oh, I don't think so, Nira. I have too much work to do, too many documents to read. My mind is swelled with the sheer volume of information that remains to be shared with the worldtrees.' She suddenly noticed the crestfallen expression on her assistant's face, and smiled. 'You, of course, may feel free to go. Please represent Theroc in my stead.' Seeing Nira's look of joy, Otema said in a gruff voice, 'Besides, I am certain the Prime Designate prefers your company to mine. He was merely asking me as a formality.'

'That's not true, Ambassador!' Nira said, but she knew not to protest too much.

*

Inside the domed jousting pavilion, Nira sat close to Jora'h in his private spectator lounge. The Prime Designate leaned over to her, his topaz eyes flashing. When he smiled at her, Nira wanted to melt.

'I am saddened that your companion Otema could not join us,' he said.

Nira couldn't stop herself from laughing. 'No, you're not.'

Jora'h was taken aback, then he chuckled as well. 'Perhaps my feelings are too obvious. You are correct. I would have played a fine host to the ambassador, but I would rather spend the afternoon with you.'

'With me . . . and five thousand Ildirans?' Nira gestured to the crowds lining the brightly lit arena. The spectators sat in designated sections, different kiths clustered together so that as Nira swept her gaze across the cheering people, she saw a spectrum of different facial features and body types.

'Ah, but you are the only person I see, Nira.' A fanfare sounded, and the crowds shouted. 'The spectacle is about to begin.' Jora'h brushed his fingers across her wrist, then chastely folded his hands in his lap.

Ildiran jousting was an important ritualistic sport performed inside covered amphitheatres. Mirrored panels alternated with transparent skylights that shone down on a sandy competition field. Warriors clad in highly polished, reflective body armour rode out of dark openings astride grey six-legged reptilian beasts that seemed to be all muscles and spines and scales. The beasts reminded Nira of Komodo dragons with rills at their throats, knobs on their bent limbs.

The heroic jousters came together slowly, the steeds leaving wide footprints in the soft dirt of the combat field. The reptilian mounts hissed and then lashed out with spined tongues, but the riders kept the creatures apart to prevent them from doing damage . . . at least until the jousting formally began.

The Ildiran knights carried throbbing laser lances, long crystal shafts couched with ruby projection rods and power sources connected to battery packs behind the saddles of the reptilian mounts.

'Are those spears used for combat?' Nira asked in a hushed voice. 'Do they stab each other or those creatures they are riding?'

Jora'h's golden hair waved about his head. 'The crystal spears can be formidable weapons, but no sophisticated Ildiran knight would use them in so crude a fashion.'

He stood, and on cue projected lights focused on him, a prismatic rainbow glow that drew the full attention of the audience. When Jora'h raised his hands, the crowd suddenly fell silent. 'Fighters! Make a good impression today!' His voice boomed out, somehow amplified, though Nira could see no microphone or speaker. 'Combatants – power your lances.'

The crystal spears shimmered with an inner jewel light, as if a tiny stellar core had just been ignited in their handles. 'Begin the joust!' Jora'h shouted.

The dazzling lights turned from the Prime Designate and illuminated the combatants' field where the huge reptiles began circling. The three jousters raised their shields in salute. Nira noticed that, though the shields were all generally the same size, each had a different shape and was inlaid with a specific pattern of mirrored patches, designs, and transparent windows.

The knights raised their crystal lances, and each fired a dazzling burst of light towards angled mirrors in the amphitheatre ceiling. The long lance shaft was actually a laser collimation path to project a coherent beam, which reflected and sparkled in a beautifully patterned webwork visible against the faint mist within the dome.

'By regulation, the knights' shields have to be exactly half-silvered,' Jora'h said to her, 'part reflective and part transparent. However, there is no requirement as to *how* the patterns must be arranged. Our greatest jousters believe there is much strategy in applying the mirror surfaces to their shields.'

Nira didn't entirely understand, but she leaned forward. 'So if they don't hold the shield just right, the laser beam can pass directly through?'

'Indeed,' Jora'h said, his eyes on the tournament. 'It can be fatal.'

The jousters urged their lizard mounts to greater speed, then shot deadly lasers at their opponents. One knight fired a beam that reflected from his challenger's shield, ricocheted off one of the ceiling mirrors, and scorched the third jouster's reptile steed. Squealing, the creature lashed out with a spined tongue, but the first jouster backed away to roars of applause.

Jora'h said, 'It is considered the greatest mark of skill to take down one's opponent by a reflected shot of his own lance.'

One of the three jousters was clearly the crowd's hero. Every time he moved, cheers and shouts rang out with increased ardour. 'Who is that?' Nira observed the knight's aloof manner, the dramatic flourish of mirrored swirls on his shield.

Jora'h smiled. 'Cir'gh is one of our greatest champions. He has won hundreds of matches, and he feels and thinks like his mount. He also knows precisely how every beam will reflect. Perfect instinct.'

Cir'gh launched a laser volley that reflected off the ceiling, struck one opponent, reflected off his armour, and grazed the second jouster, all in a single move.

'He is also blind in one eye.' Jora'h grinned at Nira's expression of shock. 'A laser spark caught him in the cornea. But though it darkened his sight, he claims it improved his overall vision.'

The jousters furiously fired their lances, tilting and slashing with their mirrors, rotating shields to prevent the lasers from blasting through the transparent patches. A flurry of beams criss-crossed the misty air. Nira was astonished that no spectators were killed by stray reflections.

'You will read about our jousting when you study the *Saga of Seven Suns*. I am no rememberer, but let me tell you a tale from our history.'

Nira laughed. 'Surely the Prime Designate of the Ildiran Empire can spin a story as well as anyone else?'

'It is about another Prime Designate from the past, so I am familiar with the poignancy and the political relevance.' He looked at her, questioning. 'You understand that before he becomes Mage-Imperator, a Prime Designate is required to have many offspring? These then become Designates on other colony worlds as well as noble leaders of the various kiths. Long ago, however, the first-born son of a Mage-Imperator was incapable of siring children. When a Prime Designate has so many mates, it becomes apparent very quickly if he is sterile.'

'That's terrible,' Nira said.

Jora'h's vibrant gold hair flickered around his face. 'If a Prime Designate were unable to bear a successor, then the future of our political rule would be in doubt. Rather than letting the other Designates intrigue and squabble over who should be the replacement heir, the sterile Prime Designate called a tournament of Ildiran jousting. All sons of the Mage-Imperator could compete to see who was best equipped to become leader of the Ildiran Empire.'

'You used a . . . a game to decide a matter of dynastic importance?' Nira wasn't sure if he was joking or not.

Jora'h's smoky eyes gleamed in the light. 'Ildiran jousting is no simple sport, Nira. It requires athletic ability, as well as speed of thought, strategy, learning how to cooperate with your enemies against a third foe.'

In the arena below, Cir'gh scored another tremendous blast. He scorched a reptilian steed so badly that its rider bowed his crystal lance and raised his mirror-painted shield in surrender, backing out

414

of the competition. The defeated knight returned to the side of the arena so that the two remaining jousters could battle out the championship.

Jora'h continued, 'The sterile Designate wanted his jousting tournament to be a grand event, a spectacular pageant that would be remembered for centuries to come. Unfortunately, it ended in tragedy.'

Nira was listening now, paying only slight heed to the laser battle going on below. 'Why? What happened?'

'The sterile Designate's most beloved brother was in the match when a mirror-shield broke in half, and the fragments sent beams flying into the audience. It killed him, his opponent, and three spectators.'

'How awful,' Nira said.

'The Designate's successor, when finally chosen, ruled under a cloud of doubt for ninety years. The sterile Designate who should have become Mage-Imperator remained an adviser in the Prism Palace for the rest of his years and never chose to be castrated, as was his right.'

Below, one-eyed Cir'gh finally defeated his opponent, and the other knight raised his shield, conceding. The crowd roared. Jora'h stood to applaud as the brilliant spotlights increased the illumination inside the arena, dazzling Nira.

'You have a strange but compellingly beautiful history, Jora'h,' Nira said.

His face seemed to diffuse with warmth upon hearing her say that. 'I hope you continue to think so, Nira, as you learn more about us.'

SEVENTY-TWO

ESTARRA

Father Idriss and Mother Alexa were surprised, then disappointed, when Beneto announced his intention to leave Theroc and devote himself to the backwater colony of Corvus Landing. They had anticipated much greater things for their second son, perhaps a primary position or a leadership role among the green priests.

But in the end, they bowed to the wishes of the worldforest. When Alexa finally realized that this was truly what her son wanted, she embraced him and announced that she would host a grand farewell celebration, complete with a full performance from the most skilled treedancers from the largest tree cities. Beneto smiled graciously, though he would have preferred no fuss whatsoever. Alexa was doing this more to fulfil her own needs than her son's, and so he accepted the planned banquet with good grace.

Upon hearing of her brother's imminent departure, Estarra was deeply hurt. With a sad expression, Beneto gave her the news directly, rather than letting her learn from her parents or from gossip. She would miss the times she had spent with him out in the forests, talking about native plants and towering worldtrees and any other thoughts that came into her head. But she could see in Beneto's face that this volunteer assignment was truly a dream that had captured his heart.

'I'll think about you often, Beneto,' she said, already lonely. 'Maybe some day I'll be able to travel and see you on Corvus Landing.'

He laughed. 'From what I can tell, there isn't much of a tourist industry, but old Talbun seems to enjoy living there. I look forward to taking his place, so that he can move on.'

On the day of the farewell celebration, Estarra wanted to contribute in a way that would make her brother proud. She considered helping with the banquet preparations, but decided instead to gather Beneto's favourite delicacy: slices of the tender outer skin of the reef fungus, found only at the topmost, uninhabitable layers of their city.

Estarra and her sister Celli climbed to the upper chambers of the fungus-reef where the walls were too young and soft to support permanent dwellings. The girls strapped pouches to their waists and lashed spikes on to their thick boots, ready to climb out on to the sloping soft layers.

'You're too old to do this,' Celli said, looking at her sister. Estarra had just turned thirteen, an awkward age that placed her among the full-grown women half the time, while at other times she was reluctant to sever her ties to childhood.

'I am not,' Estarra said, ready to punch her sister. 'Besides, I'm doing this for Beneto, and you aren't going to stop me.'

'I'll gather more mushroom meat than you will,' Celli said. 'He's my brother too.'

Yes, he is, Estarra thought, *and we'll both lose him when he leaves tomorrow.*

With Celli breathing down her neck, Estarra pushed through the rubbery-lipped opening of a natural window. Using a support hook, she clawed her way on to the outer roof. Celli scampered over the hardening mushroom to the fresh, expanding growth, her boot spikes giving her traction. The girl pulled out her knife while searching for a good spot far from scars where the children had cut the fungus. 'Careful!' she cried in a singsong voice.

Estarra climbed straight up to the highest point of knobbly growth, where she would find the tenderest flesh. 'Mind your own business.' She knew that Celli just wanted to win some imagined race, while she herself thought only of Beneto. She wanted her brother to have a good memory of her whenever he got lonely for Theroc on Corvus Landing.

Estarra pounded a metal stake at the end of her arm's reach to pull herself higher. She spread herself flat on the delicate skin of the fungus and crawled upwards, planting the heel of her foot against the stake for support. It wobbled beneath her weight.

Estarra began cutting meaty chunks and stuffing them into the pouch at her waist. She gritted her teeth with the effort, but thought of the great feast she would make for Beneto. Sarein would no doubt frown at her sister for climbing up and doing a child's work, suggesting that Estarra should find more mature responsibilities. But Estarra bit her lower lip and climbed even higher, assuring herself that no one else would do this for her brother.

She balanced precariously and leaned forward to cut another slice, though her pouch was already mostly full. Then, accidentally, she triggered one of the spore nodules, which unleashed a shower of pebbly white powder into her face.

Estarra sneezed violently as the spores caught in her nose and throat. Unable to breathe, she sneezed again, the fit sending spasms through her body. She slipped and tumbled off the smooth outer covering of the reef. Frantically, she scrambled with her spiked boots, trying to gain purchase.

The spikes ripped gashes in the soft mushroom, and when she finally hit the support stake she had pounded in, it tore free and she plunged through the roof. The soft tissue dumped more spores around her, and she dropped through fleshy walls down into another unopened chamber of the fresh growth.

'Help!' she shouted, then sneezed again and tried to catch her breath. The air was close around her, but at least she wasn't falling any more.

Wide-eyed, Celli scrambled to the gaping hole through which Estarra had broken. The little girl balanced carefully, leaning forward to look at her older sister. Then, seeing that Estarra was not hurt, she began to giggle. 'I said you were too big.'

Later, with an embarrassing crowd of her family and other spectators gathered to watch, it took several other children with ropes and pulleys to haul Estarra out. Beneto stood on a high branch to direct the rescue, calm and self-assured. The girl emerged, slick with smelly moisture from deep within the reef fungus. Her twisted braids had become tangled and loose, and her cheeks and arms were covered with grime. But all in all, the only thing injured was Estarra's pride.

When Beneto came to see her, Estarra was afraid he would be disappointed in how she had clumsily got herself into trouble doing a foolish thing for him. Instead, he hugged her. 'Thank you, Estarra. If your heart wasn't so big, maybe you wouldn't have fallen through the roof of the city.'

No matter what anyone else might say, she knew that he understood what she had been trying to do. Emotions crowded in a lump in her throat, but Estarra could only look at him with relief sparkling through her tears. After that, everything was all right.

*

She held that moment close in her thoughts throughout the long, loud banquet and farewell celebrations. The memory did not help to mitigate her sadness the following morning when she stood on the high treetops and watched Beneto's shuttle depart, taking him away to a distant world forever.

SEVENTY-THREE

RLINDA KETT

In the asteroid field between Mars and Jupiter, the EDF began the largest military construction project in human history. Space scavengers corralled metal-rich asteroids, diverted their orbits, and brought resources together into chaotic three-dimensional rubble piles.

Hundreds of thousands of sophisticated engineers moved out to the gigantic site, along with numerous shifts of workaday orbital construction jockeys. A second wave came: support personnel, resources, temporary habitation canisters, food, water, fuel. Construction never stopped for a moment.

The Terran Hanseatic League had authorized the funding and labour necessary to complete the mobilization project in the fastest possible time. King Frederick had given speeches, warning his people that they would be required to make sacrifices for the good of mankind. All of humanity must unite against the mysterious and destructive enemy.

Anger and fear ran rampant throughout the colonies. There seemed to be no pattern to the alien attacks. Two Roamer skymines, four uninhabited moons, and a technical observation platform. Political leaders demanded that the EDF mount the greatest possible resistance against the mysterious foe, regardless of cost.

Rlinda Kett, however, felt she was paying a higher price than most. Forlorn, she sat in a mobile administrative station outside the dockyards where construction engineers and inventory specialists moved among the vessels being refitted to new military purposes. Rlinda regarded the great steel whalebones of structural frameworks, new hulls being assembled, powerful engines grafted to commandeered cargo vessels like her own poor ships. She felt sick inside just to watch the butchery. Her merchant fleet would never be the same.

When a door hatch hissed open in the dim lounge, Rlinda did not turn from where she sat brooding. The last thing she wanted was polite conversation with one of the people who had confiscated, with feigned apologies, three of her four remaining merchant ships to convert them into fast reconnaissance vessels and materiel-supply craft.

The simple act – blithely ordered by King Frederick and signed by some bureaucrat who paid little attention to whatever paper was thrust in front of him – had robbed Rlinda of her dreams, and most of her livelihood. The token payment from the EDF wouldn't be enough to buy rations for more than a year.

Instead of a bureaucrat or supply expert, though, the next sound she heard was the friendly voice of Branson Roberts, whose *Blind Faith* had been among the three commandeered ships. 'The least they could do would be to offer us some strong drink.' He came forward, and Rlinda shifted in her chair, giving him a wan smile. 'A good dose of hard alcohol to help ease my heartache.'

Rlinda wrapped an arm around his waist, hugging him close. 'You're a good pilot, BeBob. Want a recommendation letter? You can get a commission flying reconnaissance surveys. The EDF will give you a pension, and you can have all the military rations you can eat.'

'All I can stomach, you mean,' he grumbled. 'Not like your cooking, Rlinda.'

'You're sweet,' she said.

He leaned over to make the hug closer, and she pecked him on the cheek. He had curly grey-black hair that had grown too long, like a tiny thundercloud over his head. His cheeks had begun to sag a bit with age, giving him an endearing hangdog look, especially with his big brown eyes. They'd had five good years as husband and wife, passionate years, but the two had learned that they just couldn't stand being together all the time.

'Glad to hear they let you keep the *Voracious Curiosity*,' BeBob said.

'A small enough consolation prize after losing the rest of my fleet.' Rlinda shrugged. 'But I'll take it, I suppose.'

She climbed to her feet, and the two looked out at the flurry of activity. Cutters and welders fetched components extruded by self-contained smelters. Military engineers scrabbled over the outer surfaces of the seized commercial spacecraft. Rlinda's heart went out as she thought of the years of investment and hard work those vessels meant to the traders who had been forced to surrender them.

'Maybe I'll sign up for one of the mapping missions to other gas giants,' BeBob muttered. 'I hear General Lanyan is calling for fast pilots to go look for those aliens. Maybe they'll give me back the *Blind Faith*.'

'Write your own ticket,' Rlinda said. 'You know I'll sign it.'

In comfortable silence with each other's company, Rlinda and BeBob remained together in the dim lounge. They stared into the darkness of space, where sunlight reflected from the metal hulls and the shiny surfaces of strip-mined asteroids. Against the black-velvet universe, the bright beacons of stars shone behind dazzling Jupiter.

Finally, Rlinda stirred. 'Time to get back to my one remaining ship. You're right, I'm lucky to still have it . . . and for now, at least, the galley is fully stocked.' She raised her eyebrows at him. 'Would you be amenable to letting me fix you a nice dinner? I've got a few interesting Theron ingredients left, and a special new recipe I've been wanting to try.'

BeBob looked at her and practically glowed. He bent his arm behind his back, comically twisting it. 'Ouch, okay, okay! I'm convinced.' Then he continued more seriously, 'Yes, Rlinda, I'd like that very much. It could be one of the last fancy meals I'll have in a while.'

Rlinda stood next to him, staring out at the stars. 'You and me both,' she said. 'I see plenty of tough times ahead.'

SEVENTY-FOUR

TASIA TAMBLYN

Though Roamer commercial ships provided vital ekti and other resources for the Terran Hanseatic League, the EDF treated the 'space gypsies' with distaste. Tasia figured the Eddies needed to have some sort of scapegoat until they got into a real fight with the enemy aliens. So she put up with it. For herself, she intended to save her energy for the right opponent.

When she'd volunteered for the space military, Tasia had been prepared for lousy treatment. She didn't let childish insults bother her and usually made a witty rejoinder that surprised Patrick Fitzpatrick (especially when he didn't understand her comment and had to pretend that he did). After his injury in the decompression exercise, she had hoped Fitzpatrick might be sent home to a desk job. Inventorying spampax, maybe . . . He hadn't been. She foiled the criticism of her fellow recruits with superior performance in all training exercises. The kleebs could make all the snotty comments they wanted, but they knew she could outshoot and outfly any one of them.

Still, any time a piece of equipment unexpectedly broke down or messages were inexplicably garbled, wary eyes turned towards her as if she were some sort of hidden saboteur. Tasia couldn't understand why Roamers would be suspect, since they had lost more than anyone else to the new enemy. But the other Eddies did not look at their suspicions rationally.

What do you expect from kleebs?

By now her father and Jess must know where she had gone. Sometimes, she allowed herself a wry smile, imagining how Bram Tamblyn would have railed and ranted at what his daughter had done. He would have shouted at the frozen ice ceiling and, bewildered, asked what he had done wrong as a parent. Jess could have given him a long litany of his parental shortcomings . . . but he wouldn't. Instead, Bram would end up riding Jess harder than ever, adding responsibilities and pressures, criticizing his every task, and unwittingly losing his only remaining child . . .

She lifted her chin with determination. One day, after she'd become a vital key to defeating the sinister aliens, her father might actually be proud of her. Tasia would not hold her breath, though.

She was on duty in the base communications centre, a domed room atop the cracked canyons of Labyrinthus Noctis, during an off-hours shift that had nothing to do with the day/night cycle of Mars. All Eddies ran on standard Earth military time, regardless of what planet or ship they served on.

A Roamer supply vessel had stopped at the EDF base on Earth's Moon to drop off much-needed tanks of ekti for military use. Upon departure from the Moon, the cargo ship had sent a loud scrambled signal at a very low frequency, far below the range of normal communication bands. When Moon-base EDF personnel demanded an explanation, the Roamer captain answered with chagrin that he'd experienced a malfunction of his pulse transmitter, that he'd merely sent a test signal in a low frequency band that would not interfere with normal EDF communications. Tasia hid her smile, not believing the excuse for a second. Even the Eddies didn't seem to be convinced.

Then the Roamer vessel had streaked away from the Moon. But rather than heading up and out of the Sol system, the cargo ship looped in a broad parabola that intersected the orbit of Mars. The red planet was a third of the way clockwise around the Sun.

In the communications centre, Tasia spotted the oncoming craft and hesitated. The Roamer ship displayed extraordinary speed as it approached the military compound on Mars. The vessel almost certainly had doctored serial numbers and a false identification beacon. Even without knowing the captain's clan, she still didn't want to get him in trouble . . . but if Tasia didn't sound the alarm fast enough, then more suspicion would be cast upon *her*. She punched the alert signal.

'Roamer captain, identify yourself. You have no authorized approach vector.' He did not answer, and Tasia signalled again, more urgently this time. 'You are not allowed to land. All supplies must be delivered to the Moon base. Mars is off-limits to unauthorized personnel.' *Especially Roamers.*

'I do not intend to land,' the captain finally answered, and she thought she recognized his voice. *Jess?* That was impossible.

'Transmitting my authorization now.' He sent a garbled burst signal that lasted barely two seconds. Then, activating his enhanced engines, the unidentified Roamer captain accelerated away from Mars faster than the Remora interceptors could hope to catch him. The speed with which the cargo ship moved astonished the EDF personnel, who expected only clunky, barely functional spacecraft from the gypsy traders. Tasia knew better.

'What the hell was that?' said the watch commander, bleary-eyed, rushing into the control room. 'Tamblyn?'

'I don't know, sir.' She looked helplessly at her fellow soldiers.

'It was a Roacher ship,' said Patrick Fitzpatrick. Somehow, she always drew shared duty with him. 'Ask Tamblyn.'

'That signal was similar to one the pilot transmitted at the Moon base,' Tasia said, knowing that if she hid that fact it would only make them wonder more. 'Can't figure out why, sir.'

'Probably some kind of spy signal,' Fitzpatrick said.

The watch commander said, 'A coded message? Get it deencrypted, pronto!' He looked at Tasia, then at the other Eddies in the communications centre. 'Put our best cryptographers on it. I want to know if that Roamer contacted a spy or a mole in our midst.'

Tasia's skin crawled, realizing what everyone must be thinking, but she sat stony-faced, bearing it. If she protested her innocence, it would only make her look worse. 'He went to the Moon base first, sir,' Tasia pointed out, 'then came here. Maybe he's looking for someone.'

'Well, for the sake of the human race, let's hope that Roacher turncoat didn't find whoever he was looking for.'

Tasia bit her lip to stop herself from defending the captain. They had no proof that the Roamer intended anything that might harm the Terran war effort. She sighed. She had worked so hard to demonstrate her loyalty, preparing to avenge Ross as soon as an opportunity presented itself, but even as she made progress, something cost her all the ground she had gained. She might have to punch a few more noses next mealtime if the kleebs got too obnoxious or rowdy.

Whatever the Roamer captain had wanted here, it was the last thing in the universe Tasia needed.

EA waited two full days, according to the command instructions in the coded transmission. Then the dutiful compy approached Tasia as discreetly as possible.

Tasia had offered her personal robot for the performance of vital EDF duties, but EA still devoted part of her time to watching over her owner. This shift she and Tasia had been assigned together to a red-walled storage bunker to take inventory of cold-environment garments for the Martian surface. The small compy worked diligently at her side, and Tasia was comforted just by the Listener robot's presence.

EA hummed, as if scanning. 'There are no eavesdroppers. It is safe for me to speak.' The voice that came out of the compy was eerie and familiar. 'Tasia, I'm so glad I found you. I have to give you some terrible news, and this was the only way I could manage it.'

It was Jess's voice! She whirled, but only the little robot stood there playing her recorded message, reminding Tasia of a demon-possessed person speaking with a different personality.

Jess's voice continued, 'Roamer compies have special programming, Tasia, and I activated it by sending a coded signal. EA knows to engage protective measures if she is ever in danger of being captured by an enemy, and she has instructions to find a time when she can talk with you. We didn't know if a message would get through by regular channels.'

Tasia's mind ran through many possibilities. What would Jess ask of her? What bad news did he bring?

'Tasia . . . Dad is dead,' Jess said through EA's vocal speaker. 'He suffered a stroke the night of Ross's funeral, the night you ran away. He never recovered. We searched for you, but you had already gone.'

Tasia reeled. Her vision blurred with sudden, stinging tears.

He paused, and his voice took on a grimmer tone. 'You've got a decision to make, and I can't really help you out now. There's been another attack on a Roamer skymine, just like Ross's. The facility at Erphano was completely destroyed, all hands lost.'

Now his voice sounded poignant and beseeching. 'You've got your own obligations and responsibilities. I understand that. But only you and I are left in the family. Our uncles are already running the water mines, as it should be. I'm helping where I can, but I need you here, little sister. Can you come home? You've made your point by joining the Eddies. You don't owe the Big Goose anything.'

Tasia stiffened to hear this, because in her heart she did owe them loyalty. She had *chosen* to enlist in the EDF, had taken her vow of service, had trained with them. And she knew that without her, the inept recruits had little chance against the enemy. She thought of the kleebs she practised with and how poorly they treated her . . . but that didn't mean she could just desert the military forces now. Wouldn't that prove they had been right about Tasia all along, that she was unreliable, not to be trusted?

Her head reeled with the sudden shift in her world. She thought of the cold but familiar ice shelves on Plumas, the water mines, the liquid geysers gushing towards pumping stations on the ice caps.

'Tasia, come back if you can,' Jess repeated. 'Or find some other way to make our family proud. I trust you to do what's right. You can figure it out for yourself.'

Tasia swallowed a lump in her throat. She stared at EA's placid metal face and imagined the features of her brother overlaid upon it.

'Shizz, I can't leave now, Jess,' she said. When no further words were forthcoming from the recording, Tasia said sharply, 'EA, do you know how to get a message back to him?'

'Back to whom, Tasia?'

'Back to Jess, in response to the message.'

'What message, Tasia?' EA asked.

'The one you just played.'

EA paused, as if reassessing her memory. 'I have no recollection of any message, Tasia. We have been here, performing inventory.'

Jess must have appended an erasure command to his recording. Ingenious, but typical. She couldn't even listen to his voice again, no matter how much she wanted to. Her brother was being very careful, knowing EA was in the vicinity of many troops who might not have Roamer interests at heart.

'Oh, never mind, EA,' she said, and looked up at the sealed containers of insulated gloves waiting for her inventory check. Her mind spinning, her heart heavy, Tasia plunged into the task with redoubled effort.

SEVENTY-FIVE

BASIL WENCESLAS

Gaping red canyons cracked open like raw wounds, stretching from the EDF Mars base in all directions. From the spherical observation cockpit of the broad-winged glider transport, Basil Wenceslas scrutinized the razor-edged canyons that accented a mercilessly rugged landscape.

Beside him, personally piloting the craft high in the vanishingly thin Martian atmosphere, General Kurt Lanyan considered the canyons to be a challenging but necessary obstacle course. Like a school of silver minnows, mismatched fighters – standard-model Remoras as well as modified private yachts recently absorbed into the fleet – streaked along. The pilots angled around sharp goosenecks, roared down blind gorges, and at the last moment pulled up to shoot straight towards the twilight of open space.

'Troop training is progressing with all due urgency, Chairman Wenceslas,' Lanyan said. 'We've had a handful of accidents so far, but certainly an acceptable ratio, considering the number and variety of non-standard civilian vessels we've incorporated into the EDF.'

'How many accidents?' Basil asked as he watched a pair of ships perform a breathtaking manoeuvre in a narrow gorge below, like two daredevil fighting fish.

'Eleven, sir.'

'Fatalities?'

Lanyan gripped the glider's controls, uncomfortable for a moment, then turned to Basil. 'Mr Chairman, sir . . . this is Mars. In any accident, fatalities are always encountered. The ships and crews were completely lost.'

They continued to observe the rigorous military manoeuvres while they discussed the growing crisis. The heavy fleet buildup had required a retooling of many Hansa industries. The EDF had been forced to scrape raw materials and finished components from widespread human colonies. The Hanseatic League had already levied higher taxes and tariffs in order to continue expanding the military. Everyone had been called upon to pull together and show the strongest possible face.

The aggressive deep-core creatures had struck again, and again.

'I could engage a much more effective preparation for this impending conflict if I had some intelligence – even basic data – of our adversary,' General Lanyan said forcefully. 'Have we received any communication yet from the enemy, any parley or demands? Do we even know what they *are*? Why they attack us?'

Basil shook his head. 'They've left no survivors.'

'Is it true they attacked a third Roamer skymine?'

'Yes, but we haven't generally released that report yet. No warning, no mercy. Complete destruction, same as before. If the Roamers are afraid to continue harvesting ekti, we'll run into fuel shortages.'

Lanyan grumbled, 'Maybe now those aloof gypsies will join with the rest of the Hansa. Have they requested EDF protection? Military escorts at their remaining skymine facilities?'

Basil frowned. 'Not in so many words, but they will eventually. The Roamers have never been keen on asking us for help.'

'Let them scrape by then.' General Lanyan descended to a wider valley where they watched space-suited marines performing ground exercises. The glider maintained too much altitude for Basil to see details other than silvery shapes moving about on the red sands. 'After executing Sorengaard's corsairs, I suspected that the Roamers might present certain difficulties of their own. These aliens might keep them in line.'

Basil scolded him. 'Don't let prejudice colour your thoughts, General. The Roamers have never committed overt violence against Hansa settlements. Rand Sorengaard himself seems to have been an anomaly.'

'A deceased anomaly,' the General said.

'We have no need of scapegoats. The Roamers have lost three skymine facilities with no survivors. We *need* ekti, General, and if the Roamers stop providing it, we don't have alternative sources readily available. Neither do the Ildirans.'

Lanyan nodded grudgingly as he watched the soldiers moving about in the impossibly dry valley of the waterless world. Basil suspected that, like himself, the General was mainly bothered that the Roamers operated as they pleased, without any Hansa oversight. Tariffs and taxes were imposed on ekti deliveries, but the actual skymines went unregulated, unmonitored. The space gypsies provided stardrive fuel and other resources desperately needed by Hansa colonies, and so Roamer eccentricities had to be tolerated.

As a military man, though, Lanyan was concerned. 'I just don't like the existence of such a large and independent group of . . . guerrillas. Nobody knows what they're doing out there, or even where they all live. Consider the potential risk they represent.'

Basil said, 'General, I myself have been troubled by certain inconsistencies. You are not aware of this, but I had my expediter,

Mr Pellidor, obtain commercial records for the past fifteen years and instructed a team of my best population statisticians to make projections as to the size of the Roamer population, based upon the resources they purchase from Hansa suppliers. At first glance, the number seemed relatively small, comfortably insignificant.'

'About what I expected.' Lanyan guided the glider, waiting for the other shoe to drop. 'But?'

'But I discovered that the Roamers have been gathering their own resources – perhaps quite extensive resources – to supplement what they purchase from us. That changes all the parameters.' He drew a deep breath. 'Therefore, since they do not depend entirely on the Hansa, Roamer settlements and populations could be *far* more extensive than we imagine.'

'Damn,' General Lanyan said, his face reddening. 'How many, exactly?'

'They could have hundreds, even thousands, of undocumented colonies. All self-sufficient, none of them paying Hansa taxes.'

'Impossible! We would know!'

The ethereal winds of Mars buffeted the glider, and Basil continued, 'I've assigned discreet spies to keep track of Roamer ships trading with Hansa outposts, compiling a catalogue of all their known vessels. When I finally began to look at the collated information, I was amazed at how many different vessels the Roamers are using. They seem to be building their own ships – lots of them.'

'And they've lost three skymines to the enemy aliens,' the General said.

'Three *that we know of*,' Basil pointed out. 'But out of how many? We don't know how many skymines the Roamers are operating, or where they are. Originally, they purchased a dozen old ekti-harvesting facilities from the Ildirans, but since that time they have built plenty more. How many? The Roamers don't report to the

435

Hansa each time they put a new one into operation. In fact, the facility that was destroyed at Erphano was completely unknown to us.'

'Bastards,' Lanyan said.

Basil shook his head. 'There are so many skymines, General, countless uninhabited systems. The Hansa's appetite for ekti is voracious — so how can we complain about their industry? Who could keep track of where all the facilities might be? No one has had the incentive before, since the Roamers keep delivering the stardrive fuel that we desperately need. They don't overcharge us, and thus we don't ask questions.'

No one had ever imagined that the seemingly aloof and disorganized space trash might in fact be part of a large hidden civilization in the back corners of the Spiral Arm. It reminded Basil of swarms of cockroaches living all unseen within the cracks of a dwelling. 'Roachers' seemed an appropriate term for them.

'Perhaps the skymine facilities should be nationalized,' Lanyan said. 'Military necessity, emergency powers act. Order them all to be placed under Hansa control and allow us to impose order. The alien attacks could serve as an effective excuse.'

Basil laughed. 'Impossible, General. Completely impossible. And if we provoke the Roamers in that way, they might well embargo all the ekti. They're the ones holding the cards, not us.'

'How about EDF spy ships? We could dispatch reconnaissance vessels, look for Roamer skymines.'

'Across the whole Spiral Arm, search for floating factories on every gas planet? Is *that* where you recommend we expend our efforts, General? The few unrecorded facilities we might discover would be an insignificant percentage, and then we'd have to take them over, occupy the facilities, and run them ourselves. *That*, General, would be an unwinnable strategy.'

Lanyan took the broad-winged glider higher, then cruised back towards the main base. They had seen enough troop demonstrations for the day.

'At the very least,' the General said, his voice showing that he had taken the time to consider his suggestion, 'we could use the crisis to call for a full census of the Roamers. Under the guise of offering to protect their skymines, we could flush them out into the open. That data could prove very useful.'

Basil refused, for now. 'Their Speaker Okiah is a clever old woman. She would see through the ruse immediately. The alien attackers are our primary concern, and I don't want to do anything to jeopardize our steady flow of ekti.' He pursed his lips. 'However . . . I will impose price restrictions, so that the Roamers can feel the effects of this war in their credit accounts as well.'

'It will be difficult enough to prosecute a war against an alien threat we don't understand.' Lanyan did not appear completely satisfied with the solution as he brought the glider in for a landing at the multiple domes of the Mars base. 'The last thing we need is a wrench in the machinery from human beings as well.'

SEVENTY-SIX

JESS TAMBLYN

An emergency clan gathering had been called at Rendezvous. But the Roamer family representatives were in such an uproar that even Jhy Okiah, with her decades of experience as Speaker, could barely maintain order.

Leaders of the various family groups sat on their designated benches in the crowded discussion chamber, jostling, talking, shouting. The air reprocessors worked double-time to keep the atmosphere fresh and breathable, because of the unusual number of people. The food, air, and water resources of the Roamer gathering point were taxed to their limits. But Speaker Okiah had deemed no other matter more important for their survival.

Jess Tamblyn sat silently on his designated bench, watching the proceedings, but deep in thought. He was now the official head of the Tamblyn clan, at least the man in the best position to represent the water mines, though his four uncles worked hard to keep the facilities running at peak production. Jess would rather be here. He had promised himself to show no weakness, to do everything expected of him.

He drew strength from looking at Cesca Peroni, beautiful in the companion chair next to the old Speaker. She looked coolly formal, a work of art, but Jess knew the fires inside her, the passions and the strength that she now directed towards protecting and managing the Roamer people. And Jess would not let his personal feelings endanger the future of the clans. Neither he nor Cesca could afford the slightest distraction now.

'We resolve nothing by shouting at each other,' Jhy Okiah said from the centre of the chamber, voice dry but strong.

'We resolve nothing by sitting here and *talking*!' Del Kellum shouted back. His starship-construction yards in the rings of Osquivel were close enough to a brooding gas planet that he felt threatened. 'Shizz, Roamers were not meant to meekly accept our fates.' Other clan representatives stomped their booted feet on the metal floors.

Jhy Okiah let them blow off steam. 'Of course not. But doing the wrong thing might be worse than doing nothing. We will follow the Guiding Star, but first we must set our course. At present, we have no information about our enemies or their reasons for attacking us. We're like a ship without a navigator flying at full speed through an asteroid field.'

Cesca moved to the Speaker's side, her dark eyes flashing. She addressed Del Kellum directly. 'Do you intend to shut down your shipyards? Are you suggesting that we withdraw all skymines from every gas giant, just to be safe? When have Roamers ever been safe?'

Grumbling, fists clenched, Kellum sat back down. 'In truth, I don't know what to do, by damn – not even what to suggest. But we've lost four skymines already – another one just days ago at Welyr! A thousand people dead, maybe more.' The middle-aged man's chest heaved as he wrestled with his anguish. Jess knew that Kellum had spent years courting Shareen Pasternak, Chief of the recently destroyed facility on Welyr.

'Yes,' the Speaker said coldly, 'and my grandson Berndt was one of the casualties at Erphano. Just like your Shareen at Welyr, Del Kellum. Don't try to convince me of the cost.'

Jess watched the discussion. Everyone at the clan gathering felt as much horror and uneasiness as he did. Everyone wanted to take direct and effective action . . . but no one knew what to do.

'Safe is one thing, foolhardy is another.' It was Crim Tylar, an ambitious blond-haired man who operated an old Ildiran skymine facility on the gas giant Ptoro. 'Perhaps we should call a temporary moratorium on ekti harvesting, pull our skymines out of the clouds until . . . until this is resolved.'

'Madness!' bellowed Cesca's father, Denn Peroni. He owned a small merchant and cargo fleet of Roamer vessels. 'Commerce in ekti is the lifeblood of Roamer civilization. Would you have us sell cometary dust?'

Cesca said, 'Ekti is vital to the Big Goose, as well as the Ildiran Empire. This crisis affects far more than just Roamer business.' She looked pensive, eyes narrowing as she turned to speak with Jhy Okiah. 'Is there a chance the EDF will mount a strong response on our behalf? The Goose has no great love for Roamers, but if we threaten to stop ekti production, they'll know they must protect their source of stardrive fuel.'

Jhy Okiah pursed her wrinkled lips. The other Roamers had fallen silent, eager to hear her answer. 'That may be asking for worse problems down the road. Roamers have always avoided requesting Hansa assistance.'

Someone shouted, 'When have we ever been able to count on them to do anything for us?'

'I, for one, don't want to be in Earth's debt,' grumbled Crim Tylar. 'They'll demand payment at the worst possible time.'

'Then our only other alternative is to protect ourselves,' Jhy Okiah said firmly.

'But how, by damn?' Del Kellum half rose to his feet, then sat back, bouncing in the low gravity. 'The Roamers don't have any military. We need the Eddies to fight the aliens.'

At the mention of the Earth Defence Forces, Jess sank deeper into his seat, concerned again about his little sister. He had been obligated to send Tasia the message about their father, but she had her own responsibilities – did the Eddies have a stronger hold on her than her clan? Her enlistment had been brash, but she had taken an oath of service. She couldn't just ignore that and run home to Plumas. No Tamblyn could. Jess knew that well enough.

He wasn't particularly concerned about his sister's ability to take care of herself. In fact, if she got into an altercation, Jess felt more sympathy for anyone who stood in Tasia's way. But he longed to have her back. Tasia's bright personality, quick wit, and sarcastic jokes would have been welcome on Plumas.

Even without Ross, or his father, or Tasia, Jess had to keep his clan business running. He would come through this, do what was right. The one anchor point that allowed him to keep his sanity – his love for Cesca Peroni – had to wait. Indefinitely.

He watched Cesca, her olive skin so smooth and perfect, her pointed chin lifted with pride and inner strength. The Roamers needed Cesca even more than Jess did. Though his heart might ache, their love could endure whatever time was necessary until they could be together . . .

Eventually, the Roamer clan gathering faded without resolution, like a dissipating cloud of smoke. Some of the family leaders promised to relocate their ekti harvesters and stop all cloud-mining operations, while others argued that the attacking aliens would likely be able to strike the facilities even in high orbit, so what was the use in withdrawing? Other clan members promised to convert their private industrial facilities and orbital construction yards to the purpose of manufacturing new weapons, if they could develop designs and plans fast enough.

Afterwards, Jess came up to Cesca and said a brief, private farewell, but he was unable to speak the things weighing on his mind. Their eyes communicated much to each other, but then other clan members came to argue with Jhy Okiah. Jess retreated quietly to his ship and flew away from the blood-red sun of Meyer.

En route to Plumas, across the lonely black vacuum, Jess had all the time in the world to contemplate plans. He was certain that with his knowledge and imagination, he could think of a way to strike against the silent aggressors, something no one else had considered. He wanted to hit them where it would hurt the most.

Jess now had access to all the resources and facilities of the extended Tamblyn family. In spite of his plea for Tasia to come home, he had plenty of competent deputies who could easily run the water-mining operations. Plumas had been self-sufficient for decades, running smoothly, providing water and air and in-system fuel. Rather than pulling all of his clan's resources together into a defensive posture, Jess would strike against the aliens instead. He had an idea.

The enemy had attacked without warning. He would do likewise, a personal vendetta. Tasia would be proud of that.

The Terran military did not know where to start. Jess, though, sat in his cockpit, calling up the detailed charts Ross had developed during years of surveying the Golgen system.

The aliens had shown that they had an interest in that particular gas giant. Jess would find the enemy lurking on Golgen, if he looked hard enough.

And as he studied the other scattered asteroids and the diffuse cometary cloud that formed a halo around Golgen's sun, Jess decided he would use the star system itself as a weapon against the enemy.

His eyes gleamed. Ross would have applauded the bold, crazy scheme – and never questioned whether it would work.

SEVENTY-SEVEN

NIRA

Even with so much work to do, Nira could hardly concentrate on her assigned tasks. The *Saga of Seven Suns* called to her, a magnificent and endless piece of descriptive poetry . . . but all the wonders of the Prism Palace and Mijistra – and yes, the attentions of Prime Designate Jora'h himself – called more strongly.

After their afternoon of Ildiran jousting, Jora'h had politely but insistently asked Nira to dine with him. She knew Ambassador Otema wanted her to devote hours to reading aloud stanzas from the *Saga*, and yet when Nira began to make excuses to the Prime Designate, his face took on such a look of open disappointment that her heart felt close to breaking. And so she had agreed.

Over a lavish and prolonged dinner, they talked more about Theroc, the green priests and the forest culture. Smiling, Jora'h raised a goblet filled with a honeyed green liqueur. 'Though he isn't here, I wish to toast my friend, Reynald, because he intrigued me. Otherwise, I might never have had the remarkable opportunity of meeting you, Nira.'

She laughed politely, not knowing how else to respond.

Though Otema had not explicitly chided her about her numerous distractions, the next day Nira promised to spend at least two-thirds of every waking period reading aloud to the treelings. The connected mind of the worldtrees drank up the Ildiran stories, growing in knowledge.

But when she decided that she had done enough work for the day, Nira allowed herself the luxury of exploring the Prism Palace. She learned how to recognize the ferocious-looking bodyguard kith, who would keep her away from where she wasn't wanted. Nira wanted to experience everything she could, but not to anger the Mage-Imperator.

As she wandered through tunnels circling the skysphere reception hall where the great leader had first received them, she ventured into a set of crystalline passageways. The halls took her past chambers with faceted walls and jewel inlays, behind which she could see the silhouettes of bureaucrats and document specialists at work.

She pressed her face close to a garnet-coloured pane, trying to make out details, but she saw only curious shapes and diligent workers. Some appeared to have odd body forms, different sizes and musculatures that she did not recognize from any familiar kith. But the garnet glass blurred the sharp outlines, and she had to squint to make out any details at all.

The halls were very quiet. The Mage-Imperator had withdrawn from his audiences to spend time in his contemplation chamber; the skysphere remained accessible to pilgrims and visitors, but without the leader present. Nira pressed her wide-eyed face against a crimson pane, trying to see more – when suddenly she heard a footstep in the corridor.

A tall man, obviously of noble kith like Jora'h, stepped out of the murky chamber and glared at her. His features were similar to the Prime Designate's, and Nira recognized a family resemblance, but this man looked harder. His face was stern, his hair shorter and spikier, as if bristling with displeasure.

'What are you doing?' he said. 'Spying?'

'No, just . . . looking. My name is Nira. I am from Theroc.' She felt embarrassed and stupid, because with her green skin and human features, she couldn't possibly be anyone else. 'You are a . . . Designate, are you not? Another son of the Mage-Imperator?'

'What were you doing there?' he said, cutting off her question. 'I am the Dobro Designate. Must I report your activities to my father?'

'I meant no harm. Prime Designate Jora'h told me I could explore wherever I wished.'

The Dobro Designate scowled at her. 'So, our *Saga of Seven Suns* has grown dull and tedious for you, and you must find other ways to occupy your mind?'

'Not at all!' She felt ashamed and perplexed, not understanding what she had done wrong or why he was so upset with her. She glanced at the thick garnet glass. 'I didn't see anything. If this is a restricted area, I will be happy to return to my own quarters.'

'Perhaps that would be wisest,' the Dobro Designate said, his voice sharp.

'I . . . meant no harm,' she said again.

His eyes narrowed, and he studied her in silence, as if dissecting her. 'Few people ever do.' Nira wondered what he meant by that.

She was about to turn and flee when he startled her with a gruff question. 'Is it true that you green priests are telepathic? That you can send thoughts through the trees and exchange information and knowledge instantaneously?'

'Y-yes, we can,' she stammered. 'The worldforest is vast and holds many thoughts. A green priest can touch all of them. Once we join with the forest, once we "take the green", we have access to telink.'

446

'Is this skill genetically based?' the Dobro Designate asked, stepping closer to her. 'How is it possible?'

'Not . . . exactly genetic,' Nira said. 'Although some Therons are better suited to the calling than others, the desire and ability does not necessarily breed true. The forest itself actually chooses. Many of our people know from childhood that they are meant to link with the worldforest. We commune with the trees, and we serve them.'

The Designate continued to scrutinize her, assessing, calculating. Then he dismissed her. 'That is all. You may go.'

Startled and disoriented, Nira retreated down the corridor. Unsettled by the encounter, she paused and turned to watch as the Dobro Designate strode in the opposite direction. The dour man walked through several security gates and past bristling guard kith until he was allowed into the private chambers of his father, the Mage-Imperator.

SEVENTY-EIGHT

MAGE-IMPERATOR

The door to the private contemplation chamber sealed behind the Dobro Designate, and the transparent magnifying walls misted over to become milky and impenetrable. No one could see them now. No one could guess what they intended to discuss.

The Designate bowed formally before the Mage-Imperator's curved chrysalis chair. 'I have arrived with my report as you commanded, Father.'

The corpulent leader sat up, his placid face slipping into an expression of malicious eagerness. 'You have brought the most remarkable examples of your experiments?'

'Yes, Liege,' the Dobro Designate said. He was the Mage-Imperator's second son, after Jora'h, but he followed the leader's thinking more closely. 'You will find them astonishing. Clearly your father's far-sighted wisdom has seized an opportunity for the Ildiran race.'

The Mage-Imperator operated a set of controls with his stubby fingers so that the cradle platform tilted him upright. The sides closed in, making the platform compact and streamlined; handles extruded from the sides. 'I wish to see these specimens with my own eyes.'

He called for attenders, and a group of small-statured helpers scurried in. They fought each other for the right to grasp the handles on the palanquin. Levitators switched on, lifting the enormous throne from the floor. The leader stroked his serpent-like braid and gestured forward with his chubby right hand. 'Follow my son. The Dobro Designate will show the way.'

Wearing a hard smile of confidence, the Designate exited through the opposite arched doorway. He led them out of the contemplation chamber and down sloping ramps to lower, more isolated rooms. He knew the Mage-Imperator would reward him for all the hard and unpleasant work he'd been forced to do on dreary Dobro. The end results of these experiments would justify all of the miserable effort.

Despite his eagerness, the Designate set a slow pace as the attenders carried the chrysalis chair, guiding it through wide passageways, always downhill. At this depth, other Ildiran workers – mainly guards and maintenance kith – stared in awe at their unaccustomed visitor under the harsh light, then they either bowed or rushed out of the way. The Designate paused on a hovering lift platform, which dropped them down several levels, through the sculptured hillside and into well-lit catacombs within the citadel. Blazers shone at every intersection.

Finally, they stopped at a private door guarded by four monstrous-looking warrior kithmen. The bodyguards stood aside, clearing the passage so the attenders could scuttle forward, hauling the floating palanquin chair. The Mage-Imperator looked around, his interest piqued, impatient with anything that got in his way.

They entered a gallery of glass-walled rooms. The transparent cells held strange humanoid creatures in an array of body types, unusual mixtures of shapes, musculatures, configurations – some of them impressive, some horrifying, some pathetic.

'As you can see, Father, our breeding programme has yielded a variety of results, as is to be expected. We collect data and then try to reproduce the cross-breed kith that we consider to have desirable traits.'

The Mage-Imperator ordered the frenetic attenders to nudge his palanquin forward so that he could float in front of the glass cells. With hard eyes, he stared at each of the mismatched creatures in turn. Some of them cowered from the immense leader, but the Mage-Imperator saw them only as specimens, not living beings. No pity whatsoever showed on his doughy face.

Certain half-breed creatures were covered with patchy scales, others had bristly fur. Several were well muscled, three having grossly enhanced arms and thighs. Two of the specimens looked broken, and huddled in misery in the far corners of the transparent cages: malformed specimens that had barely survived, genetic mixtures that were never meant to be. Every one bore some resemblance to the baseline Ildiran kiths, but the mismatched creatures also manifested a strikingly unusual quality, something alien that did not belong in Ildiran genes.

The Mage-Imperator backed off, his pasty face showing a mixture of disgust and optimism. He turned his intent gaze on his second son. 'I have never seen kith combinations such as these. The new bloodlines offer substantial new potential for our purposes.'

The Dobro Designate nodded vigorously. 'We keep trying to determine how strong the human bloodline needs to be. Our sample populations are still too small, and the time . . . it has been less than two centuries, enough for only a handful of generations.'

'Of course, my son. When my father first gave me this secret assignment, and later when I passed it on to you at the beginning of my rule, we all knew it would be a long-term task with vital consequences for our Empire.'

The Dobro Designate remained determined. 'Sometimes the third or even the fourth generation is the strongest. Our mixed-kith swimmers and architects are the best ever produced.'

'Good.' The Mage-Imperator twitched, and his attenders dragged him back from the gallery walls into the centre of the display chamber. 'Keep uppermost in your mind, however, that we must improve Ildiran *mental and communication* abilities. Now, more than ever, we must have success.'

'I am developing new avenues, Father,' the Dobro Designate said. 'Though it may take several more generations, decades at least.'

Now the Mage-Imperator looked upset. His chubby face wrinkled with a stormy expression. 'We may not have that much time. Our greatest fears have arisen. The threat has returned, and the Ildiran Empire must prepare to defend itself. We don't want to end like the Klikiss.'

Shocked, the Dobro Designate drew a deep breath to calm himself. 'Are you certain, Father? After all the legends, so many centuries upon centuries—'

'There is no question. I have seen the evidence for myself. The hydrogues have shown themselves again. Even my combined *thism* is not strong enough to accomplish what must be done. I had hoped that a cross-breed might enhance those characteristics. There is no higher priority, no greater need. We must plan, and succeed, before anyone else understands the nature of the danger.' He clenched a pudgy fist so violently that blood began to stream down his palm. 'We need at least one!'

Drawing strength and resolve, the Dobro Designate pressed forward. 'Then I must make a risky proposal. There is new information, Father. Perhaps you have seen it yourself? I just met a human, one of their green priests from Theroc – a young and obviously fertile female. Her biological connection with the worldtrees suggests some . . . very interesting genetic possibilities.'

The Mage-Imperator gestured for his chrysalis chair to move out into the corridor. The attenders pushed him backwards.

'Yes, indeed,' he said. 'I have already thought of this myself. We may have to use her, break her – and take what we need.'

SEVENTY-NINE

ADAR KORI'NH

The cohort of Ildiran warliners finally departed from the stark world of Dobro. Adar Kori'nh felt relieved to move on to the next military assignment. He could never escape a feeling of uneasiness when visiting this grim system, although he acted under the Mage-Imperator's orders. What the Dobro Designate continued to do on that planet seemed dark, horrible to him. Even humans did not deserve such treatment.

Through the all-seeing eye of the *thism*, Mage-Imperator Cyroc'h understood far more than the most well-trained Adar. A Mage-Imperator was more than any other Ildiran, the sum of their race, its pinnacle; his actions, thoughts, and decisions dictated the entire story of the Ildiran Empire. Kori'nh could not challenge the decision, but that did not make him condone the darker necessities. The Mage-Imperator knew what was best for all Ildirans, even if some people had to pay a terrible price.

It was not Adar Kori'nh's place to understand everything.

He muttered a quiet curse and sagged into the rounded seat of the lead warliner's command nucleus. Even though the Mage-

Imperator knew best, even if the outcome served the Ildiran race in some mysterious way, Kori'nh did not believe these sinister Dobro experiments could ever be viewed as heroic deeds. They would never be included in the *Saga of Seven Suns*.

'Our course is set for the Hyrillka system, Adar,' said the navigator, himself a septa commander who had been taken from his smaller grouping of ships to serve on the vanguard warliner. The navigator and all of the bridge crew looked similarly relieved to be departing from Dobro.

At Hyrillka, on the edge of the Horizon Cluster, they would perform one of the Solar Navy's more traditional duties. His full cohort of fabulous warships would engage in spectacular sky-parades to demonstrate the performance skills they had learned. The jovial Hyrillka Designate loved such spectacles and enjoyed hosting feasts and celebrations to honour Ildiran accomplishments.

Recently, the Mage-Imperator had encouraged increasingly grand exhibitions, even commanding Adar Kori'nh himself to lead the next aerial parade to commemorate the leader's birth anniversary. After so many years of flawless service, the Adar had grown bored with these childish displays of boisterous bravado. He wanted to do something more significant, more substantial.

But after seeing the unpleasantness on Dobro again, he was glad to participate in an event that was far less emotionally taxing.

The cohort of warliners cut like hatchets through space, continuing in perfect formation towards the Horizon Cluster. When the stardrives had powered up to cruising speed, he excused himself. 'I will be in my quarters, reviewing military strategy.'

His crew knew their tasks, and he expected no problems. In fact, during his full military career, he had never expected problems. The Solar Navy was a magnificent fleet, the best ever created in the Spiral Arm . . . yet for many long Ildiran generations they'd had no real enemy to fight. He had never understood why the succession of Mage-Imperators, for thousands of years, had insisted on maintaining such a huge military force when they faced no outside threat.

But a Mage-Imperator knew many things, understood much about the galaxy and the living story of their race.

Kori'nh sat in his cabin and studied the *Saga*, a private copy of certain relevant portions he always kept aboard his flagship. Many times he had been tempted to employ a rememberer for the fleet, a dedicated historian to regale the soldiers with heroic tales between their duties. But Kori'nh suspected he was the only one with such a specific and obsessive interest in military history.

The Ildiran race was a unified organism, composed of billions of people connected through the gossamer threads of *thism*. Ildirans had no outside enemies, no internal strife, no major civil wars. Except for one tragic story, which Kori'nh reread, adjusting the blazer panels in his quarters to a high brilliance that more closely simulated Ildira's seven suns.

One beloved Designate had suffered a serious head injury, and after recovering had been unable to tap into the *thism*. He could feel no connection with his Mage-Imperator, could receive no instructions. He was alone, adrift . . . separate.

The Designate had had a vision of independence. He led his hapless planet into a civil war against the Mage-Imperator, trying to break away from the Ildiran Empire, to begin his own story. The rogue Designate convinced his people that he was still receiving guidance from the *thism*, and they – knowing nothing else – had followed him. Yet his vision of independence brought only bloodshed and death. In the end, the insane son of the Mage-Imperator had been murdered, his misled people brought back into the fold of untainted *thism*. The appalling civil war had left deep psychological scars in the Ildiran psyche. For centuries, rememberers had sung ballads of the tragic event.

Feeling an oppressive sense of gloom after rereading the sad legend, Kori'nh put the *Saga* documents away. Then he opened his storage drawers and withdrew the weighty selection of medals and ribbons he had earned in his career. He took up cloths and creams and began to polish the metal and the jewels.

Disappointingly, he'd received most of the glittering awards for traditional service: presiding over spectacular test performances and military parades, successfully effecting rescue missions such as the one on Crenna, or using his soldiers to complete difficult civil-engineering feats.

The Ildirans had never met a great enemy for epic conflicts. Although the humans were somewhat troubling, they were obviously too disorganized to pose a real threat. The Klikiss had vanished eons ago, and the other life forms encountered in the Spiral Arm were still far too primitive to become spacefarers.

He wished he could one day seize significant glory for himself. Before he died, he wanted to achieve something vital and glorious that would warrant his inclusion in the epic history of his people. Adar Kori'nh had spent his entire career waiting for a worthy opponent.

For now, though, his only duty was to demonstrate the Solar Navy's prowess in order to amuse the Hyrillka Designate.

With Adar Kori'nh watching proudly beside him, the chubby Hyrillka Designate rose to his feet and applauded. In another comfortable seat in the permanent viewing stands, Thor'h, first-born noble son of the Prime Designate, also seemed to be enjoying himself. Though Thor'h was not much younger than his brother Qul Zan'nh, the noble son seemed much less mature, pampered and untested. The young man had more than a century yet before he could expect the responsibility of the chrysalis throne in the Prism Palace, and he took blithe advantage of his freedom.

In the sky, brilliant nearby stars shone like colourful jewels sprinkled across the vault of heaven, bright enough to be seen during daylight. At night, the glory of the Horizon Cluster filled the Hyrillka darkness like fireworks, showering even the deepest evening with enough light to comfort a shadow-fearing Ildiran.

Thick vines full of brilliant flowers grew in tangles around the tall buildings, filling the stands with sweet perfume. Immaculately dressed pleasure mates surrounded the Designate's observation chair, and he looked at them adoringly, though Thor'h could not tear his eyes from the aerial display.

Two big warliners hovered above the primary city. 'Have them do the last part again!' Thor'h said, his eyes bright with boyish wonder.

The Hyrillka Designate tore a pastry in half and fed the two morsels to the closest women. 'Indeed, Adar. Those flips are breathtaking. Can we have an encore?'

'As you wish, Lord Designate.' The Adar spoke into a communications link at his wrist.

The fast inter-orbital craft turned about in a long sweep and streaked back towards the primary Hyrillka city. Behind them, the vessels trailed kilometres-long streamers made of reflectorized metal that sparkled like electrified whips in the sky. The ships flew so low and fast that they rippled the colourful and gentle fields of enormous blooming nialias, making their dusty blue petals flap. The mobile male forms of the plantmoths broke from some stems and took panicked flight.

The Hyrillka Designate and young Thor'h both cheered with delight.

The Hyrillka Designate was the Mage-Imperator's third son. He bore patrician features similar to Jora'h's, but the younger Designate was more corpulent than his eldest brother, his round face more closely resembling the godlike leader. Before the arrival of the cohort of ships, the Designate had already announced a day of celebration, feasting, and dancing for all kiths across the primary city, from the Grand Citadel all the way down to the farm fields. He wanted to welcome the soldiers of the Solar Navy, to offer them music and treats and trained pleasure mates.

'Your crews have such incredible skill, Adar Kori'nh,' said young Thor'h. 'Your pilots, your weapons specialists. They are aerial acrobats!'

'They have nothing else to do but practise,' Kori'nh said, feeling oddly disappointed. 'One of my best pilots is your brother Qul Zan'nh.'

The fast vessels roared overhead again, long streamers crackling behind them. The crowd yelled; some climbed the thick vines to get a higher vantage. The ships turned about, and made one last run past the reviewing stands.

Enduring the long Hyrillka celebration proved more difficult than Kori'nh imagined a real battle could ever be. He was bored within an hour, but did his best to look entertained and appreciative. Both young Thor'h and his uncle seemed to find everything amusing.

The celebration continued in the faint twilight under brilliant jewel-tone stars from the nearby cluster. Wide irrigation canals extended in straight lines out to the nialia fields, shimmering silver from the luminous gelfish that filled the waters. Young Thor'h seemed exhausted and preoccupied, but not willing to leave the celebrations. He consumed a fair amount of stimulant extracted from the fertilized nialia seedpods, one of Hyrillka's drug exports.

The laughter, carousing, and music gave Kori'nh no enjoyment. He chose no pleasure mate for himself, though the Designate repeatedly offered the Adar his personal favourites. Finally, with good grace, the Mage-Imperator's son laughed and instructed the pleasure mates all to go to his steamy bath pools, where he promised to make up for the Adar's lack of interest.

As the celebration began to blur and fade, Kori'nh politely suggested that the Designate entertain his women, then he took a small shuttle back to his nearly empty flagship.

He spent hours in his cabin reading, but this time he put aside the *Saga of Seven Suns* and perused human military history instead. Over the past decade, Kori'nh had become quite enamoured of all the wars and holocausts the Terrans had inflicted upon themselves. The desperate strategies of human generals – Kori'nh's spiritual counterparts – surpassed the wildest imaginings of Ildiran soldiers.

He was constantly amazed that a single race, confined to one planet, had engendered such incredible strife, such terrible struggle. Humans had pursued more warfare in a handful of centuries than the Ildiran race had in all the Empire's recorded history. While Kori'nh did not envy Earth its bloodshed, he remained fascinated by the 'thought experiments' he could conduct by analysing Napoleon, Hitler, Hannibal.

While he waited for the celebration to end on Hyrillka, an idea brewed in his mind. Adar Kori'nh decided to call an important meeting of his subcommanders as soon as the Solar Navy departed from the Horizon Cluster.

The Adar gave instructions to his navigator that the cohort was to be brought to a dead halt in an empty desert of space far from any stars or planets – or observers.

Flustered, the Qul subcommanders who led the seven maniples, as well as the Tal overseer of the entire cohort, answered the Adar's summons to come aboard the flagship warliner. Kori'nh surveyed them coolly in his private briefing room under dazzling lights.

Most of the maniple commanders sat quietly, awaiting orders, but Tal Aro'nh, senior leader of all three hundred and forty-three ships, was taken aback by the unexpected change in plans. 'But Adar Kori'nh, we have a schedule. We have a new pageant to perform in two weeks' time at Kamin. The Designate has erected an entirely new arena for our arrival celebration. Volunteers from seven kiths have been recruited to sew banners and stage a welcome ballet—'

'Thank you, Tal Aro'nh,' Kori'nh said in a clipped voice. 'I will consult you if ever I have difficulty establishing priorities for the Solar Navy.'

The conservative old Tal subsided into an embarrassed silence.

Kori'nh regarded the subcommanders until he saw that he had their full attention. Through the *thism* the Mage-Imperator understood Kori'nh's general aims, and approved. The Adar could feel the all-seeing leader sensing his actions, watching the movements of the fleet like a benevolent deity.

This was an impulse, Kori'nh knew, but an important one, and he was curious to see how the Solar Navy would perform. He also dreaded what might happen.

'I have obtained several Earth military strategy games, computer simulations the humans constructed primarily for entertainment.' He handed out imprinted datacards that contained the simulations, converted to a form readable by their warliner command systems. 'You will study them for a day, and then I challenge you to play against me.'

The gathered Quls were shocked. Tal Aro'nh looked confused and alarmed. 'But Adar, what relevance do human . . . diversions have to our duties in the Solar Navy?'

Kori'nh regarded the old man sourly. They have every relevance, Tal Aro'nh. What if one day the Mage-Imperator declares war against the humans? Would it not be best to understand a bit of their strategy ahead of time?'

'A war with the humans?' the other Quls muttered to each other.

Tal Aro'nh looked angry now. 'Impossible, Adar! The Mage-Imperator would never demand such a thing.'

Kori'nh's voice was as flat and threatening as a naked blade. 'So, Tal, do you now presume to know the thoughts of the Mage-Imperator? Do you understand why and how our leader arrives at the decisions that affect his entire Empire? *K'llar bekh!* Shall I slice off your testicles and see if you suddenly have access to the *thism?*'

Tal Aro'nh backed down immediately. 'Not at all, Adar.' He snatched up the datacard. 'We will assess these simulations and play your . . . space games here, privately, without embarrassment.'

Kori'nh had already attempted the games himself, running simulations in his quarters. Most of the scenarios were simplistic and naive, with a childishly clear objective, usually to conquer a world. But the Adar insisted, and the Quls gathered up their orders and departed for their own warliners . . .

Two days later, Kori'nh engaged his subcommanders in direct human-style space combat – without pomp and tediously rehearsed manoeuvres, without a plan that every officer knew beforehand.

Every one of the subcommanders failed so miserably that even Tal Aro'nh had the good grace to be embarrassed.

EIGHTY

TASIA TAMBLYN

All EDF recruits were summoned to the Mars base's lecture hall for yet another emergency briefing. Tasia accompanied Robb Brindle into the cold, harshly lit room constructed in a domed-over crater. She felt a knot in her stomach, a growing dread about the reason for the mandatory gathering.

'This isn't going to be good,' she said.

Robb looked at her with his large, honey-brown eyes. 'Lately, these briefings are always about bad news,' he said. 'I wonder what's happened now.'

The other recruits were restless, too, talking uneasily among themselves. The trainees had spent a month practising with various configurations of attack craft, dropping bombs in the isolated red deserts, shooting at gigantic targets painted on the mile-high canyon walls.

A lieutenant now, an easy promotion thanks to the huge increase in recruits due to the military expansion, Tasia excelled in solo missions, flying her reconfigured ship fast and hard, intuitively understanding the different mechanical systems because, as a

462

Roamer, she had learned to be flexible.

Due to the sudden immense mobilization against the mysterious aliens, the Eddies had been required to take whatever vessels they could get, cobbling together a fleet from a thousand modified types. Many of the confused recruits complained bitterly about the non-standardization, but Tasia recognized the differences and capabilities of ships and kept track of each one's advantages in various situations. *Roll with it.*

The only time she'd had trouble was during regimented ground missions, when she'd been forced through nonsensical marches and choreographed infantry drills that reminded her of primitive folk dances. Tasia hadn't functioned well when asked to be a mindless part of a team. After one such assignment, Robb Brindle had joked, 'With your attitude and your independence, Tamblyn, you're on your way towards either a court martial or a general officer's commission.'

Now, when all the recruits had settled down in the domed lecture hall, the lights dimmed. Overhead, the dome showed only the night of space and the dazzling pinpoints of Phobos and Deimos racing each other across the sky.

The podium shone under a single spotlight and the EDF liaison, Admiral Stromo, stepped to the centre. Tasia's stomach sank even further. The liaison officer would not address them unless this was a matter of grave importance. The recruits muttered themselves into silence, but Tasia felt the tension grow in the crater auditorium.

The jowly admiral spoke without preamble. 'We have obtained more images of our alien enemies,' Stromo said. 'My highest tactical advisers are studying every fragment of these signals, but I want you all to see them. Understand what we are up against.'

'If those aliens ever show themselves, we'll kick their butts,' muttered one of the recruits near her. His comment was answered by rowdy chuckles from his friends.

'We have learned of three more Roamer skymines destroyed in the past month. Five total. We obtained these transmissions from the last minutes of one such facility on a gas giant called Welyr.'

In utter silence, the trainees watched a projection in the middle of the lecture hall. Spiked crystalline spheres rose above Welyr's clouds, ignoring the winds and storm systems and descending upon a skymine.

Admiral Stromo's voice echoed through the hall, adding unnecessary commentary. 'The skymine captain – a woman – sounded an immediate evacuation, and numerous scout ships attempted to escape. The captain ejected her cargo of ekti, but the invaders showed no interest in it.'

As the recruits watched, the disengaged cargo hold full of stardrive fuel tumbled away from the skymine and plunged into the ocean of coloured gases. 'The Roamers repeatedly tried to surrender, but the aliens refused to respond. They just . . . attacked.'

Shareen Pasternak – now Tasia remembered the woman's name. The Welyr Chief had met sometimes with Ross. Now they were both victims of the new enemies.

Stromo fell silent again while in the image the habitation dome detached from the skymine. Tasia knew that such an action would have been the Chief's absolute last resort, a decision no Roamer captain would make unless she was convinced all hope was gone.

'Observe. Even when the skymine captain tried to evacuate her crew, the aliens came after her. Intentionally and maliciously.'

In the projected images, the predatory crystalline spheres blasted the habitation module into molten shrapnel . . . and then returned without hurry to chop up the rest of the cloud-harvesting facility, leaving the debris to tumble down into the clouds.

All hands lost. Tasia swallowed hard, driving down the anger and impatience to do something. She hated just sitting here on Mars.

'Several of the Roamer scout ships remained aloft for a week, trying to survive in the upper atmosphere of Welyr,' Stromo finally said. 'Those vessels recorded the images you just saw, but they did not have sufficient life-support resources or long-range capabilities. When rescue finally arrived, there were no survivors aboard.'

Robb Brindle looked at Tasia, knowing the pain she felt. He reached out to squeeze her hand, but she barely felt it. Her fingers were ice-cold.

The images stopped. 'That is all,' Stromo said. 'Raw data, with no conclusions. Our experts are studying these recordings and will give you further intelligence as it arrives.'

The light on the stage faded, and the Admiral said, 'Dismissed.'

Tasia barely said a word as they filed back towards their barracks. Robb Brindle walked beside her in silence, giving his quiet support. She hoped he understood how much she appreciated it. By now he knew better than to try and cheer her up or engage her in innocuous conversation.

As they entered the communal room near the lockers and sleeping quarters, Patrick Fitzpatrick pointedly looked at Tasia and turned away, raising his voice to his companions. 'Hey, at least it was only *Roachers* who got killed.' He revelled in his callous wisecrack. 'Next time, though, it might be real people.'

Tasia bristled. Robb stepped in front of her and glowered at the young man. 'Hey, vacuum brain – maybe you missed the briefing where they told us who the real enemy is.'

'Oh shut up, Brindle,' Fitzpatrick said, annoyed that the young black man would take sides against him.

Robb shook his head. 'Your stupidity is more dangerous than those aliens are.'

With exaggerated patience and a steel-hard smile, Tasia touched Robb on the shoulder. 'Thanks, Brindle. It's nice to have a shining knight, but I have my own suit of armour – and it's pretty damn tough.' She stepped around him towards the sarcastic trainee. 'You have two choices, kleeb: either apologize, or go to the infirmary.'

Fitzpatrick just laughed at her. Therefore, he had chosen the infirmary.

Tasia used the low Mars gravity to her advantage and launched her full body weight at him, swinging simultaneously with both fists to hammer his jaw and the top of his head. She sent him into the metal wall, kicked off from Fitzpatrick's chest and heard a few ribs crack as she bounced away and rebounded from the ceiling. Tasia didn't waste her breath, concentrating all of her energy into knees, elbows, feet, and fists.

The sarcastic young recruit fought back ineffectively, as if he'd always had other people around to protect him. Tasia smacked him hard in the nose, a choice blow that caused blood to spout from his nostrils. The gushing scarlet seemed to strip all the bravado from Fitzpatrick.

As if Tasia were a matador waving a red cape, his friends joined in against her, punching from behind, landing a hard blow across the back of her head. Outnumbered, she whirled to face the new antagonists, never backing down.

And so Robb Brindle was drawn into the fray after all . . .

Both Tasia and Fitzpatrick ended up in the infirmary with bruises, contusions, cuts, and a few cracked bones. She found it ironic that she was tended by her own compy, who had been upgraded with first-aid programming to make her more useful at the base.

Both recruits received disciplinary censures – which meant nothing to her, but she could see from the squirming uneasiness on the spoiled trainee's face that he was more afraid of his rich parents than of any damage it might do to his military career.

Tasia was released from the infirmary two full days ahead of Patrick Fitzpatrick III. Both of her brothers would have been proud of her.

EIGHTY-ONE

BENETO

ecause Corvus Landing was so far from any heavily populated Hansa colonies, Beneto's roundabout passage took more than a month. The time gave old Talbun the opportunity to tidy up all the matters in his life.

Carrying a small potted treeling so that he could remain connected to the worldforest on the long journey, Beneto travelled on three different ships, transferring from a passenger vessel to a merchant ship and then to a freelance explorer, before he finally arrived at his new home. He landed at Colony Town, accompanied by cargo containers, crowded cages of noisy and uneasy livestock, supplies and equipment, as well as special gifts from Theroc. Content and smiling, Beneto stepped out and breathed the strange air, smelling the fragrances of an untamed world where Terran agriculture was only beginning to secure a stable foothold.

Corvus Landing was a young, geologically quiescent planet with a generally mild climate and minimal native vegetation. Even the seas were shallow, and the landforms were smooth, with nothing more extreme than hilly plains.

Dazzled by the clear sunlight without the shade of a dense forest canopy, Beneto drank in the details, felt the sunlight tingle his exposed green skin. Through the information he'd learned via telink, he knew that fierce storms occasionally whipped the land with hurricane-force winds that crossed the open plains. Tapping into memories related by Talbun, Beneto experienced one of these tempests secondhand, seen through the eyes of the local worldforest grove.

In consideration of the weather, Colony Town's shelters were low, aerodynamic structures. The agricultural grid of cereal grains was able to withstand the harsh storms. The resilient grasses always sprang back when the sky cleared and the sun returned.

Beneto had no qualms whatsoever about being here. Even the small tree he carried seemed delighted to reach its new home.

When Talbun came to greet him, his skin dark and decorated with a hundred tattoos of his impressive life accomplishments, Beneto felt as if he had known the aged man all his life. Talbun embraced the young man with skinny arms. 'I thank you for coming, Beneto. And the trees thank you.' He touched the small new treeling from Theroc, as if greeting it.

Beneto smiled. 'The Corvus Landing colonists would not want to be without a green priest. You have spoiled them.'

Talbun laughed. Even his gums were dark green. 'The settlers don't use my services all that much, but having access to telink and the immediate news I bring gives their colony a certain status in the Hansa.'

'Ah, status. I am the second son of the rulers of Theroc. Do you think they'll be able to handle so much importance?'

Talbun led his younger comrade away from the colony's small spaceport, which was not much more than a paved clearing used as a flea market and meeting place when no ships were due to land.

469

'They'll get over it soon enough, and then you'll want to go back to your fancy fungus-reef city. Why would you want to be a monk, when you can live as a king?' Talbun was joking, but he seemed truly concerned about the possibility. 'I am leaving them in your care, Beneto.'

'Don't worry about that. My first and truest dedication is to the trees. I want to live here, to read to the trees, to help the grove flourish. I won't flinch from getting my hands dirty, if I need to help the colonists. I am just grateful to be serving a valid purpose.'

Talbun walked in contemplative silence for a few moments, then turned back with a genuine smile on his dark face. 'I know, Beneto. Everything I've learned about you from the worldtrees tells me that my grove and the colonists are safe in your hands.' He increased his pace. 'Let us go quickly, before the mayor and a thousand colonists want to welcome you, introduce themselves, and tell you stories about me.'

'Plenty of time for that later,' Beneto said. 'For now, after being so long in space, I would rather see the trees you have planted.'

With a spring in his step, the aged priest took Beneto away from the concentric circles of low buildings. Talking comfortably, the two walked along a dirt footpath towards a shallow extended valley where the expanding grove grew in the Corvus sunlight. Beneto could sense the yearning trees even before he drew close. It was like being reunited with an old friend.

'When the first colonists came here, Corvus Landing was a blank slate ready to be converted and farmed,' Talbun told him. 'Hansa surveys had shown that there was mineral wealth in the northern latitudes, with no native forests to get in the way of strip mining. Much of the ground was bare of vegetation and composed of exposed rock.'

'I saw some native groundcover from the skies,' Beneto said.

'That's an interconnected hairy moss, not even grass. It reproduces by spreading and breaking off shoots. The largest indigenous plants here are simple ferns that grow no higher than my shoulder.' He trudged up a hillside, not even panting as the path steepened.

'Unfortunately, our grazing animals could not eat the native groundcover at first. Finally the colonists tried genetically modified goats. Those animals could digest the native mosses and grassy sprouts, as long as farmers supplemented their diet.'

Beneto chuckled. 'So it's true that goats can eat anything.'

'Just about,' Talbun said. 'And humans can eat the goats, too. For years, goats provided the only fresh meat and milk here. Such products were truly a delicacy, considering that the settlers mostly ate preserved and packaged food that they bought from passing merchants. We relied a great deal on regular supply shipments.'

From the top of the ridge bounding the valley, they looked back to see the orderly patterns of planted farmlands.

'At first, the Corvus soil structure couldn't support even the hardiest Earth plants, until the colony investors spent most of their capital on shiploads of fertilizer. Ah, it was considered a marvellous joke in the Hansa – the great manure convoy to Corvus Landing – but carrier after carrier spread it across our plains. After the colonists had stabilized the soil chemical levels, the next season they were able to make the transition to wheat and oats and barley.' Talbun sighed. 'I wish the trees had been here to record everything. Massive amounts of seeds were planted in an industrial fashion, low-flying aircraft strewing them like cropdust all across the plains.'

The old priest looked wistful as he led Beneto down the gentler slope on the other side towards the beckoning grove. 'I came here after three years, and it took the settlers five to turn Corvus Landing around. Now we're marginally self-sufficient, modestly profitable, though we have little to export. The northern mines produce enough minerals and refined metals that we can build our structures. Mayor Hendy has changed Colony Town into the thriving boom city you saw at the spaceport.'

Beneto and Talbun passed a low structure that the aged priest identified as his home. 'The women of Colony Town cook for me and insist on cleaning my house. It's important to them. They'd never let a green priest forget how much they respect and appreciate us.' Talbun gave a weary smile and continued towards the whispering fronds of the worldtree grove. 'In truth, though, I spend little time within walls. I prefer to sleep and pray out among my friends the trees.'

They walked into the grove, and Beneto immediately felt the benevolent sensation around him, the dozing, infinite mind of the worldforest. Beneto knew he would take his rest out here as well, where the grove could speak to him. The trees would whisper in his dreams, and he would whisper back to them.

When Talbun touched the scaly bark of the nearest tree, his face became wistful, as if decades had melted away from him. 'Every day, I come here and tell the trees whatever news I've learned. Not much happens on Corvus Landing, but they seem to enjoy it if I just ramble on about philosophical matters.'

'The trees love to drink in information wherever they are, regardless of the subject.' Beneto stood beside the old man in the grove, feeling as if he had come home. These worldtrees were much younger than the ancient forest that covered Theroc, but still exactly the same.

Talbun looked at his young comrade, obviously relieved – as if anticipating when he could rest at last. 'Corvus Landing is no one's dream of a paradise, Beneto, but it is a planet where hardy pioneer spirits can make a home for themselves. I hope you'll like it here.'

Together, they scooped a hole out of the soft earth and planted the new treeling from Theroc. Straightening, Beneto closed his eyes and reached out to touch the trees. He spoke aloud, answering both the old green priest and the forest itself. 'Talbun, this place is *exactly* what I had hoped for.'

EIGHTY-TWO

PRIME DESIGNATE JORA'H

Bound by cultural expectations, Prime Designate Jora'h brought an endless string of lover-applicants to his private chambers. Some of the women were exotic, some ethereal and beautiful, others strange and sturdy. They represented the variety of kiths in the Ildiran race.

However, after studying the long list of prospective mates, Jora'h could not drive thoughts of the enchanting Nira Khali from his mind. He had read the names of supplicants from his own race and viewed images of the females, a spectrum of Ildiran beauty. His assistants would consider the records of previous lovers he had chosen, so that he would not appear to play favourites among the kiths. Jora'h had to be fair to all his people.

But more than anything else, he wanted Nira. The green-skinned, beguiling woman from Theroc filled his thoughts. None of the other names in the catalogue of options could compare with her innocent, exuberant charms.

At last the Prime Designate chose at random, a singer who came to him trilling and ecstatic. Her large dark eyes were wide, her smile and smooth body eager to please him. She was called Ari't, and when she told him her name, she sang it in musical notes rather than speaking more familiar sounds.

Jora'h's delighted laugh was a harsh and guttural sound compared with the tones that flowed like honey out of Ari't's mouth. His smoky eyes gleamed with starlight reflections as he looked appreciatively at the ethereal singer.

'My deepest gratitude for choosing me, Prime Designate,' Ari't said, and ended her sentence with a flourish of wordless melody. 'I hope you find me acceptable as a mate.'

Jora'h wished for nothing more than to forget his fantasies of Nira. He sank back into his curved chair, admiring the singer's exotic form. 'You are very acceptable, Ari't.'

She looked back at him, awestruck and nervous, giddy with disbelief. Jora'h let his eyes fall half closed as he studied her body, her face. Without referring to the list, he couldn't remember if he had ever chosen a member of the singer kith before.

Ari't's chest was broad, her ribcage expanded to accommodate powerful lungs. Her throat was enlarged to contain a symphony of delicate vocal cords. She had the most beautiful voice that Jora'h had ever heard. Ari't supposedly had the ability to make her audiences weep, or laugh, or fall in love.

'Sing for me first, Ari't.' His voice went husky, a little afraid of what she might be able to do.

'It would be my honour, Prime Designate.' And out of her mouth flowed a swirling river of music, melodies and tones that needed no words or verses, only the colourful crystal of sound itself. Jora'h felt as if he had been hypnotized.

For decades now, since he had come of age, the Prime Designate's staff had maintained lists of the women who applied to become his lovers. He had done his duty with diligence, choosing carefully and spreading his noble bloodline among the lesser kiths as well. He mated with swimmers and scalies. He honoured women of the least-humanoid-looking breeds. All kiths had admirable qualities, and Jora'h found beauty and strength in each one, though other nobles might have seen only ugliness.

The Prime Designate showed kindness and deference to every one of his mates, though he was never expected to fall in love. Even with mates that he found unattractive, Jora'h took care never to allow them to feel belittled or inadequate.

He particularly remembered a tall, brutish-looking female of the warrior kith, whom he had impregnated the previous year. Mage-Imperator Cyroc'h had taken great pains to impress upon his oldest son that each breed of Ildiran had its unique role in the Empire, and it was Jora'h's duty to honour them all. Besides, the Prime Designate had enough gorgeous and exotic lovers to make up for any unpleasantness he might briefly endure. In fact, he recalled with generous optimism, that warrior female had given him some of the most exhausting and athletic sex he'd ever enjoyed.

Now in his private chambers, Ari't's song carried him through his thoughts and memories until he was no longer aware of where he was. Slowly the singer's melody changed and her tone grew richer, transforming into an incredibly erotic trilling. Jora'h found himself unbearably aroused, exactly as the singer had intended.

Ari't spoke to him with her music, seduced him with her voice. Breathless, Jora'h came to her. She continued to hum deep in her throat even as he ravenously kissed her, playing his lips down her face and her long, slender neck. His golden hair crackled and thrashed like a static storm around his head.

Oddly, despite the intensity when he and Ari't were making love, Jora'h's thoughts were once again diverted, his imagination drawn to the beautiful and unassuming Nira . . . who was so very different from any Ildiran woman.

EIGHTY-THREE

BASIL WENCESLAS

As Chairman, he never had a moment of peace.

Given the vastness and complexity of the Terran Hanseatic League, Basil Wenceslas expected and accepted a constant string of crises and emergencies. He had to make the decisions and mitigate the disasters. In moments of triumph, King Frederick gloried in the applause and accolades; whenever a plan went wrong, faceless and unnamed bureaucrats took the fall. Either way, Basil remained safely behind the scenes.

The devastating and inexplicable alien attacks, along with the massive military buildup, had preoccupied him for months, taking him from less pressing duties. Now, belatedly, he checked on the progress of the new Prince Peter. He had to make sure all the threads in the tapestry remained tightly knotted.

Sitting in a comfortable chair within a private business alcove beneath the Whisper Palace, Basil sipped hot cardamom coffee from a delicate china cup. He observed through surveillance cameras as young Raymond Aguerra underwent more training. Inside a windowless tutorial room with several chairs, benches, projection screens, and writing tables, the Teacher compy OX continued his lesson, though the Prince appeared restless and bored.

'When the Ildirans brought the *Peary* officers and myself back to Earth, the celebration and the public reaction were quite memorable,' OX was saying. 'After one hundred and forty-five years, the people on Earth had thought the generation ships gone forever, but when the Ildiran Solar Navy arrived at Earth – the first alien civilization humans had ever encountered – the public didn't know how to respond.'

The old compy paced back and forth as he related his history files. 'The Ildiran military officers dressed in dazzling uniforms and flew their streamers through our skies. The cheers were deafening!' OX actually sounded wistful. 'As the senior compy aboard the *Peary*, I had observed and recorded every moment of the initial encounter. I was able to replay my experiences for humans and download my files to other compies so they could spread the news.

'The Terran Hanseatic League immediately transferred my services to their highest corporate levels. Back then, King Ben was on the throne, but he died shortly afterwards. I trained young Prince George, just as I am training you. The Hansa gave me private quarters, an office of sorts, which was unheard of for a compy—' OX rambled, as he occasionally did when sharing his reminiscences.

Raymond tapped his fingers on a smooth writing surface and let out a loud sigh. 'OX, if your personal database is so maxed out with nostalgia, why don't you just delete some of the old memories to make room?'

Taken aback, the Teacher compy fell briefly into a flustered silence. 'Because it was history in the making. I must retain my memories, Prince Peter, because I teach by using my own life and activities, to instruct you by way of example.'

'If you want me to learn by example,' Raymond said, exasperated, 'then why won't you or Chairman Wenceslas let me meet King Frederick? I'm supposed to take his place one of these days, aren't I?'

Watching the surveillance screens, Basil pursed his lips. *I wouldn't plan on that encounter any time soon, Prince.* Not until he was able to plan the event to his own satisfaction, to make sure everyone would be happy with the situation.

In the meantime, Basil had a team of official biographers working with crack image modifiers to compile a complete pictorial 'history' of the young Prince's life: a blessing from the Unison Archfather, numerous shots of Peter with his father King Frederick, fond remembrances from his sorely missed mother who had died long ago. All in all, it would be a very nice package, all the accoutrements of a royal upbringing.

Interrupting Basil's careful study of the Prince's activities, Mr Pellidor entered the private alcove. The Chairman swallowed a sigh. Any moment of peace, however brief, was a precious respite. An interruption always came before long.

The expediter carried paperwork and an electronic report. Pellidor looked not exactly smug, but at least satisfied. He paused until Basil acknowledged him, then he spoke, intentionally keeping his voice low and confidential as he glanced at the surveillance screen, though the Prince could not possibly hear anything in his sound-proofed instruction room.

'Mr Chairman, all loose ends are now wrapped up with the young man's family.' Pellidor extended the reports.

Basil set them on a low table. He took Pellidor at his word; the man had never failed him before. 'Including Esteban Aguerra?' Raymond's father had changed his name and voluntarily converted to Islam after settling down on the new colony. 'Was he difficult to find?'

Mr Pellidor shook his head. 'My men have just returned from Ramah. Quite a peaceful planet, I'm told. They reported no special problems.'

Basil sipped his coffee again, savouring the sharp cardamom taste. 'Good.'

On the screen he saw Peter apparently arguing with the Teacher compy. Frowning, he waved Mr Pellidor to silence as he enhanced the sound to listen in on the conversation. With so much at stake, Basil intended to watch this Prince very closely to make sure no deviation was allowed to go too far.

Peter was their best hope for a well-trained, pliable successor.

Raymond Aguerra had recovered quickly from his induction into the Whisper Palace. Though he still grieved for the tragic loss of his mother and brothers, it must seem to him as if a miracle had occurred. But, like a suddenly spoiled teenager, Raymond had of late begun to show signs of unruliness and resistance, as if some deep unconscious part of him had already realized what lay in store.

Keeping the reports and documentation at hand, Basil dismissed Mr Pellidor and turned back to the observation screens. OX had displayed text across the computerized writing desk, and on the wall he projected a facsimile of the actual document. 'This, Prince Peter, is the charter of the Terran Hanseatic League. You must familiarize yourself with every amendment and all provisos.'

'I already studied that in school,' Raymond said, uninterested.

'Yes, but you must *know* it in your heart, understand the words and the concepts, give it a prominent position in your thoughts. This document is the basis by which you will rule as King.'

'Will I be given a test?' Frowning, Raymond looked at the words on his screen.

'No, but you may need to use pertinent quotations from time to time.'

The young man stood up and impatiently walked around the training room, but he found nothing else to capture his interest. 'I thought you said I would never go out in public without my speeches written for me.'

'True,' OX admitted. 'All of your public comments will be carefully scripted.'

'Then you can "carefully script" any quotations you want me to use.' Rudely, he switched off the screen. 'I want to do something else.'

Watching the young man's behaviour, Basil frowned in frustration, then became resigned. He remembered the debacle of the previous candidate, Prince Adam. Five years ago, that young man had seemed so perfect, passing every test. The Hansa executive council had unanimously chosen him, yet the ungrateful youth had soured during his instruction, even threatened to expose Basil and the underhanded activities of the Hansa – as if anybody cared! So very foolish.

Basil had led an emergency meeting of the Hansa council, and the members had determined, reluctantly, that Prince Adam could not be salvaged. At any time during his staged reign, his intransigence might come back to bite them. They could not afford that. So, Basil had seen to it that the young man was quietly eliminated. Prince Adam had never made a single public appearance or been mentioned in any news release.

He had never existed.

Now, as he watched OX's unsuccessful attempts to get his new student to participate in the assignment, uncertainty ate into Basil's resolve. If 'Prince Peter' did not work out, the Hansa had no time to start all over again.

He finished his coffee and convinced himself not to be overly concerned, even as he watched Raymond Aguerra trying to get his way. Simple petulance could be monitored and handled. This had happened before, and Basil should have expected it. 'I have to stop being such an optimist when it comes to human nature,' he said to himself.

The candidate Princes always believed they could hold out and become their own masters . . . But they never succeeded.

EIGHTY-FOUR

MARGARET COLICOS

A second wave of the storm pummelled the canyons on Rheindic Co, but Margaret was too amazed by the new Klikiss city to notice the sounds at all.

Wind and driving rain pelted the cliff face. Another surging gurgle of water crashed along the canyon floor, scouring the rocks and stripping piled sediment and dust from where the three black robots had been.

Inside, the abandoned ruins were dry and sheltered. And fascinating.

DD directed a glowing light panel into the dark tunnels as Louis and Arcas ventured deeper into the strange echoing buildings. The two men shared a boyish, fascinated grin, and Margaret joined her joy with theirs. The place was like a tomb, hushed and undisturbed.

Margaret touched the smooth walls, feeling a film of dust laid down by incomprehensible age. She feared she might damage these brittle artifacts just by breathing, but the Klikiss ruins had been built to withstand eons. Sealed inside the canyon walls, this city had remained undisturbed by intruders, weather, or time. Just waiting for them.

'This construction is similar to what we found on Llaro,' Louis said. 'Look at the walls, the arches.'

'Yes, but these are much better preserved.' Margaret looked triumphantly at Arcas. 'In fact, these are the most perfectly intact set of Klikiss ruins ever found in the Spiral Arm.'

The green priest looked proud of his role in the discovery, pleasantly surprised by Margaret's praise. DD said, 'I wish Sirix, Ilkot, and Dekyk could be here to see them. Such details might spark their memories. Do you think there is a possibility they survived intact? An ancient Klikiss robot is irreplaceable.'

'A possibility, certainly, DD,' Louis said with forced optimism. 'Keep your chin up.' The compy tilted his head upwards, taking the instruction literally.

For hours the archaeologists explored the labyrinth of buildings and rooms. The Klikiss builders had extended their smooth-walled tunnels deep into the mesa, but the outer face of this alien settlement had been walled up . . . as if intentionally hidden from view.

'I wonder if the Klikiss were afraid of something,' Margaret mused, looking at the remnants of the camouflaged cliff wall. 'Were these outer walls meant as defences?'

'We've never understood why the Klikiss race disappeared,' Louis said, speaking more for the green priest's benefit than for Margaret's.

'Do we know what the Klikiss looked like?' Arcas asked.

Louis shook his head. 'Nope. Even at the apparent battle site on Corribus where we discovered the Klikiss Torch, we didn't find so much as a single alien cadaver.'

'And the writings and hieroglyphics on the walls contain no drawings of the Klikiss people,' Margaret said.

'Perhaps we will find something here, Louis,' DD said, always optimistic. 'I will help you look.'

Louis had published a brief monograph in a prestigious xeno-archaeology journal, speculating – not entirely seriously – that the lack of Klikiss cadavers might indicate that the lost race engaged in ritual cannibalism, devouring their dead and leaving no remnants. As evidence, he pointed to the fact that there were no cemeteries, tombs or any indications whatsoever of Klikiss burial practices. Louis's conjecture had met with scepticism and a brief flurry of debate, but because of his stature in their field, no one dared call Louis a crackpot.

As they explored, the fused stone corridors widened, tending towards what seemed to be a nexus in the cliff city. DD tromped ahead with the light, and they followed into another chamber. The air in this room vibrated with a strange humming silence, as if some odd quality of the stone walls themselves absorbed echoes.

As in most of the Klikiss chambers, every smooth surface here was covered with designs, writing, hieroglyphics, and mathematical symbols – as if the insectoid race felt compelled to record thoughts and historical events for all to see. Oddly, though they were clearly a star-travelling race with colonies on many planets, the Klikiss had also never drawn any images of spacecraft or other vehicles on their walls.

Encased machinery crouched in one corner of the room, casting razor-edged shadows. As DD shone his glowpanel around the chamber, Margaret saw that a major section of the primary wall was completely blank, a trapezoidal sheet of stone like a virgin canvas, framed by a dense perimeter of symbols. The blank space was striking in contrast to the sheer density of designs and pictographs on every other clear surface of the wall.

'Well, it looks like the Klikiss weren't finished here,' Louis said. 'But why avoid that particular section? Some quality of the stone, perhaps?'

Margaret shook her head. 'No, old man. Look, it's a perfect trapezoid. This patch was left intentionally blank, as if they needed it clean and flat for something. We've seen this before in some of the other ruins.'

'Yes, now I remember. But we never figured it out, dear.'

Arcas hunkered down and contemplated the flat trapezoid, which was three metres across at its base. 'It looks to me like a broad window . . . or a door.'

Margaret could not argue with his impression, because she'd had the same eerie feeling. 'But where would it go? There's nothing but stone behind it.' She went forward to study the inscribed symbols bordering the blank space, compelled and curious. The few other 'stone windows' they had previously discovered had been surrounded by rubble or damaged in some way. This one was intact.

But its purpose was still unclear.

DD interrupted her thoughts with an exclamation. 'Excuse me! I have found something important!' He stood by the encased machinery against the wall, turning his glowpanel into the shadowy gaps between cubical modules.

There, Margaret saw a motionless shape, a smooth dusty shell with several twisted legs and a rounded body core with a dull and dusty outer covering that gave the hulk the appearance of a gigantic, squashed beetle. It looked vaguely like the Klikiss robots, but more natural, smoother.

She drew in a cold, astonished breath, reeling with excitement. She could feel the adrenaline surge through her blood. 'Is it . . . ? Louis, is it really?'

Louis trotted over, then gave a laugh of triumph. Margaret knew exactly what the thing must be even before Louis turned to her, his wrinkle-seamed face lit up in a huge grin. 'It's the first one!' he crowed. 'Good work, DD!'

With the compy shining a light upon the mummified Klikiss cadaver, Margaret bent to study it. She took extreme care not to touch the alien, because age had made it a fragile construction. 'The body is so old, it'll turn to dust if we try to move it.'

Louis pointed to a long crack along the back of the Klikiss carapace. 'It seems to have been crushed. A blow from behind . . . or maybe part of the ceiling fell in on top of him.'

'Then where's the rubble?' Margaret stepped back, drinking in every detail. The Klikiss alien bore a superficial resemblance to the hulking black robots, but was no more identical to them than DD's crudely humanoid shape was to the delicate contours of a human form.

Incautious as always, Louis reached out with a gentle fingertip to brush the alien's twisted forelimb, and a portion of the grey-brown body armour crumbled into powder. 'Well, I guess that prevents us from performing a useful autopsy, dear,' he said. 'But we had better image this specimen in every way we can.'

Margaret agreed. 'Some biological scrapings of the residue will give us something to analyse. We can develop a chemical break-down. There may even be some intact cells.' Her heart pounded with excitement. At the moment, everything seemed possible.

'What's that sound?' Arcas stood up and looked around.

Margaret heard movement in the outer tunnels: heavy footsteps, a ticking, thumping sound as of something heavy moving along. She suddenly became intensely aware of how alone and isolated they were in this abandoned ghost city. They had no weapons, no defences whatsoever.

Could something have survived after all this time?

The deserts of Rheindic Co were home to only a few small lizards and arachnids. There was no evidence of large predators. Outside, the storm had fallen to silence, enhancing the scraping sounds of ponderous movement. Margaret's throat went dry, and

Louis stood closer to her, either for emotional support or in a faint show of bravery and protectiveness.

Fearless, DD walked across the chamber, holding out his glowpanel. Then the compy said in a delighted voice, 'It is only Sirix – in fact, all three Klikiss robots. They have returned!'

The heavy black machines moved into the light, passing one at a time through the stone tunnel opening. Margaret stared in amazement, for she had seen the three robots swept away in the raging flash-flood. Clumps of clayish mud coated their exoskeletons. One of Ilkot's scarlet optical sensors had been smashed and now glinted a dull garnet. Their black carapaces looked battered and dirty, but otherwise undamaged.

'We are . . . intact,' said Sirix. The trio of grimy robots paused inside the chamber, looking around and scanning, as if recording everything they saw.

'Well, I am impressed at your indestructibility,' Louis said cheerfully. 'Come, look what we've found. A mummified Klikiss cadaver, the first we've ever seen!' He was excited, like a schoolboy anxious for show-and-tell.

Margaret, still uneasy, looked at the immense beetle-like robots. She recalled how difficult it had been for the three humans to scale the cliff wall – even with DD's ropes and automatic pitons. And that had been before the landslide. 'How did you get up here, Sirix? I thought you were incapable of climbing that cliff.'

'We managed,' Sirix said.

Then the robot turned to study the Klikiss body that had nearly fallen to dust on the floor, wedged between the strange machinery. The other two robots stared at the intact trapezoidal stone window, as if searching their scrubbed memory circuits.

EIGHTY-FIVE

OTEMA

Engrossed in her task, the old ambassador from Theroc rarely left her crystal-walled chambers in the Prism Palace. The *Saga of Seven Suns* transported her farther than any sightseeing journey could have. Otema had everything she needed, except time. The epic was far too long to read in the remaining years of her life.

Filtered light shone around her so that her photosynthetic skin felt drenched with warmth and nourishment. Two potted treelings rested on the table, each one four feet tall and thriving in the bright environment.

She read aloud until her scratchy throat forced her to pause. Otema reached for the jug of cool water she kept with her at all times. She took a long drink to soothe her dry vocal cords and sat back to rest for a moment.

At first, after surrendering her ambassadorial work to ambitious Sarein, Otema had felt uncertain about going to Ildira on this task and uncertain about what changes and concessions Sarein might make. She worried that all her careful protective labour might come to naught.

Once here on Ildira, though, after seeing the sheer potential of the *Saga of Seven Suns*, Otema realized she could contribute more to the overall well-being and knowledge of the worldforest than by engaging in political dances with a transient group of leaders on Earth.

At times, the Iron Lady was disappointed with Nira, who spent as much time with Prime Designate Jora'h as she did reading from the *Saga*. Every day now, Nira attended jousting tournaments, visited museums, or watched sky parades. But then, her assistant was young and easily impressed by new and novel things. Yet Nira was experiencing Ildiran culture in much greater depth than the old green priest could, and the girl always made a point of sharing her impressions with the treelings. Thus, the worldforest increased its knowledge in that way as well.

Otema, unable to shed her ambassadorial sensibilities, remained concerned about the political future of Theroc and the disposition of green priests throughout the Hansa. When, after endless hours, she found herself weary from reading aloud, Otema would relax, touch the treelings, and engage her telink to ask the forest for news.

She attempted to follow Sarein's activities as the new Hansa ambassador, the treaties the young woman offered and the documents she signed. So far, Sarein had effected few major changes . . . but this did not put Otema at ease. Sarein could well be working her schemes behind closed doors, away from the network of green priest communicators.

Oh, the damage she could cause!

Otema passed her concerns through the worldforest, and the other priests would maintain watch, especially those stationed on Earth. But the worldforest seemed preoccupied with a brooding uneasiness of its own – something much worse than mere Terran politics, something that no green priest could yet understand. . . .

She and many of her counterparts had tried to learn more about the troubling mystery, but the trees had yet to reveal a single warning, hint, or prophecy. And Otema's reading of the *Saga of Seven Suns* had fascinated – and agitated – the worldforest even more.

Now she picked up another portion of the document and began to relate a new story from the Ildiran epic to the listening trees.

Two potted treelings also remained in Nira's quarters, while the rest of the small trees had been lovingly planted in the vine-studded walls of the skysphere, the huge terrarium that hovered over the Mage-Imperator's reception hall.

She heard footsteps stop at her chamber, but refused to acknowledge her visitor until she had finished the legend of a deaf singer whose music was so achingly powerful it could stop the hearts of his listeners, though the singer never heard the melodies himself. Sadly, the Mage-Imperator at the time had been forced to order the singer's execution after he, with his sheer power to evoke melancholy, had caused the grief-stricken deaths of two noble listeners.

With a sigh, Otema set the document aside and turned to welcome Rememberer Vao'sh. The historian stood in the doorway, his arms burdened with scrolls and written documents. 'I doubt you are ready for more of the *Saga*, Ambassador Otema, but I have selected these particularly interesting stories. You will enjoy them.'

'And the worldtrees enjoy them as well . . . Ah, if only I had more time.'

Vao'sh laughed, a tone so friendly it warmed Otema's heart. 'I have had that problem ever since I was born a historian. For a rememberer, the most tragic death is to die young, because one can never read the complete epic, and therefore dies unfulfilled.'

'Fortunately,' the old woman said, 'the worldforest is capable of absorbing information by parallel processing. It is not *my* purpose in life to read the *Saga* from start to finish, but to ensure that the worldforest acquires the entire epic, by whatever means.'

The rememberer set his documents beside the others on Otema's study table. 'In that respect, I believe the rememberers can offer you assistance, Ambassador. You have told me that large groups of green priests and acolytes recite stories and information to the worldforest on Theroc. Why then, can we not achieve the same ends here, with other readers and other parts of the *Saga*?'

Otema brightened. 'What is it you suggest?'

'The Mage-Imperator has commanded that I help you in any way. In his name, I could assign other rememberers, singers, even courtiers to read sections of the *Saga* to the other treelings you have brought. A green priest is not required for direct input, if I understand correctly. Can we not divide the time-consuming labour into numerous shifts?'

Otema caught her breath, delighted. She had been thinking of how she could break down the task for green priests back on Theroc, but it hadn't occurred to her that Ildirans could just as easily share in the dictation. A reader was not required to be engaged in telink – after all, none of the acolytes on Theroc had yet taken the green.

'That is a perfect idea, Rememberer Vao'sh. Your method would make the reading of the *Saga* go much faster.'

With a sigh of anticipation, Otema looked at the stack of scrolls and documents Vao'sh had just delivered. She scanned the symbols and was surprised to notice a mention of the mysterious Klikiss robots. She recalled reading another long portion of the epic narrative, searching for more detailed information about the vanished race, but the insect civilization had vanished before the beginnings of Ildiran recorded history.

She turned quickly, glad to see that Vao'sh had not yet disappeared down the corridor. She called him back. 'I have a question, Rememberer. I realize that I have read only the smallest fraction of your *Saga*, but I have found little information about the Klikiss robots. Didn't Ildirans uncover the first ones on a mining moon somewhere? I have seen several of the robots here in Mijistra, and I know there are others throughout the Ildiran Empire.'

'Klikiss robots have also visited the Hanseatic League,' Vao'sh said, his expressive facial lobes colouring into different shades. Otema did not yet know how to interpret all of the alien skin signals.

'True, but the Ildiran Empire is so much older. Do you have any more stories about them? Why is there so little information about the Klikiss race? They were once an important civilization, just like yours. Were the Klikiss gone before the Ildiran Empire was formed?'

Vao'sh looked puzzled, considering how best to answer her question. By his reluctance, Otema realized that the historian had not often considered the fundamental question.

'The Klikiss and their robots are part of a different tale,' Vao'sh finally said. 'A history all their own. Perhaps they have no role in our story, or yours.' He backed away, his skin lobes flushing an unusual range of colours. 'Or perhaps that part of the tale has not yet been written.'

EIGHTY-SIX

NIRA

The view from the crystal balconies of the Prism Palace was spectacular. Prime Designate Jora'h took Nira up to an observation ledge beside the rushing gurgle of upwards-flowing streams. He left his bodyguards inside so that he and the lovely Theron woman could have a few moments to themselves.

'This is one of my favourite places,' he said.

Nira took a few moments to catch her breath. 'It's . . . beautiful.' Jora'h reached out to touch her arm, then held her hand. She let his grip linger there.

Atop its commanding hill, the Prism Palace overlooked the far-flung skyline of Mijistra. Sinuous glass-like structures crept towards the horizon, like ripples on a pond. The tall Palace towers rose high, surrounded by spherical domes of the government ministries. The viewing ledge thrust out at an angle with the support stalks bent inwards so that as Nira stood on the transparent shelf with no obvious support beneath her feet, she seemed to be floating off into space with Jora'h at her side.

Rising steps of land on the citadel hill led up to hemispherical platforms and domes that supported the Palace. Seven major streams, all of them cut into perfectly straight channels, converged to a single central point.

The Prime Designate said, 'The original designers of the Prism Palace wanted to show that all things, even the laws of nature, flow towards the all-seeing and all-powerful Mage-Imperator.' Jora'h lowered his voice and smiled warmly at her. 'Unfortunately, I defy that concept — for all of my thoughts flow towards *you*, Nira.'

Laughing with embarrassment, she squeezed his hand. At the archway behind them, the ferocious-looking bodyguards seemed completely unconcerned by their behaviour. 'Being so high . . . the sight takes my breath away. It reminds me of Theroc, when I would climb to the tops of the worldtrees.'

'Reynald described your world to me, and it sounds beautiful.' Jora'h's smoky eyes glittered as he painted the pictures in his mind. 'I will visit Theroc one day. Perhaps with you.'

'And along with an entire cadre of attenders and bodyguards and assistants,' she said with a smile. 'It would be hard to have any peace around you, once we left Mijistra.'

'Ildirans don't like to be alone.'

The two stood close together, though the viewing ledge offered plenty of room. Nira was very conscious of the Prime Designate's presence, and she did not want to move away.

She watched the small forms of people far below. An endless stream of Ildirans ascended tier after tier of the citadel hill that supported the Prism Palace.

'Pilgrims,' Jora'h said, seeing her interest, 'wishing to gaze upon the glory of the Mage-Imperator.'

Groups from various kiths climbed steadily, stopping at prescribed points along the road. They crossed bridges and circled the hill, washing themselves ritually in the seven streams as they ascended towards the entry dome. 'All citizens of the Empire have access to the Palace. My father keeps his audience gallery open to visitors. Anyone who makes the pilgrimage can observe his glorious face projected under the skysphere.'

'Is he ever worried about assassination attempts, or violence?'

Jora'h looked at her, surprised. 'Through the *thism*, the Mage-Imperator can know precisely if anyone harbours such thoughts. My father could deal with the problem long before any would-be assassin entered the Prism Palace. We Ildirans are different from you, Nira. You must understand that.'

They stood on the high vantage in silence, side by side, watching the groups of pilgrims marching reverently towards their goal. Finally, Nira said, 'We are not so very different.' She intentionally snuggled closer to him. 'In fact, Jora'h, you and I could be compatible . . . in many ways.'

Back in the Prime Designate's private chambers, Nira wondered if the charismatic man had used any hint of telepathic powers to seduce her. But she was aware of the power of outside thoughts because of her communications with the worldtrees. And at this moment Nira felt as though she was doing nothing against her will . . . nothing that wasn't absolutely *right*. This was her first time, but she was not afraid.

Her skin drank in the warm light in the room all around her, and she felt energized by his every touch. Even as she held the Prime Designate, she hungered for him, and Jora'h responded in kind. Slowly and with fascination, they removed each other's clothes, one item at a time.

'I find you so incredibly interesting and intriguing, Nira,' he whispered, his breath warm in her ear.

She felt precisely the same way about him.

Nira had been afraid he might be aloof or jaded after having had so many mates, but as she made love to him, Nira felt that she held the Prime Designate's absolute attention and devotion.

EIGHTY-SEVEN

ADAR KORI'NH

It was an old trick the Adar had learned from studying human military strategy games. He led two cohorts of warships to the outskirts of the Qronha double-star system, which held two of the seven suns in the skies of Ildira.

The Qronha system had a sparse population, a pair of habitable but insignificant planets. Its main importance derived from a very old ekti-harvesting city that floated in the clouds of the system's gas giant, one of the few remaining skymines still run by Ildirans, rather than human Roamers.

To Adar Kori'nh, this seemed a good place to engage in instructive space military manoeuvres.

He divided the two cohorts into opposing teams and ordered hundreds of ships to become artificial antagonists. Following the human tradition, Kori'nh designated the two groups 'red team' and 'blue team'. Earth strategists had developed this process during centuries of combat simulations, and the Adar thought the exercise would be interesting. More than just a game.

Tal Aro'nh, an old-school professional, led the blue cohort. The

Tal adequately performed all his assigned duties and exercises. But even so, he concerned Kori'nh the most. Innovation seemed a foreign concept to the old commander, who complained most bitterly about 'wasting time' on unorthodox exercises.

Tal Lorie'nh commanded the red team. The Adar did not consider him a better commander, but Lorie'nh had the good sense to do as little as possible, allowing his Quls, the maniple subcommanders, to perform their duties. And since Tal Lorie'nh chose talented underlings, in the final summary the cohort leader usually looked very good.

Kori'nh sat in the command nucleus of a small observation platform, where he could watch the engagement of his two opposing teams. He activated the short-range transchannel and spoke to the two Tals. 'Aro'nh, Lorie'nh – you may commence the engagement.'

Tal Lorie'nh acknowledged brusquely, while Aro'nh transmitted a final stiff-sounding objection. 'Adar, I must again ask you to cease this divisive activity. The Solar Navy is a single unit, operating together to complete the missions which the Mage-Imperator gives us. Never has maniple fought against maniple, except in the terrible civil war long ago. These exercises can only disrupt military discipline and lead to confusion, make our soldier kithmen feel as if members of their own race are the enemy—'

Kori'nh had no sympathy for the rigid old commander. 'Tal Aro'nh, I find it more divisive to hear you publicly challenging my orders. I am your Adar, blessed by the Mage-Imperator. Do as I say, or stand relieved of command.'

'Yes, Adar,' the Tal said, and switched off the channel.

Kori'nh sat back to observe the ship movements. The two cohort commanders had not been allowed to discuss their respective strategy choices. The objective of the exercise was to have one team capture and occupy a misshapen lump of asteroid, a minor planet that orbited at an extreme angle around the two Qronha suns.

Not surprisingly, Tal Aro'nh flew all the vessels of his cohort in perfect standard formation, a sphere-within-sphere arrangement familiar to all observers of Ildiran sky parades and military pageants. Warliners surrounded the outer perimeter, with escorts and cutters in layers within the circle. Aro'nh moved his ships en masse along a straight line towards the objective asteroid.

A flurry of sentry ships patrolled around the sphere-within-sphere configuration, orbiting in tight rings as they circled the main warliners. It was meant to be a defensive posture, but as the bands of fast streamers orbited in opposing directions, it created a spectacular visual image – designed to evoke cheers from distant audiences, not to demonstrate military proficiency.

Tal Lorie'nh directed his red team in a more chaotic configuration. The seven maniples of his cohort separated into individual groups of forty-nine ships, each maniple rushing forward in allied but discrete swarms. To the critical eye, red team's approach had less finesse and no artistry. Then the seven individual maniples, each containing seven septas of warliners, broke apart and advanced pell-mell towards the objective.

One by one, six of Lorie'nh's seven maniples careened into blue team's complex sphere-within-sphere grouping, sending a ripple of chaos through Tal Aro'nh's carefully choreographed vessels. The cumbersome configuration began to disintegrate, but at the old Tal's barked orders, the captains of each ship in blue team returned to formation. The giant spherical configuration pressed inexorably towards the target, disregarding any threat that red team might make.

However, while six of the red team maniples were harrying the cumbersome but beautiful group of blue team ships, Lorie'nh's seventh maniple accelerated rapidly towards the asteroid. They allowed themselves no diversion, surrendering all other considerations.

It was a simple enough tactic, and obvious in hindsight. By the time Aro'nh's lumbering spherical configuration reordered itself and began to unfold its vessels, splitting open the outer shell of warliners to dispatch the central rank of landing craft, red team's rogue maniple had already arrived at the asteroid. They dropped a rapid deployment of all cutters, releasing occupation forces of spacesuited Ildiran ground troops who planted their cohort's emblem and activated their victory beacon.

The other six maniples of red team stopped harrying the opponent and retreated to surround the asteroid, preventing Aro'nh's cohort from even approaching the objective. It was a total rout.

Before blue team managed to launch a single troop transport, Adar Kori'nh signalled the two military commanders and declared the exercise over, granting a complete victory to red team.

Tal Aro'nh looked particularly old, virtually fossilized, as he appeared before Adar Kori'nh in the command nucleus of the observation platform. He stood ramrod straight, his Solar Navy uniform impeccable, insignia and medals neatly arranged on his chest.

He had lost. Utterly.

Aro'nh's career had been a model of traditional service in the Solar Navy. Adar Kori'nh no longer considered that good enough. The old Tal waited in silence, but indignation was clear on his stony face.

The maniple subcommanders of the opposing teams waited in outer chambers. Kori'nh looked at the two Tals standing before him and let the silence hang for a moment, his face reflecting disappointment in both of them. 'Well, gentlemen? Your assessment of the exercise?' he finally said.

Tal Lorie'nh, as usual, waited for someone else to speak. Aro'nh, however, lifted his chin and sniffed. 'Adar, I must object to the tactics used by red team. No military guidebook of the Solar Navy recommends such procedures. Nowhere in the *Saga of Seven Suns* is there any mention of a commander who used such tactics. Never before! I find Tal Lorie'nh's blatant embrace of . . . of *chaos* to be beneath contempt. We are cohort commanders in the Ildiran Solar Navy. Our soldiers are not disordered herd animals to be provoked into a stampede.'

Making no comment, Kori'nh let the man's complaints run out of steam, before he said in a quiet but devastating voice, 'And yet red team managed to defeat you.'

'An invalid victory, Adar—'

Kori'nh slammed a fist on the table and stood up, his eyes blazing. 'There are no invalid victories!' His tone of voice shocked both Tals. 'Why do you insist that the Solar Navy use old, predictable techniques for *all* circumstances? What if we encounter an enemy that has no comprehension of our rules, and even less respect for them? What then?'

'This is not our way, Adar,' Aro'nh glowered. 'Ildirans have a tradition of honour. If you allow this uncivilized madness to continue, you invite the downfall of all that has made the Solar Navy proud and invincible.'

Angered at his inability to penetrate this old commander's petrified imagination, Kori'nh said, 'The Ildiran Empire will not remain invincible if we insist on being inflexible. Enemies exist, though we have been blind to them before.'

He looked at the conservative Tal and felt a stirring of pity. Aro'nh had never dreamed he would be called upon to do anything that required innovation. He was proud. He had followed all the rules and did not know what to do without the safety net of routine and tradition to catch him.

'Tal Lorie'nh,' he turned to the other commander. 'Explain to me what prompted you to devise such an unusual tactic.'

'You provided red team with a clear objective, Adar,' said the other cohort commander. 'We simply calculated the most likely manner to achieve the goal. Since this was not a public exhibition and no other Ildirans were observing our methods, I determined that we were meant to capture the asteroid . . . not put on a show.'

Aro'nh scowled. 'Blue team was not "putting on a show"—'

'Shall I replay the tapes for you, Tal Aro'nh?' Kori'nh snapped. 'What was the point of the sphere-within-sphere configuration, the orbiting sentry ships, the unfolding outer shell – if not for show? What purpose did that serve, without an audience? At the very least, Tal, you made a poor choice of a standard battle-group formation. The situation required speed above all.'

'Adar, perhaps I should show you in our military manual—'

'Enough!' Kori'nh said, disgusted. 'Tal Lorie'nh, did you conceive of your manoeuvres? If so, I commend you.'

Though embarrassed, the other commander had enough honour not to take credit for something he hadn't done. 'Not precisely, Adar. I recognized the wisdom as soon as I heard the plan . . . but the original concept can be credited to Qul Zan'nh, the Prime Designate's son. Zan'nh suggested that I break the cohort into separate maniples, each one with a different objective.'

Adar Kori'nh gave a satisfied sigh. Previously, he had seen Zan'nh do fast and imaginative things even when he led only a septa; he was not surprised to hear that the Prime Designate's eldest son was the mastermind behind red team's victory. 'Send him in,' Kori'nh said, 'immediately.'

A message was transmitted to the outer rooms where the maniple commanders waited. Moments later, the bright-eyed young Zan'nh entered, saluted the Adar and then both subcommanders. 'You asked to see me, Adar?'

'Qul Zan'nh.' Kori'nh stepped closer and clasped his hands in front of his chest, formally acknowledging the young man. 'As supreme commander of the Solar Navy it is my right to hereby promote you for exemplary service and remarkable imagination in achieving a victory during our exercises today.'

All three listeners looked astonished. Zan'nh had only recently been promoted to the rank of Qul, and traditional protocol generally laid down the career pathways. 'In light of the growing danger in the Spiral Arm, the Solar Navy vitally needs intelligent and imaginative officers like yourself. You are hereby named Tal.'

Aro'nh could not contain himself. 'This is extremely irregular, Adar! There are accepted practises—'

Kori'nh continued, ignoring the old man. 'Zan'nh, you will replace Tal Aro'nh, who is from this day forward demoted to the rank of Qul. His inappropriate command decisions would, in my opinion, place his cohort at risk in a real combat situation.'

The old Tal gasped, standing shaken as if the foundation of his entire life had been swept out from beneath him. 'I . . . I would prefer to retire, sir. My rank is—'

'Denied. This is a time of potential military crisis. I will not lose one of my experienced officers, but the lower rank is better suited to your rigid disposition. You have always taken orders well.'

Aro'nh seemed barely able to keep his feet, for a moment it seemed as if only his stiff uniform kept him from collapsing. 'Adar, I will file a formal complaint.'

'Your complaint will be dismissed. I have the Mage-Imperator's blessing, as well as his charge to make the Solar Navy into a far superior fighting force.' The disgraced commander's eyes blazed, but he refused to back down. 'You have served well during your career, Aro'nh, but you have ceased to learn. You have forgotten how to adapt, and that would be a grave danger to our Empire in the event of a conflict with an outside enemy. The Mage-Imperator has instructed me to heighten our state of preparedness.'

The Prime Designate's son stood at attention, astounded at the turn of events. Adar Kori'nh was pleased that the young man did not preen or seem overly pleased with the promotion.

'Tal Zan'nh, you are now in command of a full cohort. Under your guidance, you will lead blue team's complement of three hundred and forty-three ships. Congratulations, young man.'

Aro'nh looked broken, as if he had aged another century in the past few moments. Tal Lorie'nh also looked surprised and intimidated, fearing the possibility of another exercise. Next time, he knew he would have to face off against Zan'nh, instead of having the innovative young officer as his greatest resource.

'Gather all the ships,' Kori'nh said, tired. 'I wish to announce Tal Zan'nh's promotion and proceed with the victory ceremonies as soon as possible. Perhaps the gas miners on Qronha 3 would like to see a show.'

EIGHTY-EIGHT

GENERAL KURT LANYAN

The first new warship in the EDF's enhanced Juggernaut class sparkled in spacedock, surrounded by a festival of monitoring lights and sensors. The giant vessel hung completed in the construction yard, waiting to be formally launched.

The design and construction engineers were very proud of their work. Twelve more of the enormous vessels would be completed soon, the cornerstones of an improved fleet ready to fight the deep-core aliens.

General Kurt Lanyan and the Grid 1 liaison officer Admiral Stromo – who would captain the new ship on its maiden voyage – had arrived for the full ceremony with an honour guard of twenty combat-ready Remoras and a handful of carefully chosen news media representatives.

As far as Lanyan was concerned, all this spectacle got in the way of the efficient running of military operations, but Chairman Wenceslas disagreed. 'Such things take little time but engender a great deal of public fervour and interplanetary support, General,' Wenceslas had insisted. 'It is an investment in your long-term military capabilities. If you can make the public fall in love with you now, you won't have problems later defending your actions – whatever they may be.'

And so, to inaugurate the expanded EDF fleet, King Frederick himself made a procession out to the asteroid construction yards, where he would christen and launch the first Juggernaut. *Goliath*.

Though the name sounded fierce and powerful, General Lanyan wasn't entirely sure it was an auspicious christening. After all, the eponymous Biblical giant had been defeated by a vastly smaller and underestimated David.

Surrounded by his flock of sycophants, advisers, court politicians, and ornately uniformed royal guards, the King arrived and docked with the *Goliath*. 'Most wonderful,' he said. Robes flowing, Frederick glided down the shining metal corridors towards the bridge. The status lights and gleaming tactical displays shone impressively.

Lanyan had made sure that the crew worked doubletime to polish every floor and panel, and to make certain there wasn't a speck of dust on the thick windowports. Frivolous showmanship, when the time and manpower might better have been spent rehearsing military drills or performing target practice with the modified jazer and railgun weapons systems.

King Frederick nodded with appreciation. 'Truly, General Lanyan, this is a remarkable warship.'

The news media accompanied him, broadcasting the sheer impressiveness of the *Goliath* to their viewers.

The expanded fleet had taken shape over the past several months, incorporating a dozen new Juggernauts, each with augmented weaponry: ninety mid-size Manta cruisers, two hundred and thirty-four new Thunderhead weapons platforms, and literally thousands of fast Remora attack ships – all completed at the space construction yards and issued to new squadrons scattered across the ten tactical grids. They were ready for full-scale deployment, as soon as the deadly aliens showed themselves.

No one doubted that the insidious enemy would strike again.

In addition to the new craft, Lanyan had overseen the refit and absorption of a thousand privately owned vessels, commandeered spacecraft that had been modified for useful service to the Earth Defence Forces: couriers, supply ships, recon vessels. As commanding officer of the rejuvenated space military, Lanyan was doing his job and doing it well.

On the bridge of the *Goliath*, Admiral Stromo bent over a tactical control panel and activated the jazer banks. In a modulated, well-educated voice, he explained the weapons carefully and optimistically to the King, who appeared fascinated.

'Our new fleet is far superior to those old relics still flown by the Ildiran Solar Navy. In fact, these EDF ships are more powerful than any other war fleet ever constructed.'

'I certainly hope so, Admiral,' said King Frederick. 'We did not invite hostilities with the strange aliens, but it is my desire to finish this conflict as swiftly and cleanly as possible. Perhaps now they will parley with us.'

'We all wish that, Sire,' General Lanyan said with a tight smile. Unfortunately, he thought to himself, nobody had the slightest idea of how to proceed. The EDF couldn't even find the deep-core aliens. Many skymines and probes had skated over the high cloud surfaces, but when had anyone ever explored the furious inhospitable depths of a gas giant?

Fighting the exotic enemy, striking against diamond-hulled warglobes or pursuing them into high-pressure atmospheres was completely different from any kind of warfare that Lanyan had ever considered in his simulations. His prior plans would have been effective in any conflict with the Ildiran Empire or a rebellious Hansa colony.

The deep-core aliens, though, were something else entirely.

This would never be a war based on infantry and ground troops. It would not be won by capturing and occupying territory, probably not even through negotiation. If the enemy truly lived deep within a giant planet, where hydrogen itself could be compressed into metal, what possible overlap of resources or territorial needs could the two sides have? What could the aliens want?

Lanyan knew in his gut that this would be a war of utmost destruction, employing heavy weaponry – perhaps even doomsday bombs – as well as massive, invincible starships. Individual soldiers would be useless, infantry and handguns completely irrelevant. Instead, the EDF fleet needed trained navigators, pilots, and gunners for the integral weaponry on heavy battleships.

On the *Goliath*'s bridge, King Frederick called an end to the tour. Basil Wenceslas must have instructed him to limit his visit to no more than an hour. The Juggernaut crew had other duties to perform.

'Gentlemen,' Frederick said, 'we are most pleased and impressed. I find the *Goliath* completely satisfactory, and I declare it ready to depart. This Juggernaut will be the flagship of our awesome new Earth Defence Forces.' When he smiled, his wrinkled face reclaimed some of its youthful glow. 'I trust you'll one day honour me with a brief cruise around the solar system?'

'That can be arranged, Sire,' Lanyan said, then remembered the public-relations reminder Basil had given him. 'I'd like to take this opportunity to express my gratitude to every citizen in the Terran Hanseatic League. Their support, their sacrifices, and their continued belief will help to ensure a thorough and decisive victory. We humans are a strong race. We spit at adversity, and we always triumph in the end.'

King Frederick beamed. 'Well spoken, General. I will issue a royal command for the new, expanded fleet to launch with all due haste. Once we defeat these cowardly aliens who strike without warning, we can return to our normal and prosperous way of life in the Hansa colonies.'

The King's retinue applauded while the media representatives gulped up every image to enhance and broadcast to their viewers.

General Lanyan's heart swelled with enthusiasm and confidence, but in his mind he knew the reality would be significantly more difficult than his speech had implied. Glancing across the *Goliath*'s bridge, he met Stromo's eyes. Both men understood, held the same reservations.

The new Terran battle fleet was far superior to anything Lanyan had commanded before. Their ships were more numerous, their weapons more destructive. But in reality they knew almost nothing about the capabilities or motives of their enemy.

Lanyan feared that all this cheering and celebration amounted to little more than whistling while passing a graveyard.

EIGHTY-NINE

JESS TAMBLYN

Jess's heart still ached with cold anger, but now that he had decided what action to take, the freedom gave him a giddy sense of relief. He had never seen the Guiding Star so clearly in his life; he knew exactly what course he must set.

Jess did not intend to inform the Roamer council of what he was doing – not Speaker Jhy Okiah, not even Cesca Peroni. He had seen the squabbling and panic and indecision in the recent clan gathering at Rendezvous. They would only muddy the water.

No, this would be his personal retaliation, for good or ill. His uncles on Plumas had approved – raspy Caleb Tamblyn had even insisted on coming along – but Jess made it clear that he must be in charge. It was his clan's business, his responsibility . . . his revenge. And afterwards, there would be no one but himself to blame.

Accompanied by a group of picked loyal workers from the Plumas water-extraction facilities, Jess took several industrial ships loaded with all the resources and equipment he would need. These volunteers had known Ross, had worked for Bram Tamblyn, and would follow Jess's every instruction. Once his Uncle Caleb had learned what he meant to do and told the work crews, no force in the universe could have prevented them from helping him.

Now, the mismatched vessels rendezvoused at the edge of the Golgen system, out in the icy veil of the Kuiper belt of comets high above the ecliptic. From there, they could look down on the bright spotlight of the gas giant.

Murderous aliens lurked somewhere deep within those clouds.

Jess thought he could sense his brother down there, along with the ghosts of all those who had been slaughtered aboard the Blue Sky Mine. Had the skymine offended the aliens somehow? Or did the enemy simply see Roamers as insignificant insects to be squashed and then brushed aside?

So far, the Roamers knew of five skymines that had been obliterated, with all hands lost, on scattered and unrelated gas giants. The attacks were unprovoked and merciless . . . and thus far unpunished.

Many uneasy Roamer clans had already pulled their independent skymines from other gas giants, manoeuvring them up out of the atmospheres and mothballing them in planetary orbit. Ekti production had dropped to a fraction of what it had been before the attack on the Blue Sky Mine. The Terran Hanseatic League had not yet felt the squeeze, but Jess was certain that Chairman Wenceslas and King Frederick already understood the impending shortages of starship fuel. This crisis had to be resolved soon.

He opened the communications channel in his small ship. All of his volunteer workers listened in from their own vessels. 'My brother died down there on Golgen. So did members of many of your clans. By the Guiding Star, now it's up to us to do something about it.'

He drew a breath. Jess had not rehearsed his speech. 'Roamers are not a violent people. We don't have an impressive military force or weapons of mass destruction. But we are not to be trifled with.

We will resist these enemies and avenge our lost family members. Not one of us can shrink from this task. I certainly don't intend to.'

Growling oaths and muttered cheers came over the communications link, fierce determination that smothered an undercurrent of fear.

'Lucky for us, the universe provides its own weapons,' Jess said. 'We're going to use them.'

The system was surrounded by an arsenal of cometary shards, giant balls of ice that he would convert into bombs. Back on Plumas, he had already analysed precise mappings of the Kuiper belt, projecting millions of cometary orbits and simulating the results of perturbations. He found more than a thousand candidates, any one of which would rain incredible destruction on to Golgen.

Jess had an intuitive feel for celestial mechanics and orbital manoeuvres. He had always been particularly good at navigation and Roamer 'stargames', looking at constellations from different perspectives and backtracking to place the viewer on an objective map of the Spiral Arm. When he was younger, he'd liked to look at the maps, often with Tasia, and imagine different places where he'd never gone, exotic worlds or galactic phenomena that could not be fully appreciated through small images on a screen.

Today, Jess gritted his teeth and stared at Golgen's celestial cartography for a different purpose entirely. The ponderous and inexorable paths determined by celestial mechanics often took centuries, and he eliminated most of the alternatives, selecting only those comets that could be dropped in steep hyperbolic orbits, massive cannonballs carrying enough kinetic energy for an impact equivalent to a thousand atomic warheads. Eighteen outer comets were viable projectiles.

His Plumas commando crews – everyday water miners, pump specialists, and ice engineers – carried automated reaction thrusters that would dig out and hurl chunks of cometary mass in the opposite direction. When the constant recoil persisted for weeks and weeks, it would gradually perturb the comet out of orbit and send it down on a collision course.

'You all know your targets. Let's start rolling these big ice bombs down to smack Golgen right in the face.' Jess lowered his voice to a growl. 'Those aliens don't realize just how much trouble they've asked for.'

With a final round of acknowledgements, the Roamer ships split away from Jess and dispersed into the obstacle course of tumbling icebergs. These workers understood the minimal tolerances and the accuracies that were involved; after all, they had worked for demanding Bram Tamblyn. Any Roamer who cut corners or performed sloppy work ended up dead soon enough, usually with the blood of many innocents on his careless hands.

Jess double-checked his cargo and altered course towards his chosen target, a large comet already inbound to the inner system. He dropped out of the edge of the Kuiper belt into the neighbourhood of the ecliptic.

Inside the cockpit, Jess wore insulated work clothes, a comfortable set of overalls with dozens of pockets, clips, and gadget belts. Over the outfit he had wrapped an embroidered shoulder cloak, an old family treasure his mother had made before her death in the Plumas crevasse. On it were stylized designs and the names of Ross, Jess, and Tasia against a background of the Roamer Chain. His heart sank as he thought of how his tight clan had unravelled, how his whole family had dwindled. But things would change.

The separate crews arrived at their snowball landing points, locked down docking clamps, and emerged from their ships to begin installing equipment. Throughout the day, the Plumas team transmitted messages, updating Jess. With deceptively gentle movements, his other team members had launched a flurry of comets like a shotgun blast towards the gas giant. Now, the only thing needed was time and celestial mechanics. The bombardment would continue for years, one impact after another.

'That'll give 'em heartburn,' said his Uncle Caleb over the comm.

But Jess had in mind a more immediate strike, a blow that he could observe soon, while his anger still burned high. For Ross.

He brought his ship close to the comet dropping towards the sun on its original long-term journey. The ice mountain had passed close enough to be deviated by Golgen's gravity, hooking its orbit inwards. Sunlight had volatilized a thin mist from its surface that leaked out in a fuzzy mane that would eventually become a tail.

Jess mapped the surface topography of the comet to understand the material structure. After using scanners to investigate the internal inhomogeneities, he modified his calculations. If everything worked out right, this comet would arrive at its target within a month.

Selecting the appropriate place, Jess anchored his ship on an ice clearing where shards of vacuum-extruded pinnacles crunched under the weight of his hull. His fuel tanks and his cargo hold were filled with ekti, enough to provide a prolonged thrust with immense force. The roar echoed into the silent vacuum, and Jess grimly held on as the ship trembled with the effort. A Roamer vessel locked down, with its stardrive engines blasting at full thrust for two weeks, would be enough to drive the comet like a sledgehammer into the target planet.

Within a day, one of the Plumas crew ships would pick him up. The engines continued to blast away, nudging the giant ice mountain. Jess had plenty of time to think. He had no regrets, no reservations. He could not turn back. This was something he had to do.

He didn't care what the Big Goose or the Eddies might think. No doubt, even some Roamers might be infuriated at his provocative act, but most would cheer that he had actually done something. He didn't know if Cesca would be disappointed in him, or if she would applaud his actions. He would stand firm, either way, knowing his obligations. It wasn't as if diplomacy had been effective. The enemy had offered no communication whatsoever.

He looked through his cockpit window and saw the giant planet below him, much closer now, a bright spotlight like a bull's-eye.

Before he suited up to go wait for the pickup ship, Jess removed the embroidered shoulder covering that bore his name along with Ross's and Tasia's. He laid it gently in the captain's chair, then went to the suit locker and made ready to depart.

He did not once look back or reconsider what he was doing.

With his own ship anchored to the comet and its heavy stardrive engines blazing, adding inexorable force in a vector against the routine pull of gravity, Jess climbed aboard Caleb's pickup vessel that had arrived for him. They joined the other Roamer ships on their way out of the system.

Jess scanned the eighteen mountains of ice that had already begun their descent. Once he made certain that each one of the comet bombs was on course, he sank back into his padded chair and gave orders for his team to depart.

The die was cast.

NINETY

BRANSON ROBERTS

Some job this had turned out to be. Branson Roberts hated piloting the only human ship in an isolated godforsaken system, especially in a place where the destructive aliens were bound to be hiding. But he had his orders. Even worse, he had no choice. General Lanyan had made sure of that.

At least the EDF had given Roberts back his own ship, the *Blind Faith*, and it was good to be sitting at the old girl's controls again. The cockpit felt like home, felt like normal – except for all the modified systems, pumped-up engines, and heavy armour the EDF had installed on the ship. That had seemed like adding insult to injury.

Still, when he dropped into the Dasra system hunting alien bogeymen, Roberts was glad that no one but himself held the controls. He and the *Blind Faith* had been through a lot together.

A month ago, the deep-core aliens had emerged from the cloud decks of Dasra and destroyed Roamer ekti-harvesting facilities there, the alien's fifth such target. The Dasra attack had played out the same as all the others: huge crystalline globes attacked with no warning, no mercy, accepting no surrender. The aliens had annihilated the skymine despite transmitted pleas, leaving no wreckage or survivors.

Thus, the deep-core aliens had proved they lived within this system, and Branson Roberts had orders to find them. How many other gas giants did the enemy inhabit? Were all of them danger zones?

He thought of Rlinda Kett, with her generous body and expansive moods. She always called him her favourite ex-husband, and he called her his favourite ex-wife, though he had only been married once. Roberts had proven to be a mediocre husband but an excellent pilot, and so Rlinda kept him on with her small merchant fleet. He'd made a good profit flying the *Blind Faith*, enough to keep him content and let him pretend that he lived a playboy existence, so Rlinda would not take pity on his loneliness.

But the small fleet's easygoing success had careened to a halt when this alien trouble began. Rlinda had lost the *Great Expectations* to Rand Sorengaard's pirates, and now three of her other ships had been commandeered by the EDF. In order to keep his pilot's licence and a ship to fly, Branson Roberts found himself forced to run errands for General Lanyan.

The General had sent a specific summons to Roberts, bringing him to EDF headquarters on Mars. In a private staff office, with the door closed and broad skylights open to an olive-green sky, Lanyan had made his proposal. He had not stood when Roberts entered the office, but remained at his desk, which was piled with data reports and multiple screens that showed endless troop deployments and combat exercises.

After only a few words, Roberts realized that the General had already pulled his files, studied his piloting career and track record, and knew more about Branson Roberts than he generally wanted anyone to know.

It was going to be an offer Roberts couldn't refuse. No doubt about that.

'Your dossier suggests you are quite a daredevil pilot, Captain Roberts. I have already noted how well you comported yourself when my squad used you as bait to catch the criminal Rand Sorengaard. In addition, I see you have performed dangerous runs, black market deliveries, and risky navigation.'

Roberts felt a cold prickle of sweat along his neck. 'General, sir, I assure you I have never been convicted of or even charged with anything illegal. You can check my criminal record—'

Lanyan waved him into a seat. 'Let's not get into that, Captain. It's a red herring, and I don't have time for it.'

Roberts quickly sat down, folded his hands in his lap, and waited in silence.

'Captain, allow me to be clear. I intend to take advantage of your abilities. It would be most advantageous to recruit someone with your skills rather than sifting through these enthusiastic numbskulls to find a new cadet with only a fraction of your experience. I understand that King Frederick's new order has required you to surrender your private ship to the greater military effort, and that you are currently without a livelihood?'

The General already had that information, and both men knew it. 'I . . . recognize the Hansa's need. As the King says, we all have to make some unpleasant sacrifices.' Roberts smiled wanly, then shrugged. 'The Hansa gave me enough compensation to meet my expenses for a month or two.'

Lanyan regarded him with hard, intelligent eyes and finally the General's face broke into a knowing smile. 'I'll bet you're bored, though.'

Although the *Blind Faith* had been designed as a merchant ship and cargo carrier, she had sleek lines and fast engines. The EDF had retrofitted the ship for increased manoeuvrability and range. Roberts wasn't entirely sure the modifications would protect the *Blind Faith* against an outright attack from the enemy aliens, but it made him feel more confident.

So far on his mission, he had already been to Welyr and Erphano, known hiding places of the deep-core creatures. Like a dive bomber, he raced into each system and dropped a cargo load of robotic probes and message buoys into the murky clouds. The devices sank out of sight, relaying information back to the *Blind Faith*. The buoys transmitted demands that the aliens cease their unprovoked aggression or urgent requests for any sort of parley.

Each time, the messages were ignored, the probes destroyed.

Now, without slowing, Branson Roberts piloted the *Blind Faith* towards Dasra, approaching from the north pole. The greenish gas giant was surrounded by a stack of thin treacherous rings, like a sparkling pile of old phonograph records encircling the equator.

Needing to move quickly, Roberts did not thread his way through the crowded rubble-filled rings. Instead, he skimmed close to the atmosphere in the gap between the planet and the rings, traversing from north to south. Per General Lanyan's orders, he was required to stay long enough to gather data transmitted from the probes. But he didn't have to wait around for trouble.

Skimming above the storm systems, Roberts opened the *Blind Faith*'s cargo bay doors and dumped a string of robotic probes, self-contained transmitters, and sensors. As they fell, the message buoys bleated their recorded announcements across a spectrum of frequencies. The data probes drifted into specific storm 'levels, sending electronic surveillance intelligence as they descended.

Roberts collected every signal, recording all the data in his ship's systems. He would bring his reconnaissance packets back to EDF headquarters and deliver them personally to the General and his analysts. Maybe he'd even ask for a raise.

He listened, cruising above the silent clouds, passing over Dasra's equator and then traversing the gas giant's southern hemisphere. As before, once the probes reached a certain depth, the transmissions suddenly broke off, changing to static and then silence. Each device was destroyed far sooner than the environmental conditions could have harmed the rugged components.

Obviously, the deep-core aliens were the cause.

Gas-giant planets were common in the Spiral Arm, and many probe runners like himself were investigating them. If the probe destructions were an accurate indication, the deep-core aliens were astonishingly widespread. The EDF, as well as the human population, was beginning to realize just how prolific their enemy was, how far flung this heretofore unsuspected empire. They seemed to be everywhere.

When the last probe transmissions abruptly ended, Branson Roberts made ready for his dignified but rapid retreat, as on his two previous excursions. This time, though, flashing lights appeared deep within the pea-soup clouds. The glowing movement seemed to be tracking the rapid passage of the *Blind Faith*.

Roberts scanned the clouds and the brightening lights, feeling a glacier form in his stomach. It looked like a cluster of thunderstorms climbing deliberately towards the upper atmosphere. Lightning strikes crackled, and a windy vortex swirled, as if preparing to open up and disgorge a massive object.

As the submerged lights grew more brilliant, more ominous, Roberts leaned on his ship's controls, disengaged the safety protocols, and powered up all the enhancements the military had installed. 'Time to get the hell out of here.'

Firing the stardrive's turbochargers, he shot away from the rings of Dasra and streaked out of the system at maximum speed.

NINETY-ONE

ADAR KORI'NH

With tensions increasing among the humans and the mystery of the marauding aliens still unsolved, Adar Kori'nh kept one maniple of his fleet in the vicinity of Qronha 3. The Mage-Imperator gave him explicit orders to place a ceremonial protection fleet at the ancient Ildiran ekti-harvesting city, and so, for appearances, Kori'nh remained with the forty-nine ships led by the recently demoted Qul Aro'nh. By their very visibility, the warships would ease the unreasonable fears of the cloud miners.

The rest of the vessels, commanded by Tal Zan'nh and Tal Lorie'nh, continued back to their home port, ready to respond to any real emergency.

Qronha 3 was the nearest gas giant to Ildira, a large planet bright enough to be visible by telescope even in Mijistra's permanent daytime. Ages ago, the Ildirans had built their first cloud-harvesting facility here. The scoops and reactors had operated continuously for dozens of centuries, producing the hydrogen allotrope, though, in recent years, it was only a token amount.

Human Roamers had taken over most of the ekti-processing business, selling stardrive fuel to the Ildiran Empire and the Terran Hanseatic League. However, the Mage-Imperator Cyroc'h and his predecessor had kept the Qronha 3 facility under Ildiran control, as a minor gesture to prove that they *could* produce their own ekti, if they wished.

Now the Mage-Imperator feared the creaking old Qronha 3 cloud harvester might be threatened. This was to be a formal mission, flying the colours and demonstrating the might of the Solar Navy. The operation would be by the book, with no innovation required – exactly the kind of assignment Qul Aro'nh could perform to perfection. Perhaps the old officer would see that despite his shame, he could still be a valuable component of the Solar Navy.

Because the skittish Roamers were curtailing their ekti production and exports, the Mage-Imperator had commanded that the Qronha 3 skymine be brought up to full capacity. The Empire needed an uninterrupted supply of stardrive fuel. Only now was the Empire beginning to understand the weak link in their economy: how much they depended on Roamers to provide the necessary resource.

Long ago, when Ildirans had first allowed the outcast human clans to take over operations on old ekti-harvesting facilities, the Roamers had taken out long-term loans to build additional skymines. Recently, sensing the economic shift, the uneasy Mage-Imperator had warned the Roamers not to default on their loans; surprisingly, the nomadic humans had continued to pay their expected instalments, tapping into hitherto unsuspected cash reservoirs. No one knew how the Roamers had acquired such liquid wealth or how long they could continue to make their regular payments.

For the time being, the Ildiran Empire's deliveries of ekti had been slashed by thirty per cent, and even the Mage-Imperator could do nothing about it. Through the *thism*, Adar Kori'nh could sense his leader's distress. The outmoded Qronha 3 cloud harvester had no hope of making up for the shortfall, but the workers would make a dramatic, symbolic effort.

Guided by Qul Aro'nh in a formal wedge formation, the forty-nine warliners and escorts had made a circuit of the Qronha system. The battleships would impress upon Ildiran workers and potential enemies alike the awesome might of the Solar Navy. From high orbit above the gas giant, the maniples dispatched cutters and streamers to patrol the skies for any alien intrusion.

Adar Kori'nh took an escort down to the floating skymine city. As supreme commander, it was his responsibility to be visible, standing tall and brave in order to reassure the ekti harvesters.

The long-established Qronha 3 colony had a place in Ildiran lore, mentioned no fewer than a thousand times in the *Saga of Seven Suns*. Riding high above the thick vapours and cloud banks, this was an enormous facility. Huge structures, distillers, and reaction chambers protruded in all directions. Its industrial systems were outdated and inefficient by now, but processing of the hydrogen allotrope continued.

The ekti factory held enough inhabitants to qualify as a genuine splinter colony. The Ildirans, though isolated from their planet, were crowded enough for their comfort. And because of their proximity to Ildira, the Qronha 3 miners often received furloughs to return home, as soon as replacement crews came to continue their work.

Still, as Kori'nh saw the size of the Qronha 3 facilities and the sheer number of workers required to maintain the population at its critical density for the *thism*, he understood how the Roamers, given their willingness to live and work with skeleton crews, could be far more efficient.

Five other cutters landed on the docking platforms after the Adar had stepped out. The ekti harvesting crews and their extended families greeted the military with a grand reception. Kori'nh could see that the Qronha 3 workers were also nervous about unseen aliens lurking within the clouds below, though they had never witnessed any sign or threat in their many centuries of operation here. Despite their uncertainty, the Solar Navy gave them all the confidence they needed.

The fleet had been settled in for less than a day when the attack occurred.

Without warning, dazzling acid-bright lights appeared in the clouds beneath the giant industrial city. Kori'nh's ever-vigilant patrol streamers noticed the change almost immediately and sounded the call to arms. After reviewing images the Earth Defence Forces had retrieved from Oncier and the destroyed skymine at Welyr, the Adar knew how such an attack would begin. His soldiers had drilled sufficiently and reacted with due speed.

Even so, they could not be prepared enough.

Kori'nh summoned an emergency brigade of escort ships to drop down on to the large harvester complex and evacuate all personnel. Alarms rang throughout the industrial city, and Ildiran workers scrambled to their emergency checkpoints, queuing up in preparation for escape.

Leaving a Septar to manage the on-site evacuation efforts, Adar Kori'nh boarded the first outbound cutter. 'I need to get back to my fleet,' he said, concerned about Qul Aro'nh's lack of ingenuity in the face of a crisis. He would have to take command of the maniple himself.

As his cutter rose above the last wisps of atmosphere and into the indigo of space, he looked down to see the first of the fearsome diamond warglobes emerge from the depths of Qronha 3. Broken electrical arcs crackled from the blunt spikes protruding through its hull. Crewmen shouted from the deck; the cutter's pilots engaged emergency thrusters. The Adar could only stare in awe for several seconds until he finally grabbed for the communications systems.

Old Qul Aro'nh was already broadcasting angry threats to the emerging deep-core aliens. 'Leave our facility unharmed or risk grave consequences.'

Adar Kori'nh knew that such warnings would do no good. The aliens had always refused to communicate before. This time, though, the deep-core enemy faced more than an unarmed Roamer skymine. The well-armed Ildiran Solar Navy stood against them.

'Get me back to the lead warliner,' Kori'nh called to the pilot. 'I must guide our response.' The cutter pilot flew faster, recklessly, but they closed the distance to the enormous Solar Navy flagship.

As the maniple subcommander repeatedly broadcast his stern threats, the ominous crystal globe continued to emerge from the clouds, blue-lightning weapons building up to a giant discharge. Kori'nh opened a channel to the lead warliner. 'Don't waste time, Qul Aro'nh. These aliens have already proved their aggressive intent on numerous occasions.' He drew a deep breath, committing himself and the Solar Navy. 'Open fire!'

As escorts continued to stream down to the floating city, intent on evacuating as many inhabitants as possible, a second warglobe broke through the clouds, rising towards the mining facility. Deep below, the Adar saw a third phosphorescent patch glowing, emerging. How many were there?

'As you command, Adar,' Qul Aro'nh said and drove the front ranks of warliners in. They launched a full spread of kinetic missiles that impacted in flashes of fire against the diamond hull, leaving only slight discolorations. Then Aro'nh shot his banks of high-energy cutting beams, spears of orange fire that scorched tracks

526

along the crystalline hull. One warliner pushed forward for a closer strike.

In response, blue lightning bolts crackled from the spikes on the two alien warglobes. With a jagged blast of pure energy, the deep-core aliens completely vaporized the nearest warliner. The other battleships reeled.

A gasp of sick dismay went though all the Ildiran troops. Adar Kori'nh could not believe what he had just witnessed, the utter ease with which the enemy had destroyed one of the most powerful vessels in the Ildiran Solar Navy! Qul Aro'nh shouted for his remaining warliners to regroup.

Escort ships loaded with refugees began to rise from the Qronha skymine, while other transports landed. The workers onboard the mining city were panicking. Kori'nh could hear their cries for help across the communications channels, but he could not evacuate them any faster. Already the maniple's docking bays were filled to capacity.

Small private ships began to fly away, personal leisure craft and tiny supply vessels designed to make regular shuttle runs back to the main Ildiran system. But those spacecraft would never be sufficient to remove all of the people in the crowded splinter colony.

A third diamond warglobe finally emerged from the clouds, and now the triad of enormous spheres hovered high above Qronha 3's storms, blistering with lightning. They opened fire on the cloud city. The first shot blasted a reactor dome and vaporized one of the crowded dwelling modules, murdering hundreds. Flames spread quickly.

The Adar felt a sick pain in his heart, a wrench through the *thism* for all the people who had just died. 'Get me aboard my flagship!'

'Almost there, Adar.'

Up in orbit, Qul Aro'nh had focused five of his warliners,

closing in on the nearest warglobe. The individual captains launched every weapon on their defensive boards: high-energy beams, kinetic projectiles, even powerful planet-splitters.

The alien globes crackled with blue lightning again, striking six of the unarmed refugee-laden escorts, shattering them into molten debris. Then, with another shot, the aliens took out a second section of the ekti-processing facility. The giant industrial city reeled in the sky, already mortally wounded.

When his cutter finally docked in the flagship warliner, Adar Kori'nh raced to the command nucleus. In his own battleship, Qul Aro'nh continued to drive forward, still firing, but causing no discernible damage to the warglobes.

The pilots of his escort ships, still involved in desperate evacuation activities, begged to be recalled now that they had seen the hostile aliens blow up the refugee ships. Kori'nh sharply countermanded them. 'I will not cease this rescue mission.'

Twenty escorts, overcrowded with panicked Ildiran escapees, docked inside the warliners and disgorged their passengers into holding areas. Hundreds of cloud miners had been saved so far, but the total was barely a third of the splinter colony's population. The Qronha 3 floating factory was now completely in flames, its habitation spheres broken, its industrial facilities, condensation towers, and distillers smoking, bent, and tangled.

Kori'nh demanded an update from all the maniple's subcommanders. Five more escorts had lifted off from the doomed ekti-processing facility. More than fifty small private ships had already escaped above Qronha's atmosphere and requested to be picked up by the warliners.

Ignoring the furious resistance of the Ildiran Solar Navy, the three alien warglobes closed in on the smoking factory. Maliciously, with a concerted blast of jagged blue lightning, they demolished the entire sky city, blasting it into a dispersing cloud of debris that dropped like meteors down into the planet's milky storm systems.

Everyone onboard was dead.

Kori'nh summoned all the surviving ships in his maniple. 'Gather up all the refugees you can. Escorts, return to your warliners immediately.' His voice caught in his throat. Never in his life had he read of such an ignominious defeat, not in the long glorious history of the Ildiran Empire! This debacle would be recorded in the *Saga of Seven Suns* for all later generations. 'We must retreat. We must fly to safety.'

'But Adar!' Qul Aro'nh said over the communications system. 'The Solar Navy does not flee. The shame of it—'

'*K'llar bekh!* We have just rescued as many survivors as possible from the complex and we are bringing them aboard our warliners. I will not see them all murdered now because of our bravado or pride. Our first duty is to bring the civilians back to Ildira and deliver our report to the Mage-Imperator.'

Without comment, Qul Aro'nh ordered six of the seven warliners in his foremost septa to return to the maniple's main grouping. But the old subcommander's own battleship continued to drive forward.

Sitting in his command nucleus, the Adar saw from his sensor readings that the conservative old Qul had set the power of his stardrive reactors high enough to trigger a cascade overload. The lone warliner plunged towards the three diamond warglobes that still hovered over the smouldering wreckage of the mining facility.

Kori'nh spoke sharply. 'Qul Aro'nh, what is your intention?'

'As you instructed during our training exercises, Adar, I am attempting to employ nontraditional tactics. Perhaps this manoeuvre will eventually become a standard routine in desperate situations such as this.'

Then the old subcommander cut off communication entirely.

He had made up his mind and seen his path. Kori'nh could only watch helplessly as the warliner's rear ports glowed cherry red. The reactors would go supercritical within a few seconds.

All the people aboard, the Ildiran crew, the soldiers, the engineers . . . Kori'nh sensed their brooding terror, their determination, their grim acceptance as the battleship headed towards oblivion. The Adar stood inside his command nucleus, knowing he was responsible for the Qul's actions. He had disgraced the man, yanked away his solid reason for existence, pushed him to this extreme solution.

If only it works . . .

Qul Aro'nh drove his battleship towards the first warglobe. As he approached, the ship launched all of its remaining kinetic projectiles and planet-splitters, while continuing a relentless bombardment with high-energy weapons. Already, Kori'nh could see damage being inflicted. The other two warglobes rose up, blue lightning intensifying.

But before the alien weapons could lance out, Aro'nh's ship collided head-on with the warglobe. Simultaneously, the stardrive reactors reached their overload point, and the impact created a brief, intense new sun above the Qronha 3 clouds.

Kori'nh felt the blow like a dagger to his heart. But after all the casualties the enemy aliens had inflicted, at least the brave martyrs aboard that warliner had not been helpless. Qul Aro'nh had chosen their fates for them, and – if the Adar had anything to say about it – their sacrifice would be memorialized forever in the *Saga of Seven Suns*.

Aboard the flagship, as the sensor screens readjusted from the blinding overload, Adar Kori'nh saw that the first alien warglobe was now a blackened husk, plummeting downwards in the clutches of the gas giant's gravity. Mortally wounded.

The other two diamond-hulled spheres reeled as if stunned.

They appeared cracked and damaged from the shockwave, white jets of high-pressure atmosphere bursting out from breaches in the spherical hulls. But they seemed to be recovering quickly.

Kori'nh knew the rest of his maniple and the rescued miners were doomed if he did not move immediately.

He had to think of the people first. Opening a channel to the surviving Solar Navy ships, he ordered a swift and complete withdrawal of the forty-seven defeated warliners.

Kori'nh was in shock. He had just watched the utter rout of his battle fleet – the first such humiliating defeat ever recorded in their epic history. But beyond even this shameful debacle and the unconscionable loss of life, the Adar felt a deeper despair. He knew this was likely just the beginning.

Now the enemy aliens had declared war on the Ildiran Empire too.

NINETY-TWO

MAGE-IMPERATOR

Reclining in his chrysalis chair beneath the Prism Palace's skysphere, the Mage-Imperator basked in the focused sunlight that shone through the curved walls. Overhead, birds and colourful insects flitted inside the giant open terrarium, held captive by discourager fields. Sprayed mists congealed into a cloud on to which a hologram of the leader's benevolent features was projected at the top of a column of light from his enormous throne. His face looked down like a deity upon the pilgrims and petitioners who came to see and worship him.

As it should be.

Through the *thism*, the Mage-Imperator sensed the tangled web of major events across the Empire. Such widely scattered thoughts and feelings were most distinct when funnelled through his sons, the Designates of other Ildiran colonies, but he could also feel the glittering lights of other important people across the Empire: his military commanders, researchers, architects, even occasional pairs of lovers whose passion sparked a glow bright enough to be noticed in the noise of billions of Ildiran souls. As Mage-Imperator, he could juggle those sensations in the background while he concentrated on his benevolent duties at court.

Only he understood the priorities, the unpleasant necessities. Everyone else could remain in the dark, as far as he was concerned. The Ildiran race served him in whatever he chose to do. He was the centre of the Empire, and all lifelines radiated from him.

As he brooded, a delegation of five scalies came forward, heads bowed and backs bent. They had angular faces and long snouts and moved with a fluid rapidity that gave them a reptilian flicker. The scalies were an Ildiran kith that worked in the equatorial zones, maintaining arrays of shimmering solar-power collectors under always-glaring skies. They built windmill power generators within narrow canyons that channelled the gusty breezes. Some scalies also worked in mines and quarries, excavating treasures from rugged cliff bands.

Sitting forward in his chrysalis chair, the Mage-Imperator acknowledged the delegation. Their leader, wearing an oiled leathery jerkin, approached with reverence. He wheezed, uncomfortable with the humidity in every breath he drew, and kept his head bowed low.

'My Mage-Imperator,' he said in a raspy voice, 'we have brought you a gift, our greatest discovery in the cliff quarries. Our kith presents this offering to you in praise of your wisdom and the paternal care that makes our Empire thrive.'

The corpulent leader sat up with interest as burly labourers opened the doors at the far end of the reception hall. Working together, they began to drag an enormous, heavy stone. Strong as they were, the workers seemed to have difficulty with such a massive object.

The Mage-Imperator wondered if the scalies might have found a great meteorite buried out in the sands, but when the labourers rotated the giant boulder, he could see that the face had been sheared off to reveal a raw bowl of stone encrusted with beautiful crystals, coloured with watery bands of amethyst and aquamarine.

'The most massive geode we have ever uncovered, Liege,' said the scaly representative. 'Taller than the largest soldier kithman, a treasure beyond compare. We offer it to your glory.'

The nobles, bureaucrats, and court functionaries gasped and twittered. Even the Mage-Imperator smiled. 'I have never seen a natural object so wondrous.'

He raised a plump hand, his face satisfied but humble. It was time now to show his generosity, his paternal benevolence. 'I do my task only as well as you do yours, as do all of my Ildirans. A Mage-Imperator is no more responsible for the prosperity of the Empire than is the lowliest servant of any kith.' He nodded to the scaly delegate. 'Your offering is appreciated, but your loyalty is a far more valuable treasure to me.'

All the scalies bowed to the throne room floor as if overwhelmed by this reaction. 'But truly even I do not deserve such an incomparable gift,' the Mage-Imperator continued. 'It is my command that you display this wondrous object in your equatorial zones, for your kithmen, in commemoration of your own prowess. As it dazzles under our seven suns, let it remind all of us of your efforts on behalf of the Ildiran Empire.'

Still kowtowing, the scalies backed up in unison. The Mage-Imperator could feel the warmth in their hearts, the worshipful devotion, and he knew he had made the right decision. Their loyalty was enhanced, and his control was strengthened.

Before he could say another word, though, a horrific tidal wave of pain and despair swept through him. He spasmed in his chrysalis chair. Jolts shot along his links with the *thism*. He cried out in pain, rocking backwards, his enormous soft body twitching.

His personal bodyguard rushed forward, deadly crystal katana drawn, ready to fight any foe. Bron'n glared at the scaly delegation, as if they had somehow poisoned the Mage-Imperator. The scalies wailed in sudden apprehension.

The Mage-Imperator writhed again. The chattering small-statured attenders fled shrieking. The Ildirans close to their leader also flinched, thanks to the tenuous *thism* link, feeling a strong echo of his anguish. He became lost within himself, falling into the tapestry of other lives across his Empire, drawn like a moth to the hot flame of disaster blooming at Qronha 3.

Through the mental connection, he experienced the horror and pain, the astonishing and unwarranted destruction, the obliteration of the splinter colony. He felt the ekti-processing facility devastated by the hydrogues, and then the further massacre as Qul Aro'nh drove his fully-crewed warliner on a suicide mission to destroy one of the alien warglobes. The Mage-Imperator endured the deaths of the soldiers and crew, and all of the slaughtered workers who had not been evacuated from the sky city.

He felt the defeat of the Ildiran Solar Navy.

And when he came back to himself, surrounded by stunned silence and confused fear in the throne room, the Mage-Imperator remained speechless. He was appalled by what the hydrogues had done. He wanted to howl his anguish, his anger and helplessness.

He had read the signs and known of the increasing threat from the legendary enemy, but he had looked upon the reappearance of the strange aliens as an opportunity. If managed correctly, the hydrogue aggression could have been used to rekindle the waning golden age of his Empire. But the Dobro experiments were not yet complete, and the Mage-Imperator doubted his plans could ever come to fruition now.

Ah, the agony in his soul!

With their attack on Qronha 3, the hydrogues had struck him

to the heart. Now he feared that this war would bring about the destruction of not only the upstart Terrans . . . but the Ildiran Empire as well.

NINETY-THREE

RAYMOND AGUERRA

OX had saturated Raymond's brain with so much information the young man felt that his skull would explode. And there seemed to be no end in sight. So much to learn, absorb, and memorize. If anything, the urgency of his training seemed to have increased.

After enduring so much tedious instruction and review, the wonders of the Whisper Palace had begun to fade, and Raymond's restlessness was growing. He had not been outside to breathe fresh air or run through the streets in months. Though the Palace was vast, with many remarkable chambers and diversions, he thought longingly of the days when he had been able to slip unseen through the crowds that gathered for the King's speeches. He liked to sneak a treat from a vendor's stand, or walk home with a bouquet of fresh flowers for his mother.

His heart ached at the thought of her, not only because of the accustomed sadness, but because – with this one reminder – he realized that OX's lessons, the entertaining toys and games and fine food had made him *forget* about his family. His mother and brothers had died in the terrible fire and explosion, and Raymond did not want to be distracted from the tragedy. Perhaps that had been the Chairman's intention all along.

Recently, he had acted petulant, resisting assignments the Teacher compy gave him. He had refused to perform simple tasks Basil had requested, for no reason other than to be difficult. But OX and the Chairman had made it clear that Raymond's continued pleasure and his future depended entirely on the benevolence of the Hansa. What was it worth to him?

Basil had scolded him. 'You're an intelligent young man, Peter. Don't act childish. Your behaviour is disappointing, like a little boy throwing a tantrum.'

Raymond had sat across from the Chairman. He remembered when his little brothers had thrown tantrums. Rita Aguerra had always known how to deal with them. He wished she was here now. He couldn't seem to control his own behaviour.

'Consider what your life would be like if we hadn't intervened on the day of the disaster. Such rewards do not come for free.' Basil had sounded paternal as he leaned across the table, his face softening. 'We don't ask so very much of you. Perhaps you resent being told what to do at times, but you must understand that no one in the Hansa – not a factory worker, nor an artist, nor even myself as Chairman – is completely free to do what he wishes to do. You must make concessions in order to reap the benefits.' Basil sat up straight, like a businessman finishing a meeting. 'Now, do you understand?'

Raymond had nodded, still resentful, still confused, but now he realized he would have to take a different approach. He'd need to play along.

That morning, OX had been delighted when Raymond asked to work independently for a while, to scour the databases accessible inside the Whisper Palace. 'I promise not to go into any restricted areas,' he said contritely. 'I'm just curious about the other planets in the Hansa. There are so many colonies on so many worlds. Maybe when I'm King, I'll be able to visit them.'

The small Teacher compy made an appreciative noise. 'Even as King, it would require many years to visit all sixty-nine of the Hansa colony worlds.'

'Then can I at least look through the databases?' he asked, not trying to cover his eagerness.

'That would be a most constructive use of your time, Prince Peter. Because you are to be King, very few data files are restricted to you.'

The weight of responsibility felt heavy on Raymond's shoulders. At the moment he wasn't sure he wanted to know what state secrets he might find.

So, he spent hours with the polite interactive computer systems, studying the geographical files of world after world, some of them rich and exotic, others hardscrabble places that Raymond had never heard of before: Palisade, Boone's Crossing, Cotopaxi.

By accident, he stumbled upon planetary files for the primarily Islamic world of Ramah. He hesitated before he remembered why the name sounded familiar. Long ago, his father had fled there, running away from wife and family, never to be heard from again.

Curious to test how much freedom he really had, Raymond pulled up detailed population records for Ramah. On the entire planet he saw no listing for a man named Esteban Aguerra. Ramah's relatively small population observed a traditional Islamic way of life, and the world was not high on anyone's list of memorable Hanseatic colonies. When he realized that nearly all of the names were of Arabic extraction, he wondered if his father had changed his name. In that case, Raymond would have no way of finding him.

After further thought, however, he recalled the month and year his father had left home, after Esteban and Rita Aguerra had spent the night arguing and shouting. From there, it was a simple matter to discover which colony recruitment ship had departed for Ramah in that timeframe.

Next, he acquired the passenger manifest and the colonist number assigned to Esteban Aguerra, which allowed Raymond to track his father through the number instead of his name. Following him to Ramah, Raymond discovered that Esteban Aguerra had converted to Islam and changed his name to 'Abdul Mohammed Ahmani'.

Delighted with his cleverness, the young man then went back to the Ramah population records and tracked where his father had lived with moderate success as a metal worker. Raymond frowned when he learned that Abdul Mohammed Ahmani had remarried and fathered two more children.

Much more unsettling, though, was the discovery that his father had died recently. He stared at the record, feeling strange and unsettled, trying to remember the man. Raymond had never much cared for his father, but now he had reached a dead-end. Esteban had been killed in a backstreet brawl, apparently by muggers who had never been caught. The case had been closed, drawing little attention whatsoever.

Suddenly Raymond realized that the date of his father's death was within days of the apartment fire that had claimed the lives of his mother and brothers. The young man sat back heavily, feeling cold prickles of sweat on his back. A coincidence? Perhaps, but an awfully big one.

He remained motionless for several minutes, feeling weak. When he finally returned to the database, he began to address the questions he had dreaded asking all along . . .

He called up news clips, then written records, then finally the accident investigation reports about the disastrous explosion that had claimed the lives of so many people. As Raymond knew, illicitly stored contaminated stardrive fuel had been hidden in sublevels under an innocent-looking dwelling complex. Containers had cracked, volatile fumes leaked. The explosion had ripped out the foundations of the building, and sent an eruption of flames and toxic vapours through all levels.

Private reports of the accident investigation, however, highlighted certain irregularities in the identity of the building owner, a man with supposed black-market connections, the origin of the siphoned and stolen fuel.

One of the rescue engineers injured in the fire had insisted during an interview that the doors beyond level sixteen had been blocked so that no one could have escaped, even those who might have survived the initial explosion. He even suggested that the evacuation doors had been welded shut on purpose. Oddly, the man had not been interviewed in any other accident investigation. According to the records, after his recuperation the rescue engineer had been transferred to municipal duty in a small emergency-response department on the planet Relleker.

Raymond found other discrepancies when he compared interviews and reports from different sources. He was not surprised to find his own name tallied among the casualties. Basil Wenceslas had warned him that they would cover up his disappearance to prevent anyone from suspecting 'Prince Peter's' humble origin. He swallowed hard when he read the names of his mother and three brothers beside his own, listed in small type among so many other casualties.

His heart turned to ice, however, when he uncovered greater detail. According to precise time codes, his own name and the names of his family had been entered on to the list of victims *first* — before the fire had been extinguished, before the first bodies were identified, and before the accident investigation had begun. He compared the precise filing time of the report with the chronometer readings on the fire images and the news coverage. There could be no question.

They had known all along. The Hansa had recorded the deaths *beforehand*.

Coldly horrified, Raymond deleted all record of his search, hoping that his caretakers had not bothered to watch his specific movements. He had been innocently busy for hours before he'd looked at anything that might have been construed as suspicious.

Raymond's entire world had changed again, as much as it had on the day of the fire. Now he knew for certain that his family had been assassinated, including his estranged father – all to tie up loose ends in order to stage Raymond's death. The stakes were high.

Chairman Wenceslas and the Terran Hanseatic League were willing to pay any price so that a young man named Raymond Aguerra could vanish completely and reappear as Prince Peter, their willing puppet.

None of it had been an accident.

Infuriated and sickened, Raymond vowed to resist the indoctrination. No matter what his handlers told him, no matter what OX taught, no matter how much Basil Wenceslas tried to be oh-so-paternal, Raymond silently swore he would remain independent, though he might act cooperative on the outside. In his secret heart, he would refuse to fill the role forcibly laid out for him.

But he would have to be very, very careful.

NINETY-FOUR

TASIA TAMBLYN

After logging fifty-eight cumulative hours in the enclosed cockpit, Tasia Tamblyn felt as if the Eddies' fastest fighter was almost as efficient and manoeuvrable as a standard Roamer vessel. She could get used to it.

EDF engineering seemed to require two steps where only one was necessary, but once Tasia stopped complaining about the cumbersome routines and concentrated on *learning*, she stopped expecting streamlined finesse and got used to the brute-force approach. She could still fly circles around anyone else.

Her Remora bobbed and dipped as she moved her fingers, adjusted thrusters, nudged attitude-control jets. The sleek ship raced through the obstacle course of space rubble at one of the Trojan points between Jupiter and Mars. Her reflexes singing, Tasia played a game of high-speed touch-tag in the asteroid belt. 'This is fun, Brindle.'

His response came over the cockpit radio. 'You have psychological problems, Tamblyn.'

Her arms were stiff and her legs beginning to cramp after four hours of high-tension acrobatics. Most of the other EDF trainees had dropped out of the challenge, but Tasia continued to thread her needle through the course. The drill sergeants would scold her for showing off, but behind their stern expressions they'd be smiling with grudging admiration. No one had expected this young Roamer to do so well.

But then, none of them knew the determination of a Tamblyn.

Throughout the exercise, Robb Brindle doggedly kept up with her. He followed her every move, chasing her ship's exhaust stream through the dangerous navigational hazards. 'Hey, you intend to leave your footprint on every one of these rocks, or can we go home soon?'

'Turn around any time you want, Brindle. Just make it back to base in time to make me a nice dinner.'

'And if I keep up with you, we both have to eat mealpax?' he said. 'Shizz, what a wonderful choice you offer.'

She flew straight towards an angry-looking cluster of rocks, like a swarm of wasps waiting to sting her ship.

'Tamblyn, watch out!'

'Don't bother with a lacklustre little obstacle,' she said, powering up her weapons. 'Somebody's always trying to put up roadblocks.'

She fired a spread of her upgraded jazers, a high-powered laser beam jacketed with a tightly wound magnetic sheath. The beam's double-whammy could scramble most solid matter. She cleared a path through the space rocks, vaporizing them into tiny speckles of dust, and ploughed right through with a reckless whoop. 'That'll pepper your windshield, Brindle.'

Already she had trained on many different models of military spacecraft, from sluggish former tankers to fast Remoras to middle-weight Manta cruisers to powerful Thunderhead weapons platforms. She had met every challenge and was sniffing for a real fight.

Many of the other recruits had groaned at the exhausting training: a dozen or so even dropped out and accepted dishonourable discharges. But so far, Tasia had never been pushed beyond her limits. Thanks to years spent honing her skills, she was accustomed to trials as part of her daily life. It disappointed her that the vaunted EDF did not demand higher standards of excellence.

Tasia found herself at the top of her class, her scores almost perfect. She was hindered only by her impatience with military protocol.

Robb Brindle helped her run those political and personal gauntlets, and Tasia flirted with him just enough that he probably lost a little sleep at night (and so did she, at times). Tasia toyed with the idea of a romance with Brindle, though she'd never before have considered the son of two Earth military officers as a potential mate. As the daughter of a clan leader, Tasia had always been prepared for a well-placed marriage alliance with another important Roamer family, just like Jess and Ross.

As she thought of her brothers, she clenched her jaw with steely resolve. While growing up, she had hero-worshipped Ross and Jess. They had protected their sister, without smothering her. They let Tasia fight her own battles and rescued her only when it was necessary. It usually hadn't been necessary.

When she and Robb had dinner together, Tasia often talked about her brothers, and about her rigid old father. She had been stung by Bram's death, remembering her last fight with him, wishing they could have parted under better circumstances. But she knew she had made the right choice, following her own Guiding Star.

Considering the clumsy performance of the other kleebs, Tasia wondered if she might be Earth's best hope for fighting the deep-core aliens. With the loss of her father and Ross, Tasia wanted to make her clan proud. Only Jess was left . . .

She decided she'd had enough of this silly exercise. She opened the comm channel again. 'I'm done playing hide-and-seek, Brindle. My butt is sore from this cockpit chair. Let's go back.'

She spun her Remora in a backwards arc away from the asteroids. With Brindle keeping close pace, they raced back to the EDF base, confident they had achieved the best score in the piloting exercise.

In the hangar bay on the Mars installation, Tasia climbed out of her Remora, groaning from a stiff back and legs. She wished she could install her own pilot's chair from the Tamblyn clan shuttle she had flown to Earth. Or maybe she could talk Brindle into giving her a massage. That wouldn't take much convincing . . .

Grinning, Robb jumped out of his craft and came over to her. 'Who taught you to fly like that without killing you first, Tamblyn?'

'Some of us just have inborn skill, Brindle . . . and some people will never learn, no matter how much they practise.'

The drill sergeants congratulated them on their score. Many of the trainees grudgingly admitted defeat, while others still gave the Roamer girl a cold shoulder. Brindle accompanied her towards the mess hall, though Tasia wanted to use her water ration and shower first.

'Those exercises are too damn long,' he said, heaving a big sigh.

'They won't always be just games, you know.' Her gaze hardened. 'General Lanyan is pushing us hard for a major assault. Count on it. It's bound to come soon.'

Robb seemed unsettled by the prospect. 'The EDF is still gathering intelligence. We won't fight the aliens until we have the best chance of winning.'

Tasia scratched her shaggy hair and thought again of Ross and the Blue Sky Mine and how the enormous facility had been so mercilessly destroyed.

'The sooner the better,' she said.

NINETY-FIVE

MARGARET COLICOS

I n the silent desert night on Rheindic Co, Louis Colicos and the
green priest Arcas engaged in a card game, using DD as a third
player. Margaret sat by herself in her sleep tent, listening to the
tinny music of 'Greensleeves' from the music box her son had given
her.

For hours she had pondered the Klikiss hieroglyphics from the
newly discovered city. Although the first abandoned metropolis
held many wonders, this isolated section offered more
opportunities, more mysteries, and more clues.

The trapezoidal 'stone window' intrigued her most of all. She'd
been unable to translate the markings on the separate tiles that ringed
the blank sheet of rock. The symbols bore no correlation to the
mathematics or storytelling words she had previously deciphered.

Inside the quiet tent, the music box finished its tinkling tune.
Out of habit, Margaret reached over to rewind it, but stopped.
Instead, she listened to the gentle darkness outside. Nearby, she
heard Louis laughing, Arcas rattling game tokens, and DD's
mechanical voice repeating the score.

Restless in her frustration but not wanting to join the silly games that kept her husband sane, Margaret finished her cup of tepid tea, stood up, and stretched. She stepped out of her tent into the starlight.

The night was warm and motionless, the air like a transparent blanket. As she walked out into the shadows, Margaret suddenly stopped, seeing an ominous silhouette in front of her. It looked like a hole in the night, a shape that dully reflected the stars. She heard smooth movements, a hard clacking sound, articulated joints . . . then, with a flash, scarlet optical sensors ignited, shining out like demon's eyes.

'Margaret Colicos, do not be alarmed. I was conserving energy,' the robot said, 'and reassessing my database.'

With a nervous laugh, Margaret said, 'Just what I was doing. Which one are you?'

'I am Sirix.'

They fell into silence, Margaret not certain she wanted to be alone in the dark with the beetle-like machine. Though Sirix was no conversationalist, she decided to take advantage of the opportunity. 'Do you have any idea, any speculation, about those symbols around the trapezoidal "stone window" we found in the new ruins?'

'All of my memories were wiped during the holocaust that destroyed my parent race, Margaret Colicos.'

'Yes, yes, you've told me that before,' she said. 'But you obviously retain some subset of skills, otherwise you could not function or communicate. I'm sure you've uploaded all the summaries of what we've found on other digs, just to fill in the blanks in your own memory.'

'Many significant blanks remain, Margaret Colicos.'

She frowned, promising herself not to sigh out loud, though she doubted that Sirix could have interpreted the human response. 'I'm wondering if those designs on the tiles are perhaps location indicators, like coordinates on a map. Maybe the entire grid around the stone wall is like a . . . directory or a phone book.'

'I do not understand the reference,' Sirix said, but somehow Margaret was sure he did. Silhouetted against the dim starlight, the black robot remained implacable, volunteering neither information nor suggestions.

'Are you avoiding the answers?' she finally asked. 'You're not being very helpful.'

'I am telling you what I can, Margaret Colicos. My companions and I have already pondered and discussed this mystery in great depth for several centuries. We have no answers for you.'

'I . . . I'm sorry for doubting you, Sirix. Please don't take offence.'

'We do not take offence,' said the Klikiss robot. 'Even without clear memory files, I do understand that all Klikiss robots were once part of a vast civilization, which is now completely dead. Our creators were wiped out, as were our memories.'

'As if everything was systematically deleted,' Margaret added.

'Perhaps that is the explanation,' Sirix said.

Unsettled and feeling as if she had made no progress, Margaret bade Sirix goodnight and walked towards the light shining out of the other tent. Though she liked to be alone where she could concentrate, right now Margaret wanted the company of her husband.

She entered the tent, saw that Louis had begun another game of cards with Arcas and DD. Louis's face lit up when he saw her. 'Come inside, my dear. Join us. I'll deal you in.'

Before she could answer, he added a pile of cards at the table's empty place. Margaret seated herself and quickly summarized her conversation with Sirix and turned to their Friendly compy. 'DD, you've talked with the robots. Have you been able to learn anything from them that we don't know?'

'Not at all, Margaret. I have done my best to explain to them how compies function and how our design is different from their own. But I have learned nothing about the original Klikiss race.'

'He tried, dear,' Louis said.

DD's mood changed, becoming sad, almost distraught. 'It is distressing that all of their lives, all of their stored experiences have vanished. One can only imagine what amazing wonders the Klikiss robots must have experienced. Such a shame.'

Margaret picked up her cards and studied the hand, though she hadn't yet figured out which game they were playing. 'We're doing our best to uncover it all, DD.'

NINETY-SIX

BASIL WENCESLAS

The Mage-Imperator of the Ildiran Empire and Chairman Basil Wenceslas of the Terran Hanseatic League were the two most powerful men in the Spiral Arm, but they had never met in person. It was about time.

Basil boarded a diplomatic ship and headed towards Ildira to take matters into his own hands. This was not a time for ambassadors or diplomacy: the circumstances demanded an immediate and frank discussion of the alien crisis.

The devastating attacks on Roamer facilities had drastically curtailed ekti production. Many skymines had been shut down and abandoned. And who could blame the Roamers? Now, after the destruction of the Ildiran cloud-harvesting complex on Qronha 3, Basil was sure the Mage-Imperator would be willing to join forces with the EDF against the common enemy. He hoped the Ildiran leader understood that he, as Hansa Chairman, could make whatever decisions might be required on behalf of humanity.

Early in his career, he had listened to his father's insight: 'Learn from mistakes, Basil – preferably someone else's.' Using the Ildiran stardrive to spread colonies and increase the Hansa's economic power, human civilization had finally reached a point at which it could achieve its true potential.

Now, as his ship descended towards Mijistra and his staff broadcast a request for an immediate audience with the Mage-Imperator, Basil steepled his fingers and drew a deep breath, considering possible ways to handle the discussion. There were many alternatives, and a multitude of unknown factors.

Before his departure to Ildira, Basil had met again with General Lanyan to receive a final briefing on the readiness of the revamped Earth Defence Forces and how best they could make use of the Solar Navy. Frowning, the General had called up surveillance images on his display screens. In a precise voice, he said, 'I have my doubts, Mr Chairman, about the military efficacy of the Ildiran Solar Navy. In my assessment, I question their ability to perform adequately in a genuine conflict.'

Basil had looked at images of the immense warliners without arguing. 'According to reports from Qronha 3, Ildiran warliners successfully destroyed at least one and possibly several enemy spheres.'

Lanyan pursed his lips. 'Sir, that was a fluke. A suicide mission that cost an entire Ildiran battleship. It is not standard practise for the Solar Navy.'

'Explain yourself, General.'

'They're all thunder and no lightning, sir. It has been so long since the Ildirans confronted an actual enemy – if ever – they are so deep in a rut they cannot even see the top edges.'

Basil had pondered this. 'Do you recommend that I cancel my trip to Mijistra? Should I not bother to attempt an alliance?'

Lanyan had switched off the display screens. 'Oh, I'll be glad for Ildiran support, don't misunderstand me – we can use their pretty ships for cannon-fodder, if nothing else.' He tapped his fingers on the desktop. 'But don't be fooled. The Solar Navy is composed of peacocks. Right now, what we need are hawks.'

When he stood face-to-face with the alien leader, though, Basil Wenceslas would be careful to keep this information to himself.

He took a moment to groom himself in his private cabin, making certain that his formal suit was impeccably clean, every steel-grey hair in place, his manicured hands carefully scrubbed. He peered into a mirror and was pleased to see no bloodshot lines in his grey eyes, though he had not slept well for many nights. Even in private meetings, appearances were vitally important.

As he looked out upon the alien metropolis, Basil's heart pounded. Despite his various briefings, he still considered the Ildirans a vast mystery. Before leaving Earth, Basil had received another detailed report from his socio-cultural spy on the abandoned colony of Crenna. Davlin Lotze had been sent there to comb through the remnants of the plague-stricken settlement but, expert though he was, Lotze had gleaned only a few titbits, no revelations of great economic or military significance.

The empty Crenna town had yielded a blurry glimpse into the mundane parts of Ildiran society, the way some kiths lived, how they designed and built their structures, what old-fashioned communal agricultural methods they used. Unfortunately, the anthropological spy had been unable to discover any weaknesses or flaws that the Hansa could exploit against the Ildirans.

And now they had to work together. Basil steeled himself to proceed, despite the level playing field.

When he caught his first breathtaking glimpse of the curves and pinnacles of the Prism Palace dazzling under the light of seven suns, Basil understood why some Ildirans joked that the name of the Whisper Palace was fitting, since it was only a whisper of their Mage-Imperator's citadel.

When he and his delegation entered the Prism Palace, a

uniformed Ildiran military officer quickly met them. Basil recognized Adar Kori'nh of the Solar Navy, who had flown formal observation ships to Oncier for the Klikiss Torch experiment.

Basil spoke quickly. 'I am pleased that a leader of your stature has come to greet us, Adar Kori'nh. We have important things to discuss with your Mage-Imperator, and I would be honoured if you would join us. We are faced with substantial military implications.'

Kori'nh bowed his head. 'Agreed, Chairman Wenceslas. I have unfortunately had recent first-hand experience with the enemy.'

Basil's eyes widened. He had not known this. 'You were present at the Qronha attack?'

'Yes, Chairman. I . . . survived. Many others did not.'

Their pace quickened. 'We must discuss how the Earth Defence Forces may combine with your Solar Navy in defence against these terrible aliens.'

'If the attacks continue,' Kori'nh said.

Basil drew a deep breath. 'Adar, you know as well as I that the attacks will continue.'

Kori'nh led them to a private grotto with stained-glass walls that glowed like jewels on fire. Diminutive attender kithmen hurried into the room bearing the levitating chrysalis chair, as if it were a palanquin. Basil assessed the grub-like Mage-Imperator, an obese man who had, by all accounts, never left the womb-like throne since his ritual castration nine decades earlier.

After introductions, Basil folded his hands in front of him. 'Mage-Imperator Cyroc'h, I apologize for not knowing the expected conventions in your culture. What is the appropriate greeting for a leader of your stature?'

The Mage-Imperator's chubby face was like a baby's, completely unreadable – seemingly gentle, yet somehow intimidating. 'In Ildiran culture, supplicants endure many days of purification and make a ritual ascent around the citadel hill of the Prism Palace, washing themselves in the blessed canals. That is how my people come to request an audience with me.'

His eyes narrowed into folds of fat. 'However, Chairman Wenceslas, our time is short. I expect only that you greet me with respect, as you have done. It is best if we do not attempt frivolous imitations of each other's culture.'

'Thank you for that concession, sir,' Basil said. Did the Ildiran leader truly expect the Chairman of the Hanseatic League to treat him as a god? 'I wish our meeting were taking place under better circumstances.' He decided to move quickly, speak bluntly. Behind closed doors in private conferences such as this, powerful men usually had little patience for flowery evasions. 'The Ildiran Empire and the Terran Hanseatic League are faced with a common enemy, and the time has come for us to discuss cooperation and mutual assistance.'

The Mage-Imperator studied him. His voice was wary. 'I am listening, Chairman.'

'Both of our civilizations have grown large and powerful,' Basil said. 'Although we took different paths to our success, we each still build upon the greatness that already exists.'

The Mage-Imperator looked sceptically at his human counterpart. He seemed annoyed. 'Ildirans have already reached our pinnacle of culture, and we are content. We have no desire to climb upwards into an empty sky.'

The alien leader seemed to be testing the Chairman's mettle. Basil responded, 'How else does one reach the stars, Mage-Imperator, but through continued climbing?'

The Chairman had studied decades of observations on the Ildiran Empire and analysed the aliens' potential flaws to make certain the human race could surpass them. While Terrans continued to look forward and push ahead, Ildirans preferred to gaze backwards, dwelling upon their past accomplishments. While the Hansa expanded into more and more new colonies, the Ildiran Empire had begun to shrink. Even the unruly Roamers had usurped the Ildiran ekti-processing industry, with the aliens' complete blessing. Basil thought the Mage-Imperator was a fool to allow such weakness. But right now the two races needed each other.

The corpulent Mage-Imperator shifted in his chrysalis chair and seemed to draw himself up, swelling his body size, making himself more intimidating.

'Before I consider an alliance, I must speak to you with blunt clarity, Chairman. I find to my dismay and annoyance that the Ildiran people have been drawn into this conflict against our wishes. The enemy aliens do not distinguish between humans and Ildirans. I resent the fact that you have inadvertently dragged us into a war in which we wanted no part.'

Surprised at this, Basil took two breaths to calm himself so as not to react precipitously. 'Excuse me, Mage-Imperator, but no one knows why these aliens launched their aggression. They have attacked Roamer skymines, our scientific observation station, and now your floating city on Qronha 3. It makes no sense. Our skymines operated without incident for well over a century. Ildiran ekti factories have been in operation far longer than that. Why should this enemy choose to strike *now*, without warning?'

The Mage-Imperator looked angry. Many years of experience were clearly apparent in his gaze, and Basil looked at him from across an age-gulf of more than a century. The Ildiran leader stared at him in disbelief, then seemed to realize that the Chairman's puzzlement was not feigned.

'*Kllar bekh!* How can you not know? You humans caused all of this. You! You murdered millions of hydrogues.' His long braid thrashed at his side. 'Tell me, Chairman Wenceslas – is that not a sufficient provocation to war?'

NINETY-SEVEN

KING FREDERICK

A spike-studded warglobe the size of a small asteroid streaked into the solar system and entered Earth orbit as fast as the distant early-warning sensors could respond. Before the EDF could rally its troops, the gigantic diamond-hulled sphere disgorged a much smaller globe, like a droplet of dew, that made its way directly to the Hansa capital.

The crystal sphere hovered like an unexploded warhead above the sunlit towers of the Whisper Palace. While the military scrambled, the ball dropped down, crossed the Royal Canal, and hung in front of the immense arched Palace doorways.

Words thrummed out, vibrating from the murky soup inside the small liaison sphere, four metres in diameter. The voice, though not human, produced speech that was clearly understandable. 'I speak for the hydrogues. I bring a message to the King of the rock dwellers.' With a hissing blast, excess steam vented from tiny holes in the pressure vessel.

The royal guards moved about in a frenzy with weapons drawn, looking pathetically ineffective. Ground-based military units rushed into place, but none of them wanted to open fire on the small diamond ball. High overhead, the immense alien mothership waited, silent and threatening.

When no one moved to open the Whisper Palace doors, the alien voice pulsed again. 'I am the hydrogue emissary. I demand to speak with your King.'

Inside the Throne Hall, Old King Frederick squirmed in anxious confusion. What was he to do? Basil Wenceslas was not here. The Chairman had gone to Ildira to meet with the Mage-Imperator, leaving him to sit on his throne and maintain the appearance of stable government.

'I've looked over your calendar, Frederick,' Basil had said before departing. 'There is nothing that requires immediate attention, and if anyone should demand that you make a decision, stall them. Send me a message. I won't be gone more than a week.'

Who could have guessed that after so many ignored demands for parley, that the deep-core aliens would choose this moment to appear in person?

'Get me a green priest,' King Frederick said. 'We must send a message immediately.' He would ask Basil what he should do. Unfortunately, on Ildira there would be few, if any, green priests to respond in kind. The King had to hope his message would get through, that someone in the Mage-Imperator's palace could use telink for instant communication.

Nearby, the minor court advisers, equally terrified, pressed close to the throne, drawing upon the King's imagined strength, hoping Frederick would keep control of the situation.

Outside, the emissary's enclosed sphere hovered impatiently in front of the barred doors. Thin, ominous wisps continued to hiss from the sphere's vents, like a fuming and impatient dragon.

'Tell him we're considering the request,' Frederick said, stalling, and the message was relayed. He felt desperate for someone to lean on. 'And find my old Teacher compy OX. I might need to tap into his information.'

The alien's liaison tank reminded King Frederick of a diving bell. Recalling that these — what had they called themselves, *hydrogues*? — lived at incredible pressures deep within gas giants, he realized the crystalline sphere must be an environment chamber. Any alien emissary would have had to enclose himself like that, just to survive in Earth's atmosphere. He couldn't imagine the pressure it must contain.

'That small tank could be filled with weapons, Sire,' said one of the court guards.

'Probably.' King Frederick heaved a deep breath. 'We've seen that those large warglobes can obliterate entire moons. If the aliens wanted to, they could have launched an outright attack on Earth. Instead, their emissary decided to knock on our door. I think . . . I think we should hear what he has to say.'

'I still don't trust them, Sire,' said another adviser. King Frederick kept forgetting all their names, since the people changed so often.

His stomach in knots, Frederick shifted uncomfortably on his large throne. Now of all times, Basil was not there to whisper words into his ear. Frederick would have to play this on his own terms. After decades of acting experience mouthing the niceties of diplomacy, today he would have to be a real King. He steeled himself, sat up straight, and raised his right hand. 'Very well. I command you to let the alien emissary enter my Throne Hall.'

The court guards and advisers muttered disapproval, but the old King glowered at them. 'I must hear him out. Perhaps he wishes to sue for peace! For months we have begged them to communicate with us. We have repeatedly requested negotiations or peace talks, and until now the aliens remained silent. How can I refuse to see this emissary simply because he has not arrived at my convenience?' He clenched his ringed fist and slammed it down on the arm of his throne. 'No! If we hope to put an end to this conflict, I must have words with this creature.' He raised his chin. 'Let the aliens explain themselves and their actions.'

The arched outer doors, which had been hastily barricaded upon the arrival of the emissary's tank, were unbarred. Royal guards sweated and strained to pull the massive barriers open again. Finally, they swung wide enough that the delegate's spherical environment chamber could pass through.

Mustering all his dignity, the King stared at the strange, perfectly round container. The chamber contained milky vapour, probably a thick high-pressure concentration of gases that the hydrogue creature breathed. A burst of steam emitted loudly from the diving-bell sphere, startling the royal guards.

Finally, one of the court green priests came in from a back alcove, stumbling under the weight of a potted treeling, much larger than was meant to be conveniently moved. Frederick belatedly realized that it was foolish not to have several worldtrees waiting in the Throne Hall at all times, though Basil had feared the Therons could use them to eavesdrop on the activity at court.

'Have you got through to the Chairman?' he said harshly out of the corner of his mouth. He could not tear his eyes from the fearsome environment sphere that glided towards him on some sort of levitating mechanism.

'Not yet,' said the green priest, setting the heavy pot down on the step beside the ornate throne. He crouched next to the treeling and wrapped his hands around the scaly bark. 'Other green priests in your connecting chambers have been trying to track him down. They spoke with our counterparts in Mijistra. But locating the Chairman in his private meeting with the Mage-Imperator is more difficult.'

'Keep trying,' the King said, trying to be strong and noble, not wanting to show how much he relied on Basil.

The hydrogue emissary approached, his pressure vessel looming large and ominous. A handful of court bureaucrats sent in musicians to play a bold fanfare, as if the deep-core alien might enjoy such a reception. Protocol ministers raced in with colourful banners and flags, presuming that their symbols and pennants would be recognizable to an alien species. King Frederick thought them ridiculous.

Thrumming with power, the translucent sphere came to a halt, an overwhelmingly large presence even in the giant Throne Hall. Murky clouds inside churned like a living opal.

King Frederick thought of a child's snowglobe and desperately struggled to stop himself from giggling at the mental picture. He had to appear brave and resolute. He would make Basil proud by demonstrating that he had learned true diplomacy after so many years in the Whisper Palace.

In his dread-filled heart, Frederick knew that this was the most important meeting of his long reign. He stood, not out of deference to the hydrogue emissary, but to keep himself from feeling so small and insignificant in front of the hovering crystal sphere.

He waited in silence, but the pressure vessel tank had emitted no words since the initial demands for an audience. Finally, in an effort to maintain a semblance of control over the situation, Frederick decided to speak first. While the green priests kept trying to contact Basil, the King would draw out this encounter, make no rash decisions – and, above all, do nothing to provoke the aliens. The gigantic hydrogue warglobe in orbit no doubt had its weapons fully charged, ready to level all the cities on Earth.

'I am King Frederick of the Terran Hanseatic League.' He squared his shoulders and spoke with pride, though he doubted the hydrogues had any sense of human expressions. 'I represent all humans throughout the Spiral Arm, on Earth, on our colony worlds, and also on the space stations and skymines that you have destroyed.'

Frederick waited, certain that his words would spark some sort of reaction from the alien emissary.

Finally, a shadow congealed in the centre of the globe's compressed gases. The mists thinned, as if solidifying into a form, and a quicksilver silhouette became a shimmering humanoid shape – a perfectly formed man, complete down to every eyelash, every hair on his head, and a uniform of clothes with many pockets, clan emblems embroidered on a flowing cape, every wrinkle preserved.

Yet the emissary was fashioned out of a flexible liquid crystal that looked like thick mercury. The creature moved towards the transparent curved wall of the environment chamber. The eerie molten features moved, the lips formed words. 'I bear a message from the hydrogues to you, Frederick, King of the rock dwellers.'

'He's dressed like a Roamer,' said one of the awestruck protocol ministers. Some of the royal guards and court attendees crowded into the Throne Hall now murmured with anger, wondering what that might mean.

The deep-core aliens could not simply have chosen a generic approximation of a human form. This image included too many exact details, too many precise contours. It was an identity stolen or copied from somewhere. Since the hydrogues had destroyed at least five Roamer skymine installations, perhaps they had duplicated one of their victims, absorbed or mimicked his body and clothing in every detail.

King Frederick calmed himself, knowing how much was at stake. 'You call yourselves hydrogues?' He tried to keep the quaver from his voice. 'We know nothing about your civilization or your species. We did not even know of your existence. From such ignorance, mistakes are made.'

Always be careful. Choose your words. Be vague. Do not assign blame. He had learned the tenets of diplomacy, but such techniques had been developed for humans to deal with humans. Who could tell how a liquid crystal alien from a gas-giant planet would interpret them?

The Teacher compy OX entered the Throne Hall, unnoticed in the tension, and stood patiently near the green priest and his potted treeling. OX took in all the details, but remained silent until the King should ask him for advice.

'Hydrogue civilization has existed longer than any rock-dwelling settlement,' the alien emissary said, its expressions shifting sluggishly, like solder melting into a pool and then hardening again. 'Within our worlds, mobile cities are encased in diamond. Our people move from planet to planet in our empire through transgates, only rarely travelling across space in self-contained vessels.' The emissary paused.

King Frederick asked the expected question. 'What are transgates? We are unfamiliar with your technology.'

'Dimensional doorways that allow instantaneous journeys from world to world. Though our warglobes and some of our cities are capable of space travel, we find it an inefficient method of making a journey from point to point.'

Frederick tried to grasp the information. Beside him, the green priest droned quietly into the tree, speaking through telink like a stenographer repeating everything he saw and heard. Other green priests across the Spiral Arm would pass on the new information.

These deep-core aliens, these hydrogues, had an entire hidden network of civilization that spanned at least as much area as the Hansa or the Ildiran Empire. But since they lived deep within 'uninhabitable' gas giants, travelling through dimensional gates rather than across open space, no human had ever suspected their existence. The depths of his ignorance astonished him.

Frederick decided it was time to press for more vital information. 'If you have inhabited and colonized so many gas giants, why are our rocky worlds significant to you? What do we

563

have that you could possibly want?'

The alien emissary shifted inside his vessel. 'You have nothing we want.'

The King ignored the buzz of conversation around him. 'Then why do you attack us? Why do the hydrogues provoke a war with the humans and Ildirans? Thousands of innocent people have already died because of your aggression.'

'The hydrogues started no war,' said the emissary. 'All was at peace for millennia. We had no interest in insignificant outsiders. We had no needs in common with rock dwellers, no overlap of interests or territory.'

The King was so frustrated he wanted to scream. Then *why?* He felt the weight of all those deaths upon him, even the Roamer and Ildiran casualties, every victim slaughtered by these hydrogues.

The alien emissary's features shifted as if replaying a sequence of images it had captured from observing the terror and death of the human model it had used as the basis for its appearance. 'In an unspeakable act of destruction, you set fire to one of our finest worlds. You ignited a heavily populated planet. Hundreds of cities and tens of millions of hydrogues were destroyed when you turned our world into a star. Very few of us escaped.'

The liquid-crystal envoy pressed close to the thick wall of the high-pressure environment chamber. 'It was *you*, King of all rock dwellers, who declared war on us.'

NINETY-EIGHT

OTEMA

Basking in the half-slumbering presence of the all-connected worldforest, Otema sat at her writing desk within the Prism Palace. She wrapped a gnarled hand around the flexible trunk of the potted treeling and recited aloud the beautiful cadences of the *Saga of Seven Suns*.

She told the frightening tale of a horrific wildfire that had swept across the conifer forests of Comptor, and how the Comptor Designate, the youngest and most beloved son of a former Mage-Imperator, was trapped in his rustic private dacha. As the ravenous fire surrounded the dwelling, the young Designate had brought his family together, to stare out at the bright flames. The Designate told his children that they must never be afraid of the light, that the brilliant glare reminded him of the seven suns that shone down upon Ildira. Then through the *thism*, he had communed with his father during the last awful moments, telling the Mage-Imperator how much he loved and worshiped the godlike leader. And then the *thism* had snapped . . .

The legend deeply moved Otema, and she read stanza after

stanza to the worldforest, which had its own innate fear of fire. The sentient interlinked trees brooded with terrible half-hidden memories of another ancient conflagration, a sweeping conflict that had engulfed many worlds – long, long ago. She tried to tap into the history, but the trees would not share it with her . . .

The unexpected mental shout that broke through via direct telink startled Otema out of her prayerful reverie. The insistent contact had been sent by one of her colleague priests at the Whisper Palace, calling for her.

With a surge of comprehension, the old ambassador suddenly grasped the situation: the arrival of the hydrogue emissary on Earth, his demand to speak with King Frederick, and the King's urgent need to communicate with Chairman Wenceslas, who had come to Mijistra. Otema knew full well from her time spent on Earth that the aged monarch made no decisions for himself, could not even legitimately speak for the Hansa unless the Chairman gave him permission to do so.

She sent a telink acknowledgement of the request and, grabbing up the nearest treeling, hurried out of her chambers as fast as her weary legs could carry her. As she raced down the crystalline halls, she bumped into Nira emerging from her room, wide-eyed and frightened. While reading the *Saga* into the worldtrees, her young assistant had also heard the emergency telink message, as had all green priests across the Spiral Arm. The news of the hydrogue arrival on Earth had spread as quickly as the worldforest learned of it.

'Come with me, Nira,' she said, cutting off the girl's question. 'I may need you to call the Prime Designate if we must interrupt a meeting between the Mage-Imperator and the Chairman.'

The two priests hurried to the skysphere audience chamber, but only a few low-level workers and court nobles were there. Otema spoke harshly to the first bureaucrat she encountered. 'Where is the Mage-Imperator?'

'He must not be disturbed,' said the bureaucrat and turned away.

Otema snatched at his shimmering striped garment with an iron grip. 'I have an urgent communiqué for Chairman Wenceslas from the Terran Hanseatic League. The Mage-Imperator will want to hear my news as well.'

Alarmed and disturbed, the bureaucrat hesitated. His eyes glazed over for a moment, as if the Mage-Imperator sensed something through the *thism*. The bureaucrat finally said, 'This way.'

The two women hurried, sharing the burden of the heavy treeling. Otema continued to rest her fingers against the scaly trunk, primed to receive further news as it occurred. Her counterpart inside the Whisper Palace described each event as it unfolded, and the words were instantly transmitted to her. In her imagination, Otema saw the hydrogue emissary's crystalline environment sphere enter King Frederick's Throne Hall.

When she and Nira burst into the private meeting room, Basil Wenceslas was interrupted in mid-sentence. Turning to see Otema's wrinkled and tattoo-marked face, he frowned with impatience.

'I have a message for both Chairman Wenceslas and the Mage-Imperator.' Without being welcomed, Otema stepped into the chamber. Nira set the potted treeling on a small table, moving aside a smooth onyx statuette.

Otema and the Chairman had a great deal of history together, much of it frustrating and combative. As the Theron ambassador to Earth, Otema had stonewalled Basil at every turn, and the Chairman resented her for it, calling her old-fashioned and needlessly restrictive, hindering progress and commerce that would benefit all humanity. She suspected that he had engaged in numerous manipulations to see that she retired, and a much more cooperative Sarein took her place . . .

'These events are unfolding at this very moment.' The old woman rapidly summarized the warglobe appearance at Earth and the sealed environment tank that held the hydrogue emissary.

An annoyed, then astonished Basil Wenceslas heard her words. The Mage-Imperator reclined in his chrysalis chair, also intent. Adar Kori'nh looked from his leader to the green priest, absorbing the necessary information.

Basil said, 'King Frederick can't handle this situation himself. He's never done such a thing before.' He looked up at Otema, all business now. 'He needs my guidance. Can you relay instructions? Does he have a green priest nearby?'

'He has a priest and a tree beside his throne.'

Basil clenched his fists so hard his nails left half-circle marks in his palms. 'Good. Tell him that—'

Otema held up her hand. 'The alien emissary is speaking.' She listened to echoes of repeated words through the forest telink. 'He says the hydrogues will no longer tolerate trespass by dangerous rock dwellers – that's what he calls us.'

'What does that mean?' Basil said.

Otema repeated words that the hydrogue emissary spoke. 'He says, "We will no longer allow parasites on our worlds."'

'Frederick, you'd better not muddle this one up,' Basil muttered. 'Has the King responded?'

'I think he is as astonished as you are,' Otema said.

'Tell him to stall,' the Chairman said urgently. 'Don't agree to anything.'

Otema repeated this through telink, but she added her own comment back to Basil. 'Mr Chairman, I do not believe the hydrogues are seeking any sort of concessions from us. The emissary is simply delivering an ultimatum.'

Basil looked aghast. They won't let us near any gas-giant planets? Preposterous! That means no more skymining, no more ekti—'

Adar Kori'nh turned to the Mage-Imperator. 'Liege, without ekti for our stardrives the Ildiran Empire will crumble.'

Basil interjected, 'And the Hansa will fall apart as well. The hydrogues will starve us out. Trillions will be isolated and die. We cannot comply.' He pointed a finger at Otema. 'Tell that to King Frederick. He has to say it to the alien ambassador.' The Chairman lowered his voice. 'Damn, I wish I could put words in his mouth.'

After Otema relayed the message, she observed genuine fear on Basil's face. Neither Ildirans nor humans could tolerate the restrictions the deep-core aliens had just imposed. A shutdown of ekti processing would effectively destroy space travel in the galaxy.

Otema repeated another message from the hydrogue emissary, word for word. Her voice was dry and she was unable to believe what she said. 'He says, "We hereby declare all gas planets off-limits. Any facilities processing the hydrogen reservoirs in our clouds are henceforth forbidden and must be removed or destroyed."'

She closed her eyes, trying to drown out the gasps she heard in the room. As if granting a benevolent favour, the hydrogue emissary continued, '"We will allow a brief but sufficient time for the withdrawal of all skymines. After that, any parasite we discover within our clouds will be annihilated."'

569

NINETY-NINE

KING FREDERICK

A very nervous King sat on his throne, cold and overwhelmed. He glanced sideways to the green priest, who relayed a few words that – unfortunately – did not comfort him.

He'd been enormously relieved to hear from Basil, foolishly imagining that the Chairman would instantly know how to respond, would tell him how to fix the situation. But the hydrogue emissary had delivered his appalling ultimatum, and Frederick still didn't know what to say. He couldn't believe what he had heard.

The liquid-crystal alien hung in its high-pressure vessel before the King. Having delivered his message, the creature fell silent.

King Frederick, fearing that the containment globe would now withdraw and the alien representative would not parley at all, spoke quickly. 'Wait! This is . . . unprecedented. And unnecessary! You are overreacting.'

The perfectly sculptured face shifted its human expression to an inappropriate reflection of an open-mouthed scream of terror. No doubt the deep-core aliens had no understanding of facial subtleties. 'You have destroyed one of our worlds. There can be no peace between us.'

'But your gas planets contain a vital resource that our civilization requires.' King Frederick prayed that his voice wouldn't crack with fear. 'To my knowledge, our skymines have caused no damage to your worlds, nor have they harmed your ecosystems or weather patterns. But we must process vast volumes of hydrogen to obtain sufficient ekti for our stardrives.'

'Your request is denied,' the hydrogue emissary said from his chamber. 'Remove all rock-dweller parasites from our clouds, or we will eliminate them.' Another squealing release of steam belched from a tiny vent.

The King looked quickly down at his ancient Teacher compy OX, hoping for some small flicker of stability and confidence. Back when he'd first begun training to become the next Great King, young Frederick had spent months with OX, learning from the compy's great store of wisdom and experiences. Now, unfortunately, Frederick doubted that even wise OX could provide diplomatic assistance against this incredibly strange alien.

'Please, listen to me.' The King rose from his throne and stepped down one of the levels of his dais, closer to the emissary's containment sphere. He gripped his sceptre as if it were a cane. 'On behalf of our entire population and all governments of the Hansa worlds, allow me to express my deepest regrets and my most sincere apologies.' *There, that sounded good.*

'You must understand that this has been a terrible mistake. Our test of the Klikiss Torch at Oncier was not meant as an attack against your people. We had absolutely no knowledge of your hidden empire. I give you my word as King that we will never undertake another such test. Surely there can be some reparations made?' His voice had a pleading tone, and he stood straighter, tried to sound firmer.

'Rock dwellers have nothing the hydrogues want or require,' the emissary said. 'You could not possibly provide reparations.'

The King felt more desperate. He tried to sound benevolent, to play upon any glimmer of feelings these aliens might experience. 'You do not understand just how much damage such an embargo would cause. Without stardrive fuel, commerce across the Hanseatic League will grind to a halt, and our colony worlds will starve. Think of the suffering! There must be room for negotiation. Please, let us find some compromise.'

Wearing the silvery face of a dead Roamer, the alien emissary stared straight ahead. 'I was not sent here to negotiate, merely to deliver my message. Has the statement been recorded and transmitted, so that all may hear my words?'

King Frederick looked over at OX, who would be preserving every nuance of the encounter. On the other side of his throne, the green priest finished sending his summary through telink to Basil Wenceslas and the Mage-Imperator on Ildira. Local media representatives broadcast these events as they happened, uploading signals to widespread information networks for eventual distribution via commercial spacecraft across the Spiral Arm.

Frederick felt defeated. 'Emissary, your words have already been heard by millions. An account of this meeting will spread to the other worlds of the Terran Hanseatic League as well as the Ildiran Empire.'

'Then my mission is complete.' The hydrogue sank back into his thickening opal clouds. His liquid crystal humanoid form became fluid again, dispersing.

One of the royal guards touched a transmitter pickup to his ear, listened to a report, and quickly took a step closer to the throne. 'Sire! The main warglobe has just withdrawn from Earth orbit.'

Frederick couldn't believe what he had heard. 'Then how will the emissary get back to his mothership?'

The green priest suddenly jerked his head up, looking away from his tall treeling, as if he'd been burned. 'Sire, Chairman Wenceslas expresses extreme concern. He advises your highest level of caution.'

OX spoke, his words overlapping the green priest's. 'The emissary does not expect to return.'

The King backed away from the hovering containment sphere, stumbling up a step to the throne. The sphere's curved walls were opaque now, and he could no longer see the liquid crystal form of the hydrogue emissary.

'Evacuate the Throne Hall!' he said. 'Get everyone to safety! I want—'

Thin cracks appeared along the outer skin of the environment sphere, a pattern of lines that had been laid down within the thick diamond walls. A series of apparent circular hatches were surrounded by a jagged starburst of stress-fractures, cracking, splitting . . .

The hydrogue emissary blew open the armoured seals of his containment vessel unleashing an atmosphere dense enough to crush hydrogen gas into metallic form, to rearrange carbon into diamond. The sudden, complete release of pressure sent a shock wave through the Throne Hall.

A hammer of overpressure obliterated the opulent room, demolished the ornate stained-glass windows, pulverized the hapless spectators. The explosion crushed the Whisper Palace throne and hurled the Teacher compy OX into a stone wall.

The blast wave turned Old King Frederick – the man who had ruled the Terran Hanseatic League for forty-eight years – into boneless jelly. And forever changed the course of history.

ONE HUNDRED

MARGARET COLICOS

After weeks of combing through the cliff-side Klikiss city, Margaret and Louis Colicos finally made their breakthrough.

DD diligently strung lights throughout the tunnels. The Friendly compy wired up illumination systems and installed a small power generator to provide heat and air exchange inside the inner chambers.

Now that the initial archaeological excitement was over, Arcas frequently remained back in camp, tending the now-thriving treelings. He spent hours summarizing the Klikiss discoveries for the benefit of the worldforest and anyone else who could tap into it.

The three Klikiss robots often wandered off without reporting their whereabouts. One early morning, Louis pointed out what he thought were faint changes in the first set of ancient ruins, scuffed caterpillar-like foot-treads and subtly rearranged equipment. From this, he surmised that the black robots must have returned to the abandoned buildings, looking for hints and trying to reassess their past.

'I guess I'd do the same if I had complete amnesia, dear,' Louis had said. 'Exploring one of your old cities, who knows what tiny thing might trigger a revelation? Maybe they're getting closer to a memory flash.'

Margaret agreed, though she remained disturbed. 'I wish they weren't so secretive about it. We certainly aren't hiding anything from *them*.'

She had stored copies of their tangible images and reports. Detail-oriented as usual, Margaret kept files back in her tent and stashed a duplicate datawafer inside the ghost city. The brutal flash-flood that had swept through the canyon demonstrated how even a seemingly secure location could suffer catastrophic damage.

While Louis was tinkering with the incomprehensible machinery inside the stone-window chamber, he finally discovered a way to remove the outer casing of the strange geometric generator. 'Eureka!' he cried. 'To quote another famous scientist.'

Margaret hurried over to see what he had found. Her husband peered into the clean components of the alien device, studying how the connections engaged other sub-systems. 'Ah, I see how it fits together now! This . . . must be a power source, and it's been disengaged from the conduit here. Almost as if the system has been put in a standby mode.' He ran his fingers along the metallic and polymer components, checking linkages, letting his intuition flow.

Inside the discarded casing Margaret spotted a detailed diagram drawn in Klikiss symbols, showing specific connections with the components of the alien device. To her pleased astonishment, the symbols matched the markings on individual tiles surrounding the trapezoidal stone window. Each one seemed to correspond to a set of coordinates targeted by the exotic Klikiss machinery. The linkages ran into the blank stone wall itself, weird organic circuitry lines laid down like insect pheromone trails and covered over with layers of rock.

'These are . . . *locations*, old man. It's a map, or maybe more like a catalogue or a directory.'

Her husband tore his attention away from studying the machinery. 'Ah, like the pulsar coordinates in the Klikiss Torch plans.'

Hearing their excited shouts, DD moved into the room and absorbed what had changed. 'Those are marvellous conclusions, Margaret,' the compy said. 'You can use this as a basis for extrapolating other theories about the Klikiss.'

'Absolutely, DD! We've got a handle on this now.' Louis gave Margaret such a vigorous hug that he embarrassed her, even after so many years of marriage, although no one was there to see it. 'This is the best discovery since the Klikiss cadaver.'

'Maybe even better in the long run, old man,' Margaret offered. 'Remember that we found similar stone windows in every other Klikiss ruin we've studied, but many of them were damaged, especially on some of the coordinate tiles. Never have we come this close to understanding the system or the technology. I have faith that you can figure it all out, old man.'

'Have you attempted to engage the power source, Louis?' DD asked.

With a scuffling noise, the black Klikiss robots entered the chamber, their optical sensors bright and curious. DD looked up and said brightly, 'Sirix, Ilkot, Dekyk! You must see what Louis has found.'

The trio of beetle-like machines scuttled forward to hover over the exposed machinery and scan the diagram and components. Margaret stared at the coordinate symbols imprinted in the machinery, noted identical hieroglyphics repeated on small tiles around the trapezoidal window . . . like selector buttons.

'Well, I think the power system is still intact.' Louis squatted and tinkered with the machinery. 'Should be able to fix this without too much trouble.'

'Could this stone window be part of an alien transportation system, old man? Each tile seems to indicate a place – a destination, perhaps?'

Louis looked sceptically at his wife. 'And colleagues say *my* ideas are strange. Do you think the Klikiss could walk through solid rock walls?'

Margaret turned to Sirix. 'What do you think?'

'I can offer no input, Margaret Colicos.'

Louis looked up with his crooked grin. 'You three robots must be excited! Now we've finally got a very real possibility of learning what happened to your creator race and why all your memories were wiped so long ago.'

'Don't overestimate what we've just found, old man,' Margaret cautioned. 'This isn't the equivalent of a Rosetta stone.' But if it did offer the key to a Klikiss transportation system, perhaps it would provide all the information they needed.

Louis knelt on the hard stone floor again as he contemplated the maze of mechanical components before him. 'Ah, I see what to do with this now, but the power source is corroded. I'll need to jump-start it using some of our own equipment back in camp.' He looked up at Margaret. 'Could take hours, dear.'

DD interrupted. 'In that case, might I call attention to the time? The sun has gone down, and we are already an hour beyond our usual mealtime. Perhaps this would be a good point to break for the day? We can begin our labours fresh tomorrow morning.'

'I hate to stop when I'm so close . . .' Louis said.

Margaret frowned wryly at him. 'Old man, you're always too optimistic. You're never as "close" as you think you are.'

They arrived at the tents after a trudge through gathering darkness. Arcas sat by himself near the water pump and the prefabricated storage sheds, surrounded by glowing light panels. He looked stunned and speechless.

Margaret immediately sensed something deeply wrong. 'What is it? What's happened?'

The green priest looked at the palms of his hands and then stared up at her. 'When I linked with the trees, I . . . I watched the events as they happened on Earth . . .'

Louis came forward. 'Well, tell us, Arcas! You look like you've seen a ghost.'

'The deep-core aliens declared war on all of humanity and said it was because of the Klikiss Torch!' His voice sounded strangled. 'By turning Oncier into a sun, we killed millions of their people.'

Louis stammered, 'But the Torch was . . . just an experiment. We only wanted to warm up those moons for new colonies.'

Margaret understood immediately, though. 'The aliens *live inside* gas giants, old man. We incinerated their home world.'

Louis dropped to his knees in the dirt beside Arcas. 'We didn't know. How were we to know? The aliens never showed themselves.'

'Now they have,' Arcas said. His breath hitched. 'And then . . . and then there was an explosion. The emissary killed Old King Frederick and fifty-three others in the Throne Hall.'

'That is indeed terrible news,' DD said.

The three Klikiss robots silently absorbed the green priest's words. But Sirix and his two companions made no comment at all.

ONE HUNDRED AND ONE

JESS TAMBLYN

J ess returned to Golgen, alone, to watch the personal holocaust
he had set in motion. He didn't expect to feel any smugness or
joy, but he hoped for a sense of closure at least . . . or satisfaction. Accomplishment. Triumph. Release?

Back in his family's ice-mining facilities, Jess maintained a
careful map with programmed dots that displayed the courses of
each plunging comet he and his Roamer engineers had shoved out
of a stable orbit. As the celestial missiles careened towards the gas
giant, Jess knew that Golgen would soon become far more than his
brother's grave.

Bram Tamblyn had trained his Plumas foremen well. The
pumps that brought water through the ice sheath to the surface
wellheads operated so efficiently that Jess had little to do. His old
father had kept himself busy by micromanaging his employees,
maintaining a careful watch on their every activity. Jess preferred to
trust the workers and let them do their jobs while he planned his
revenge.

The anxious Roamers had called three more clan gatherings.

Jess had attended every one and stayed on the sidelines, knowing that his comets were on their way. During the inevitable shouting matches, he kept his own counsel, sitting back in the group and watching the old Speaker struggle to lead the clans.

At least he was *doing* something.

While other family heads discussed politics and emergency measures, Jess observed Cesca, devouring the sight of her like a starving man, watching her every move, catching a flash of her dark eyes. *Someday, Cesca. Someday we can be together. We will have our time . . . but right now, these months without you, waiting for you, seem to last forever . .*

Now his small ship hovered close enough to Golgen that he could observe the storms across its churning face. He thought of the other times he had been here, he and Ross together on the Blue Sky Mine, looking down into the clouds. Back then, his older brother had thought that his greatest danger was missing a debt payment. But those alien murderers had chosen him, had destroyed a cloud-harvester that had harmed no one.

And now they would regret it.

With grim fascination, Jess watched the first enormous comet riding downwards, caught within Golgen's gravitational pull. Surrounded by a greyish-white halo of evaporating gases, the largest comet somehow seemed silent and motionless against the stars, but Jess knew it was hurtling at incredible speed, a bullet already aimed. Unstoppable. According to his calculations, the impact would occur within hours.

A beginning.

The changed trajectory and gravitational stresses had fractured the gigantic ball of ice and rock. Mountain-sized shards spread out in a line of frozen cannonballs, each one with enough force and momentum to deliver a blow equivalent to a thousand atomic bombs.

With a hardened heart and eager eyes, Jess sat back to watch the show.

The first fragment struck like a cosmic hammer blow, slamming into the clouds of Golgen. The impact was bright, sending slow, titanic ripples across the atmosphere, fiery shock waves that continued to spread as the icy projectile sped into the deepest layers.

Jess hoped the impact would be a mortal blow, an extinction event for the aggressor aliens. He set his mouth in a grim line and enlarged the view.

When others learned of this reckless blow he had struck to avenge his brother, they would be horrified. No doubt the action would heat up the war between humans and the gas-giant aliens. Jess was convinced, however, that despite any Roamer outrage or Hansa condemnations, all humans would secretly be pleased at his sudden significant strike against their enemies . . .

Jess remained in position for three days, watching comet fragments slam into Golgen. The soupy pastel clouds became a turmoil of glowing bruises, making the bloated world look like a piece of rotting fruit.

As the immense wounded planet continued its daily rotation, Golgen turned a different face towards the oncoming fragments, exposing more vulnerable areas.

With his jaw set, Jess called up his orbital diagrams again, saw that the second huge comet would strike Golgen within a month. The string of missiles, one after another after another, would continue to rain mercilessly upon the alien stronghold for the next two years – and there was nothing he, or anyone else, could do to stop it.

More fragments struck. And struck.

ONE HUNDRED AND TWO

CESCA PERONI

Back on Rendezvous, unable to hide the proud defiance in his eyes, Jess Tamblyn announced to Cesca what he had done. Though no one could be sure how much damage each explosion had done to the deep-core aliens on Golgen, he was certain he had hurt the enemy – and hurt them badly.

They were alone in Cesca's private office within the asteroid cluster. After a moment's hesitation and longing, she allowed herself to come forward and give him a brief but warm hug. Jess seemed reluctant to return the embrace, afraid to let himself go.

She, too, had to put her personal feelings aside for the foreseeable future. The Roamers were at war, their livelihood threatened, the clans in turmoil. It was no time for fluttery hearts and dreamy romance. She and Jess both knew that they must remain apart for now. Cesca rested her head on his shoulder, then chastely returned to her desk, heaving a sigh. 'You have done a brave but terrible thing, Jess. We can only hope it turns out for the best.'

She would have to tell Jhy Okiah immediately. She and the

Speaker would determine an official Roamer response, because Jess's impetuous destruction would force them to call yet another clan gathering. At least the Roamers need no longer feel so completely helpless.

The cometary bombardment would send an implicit message to the Terran Hanseatic League as well. The Hansa had a history of underestimating Roamers, imposing capricious new tariffs and dismissing them as disorganized riff-raff with little power. But Jess Tamblyn had demonstrated exactly what kind of Armageddon a crack team of Roamers could cause.

Before he could leave or Cesca had a chance to seek out Jhy Okiah, more dire news arrived from a trader; he had reviewed the media recording he had brought many times, but could not yet believe everything it implied.

Cesca and Jess watched the preserved transmissions from the Whisper Palace. When the hydrogue emissary appeared within the transparent chamber and humanity received its first glimpse of the enigmatic deep-core aliens, Cesca gasped, and Jess let out a low groan. 'It's Ross!' he said. 'They've taken my brother!'

Cesca stared in disbelief at the flowing quicksilver features of the man she had promised to marry. 'Or at least they've copied him. Ross was one of their first targets. Perhaps the hydrogues are using his image to communicate.'

Jess slumped into a wall-mounted slingchair, as if the low gravity had suddenly become unbearable. He leaned his head against the rough wall. 'Haven't they hurt my family enough? What did we ever do to these creatures?'

When they heard the emissary's ultimatum, Jess and Cesca looked at each other, angry now. The explosion and the murder of Old King Frederick took them entirely by surprise. Cesca bit back a moan. Although the Roamers had never signed the Hansa Charter and did not consider Frederick to be their King, the hydrogue emissary's final act went beyond the bounds of comprehension.

Jess was white-lipped. 'All this is in response to a Hansa experiment? Roamers had nothing to do with igniting Oncier!'

'Neither did the Ildirans.' Cesca's mind spun, grasping the implications. 'These . . . hydrogues don't comprehend our social groupings or politics. Apparently, they don't even know the difference between humans and Ildirans.'

Jess sighed. 'Or maybe the distinction doesn't matter to them.'

The shaken trader scuttled off to spread the word. Cesca told him where he would find Speaker Okiah, since the old woman needed to hear the news before gossip and horrific rumours reached her.

Weary and torn, Cesca wanted nothing more than to run off with Jess to somewhere they could be together and not have to worry about galactic warfare and alien antagonists. But that would not happen for a long time, now. She placed a gentle hand on Jess's shoulder. 'Go home, Jess. There's nothing you can do here.'

He looked up at her, as if too many thoughts warred within him, struggling to get out. 'There's always something I can do, some way to fight, to survive. Isn't that what Roamers have always done?'

Before he left, he folded her in a long, warm, desperate embrace. 'Yes, the clans need us, each in our own way,' she said. 'Roamers must prepare. You know this will get worse.'

Jess nodded grimly. 'Yes, that's one of the few things I *do* know.'

She found Jhy Okiah in the zero-G nursery on one of the outlying asteroids of the Rendezvous complex. The Speaker had heard the news and by now also knew about Jess's cometary bombardment of Golgen, but she had not yet responded. In all her years involved in Roamer politics, the old woman had learned not to react too quickly.

'A moment of consideration often prevents a thousand apologies, Cesca,' she had once said. Because of the vast distances between the scattered Hansa colonies and uncharted Roamer settlements, no action ever had instant counter-effects. Sometimes, years were required before consequences made themselves known.

Jhy Okiah drifted against a wall, her brittle old legs bent into a lotus position. The Speaker had placed her thin wrist in a tether loop that anchored her in the weightless environment. Here in the nursery, she loved to watch the Roamer children play and laugh while learning movement skills in the gravity-free environment. The painted chamber walls were padded so the children could bounce balls, or themselves, off of different targets.

In the centre of the nursery, equipped with a canister of compressed air that she used for manoeuvring, the matronly Governess-model compy UR kept a careful attentive eye on her charges. UR had a full suite of first-aid skills and discipline programming, and a great deal more patience than any human. With her maternal-based psychology, the compy could tend many Roamer children at once.

When Cesca entered the gravityless nursery asteroid, the Governess recognized her before Jhy Okiah came out of her deep reverie. 'Cesca Peroni, it has been far too long since you've come to visit me. Are you behaving yourself, as I instructed?'

Cesca smiled at the motherly compy. 'I haven't forgotten any of the things you taught me, UR.'

'See that you do not.' Then the Governess jetted off to interpose herself between two boys who were wrestling and tumbling a bit too roughly. UR had watched over several generations of Roamer children, and though stern and meticulous, she also knew how to inspire devotion and love.

While the old Speaker continued to gaze at the rambunctious children, Cesca pulled herself along the wall handholds and took up a position next to her. Jhy Okiah said, 'It may seem odd, with all the chaos and noise here in the nursery, but I come here for peace so I can think.'

Cesca looked at the carefree boys and girls. 'It's not difficult to understand, Speaker Okiah. Where better to see that there are still people who have no concerns and are delighted with life? People who envision the whole future bright around them?'

The old woman turned to look at her protégé. 'I have taught you well, Cesca. If only everyone else could be so clever.'

They sat in a comfortable silence until Cesca could no longer withhold her questions. 'So you have heard the news? About the hydrogue emissary, and about . . . Jess and Golgen?'

Jhy Okiah nodded. 'We did not bring this upon ourselves. Frederick was not our King. The Klikiss Torch was not our idea. But now, thanks to brash Jess Tamblyn, we are thoroughly involved in the conflict – no longer innocent bystanders.'

Cesca's expression grew sterner. 'We were involved from the outset, Speaker Okiah, when the hydrogues attacked the Blue Sky Mine. When they took Ross. When they murdered your grandson Berndt, and many many more. And now the aliens have issued an ultimatum against ekti harvesting, the very foundation of our economy! Jess's comets had nothing to do with that.'

The old woman agreed. 'True. And all of us will suffer . . . not just those closest to us, like your Ross or my dear Berndt. Even the farthest-flung Hansa colony worlds will feel the sting, since the ekti embargo will shut down interstellar travel. But, as usual, we Roamers will be hurt more than anyone else.'

ONE HUNDRED AND THREE

BENETO

Inside their small but comfortable dwelling, Beneto observed the green priest Talbun closely – the deep weariness that clung to him, the eyes dark and nested in wrinkles, the way that age seemed to seep out of his emerald skin. Yet today the ancient man's expression was bright and eager, sparkling with a youthful excitement that Beneto was seeing for the first time since he'd arrived on Corvus Landing two months earlier.

'I have shown you everything you need to understand here, Beneto,' Talbun said. 'You have spoken to the mayor, met all the people, seen their work. With the assistance of the worldforest, you are as prepared as you will ever be.'

Beneto clasped the old green priest's hand. 'I feel very much at home, Talbun. Before long, I will come to love Corvus Landing as much as you do.' He swallowed hard, not wanting to shroud this moment with any veil of grief. 'You are ready. I can tell. And so am I.'

All of the settlers in Colony Town had welcomed Beneto, accepting him without reservation. Mayor Hendy, the colony labourers, the businesspeople and their families went out of their way to emphasize how much they appreciated the younger priest's willingness to settle there. They had feared that no one would replace Talbun, despite the old man's repeated assurances that he would not leave the settlers – his surrogate family – without a telink contact.

Today, Mayor Hendy had declared an afternoon of celebration, with an extended banquet of their most wholesome, if not precisely sumptuous, foods: goat stew, feta cheese, heavy breads. The children had run around the dusty Colony Town streets, and the farmers had come in from their fields wearing clean clothes. Laughing, the settlers reminisced about kindnesses Talbun had shown them, sending birthday greetings or congratulatory poems to family members on distant Hansa worlds.

Beneto listened to their amusing recollections of how Talbun had once huddled among his treelings during a rough storm just so he could communicate human impressions of the local bad weather to the worldforest. They said their awkward farewells as best they knew how.

As the darkness deepened on Corvus Landing, the winds picked up; brisk breezes rattled across the grain fields and swept over the aerodynamic houses in Colony Town. 'Looks like a storm approaching,' Beneto said, walking with the ancient green priest towards the door of their dwelling.

Talbun smiled. 'Not a bad storm. Just enough wind to make the trees talk.'

Now outside, Beneto could hear the worldtree fronds scraping together like whispering voices, laughing at shared conversations. Talbun looked out into the darkness.

'Let me embrace you before you go,' Beneto said, his voice quiet.

The old man wrapped his wiry arms around the younger priest.

Beneto thanked him for sharing his knowledge, for showing him everything he needed to know.

'You were a natural student, Beneto. You already understood anything I could have taught you. I just helped speed the process. I have no qualms about leaving you here. My people and my trees are in good hands.'

Then Talbun turned, his eyes alight with serene confidence, and left the dwelling. He moved with a remarkable spring in his step as he hurried towards the dark grove of worldtrees he had planted years before. As Beneto watched, the old man shed his lightweight robe and dropped it on to the ground, then proceeded naked and barefoot into the darkness . . .

Talbun savoured the touch of a breeze against his skin, the crunching ground beneath his feet, and the soft strands of the hairy matted groundcover. He walked into the grove – by himself, but not alone, as the worldforest encompassed him.

The treelings had rapidly matured into a tall stand, spreading to become a verdant anchor on this far-away planet. He glided between the whispering trunks, touching fingertips against the soft, scaly bark. He greeted each tree individually, even the new treeling Beneto had brought from Theroc, though they were all connected, all part of the same immense mind.

Returning to the centre of the grove, Talbun lay down on the soft ground. He leaned back and rested his bony shoulders against the nearest trunk. He looked up to see patches of the sky speckled with stars, criss-crossed by waving fronds that moved as if applauding him . . . or beckoning.

Through his skin, Talbun initiated a deep telink prayer with the trees. He closed his eyes, sent his mind deep into the wood, into the roots, and out into the overall worldforest.

Summoning his last thoughts, the old man willingly died and

surrendered his spirit so that, as it lifted, it could be caught in the welcoming boughs of the golden semi-sentient trees.

The wind increased later on in the night, but the storm passed with only a brief, welcome rain shower. The next morning when Beneto emerged from Talbun's dwelling – his dwelling now – he looked up into blue skies and nourishing sunlight. His green skin tingled, drinking up the photons. He consumed a litre of water, then walked into the worldforest grove to perform his last duty for the old green priest.

Beneto found the old man lying peacefully in the morning shade under the tallest worldtree. He smiled to see the smooth expression of utter contentment on the tattooed face.

Beneto used no shovel, so as not to damage the nervelike roots of the worldtrees. He required no tools other than his bare callused hands to scoop soft soil from between two widely spaced trees. In less than an hour he managed to excavate a shallow grave. Then he picked up the old man's body as if it weighed no more than kindling and placed it into the soil close to the roots. Beneto covered Talbun, enfolding him in the earth where he had longed to be for so many years.

The young man spoke silent prayers, and the trees themselves whispered. All green priests with access to the worldforest could witness this funeral of one of their own.

Satisfied, Beneto finished and returned to his dwelling to wash. Later in the day he would go into Colony Town and deliver the news to the settlers. He knew there would be much mourning, for Talbun had been a dear friend to them, but Beneto would do his best to comfort them and follow in the old green priest's footsteps.

By tradition, an hour after the burial, Beneto returned to the grove and carefully selected a worldtree that grew tall and straight. He removed a viable treeling, a thin flexible outgrowth that protruded from an intersection of the widest fronds. Its delicate, moist roots still glistened with a varnish of sap and tree juices. Cradling it gently, Beneto went back to the mound of fresh dirt that marked Talbun's grave and, in the centre, dug down so that he could plant this new treeling in honour of the old green priest.

He had covered the old man's body here to let Talbun's molecules rejoin the worldforest. As he dug down, Beneto found that the green priest's physical form had vanished completely. Old Talbun had already been absorbed into the soil, incorporated into the network of the burgeoning worldforest.

Beneto planted the treeling there, wearing a bittersweet smile. When he was finished he stood up and looked around the lush grove.

Silently to himself, and then through telink by touching the trunk of the nearest tree, he promised to plant more and more treelings on Corvus Landing, doing his sacred labour so the worldforest could spread across the universe.

ONE HUNDRED AND FOUR

NIRA

More and more each day, Nira found herself in the mood for singing. Though old Otema seemed disappointed with how little progress her assistant had made in reading the *Saga* to the trees, Nira's complete happiness deflected even the Iron Lady's inclination to scold her. And Rememberer Vao'sh had offered a group of dedicated readers to help with the project. Otema was satisfied with the progress.

Nira's affair with Prime Designate Jora'h had already lasted for months – very unusual for him, and they both knew it. She found him exciting and compassionate, gentle and intelligent. Not surprisingly, he proved to be an excellent lover, caring for her and pleasuring her, and she did her best to please him in return.

Though Jora'h had already stayed with her far longer than he'd spent with any of his other carefully selected lovers, he kept returning for her kisses. The Prime Designate seemed more captivated by the green-skinned Theron woman than he had ever been with the most exotic of Ildiran kiths. He saw Nira as innocent and refreshing. Though respectful of his noble rank, she was not paralyzed with reverence for the eldest son of the godlike Mage-Imperator. Jora'h found that liberating.

But in spite of the numerous times they had made love, and even well aware as she was of the Prime Designate's proven virility, Nira was completely astonished to find herself pregnant with his child.

She had suspected for weeks, but could hardly believe the miracle. A trans-species child implied an extraordinary compatibility between the genetics of the two races. Finally, though, after she missed her period and recognized the changes in her body – unexpected nausea, troublesome fatigue even in the bright Ildiran sunlight, slight weight gain – Nira could no longer deny the possibility. The sheer wonder placed her in a daze.

She recalled lying on colourful cushions beside Jora'h in an enclosed atrium that looked out upon the upwards-flowing waterfalls. They had finished making love, yet still held each other with just as much passion, still kissing, moving on to another phase of sex. She had asked him about Ildiran kiths, how the different breeds related to each other.

'Ah, Nira,' he said, smiling, 'the Ildiran genome is very . . . undiscriminating. Our species is adaptable, incorporating any trait that might be useful, finding common segments of DNA and joining them to make a stronger half-breed. We take the best of every kith.'

'The different races of humanity have subtle variations in appearance,' Nira explained, 'but genetically we are all the same.'

Jora'h had laughed at that, kissing her again. 'Nira, even *I* can see that not all humans are the same. Especially not you.'

Now, alone, she touched the smooth skin of her flat abdomen. Nothing showed yet, of course, but as she closed her eyes Nira tried to imagine the baby growing inside her, an individual life form. Partly hers, partly Jora'h's. She wondered how soon she would be able to sense its stirring presence.

'What will you be like? A son or a daughter?' she whispered aloud, thinking of the mixed genetics of a telepathic green priest and the Mage-Imperator's son. The possibilities seemed limitless and she smiled, impressed at the potential this child held.

When he became Mage-Imperator, Jora'h would have full access to *thism*, a telepathy completely different from Nira's own connection with the worldforest. Through the *thism*, a Mage-Imperator sat at the top of a diffuse mind, sensing all of the subjects in his Empire. When that happened, Nira would lose her lover entirely. Jora'h would become something else, something that was both more and less than what he was now.

'Are you eager for that day?' Nira had asked him.

'That day will come regardless of my enthusiasm or trepidation. I am the Prime Designate. My destiny is to be the next Mage-Imperator. The *thism* will be my canvas, on which I can continue the masterpiece of the Ildiran Empire. I will know everything, and the people will treat me like a god.' He kissed her. 'I don't have a choice in the matter.'

Nira had felt afraid as she held the Prime Designate naked against her, feeling his warm skin, the topography of his muscles, the pleasantly hot stirring of his breath against her face. His tiny golden chains of hair crackled like living static. 'But before that can happen, Jora'h, you must . . . they will have to—'

He brushed his fingertips over her lips. 'No man would ever look forward to ritual castration, but I have been prepared for that since I was a child. For now, my duty is to spread my bloodline among the various Ildiran kiths. Later, my duty will be to manage the web of *thism* so that I can be the heart and mind of the Ildiran race.' He stroked her smooth shoulders. 'But that will not occur for half a century or more. Don't worry about it, Nira. Does not the transience itself make our love sweeter?'

How could she disagree?

Astonished but incredibly happy to learn that she carried his child, Nira longed to see Jora'h, needed to talk with him, but he had been exceptionally busy. Since the hydrogue attack on Qronha and the alien emissary's ultimatum against ekti production, the Mage-Imperator had been keeping his son close beside him. Such dire circumstances had forced the Prime Designate – indeed all the Designates, as well as Adar Kori'nh and the other commanders of the Solar Navy – to address the emergency.

Nira knew this was not a time for love-making, and comforted herself with the knowledge of her precious secret, looking forward to the time when she would be able to reveal it to Jora'h. One day, when his duties and obligations as heir to the great Empire weighed too heavily upon him, she would tell him, offer him a bright spot in an otherwise troubled day. She felt sure he would consider it a miracle.

Reluctant to confide in stern Otema, though, Nira kept the information to herself and concentrated on reading the *Saga* to the treelings. Nira wondered whether she might have earned a place in the epic herself, by carrying the first child of an Ildiran and a human. Her baby, a hybrid with such monumental potential, might some day perform great deeds.

Soon she would have to tell Otema about the baby, if the old woman didn't already know through the worldforest. For now, Nira justified her love for the Prime Designate, sorting out her feelings for him and speaking them aloud. Having no one else to talk to, she shared her thoughts with the non-judgemental treelings, telling them everything.

And the always-curious worldforest absorbed the information with benevolent fascination.

ONE HUNDRED AND FIVE

MAGE-IMPERATOR

After a noticeably agitated Chairman Wenceslas raced back to mitigate the disaster on Earth, the Mage-Imperator knew it was time to launch his own plans. In the end, it did not matter how many people were hurt, because the Empire was at stake. He could no longer delay.

As the focal point of an entire race, the Mage-Imperator had no qualms about making the necessary decisions, no matter how grim and unpleasant they might be. Someday, his son Jora'h would also understand – *after* the Mage-Imperator was dead. The Prime Designate had no choice, and he suspected nothing.

Under bright sunlight on the rooftop of the Prism Palace, the Prime Designate and his large assigned retinue stood in travelling clothes, ornately dressed in a combination of traditional Ildiran stripes and looping scarves made from Theron cocoon fibres.

The Mage-Imperator had ordered teams of attenders to carry the chrysalis chair to the rooftop landing platform so he could bid his eldest son farewell. Getting Jora'h out of the way was the important first step, before the leader could issue his more unpleasant orders.

'I hope you will learn much from this diplomatic trip, my son,' he said with a beatific smile. The Prime Designate seemed untroubled; it was easy to manipulate him.

Jora'h's tiny gold braids floated in a nimbus around his head as he nodded. 'I will be pleased to view Theroc with my own eyes, Father. And I look forward to meeting with Prince Reynald again. I believe he will be a friend to our Empire.'

The Mage-Imperator nodded, feigning contentment in his reclining chair though fully aware of the desperate, growing danger from the ancient hydrogue enemies. 'Yes, we must make sure that our alliances are secure.'

Jora'h glanced at the green-skinned female, Nira, who waited with spectators outside the cordon, where Bron'n and other bodyguards kept them at a safe distance. 'Still, Father . . . are you convinced you don't require my counsel and assistance here? What if the hydrogues attack another Ildiran facility?'

The Mage-Imperator nudged his chrysalis chair closer to where his son stood. 'Jora'h, because of your friendship with Reynald, no one can treat with the Therons as well as you. At present, this is the most important duty you can perform for the Ildiran Empire.'

The Prime Designate bowed, pleased to be given such a responsibility. 'As you command, my Mage-Imperator. You see all and know all.'

Waving to the spectators, he cast a lingering gaze towards the female green priest, to whom he had never said his private goodbye. Jora'h led the bureaucrats and nobles into the transport ship that would take them to Theroc, where he would be conveniently preoccupied for some time. The Mage-Imperator's faithful and unquestioning minions would cover up the mess and concoct appropriate excuses and alibis, if necessary. Jora'h need never know.

He had worried that his son would ask Nira to accompany him

on this journey – which would have forced the corpulent leader to make an awkward refusal, based on some pretext or other. But the old green priest had preempted Jora'h's request, saying that their work on the *Saga of Seven Suns* was not proceeding as rapidly or efficiently as it should. Before Nira could ask to join the Prime Designate, Otema had made it very clear that her assistant must remain in Mijistra and do her work.

That was perfect, the Mage-Imperator thought. *The young woman is mine.*

As the Prime Designate departed into the dazzling sky, the spectators cheered and raised their arms. The Mage-Imperator's restless braid twitched at his side as he scrutinized the green-skinned young woman, analysing her and deciding how best Nira could be used . . . how long she could last under the harshest circumstances.

With his chambers guarded by Bron'n and four other muscular sentries, the Mage-Imperator sat propped upright in his chair, sorting and assessing all the information the *thism* delivered to him. He observed the widespread citizens of his Empire, looking for clues and reactions to the brewing events, the darkening hydrogue threat. Only by understanding the totality of his race could he comprehend the steps he must take.

Jora'h was his first-born son, destined to become the next Mage-Imperator, and he would come to understand. If he found out what was to become of the two green priests, the shock would be a painful revelation to him, a more dramatic shift in his life than the eventual ritual castration. But in time he would learn what had happened . . . and how to live with it.

The Mage-Imperator picked up some of the densely written documents at hand: carefully censored stanzas from the *Saga of Seven Suns*. These stanzas, lines of grim poetry unfamiliar even to the greatest rememberers, were a hidden piece of history, deemed by a former Mage-Imperator to be too horrendous for the Ildiran people to hear.

When the rediscovery of these events had brought Rememberer Dio'sh to him, the Mage-Imperator had been forced to kill the young historian to keep that information hidden, especially in these dire times. He had easily covered up the young rememberer's disappearance by saying that Dio'sh had been sent to a distant splinter colony. No Ildiran would doubt the word of the Mage-Imperator.

Now, he reread line after line of the records from so long ago to refresh his memory of the hydrogues. *The ancient enemy*.

From his perspective of nine decades of rule, the Mage-Imperator understood far more than the frenetic humans did. He realized just how incredible this war would be – a conflict that could shatter the cosmos. If only Jora'h could understand as well . . .

He wished his eldest son grasped the consequences and interconnections involved in long-term planning, but the Prime Designate remained too naive and optimistic. Not yet prepared to lead an empire. Jora'h's hands were far too clean – for the moment.

In the forgotten stanzas, the Mage-Imperator searched for a way to turn the situation to Ildira's advantage. At the very least, this new and escalating war against the hydrogues promised to take up a million lines in the ever-growing *Saga of Seven Suns*. And, if the struggle could be managed correctly, the Mage-Imperator might bring back a new golden age for his waning empire.

His only hope was to make some form of alliance with the alien enemy. He would have to make the necessary sacrifices, as would many others. But even the simplest negotiations with the hydrogues would be impossible unless the extended Dobro experiments finally came to fruition. The Mage-Imperator could think of only one way to communicate *directly* with these deep-core creatures, on their own terms.

The overall plan might take as long as a decade or two. The Mage-Imperator must do it correctly. If he succeeded, the hydrogues would listen to him. But, oh, the death and mayhem his people would endure in the meantime!

Bron'n entered the chamber, interrupting the Mage-Imperator's thoughts, and bowed his bestial head. 'Liege, the Dobro Designate has arrived, according to your summons.'

'Good. Remain close, Bron'n. I have an important task for you, as well.' As the Mage-Imperator set aside his secret documents, his long braid began to jerk and thrash with agitation. 'We all have much work to do.'

ONE HUNDRED AND SIX

BASIL WENCESLAS

The Throne Hall of the Whisper Palace was a wreck. Walls had fallen down, windows shattered, support beams collapsed in the hydrogue explosion. At least there hadn't been a fire.

Basil Wenceslas stood speechless amidst the destruction, jaw clenched tight, lips pressed together, though his hands trembled with the sheer buildup of rage and shock.

Surrounded by grim-faced royal guards, Basil inspected the areas where engineers had shored up the support walls and verified the safety of that portion of the Palace. After the attack, the Throne Hall was declared completely off-limits until Basil returned from Ildira. No one else had been allowed to see the destruction – nor would they.

Basil turned to Franz Pellidor, who had remained silent and unobtrusive while the Chairman made decisions and chose his priorities. 'Give me an assessment, Mr Pellidor. You've been watching the public reaction for the past several days. Have you controlled the media coverage?'

The blond man seemed surprised. 'How could we control the coverage, Mr Chairman? From start to finish, the meeting with the hydrogue emissary was a matter of public record. Are you suggesting that I should have tried to suppress information after the fact? Very dangerous, sir.'

'No, no, much too late for that. But we do need to channel the public reaction. Encourage the people to think what we want them to think.'

Pellidor gave a flat, unemotional assessment. 'Rumours are running rampant. The populace is still in a state of disbelief. Some are outraged, others are terrified at the prospect of a hydrogue invasion. What is it that we want them to think? Most citizens haven't yet grasped the long-term hardships we may face if ekti production is halted indefinitely.'

'We'll get our ekti,' Basil said, his voice close to a growl. 'We've got to take advantage of public outrage, rally our citizens, and prepare an immediate response. If we form an alliance with the Ildirans, our combined might will certainly be enough to resist these aliens.'

Basil frowned, though, recalling his meeting with the Mage-Imperator. During the journey back to Earth, a thought had repeatedly nagged him. At the time, events had been so dramatic and horrifying that he'd forgotten the Mage-Imperator's exact words immediately before the green priest Otema had arrived. But now he remembered.

While insisting that he knew nothing about the mysterious enemy, the Mage-Imperator had referred to the deep-core aliens as 'hydrogues' – before the emissary had ever arrived at the Whisper Palace. How had the Ildiran leader known what they called themselves? What knowledge was he keeping secret from the Hansa?

Basil stepped over chunks of broken marble that had once been a pillar. Dagger-shards of silvery mirrors and coloured window glass lay strewn about like the contents of some pirate's overturned treasure chest. He turned to Pellidor. 'What about Frederick's body? What condition is it in?'

Pellidor frowned. 'Unrecognizable, Mr Chairman. The pressure wave didn't leave much more than a stain on the wall . . . and then the wall collapsed.'

Basil nodded sadly. 'Find us an appropriate corpse, then. With the proper makeup and prosthetics, the public will never know the difference. We need to stage a glorious royal funeral, pronto. Old King Frederick must look peaceful and beatific, lying in state. Not a scratch on him. A closed coffin would send entirely the wrong signal.'

'Yes, Mr Chairman,' Pellidor said. 'Leave that to me.'

Basil looked around the shattered Throne Hall, at the bloodstains pounded into the glossy walls. Drafts whistled through breaches in the wall of what had been the most opulent room in the Whisper Palace. For the first time in decades, Basil felt tears sting his eyes. A rush of angry thoughts drove them away.

With an ungainly gait that hinted at how much damage he had suffered, OX entered the Throne Hall. Basil looked at the small-statured old compy, taking in the twisted arm and the bent support strut in his left leg. Flashes of bright silver showed where new components had been grafted on. Many portions of the compy's hull were still scratched and damaged.

'I will present my eyewitness report whenever you wish it, Chairman Wenceslas,' OX said. 'Although I alone survived the explosion, I can provide little information beyond what has already been recorded and transmitted.'

Basil pursed his lips. 'OX, you have a far more important mission. Our timetable has been dramatically accelerated. Prince Peter must be introduced to the citizenry as soon as possible. We have no choice.'

OX showed no surprise, though his response expressed a thread of doubt. 'His training is not yet complete, Mr Chairman.'

'We will have to make do. The Hansa desperately requires continuity, and a new Crown Prince will provide much-needed reassurance. And because of his youth, the people will be inclined to overlook any initial missteps he might make.' He turned, and the guards stiffened to attention, ready to respond the moment Basil issued commands.

'I want the Throne Hall cleaned up and repaired *instantly*. Spare no expense. Bring in all the materials you need, but release no images of the damage. I don't want the public to see it. Not ever. The next time we show the Throne Hall, it should look good as new – in fact, more impressive than ever before. King Frederick is dead, but we cannot let anyone know how deeply the hydrogues wounded us. Public dismay would cause more damage in the long run.'

Pellidor's eyes were distant as he considered how best to assemble discreet work teams of architects and engineers.

'Immediately following the state funeral,' Basil continued, 'we will host a glamorous coronation for King Peter. And I want a genuine celebration. You know, "long live the new King!"' He took one step ahead of the Teacher compy. 'Come, OX. You and I have to write the first public speech Prince Peter will give. I think I have exactly the right announcement for him to make.'

When Peter stepped out on to the oration balcony of the Whisper Palace, Basil watched him with all the critical scepticism of a perfectionist director of an expensive entertainment production.

Prince Peter's hair and clothes were immaculate, his posture and poise admirable. Looking at him now, Basil could see almost no remnant of the streetwise Raymond Aguerra. Peter looked like images of a young King Frederick, though many of those photographs and holograms had been subtly doctored in recent months to enhance the resemblance between the two.

The public was surprised to learn of the young Prince's existence, for King Frederick's family life had been a closely held secret. But in such trying times, they expressed neither shock nor complaint, only relief that the Hansa crown would be passed smoothly to a new ruler and sympathy towards Peter for the loss of his revered 'father'. Old Frederick had been pleasant and benevolent, and his reign had spanned calm waters. Now, with the hydrogue depredations, a stronger monarch was required.

At the start of the well-rehearsed speech, Prince Peter raised his hands, as he had been instructed to do. The crowd swarming across the plaza roared with approval. 'To all my people on Earth and all my subjects in Hansa colonies, allow me to introduce myself.' Peter gave them a cocky smile. 'In the times to come, we'll probably be seeing a lot of each other.'

Basil frowned at the Prince's casual ad-libbed comment. His speech hadn't been scripted in that way, but the people chuckled – they actually *chuckled* – which was a heartening sound and a great relief after their shock and grief. While Basil was annoyed that Peter had already departed from the script, perhaps the young man's instincts weren't so bad. A warm-hearted and beloved leader could draw the population together more effectively than a stony, aloof idol.

'My father is dead, and I must become your new King far sooner than I had hoped. The Archfather has counselled me through this difficult time, giving me the blessings of Unison, and now I am ready. I promise you I will never serve with less than my utmost ability . . . if you will promise to do the same for all of humanity.'

The crowd cheered, and Basil nodded to himself. *These times call for a strong and decisive leader. And a likeable one wouldn't hurt, either.*

The coronation date was already scheduled, as was the funeral of Old King Frederick. Such spectacles would distract the people from their fear of further hydrogue strikes. The deep-core aliens could return at any time.

'As my first duty to you,' Peter continued, his strong voice echoing across the torch-lit plaza, 'I must issue orders to General Kurt Lanyan, the leader of our Earth Defence Forces. The hydrogues have committed an unforgivable aggressive act, not only by assassinating my father and your King, but by threatening to cripple the Terran Hanseatic League. We cannot tolerate this!' He raised a fist and the people roared their approval. 'We must stand up to our enemies. They are gravely mistaken if they think the human race will cower from an unwarranted threat. They cannot deny us the stardrive fuel our civilization requires!'

Basil was astounded to hear the shouts and cheers of absolute conviction. Prince Peter had the crowd in the palm of his hand.

'Therefore, I command the launch of a full-scale military assault using our newly upgraded battleships. Hansa cloud harvesters will proceed under full EDF escort *and take all the ekti we need!* Our first target will be Jupiter, right here in our home system. The hydrogues have no right to deny us our own resources.'

Basil smiled. The population, though grief-stricken, was enthusiastic, and apparently willing to sacrifice anything.

'In the face of hydrogue posturing and threats, all of humanity must remain brave. We have never intended these aliens any harm – but harm is certainly what they will find if they interfere with us in any way.' Peter raised his voice, hurling his words into the tidal wave of the crowd's response. 'I command that the ships be launched immediately!'

Basil sat back in his alcove, pleased at how well the speech had turned out. Peter had changed a few words to make his mark, probably a petty gesture to resist where he could. This Prince was perhaps just a bit too much his own man still, but that could be taken care of.

Basil would knuckle him under by the time of the coronation.

ONE HUNDRED AND SEVEN

TASIA TAMBLYN

As in all exuberant new fleets going off to battle from every war in human history, the mood in the Earth Defence Forces was upbeat and patriotic. Even those cadets who had previously given Tasia the cold shoulder, now gave her a comradely slap on the back, grabbed their equipment, and ran for their assigned vessels. She hadn't been called a 'Roacher' in days.

After waiting for so long, Tasia would soon get her chance against the alien bastards. The hydrogue emissary that had killed King Frederick had had the audacity to disguise himself as Ross. She wanted to kill them for that – among other things.

They had received unconfirmed reports about a massive, intentional cometary strike against the gas giant Golgen, the site of the first hydrogue attack. While no one could be certain how much damage the celestial bombardment had inflicted on the enemy, the sheer audacity of the spectacle lit up the imaginations of the Terran soldiers. They seemed startled, even amused, that a mere Roamer could have done such a thing. And it stood to reason that the EDF 'professionals' could do even more damage.

Tasia knew in her heart that Jess had been behind the cometary scheme. He had chosen Golgen intentionally, to retaliate for the destruction of the Blue Sky Mine. 'Now it's my turn, big brother,' she said to herself.

Swept along by enthusiasm and her own plans, she gave Robb Brindle a swift, hard hug followed by a startlingly hot kiss, then rushed off before her grinning friend could react.

With her kit and her uniform, and a few Roamer survival items she had managed to stuff into her jumpsuit pockets, Tasia ran towards the shuttle bay where troop carriers ferried crews up to the waiting battleships. Admiral Stromo, in command of the Grid I battlegroup, would captain the magnificently armoured *Goliath*, first of the new enhanced Juggernauts. The *Goliath* had already completed its initial shakedown routine and tested out perfectly. Ready for battle.

When Tasia saw the congregation of enormous ships, the sheer massed firepower about to launch for Jupiter, she felt the same confidence and optimism as all the other recruits. But she also knew that such things could change in a heartbeat. After studying intelligence files of the hydrogue attack against the Ildiran Solar Navy at Qronha 3, they all knew the alien warglobes would be tough nuts to crack.

Because of her excellent scores, Tasia had been promoted in rank again, to Platform Commander, or Platcom, and given command of her own Thunderhead weapons platform; such rapid promotions were possible only because of the huge war buildup, but she knew she had earned her place. Robb Brindle, who had demonstrated effective teamwork with Tasia, was assigned as her first officer, given full command of the Remora squadrons that would bear the brunt of space combat should the hydrogues appear.

When all the EDF ships had been manned, their engines

powered up, their weapons fully charged, Remora squadrons prepped and in position for immediate launch, Admiral Stromo broadcast on the channel linking the expeditionary fleet.

'This is our first direct mission against the enemy, more important than any other action the EDF has taken. This is not just a brushfire conflict with a rebellious colony or a punitive strike against a few unruly Roamer pirates preying upon innocent colonists—'

On the bridge of her Thunderhead, Tasia glowered at hearing the reminder of Rand Sorengaard. 'Shizz, thanks a lot, sir,' she muttered quietly enough that no one would hear her. With his dismissive comment, Stromo had just weakened her ability to command.

'This mission has direct consequences for the future of the Terran Hanseatic League, and for all of humanity,' the Admiral continued.

Tasia's bridge crew made rowdy catcalls. 'Let's go kick some hydrogue butt!'

'Only one way to deal with a bully – kick him in the balls!' Tasia recognized the voice of Patrick Fitzpatrick, who had demonstrated his own willingness to bully, until she had shown him the error of his attitude. He had not received a promotion and remained assigned to her Thunderhead's bridge crew.

Tasia just wished they would get on with it and launch already, but Stromo droned on. 'This will not be a direct offensive strike, since we do not know the location of our enemy. We must, however, stand up to the hydrogue ultimatum. We will take the ekti we need by main force.'

The fleet finally departed from the swarming construction yards in the asteroid belt and chased after the enormous ball of Jupiter. It was a striped sphere of clouds; grey and tan and yellow bands girdled the planet with enormous hurricanes. Had hydrogues always lurked here, throughout the millennia of human history, even before Galileo had first looked through his crude telescope?

Four massive Hansa ekti harvesters had been put into service, assembled from cannibalized components in the asteroid construction yards. The gigantic facilities moved under their own power, escorted by the EDF battle group.

On the Thunderhead's bridge, Tasia could not help smiling at the primitive Hansa-design skymines. Roamers had made the harvester systems so much more sophisticated, streamlined, and efficient. While these jerry-rigged factories might serve the purpose, after learning the questionable skill of the local ekti miners, she understood how her people had managed to keep a corner on the market.

But without EDF protection against the hydrogues, the Roamers were effectively cut off from their livelihood. Eventually, given the inefficiency of their own facilities, the Hansa might contract with Roamers, providing enough military support to guard their skymines. But being put over a barrel made Tasia deeply uneasy, and it would force an uncomfortable partnership with the Big Goose, which the Roamers had avoided for their entire existence.

The cross-orbit journey was brief. The Juggernaut *Goliath*, three Manta cruisers, and a cluster of Thunderheads shepherded the ekti harvesters down into the Jovian atmosphere. Tasia was impressed with the beauty of Jupiter's fingerpainted cloud bands, but she had seen many other planets, had stood on the observation deck of the Blue Sky Mine with Ross . . .

Now she was spoiling for a fight, for direct payback against the hydrogues. If the deep-core aliens dared to show up, Tasia hoped to get in the first shot.

A resounding cheer went through her crew as the ekti

harvesters began to skim along the clouds, sucking up a huge volume of hydrogen and processing it through their ekti reactors.

The slow facilities would have to remain on-station at the gas giant for weeks before they produced enough of the rare allotrope to make a worthwhile cargo. But simply by putting the operations in place the EDF had scored a psychological victory for humanity. They had proved they would take the stardrive fuel, in spite of alien threats. They had called the hydrogues' bluff. They had stood up to the enemy, thumbed their noses at them.

Tasia's crew was joking, making bets, sounding even more enthusiastic than they had before the fleet's launch. Manta cruisers flaunted their military manoeuvres where other ships could see them. Robb Brindle stood beside her, though not too close, because he was on the bridge and she was the Platcom. But he caught her gaze with his honey-brown eyes. 'Far be it from me to request a reality check,' he said in a low voice, for her alone, 'but I have a feeling that we're mooning a mean junkyard dog, all brave and laughing – until the dog's leash breaks.'

Tasia looked at him with a bemused expression. 'Sometimes, Brindle, you speak a language completely foreign to me.'

But in truth, she understood exactly what he meant . . . understood it all too well. She just wondered how long they would have to wait.

ONE HUNDRED AND EIGHT

MARGARET COLICOS

A function diagram inside the Klikiss machinery provided the clue Margaret had been looking for. Using her new intuition that the symbol tiles around the trapezoidal window represented coordinates of the lost race's planets, Margaret hurried through nearby rooms. She stared at the clearest records – testaments or desperate messages hastily scribed on the wall surfaces.

While Louis tinkered with the machinery itself and DD rigged more lights around the writing, Margaret stood for hours, concentrating. She quickly documented her suspicions, translating one section at a time. Whenever she encountered stumbling blocks of indecipherable pictographs, she skipped to a different section. Each newly translated segment gave her insight into the more difficult parts, and she went back and forth.

Understanding each wall segment was like peeling back the layers of an onion, yielding some answers while revealing new mysteries, filling in Klikiss history yet demonstrating how much still remained to be learned. Finally, she pieced together a rough summary.

Two of the black robots lumbered into the stone-window chamber to observe the archaeologists' progress. In an adjacent chamber, where Margaret stared at the alien words, she started the tiny music box Anton had given her, its tinkling tones helping her subconscious. The metallic melody encouraged her eyes to wander up and down over the symbols. In fact, the way the Klikiss chroniclers laid down their notation actually seemed to have a rhythm, a linguistic 'cadence' that human language did not have.

Moving on their clusters of finger-like legs, Sirix and Dekyk entered her chamber and scanned the walls with their optical sensors. The plinking melody seemed to unsettle them somehow. The black robots remained motionless until the music box wound down and the melody slowed to a stop in mid-measure.

DD turned to the two Klikiss robots. 'We have good news for you today, much progress made. Margaret, would you share your translation so far?'

She traced her finger along compact groupings of hieroglyphics. 'I'm still putting pieces together, but it's going much faster now. Each bit I understand helps me unravel something else. Here, it talks about a great war, an enormous conflagration that swept across the galaxy. That's probably what wiped them out. We suspected as much, especially after seeing Corribus, but this is the first outright Klikiss documentation of the event.'

She pointed to a broad section of the wall. 'This part is incomprehensible, so far, though the few words I can identify make me suspect this talks about an enemy of the Klikiss. And look, here and here.' She walked forward, indicating several pictographs in the dense clusters of markings, 'I believe these are notations about the Klikiss robots.'

Sirix and Dekyk flashed their optical sensors and buzzed to each other. Margaret put her hands on her hips and smiled. 'It's going so well, I wouldn't be surprised if I finished this wall today. We'll know the answers soon.'

Sirix said, 'Knowing the answers will change many things.'

They were interrupted by an excited whoop from Louis in the other room. Margaret and DD hurried to him with the two black robots following more sedately. Louis stood by the ancient machinery, which now throbbed and hummed. The stone window seemed different somehow, as if it had transformed from solid rock to a pliable clay.

'I've got the power source working!' he crowed, and Margaret came forward to kiss him on the cheek. 'It's still fluctuating, but I can make a definite guess about the purpose of this and all the similar stone windows.'

'Well, old man? Is it a transportation system?' Margaret asked.

'These trapezoidal stone windows are . . . portal walls. Klikiss mathematics and engineering are completely amazing. Using what we already learned from the Torch, I was able to back-calculate and fill in some of the equations.' He placed one hand atop the humming machinery, gesturing with the other towards the compelling blank trapezoid. 'These portal walls are a completely different type of star travel. According to the equations, this machinery makes the variable of distance go to zero. They shift the reference frame, overlapping coordinates of different destinations.'

Margaret stared in amazement. 'In other words, they could travel through these portal walls from Klikiss city to Klikiss city without even climbing aboard a spaceship.'

'And without ekti, and without wasting any time.' He turned to the Klikiss robots. 'Isn't that right? Do you remember anything yet?'

Sirix answered, 'Your conjecture appears to be reasonable. Unfortunately, we cannot confirm or deny with certainty.'

'If you're right, that explains why they never bothered to leave any records of spaceships, though they obviously travelled from planet to planet.' Margaret turned to her husband, holding out a stern finger. 'You'd better not even begin to *think* about testing one of these portals, old man. That machinery has been non-functional for thousands of years. You may be a genius, but you don't really understand how it works yet.'

'No, dear.'

Abruptly, the two black robots swivelled on their ellipsoidal body cores and scuttled towards the exit of the chamber.

'Where are you going?' DD asked.

'We must inform Ilkot of this development,' Dekyk said.

Louis called after them, 'Well, if you remember anything, come back and tell us right away.'

The Klikiss robots vanished, leaving Margaret and Louis alone with DD. Margaret turned to the compy. 'When the robots talk to each other in their electronic language, can you understand any of it?'

'Not all of it, Margaret, but a substantial portion.'

'And? What were they just saying to each other?'

'Sirix and Dekyk seemed quite excited by your translations and deductions.'

She frowned. 'Were they excited, as in "thrilled and happy"? Or were they more . . . agitated.'

'Those nuances are beyond my capabilities of interpretation,' DD said. 'I am very sorry, Margaret.'

Louis's enthusiasm and good cheer could not be diluted. He placed his bony arm around his wife's shoulders and gave her another hug. 'We still have that dusty old bottle of champagne we brought with us, don't we, dear? Tonight we have plenty of cause to celebrate.'

Margaret smiled. 'Absolutely right, old man – if I can just finish translating this section of the wall. I think the Klikiss have a few more surprises in store for us.'

'Incredible!' Her voice was husky in her dry throat. At last, after staring for hours and crouching until her muscles cramped, Margaret couldn't believe what she read.

Beside her, DD said brightly, 'I am sure it is incredible, Margaret.'

She had meticulously transcribed every portion of the scrawled messages. But now, cold and distracted, Margaret felt reluctant to share her secret. The implications weighed upon her.

Out of habit, she stored a backup of her work in an alcove, then took the original datawafer and hurried into the chamber where Louis continued to tinker with the portal wall machinery.

Though her skin was pale and her eyes wide, he was too focused on his own exciting discovery to notice anything wrong. 'Well, dear, I think I've got this now. I compared this setup with the other portal walls we discovered on Llaro, Pym, and Corribus. If we dig deep enough into the database we'll find at least one portal wall inside every Klikiss city. But this one is different.'

Pressing a hand to the small of his aching back, he went over to the wall and pointed to coordinate tiles near the upper left corner of the trapezoid. 'At the other sites, some of the destination tiles were destroyed, as if someone smashed them before departure. Whatever happened to the Klikiss, whoever sent them away or destroyed them . . . never finished here on Rheindic Co.'

'It was a war, Louis,' Margaret said. 'An incredibly destructive war between titanic forces. The Klikiss race was a powerful empire, yet they were insignificant players on such an immense battleground. Their robots took part in some manner, though the details are unclear.'

Louis was fascinated. 'But what kind of war? Who were the Klikiss fighting against?'

617

She drew a deep breath. The *hydrogues*, Louis! The deep-core aliens. This isn't the first time they've attacked.'

Louis gasped, his astonishment melting into a boyish grin. 'That's incredible, Margaret. First, the portal wall discovery and now this ancient war between the Klikiss and the hydrogues – not even the Klikiss Torch can match such a breakthrough!' He hugged her again. 'We have to send news right away. Everybody needs to know.'

Margaret grabbed her husband by the shoulders, squeezing hard enough that his smile faded. 'Louis, don't you understand? The hydrogues *completely wiped out* the Klikiss. They caused the race's extinction across the Spiral Arm.' She looked hard at him, but he still didn't seem to see. 'And now they've begun to attack humans!'

Margaret glanced into the other word-filled tunnels where the Klikiss ideographs were messier and harder to decipher, as if someone had scribbled them in a rush. 'DD, go string lights back in the deep passages. I think I can unravel the last of those records now.'

'We need to get back to Arcas,' Louis said. 'He can send the details to everyone in the Hansa.'

'I will be happy to do the work here while you return to camp, Margaret and Louis,' DD said.

Leaving the compy behind, the two xeno-archaeologists descended the scaffolding stairs along the canyon wall. They could write more detailed reports later, but because of their new understanding of the hydrogue threat they wanted to send an immediate summary of their discovery via the green priest.

In Rheindic Co's night, the desert heat had dissipated after sunset. The breezes that whistled across the barren ground carried a chill. When they arrived at the encampment, their tents and huts were dim.

Margaret saw no sign of the green priest. The mechanical water pump hummed in the stillness. An automatic light had switched on inside Margaret's and Louis's tent, and another one shone dimly within Arcas's dwelling, but she could see no shadow of the green priest inside.

'Arcas!' Louis called. 'Boy, do we have news for you. We need to send a telink message right away.'

But no answer came to him in the night. The camp remained silent and brooding. Nothing stirred. Uneasy, Margaret looked around, peering into the shadows.

As always, Louis remained optimistic. 'He's probably over by his trees, and that's where we need to go anyway to send our message.' But when Margaret followed her husband to the stand of treelings, she stopped short. She saw the details in the moonlight even before Louis switched on his handlight to verify what she had feared.

All of the worldtrees were destroyed.

Each one had been uprooted, its trunk severed. Some had been chopped off neatly, as if with shears; others had been ripped apart, leaving ragged ends that still dripped sap like golden blood. The dead fronds drooped into the dust.

'What – what . . .'

Margaret turned, her face set. 'Arcas,' she said, not calling his name as much as uttering her fear.

She ran back towards the camp where she still saw the faint glow inside the green priest's tent. Louis followed her.

Margaret was already terrified, her stomach queasy. She reached the tent first, yanked open the door flaps, and stared. Louis followed her, then stopped abruptly.

Inside, Arcas lay brutally murdered on the floor of his tent. His green-skinned body had been broken, lacerated, pummelled, and crushed. A hundred fatal injuries covered him, as if his attacker had not understood what constituted a mortal wound and had chosen to guarantee the result.

619

Sickened and horrified, Louis crept out on wobbly legs, unable to believe what he had seen. From the entrance to the tent, Margaret looked out into the night, knowing how completely alone and defenceless they were.

ONE HUNDRED AND NINE

NIRA

The Mage-Imperator's brutal raid came while Nira was asleep. She had no chance whatsoever to defend herself.

During rest periods inside the bright Prism Palace, under the always-dazzling light of the seven suns, Nira had grown accustomed to wearing an opaque mask. The blindfold allowed her to sleep in darkness while her green-tinted skin continued to tingle with the constant nourishment of sunshine.

She was resting well, weary but content. With Prime Designate Jora'h gone to Theroc on his diplomatic mission, Nira had plenty of time to think here in the Palace. She could feel her body's changes with the growing pregnancy. As soon as Jora'h returned home after seeing the worldforest, she would tell him the joyous news. Although he already had numerous sons and daughters, this one would be different from all the others, and she hoped he would be pleased. Together they could decide the best possible future for their hybrid baby, a child that was sure to have remarkable potential.

Nira did not expect any lifelong commitment, such as human

marriage, from the Prime Designate – that was impossible. But she had already seen how devoted Jora'h was to his other children, how kind he remained to his brief lovers. And Nira knew that the two of them shared something special.

Now that her handsome prince was gone, however, Nira concentrated on reading the *Saga of Seven Suns* to the potted treelings. Today she and Otema had recited one stanza after another, enjoying the magical Ildiran legends for hours and hours. At the end of the day, Otema smiled at her assistant, complimented her on a job well done, and sent her to bed . . .

In silence, seven muscular guards pushed their way into Nira's quarters, startling her from a deep sleep.

'Take her,' said a gruff voice as she fought her way back to wakefulness. Strong arms gripped her, and she bumped into thick body armour, smelled pungent bristling hair and the odour of penned animals. She clumsily peeled off her blindfold and blinked in the dazzling light, trying to focus on the rough features of Bron'n and other guards she had seen around the Mage-Imperator.

'What's wrong?' she said.

'Take her,' Bron'n repeated, and the burly guards yanked her to her feet. They held throbbing katana spears with white blades and chipped, faceted edges.

Nira squirmed and thrashed. 'What have I done?' She reached behind her, fingers extended, trying to touch a nearby treeling in its pot.

'Don't let her close to the plant!' Bron'n snarled. With a jerk they tugged Nira away. Her soft fingertips barely brushed the ornate enameled pot. The treeling wobbled, but did not fall and shatter on the floor.

'The Mage-Imperator ordered us to be quiet and efficient,' Bron'n said. 'Others will return to these corridors soon.'

When words and actions failed her, Nira finally screamed.

Bron'n cuffed her hard on the cheek, and she crumpled. Terror turned her limbs to water as the guards hauled her out into the corridor.

'Do not damage her,' Bron'n ordered. 'She is fertile and necessary.'

To her shock and deeper dismay, she saw that another group of bestial guards had broken into Otema's private chamber and taken her captive as well. The old green priest stood rigid, her expression hard and stormy, but she did not squirm and thrash, seeing the futility of resistance.

Wrapping dignity around herself like a shawl, Otema glared at Bron'n. 'I challenge what you are doing. If we are accused of some crime, name it. If we have been summoned to the Mage-Imperator, we will go willingly.'

Bron'n pressed close to the old woman. 'I follow my Mage-Imperator's orders.'

Otema looked at Nira, then back at Bron'n. 'If you harm us, there will be dire diplomatic consequences. We are legitimate representatives of Theroc, invited here by the Prime Designate and your own Mage-Imperator. I demand—'

From his thick vest, Bron'n removed a jagged knife made of smoky grey glass. 'Old woman, you are long past breeding age, and therefore of no use to us.'

Before Nira could even scream, the brutish guard struck down with the dagger, plunging it deep into Otema's heart. He yanked the glass blade back, and her captors let the old woman fall to the floor. Each of the guards raised his spear. Each stabbed the already-dead ambassador. Then they stepped away from her bleeding body.

Bron'n gave a signal. Five scuttling servant kithmen hurried forward to clean up the mess, as the Mage-Imperator had commanded.

Sobbing with revulsion and horror, Nira sagged. Her knees buckled, and black specks swam in front of her eyes. She couldn't believe what she had seen, prayed that it was some bizarre nightmare, but the guards grasped her and held her up. She felt the hard grip of their callused hands, smelled their musky, violent scent.

Wrestling her arms behind her, exerting pain but careful not to break her wrists, they bound Nira tightly, strapped a gag across her mouth, and hustled her down dim and winding corridors deep within the Prism Palace.

They tossed her into a stiflingly hot chamber with thick curved walls of blood-red stained glass. The shadows here were darker, the blazers turned low, the air almost too thick to breathe. Bron'n stood blocking the doorway behind her. Nira fell to her knees, unable to move her arms because of the bindings.

Another man came forward. He grasped her chin and tilted her smooth head up towards him. The Dobro Designate glared at her with dull eyes, as if he saw nothing living or intelligent there, only a specimen for a collection. Nostrils flaring, he sniffed her, then released her chin and stepped back with a cruel but approving smile to Bron'n.

'Perfect material,' he said. 'She is healthy and strong. I can *smell* the possibilities in her genes. Take her to my ship and be certain that all evidence is gone well before the Prime Designate returns from Theroc.'

Bron'n acknowledged the instructions. Nira couldn't even find the strength to struggle. The Dobro Designate looked down at her, eyes glittering.

'The potential you give us,' he said, 'is the only hope the Ildiran Empire has of surviving the hydrogue war.'

ONE HUNDRED AND TEN

CESCA PERONI

After all the terrible news the Roamers had heard in recent months, Jhy Okiah's announcement still managed to astound the clans.

The old Speaker waited for silence to fall in the speaking chamber at Rendezvous. She stood at the pedestal on her oratory platform in the middle of the vault. Lights shone down upon her, commanding the focus of the gathering.

She exercised her veto power, putting an end to arguments and discussion and waited for the clans to hear what she had to say. 'The future will require extraordinary strength and vision – more than I have left within me.' Her firm voice cut through the cries of dismay and shouts of dissent. 'I have led you through many productive years, but now the rules have shifted. My predictable ways are no longer appropriate. We Roamers must change in order to deal with the hydrogues.

'And therefore, for the good of Roamer society, and for the human race itself,' she said, 'I have no choice but to resign my position as Speaker for all Roamer clans.'

She stopped and waited a second. Then the uproar began.

During the worsening crisis, the Speaker had seemed to be the only bastion of stability for the Roamers. Jhy Okiah had represented the clans impartially for years and directed their discussions with an even hand. She was considered a fair and reasonable leader, even by those who disagreed with her decisions.

The aliens had followed through on their threat against all trespassers after delivering their ultimatum and assassinating King Frederick on Earth. Intimidated, most Roamers had withdrawn their skymines from the gas planets, but a few had lingered too long. Within a week, fifteen more ekti-harvesting facilities had been obliterated by hydrogue warglobes. Fewer than a hundred Roamer refugees had survived, bringing back horrific tales and images. The enemy was efficient, thorough, and completely merciless.

'We need a new Speaker, a stronger Speaker,' Jhy Okiah continued. 'Someone with more imagination and energy than I.'

Seated in her private booth near the podium, Cesca Peroni could barely keep from weeping. She had known the old woman's plans and argued with her privately, but Jhy Okiah was stubborn and implacable.

'This conflict may go on for a long time, Cesca,' she had said. 'Things could get difficult . . . and very ugly. I apologize for the ordeal I'm about to put you through. But in my bones I sense that I may not see this war through to its end. It is better to begin with a strong Speaker at the outset, rather than increase turmoil later on, when more harm may result.'

'But I'm not ready. You know how much I have yet to learn.'

'More important, I know you are *capable* of learning.' The old woman touched a gnarled finger against Cesca's lips to silence her. This is the most important secret I can teach you: no one is ever ready. You cannot be less qualified than I was when I took on the role. And I haven't done too badly.' She chuckled softly. 'You are capable, Cesca, and you have no delusions of infallibility. Frankly, those are all the requirements you need. Just follow your Guiding Star.'

Now that she had made her announcement in public, Jhy Okiah allowed no further discussion. In her life she'd had all too much discussion. She stepped down from the podium and motioned for Cesca to take her place, both now and for the years to come.

Cesca paused at the oratory podium, feeling insubstantial in the asteroid's low gravity, though her heart was heavy inside her. Her shoulders bowed under the weight of the immense burden she now carried. *Just follow your Guiding Star.* She wanted to laugh. The Roamers liked to believe their paths were set, if only they could see the proper course. But she had already strayed many times.

Now she looked into the audience, found the seating area reserved for clan Tamblyn, and spotted Jess watching her, his face intent and supportive, as he sat beside his four uncles. A different path, a different course would have steered them together. But now she couldn't see a way to join him. Not yet. Their eyes met, and he gave her a smile, which was all the strength she needed.

Jess's cometary bombardment of Golgen had indeed sent cheers through the Roamer community. Having struck back, however fruitlessly, they no longer felt so helpless. Already, orbital specialists were mapping the Kuiper belts in other solar systems to continue the silent gravity-driven war against other gas giants where Roamer skymines had been attacked. Sadly, there were many graveyards to choose from.

Cesca had rehearsed her speech over and over again, but now the words tasted flat and lifeless in her mouth. How could she possibly lead all these people, so many disparate clans? How could she inspire them to do the necessary things, make the uncomfortable sacrifices that would help Roamer society survive?

627

'I did not want to be your Speaker so soon,' she said softly. Then her voice grew bitter, almost strident. 'Nor did I *want* the hydrogues to murder my fiancée and destroy his skymine on Golgen. I did not *want* the enemy aliens to engage us in a war we did not start. I did not *want* our ekti harvesting to be violently cut off.'

Cesca paused, staring at the audience. 'Unfortunately, we do not always get what we want. And so I am here as your new Speaker. All Roamers are tied together by this terrible crisis.' She held out her hands. 'So, what are we going to do?'

No one dared to make a suggestion, though the Roamer clans had never been reluctant to speak their minds. Cesca continued. 'Throughout our history, Roamers have never had an easy time. We have crashed headlong into adversity, and we have survived. We know how to adapt. We know how to innovate. And we know how to remain what we are.'

Cesca had been trained to be firm and unwavering, as well as a caring and nurturing leader. She would devote her heart and mind to this job. 'I intend to see us through this crisis, and I do not speak lightly of the hydrogue threat. This war could either destroy all of human civilization . . . or finally give Roamers our independence at last.'

This sent mutters through the audience hall, and she let the gathered people express themselves, building upon each other's confidence.

'So, what are we to do, if we can no longer harvest ekti from gas giants? Our entire economy is based on this. Should we just surrender to the inevitable – maybe join the Big Goose after all?' She shook her head. 'We dare not become more dependent upon the Hansa, after working for more than a century to wean ourselves from suffocating ties with Earth.'

'Then how do we survive?' shouted someone from the audience. 'Without ekti we—'

She cut him off with a sharply raised palm. 'Since when have the Roamers been bound to a single option? Gas giants are merely the most convenient reservoirs of hydrogen. But it is the most abundant element in the galaxy. We must look at alternatives and begin to harvest ekti in other ways.'

Cesca smiled down at a man seated in the front row of audience benches. 'I have recalled Kotto Okiah, one of our best inventors from Isperos, where he was building a new Roamer colony there in the heat and lava. I have asked him to apply his ingenuity to this new problem. It may prove more difficult to harvest ekti elsewhere in the Spiral Arm . . . But will that stop us?'

She forced a laugh. 'I don't think so! We are *Roamers*. Let us apply our imaginations, our creativity, and face down this challenge. Look towards the Guiding Star we all know is out there. We can come out stronger if we work hard enough and demonstrate our true brilliance. We've always been good at considering long-term plans, haven't we?'

Cesca lifted both hands, looking at all her people. 'Every one of our inventors and designers and engineers must join in. We have no time to lose.' Relieved but giddy, she took a step back from the podium and raised her voice. 'We will find new ways.'

ONE HUNDRED AND ELEVEN

TASIA TAMBLYN

The *Goliath* rode in a stationary orbit, while Platcom Tasia Tamblyn's Thunderhead crouched close to the Hansa mines ploughing through the colourful Jovian skies. The enormous factories sprayed exhaust plumes shaped like anvils high into the rarefied air.

Day after day, the EDF escorts stayed at high alert. The Juggernaut loomed at the edge of orbit; Manta cruisers soared above the skymining operations. Survey flights of Remoras streaked through the cloud layers while Thunderheads hovered overhead, scanning Jupiter's storm systems and weather patterns for any anomalies. The cloud patrols returned to their base ships at hourly intervals, reporting nothing unusual. The edgy suspense never waned, though many crewmembers began to doubt that hydrogues lived at the core of Jupiter.

Tasia did not allow herself to stop watching, though. The cloud harvesters were like fishing boats drifting on the sea, while the hydrogues were monsters lurking at the bottom of the deepest ocean trenches. Admiral Stromo, aboard the *Goliath*, continued to stage response drills and weapons practises. Everyone remained ready.

Robb Brindle, who commanded the Thunderhead's surveillance Remoras, grew more optimistic. He stood beside Tasia, looking down at the lumbering ekti factories like fat cattle grazing on the upthrust storm systems.

'Two possibilities, Tamblyn. Either the hydrogues don't live here, and we can keep processing ekti to our heart's content. Or,' he turned to glance behind him at the bridge crew, 'our kick-ass fleet has scared the aliens away.'

Tasia didn't offer the third explanation that came to mind: that the hydrogues simply hadn't shown themselves yet. She did not want to shatter his confidence, knowing that the happy bravado was, in part, a response to extended anxiety. 'I hope you're right, Brindle.'

Within three hours, however, the first alarms started to ring.

A Remora survey squadron returned, signalling instant alerts after they detected a flurry of deep lightning and fast-moving meteorological disturbances.

Aboard the *Goliath*, Admiral Stromo wasted no time before declaring red-alert status. Terran skyminers aboard the cloud harvesters were instructed to stand down and prepare for immediate evacuation, if so ordered. Tasia issued quick commands to her bridge staff and sent all Remora crews racing to their ships.

Robb Brindle squeezed her arm. 'Show time!' Without a further farewell, he raced down to the Thunderhead's hangar bay to take command of his squadrons.

Deep below, Jupiter's sky ripped apart to disgorge eleven diamond-hulled hydrogue battleships. The fearsome spiked warglobes rose above the clouds in a show of alien force that dwarfed even Admiral Stromo's proud escort fleet.

'Here they come!' Patrick Fitzpatrick shouted, losing his usual arrogance.

When stunned curses echoed from the astounded bridge personnel, Tasia whirled and snapped at them. 'Everybody focus! Save the whining 'til you get home and complain to your mothers.' She pointed to individual stations. 'Every soldier at your weapons consoles! Power up all jazer banks. Charge the railguns and load the kinetic projectiles.'

'Do we let the aliens take the first shot, Platcom?' one of the men asked.

'Shizz, not on your life. We've all seen what they do.' She gritted her teeth. At last she would get a chance to avenge her brother.

But Admiral Stromo sent an all-fleet signal, countermanding her orders. 'Mantas, Thunderheads, and Remoras – hold your fire!' He switched to a broad-band channel. 'Attention, hydrogues! I request an open dialogue with your commander.'

'As if that'll do any good,' Tasia muttered. 'They already blew up King Frederick. They don't want to talk – they want us dead.'

Stromo waited a second, received no response. 'Our mission is peaceful, intended only to acquire vital resources for the Terran Hanseatic League. We are mining in our home solar system. We mean no harm to any hydrogue. But we will not be denied the resources we need for our survival.'

The spiked warglobes climbed higher and moved towards the first Hansa ekti harvester. At the warglobe's approach, the panicked cloud miners launched their lifepods, which sprayed outwards like spores from a mushroom. Without transmitting a word of response to the *Goliath*, the deep-core aliens unleashed their crackling blue lightning. Hydrogue energy bolts ripped though the evacuated gas-harvesting facility, detonating the ekti reactors and stored fuel tanks. The explosion set up a chain reaction, ripping from module to module. No Roamer skymine could have been breached so easily, Tasia knew, but the end result would have been the same.

'That's it!' she shouted in disgust. Not caring about insubordination, she turned to her weapons officers without waiting for orders from the astonished Admiral Stromo. 'All jazer banks open fire. Target that damned warglobe.'

The hydrogues continued their destruction against the first cloud harvester. A second warglobe fired on the Earth battleships. The EDF subcommanders screamed for orders, while some defended themselves. Admiral Stromo refused to respond.

Tasia stabbed her finger towards the screen. 'Everybody on the same page, same bull's-eye. Aim just below that spike there. Let's not dilute our firepower. *Now*.'

With an angry whoop and snarled threats, the Thunderhead bridge crew fired lasers wrapped in sheaths of high-energy particles. Jazer bolts hammered into the foremost crystalline warglobe, scratching it, scarring it.

'Kinetic projectiles next! Shoot the railguns – a full volley. Aim for the same weak point we just hit with the jazers.'

Electromagnetic rails in the underdeck crackled, firing a pulsed salvo of solid projectiles made of superdense depleted uranium. Travelling at near-relativistic speeds, they slammed into the diamond hull, each one with the kinetic energy of a small nuclear warhead.

The other Thunderheads hesitated less than a second after Tasia gave her order to fire, while Stromo remained frozen and speechless. Full of new recruits who had never seen battle and nervous commanders with itchy trigger fingers, the EDF escort group retaliated when the hydrogues opened fire. Manta cruisers dived into the fray. Squadrons of Remoras shot out of their docking bays like a hail of huge bullets. Each fast fighter drove in, targeting the enemy warglobes with their smaller but more precise ship-to-ship defences.

Over the EDF comm channel, Stromo spluttered orders and finally tried to regain control of the situation. In a moment, though, he realized the futility and changed his mind. 'All ships, all commanders. Fire at will! Let's get these bastards.'

The huge *Goliath* descended into the midst of the firestorm, readying the fleet's heaviest weapons. The Juggernaut, with ten times the weaponry and armour of any Manta or Thunderhead, quickly demonstrated its enhanced abilities.

The crews of the other three Hansa cloud harvesters launched their evacuation pods without instructions from the Admiral. Tasia didn't blame them one bit, but in the free-for-all of weapons fire that criss-crossed Jupiter's cloud decks, she saw the peril to the fleeing workers. She opened her channel. 'Lieutenant Brindle, tell your Remoras to haul ass towards the harvesters. Rescue as many lifepods as possible. Round 'em all up.'

Brindle hesitated just a moment. 'My whole squadron? Shouldn't we save a few Remoras to—'

'Lieutenant, if we don't rescue those cloud miners, then we can't claim much of a victory, can we?'

'No, Platcom.'

Trying to ease his frustration, she added, 'As soon as you round up the evacuation pods, I'll let you get back and cause as much damage as you want – if the battle lasts that long.'

'Acknowledged.'

The first warglobe she'd targeted had suffered visible damage. All of the jazer strikes and kinetic-projectile impacts seemed to have slowed it down. But the other ten hydrogue battleships approached without hesitation and opened fire on the Terran escort fleet. One of the Mantas fell almost immediately, without scoring a single hit.

Enemy lightning swept across two Thunderheads, ripping through armoured hulls, spilling hundreds of crew members to their deaths. Other strikes vaporized entire flights of Remoras like seeds in a blast furnace. The small EDF attack ships had insufficient shielding or manoeuvrability to avoid the hydrogue weapon. Tasia prayed that Brindle's squadrons had not been among the first victims.

When Admiral Stromo brought the *Goliath* into the fray, shooting jazers and kinetic projectiles, launching all of his Remoras, the Juggernaut resembled a terrible hurricane. But the diamond-hulled warglobes concentrated their attack on the largest Terran battleship.

Brindle's first Remoras began limping back to the Thunderhead, using tractor beams to drag lifepods salvaged from the ekti harvesters. 'Open our ship bays,' Tasia commanded. 'Get all those refugees in before it's too late.'

The Admiral shouted empty threats and warnings at the hydrogues over his broad-band frequency, but Tasia could already see how much damage the Eddie ships were suffering. Within seconds, the hydrogues obliterated another weapons platform, and all the Remoras retrieving lifepods suddenly had to find another sanctuary.

Tasia turned to Patrick Fitzpatrick, who manned the comm station. 'Signal those Remoras. Tell them to bring all the lifepods here, if they can.' Fitzpatrick looked at her, unable to believe what was happening around him. 'Do it *now*, dammit!' He bent over his transmitters, annoyed and abashed.

The warglobes opened fire and struck one set of the *Goliath*'s stardrive engines, melting the thick hull plating. Aboard the enhanced Juggernaut, Admiral Stromo yelled for damage reports, demanded that all crews shore up life support and recharge the weapons systems.

The hydrogues shot once again, inflicting even more harm to the *Goliath*. Another Manta suffered severe damage from a blast and could barely crawl out of the war zone.

Tasia realized that the battle had turned into a rout. No amount of Terran defences could stand against these eleven hydrogue warglobes. Unless the Admiral came to the same conclusion – and soon – the *Goliath*, Earth's greatest new battleship, would be destroyed.

Incomprehensible screams of panic filled the comm channels. Tasia contacted her surviving Remoras, recalling all squadrons. 'Lieutenant Brindle! Bring whatever survivors you can, but get your butt back here.'

Salvaged lifepods continued to pour into the Thunderhead's docking bays. If Tasia didn't get her ship out of there before long, they could all be destroyed in one blast by the hydrogues. Even so, she could not let the *Goliath* flounder.

She issued a call to the other Thunderheads, hoping that their platcoms would listen to common sense. 'All weapons platforms! We need to fall back and defend the *Goliath*.' She changed to a different channel. 'Admiral Stromo, sir, I recommend that you withdraw your battleship while the engines still function. We will cover your retreat.'

Four Thunderheads, still looking puny in relation to the diamond-hulled warglobes, clustered around the wounded Juggernaut. Another Manta disengaged to assist in defending the flagship.

Checking her weapons status, Tasia saw that three-quarters of her kinetic projectiles had already been expended, and her jazer banks were drained to ten per cent of nominal energy reserves. 'Keep firing! No sense saving anything for a rainy day.'

The surviving weapons platforms and cruisers bombarded the warglobes as they closed in on the *Goliath*. Two of them appeared sluggish and damaged, but the other nine remained just as deadly. The warglobes could easily pursue them all the way to Earth, but Tasia hoped the deep-core aliens would break off as soon as the EDF fleet retreated.

Tasia didn't think Admiral Stromo knew who had contacted him and issued the unauthorized but sensible order to withdraw, but the Juggernaut's engines fired up, using their remaining propulsion power to withdraw from Jupiter and into space.

'We have rounded up most of the lifepods, Platcom,' said her tactical subcommander, scanning screens to see how many of the Remoras had returned.

'Then prepare to get us out of here,' Tasia said. She turned, her brows furrowed with concern. 'Has Lieutenant Brindle reported back in?'

'No, sir,' said the subcommander. Tasia ran to the comm station herself, opening up a direct ship-to-ship channel. 'Brindle, where the hell are you?'

'Coming!' His voice sounded cheerful but with a ragged edge. 'I had some business to take care of first.'

Below them in the clouds, two hydrogue warglobes broke away to continue their systematic attack on the remaining cloud harvesters, destroying even the debris.

'All right, dammit. You've made your point,' Tasia growled at the aliens.

The *Goliath* pulled farther away, and the surviving Thunderheads and Mantas clustered around the damaged Juggernaut, collectively retreating from Jupiter. As they fled towards the orbits of the innermost moons, she saw Robb Brindle and his last four Remoras struggling upwards from the fringe of atmosphere, heading towards them. With a combined tractor beam, the small ships hauled a large spherical tank, dragging it up and away from the hydrogue cordon.

'What the hell are you doing, Brindle?' she transmitted.

'We salvaged the ekti storage tank from one of the cloud harvesters!' he said. 'Couldn't just let it go to waste.'

She dispatched other Remoras to assist him, ushering Brindle and his ships into the Thunderhead landing bay. Later, in private, she would upbraid him for his foolishness. A full skymine cargo tank contained only enough stardrive fuel to service the EDF for a week. Not worth risking anyone's life for.

Disastrously beaten, the Earth Defence Forces fell back from Jupiter. As they pulled out to the orbit of the innermost moons, still accelerating towards open space, the damaged ships maintained watch on the huge planet. The rusty clouds now looked bloodstained.

The numerous warglobes hovered among the sky wreckage, still threatening. Stromo ordered all possible speed, and Tasia stared at the alien warships, still visible in the Thunderhead's long-range scans. The aliens waited, watched, but did not pursue them into interplanetary space.

When they limped back to Earth, Admiral Stromo and the survivors of his escort fleet would have no joyous homecoming. The hydrogues had proved far more devastating than even the most drastic predictions.

The Jupiter debacle had crushed all hope for a swift and gratifying resolution to this war.

ONE HUNDRED AND TWELVE

KING PETER

On the day of his coronation, Raymond found all the colours too bright, the sounds too sharp. Yet his inner feelings — from elation to rebelliousness — were dulled and distant.

He realized that Basil Wenceslas must have drugged him.

The puppet Prince felt oddly cooperative as teams of experts dressed him, wrapped his shoulders in flowing velvet robes, draped medallions on heavy chains around his neck. Every garment was trimmed with golden lace, studded with luminous flatgems. His blond hair was carefully styled, his skin made up to cover the slightest blemish or freckle. From the outset of his reign, King Peter must appear perfect.

Beneath the fuzzy warmth of the drugs, Raymond felt a swell of helpless anger, while a detached and logical portion of his mind considered the consequences. Some chemical had probably been slipped into his breakfast. Chairman Wenceslas naturally wanted to have a tame and contented Prince walk down the carpeted aisle and accept his glorious crown from the Archfather of Unison. Any sign of intransigence would ruin the entire effect.

Did the Hansa suspect his grave reservations already? Did Basil know that young Raymond had discovered his crimes and lies?

If the Hansa was willing to drug and manipulate him, even when he had given them no overt reason to distrust him, it did not bode well for his future as King. But he had already learned how evil these men were, the day he'd discovered the truth behind the deaths of his family. The Hansa would do anything to ensure their success.

Outside the Whisper Palace, a spectacular celebration had been under way for hours. Extra torches had been lit on all the cupolas and domes, on the pillars and lampposts around the Palace District. Every hour, colourful fireworks shot into the air, exploding in glittering plumes. Commemorative coins, specially minted for the occasion, were distributed to anyone in the crowd who had made the pilgrimage to see the coronation of their new King.

For an entire day OX, now completely repaired and polished, had drilled Raymond upon the protocol and practises of the ceremony. The Teacher compy rehearsed the speech with his young ward; he explained the honours and medals Raymond must bestow as part of the grand jubilee.

Though he had grown close to the old robot and discussed many intellectual and philosophical matters with him, Raymond had never admitted his discoveries about the Hansa plot. He would hold that secret deep within his heart and use the information when the time was right, as he saw fit.

After Raymond was fully dressed and prepared – and comfortably, unwillingly numb – OX escorted him like a little tin soldier, taking slow, careful steps to the presentation stage. Raymond suspected that OX had clear orders to be his guard and keeper, not just a friend.

Trying to focus through the drug haze, Raymond looked down the long river of crimson carpet that flowed across the courtyard, through the arched doorway, and up into the pristine Throne Hall.

Dressed in an expensive formal business suit, but without gaudy trappings since he would appear on no media screens, Chairman Wenceslas met Raymond in the alcove from which he would begin his sedate procession towards the throne.

'This ceremony must go off without a hitch, Peter,' he said with a paternal smile that was cheapened by Raymond's knowledge of how Basil had lied to him. 'We must make the coronation spectacular enough to ignite a greater fire of patriotic fervour. Already, our citizens are in an uproar against the hydrogues. We must keep it that way.'

'I'll do my best, Chairman Wenceslas,' Raymond said. His voice was smooth and calm. Thanks to the dulling effect of the drugs, he could not infuse the words with the anger and resistance he truly felt.

'Wars provide the best circumstances for cementing unity and increasing governmental control,' Basil continued. 'A war is also the best time for invention and innovation. When this is all over, the Hansa's power will be greater than ever.' He patted Raymond on the shoulder. 'Perhaps that will be our silver lining . . . provided the hydrogues don't cause too much destruction in the meantime.'

On schedule, the fanfare began, music roaring to the clouds. The tourist zeppelins floated closer. Another round of fireworks went off, larger than any before, and colours blossomed in the sky.

Before Raymond could begin his procession, though, two military officers rushed in, ruddy-faced and breathless. They elbowed royal guards aside and raced towards the Chairman. Bending close to him, the officers quickly delivered what was obviously bad news. Basil stared at them, his face white. He snapped back, repeating his questions, and the military officers responded as if ashamed. Basil could barely keep his emotions in check. Dismay etched itself plainly on his face.

Outside, the fanfare reached its crescendo, and Raymond knew he was expected to begin the long slow walk along the crimson carpet. Instead, he stepped backwards. 'What is it, Chairman Wenceslas? What has happened?' Basil tried to brush him away as if he were an annoying insect, but Raymond managed to put surprising vehemence into his voice, even through the blurring effects of the drug. 'I should know, if I am to be King.'

Off balance, the Chairman turned to him, not yet recovered enough to keep control of his words. 'The hydrogues attacked our fleet at Jupiter. They've wrecked our ships and harvesters. I don't know how many are dead.' He turned to glare at the two military couriers. 'You are certain of this?'

Both officers nodded vigorously. 'Absolutely. Admiral Stromo is bringing the *Goliath* back now, but it's severely damaged. Many of his ships were destroyed. Our best weapons, our strongest defences, amounted to nothing against—'

The fanfare dropped into an awkward silence, waiting for Prince Peter to appear. Basil suddenly came to himself and whirled like a cobra to Raymond. 'Go! You have a job to do.'

The young man was surprised. 'Even after this? Shouldn't we change our response somehow? What if I make an announcement—'

'No! Now, more than ever, we need you to bring them together, to show your strength. Go take the crown and give them all hope. You alone, Peter, can save our population. They believe it.'

In a daze, his faint resistance further dampened, Raymond stepped with OX towards the arched gate. The crowds had fallen silent. The rich carpet stretched around the lavish courtyards, so the media could capture his every slow and careful step. Impeccably uniformed royal guards lined the pathway, protecting him. Raymond raised his chin, then took one measured step and another and another.

The coronation passed in a dream. It seemed to take forever to walk the length of the crimson aisle. Entering under the ornate arches, he passed into the reception hall leaving behind a chorus of deafening cheers. As he strode forward, the ranks of packed spectators grew in importance: corporate heads, visiting dignitaries, celebrities, and vocal supporters of King Frederick.

When he finally reached the Throne Hall, feeling isolated in spite of the overwhelming number of supporters, Raymond was dazzled by the sheer wonder of the chamber. Along with the new King himself, the people on Earth and the Hansa colony worlds got their first glimpse of the restored Throne Hall.

All reconstruction had been completed at a breakneck pace, erasing every vestige of damage. The restored throne looked identical to the one King Frederick had used, though it was perhaps even a bit larger, a hint more magnificent. More mirrors and prisms and stained glass had been added to the Hall. Not a stain or scar remained, not a smudge to remind the population of the recent devastating event.

The cheering and applause increased. Nothing had changed. The Hansa had shrugged off the destruction caused by the alien emissary.

Raymond plodded towards the raised dais and the waiting throne. Around the impressive chair stood a group of the Hansa's most important people – the governors of the ten most powerful colony worlds, and the robed and dominant Archfather of Unison, Spokesman of All Faiths. His voluminous purple cape and robes bore diamond stitchery, a constellation of designs incorporating the symbols of all the diverse religions from Earth's history –

crosses, circles, crescents, trees, meshed into a tangled maze that no longer meant anything at all. The Archfather was an empty and symbolic religious figurehead . . . with a role similar to the one Raymond would fill.

As the young man ascended the first step, the first of the colony governors held the revered crown and passed it to the next man, who handed it to a governor one step up, and so on, from hand to hand. Each of the important spokesmen touched the crown and passed it upwards, showing symbolically that King Peter's reign derived from the support of all factions, businesses, and creeds. Finally, the blank-faced Archfather smiled at Raymond, his eyes glittering, and intoned congratulations and blessings in eight different languages, ending with Trade Standard.

Raymond stared straight ahead, fighting the odd displacement and numbness. The Archfather reached forward, bowing, then completed the ceremony. With the crown finally settled on his blond head, Raymond didn't feel its weight at all. Not yet.

He had rehearsed his acceptance speech so many times he didn't even remember giving it. He flowed with the event, and the coronation went perfectly, with no mention of the hydrogue attack at Jupiter. That news would break soon enough. Such a disaster should not mar the day that a Prince became King.

When he returned to Chairman Wenceslas for a brief respite before he was expected to attend further celebrations and banquets, Raymond felt the drug's effects wearing off. At last, he could think for himself again.

By now the Chairman had digested the news of the humiliating EDF defeat. He had passed beyond disbelief and had begun to plan the best response and the most appropriate spin on the situation. Raymond chose not to ask for his reaction just yet. As King Peter, he would no doubt become the mouthpiece for the Hansa's outrage.

Basil came up to him, nodding in satisfaction. 'At least one thing went well today,' he said. 'King Peter, you have the potential to be a good ruler. We'll wait a few years . . .' He smiled at Peter, as if he thought he was delivering good news. 'And then we will find you an appropriate queen.'

ONE HUNDRED AND THIRTEEN

MARGARET COLICOS

In the silent base camp, backing away from the uprooted worldforest grove and leaving the dead body of Arcas inside the dim tent, Margaret and Louis crept towards their own temporary hut.

Louis was stunned, his skin pale and greyish. Margaret's vision contracted into a narrow point as she hurried him along. She simply had to *move*. She needed to discover information – and see how bad their situation might be, though she was afraid she didn't want to know.

Inside their tent, all of her records were torn apart, the tables and study screens overturned and crushed. Computers and datawafers had been melted into slag. Their standard communications transmitter had been smashed, leaving nothing but ruined metal casing, torn-apart wires, destroyed pulse nodes. A standard electromagnetic signal would have taken months to travel at the speed of light before it could be intercepted by the nearest Hansa colony or spacecraft. Much too long for a rescue. Even so, their enemy was taking no chance that Margaret and Louis would call for help.

'But . . . why? What is this for?' Louis stared up at her. 'Who could have done this to us?'

Margaret's expression turned hard. He honestly hadn't figured it out. 'Not much question about that, Louis.' She saw that her translations of the Klikiss hieroglyphics, all of their new discoveries, had been systematically obliterated, even the hand-written notes. She took her husband's arm, felt him shaking, and led him out into the open again. The tents were flimsy, the light meagre, and their defensive possibilities few. 'We're too vulnerable here.'

Out in the brooding darkness she saw no sign of the three Klikiss robots. She hushed Louis and listened, but heard no sound of moving centipede-like legs. 'We should go back to the cliff city. We can protect ourselves there, and DD's waiting for us.'

Louis started to question her, not intending to argue as much as to work through the confusion in his mind. 'Are you really suggesting that Sirix and the other two robots—'

'Give me a more reasonable possibility, Louis, and I'll listen. But for now, we've got to move. We're completely exposed here in the camp.'

The two backtracked into the narrow canyons. Margaret felt weary, her muscles sore. Louis panted heavily, and she worried about him. But the possibility of getting a few strained muscles and aching joints were the least of their problems.

As the cold stone walls folded inky shadows around them, they could see the twinkling, hopeful lights that DD had rigged inside the cliff overhang. Breathing hard, Margaret looked around her, smelled the dry air and foolishly wished for another flash flood to scour away any approaching black robots.

The three ancient machines were probably following them, even now.

Margaret did not doubt that she and Louis would be their next victims. During their stumbling flight, Louis seemed to have worked through his questions, but found no acceptable answers.

At the metal scaffolding that leaned against the sheer walls, allowing them easy access to the cliff city, Margaret urged Louis to ascend first. His footfalls were heavy, and she understood how utterly exhausted he was, not only from the exertion but from the toll of fear.

Hearing them climbing the metal staircase, DD came to the open overhang. His silvery body glinted in the light, and the Friendly compy seemed quite enthusiastic. 'Ah, Margaret and Louis, you have returned. Come, I have found something—'

'DD, help us up. Have you seen the Klikiss robots?'

'No, Margaret, not since this afternoon. Do we need their help?'

Louis reached the cave opening and collapsed to his knees, wheezing. Margaret hurried after him. 'No. DD, help me. We've got to tear down the staircase.'

Louis looked at her, then nodded grimly. 'May as well make it a siege.'

'Whatever for?' DD asked. 'We will have a much harder time getting down, although there are some ropes back with our equipment.'

'Just do it, DD!' Margaret snapped.

She and Louis worked with the small-statured compy to disengage the anchor bolts from the cave mouth. With a powerful shove and a loud clamour of bent metal and struts, the scaffolding crashed into the narrow canyon. Rubble pattered down the walls, and the clatter shot into the night with all the subtlety of a brass band.

Louis gazed down the long cliff as if he were an ancient knight standing atop a castle wall, assessing the defences of their moat and preparing for a siege. 'Well, are we safe now, dear?'

Margaret shook her head. 'I doubt it, old man.' Now that she could pause, the furious panic and the avalanche of questions roared around her, overwhelming her imagination. She held Louis close.

'Please explain what has happened, Margaret,' DD said.

'Arcas is dead.' The words sounded unreal in her mouth. 'The worldtrees have all been destroyed. Our records and our communications transmitter have been smashed. The camp is a wreck.'

'The Klikiss robots did it,' Louis said, as if admitting it to himself for the first time.

The Friendly compy was taken aback, and he remained silent as his computer brain processed the radical new information. 'Then we are stranded here on Rheindic Co.'

'Of course,' Margaret said, shoring up her helplessness with a veneer of anger.

'I have discovered new information that might shed light upon this mystery,' DD said. 'A section of hieroglyphics that were covered up on a wall not far from the stone-window chamber.'

Intensely interested in whether it had some bearing on their survival, Margaret stood up, glad for the distraction, for something positive she could do. 'I'll go look at it.' She glanced at her husband, who seemed too distraught to move. 'Louis, stay here and keep watch. Shout if you see anything.'

Louis swallowed hard and leaned against the overhang wall, looking out into the night. Without question, Sirix, Dekyk, and Ilkot would come for them. And since the archaeologists were stranded here on the ghost planet, the black robots had all the time in the world.

In a tunnel deeper within the cliff-side, away from the portal wall chamber, DD had scraped away a broad section of powdery, resinous covering. 'It was similar to plaster, obscuring the hieroglyphics. When I scanned the wall, I discovered the markings underneath. I thought you would like to inspect them, Margaret, so

I carefully cleaned the overlay. Notice several instances of the symbol that corresponds to the Klikiss robots.'

Margaret drank in the information. 'Good work, DD. You'll make a fine xeno-archaeologist some day.'

Tracing her fingertip along the symbols, she read quickly from what she knew of the language. She'd had enough practise by now that she could interpret the general meaning without recourse to her carefully compiled databases and dictionaries. No wonder some ancient Klikiss survivor – perhaps the cadaver they had found in the machine room – had wanted to hide this last testament.

'Is it important information, Margaret?' DD asked.

Her heart grew colder as she understood the markings. 'Yes, DD. This might just be the last piece of the puzzle.' She began to walk numbly back towards the main overhang. Louis had to know what she had learned.

As she passed the portal wall chamber, she glanced inside and saw the clutter of their day's work. Next to her notes lay part of a sandwich and a protein wafer, and the small but beautiful music box Anton had given her. Feeling a pang, Margaret snatched the music box and pocketed it.

Louis's shout rang out before she could make her way back to him. 'Margaret, here they come!'

Her instincts were torn between confronting the treacherous black robots, and just taking her husband and fleeing deeper into the catacombs. Perhaps they could find some escape, some protection inside the empty Klikiss city.

But it was not, after all, a difficult choice. She went to stand beside Louis.

At the edge of the overhang, he looked down into the dark canyon, his seamed face fearful but his eyes flashing. The scaffolding lay smashed on the ravine floor. Far below, the three beetle-like shapes crunched along the dry riverbed. Their optical sensors glowed like malevolent fireflies in the shadows.

'I don't see how they can get up here,' Louis said, but Margaret had her doubts about how impregnable this empty city would be. 'Did you learn anything, dear?'

'I found the answer to all of our questions,' she said.

Louis Colicos, the lifelong xeno-archaeologist, managed to summon enough enthusiasm for his passion in life that he actually looked up with interest. 'Well, a lot of good it'll do us if we can't tell anybody.'

'You and I will know, old man,' Margaret said, patting him on the arm.

Down below, Sirix and the other two robots stopped, swivelling their geometric heads upwards. 'Margaret and Louis Colicos, we know you are up there.'

'And we know you're down there,' Louis said. 'Now leave us alone.'

'We wish to discuss our creators with you. We want to learn everything you have discovered.'

'And then kill us afterwards?' Margaret called down, challenging.

The three black robots fell silent for a long moment, then they buzzed and chattered with each other in their strange electronic language. Sirix finally looked back upwards. 'Yes, and then kill you.'

Margaret was surprised the robot would be so blunt. 'Well, at least they're honest,' Louis said.

Margaret called, her words clear and sharp in the silent canyon. 'We know all about the first hydrogue war. I read hidden descriptions of the ancient battle between the Klikiss and the hydrogues, and even the Ildirans.' Louis looked at her, astonished, while the three black robots pondered the information.

'Then you know that we robots fought in that war,' Sirix said.

'I know that you turned against your creators.' She looked at

Louis. 'Their own robots are what destroyed the Klikiss race. That's why we see no living remnants of an entire species.'

Louis looked down, hoping the revelation would shock some sense into Sirix, Ilkot, and Dekyk. The trio of black robots paused, waiting at the base of the sheer cliff. 'Well, what do you have to say about that? Why did you do it?' he shouted, taunting. 'Does it jar any memories loose?'

'We already know,' Sirix answered in a chillingly flat tone.

Margaret realized deep in her heart that the Klikiss robots could never allow any of that damning information to reach the other civilizations in the Spiral Arm.

'Now what?' Louis whispered to his wife. 'Are they just going to stay down there and keep us treed like squirrels?'

As if they had heard him, the three Klikiss robots stood apart at the base of the cliff. Their black carapaces split open at the back to reveal emerging wings. Ignoring the broken scaffolding and discarded stairs, the Klikiss robots easily took flight and rose towards the cliff city.

ONE HUNDRED AND FOURTEEN

BASIL WENCESLAS

Devastating reports came to Basil Wenceslas, one after another, like a succession of death sentences.

From his executive suite atop Hansa headquarters, he stared out into the setting sun. He received each message with growing dread. He read the war reports, watched the scant but terrifying footage. The hydrogues were unstoppable.

For the first time in his successful career – in his entire life – Basil Wenceslas wanted nothing better than to hide, to find a place of safety where he could avoid the responsibility and the dangerous times ahead. He didn't have the slightest idea what to do. More than anything else, Basil hated to feel helpless.

After the EDF debacle on Jupiter, the deep-core aliens had launched repeated attacks with a vengeful thoroughness, emerging from dozens of gas giants. Crystalline warglobes had destroyed all ekti-harvesting operations across the Spiral Arm, everything from the outdated Ildiran factories, to the cumbersome processing facilities the Hansa had fielded, to the remaining Roamer skymines that had refused to evacuate.

More than any other group, the Roamers were suffering from the full-scale crackdown, unable to obtain or market stardrive fuel . . . but they would merely be the first victims. As word spread of the complete futility of attempted cloud mining, the hydrogue attacks had slackened. There was no one left to threaten.

Without ekti, all Hansa commerce, all interaction with the Ildiran Empire would grind to a halt. The business of the Spiral Arm, and then the livelihood of the scattered colonies, would slowly wither.

Most of the settlements had come to depend on regular shipments, resources, foodstuffs. Travel between the nearest star systems would now require years, decades, at top speeds available to conventional propulsion systems. No colony was an island, cut off, meant to exist all on its own. The infrastructure of many worlds simply did not allow them to be self-sufficient. Now they would have to learn – or die.

On the images transmitted to his table update screens, Basil looked down to watch newly crowned King Peter on his throne, delivering well-scripted proclamations, demanding increased weapons development, calling upon the population for additional EDF recruits.

Basil did not know what such measures would actually accomplish, but he would never let it appear that the Hansa did not know what to do. The people must continue to have hope. The EDF had already confiscated most stockpiles of ekti for military use, though some colonists on the more distant Hansa planets were hoarding the fuel themselves, saving it for what they knew would be terrible times ahead.

The citizens had accepted King Peter. His coronation had been embraced with the full enthusiasm of a family sharing grief. Peter had done well enough so far. He was a likeable young man, charismatic and strong, very attractive, with a good, sonorous voice. But in spite of being surrounded with all the opulence of the Whisper Palace, the fine foods, the pleasures and trappings of power, Peter would not enjoy his rule for a moment.

A lesser man might have felt a pang of guilt and sadness for what Basil had done to bright-eyed young Raymond Aguerra. But some people could not choose their responsibilities – neither he, nor the young orphan. However, he did not envy King Peter the difficulties he would face in his new reign.

At least Sarein had been appointed the new ambassador from Theroc, a kindred spirit, someone who would listen to rational debate about the uses of green priests in the growing war effort. That might be an advantage – though a minimal one. She had used him to gain her position. He wondered if Sarein would choose to be his lover again, now that she had Otema's coveted position, now that she'd found her prestigious place on Earth.

With the ready supply of ekti cut off for the foreseeable future, all space travel must henceforth be severely restricted. The Terran Hanseatic League and the ancient Ildiran Empire were effectively shut down.

The nightmare was only beginning.

ONE HUNDRED AND FIFTEEN

LOUIS COLICOS

Margaret grabbed his wrist. With DD hurrying to follow, they ran down the stone corridors, deeper into the abandoned cliff city. From outside, they heard the hum of mechanical wings, like a swarm of giant locusts as the Klikiss robots rose into the air and flew towards them. Louis could think of no way to block off the black machines.

Louis recalled the configuration of the empty city, trying to figure out the best place to hide, a chamber in which they could seal themselves. His mind raced over the layout of tunnels and passages, remembered where they narrowed.

Louis's face lit with forced hope. He pretended to be optimistic for Margaret's sake. 'Back to the stone-window chamber! The corridor outside is fairly small. Maybe we can find enough material to make a barricade.' He doubted the Klikiss robots would be deterred by any barrier they could construct.

Following the lights that DD had strung, they ran through twists and turns, finally arriving at the large stone room where Louis had spent so much time.

The hall held some rubble, as well as the resinous plaster debris DD had scraped from the last hastily written hieroglyphics. Louis worked with his bare hands, piling iron bars and rubble across the threshold, trying to build up a barrier. The hulking black robots would smash through it in seconds.

Outside, they heard the thump and skitter as Sirix, Ilkot, and Dekyk landed inside the overhang. The robots began to make their way through the corridors of the abandoned city, moving with a ponderous heaviness, their machine bodies cumbersome but relentless.

'Damn, I wish the Klikiss used *doors*.' Margaret looked in dismay at the open hall, the passage leading towards the stone-window chamber. The power source still hummed in the portal-wall machinery, though neither Louis nor his wife understood yet how the device functioned.

DD dutifully added to the meagre blockade using boxes of supplies, small pieces of equipment. Louis shook his head in disbelief at their pathetic effort. The Friendly compy looked back at them. 'Is there anything else I can do, Louis? I would be glad to assist in any way you deem appropriate.'

Louis frowned. 'Well, I don't suppose you have any defensive programming? Can we change you into a combat robot?'

'Perhaps if there were a programming module on hand,' DD said. 'However, I am not certain how effective I could be, since I have no built-in weapons or armour.'

'Not to mention the fact that you're about a third the size of a Klikiss robot.'

Margaret looked over her shoulder. 'You can't harm humans, is that correct, DD?'

'I cannot harm humans, Margaret.'

'And I presume a necessary corollary is that you cannot allow humans to come to harm?'

657

'I will do everything in my power to prevent that, Margaret.'

Louis looked sadly at the silvery compy, knowing he was about to give DD a suicide order. 'Then you've got to stand against the Klikiss robots, DD. Stay in the corridor and prevent them from reaching us.' He swallowed hard. 'Delay them . . . however you can.'

DD accepted his orders bravely and stood in the centre of the narrow, rock-walled passageway. The silver-skinned compy looked laughably weak compared with the enormous Klikiss robots. Louis thought of a heroic little guard dog barking furiously at a brutal intruder.

Margaret grabbed her husband's arm and pulled him deeper into the chamber. 'Louis, I need you. We've got only a few minutes to figure out this transportation system.' He was amazed she would suggest such an option. She saw that his doubt reflected her own, but she said, 'It's the only non-zero chance we have, old man.'

'All right.' He hurried over to the machinery. 'This is why I wanted a career in xeno-archaeology, to see strange new places. Usually though, I have some inkling of where I'm going.'

The energy pack was at full power, connected to the still-functioning alien systems. The exotic engines throbbed. The embedded circuit lines in the rock walls carried the necessary power to the flat trapezoid that held only an opaque stone surface.

Margaret hurried to the symbol tiles that framed the smooth trapezoidal plane. She thought out loud as she ran her fingers along the tiles, tracing the individual symbols. 'If each one of these indicates the coordinate of a Klikiss world, then perhaps we can travel to Llaro or Corribus. Did we leave any equipment there, transmitters or supplies?'

Louis shrugged in dismay. 'You're the organized one, dear. I never keep track of details like that.'

Outside in the corridor he heard the Klikiss robots approaching, treading heavily on clusters of finger-like legs. Louis saw DD standing all alone, pitifully small as he blocked the way against the three ominous machines.

At the portal wall, Margaret looked at the coordinate tiles. 'According to the records on the other Klikiss worlds, some of the tiles were destroyed, especially the ones containing these particular symbols.' She pointed to a convoluted glyph high on the frame. 'Were the robots trying to hide something to prevent travel somewhere?'

'Well, they missed this one,' Louis said. 'Until now.'

In the tunnel, DD took a step forward and held up his metal arms. Sirix paused, surprised at the boldness of the Friendly compy. 'I cannot allow you to harm my masters,' DD said. 'Please go away.'

In response, Ilkot lurched forward. With four segmented insect-like forelimbs, he grabbed the small compy and lifted him bodily out of the way. DD struggled uselessly. A bright red fire blazed in the ruby-crystalline eye in the centre of Ilkot's black head. He looked ready to destroy DD by ripping his body core into small components.

Sirix interrupted, though. 'Do not harm the compy. He has no choice. He does not understand his own bondage.'

The three Klikiss robots buzzed and hummed as if in argument, and then Ilkot turned. Gently, but with firm command, he carried DD away, taking the struggling compy prisoner. DD's protests and struggles grew fainter as the black beetle-like machine moved back towards the cave overhang.

Within seconds, Sirix and Dekyk had knocked aside the insignificant makeshift barricade and lumbered into the stone-window chamber.

Margaret did not turn around, though she must have heard the struggle in the corridor. She stared with her hands on her hips as if demanding an explanation from the portal wall. 'Come on! There must be some way to open this window.'

Finally, she stood on her tiptoes, stretched out her arm, and pushed hard against the tile containing a symbol that had been routinely obliterated in the other Klikiss ruins.

The portal wall hummed and crackled. The grey-stone plane shimmered. 'Louis! Something just happened!'

The two black Klikiss robots strode forward, their clawlike arms extended and clacking. With sick revulsion Louis saw the splatters of scarlet on their metal appendages. *Arcas's blood*.

Rushing to their tools strewn against the wall, he grabbed a pickaxe resting on one of the stone shelves. They had used the tool to chop through crumbling walls and clear away debris. Louis hefted it. The pickaxe was heavy in his arms, but the handle felt strong. He brandished it, knowing the weapon would do little good against these powerful machines.

Meanwhile, Margaret stared as the stone trapezoid crackled and fuzzed with static. Then the smooth rock faded away, suddenly replaced with another scene – an opening that gave her a view of a different place entirely, a new world.

'Louis!' she shouted.

The Klikiss robots converged towards the two archaeologists, their articulated arms extended. Louis swung the pickaxe from side to side. He looked over his shoulder at his wife, took a brief but significant gaze, like a snapshot in his memory. He memorized the determined face he had loved for so long, the inner beauty and the weathered features that had made her more attractive to him than any other woman he had ever met. 'Go!' he shouted. 'Just go!'

Margaret hesitated. 'I'm not leaving you!'

'Well then, I'm coming right after you.' The pickaxe slammed into Sirix's black body core with a loud clang, and the impact sent a jolt through Louis's arms, hurting his shoulders. The point of the digging tool left only a small scratch on the black carapace.

The Klikiss robot rocked back in surprise, then reached out with a segmented insect-like forelimb. Louis dodged, yanking the tool away and hefting it over his shoulder.

'Now, Louis!' Margaret called. Then, without hesitation, she stepped into the image that had been only flat stone moments before. The portal wall crackled – and Margaret vanished.

Elated to see that his wife had escaped, Louis hurled the pickaxe at the advancing Klikiss robot. It clattered against the dark casing. Sirix knocked it aside with his bloodstained limbs, and the pickaxe crashed to the floor.

Turning, Louis raced towards the trapezoidal portal wall where the window looked out upon a sanctuary. Another planet . . . somewhere foreign and far away.

But in front of his eyes, the stone window shimmered, then solidified again, sealing itself into a blank and impenetrable rock barrier.

Louis skidded to a halt, his heart sinking, despair etched across his face. 'No,' he moaned. He had not seen which tablet Margaret had pushed, didn't know what she had done to activate the system.

Sirix and Dekyk closed in on him now. Having seen Margaret escape, they would not give him the same opportunity. Deadly weapon arms extended from hidden openings in the robots' bodies, claws clacking.

Louis was cornered against the stone wall, trapped. He raised his hands in useless surrender, using his old lecturing voice. 'Sirix, why are you doing this? We mean you no harm. We were just trying to help. We wanted to find the answers for you.'

'We did not want the answers,' Sirix said.

Louis, leaning against the cold and all-too-solid stone wall, did not understand. 'But you said you had lost all your memories, that you didn't know what happened long ago.'

'We did not lose our memories,' Sirix said. The Klikiss robots fell upon the doomed archaeologist, their weapon-arms extended. 'We *lied*.'

To read an exclusive extract from
A FOREST OF STARS, book two in
THE SAGA OF SEVEN SUNS series,
turn to page 681!

TIMELINE

Ca.1940s	Ildirans discover Klikiss robots on Hyrillka ice moons.
2100	*Peary, Balboa, Marco Polo* – first generation ships depart from Earth
2103	*Burton, Caillié* depart
2104	*Amundsen* departs
2106	*Clark, Vichy* depart
2109	*Stroganov* departs
2110	*Abel-Wexler* departs
2113	*Kanaka* departs, last generation ship
2196	*Kanaka* leaves colony at Meyer rubble belt; becomes Rendezvous
2221	King Ben crowned on Earth
2230	Mage-Imperator Yura'h ascends
2244	Ildirans encounter *Caillié*; Theroc established as colony
2245	Ildirans come to Earth, search for other generation ships
2247	*Kanaka* found, settlers taken to Iawa

2249	Compy OX returns to Earth
	Thara Wen (14 years old) becomes the first to take the green
2250	Roamers begin skymining operations on Daym and elsewhere
2254	Dobro experiments begin
	First Klikiss ruins (Llaro) reported by Madeleine Robinson
	Theroc officially declares its independence from the Hansa
	King Ben poisoned; King George crowned
2274	King Christopher crowned
2307	King Jack crowned
2323	King Bartholomew crowned
2337	Mage-Imperator Yura'h dies; Cyroc'h ascends.
2373	Uthair and Lia Theron become Father and Mother of Theroc
2381	King Frederick crowned
2390	Margaret and Louis Colicos married
2397	Ross Tamblyn born
2400	Idriss and Alexa married
2402	Reynald Theron born
	Jess Tamblyn born
2403	Beneto Theron born; Uthair and Lia Theron retire
2406	Sarein Theron born
2408	Nira Khali born
2411	Tasia Tamblyn born
2413	Raymond Aguerra born
2415	Estarra Theron born
2427	Oncier ignited with Klikiss Torch

THE GREAT KINGS OF THE
TERRAN HANSEATIC LEAGUE

2221–2258   Ben
2258-2274   George
2274–2307   Christopher
2307–2323   Jack
2323–2381   Bartholomew
2381–2427   Frederick
2427–   Peter

CHAIRMAN OF THE TERRAN HANSEATIC LEAGUE

2200–2215	Christian Geller
2215–2223	Roseanna Burke
2223–2243	William Danforth Pape
2243–2253	Malcolm Stannis
2253–2270	Francine Meyer
2270–2291	Adam Cho
2291–2298	Bertram Goswell
2298–2299	Regan Chalmers
2299–2315	Sandra Abel-Wexler
2315–2338	Clare Faso
2338–2347	Miguel Byron
2347–2359	Tam Charles Wicinsky
2359–2367	Robert Roberts II
2367–2380	Kelly Kirk
2380–2389	Maureen Fitzpatrick
2389–2406	Ronald Palomar
2406–	Basil Wenceslas

GLOSSARY

ABEL-WEXLER – one of the eleven generation ships from Earth, tenth to depart.

ADAM, PRINCE – predecessor to Raymond Aguerra, considered an unacceptable candidate.

ADAR – highest military rank in Ildiran Solar Navy.

AGUERRA, CARLOS – Raymond's younger brother, nine years old.

AGUERRA, ESTEBAN – Raymond's estranged father.

AGUERRA, MICHAEL – Raymond's youngest brother, six years old.

AGUERRA, RAYMOND – streetwise young man from Earth.

AGUERRA, RITA – Raymond's mother.

AGUERRA, RORY – Raymond's younger brother, ten years old.

AHMANI, ABDUL MOHAMMED – name taken by Esteban Aguerra after his conversion to Islam.

ALEXA, MOTHER – ruler of Theroc, wife of Father Idriss.

ALTURAS – Ildiran world

AMUNDSEN – one of the eleven generation ships from Earth, sixth to depart.

ANDEKER, WILLIAM – human scientist, specialist in robotics.

ARCAS – green priest.

ARCHFATHER – symbolic head of Unison religion on Earth.

ARI'T – Ildiran singer female, a lover of Prime Designate Jora'h.

ARO'NH – a Tal in the Ildiran Solar Navy.

ATTENDERS – diminutive personal assistants to the Mage-Imperator.

BALBOA – one of the eleven generation ships from Earth, second to depart.

BARTHOLOMEW – Great King of Earth, predecessor to Frederick.

BEBOB – Rlinda Kett's pet name for Branson Roberts.

BEKH! – Ildiran curse, 'Damn!'

BEN – first Great King of the Terran Hanseatic League; also, a large moon of Oncier.

BENETO – green priest, second son of Father Idriss and Mother Alexa.

BIG GOOSE – Roamer derogative term for Terran Hanseatic League.

BIOTH – father of Arcas.

BLAZER – Ildiran illumination source.

BLIND FAITH – Branson Roberts's ship.

BLUE SKY MINE – skymine facility at Golgen, operated by Ross Tamblyn.

BOBRI'S – comedic figure in *Saga of Seven Suns*.

BOONE'S CROSSING – Hansa colony world.

BRINDLE, ROBB – young EDF recruit, comrade of Tasia Tamblyn.

BRON'N – bodyguard of the Mage-Imperator.

BURL – young bully on Earth.

BURR – Roamer clan.

BURTON – one of the eleven generation ships from Earth, fourth to depart. Lost en route.

BYRON, MIGUEL – hedonistic former chairman of Terran Hanseatic League.

CAILLIÉ – one of the eleven generation ships from Earth, fifth to depart and first to be encountered by the Ildirans. Colonists from the *Caillié* were taken to settle Theroc.

CARGO ESCORT – Roamer vessel used to deliver ekti shipments from skymines.

CELLI – youngest daughter of Father Idriss and Mother Alexa.

CHRISTOPHER – third Great King of the Terran Hanseatic League; also, a large moon of Oncier.

CHRYSALIS CHAIR – reclining throne of the Mage-Imperator.

CIR'GH – Ildiran jousting champion.

CLARIN, ELDON – Roamer inventor.

CLARKE – one of the eleven generation ships from Earth, seventh to depart.

CLEE – a steamy, potent beverage made from ground worldtree seeds.

COHORT – battle group of Ildiran Solar Navy consisting of seven maniples, or 343 ships.

COLICOS, ANTON – the son of Margaret and Louis Colicos, translator and student of epic stories.

COLICOS, LOUIS – xeno-archaeologist, husband of Margaret Colicos, specializing in ancient Klikiss artifacts.

COLICOS, MARGARET – xeno-archaeologist, wife of Louis Colicos, specializing in ancient Klikiss artifacts.

COLONY TOWN – main settlement on Corvus Landing.

COMPETENT COMPUTERIZED COMPANION – intelligent servant robot, called compy, available in Friendly, Teacher, Governess, Listener, and other models.

COMPTOR – Ildiran colony world, site of a legendary forest fire.

COMPY – shortened term for 'Competent Computerized Companion'.

CONDORFLY – colourful flying insect on Theroc like a giant butterfly, sometimes kept as pets.

CONGRESS OF FAITHS – Hansa religious body, similar to United Nations, comprised of representatives from many religions.

CONSTELLATION – Hansa diplomatic ship.

CORRIBUS – abandoned Klikiss world where the Colicos discovered the Klikiss Torch.

CORVUS LANDING – Hansa colony world, mainly agricultural, some mining.

COTOPAXI – Hansa colony world.

CRACKLE – Theron nut.

CRENNA – Ildiran splinter colony, evacuated due to plague.

CUTTER – small ship in Ildiran Solar Navy.

CYROC'H – original name of current Ildiran Mage-Imperator.

DANGO – Theron fruit.

DASRA – gas-giant planet suspected of harbouring hydrogues.

DAYM – blue supergiant star, one of the Ildiran 'seven suns'; also the name of the primary gas-giant planet, site of abandoned Ildiran ekti harvesting operations.

DD – compy servant assigned to Rheindic Co xeno-archaeology dig.

DEKYK – Klikiss robot at Rheindic Co xeno-archaeology dig.

DESIGNATE – pure-bred son of Mage-Imperator, ruler of an Ildiran world.

DIO'SH – Ildiran rememberer, survivor of Crenna evacuation.

DOBRO – Ildiran colony world.

DREMEN – Terran colony world, dim and cloudy.

DURRIS – trinary star system, close white and orange stars orbited by a red dwarf; three of the Ildiran 'seven suns'.

EA – Tasia Tamblyn's personal compy.

EARTH DEFENCE FORCES – Terran space military, headquartered on Mars but with jurisdiction throughout the Terran Hanseatic League.

EDDIES – slang term for soldiers in EDF.

EDF – Earth Defence Forces.

EKTI – exotic allotrope of hydrogen used in Ildiran stardrives.

ERPHANO – gas-giant planet, site of Berndt Okiah's skymine.

ESCORT – mid-sized ship in Ildiran Solar Navy.

ESTARRA – second daughter, fourth child of Father Idriss and Mother Alexa.

FIREFEVER – ancient Ildiran plague.

FITZPATRICK, PATRICK, III – spoiled cadet in the Earth Defence Forces.

FLATGEMS – layered artificial gems, rare and expensive.

FREDERICK, KING – figurehead ruler of the Terran Hanseatic League.

FUNGUS REEF – giant worldtree growth on Theroc, carved into a habitation by the Therons.

GARRIS – Nira's father.

GEORGE – second Great King of the Terran Hanseatic League; also, a large moon of Oncier.

GLYX – gas giant, site of Berndt Okiah's first skymine command.

GOLGEN – gas giant, harvested by the Blue Sky Mine.

GOLIATH – first enhanced Juggernaut in EDF fleet.

GOOSE – Roamer derogative term for Terran Hanseatic League.

GOSWELL, BERTRAM – early Chairman of the Terran Hanseatic League; originally tried to force Roamers to sign Hansa Charter.

GREAT EXPECTATIONS – one of Rlinda Kett's merchant ships, captured by Rand Sorengaard's pirates.

GREAT KING – figurehead leader of Terran Hanseatic League.

GREEN PRIEST – servant of the worldforest, able to use worldtrees for instantaneous communication.

GUIDING STAR – Roamer philosophy and religion, a guiding force in a person's life.

HANSA – Terran Hanseatic League.

HANSA HEADQUARTERS – pyramidal building near the Whisper Palace on Earth.

HENDY, SAM – Mayor of Corvus Landing Colony Town.

HIVE WORMS – giant nest-making invertebrates on Theroc.

HORIZON CLUSTER – large star cluster near Ildira.

HYDROGUES – alien race living at cores of gas-giant planets.

HYRILLKA – Ildiran colony in Horizon Cluster, original discovery site of Klikiss robots.

IAWA – colony world, once inhabited by predecessors of the Roamers.

IAWAN SCOURGE – botanical plague on Iawa.

IDRISS, FATHER – ruler of Theroc, husband of Mother Alexa.

ILDIRA – home planet of the Ildiran Empire, under the light of seven suns.

ILDIRAN EMPIRE – large alien empire, the only other major civilization in the Spiral Arm.

ILDIRAN SOLAR NAVY – space military fleet of the Ildiran Empire.

ILDIRANS – humanoid alien race with many different breeds, or kiths.

ILKOT – Klikiss robot at Rheindic Co xeno-archaeology dig.

IRON LADY – nickname for Ambassador Otema.

ISIX CAT – small feral feline on Ildira.

ISPEROS – hot planet, site of Kotto Okiah's test colony.

JACK – fourth Great King of the Terran Hanseatic League; also, a large moon of Oncier.

JAZER – energy weapon used by Earth Defence Forces.

JIGGLEFRUIT – Theron fruit.

JONNA – young friend of Celli.

JORA'H – Prime Designate of the Ildiran Empire, eldest son of Mage-Imperator.

JORAX – Klikiss robot, often seen on Earth.

JUGGERNAUT – large battleship class in Earth Defence Forces.

KAMIN – planet in the Ildiran Empire.

KANAKA – one of the eleven generation ships from Earth, last to depart. These colonists became the Roamers.

KELLUM, DEL – Roamer, ekti cargo driver.

KETT, RLINDA – merchant woman, captain of the *Voracious Curiosity*.

KHALI – Nira's family name.

KITH – a breed of Ildiran.

KLEEB – derogatory term.

KLIKISS – ancient insect-like race, long vanished from the Spiral Arm, leaving only their empty cities.

KLIKISS ROBOTS – intelligent beetle-like robots built by the Klikiss race.

KLIKISS TORCH – a weapon/mechanism developed by the ancient Klikiss race to implode gas-giant planets and create new stars.

KLIO'S – Ildiran Minister of Commerce.

K'LLAR BEKH! – strenuous Ildiran curse, 'God damn!'

KORI'NH, ADAR – leader of the Ildiran Solar Navy.

LANYAN, GENERAL KURT – commander of Earth Defence Forces.

LLARO – abandoned Klikiss world.

LORIE'NH – cohort commander in the Ildiran Solar Navy.

LOTZE, DAVLIN – Hansa exosociologist and spy on Crenna.

MAGE-IMPERATOR – the god-emperor of the Ildiran Empire.

MALPH – young bully on Earth.

MANIPLE – battle group of Ildiran Solar Navy consisting of seven septas, or forty-nine ships.

MANTA – mid-sized cruiser class in EDF.

MARATHA – Ildiran resort world with extremely long day and night cycle.

MARCO POLO – one of the eleven generation ships from Earth, third to depart.

MAYLOR – Roamer clan.

MEENA – Nira's mother.

MESTA, GABRIEL – Captain of *Great Expectations*, killed by Rand Sorengaard's pirates.

MEYER – red dwarf sun, location of Rendezvous.

MIJISTRA – glorious capital city of the Ildiran Empire.

MOON STATUE GARDEN – sculpture exhibit and topiary at Whisper Palace.

NAPPLE – Theron fruit.

NIALIA – 'plantmoth' grown on Hyrilka.

NIRA – young green priest acolyte; accompanies Otema to Ildira.

ONCIER – gas-giant planet, test site of the Klikiss Torch.

OKIAH, BERNDT – Jhy Okiah's grandson, chief of Erphano skymine.

OKIAH, JHY – Roamer woman, very old, Speaker of the clans.

OKIAH, JUNNA – Berndt Okiah's daughter.

OKIAH, KOTTO – Jhy Okiah's youngest son, brash inventor who designed Isperos colony.

OKIAH, MARTA – Berndt Okiah's wife.

OSQUIVEL – ringed gas planet, site of secret Roamer shipyards.

OTEMA – old green priest, ambassador from Theroc to Earth; later, sent to Ildira.

OX – Teacher compy, one of the oldest Earth robots. Served aboard *Peary*.

PAIR-PEAR – Theron fruit, grows double on trees.

PALISADE – Hansa colony world.

PASTERNAK, SHAREEN – chief of Welyr skymine.

PEARY – one of the eleven generation ships from Earth, first to depart.

PELLIDOR, FRANZ – assistant to Basil Wenceslas, an 'expediter'.

PEPPERFLOWER TEA – Roamer beverage.

PERONI, DENN – Cesca's father.

PERONI, FRANCESCA – Roamer woman, in training to become next Speaker, betrothed to Ross Tamblyn.

PERRIN SEED – Theron nut.

PETER, PRINCE – successor to Old King Frederick.

PETROV – Roamer clan.

PLATCOM – Platform Commander, chief's rank aboard Thunderhead weapons platform in EDF.

PLUMAS – frozen moon with deep liquid oceans, site of Tamblyn clan water industry.

PRIME DESIGNATE – eldest son and heir-apparent of Ildiran Mage-Imperator.

PRISM PALACE – dwelling of the Ildiran Mage-Imperator.

PTORO – gas-giant planet, site of Crim Tylar's skymine.

PUCKER – sour Theron fruit.

PYM – abandoned Klikiss world.

QRONHA – a close binary system, two of the Ildiran 'seven suns'. Contains two habitable planets and one gas giant (Qronha 3).

QUL – Ildiran military rank, commander of a maniple, or forty-nine ships.

RADA – Nira's younger sister.

RAMAH – Terran colony world, settled mainly by Islamic pilgrims.

RECONNAISSANCE OUTRIGGER – fast intelligence-gathering ship in Earth Defence Forces.

RELLEKER – Terran colony world, popular as a resort.

REMEMBERER – member of the Ildiran historian kith.

REMORA – small attack ship in Earth Defence Forces.

RENDEZVOUS – inhabited asteroid cluster, hidden centre of Roamer government.

REYNALD – eldest son of Father Idriss and Mother Alexa.

RHEINDIC CO – abandoned Klikiss world, site of major excavation by the Colicos.

RINDBERRY – Theron fruit.

ROACHERS – derogatory term for Roamers.

ROAMERS – loose confederation of independent humans, primary producers of ekti stardrive fuel.

ROBERTS, BRANSON – former husband of Rlinda Kett.

ROBINSON, MADELEINE – early planetary prospector; she and her two sons discovered Klikiss ruins and activated robots on Llaro.

SAGA OF SEVEN SUNS – historical and legendary epic of the Ildiran civilization.

SALTNUT – Theron nut.

SAREIN – eldest daughter of Father Idriss and Mother Alexa.

SCALY – Ildiran kith, desert dwellers.

SEEDBERRY – Theron fruit.

SEPTA – small battle group of seven ships in the Ildiran Solar Navy.

SEPTAR – commander of a septa.

SERIZAWA, DR GERALD – scientist in charge of the Klikiss Torch experiment at Oncier.

SHANA REI – legendary 'creatures of darkness' in *Saga of Seven Suns*.

SHIZZ – expletive.

SIRIX – Klikiss robot at Rheindic Co xeno-archaeology dig.

SKYMINE – ekti-harvesting facility in gas-giant clouds, usually operated by Roamers.

SKYPEARL – rare metallic black gems found inside ekti reactors.

SORENGAARD, RAND – renegade Roamer pirate.

SPEAKER – political leader of the Roamers.

SPIRAL ARM – the section of the Milky Way galaxy settled by the Ildiran Empire and Terran colonies.

SPLINTER COLONY – Ildiran colony that meets minimum population requirements.

SPLURTBERRY – Theron fruit.

SPREADNUT – Theron nut.

STARGAMES – a navigational-challenge game popular among Roamers.

STREAMER – fast single ship in Ildiran Solar Navy.

STROGANOV – one of the eleven generation ships from Earth, ninth to depart.

STROMO, ADMIRAL LEV – Admiral in Earth Defence Forces.

SWEENEY, DAHLIA – DD's first owner, as a young girl.

SWEENEY, MARIANNA – Dahlia's daughter, DD's second owner.

SWIMMER – Ildiran kith, water dwellers.

TAL – military rank in Ildiran Solar Navy, cohort commander.

TALBUN – old green priest on Corvus Landing.

TAMBLYN, BRAM – Roamer, old scion of Tamblyn clan, father of Ross, Jess, and Tasia.

TAMBLYN, CALEB – one of Jess's uncles, brother to Bram.

TAMBLYN, JESS – Roamer, second son of Bram Tamblyn.

TAMBLYN, ROSS – Roamer, estranged oldest son of Bram Tamblyn, chief of the Blue Sky Mine at Golgen.

TAMBLYN, TASIA – Roamer, young daughter of Bram Tamblyn.

TELINK – instantaneous communication used by green priests.

TERRAN HANSEATIC LEAGUE – commerce-based government of Earth and Terran colonies.

THEROC – jungle planet, home of the worldforest.

THERON – a native of Theroc.

THISM – faint racial telepathic link from Mage-Imperator to the Ildiran people.

THOR'H – eldest noble-born son of Jora'h, destined to become the next Prime Designate.

THRONE HALL – the King's main receiving room in the Whisper Palace.

THUNDERHEAD – mobile weapons platform in Earth Defence Forces.

TRADE STANDARD – common language used in Hanseatic League.

TRANSGATE – hydrogue point-to-point transportation system.

TREELING – a small worldtree sapling, often transported in an ornate pot.

TROOP CARRIER – personnel transport ship in Ildiran Solar Navy.

TYLAR, CRIM – Roamer skyminer on Ptoro.

UNISON – standardized government-sponsored religion for official activities on Earth.

UR – Roamer compy, Governess-model at Rendezvous.

VA'OSH – Ildiran rememberer.

VICHY – one of the eleven generation ships from Earth, eighth to depart.

VORACIOUS CURIOSITY – Rlinda Kett's merchant ship.

WARGLOBE – hydrogue spherical attack vessel.

WARLINER – largest class of Ildiran battleship.

WELYR – gas giant, site of Roamer skymine destroyed by hydrogues.

WEN, THARA – early settler on Theroc, from generation ship *Caillié*. First person to become linked with worldforest.

WENCESLAS, BASIL – Chairman of the Terran Hanseatic League.

WHISPER PALACE – magnificent seat of the Hansa government.

WORLDFOREST – the interconnected, semi-sentient forest based on Theroc.

WORLDTREE – a separate tree in the interconnected, semi-sentient forest based on Theroc.

WORM HIVE – large nest built by hive worms on Theroc, spacious enough to be used for human habitation.

WYVERN – large flying predator on Theroc.

YARROD – green priest, younger brother of Mother Alexa.

YREKA – fringe Terran colony world.

YURA'H – previous Mage-Imperator, ruled at time of first encounter with human generation ships.

ZAN'NH – Ildiran military officer, eldest son of Prime Designate Jora'h.

A FOREST OF STARS

the saga of seven suns

BOOK TWO

KEVIN J. ANDERSON

ONE

JESS TAMBLYN

cross the Spiral Arm, the gas-giant planets held secrets,
dangers, and treasure. For a century and a half, harvesting
vital stardrive fuel from the cloud worlds had been a
lucrative business for the Roamers.

Five years ago, though, that had all changed.

Like vicious guard dogs, the destructive hydrogues had
forbidden all skymines from approaching the gas giants they
claimed as their territory. The embargo had crippled the Roamer
economy, the Terran Hanseatic League, and the Ildiran Empire.
Many brave or foolish entrepreneurs had defied the hydrogues'
ultimatum. They had paid with their lives. Dozens of skymines
were destroyed. The deep-core aliens were unstoppable and
ruthless.

But when facing desperate situations, Roamers refused to give
up. Instead, they changed tactics, surviving – and thriving –
through innovation.

'The old Speaker always told us that challenges redefine the
parameters of success,' Jess Tamblyn said over the open comm,

taking his lookout ship into position above the deceptively peaceful-looking gas giant Welyr.

'By damn, Jess,' Del Kellum transmitted with just a touch of annoyance, 'if I wanted to be pampered, I'd live on *Earth*.'

Kellum, an older clan leader and hands-on industrialist, signalled to the converging fast-dive scoop ships. The cluster of modified 'blitzkrieg' skymines and a hodge-podge of small lookout craft gathered at what they hoped was a safe distance above the coppery planet. No one knew how far away the hydrogues could detect trespassing cloud thieves, but they had long since given up playing it safe. In the end, all life was a gamble, and human civilization could not survive without stardrive fuel.

The ekti-scavenging crew powered up their huge scoops and containers, ready for a concerted plunge into the thick cloud decks. Hit and run. Their supercharged engines glowed warm. Their pilots sweated. Ready.

Alone in his lookout ship, Jess flexed his hands on the cockpit controls. 'Prepare to come from all sides. Move in fast, gulp a bellyful, and head for safety. We don't know how long the drogue bastards will give us.'

After the big harvesting ships acknowledged, they dropped like hawks after prey. What once had been a routine industrial process had become a commando operation in a war zone.

When presented with the hydrogue ultimatum, daring Roamer engineers had redesigned traditional skymining facilities. They had accomplished a lot in five years. The new blitzkrieg scoops had giant engines, super-efficient ekti reactors, and detachable cargo tanks like a cluster of grapes. Once each tank was filled, it could be launched up to a retrieval point, passing off the harvested ekti a bit at a time without losing a full cargo load if – *when* – the hydrogues came after them.

Kellum transmitted, The Big Goose thinks we're shiftless

bandits. By damn, let's give the drogues the same impression.'

The Hansa – the 'Big Goose' – as well as the Ildiran Empire paid dearly for every drop stardrive fuel. As ekti supplies dwindled year after year, prices skyrocketed to such a point that Roamers considered the risk acceptable.

Five of the modified scoops now dispersed across the atmosphere, then plunged into Welyr's clouds, storm upwellings, and vanishingly thin winds. With giant funnel-maws open, the blitzkrieg scoops roared through storm systems at top speed. They gobbled resources, compressing the excess into hydrogen holding tanks while secondary ekti reactors processed the gas.

As he flew his lookout mission, like a man in the crow's-nest of an ancient pirate ship, Jess deployed floating sensors into Welyr's soupy clouds. The buoys would detect any large ships rising from the depths. The sensors might give only a few minutes' warning, but the daredevils could retreat quickly enough.

Jess knew that it did no good to fight. The Ildiran Solar Navy and the Hansa EDF had demonstrated that lesson often enough. At the first sign of the enemy's arrival, his renegade harvesters would turn and run with whatever ekti they'd managed to grab.

The first blitzkrieg scoop filled one cargo tank and rose high enough to jettison it, leaving a smoke trail in the thin air. A resounding cheer echoed across the comm, and the competitive Roamers challenged each other to do better. The unmanned fuel tank soared away from Welyr towards its rendezvous point. *Safe*.

In times past, leisurely skymines had drifted over the clouds like whales feeding on plankton. Jess's brother Ross had been the chief of Blue Sky Mine on Golgen; he'd had dreams, an excellent business sense, and all the hopes in the world. Without warning, though, hydrogues had obliterated the facility, killed every member of the crew . . .

Jess monitored his scans. Though the sinking sensor buoys

detected no turbulence that might signal the approach of the enemy, he didn't let his attention waver. Welyr seemed much too quiet and peaceful. Deceptive.

Every crewman aboard the blitzkrieg scoops was tense, knowing they had only one chance here, and that some of them would likely die as soon as the hydrogues arrived.

'Here's a second one, highest quality ekti!' Del Kellum's harvester launched a full cargo tank. Within moments, each of the five blitzkrieg scoops had ejected a load of ekti. The scavengers had been at Welyr for less than three hours, and already it was a valuable haul.

'Good way to thumb our noses at the drogues,' Kellum continued, his anxiety manifesting itself as chattiness over the comm band, 'though I'd prefer to slam them with a few comets. Just like you did at Golgen, Jess.'

Jess smiled grimly. His cometary bombardment had made him a hero among the Roamers, and he hoped that the planet was now uninhabitable, all the enemy aliens destroyed. A strike back. 'I was just following my Guiding Star.'

Now many clans looked to Jess for suggestions on how they might continue their retaliation against the aliens' nonsensical prohibition.

'You and I have a lot in common,' Kellum said, his voice more conspiratorial now that he had switched to a private frequency. 'And if you ever do another bombardment, might I suggest this place as a target?'

'What have you got against Welyr? Ah, you had planned to marry Shareen of the Pasternak clan.'

'Yes, by damn!' Shareen Pasternak had been the chief of a skymine on Welyr. Jess recalled that the woman had an acidly sarcastic sense of humour and a sharp tongue, but Kellum had been delighted with her. It would have been the second marriage for both of them. But Shareen's skymine had also been destroyed in the early hydrogue depredations.

Now, three more ekti cargo tanks launched away from the racing blitzkrieg scoops.

Trish Ng, the pilot of a second lookout ship, frantically radioed Jess, cutting off the conversation. 'The sensor buoys! Check the readings, Jess.'

He saw a standard carrier wave with a tiny blip in the background. 'It's just a lightning strike. Don't get jumpy, Ng.'

'That same lightning strike repeats every twenty-one seconds. Like clockwork.' She waited a beat. 'Jess, it's an artificial signal, copied, looped, and reflected back at us. The drogues must've already destroyed the sensor buoys. It's a ruse.'

Jess watched, and the pattern became apparent. 'That's all the warning we're going to get. Everybody, pack up and head out!'

As if realizing they had been discovered, seven immense warglobes rose like murderous leviathans from Welyr's deep clouds. The Roamer scavengers did not hesitate, retreating pell-mell up through the gas giant's skies.

A deep-throated subsonic hum came from the alien spheres, and pyramidal protrusions on their crystalline skins crackled with blue lightning. The Roamer daredevils had all seen the enemy fire their destructive weapons before.

Kellum ejected four empty ekti cargo tanks, throwing them like grapeshot at the nearest warglobes. 'Choke on these!'

Jess shouted into the comm. 'Don't wait. Just leave.'

Kellum's diversion worked. The aliens targeted their blue lightning on the empty projectiles, giving the blitzkrieg scoops a few more seconds to escape. The Roamers fired their enormous engines, and four of the five harvester scoops lifted on an escape trajectory.

But one of the new vessels hung behind just a moment too long, and the enemy lightning bolts ripped the facility to molten shreds. The crew's screams echoed across the comm channel, then cut off instantly.

'Go! Go!' Jess yelled. 'Disperse and get out of here.'

The remaining commando harvesters scattered like flies. The automated cargo tanks would go to their pickup coordinates, where the commandos could retrieve the haul at their leisure.

The warglobes rose up, shooting blue lightning into space. They struck and destroyed a lagging lookout ship, but the others escaped. The enemy spheres remained above the atmosphere for some time, like growling wolves, before they slowly descended back into the coppery storms of Welyr, without pursuing.

Though dismayed at the loss of one blitzkrieg scoop and a lookout ship, the raiders were already tallying the ekti they had harvested and projecting how much it would bring on the open market.

Alone in the cockpit of his scout ship, Jess shook his head. 'What has happened to us, if we can cheer because our losses were "not too bad"?'

TWO

KING PETER

It was an emergency high-level staff meeting, like many others called since the hydrogue attacks had begun. But this time, King Peter insisted that it be held within the Whisper Palace, in a room of his own choosing. The secondary banquet room he selected had no particular significance for him; the young King simply made the move to demonstrate his independence . . . and also to annoy Chairman Basil Wenceslas.

'You keep telling me my reign is based upon appearances, Basil.' Peter's artificially blue eyes flashed as he met the Chairman's hard grey gaze. 'Isn't it appropriate that I meet with *my* staff in the Palace, not at your convenience in Hansa HQ?'

Peter knew that Basil hated it when the young King used his own tactics against him. The former Raymond Aguerra had learned to play his part better than the Hansa ever expected.

Basil's studiously blasé expression was clearly meant to remind Peter that, as Chairman of the Terran Hanseatic League, he had dealt with crises far worse than a petulant young King. 'Your presence is merely a formality, Peter. We don't really require you in the meeting at all.'

By now, though, Peter knew a bluff when he saw one. 'If you think the media won't notice my absence at an emergency session, then I'll go swim with my dolphins instead.' He understood his tenuous importance and pushed, just a little, whenever he could. Peter rarely misjudged Basil's limits, though. He approached each small battle with finesse and subtlety. And he knew when to stop.

In the end, Basil pretended that it didn't matter. His primary advisers – Basil's hand-picked but diverse inner circle of representatives, military experts, and Hansa officials – gathered behind closed doors around a chandelier-lit table as a light luncheon was served. Silent servants hurried to place bouquets on the table, damask napkins, silverware; fountains trickled in three alcoves.

Peter seated himself in an ornate chair at the head of the table. Knowing his role, however, the young King listened in respectful silence while the Chairman went through the agenda items.

Basil's iron-grey hair was impeccably trimmed and combed. His perfect suit was expensive, yet comfortable, and he moved with a lean grace that belied his seventy-three years. So far today, he'd eaten sparingly, drinking only ice water and cardamom coffee.

'I require an accurate assessment of the state of our Hansa colonies.' He swept his gaze around his advisers, admirals, and colony envoys. 'In the five years since the hydrogues killed King Frederick and issued their ultimatum against skymining, we've had considerable time to draw conclusions and make realistic projections.' He looked first to the commander of his Earth Defence Forces. Since he was Chairman of the Hansa, Basil was also the technical leader of the EDF. 'General Lanyan, what is your overall evaluation?'

The General waved aside the numbers and statistics that an aide called up for him on a document pad. 'Easy enough, Mr Chairman: we're in deep trouble, though the EDF has rigorously rationed ekti since the beginning of the crisis. Without those highly unpopular measures—'

Peter interrupted. 'Riots have caused as much damage as the shortages, especially on new settlements. We've already had to declare martial law on four colonies. People are hurting and hungry. They think *I've* abandoned them.' He looked at the sliced meats and colourful fruit on his plate and decided he had no appetite, knowing what others were suffering.

Lanyan stopped in mid-sentence, looked at the King without responding, then returned his attention to Basil. 'As I was saying, Mr Chairman, austerity measures have allowed us to maintain most vital services. However, our stockpiles are dwindling.'

Tyra Running Horse, one of the planetary envoys, pushed her plate aside. Peter tried to remember which colony she represented. Was it Rhejak? 'Hydrogen is the most common element in the universe. Why don't we just get it somewhere else?'

'Concentrated hydrogen is not *as accessible* elsewhere,' said one of the admirals. 'Gas giants are the best reservoirs.'

'The Roamers continue to supply some ekti through their high-risk harvesting techniques,' said the Relleker envoy, trying to sound optimistic. With his pale skin and patrician features, he looked just like one of the faux-classical statues against the wall of the small banquet room. 'Let them keep taking the gambles.'

'And there is simply no other fuel alternative for the faster-than-light stardrive. We've tried everything,' said yet another envoy. 'We're stuck with what the Roamers provide.'

Scowling, Lanyan shook his head. 'Current Roamer deliveries don't match even our bare-bones military requirements, not to mention public and civilian needs. We may need to impose further austerity measures.'

'What further measures?' said the dark-faced envoy from Ramah. 'It has been months since my world received a supply

691

delivery. No medicine, no food, no equipment. We have increased our agriculture and mining, but we do not have the infrastructure to survive being completely cut off like this.'

'Most of us are in the same situation,' the ghostly pale Dremen representative said. 'And my colony has entered its low weather cycle, more clouds, lower temperatures. Crop yields are traditionally down thirty per cent, and it'll be the same this time. Even in the best years, Dremen would need aid to survive. Now—'

Basil raised his hand to cut off further complaints. 'We've had this discussion before. Impose birth restrictions if your agricultural capabilities can't support your population. This crisis isn't going to end overnight, so start thinking in the long term.'

'Of course,' Peter said with thinly veiled sarcasm. 'Let's take away the rights of fertile men and women to decide how many children they need to sustain a colony they've risked *their* lives to establish. Now that's a solution the people will like. I suppose you'll want me to put on a happy face and make them accept it?'

'Yes, I will, dammit,' Basil said. 'That's your job.'

The grim news seemed to diminish everyone's appetite. Servants came around pouring ice water, using delicate silver tongs to offer wedges of dwarf limes. Basil sent them away.

He tapped his fingers on the tabletop with uncharacteristic impatience. 'We need to do a better job of making the people see just how dire the situation is. We have minimal fuel, not to mention very limited communication abilities, thanks to the continuing lack of green priests from our short-sighted friends on Theroc. Our fast mail drones can do only so much. Now, more than ever, we could use more green priests just to maintain contact between isolated colony worlds. Many planets don't have a single one.'

He looked over at Sarein, the dusky-skinned ambassador from the forested world. She was lean and wiry, with narrow shoulders and small breasts, high cheekbones and a pointed chin.

'I'm doing the best I can, Basil. You know that Therons have never been good at seeing the forest for the trees.' She smiled to emphasize her clever choice of words. 'On the other hand, Theroc has received no routine supplies, no technology, no medical assistance since this crisis began. It's difficult for me to ask my people for more green priests if the Hansa dismisses our own needs.'

Peter watched the interaction between Basil and the pretty Theron woman; from the first days of his reign, he'd recognized the mutual attraction. Now, before the Chairman could respond, Peter squared his shoulders and spoke in the rich voice he had practised during many speeches. 'Ambassador, considering the hardships faced by many of our Hansa colonists, we must allocate our resources, giving our own colonies highest priority. Theroc, as a sovereign world, is already much better off than most.'

While Sarein fumed at the verbal slap, Basil nodded appraisingly at Peter, relieved. 'The King is correct, of course, Sarein. Until the situation changes, Theroc will have to take care of itself. Unless, perhaps, Theroc would care to join the Hansa . . . ?'

Sarein's face flushed, and she gave a barely perceptible shake of her head.

General Lanyan drew his glance like a scythe across the envoys. 'Mr. Chairman, our only choice is to take certain extreme measures. The longer we wait, the more extreme those measures will have to be.'

Basil sighed, as if he had known this choice would fall upon him. 'You have the Hansa's permission to do what is necessary, General.' He skewered Peter with his gaze. 'And you will do it all in the King's name, of course.'

THREE

ESTARRA

I have seen many fascinating worlds,' Estarra's older brother said as their flitter-raft travelled across the densely wooded continent. 'I've been to the Whisper Palace on Earth, and stood under the seven suns of Ildira.' Reynald's tanned face lit with a smile. 'But Theroc is my *home*, and I'd rather be here than any other place.'

Estarra grinned, looking around her at the new, but always familiar, landscape of whispering worldtrees. 'I've never seen the Looking Glass Lakes, Reynald. I'm glad you brought me along.'

As a girl, she had slipped out before dawn, running through the forests to investigate whatever caught her curiosity. Fortunately, a wide variety of subjects piqued her interest: nature, science, culture, history. She had even studied records from the original generation ship *Caillié*, the story of Theron settlement and the origin of the green priests. Not because she had to, but because she was interested.

'Who else would I bring?' Reynald playfully rubbed his knuckles on his sister's tangle of hair twists. He was broad-shouldered, his arms muscular, his long hair done up in thick braids. Though a sheen of sweat covered his skin, he didn't seem uncomfortable in the forest warmth. 'Sarein is an ambassador on Earth. Beneto is a green priest on Corvus Landing, and Celli is . . . well—'

'She's still too much of a baby, even at sixteen,' Estarra said.

Years before, as part of his preparation for becoming the next Father of Theroc, Reynald had travelled around the Spiral Arm to learn different cultures. It was the first time any Theron leader had diligently investigated other societies. Now, with travel restricted, stardrive fuel strictly rationed, and interplanetary tensions high, Reynald had decided to visit the main cities on his own world. His parents had made no secret that they intended to step down and turn over the throne to him within the year. He had to be ready.

Now their flitter-raft flew above the treetops, passing from one settlement to another. Laughing followers, pretending to be part of a procession, swooped around them on gliderbikes, small craft composed of rebuilt engines and fluttering wings scavenged from native condorflies. Rambunctious young men circled above and behind them, showing off aerial manoeuvres. Some flirted with Estarra, who had reached marriageable age. . . .

Ahead, she saw a gap in the thick canopy and a glint of azure water.

'Those are the Looking Glass Lakes, all deep, all perfectly round,' Reynald said, pointing. 'We'll stay the night at the village.'

Around the first beautiful lake, worldtrees supported five worm hives, the empty nests of immense invertebrates. When Reynald landed the flitter-raft on the lakeshore, people rapelled, jumped, climbed, or swung down from their hive homes to greet the visitors. Four green priests emerged with the grace of gently waving branches, their skin tinged emerald by photosynthetic algae.

The green priests were capable of communication more sophisticated than the most complex technologies either the Hansa or the Ildirans had invented. The problem had frustrated scientists for generations, and the green priests had been unable to help them – not because they were keeping secrets, but because they didn't know the technical basis for what they did. Many outsiders offered to hire them for their telink skill, though the self-sufficient Therons had little need or interest in what the Hansa had to offer. The worldforest itself seemed intent on keeping a low profile.

On the other hand, the Hansa representatives were very insistent and persuasive.

Balancing such issues was a difficult job for any leader. Watching her brother interact with the green priests and smiling villagers, Estarra could see how well he would fill his role as the next Theron Father.

After an evening banquet of fresh fish, riverweed, and fat water bugs baked in the shell, they ascended to platforms high in the lakeside trees. Reynald and Estarra watched a performance of skilled treedancers, lithe acrobats who ran, danced, and bounced across the flexible boughs. Treedancers used the bending limbs and matted leaf fronds as springboards, soaring into the air, turning somersaults, catching branches and swinging by their arms in a choreographed ballet. At the end, in unison, all the treedancers launched themselves out over the water and dropped in perfect arcs to the mirror lake below, plunging into the water like heavy raindrops.

Following the performance, Estarra let Reynald talk business with the villagers while she happily accepted an invitation to splash in the warm water with a few local girls. She loved the sensation of floating and swimming, though she had the opportunity to do so only a few times a year.

Treading water in the Looking Glass Lake, Estarra gazed up into the night, marvelling at the sight of open sky from ground level. In her own city, the forest canopy was so thick she had to climb to the top just to see constellations. Now, floating in the open, the view overhead dazzled with billions of gleaming lights, a veritable forest of stars in the vault of space, full of people, worlds, possibilities.

When she returned to the brightly lit worm hives, dripping and invigorated, she found her brother speaking with a young priest named Almari. The woman's eyes were bright with intelligence and curiosity; Almari had spent years as an acolyte singing to the trees, adding to the musical knowledge stored in the botanical database. Like all green priests, she was hairless, her head smooth, her face adorned with tattoos denoting various accomplishments.

Reynald was gracious and polite, leaving his options open. 'You are beautiful and clever, Almari. No one can deny that. I'm certain you would make a fine wife.'

Estarra knew the discussion, for she had seen it several times already on this brief peregrination.

Almari spoke quickly, as if to cut him off before he could turn her down. 'Especially in these difficult times, is it not appropriate that the next Mother of Theroc be a green priest?'

Reynald reached to touch the delicate green skin on Almari's wrist. 'I can't argue with that, but I see no need to rush.'

Noticing Estarra, Almari got up and took her leave, looking embarrassed.

Grinning impishly, Estarra gave her brother a playful punch in the shoulder. 'She was pretty.'

'She was the third one tonight.'

'Better to have too many choices than none at all,' Estarra said.

He groaned. 'Then again, there's something to be said for having a clear-cut decision.'

'Poor, poor Reynald.'

He gave his sister a playful punch in return. 'At least I'm not the Ildiran Prime Designate. He's required to have thousands of lovers and as many children as he can possibly breed.'

'Ah, the terrible responsibilities of leadership.' Estarra flung her wet hair to splash him. 'Since I'm merely the fourth child, my only worry is when I'll have a chance to go swimming again. How about now?'

Giggling, she ran off, and Reynald looked after her with envy.

FOUR

PRIME DESIGNATE JORA'H

As the eldest noble-born son of the Mage-Imperator, Prime Designate Jora'h filled his days with dutiful distractions. Fertile women from across the spectrum of Ildiran kiths applied for mating privileges, and the lists grew long with more female volunteers than he could possibly service.

The Prime Designate's next assigned lover was named Sai'f. Whip-thin and alert, she was from the scientist kith, an expert in biology and genetics. Sai'f was interested in botany, developing new crop strains for diverse splinter colonies.

She came to Jora'h in his contemplation chamber in the Prism Palace, where constant daylight shone through gem-coloured crystal panels. Her brow was high, her head large, and her eyes sharp and attentive, as if she were capturing every detail for later study.

Jora'h stood before her, tall and handsome, his face defining the Ildiran ideal of beauty. Golden hair drifted in a nimbus around his head like a halo, knotted into ten thousand fine strands. 'Thank you for asking to be with me, Sai'f,' he said, meaning it – as he always did. 'May our shared gift today produce a gift for the entire Ildiran Empire.'

In nimble hands, Sai'f held a ceramic pot that contained a twisted, woody-stemmed shrub. Its thorned branches were bent, constrained, massaged into an unnatural shape. Shyly, she extended the pot. 'For you, Prime Designate.'

'How poignant and fascinating.' Jora'h took it, intrigued by the labyrinthine tangle of branches and leaves. 'It looks as if you've done weaving work with a living plant.'

'I am exploring the potential of our quilltrees, Prime Designate. It is a human technique called *bonsai*. A way of compressing a plant to turn its biological efforts inwards, yet enhancing its beauty. I began growing this one a year ago when I first filed my application to mate with you. It has required a great deal of attention, but I am satisfied with the results.'

Jora'h did not have to pretend his enjoyment. 'I have nothing like it. I will keep it in a special place . . . but you must instruct me on how to care for it.'

Sai'f smiled at him, relieved and thrilled to see his obvious pleasure. He set the bonsai quilltree on a translucent shelf on the wall, then came forward to her, opening his tunic to reveal his broad chest. 'Now allow me to give you a present in return, Sai'f.'

She had been tested by his staff before she'd entered the Prism Palace. All women who came to him were certified fertile and receptive. Such tests did not guarantee that he would impregnate every lover, but the odds were good.

Sai'f disrobed, and Jora'h admired her. Each Ildiran kith had a different bodily configuration. Some were willowy and ethereal, others squat and muscular, angular and sinewy, or plump and soft. But the Prime Designate saw beauty in all kiths. While some were more lovely to him than others, he never played favourites, never insulted the volunteers or showed any disappointment.

Sai'f reacted to his caresses as if she were following a programme or a suggested procedure. As a scientist, she had probably studied the variations of sex like a scholar, attempting to become an expert so that she could excel in her encounter with him. Right now, Jora'h felt as if he was doing the same for her, following a programme, a familiar task like any other.

As he thought of the fascinating *bonsai* tree Sai'f had brought him, Jora'h could not help but recall Nira. And his heart ached with the old sadness for the lovely green priest. It had been five years since he'd last seen her.

Nira's innocence and exotic beauty had charmed him more than any adoring Ildiran female ever had. When she'd first arrived in Mijistra, her wide-eyed wonder at the architecture and museums and fountains had made him look at his own city with fresh eyes. Her innocent excitement in Ildiran accomplishments had made him feel more pride in his heritage than the most stirring passages from the *Saga of Seven Suns*.

After shy months of enjoying each other's company, when they'd finally made love for the first time it had seemed entirely natural. The warm familiarity that grew into a bond with Nira was unlike anything the Prime Designate had ever experienced before. His relationship with her had been entirely separate from these routine matings scheduled by his assistants. Jora'h and Nira had spent many afternoons delighting in each other's company, knowing the relationship must eventually end, but enjoying each day. And the Prime Designate had kept calling her back to him.

But at the beginning of the hydrogue crisis, when Jora'h had gone to visit Prince Reynald on Theroc, Nira and her mentor Otema had been tragically killed in a fire in the greenhouse that held the gift of worldtrees from Theroc. According to the Mage-Imperator's report, the two visiting green priests had rushed in to save their treelings and had perished in the blaze.

Long ago, sweet Nira had come to the Prism Palace bearing potted treelings, small offshoots of the worldforest. Now, years after her death, the woman Sai'f had brought Jora'h a *bonsai* tree, and the memories all came flooding back to him . . .

Jora'h refocused his attention on the scientist woman. He did not want her to note his troubled thoughts, or to leave dissatisfied. He made love to her with an intensity that, for a while at least, drove back the ache of memories.

Jora'h requested an audience with his father. The Mage-Imperator's bright eyes were set within folds of fat, and his plump lips smiled when he saw his son. Bron'n, the fierce personal bodyguard, stood at the doorway to the private chamber so the leader and his eldest son could speak privately.

'I wish to send another message to Theroc, Father.'

Mage-Imperator Cyroc'h frowned, leaning back in his chrysalis chair, as if relaxing into the telepathic connection of *thism*. 'I sense you thinking of that human female again. You should not allow her to kindle such an obsession in you. It can only disrupt your more important duties here. She is long dead.'

Jora'h knew the corpulent leader was correct, but he could not forget Nira's smile and the joy that she had brought him. Before coming here, he had gone to the skysphere arboretum. One particular chamber had been used to house the Theron treelings. By now, the greenhouse had been replanted with salmon-pink Comptor lilies and crimson poppies, swelling the humid air with heady perfumes. Five years ago, when he had returned from Theroc to learn the terrible news, he had stared in horrified awe at the scars from the inexplicable conflagration.

There had been no bodies left to send back to Theroc. And the worldtrees were already burning by the time Nira and Otema arrived to fight the fire, so they had been unable to send any last messages through telink. Everything had been lost. Grieving, Jora'h had explained the tragedy to his friend Reynald in a special communiqué delivered by a Solar Navy ship.

The ashes and soot stains had been scoured clean, but the memories and the sadness remained. In his heart, Jora'h had never accepted that Nira was dead. If only he had been here, he would not have let any harm come to her. . . .

Sensing his son's sadness through the web of *thism*, Cyroc'h nodded sombrely. 'You will carry many burdens when you ascend to take my place. It is your destiny, my son, to feel the pain of all our people.'

Jora'h's tiny golden braids flickered like tendrils of smoke. 'Nevertheless, I would like to send a new message to Reynald, in memory of the two green priests. We did not send the ashes or the skulls back to them.' He spread his hands. 'It is such a small thing, Father.'

The Mage-Imperator smiled indulgently. 'You know I cannot deny you.' The rope-like braid that hung from his head coiled around his pudgy stomach and twitched, as if the great leader were annoyed.

Relieved, Jora'h held out an etched-diamondfilm plaque. 'Here, I have composed another letter for Reynald to share among the green priests on Theroc. I would like to dispatch it with one of our commercial vessels.'

The leader reached out to take the message. 'It may require some time and a roundabout route. Theroc is not a frequently visited world.'

'I know, Father, but at least it's something I can do. It is my way of maintaining contact.'

Cyroc'h held the shimmering glassy plaque. 'You must not think of the human woman again.'

'Thank you for granting me this favour.' Jora'h backed out of the chamber and departed with a spring in his step.

As soon as he was gone, the Mage-Imperator summoned his bodyguard forward. 'Take this and destroy it. Make certain Jora'h is not allowed to send any message to Theroc.'

Bron'n took the diamondfilm letter in his clawed hands and, with great strength, snapped it in half. He would incinerate the pieces in a power plant furnace. 'Yes, Liege. I understand.'

Available now
from Pocket Books

POCKET
BOOKS

Also by Kevin J. Anderson

A Forest of Stars
The Saga of Seven Suns – Book Two

It has been five years since humanity's heady expansion among the stars came to an abrupt, and violent, halt. With space travel heavily curtailed, and supplies of fuel dwindling, young King Peter has no choice but to impose strict rationing.

But the Hydrogues are not the only enemies of humanity. The Leader of the Ildiran Empire forges tangled alliances among all the combatants in order to protect his failing civilisation. The mysterious Klikiss robots continue to work their sinister plans. And archaeologists Margaret and Louis Colicos vanish. Rlinda Ketta and Davlin Lotze are sent to investigate and soon realise that the Colicos's discoveries may lead to an incredible new way to travel between worlds . . . or to the awakening of enemies even more fearsome than the Hydrogues.

ISBN 0 7434 3066 2
PRICE £6.99

POCKET BOOKS

Kevin J. Anderson

Horizon Storms
The Saga of Seven Suns – Book Three

The titanic war between the elemental alien hydrogues and faeros continues to sweep across the Spiral Arm, extinguishing suns and destroying planets. Chairman Wenceslas and King Peter must now unify the human race with iron-fisted policies in a final bid to stand together – or face total annihilation. But disparate civilizations are forging new alliances that threaten the old order. The Roamer and Theron clans will not yield their independence, and the new Mage-Imperator Jora'h now faces a threat that no other Ildiran leader has ever seen – a civil war that could break apart the entire Empire.

'Space opera at its most entertaining' *Starlog*

ISBN 0 7434 3067 0
PRICE £6.99

POCKET
BOOKS

Kevin J. Anderson

Scattered Suns
The Saga of Seven Suns – Book Four

The destructive hydrogues continue their war against humans and the fiery entities, the faeros – a struggle that kills planets and extinguishes whole stars. Newly crowned Mage-Imperator Jora'h, the leader of the ancient and vast Ildiran Empire, struggles with new knowledge he has learned: an ancient bargain and long-standing treachery that may finally bring peace with the hydrogues . . . though it could mean the extermination of the human race. But Jora'h's empire is destroying itself from within, when his mad brother launches a bloody rebellion across the Ildiran planets, appointing Jora'h's own first-born son as its leader. In a galaxy torn by war, treachery, and shifting alliances, no one can know the truth about their friends or enemies.

ISBN 0 7432 7544 6
PRICE £10.99

**POCKET
BOOKS**

These Kevin J. Anderson titles are available from your
bookshop or can be ordered direct from the publisher.

0 7434 3065 4	HIDDEN EMPIRE	£6.99
0 7434 3066 2	A FOREST OF STARS	£6.99
0 7434 3067 0	HORIZON STORMS	£6.99
0 7432 7544 6	SCATTERED SUNS	£10.99

Please send cheque or postal order for the value of the
book, free postage and packing within the UK; OVERSEAS
including Republic of Ireland £1 per book.

OR: Please debit this amount from my

VISA/ACCESS/MASTERCARD:. . . . .

CARD NO: . . . .

EXPIRY DATE: . . . .

AMOUNT: £ . . . .

NAME: . . . .

ADDRESS: . . . .

. . . .

SIGNATURE: . . . .

Send orders to SIMON & SCHUSTER CASH SALES
PO Box 29, Douglas Isle of Man, IM99 1BQ
Tel: 01624 677237, Fax: 01624 670923
Email: bookshop@enterprise.net
www.bookpost.co.uk
Please allow 14 days for delivery. Prices and availability
subject to change without notice